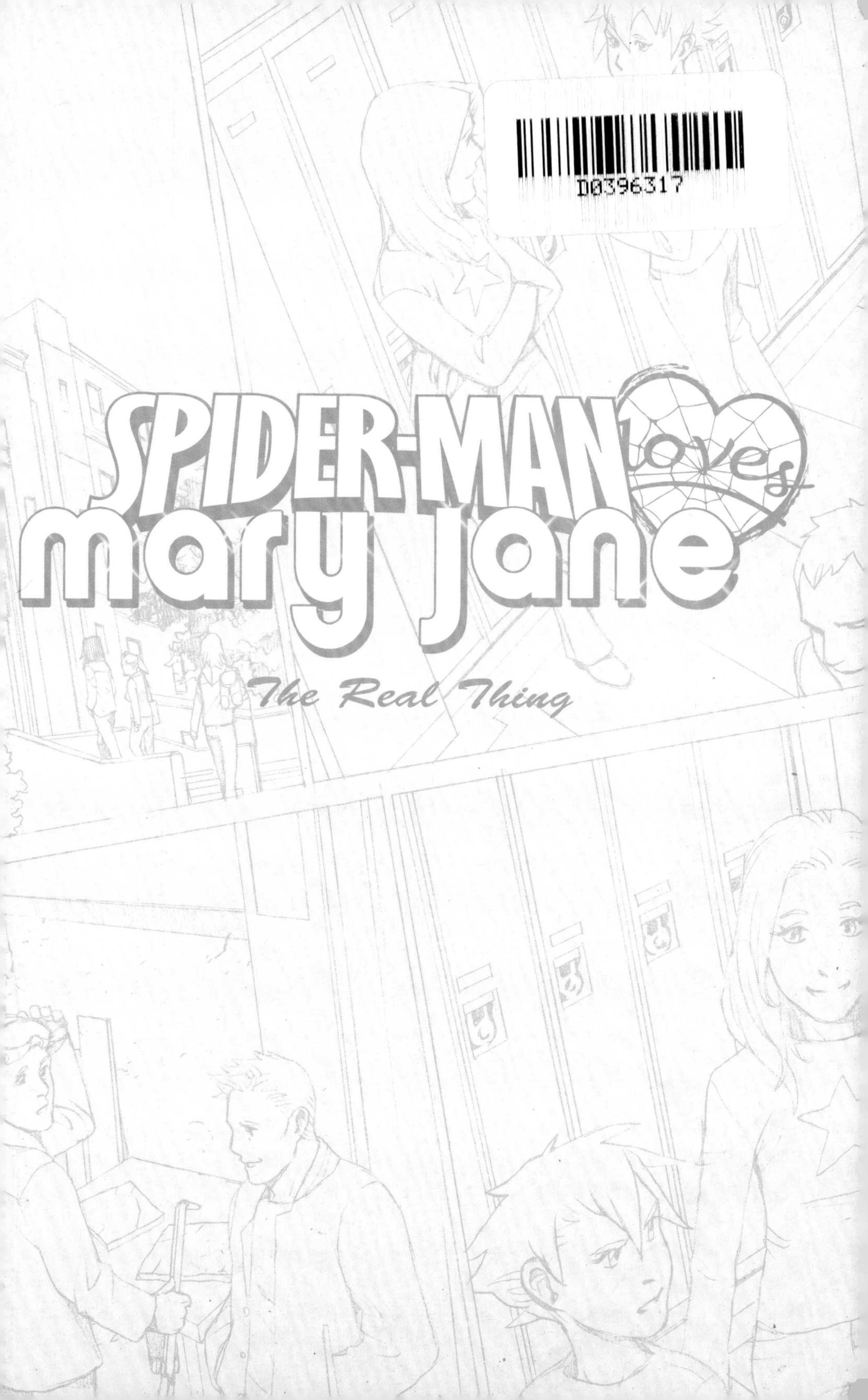
SPIDER-MAN loves
mary jane
The Real Thing

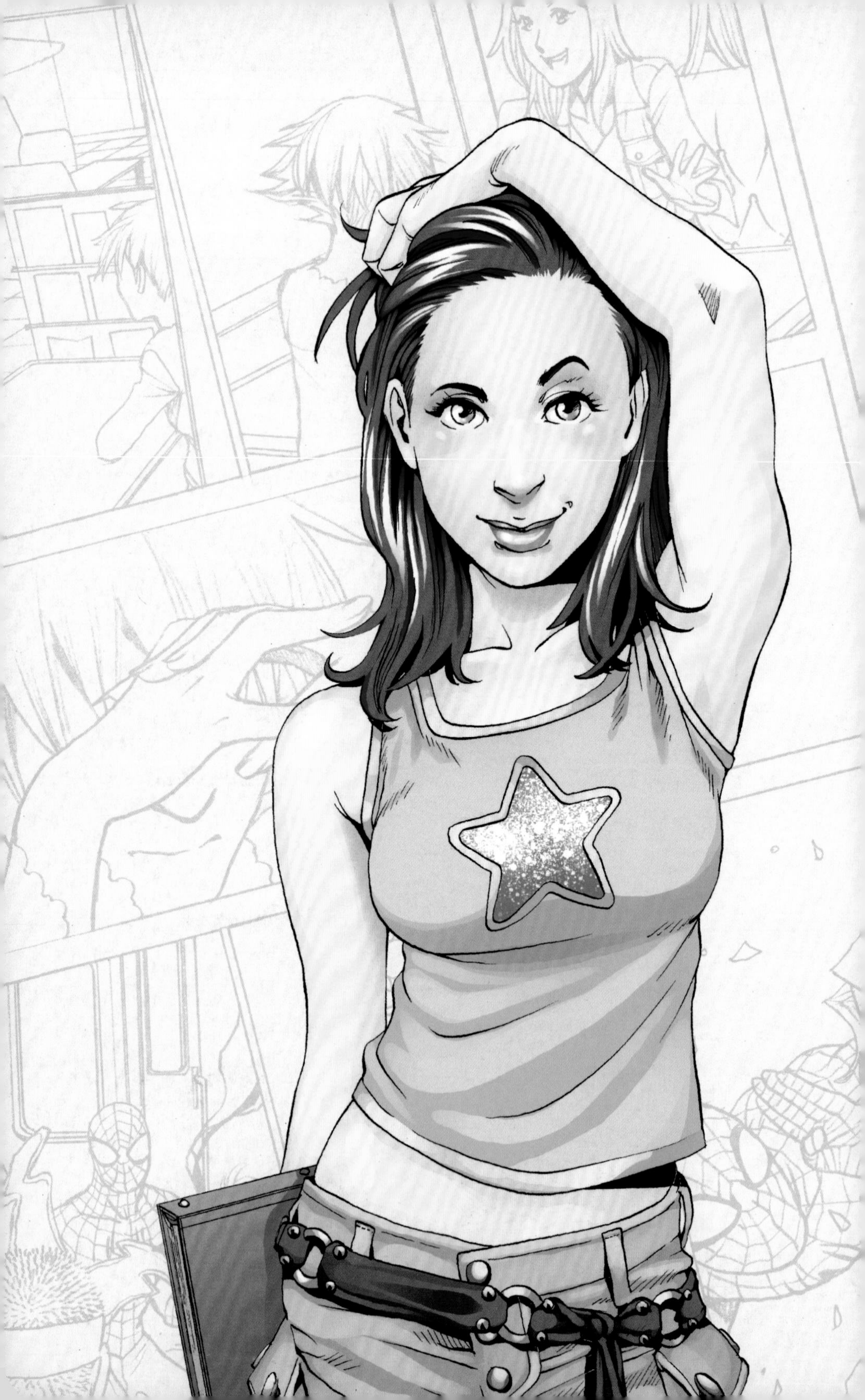

SPIDER-MAN loves mary jane

The Real Thing

WRITER
Sean McKeever

ARTIST
Takeshi Miyazawa

INKER, *MARY JANE #1-4*
Norman Lee

COLORIST
Christina Strain

LETTERERS
VC's Randy Gentile & Dave Sharpe

COVER ART
Takeshi Miyazawa, Norman Lee & Christina Strain

ASSISTANT EDITOR
Nathan Cosby

EDITORS
MacKenzie Cadenhead with Mark Paniccia

CONSULTING EDITOR
C.B. Cebulski

SPIDER-MAN CREATED BY STAN LEE & STEVE DITKO

collection editor JENNIFER GRÜNWALD
assistant editor CAITLIN O'CONNELL
associate managing editor KATERI WOODY
editor, special projects MARK D. BEAZLEY
vp production & special projects JEFF YOUNGQUIST
research JESS HAROLD

svp print, sales & marketing DAVID GABRIEL
director, licensed publishing SVEN LARSEN
editor in chief C.B. CEBULSKI
chief creative officer JOE QUESADA
president DAN BUCKLEY
executive producer ALAN FINE

SPIDER-MAN LOVES MARY JANE: THE REAL THING. Contains material originally published in magazine form as MARY JANE #1-4, MARY JANE: HOMECOMING #1-4 and SPIDER-MAN LOVES MARY JANE #1-3. First printing 2019. ISBN 978-1-302-91873-6. Published by MARVEL WORLDWIDE, INC., a subsidiary of MARVEL ENTERTAINMENT, LLC. OFFICE OF PUBLICATION: 135 West 50th Street, New York, NY 10020. © 2019 MARVEL No similarity between any of the names, characters, persons, and/or institutions in this magazine with those of any living or dead person or institution is intended, and any such similarity which may exist is purely coincidental. **Printed in Canada.** DAN BUCKLEY, President, Marvel Entertainment; JOHN NEE, Publisher; JOE QUESADA, Chief Creative Officer; TOM BREVOORT, SVP of Publishing; DAVID BOGART, Associate Publisher & SVP of Talent Affairs; DAVID GABRIEL, SVP of Sales & Marketing, Publishing; JEFF YOUNGQUIST, VP of Production & Special Projects; DAN CARR, Executive Director of Publishing Technology; ALEX MORALES, Director of Publishing Operations; DAN EDINGTON, Managing Editor; SUSAN CRESPI, Production Manager; STAN LEE, Chairman Emeritus. For information regarding advertising in Marvel Comics or on Marvel.com, please contact Vit DeBellis, Custom Solutions & Integrated Advertising Manager, at vdebellis@marvel.com. For Marvel subscription inquiries, please call 888-511-5480. **Manufactured between 4/19/2019 and 5/21/2019 by SOLISCO PRINTERS, SCOTT, QC, CANADA.**

10 9 8 7 6 5 4 3 2 1

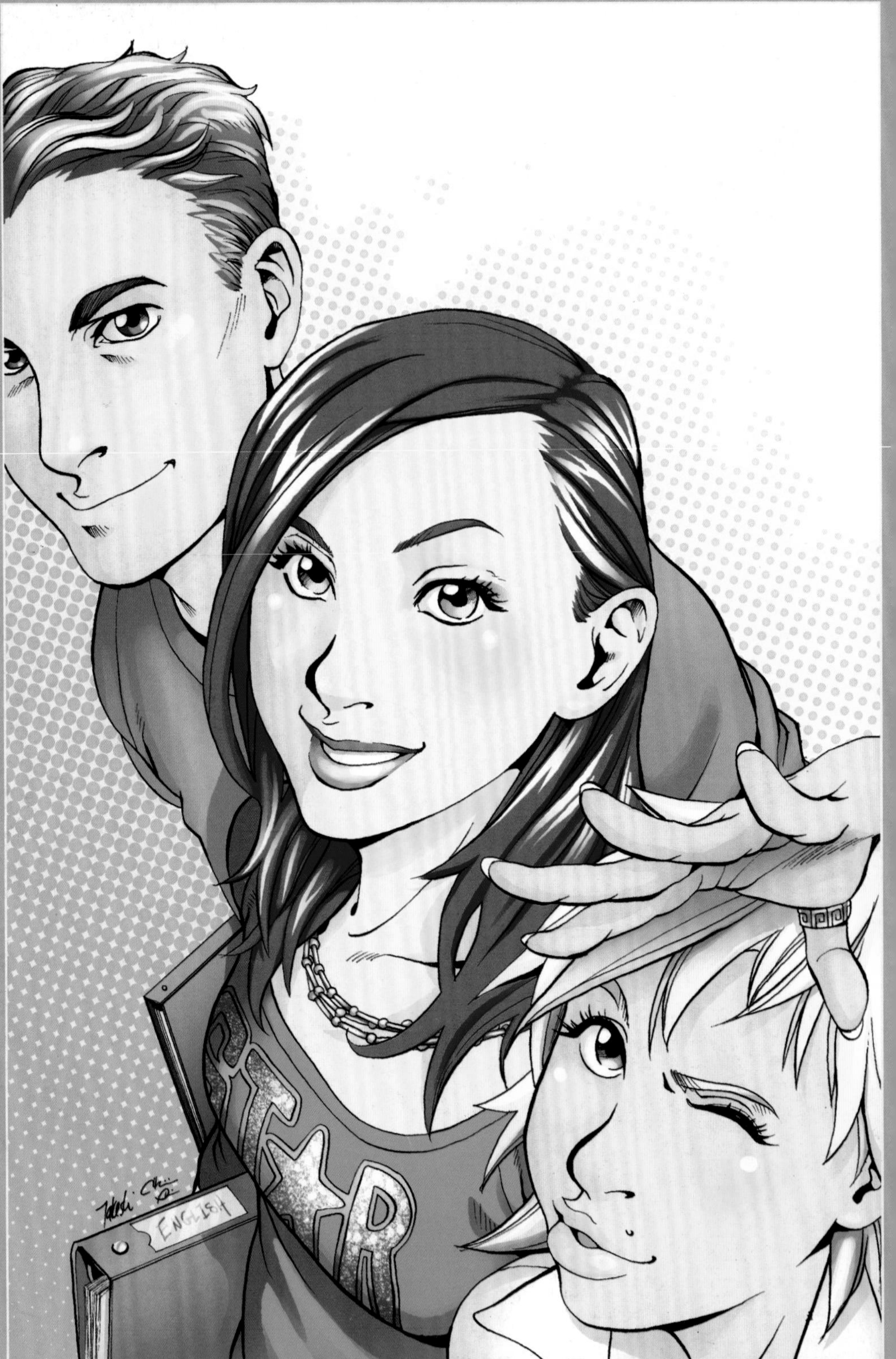
ENGLISH

Mary Jane #1

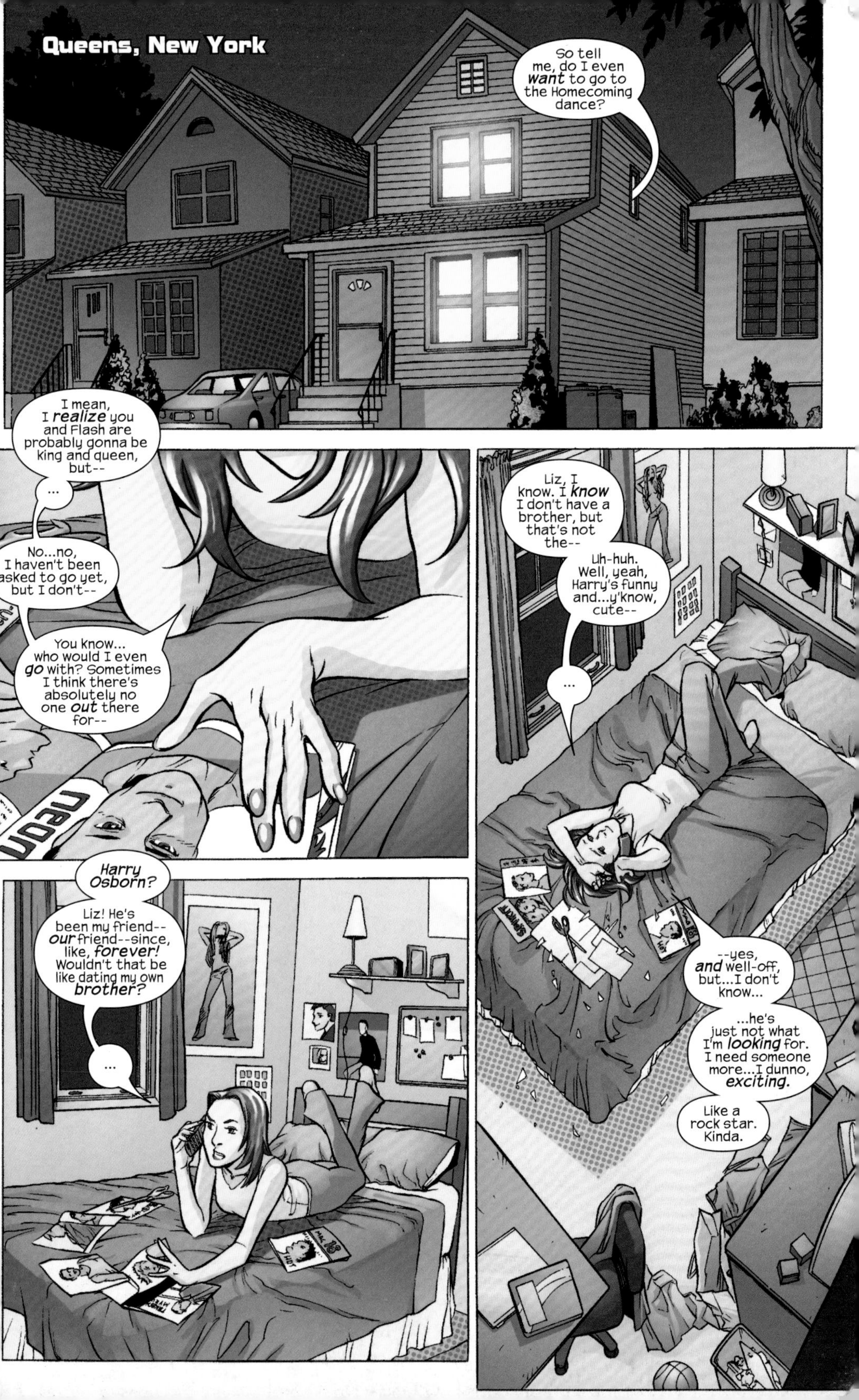
Queens, New York
So tell me, do I even *want* to go to the Homecoming dance?
I mean, I *realize* you and Flash are probably gonna be king and queen, but--
...
No...no, I haven't been asked to go yet, but I don't--
You know... who would I even *go* with? Sometimes I think there's absolutely no one *out* there for--
neon
Harry Osborn?
Liz! He's been my friend-- *our* friend--since, like, *forever!* Wouldn't that be like dating my own *brother*?
...
Liz, I know. I *know* I don't have a brother, but that's not the--
Uh-huh. Well, yeah, Harry's funny and...y'know, cute--
...
--yes, *and* well-off, but...I don't know...
...he's just not what I'm *looking* for. I need someone more...I dunno, *exciting.*
Like a rock star. Kinda.

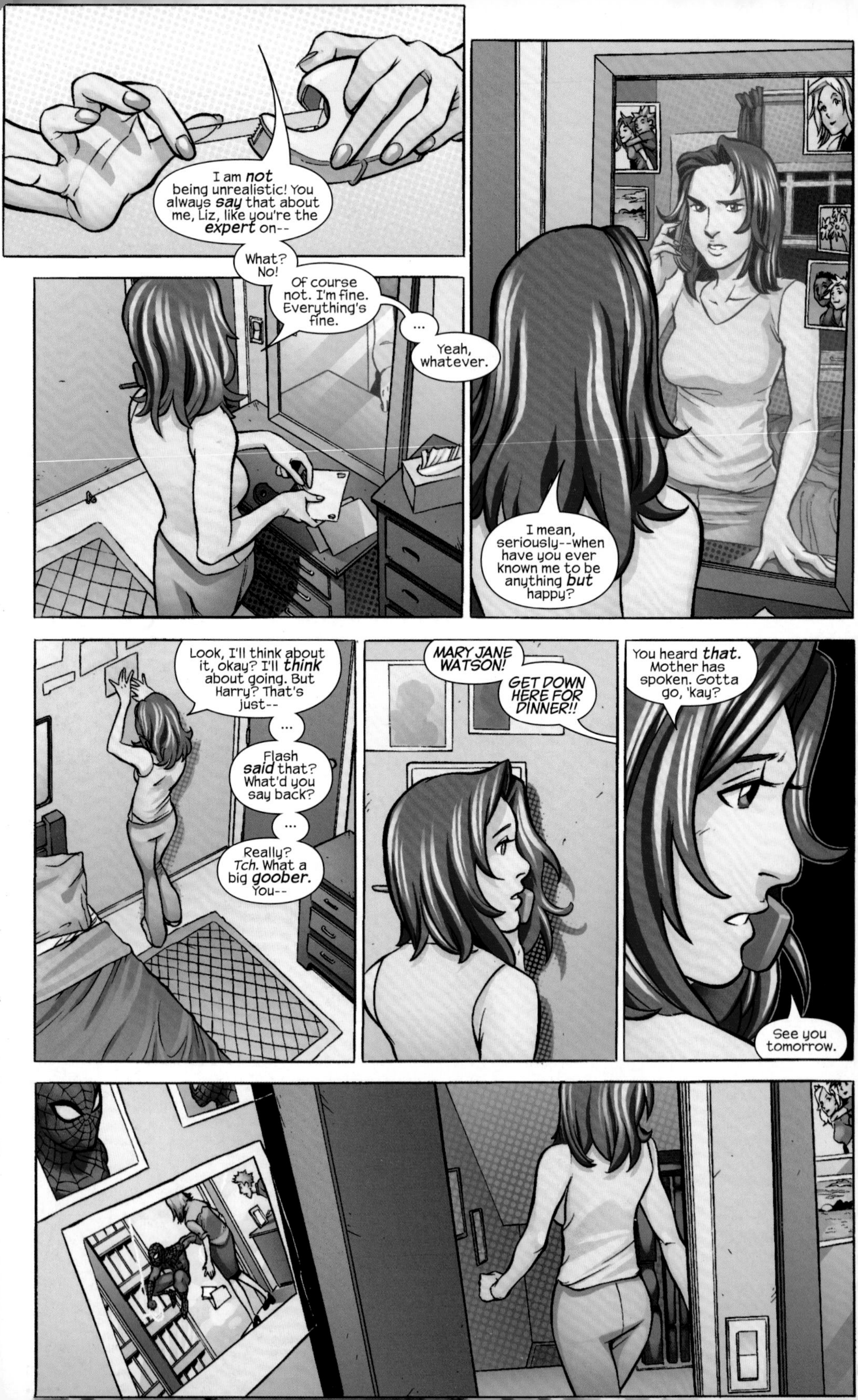
I am *not* being unrealistic! You always *say* that about me, Liz, like you're the *expert* on--
What? No!
Of course not. I'm fine. Everything's fine.
...
Yeah, whatever.
I mean, seriously--when have you ever known me to be anything *but* happy?
Look, I'll think about it, okay? I'll *think* about going. But Harry? That's just--
...
Flash *said* that? What'd you say back?
...
Really? *Tch.* What a big *goober.* You--
MARY JANE WATSON!
GET DOWN HERE FOR DINNER!!
You heard *that.* Mother has spoken. Gotta go, 'kay?
See you tomorrow.

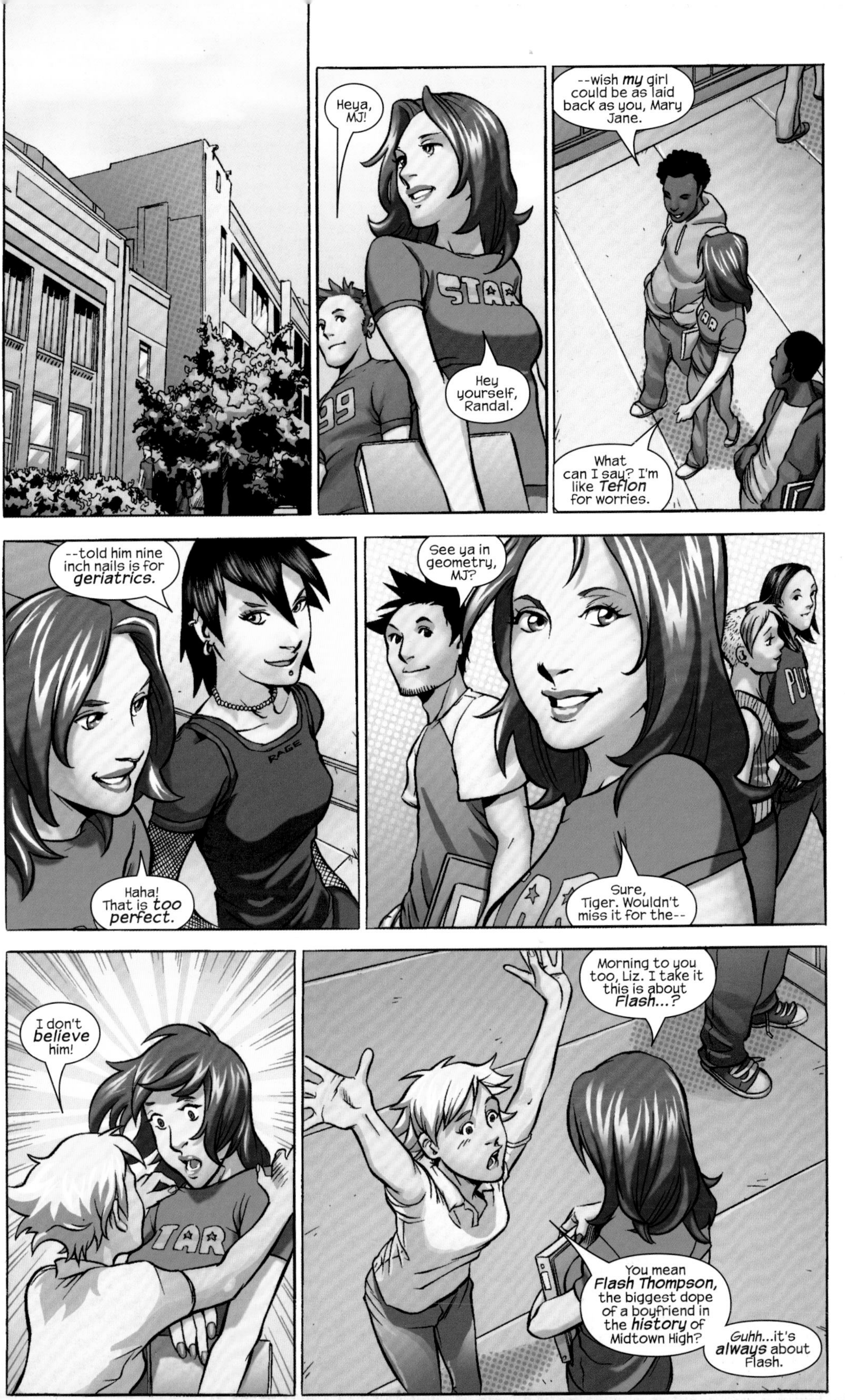
Heya, MJ!
Hey yourself, Randal.
--wish my girl could be as laid back as you, Mary Jane.
What can I say? I'm like Teflon for worries.
--told him nine inch nails is for geriatrics.
Haha! That is too perfect.
See ya in geometry, MJ?
Sure, Tiger. Wouldn't miss it for the--
I don't believe him!
Morning to you too, Liz. I take it this is about Flash...?
You mean Flash Thompson, the biggest dope of a boyfriend in the history of Midtown High?
Guhh...it's always about Flash.

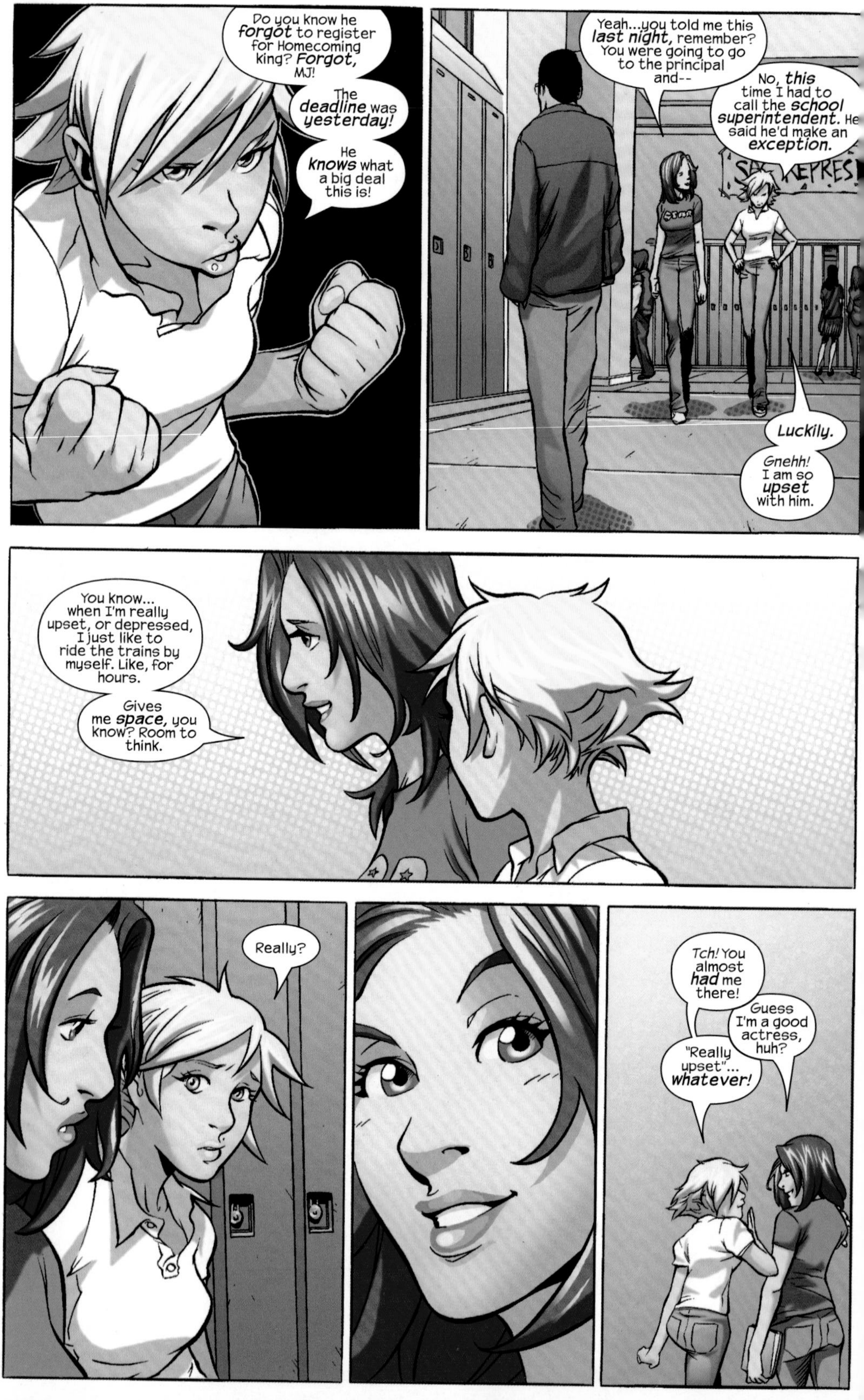
Do you know he forgot to register for Homecoming king? Forgot, MJ!
The deadline was yesterday!
He knows what a big deal this is!
Yeah...you told me this last night, remember? You were going to go to the principal and--
No, this time I had to call the school superintendent. He said he'd make an exception.
Luckily.
Gnehh! I am so upset with him.
You know... when I'm really upset, or depressed, I just like to ride the trains by myself. Like, for hours.
Gives me space, you know? Room to think.
Really?
Tch! You almost had me there!
"Really upset"... whatever!
Guess I'm a good actress, huh?

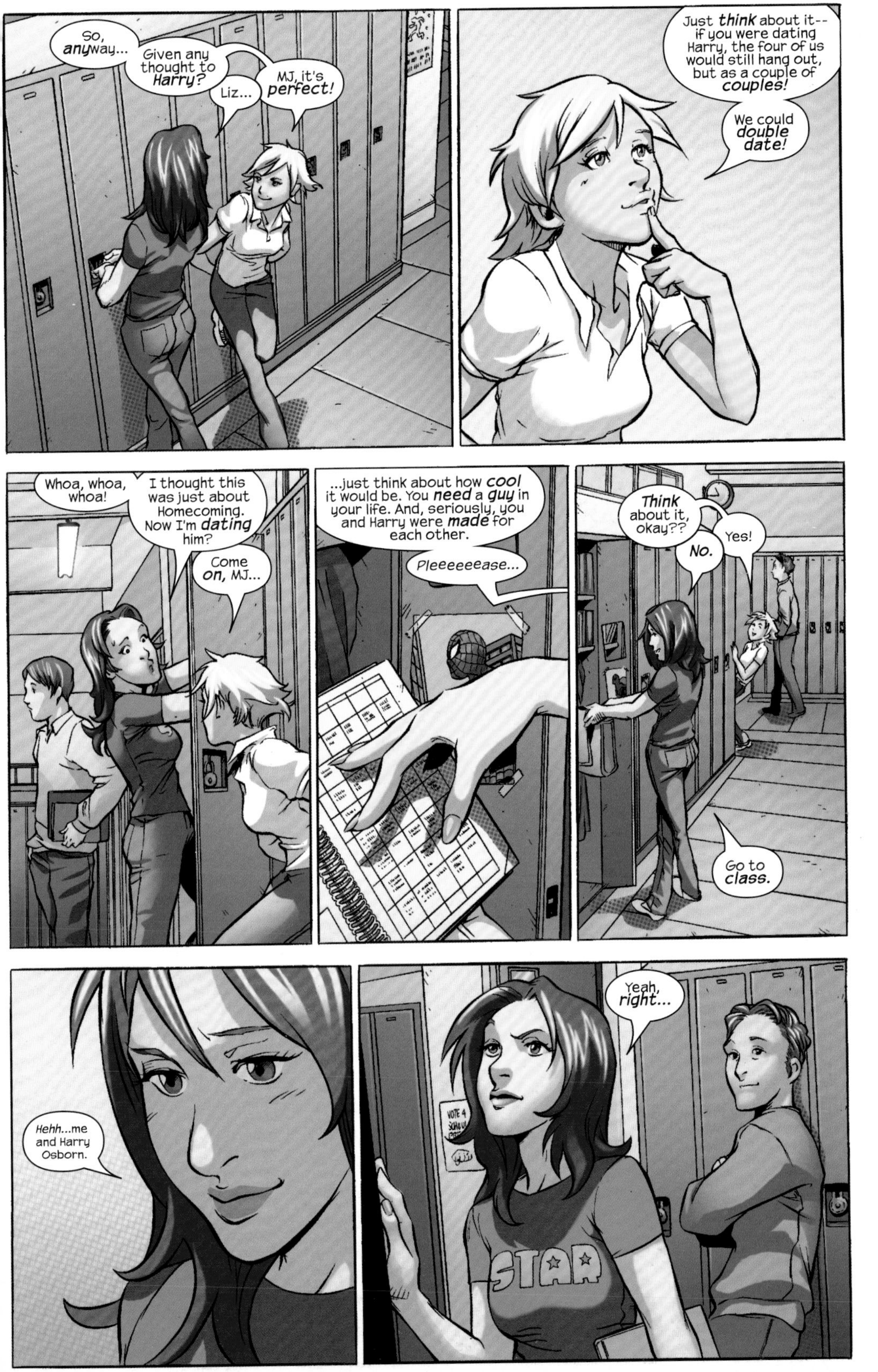
So, anyway...
Given any thought to Harry?
Liz...
MJ, it's perfect!
Just think about it-- if you were dating Harry, the four of us would still hang out, but as a couple of couples!
We could double date!
Whoa, whoa, whoa!
I thought this was just about Homecoming. Now I'm dating him?
Come on, MJ...
...just think about how cool it would be. You need a guy in your life. And, seriously, you and Harry were made for each other.
Pleeeeeease...
Think about it, okay??
No.
Yes!
Go to class.
Hehh...me and Harry Osborn.
Yeah, right...
VOTE 4
STAR

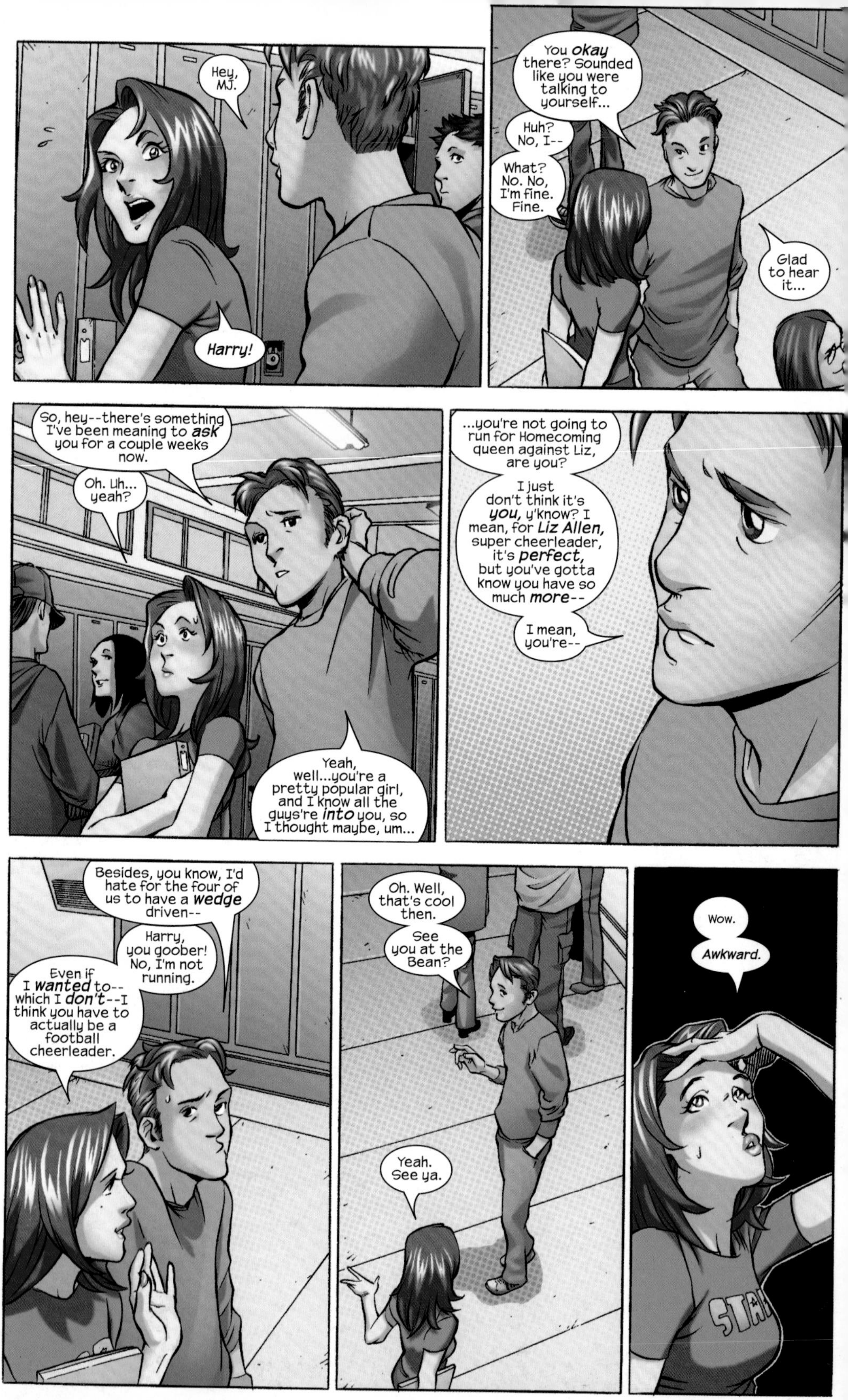
Hey, MJ.
Harry!
You okay there? Sounded like you were talking to yourself...
Huh? No, I--
What? No. No, I'm fine. Fine.
Glad to hear it...
So, hey--there's something I've been meaning to ask you for a couple weeks now.
Oh. Uh... yeah?
Yeah, well...you're a pretty popular girl, and I know all the guys're into you, so I thought maybe, um...
...you're not going to run for Homecoming queen against Liz, are you?
I just don't think it's you, y'know? I mean, for Liz Allen, super cheerleader, it's perfect, but you've gotta know you have so much more--
I mean, you're--
Besides, you know, I'd hate for the four of us to have a wedge driven--
Harry, you goober! No, I'm not running.
Even if I wanted to--which I don't--I think you have to actually be a football cheerleader.
Oh. Well, that's cool then.
See you at the Bean?
Yeah. See ya.
Wow.
Awkward.

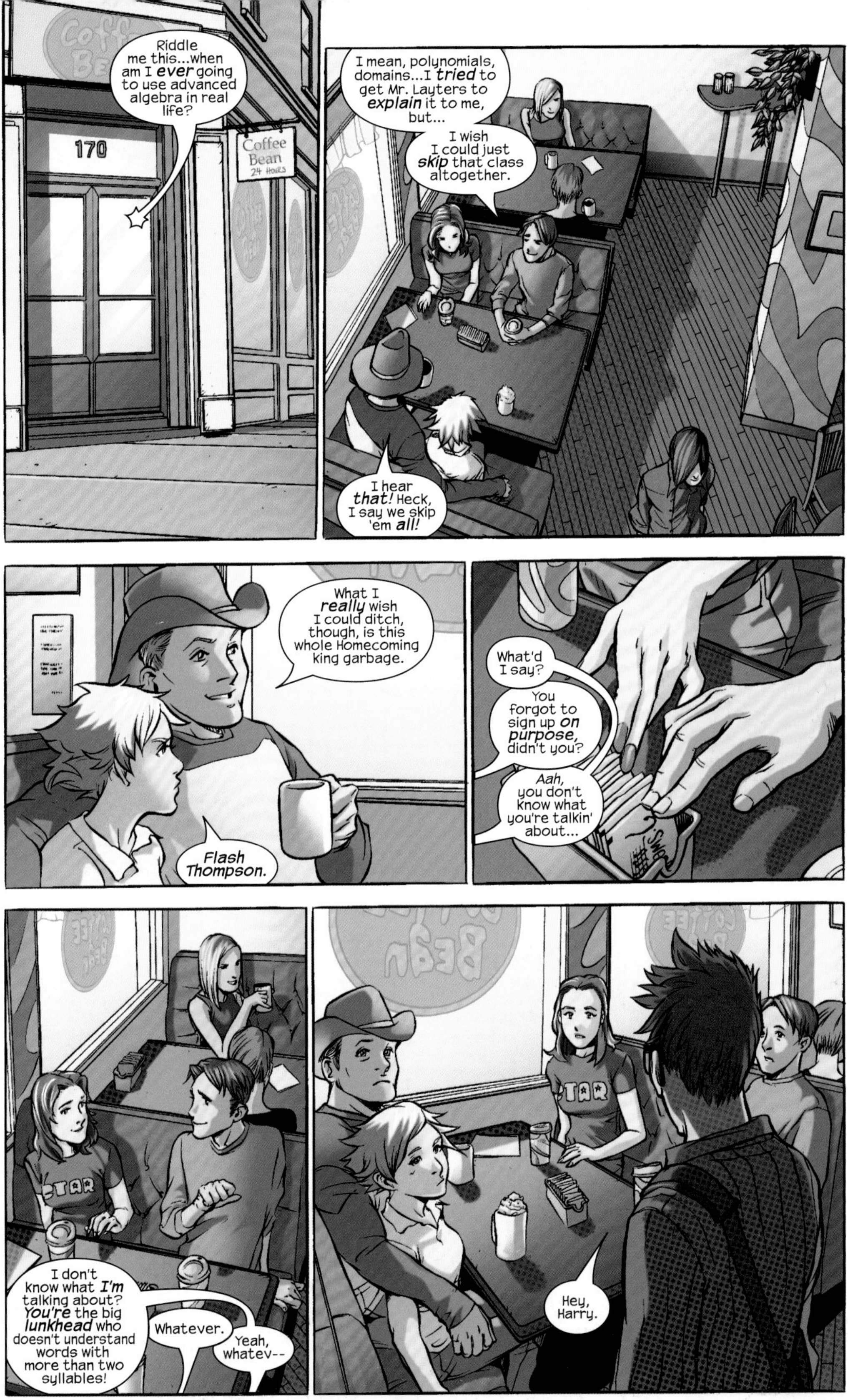
Riddle me this...when am I ever going to use advanced algebra in real life?
170
Coffee Bean 24 HOURS
I mean, polynomials, domains...I tried to get Mr. Layters to explain it to me, but...
I wish I could just skip that class altogether.
I hear that! Heck, I say we skip 'em all!
What I really wish I could ditch, though, is this whole Homecoming king garbage.
Flash Thompson.
What'd I say?
You forgot to sign up on purpose, didn't you?
Aah, you don't know what you're talkin' about...
I don't know what I'm talking about? You're the big lunkhead who doesn't understand words with more than two syllables!
Whatever.
Yeah, whatev--
Hey, Harry.

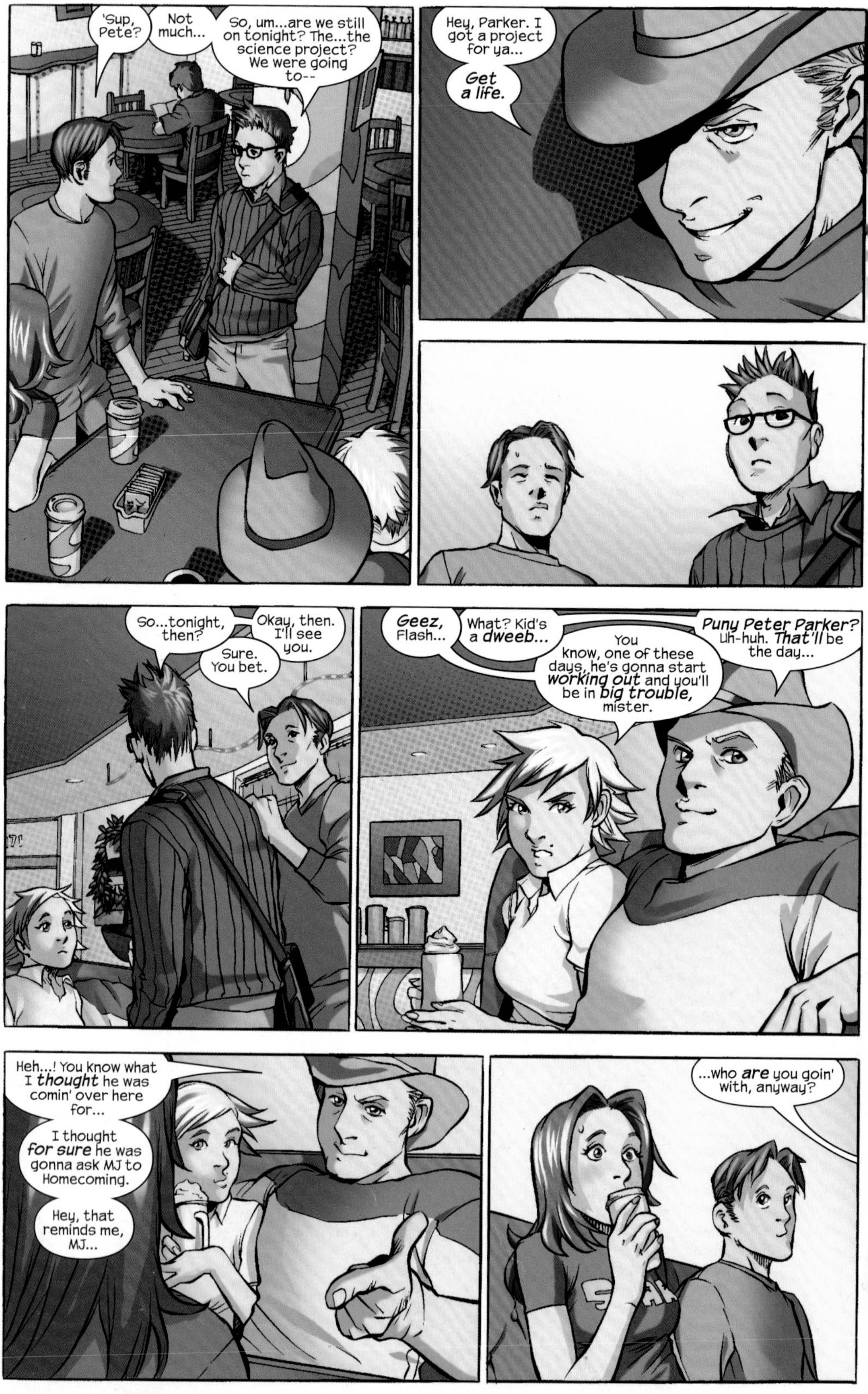
'Sup, Pete?
Not much...
So, um...are we still on tonight? The...the science project? We were going to--
Hey, Parker. I got a project for ya...
Get a life.
So...tonight, then?
Okay, then. I'll see you.
Sure. You bet.
Geez, Flash...
What? Kid's a dweeb...
You know, one of these days, he's gonna start working out and you'll be in big trouble, mister.
Puny Peter Parker? Uh-huh. That'll be the day...
Heh...! You know what I thought he was comin' over here for...
I thought for sure he was gonna ask MJ to Homecoming.
Hey, that reminds me, MJ...
...who are you goin' with, anyway?

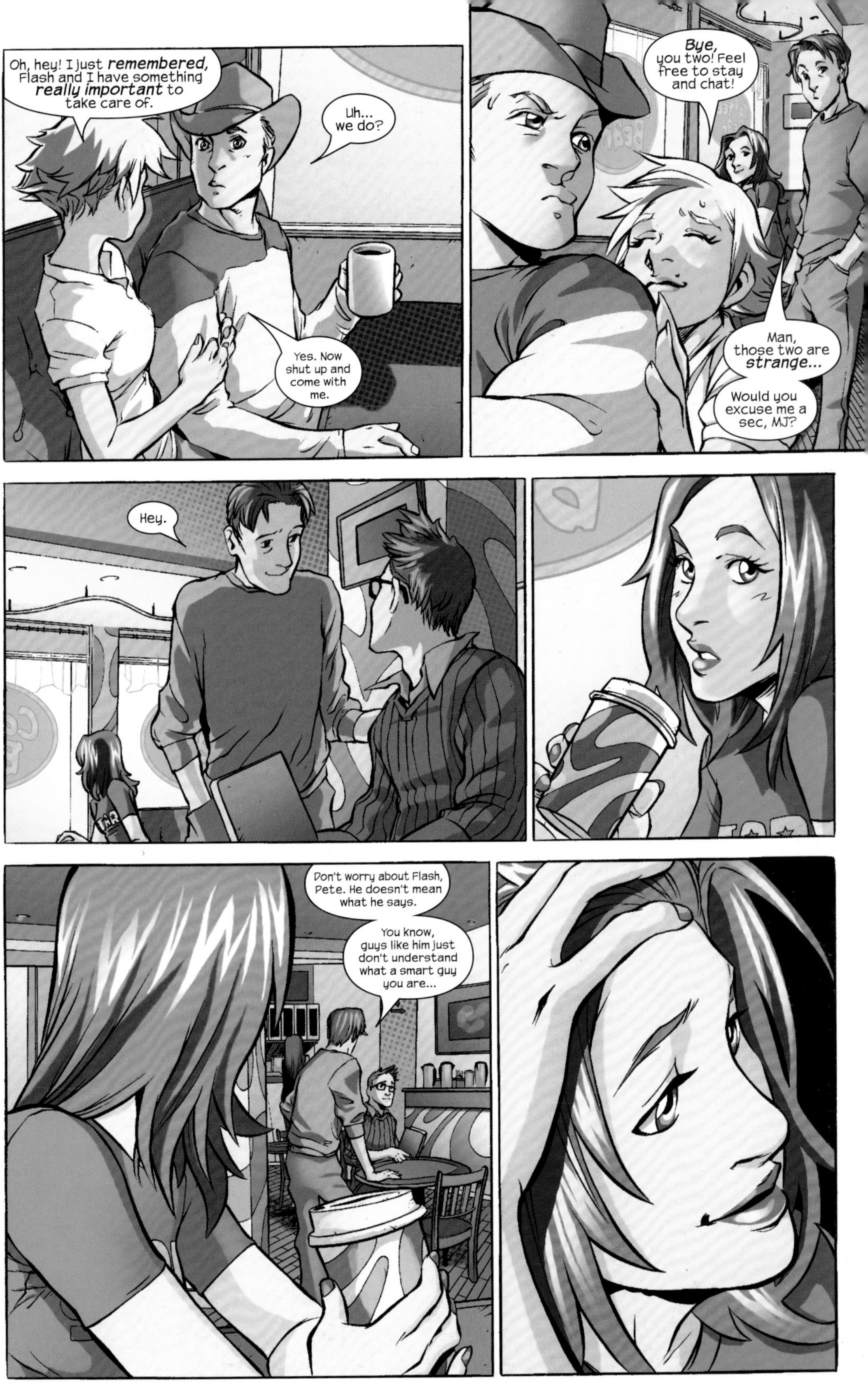
Oh, hey! I just **remembered,** Flash and I have something ***really important*** to take care of.
Uh... we do?
Yes. Now shut up and come with me.
Bye, you two! Feel free to stay and chat!
Man, those two are ***strange...***
Would you excuse me a sec, MJ?
Hey.
Don't worry about Flash, Pete. He doesn't mean what he says.
You know, guys like him just don't understand what a smart guy you are...

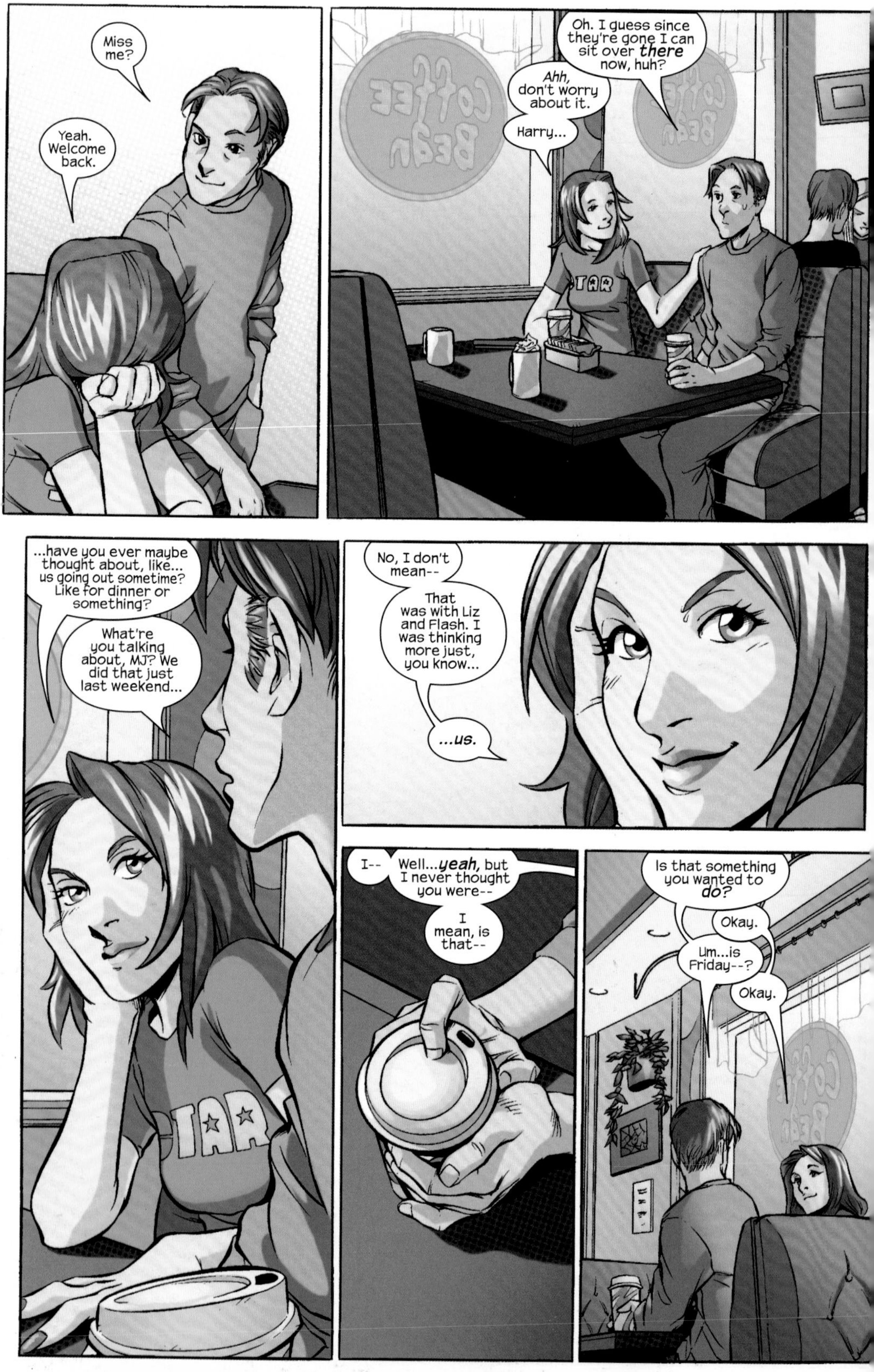

Miss me?
Yeah. Welcome back.
Oh. I guess since they're gone I can sit over *there* now, huh?
Ahh, don't worry about it.
Harry...
...have you ever maybe thought about, like... us going out sometime? Like for dinner or something?
What're you talking about, MJ? We did that just last weekend...
No, I don't mean--
That was with Liz and Flash. I was thinking more just, you know...
...us.
I--
Well...*yeah,* but I never thought you were--
I mean, is that--
Is that something you wanted to *do?*
Okay.
Um...is Friday--?
Okay.

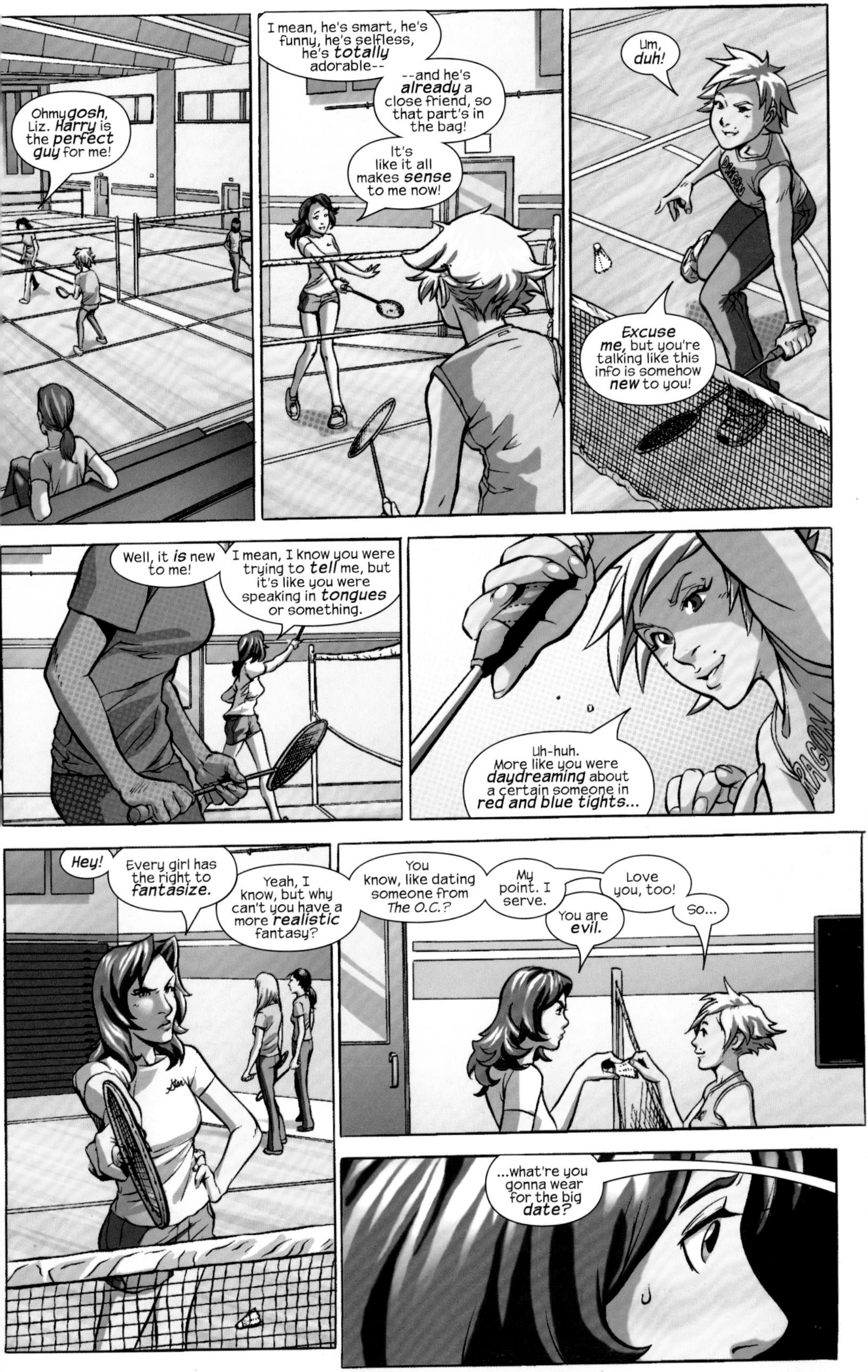

Ohmy gosh, Liz. Harry is the perfect guy for me!
I mean, he's smart, he's funny, he's selfless, he's totally adorable--
--and he's already a close friend, so that part's in the bag!
It's like it all makes sense to me now!
Um, duh!
Excuse me, but you're talking like this info is somehow new to you!
Well, it is new to me!
I mean, I know you were trying to tell me, but it's like you were speaking in tongues or something.
Uh-huh. More like you were daydreaming about a certain someone in red and blue tights...
Hey!
Every girl has the right to fantasize.
Yeah, I know, but why can't you have a more realistic fantasy?
You know, like dating someone from The O.C.?
My point. I serve.
You are evil.
Love you, too!
So...
...what're you gonna wear for the big date?

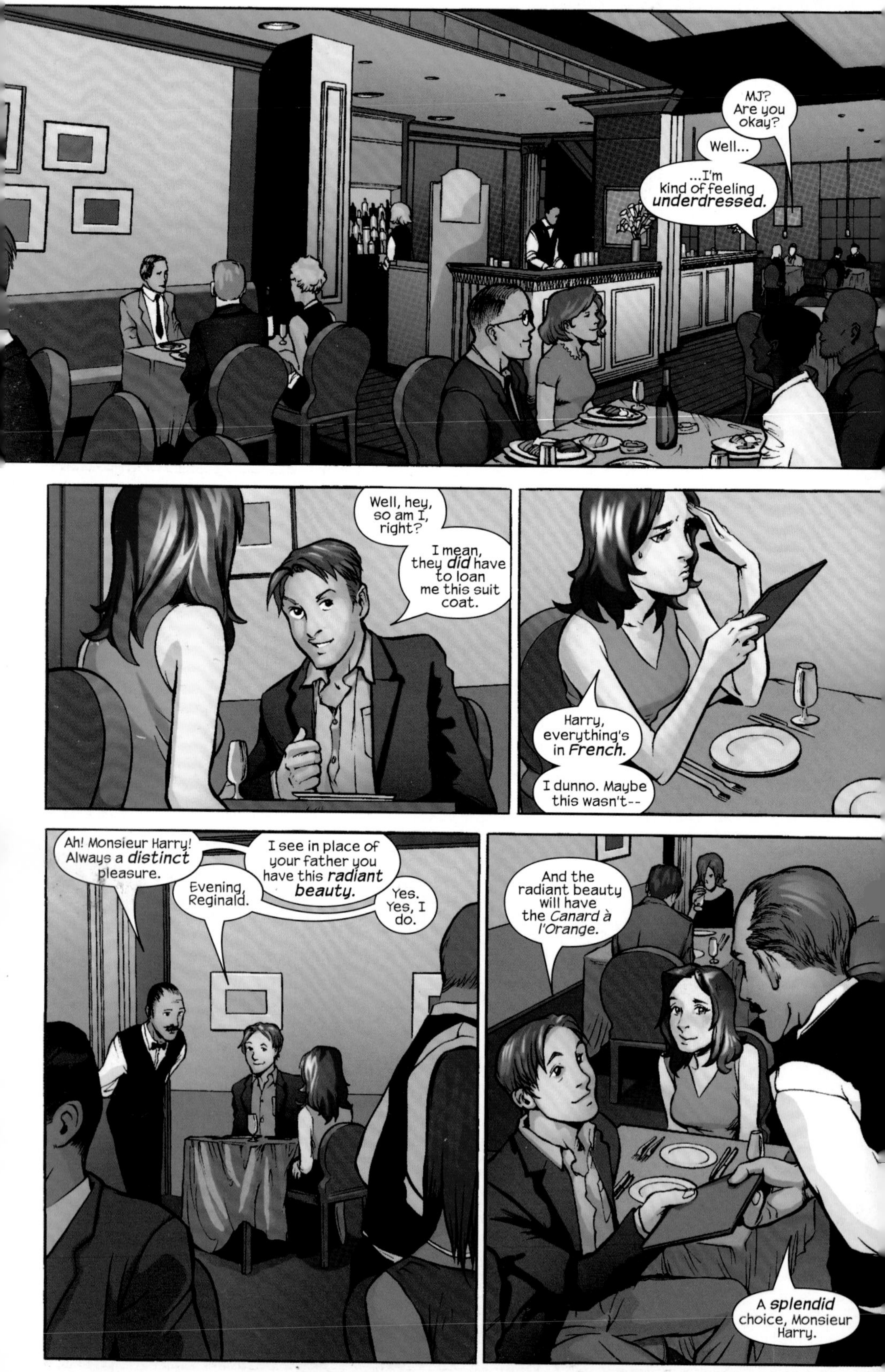

MJ? Are you okay?
Well...
...I'm kind of feeling *underdressed.*
Well, hey, so am I, right?
I mean, they *did* have to loan me this suit coat.
Harry, everything's in *French.*
I dunno. Maybe this wasn't--
Ah! Monsieur Harry! Always a *distinct* pleasure.
Evening, Reginald.
I see in place of your father you have this *radiant beauty.*
Yes. Yes, I do.
And the radiant beauty will have the *Canard à l'Orange.*
A *splendid* choice, Monsieur Harry.

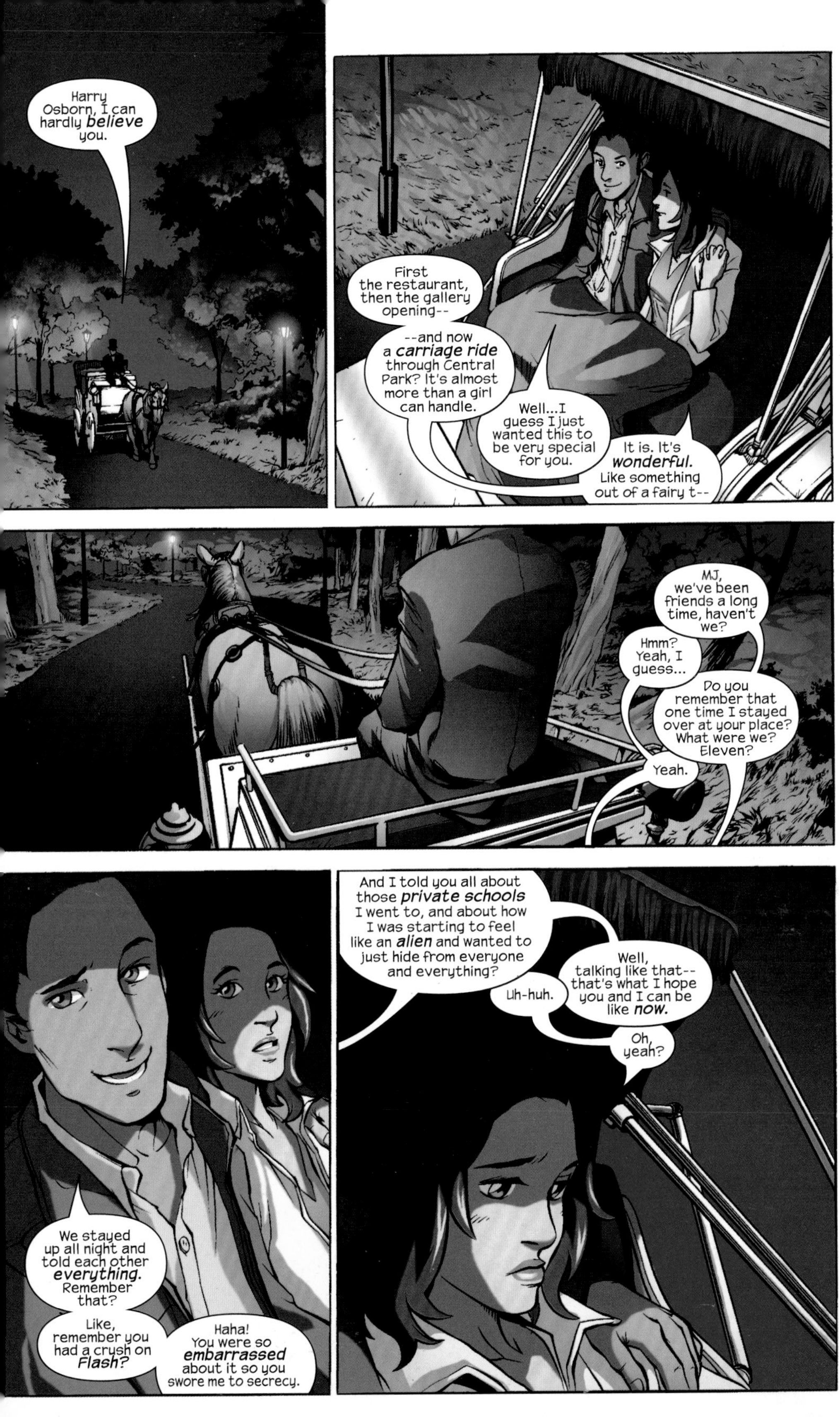
Harry Osborn, I can hardly *believe* you.
First the restaurant, then the gallery opening--
--and now a *carriage ride* through Central Park? It's almost more than a girl can handle.
Well...I guess I just wanted this to be very special for you.
It is. It's *wonderful.* Like something out of a fairy t--
MJ, we've been friends a long time, haven't we?
Hmm? Yeah, I guess...
Do you remember that one time I stayed over at your place? What were we? Eleven?
Yeah.
We stayed up all night and told each other *everything.* Remember that?
Like, remember you had a crush on *Flash?*
Haha! You were so *embarrassed* about it so you swore me to secrecy.
And I told you all about those *private schools* I went to, and about how I was starting to feel like an *alien* and wanted to just hide from everyone and everything?
Uh-huh.
Well, talking like that--that's what I hope you and I can be like *now.*
Oh, yeah?

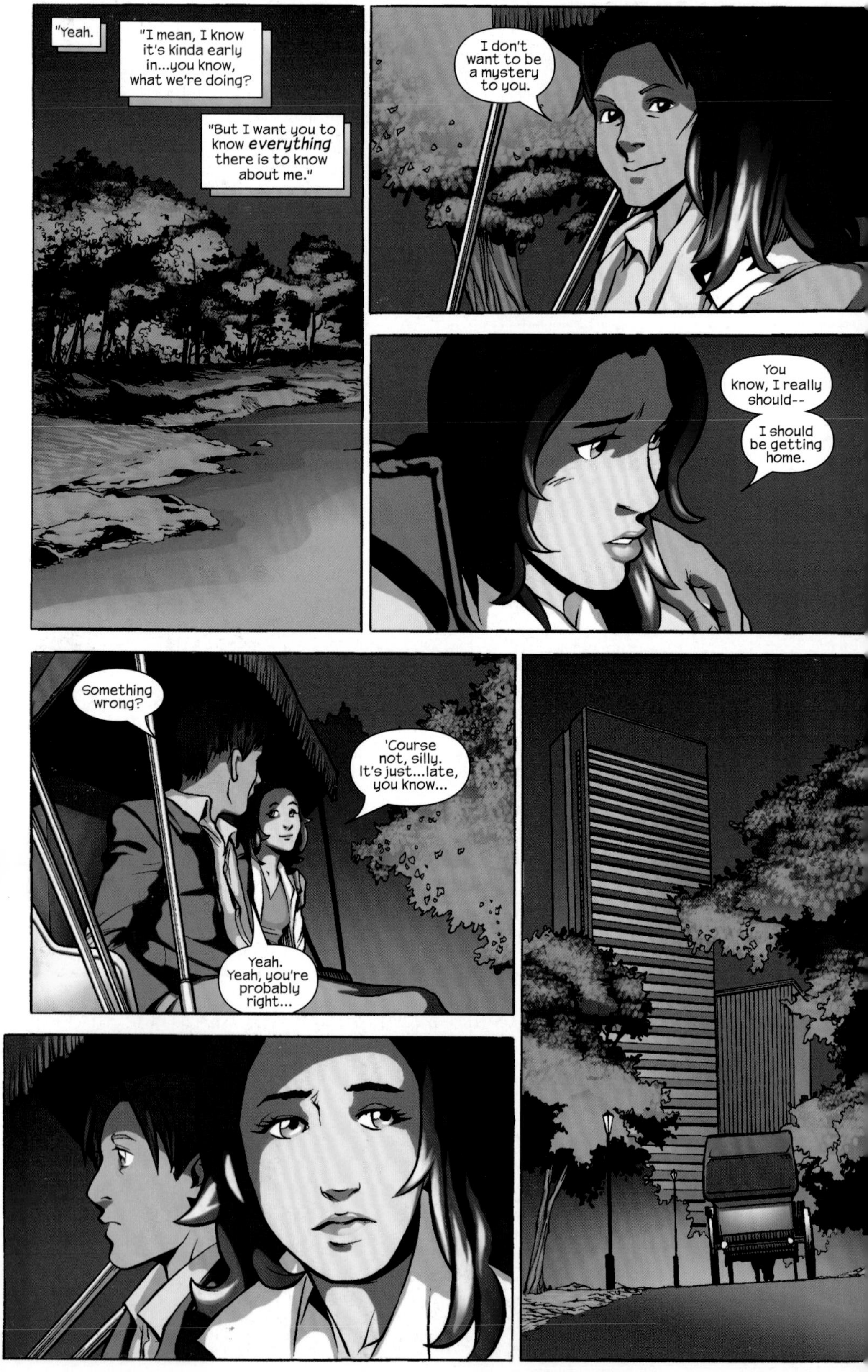
"Yeah.
"I mean, I know it's kinda early in...you know, what we're doing?
"But I want you to know *everything* there is to know about me."
I don't want to be a mystery to you.
You know, I really should--
I should be getting home.
Something wrong?
'Course not, silly. It's just...late, you know...
Yeah. Yeah, you're probably right...

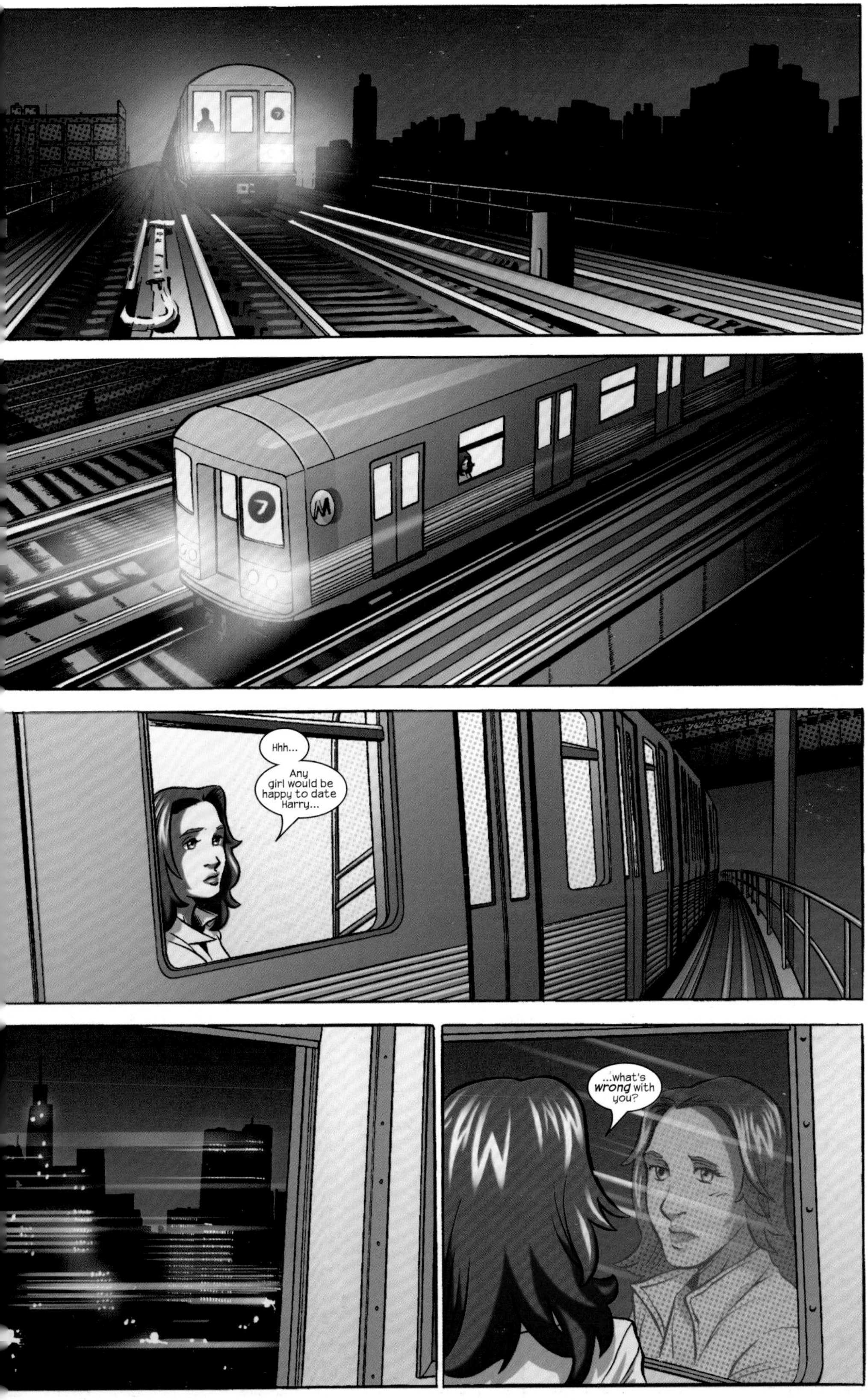
Hhh...
Any girl would be happy to date Harry...
...what's wrong with you?

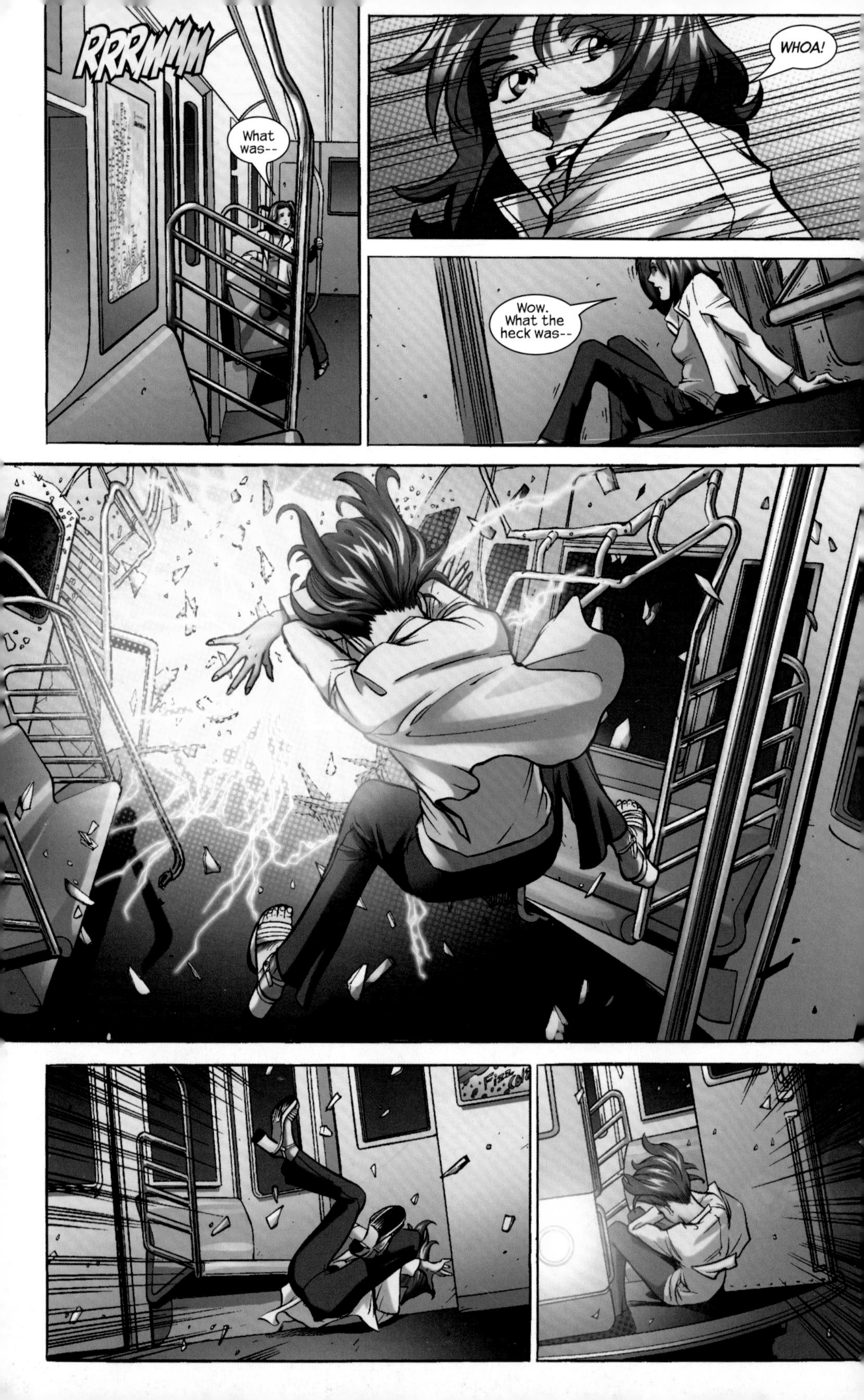
RRRMMM
What was--
WHOA!
Wow. What the heck was--

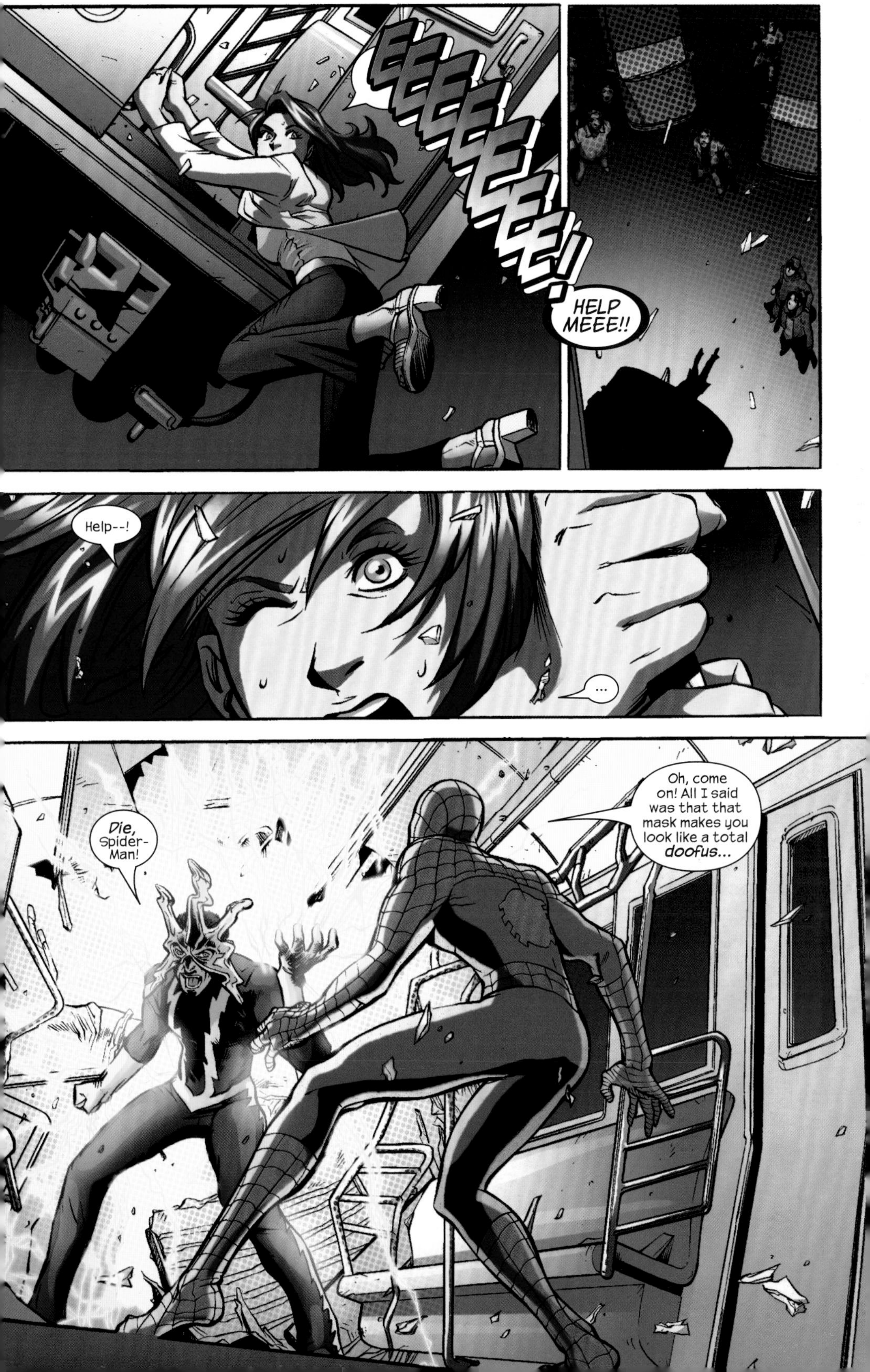
EEEEEEEEEE!!
HELP MEEE!!
Help--!
...
Die, Spider-Man!
Oh, come on! All I said was that that mask makes you look like a total doofus...

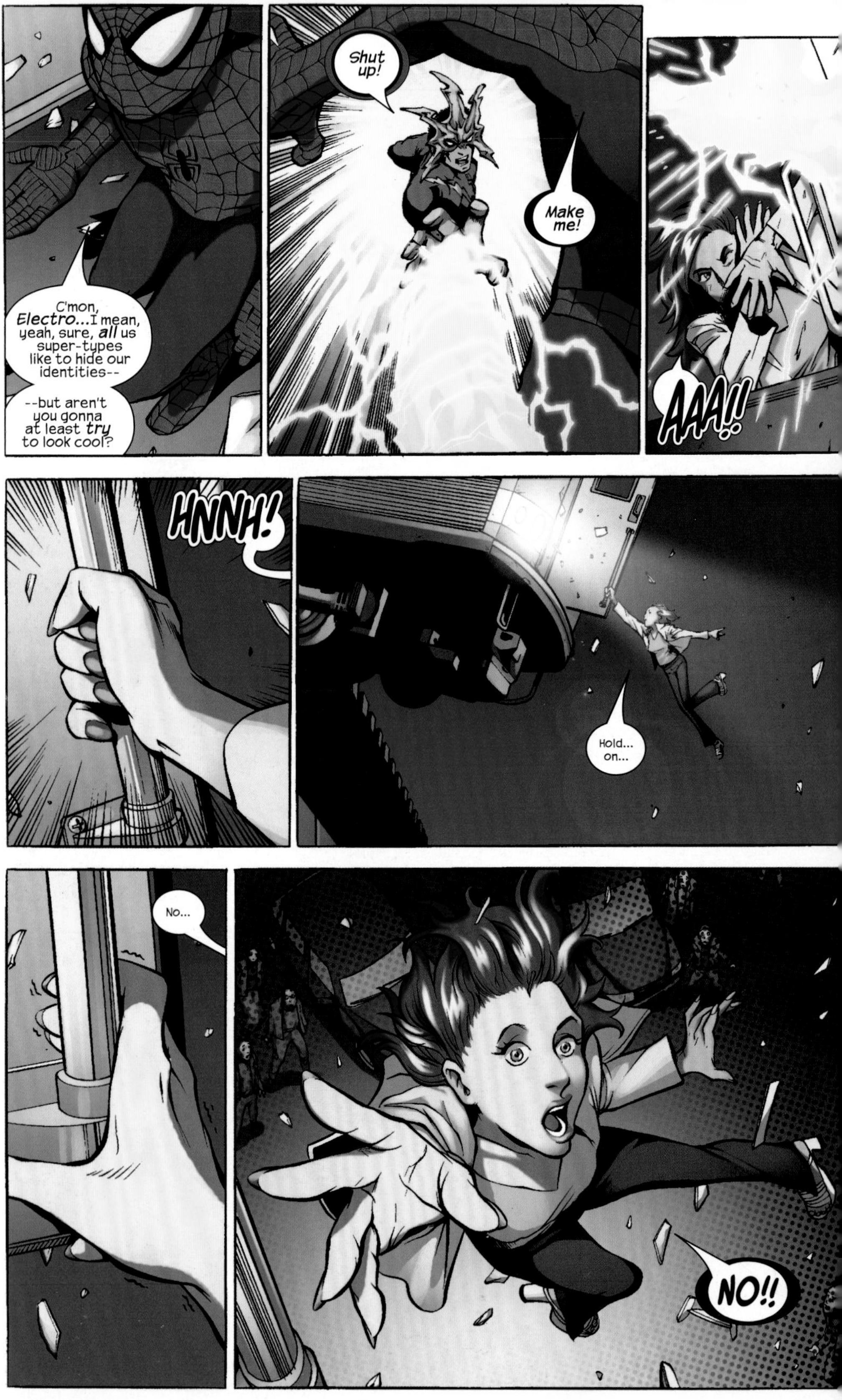
C'mon, Electro...I mean, yeah, sure, all us super-types like to hide our identities--
--but aren't you gonna at least try to look cool?
Shut up!
Make me!
AAA!!
HNNH!
Hold... on...
No...
NO!!

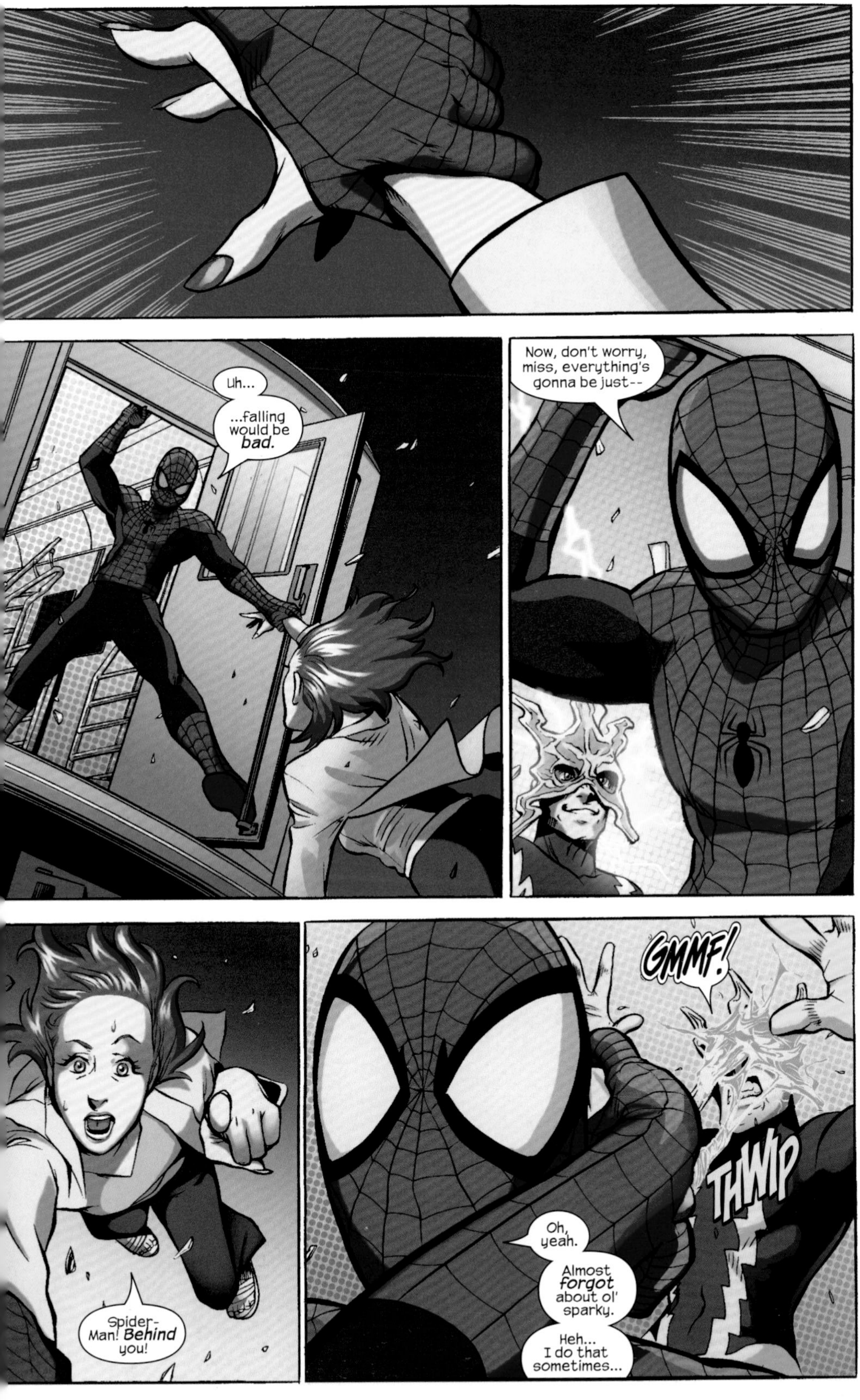
Uh...
...falling would be *bad.*
Now, don't worry, miss, everything's gonna be just--
Spider-Man! *Behind* you!
GMMF!
THWIP
Oh, yeah.
Almost *forgot* about ol' sparky.
Heh... I do that sometimes...

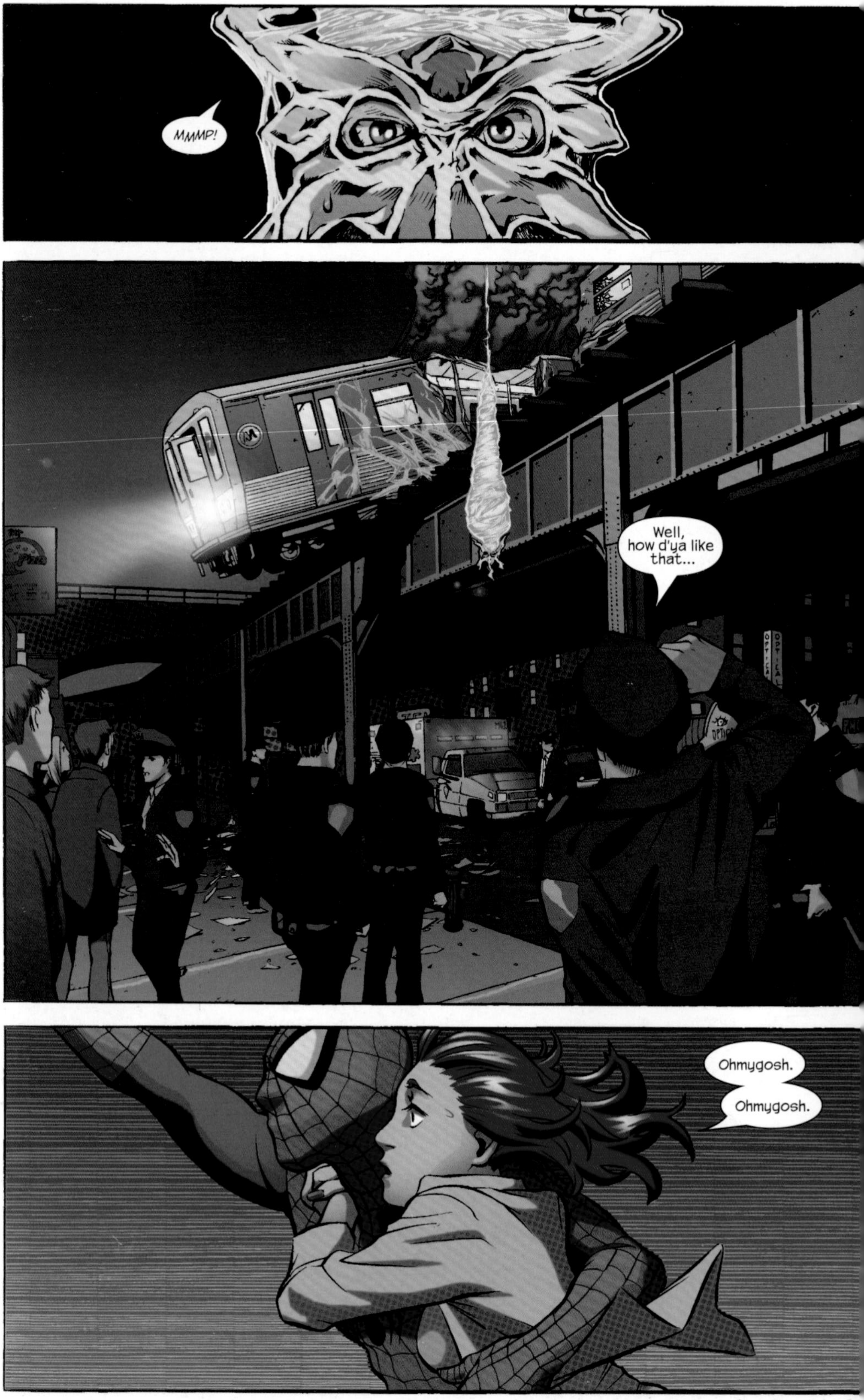
MMMP!
Well, how d'ya like that...
Ohmygosh.
Ohmygosh.

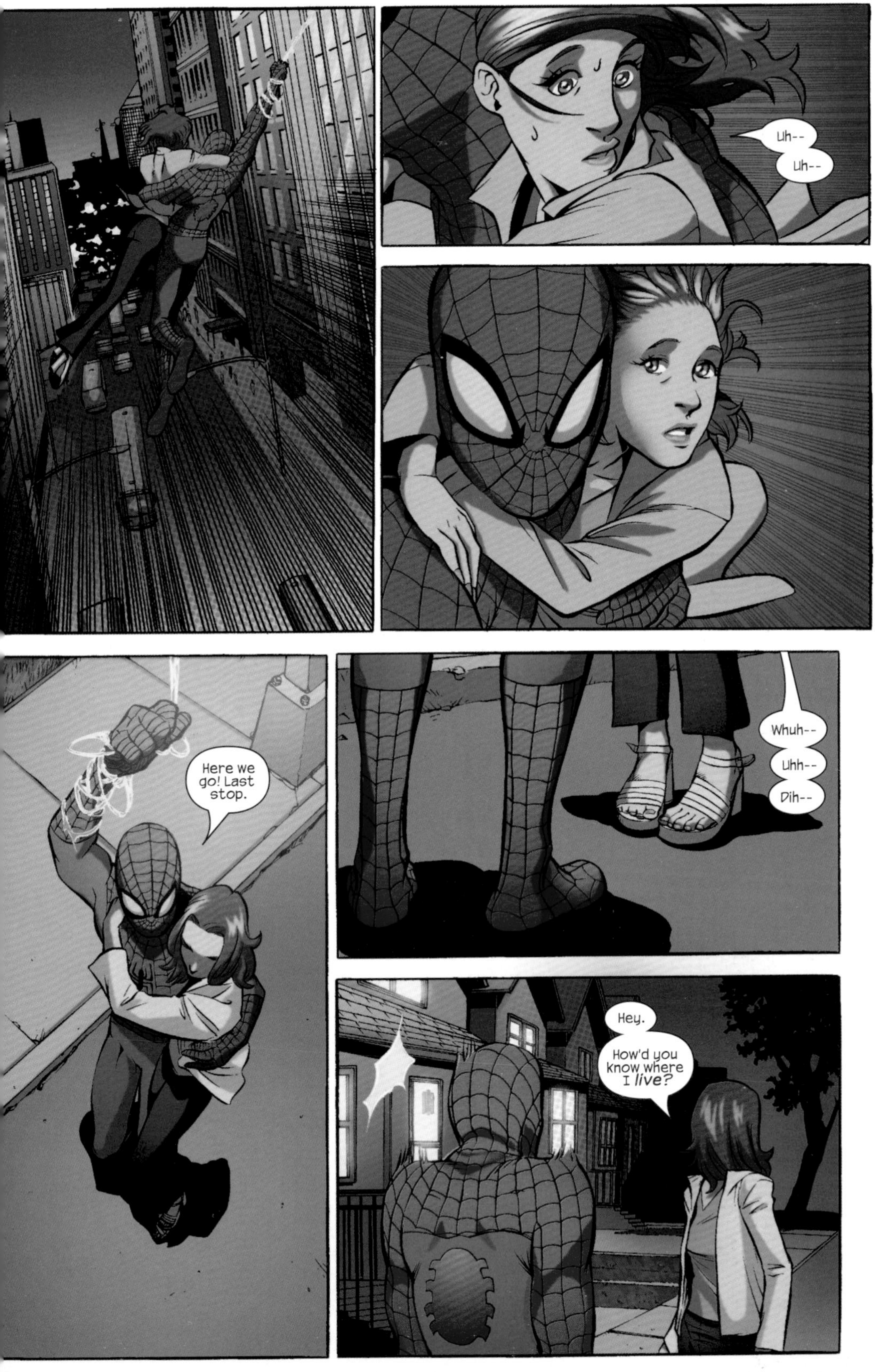
Uh--
Uh--
Here we go! Last stop.
Whuh--
Uhh--
Dih--
Hey.
How'd you know where I *live?*

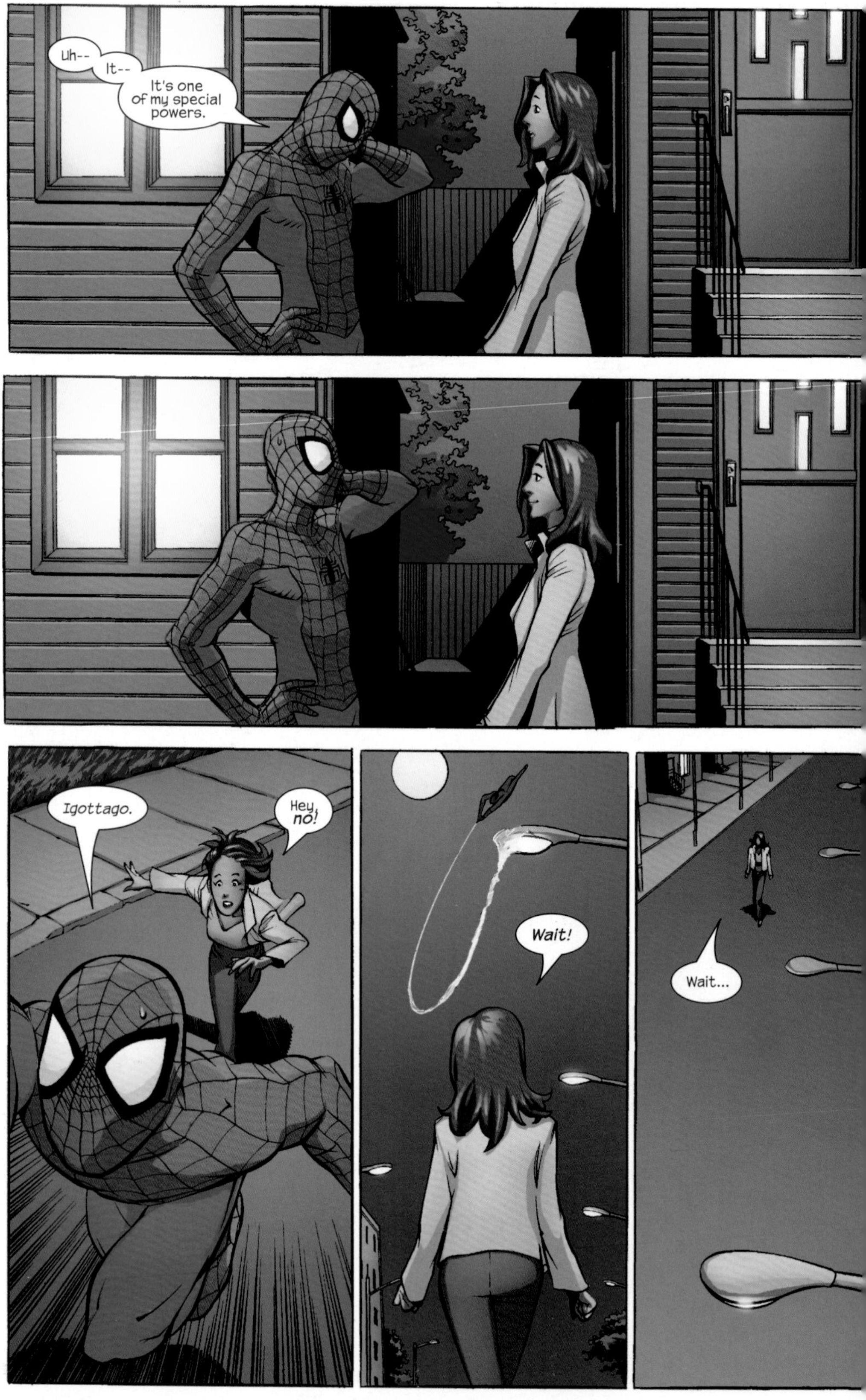
Uh--
It--
It's one of my special powers.
Igottago.
Hey, no!
Wait!
Wait...

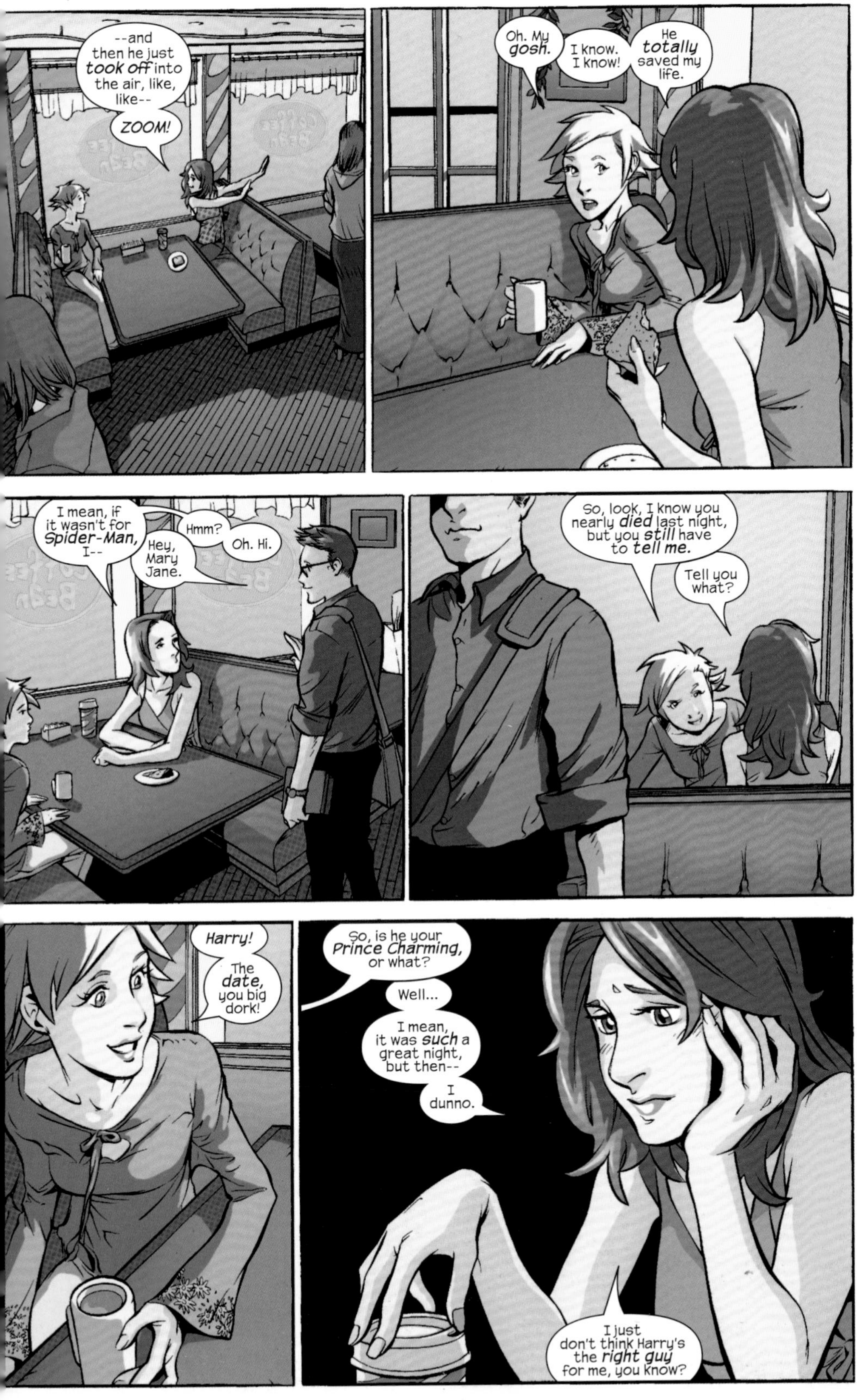
--and then he just took off into the air, like, like--
ZOOM!
Oh. My gosh.
I know. I know!
He totally saved my life.
I mean, if it wasn't for Spider-Man, I--
Hmm?
Hey, Mary Jane.
Oh. Hi.
So, look, I know you nearly died last night, but you still have to tell me.
Tell you what?
Harry!
The date, you big dork!
So, is he your Prince Charming, or what?
Well...
I mean, it was such a great night, but then--
I dunno.
I just don't think Harry's the right guy for me, you know?

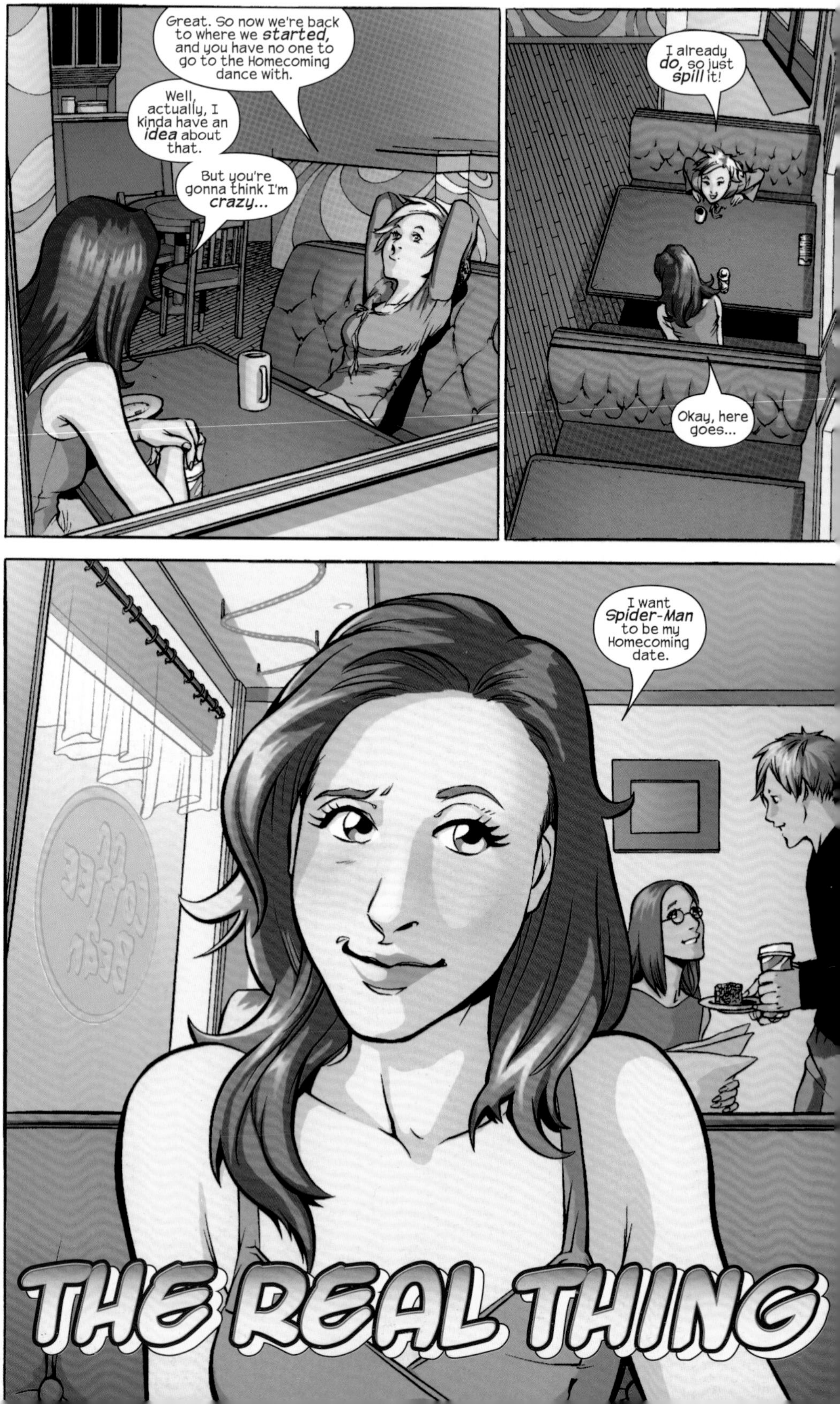
Great. So now we're back to where we *started,* and you have no one to go to the Homecoming dance with.
Well, actually, I kinda have an *idea* about that.
But you're gonna think I'm *crazy...*
I already *do,* so just *spill* it!
Okay, here goes...
I want *Spider-Man* to be my Homecoming date.
THE REAL THING

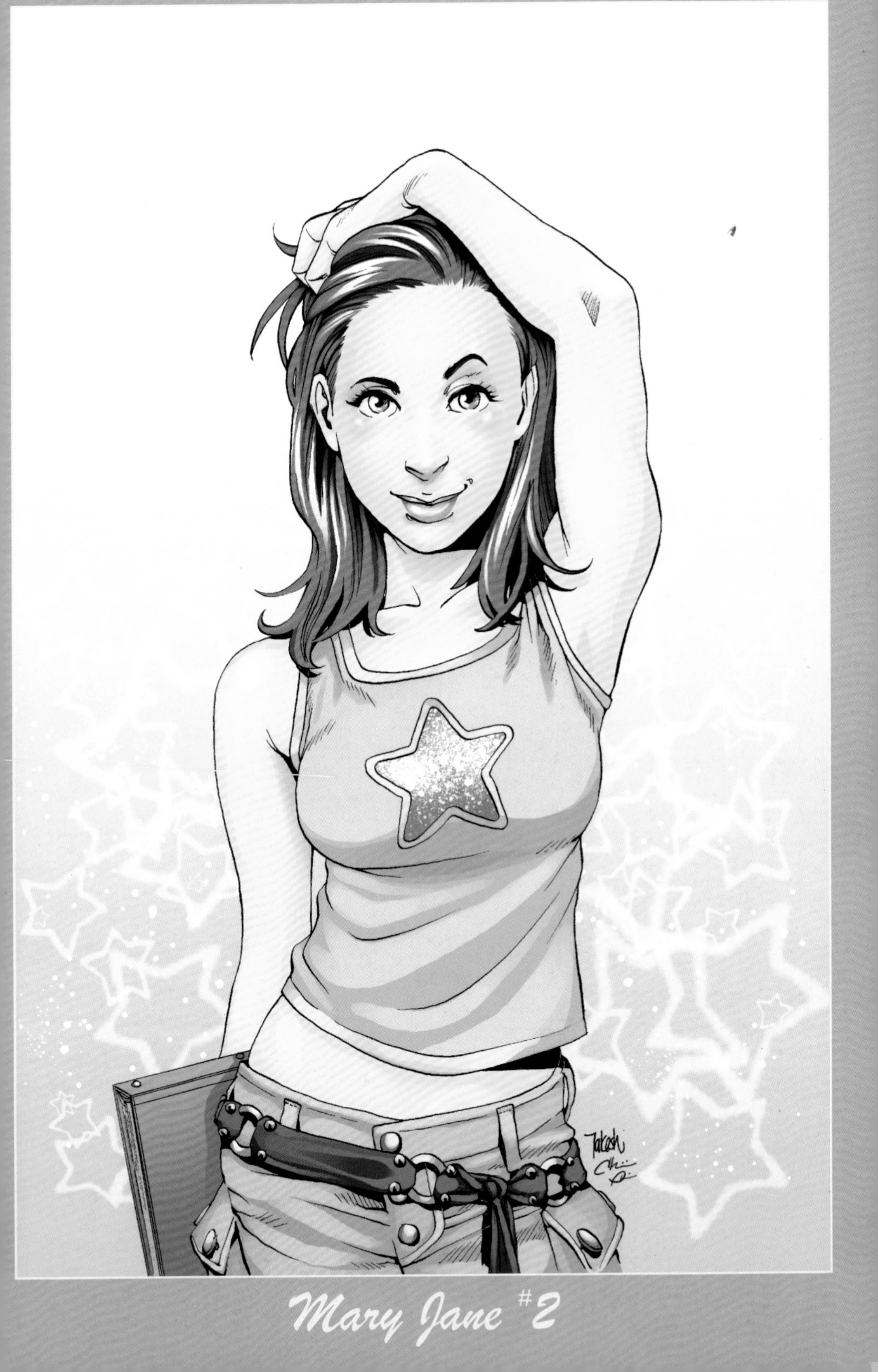

Mary Jane #2

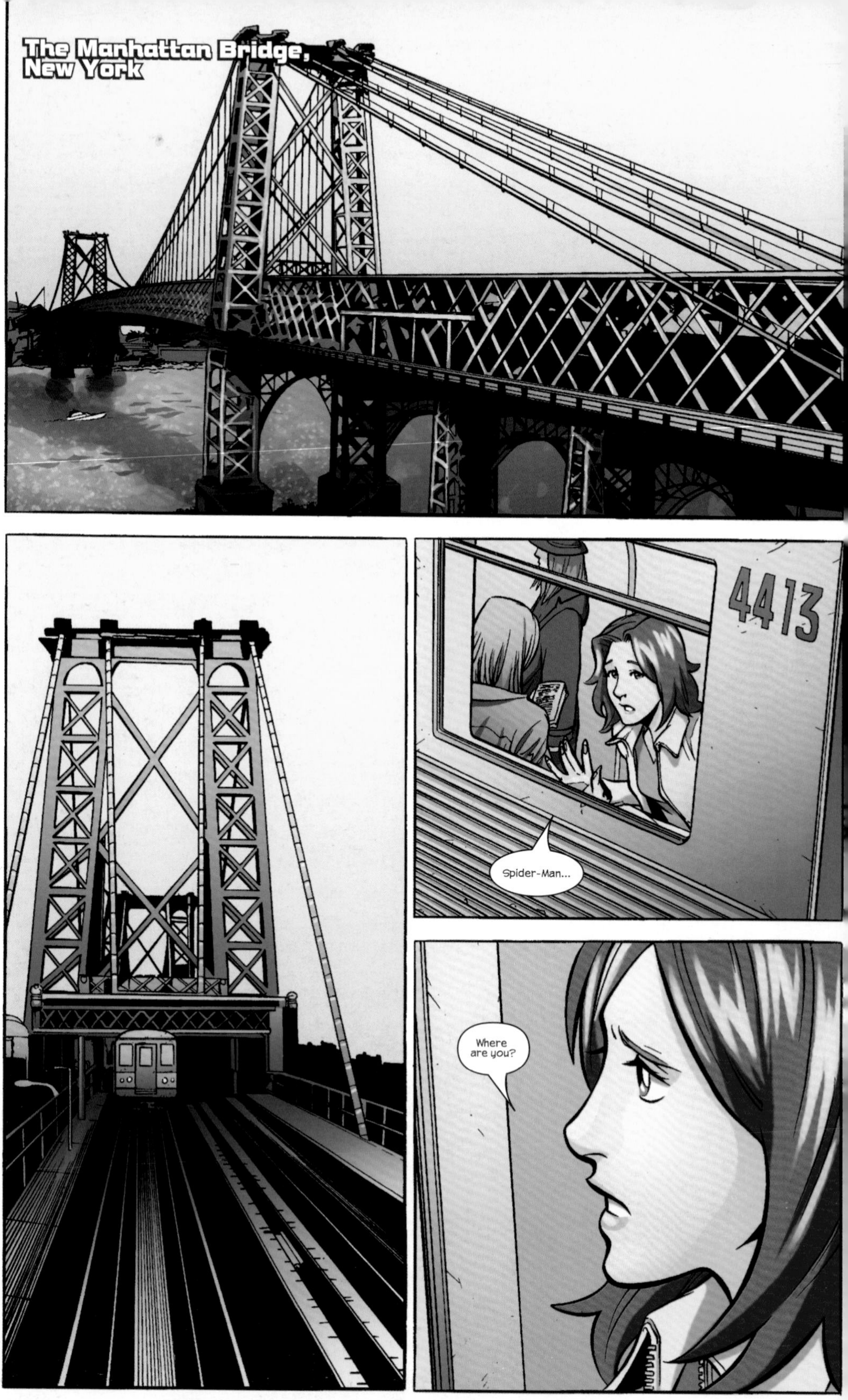
The Manhattan Bridge, New York
4413
Spider-Man...
Where are you?

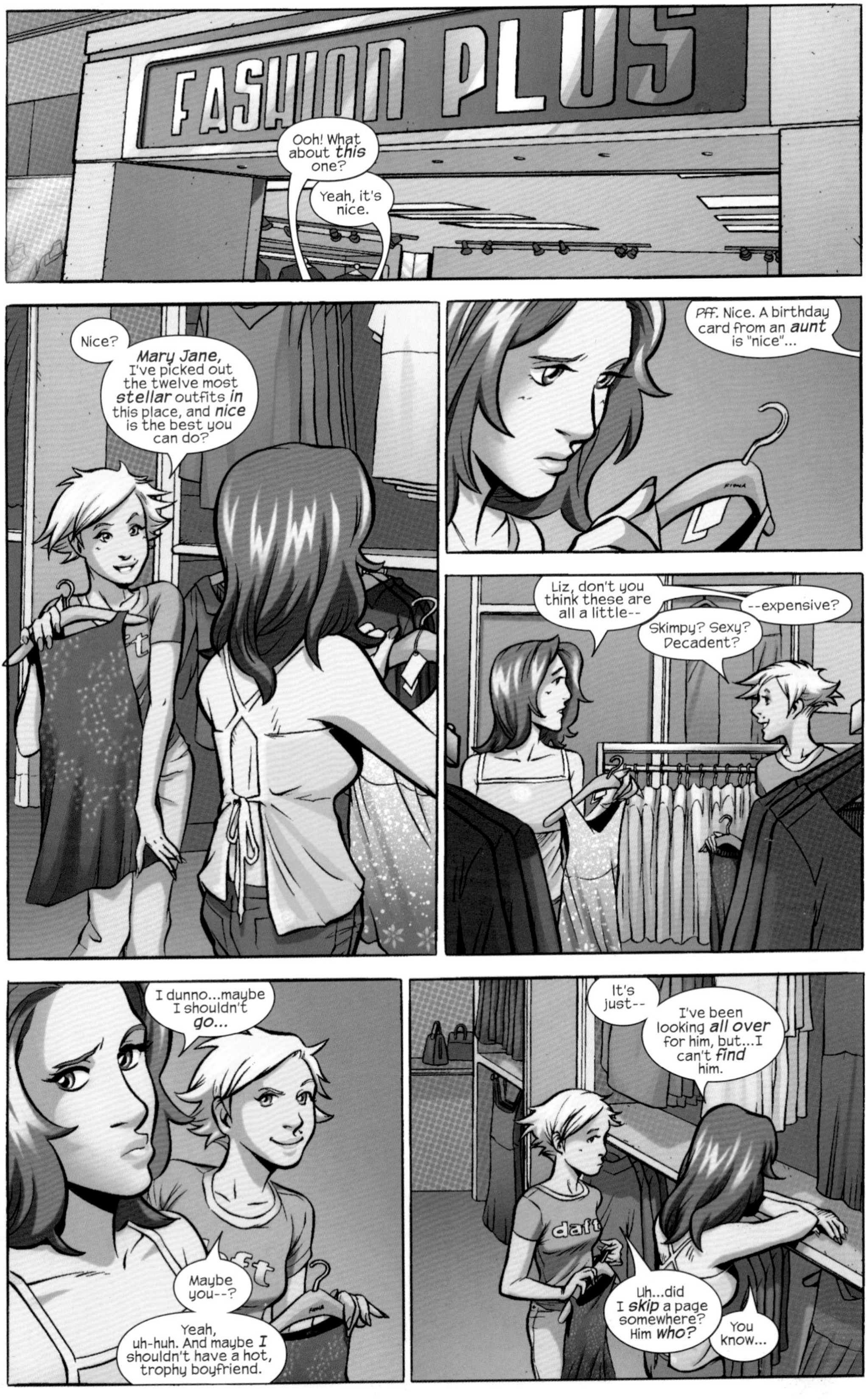
FASHION PLUS
Ooh! What about this one?
Yeah, it's nice.
Nice?
Mary Jane, I've picked out the twelve most stellar outfits in this place, and nice is the best you can do?
Pff. Nice. A birthday card from an aunt is "nice"...
Liz, don't you think these are all a little--
--expensive?
Skimpy? Sexy? Decadent?
I dunno...maybe I shouldn't go...
Maybe you--?
Yeah, uh-huh. And maybe I shouldn't have a hot, trophy boyfriend.
It's just--
I've been looking all over for him, but...I can't find him.
Uh...did I skip a page somewhere? Him who?
You know...

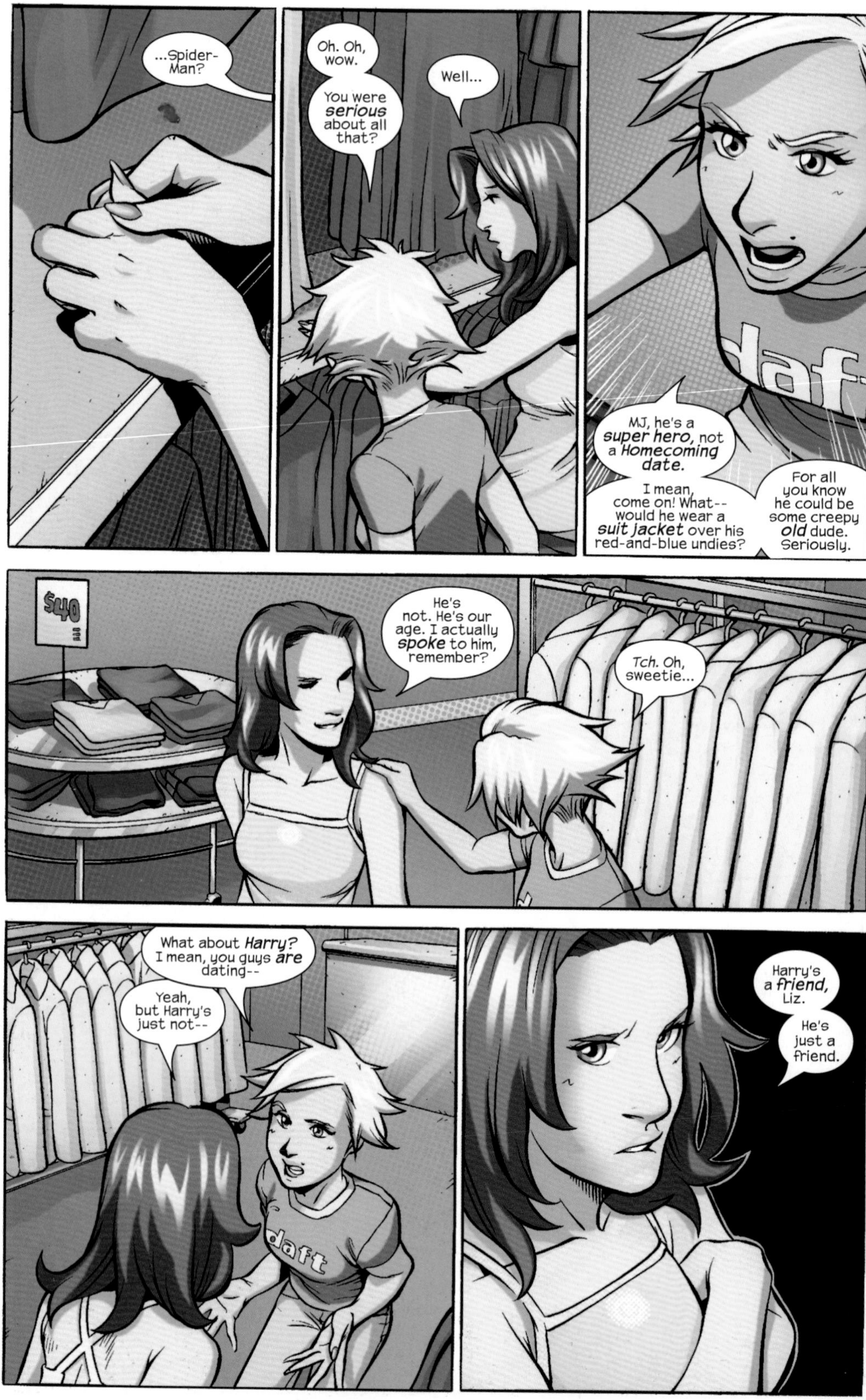
...Spider-Man?
Oh. Oh, wow.
You were serious about all that?
Well...
MJ, he's a super hero, not a Homecoming date.
I mean, come on! What--would he wear a suit jacket over his red-and-blue undies?
For all you know he could be some creepy old dude. Seriously.
$40
He's not. He's our age. I actually spoke to him, remember?
Tch. Oh, sweetie...
What about Harry? I mean, you guys are dating--
Yeah, but Harry's just not--
daft
Harry's a friend, Liz.
He's just a friend.

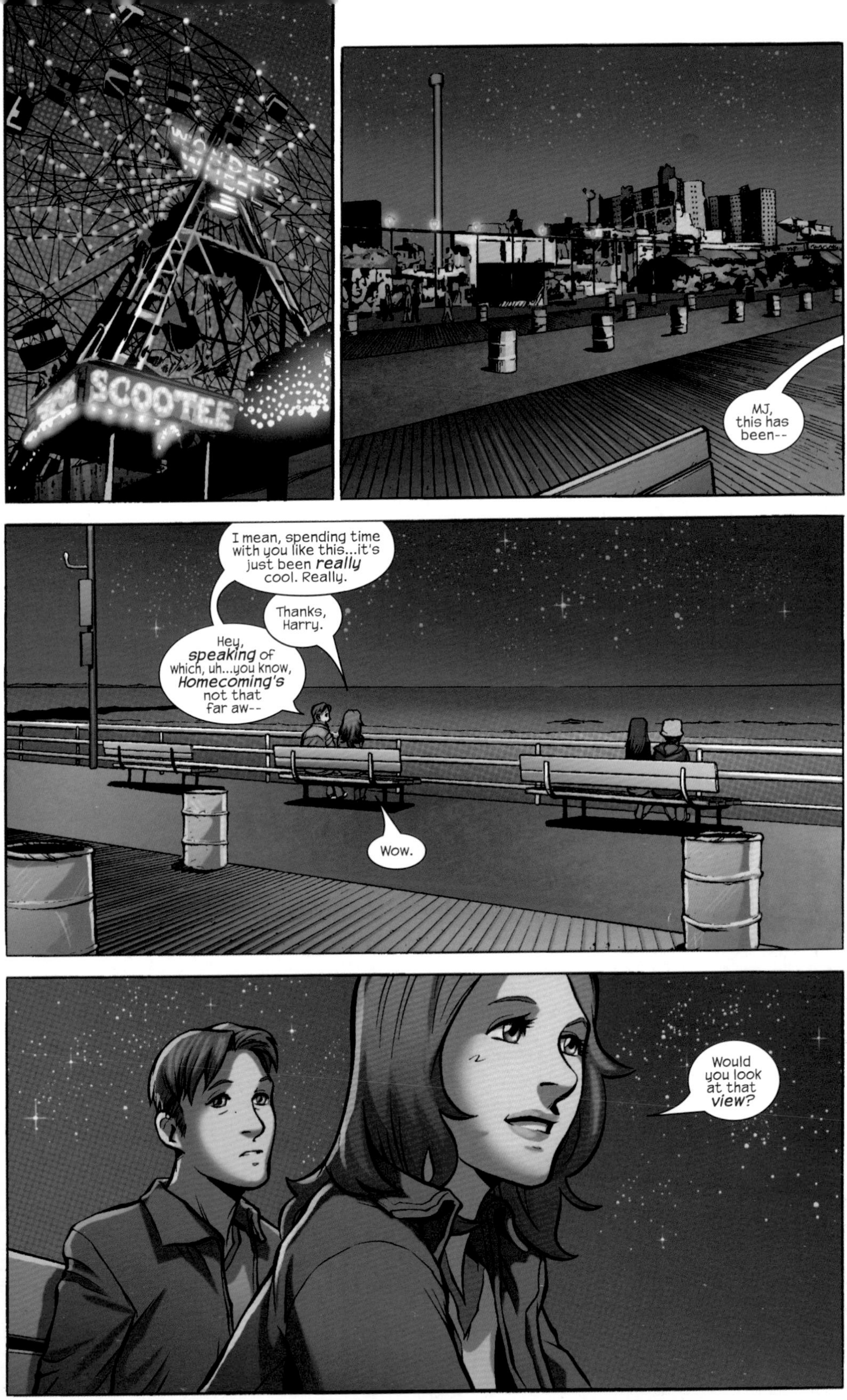

MJ, this has been--
I mean, spending time with you like this...it's just been *really* cool. Really.
Thanks, Harry.
Hey, *speaking* of which, uh...you know, *Homecoming's* not that far aw--
Wow.
Would you look at that *view?*

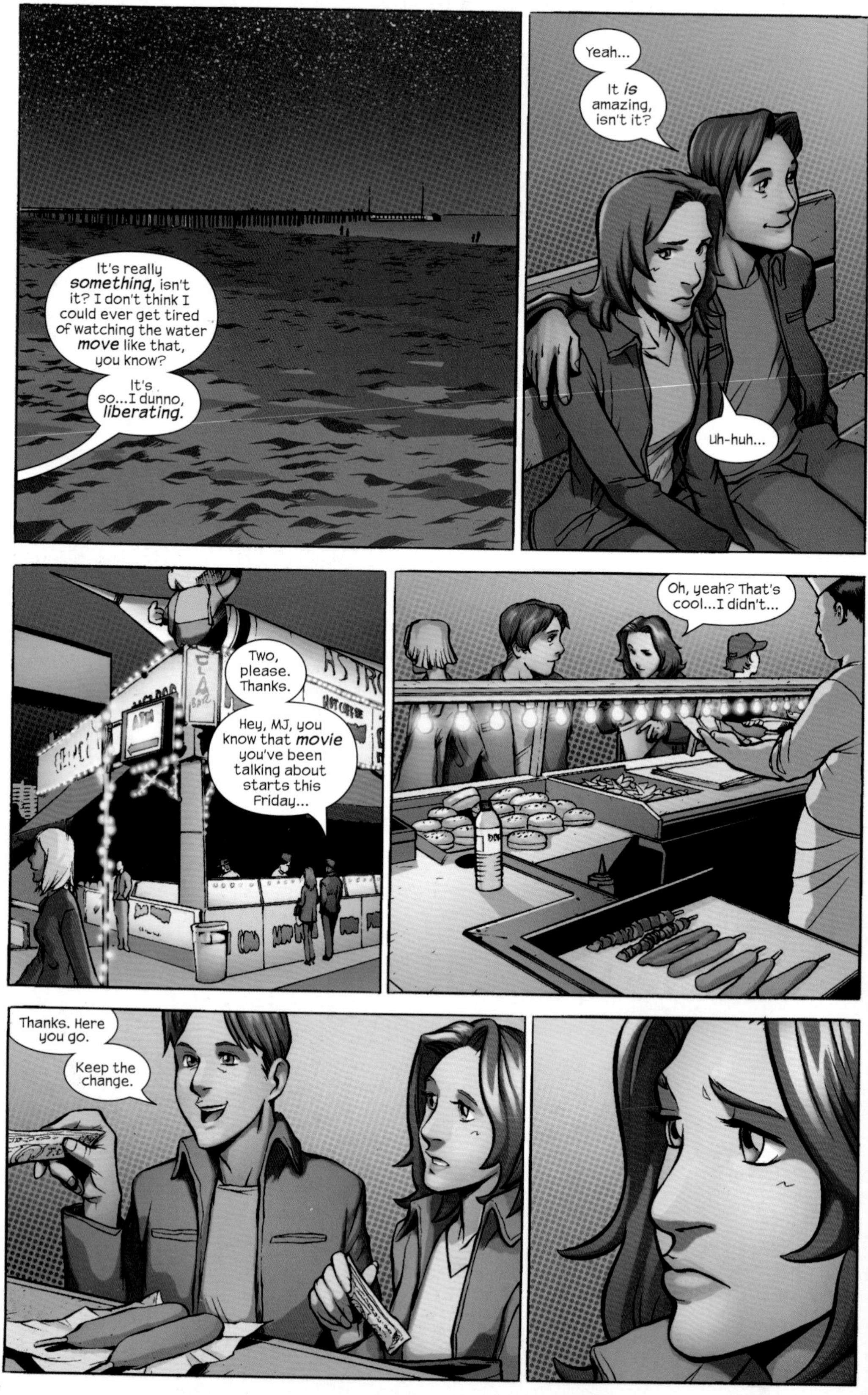
It's really something, isn't it? I don't think I could ever get tired of watching the water move like that, you know?
It's so...I dunno, liberating.
Yeah...
It is amazing, isn't it?
Uh-huh...
Two, please. Thanks.
Hey, MJ, you know that movie you've been talking about starts this Friday...
Oh, yeah? That's cool...I didn't...
Thanks. Here you go.
Keep the change.

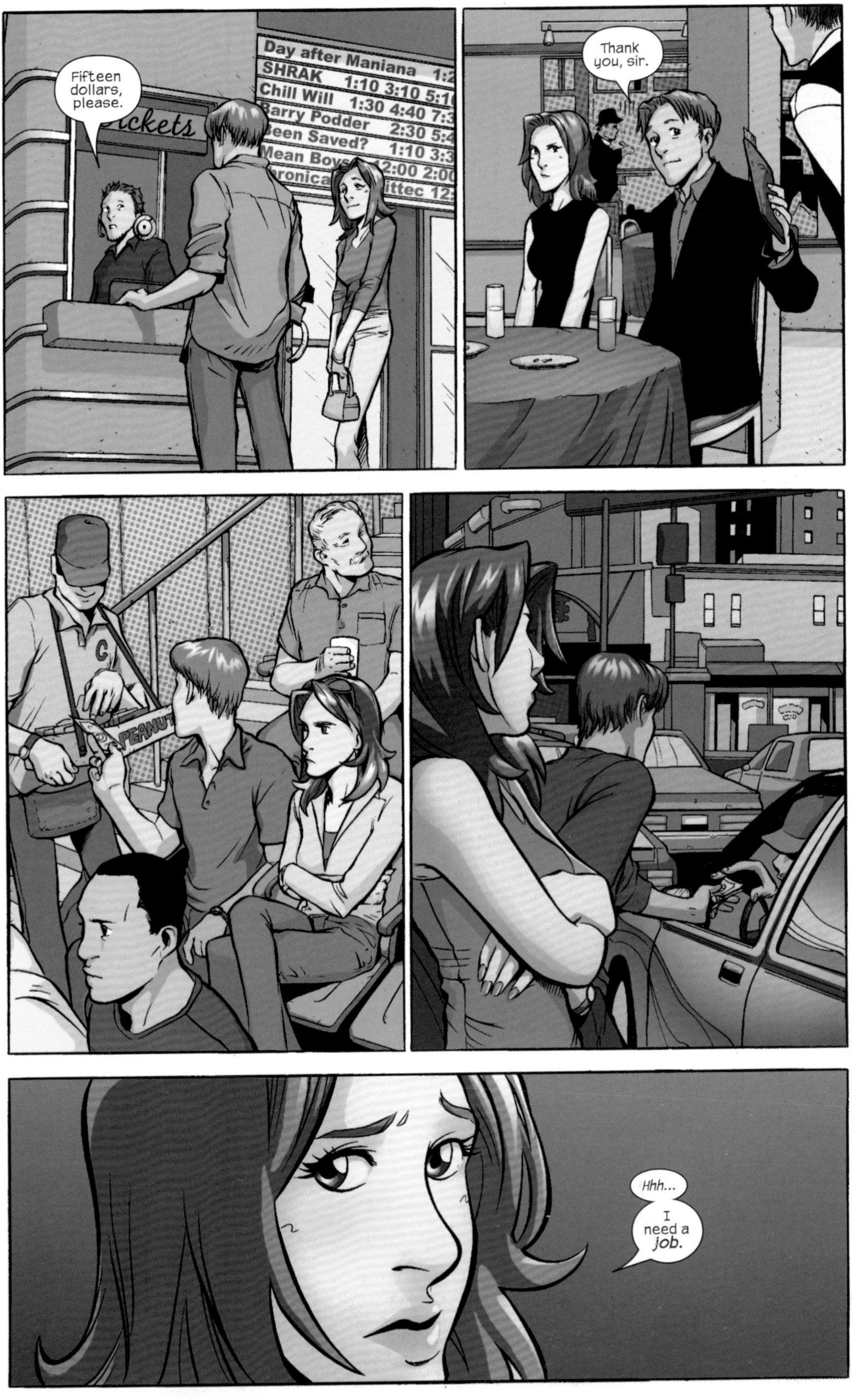
Fifteen dollars, please.
Day after Maniana
SHRAK 1:10 3:10
Chill Will 1:30 4:40
Barry Podder 2:30
Been Saved? 1:10
Thank you, sir.
PEANUT
Hhh...
I need a *job.*

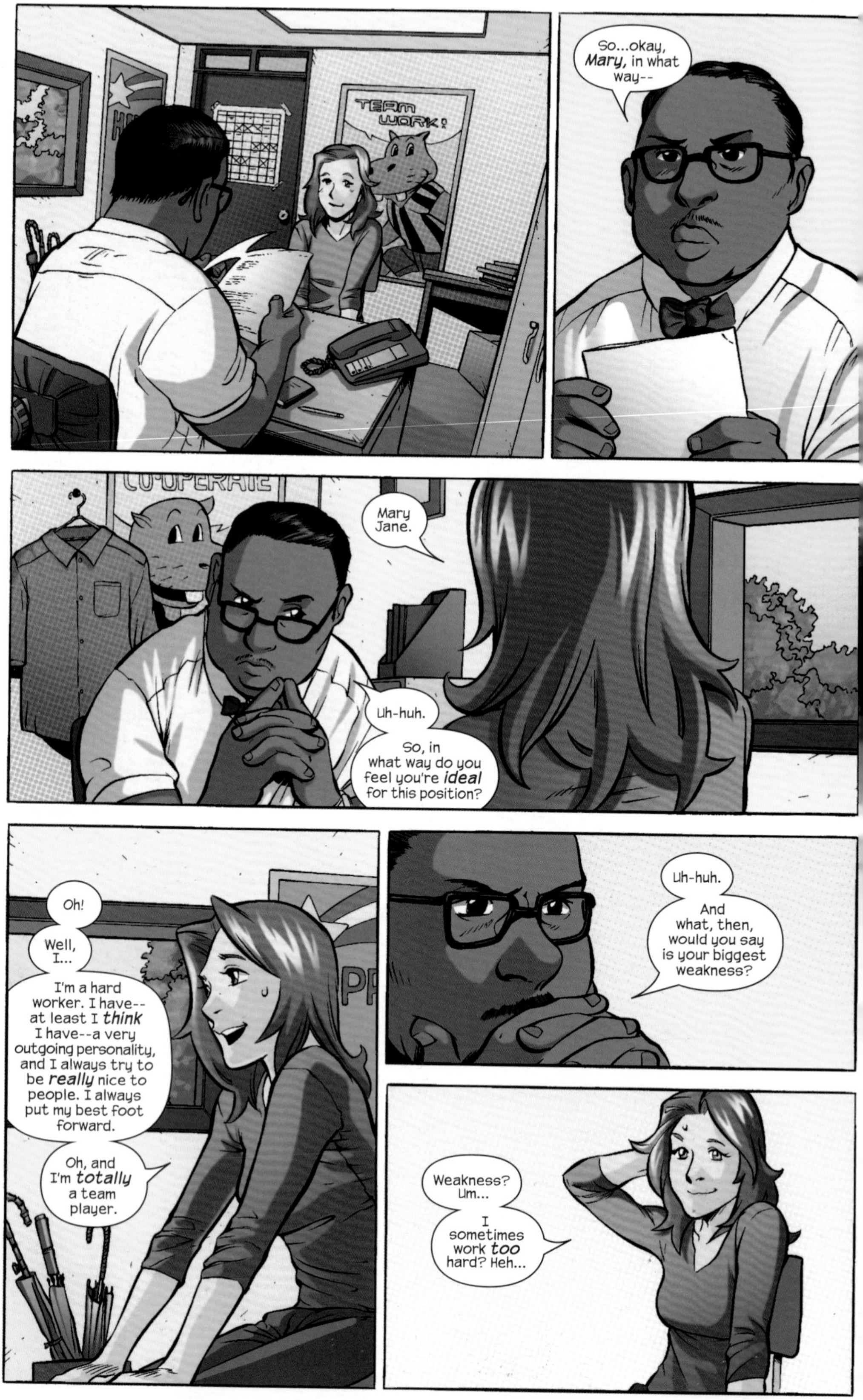
TEAM WORK!
So...okay, Mary, in what way--
CO-OPERATE
Mary Jane.
Uh-huh.
So, in what way do you feel you're ideal for this position?
Oh!
Well, I...
I'm a hard worker. I have--at least I think I have--a very outgoing personality, and I always try to be really nice to people. I always put my best foot forward.
Oh, and I'm totally a team player.
Uh-huh.
And what, then, would you say is your biggest weakness?
Weakness? Um...
I sometimes work too hard? Heh...

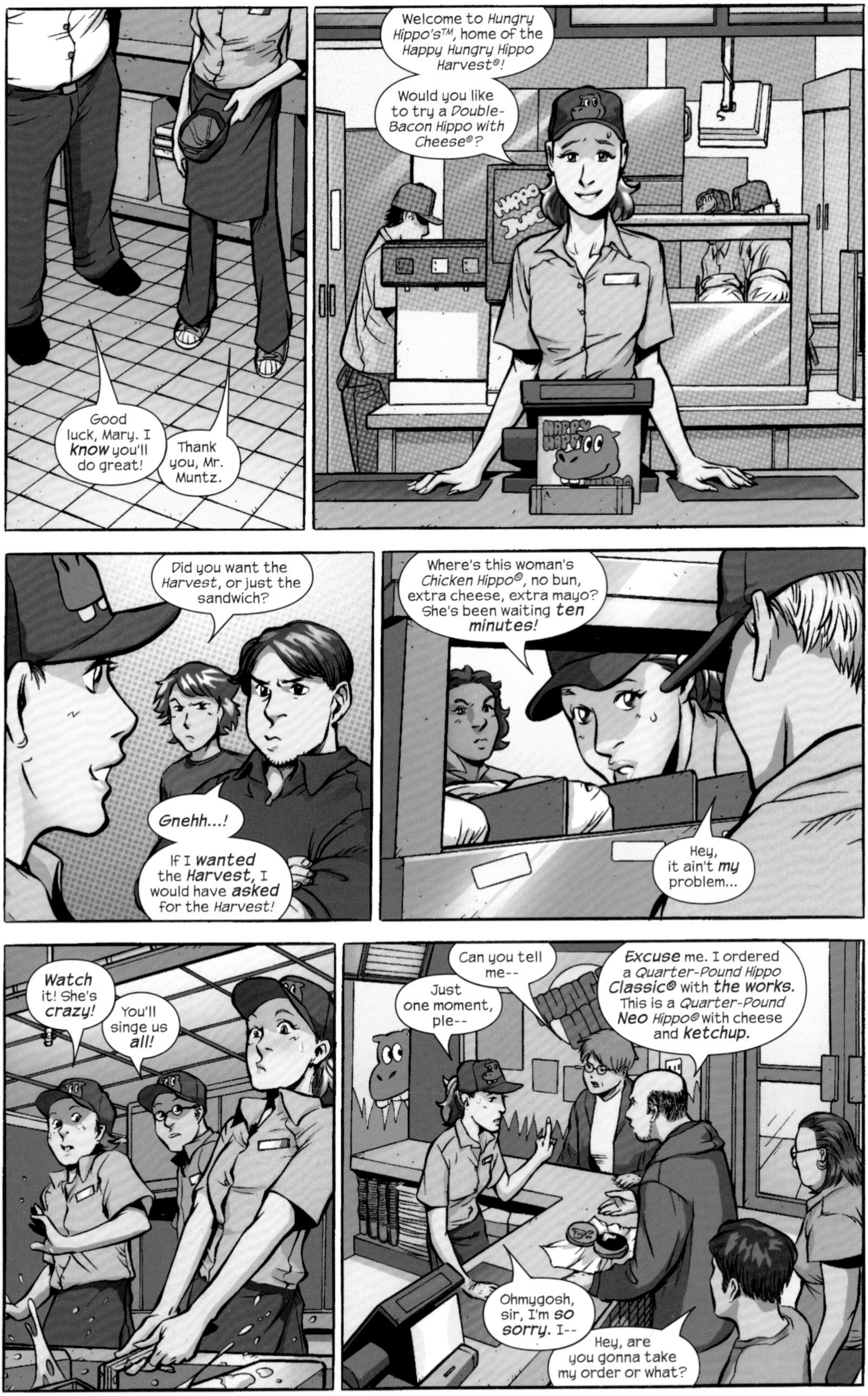
Good luck, Mary. I KNOW you'll do great!
Thank you, Mr. Muntz.
Welcome to Hungry Hippo's™, home of the Happy Hungry Hippo Harvest®!
Would you like to try a Double-Bacon Hippo with Cheese®?
HAPPY HIPPO
Did you want the Harvest, or just the sandwich?
Gnehh...!
If I wanted the Harvest, I would have asked for the Harvest!
Where's this woman's Chicken Hippo®, no bun, extra cheese, extra mayo? She's been waiting ten minutes!
Hey, it ain't my problem...
Watch it! She's crazy!
You'll singe us all!
Just one moment, ple--
Can you tell me--
Excuse me. I ordered a Quarter-Pound Hippo Classic® with the works. This is a Quarter-Pound Neo Hippo® with cheese and ketchup.
Ohmygosh, sir, I'm so sorry. I--
Hey, are you gonna take my order or what?

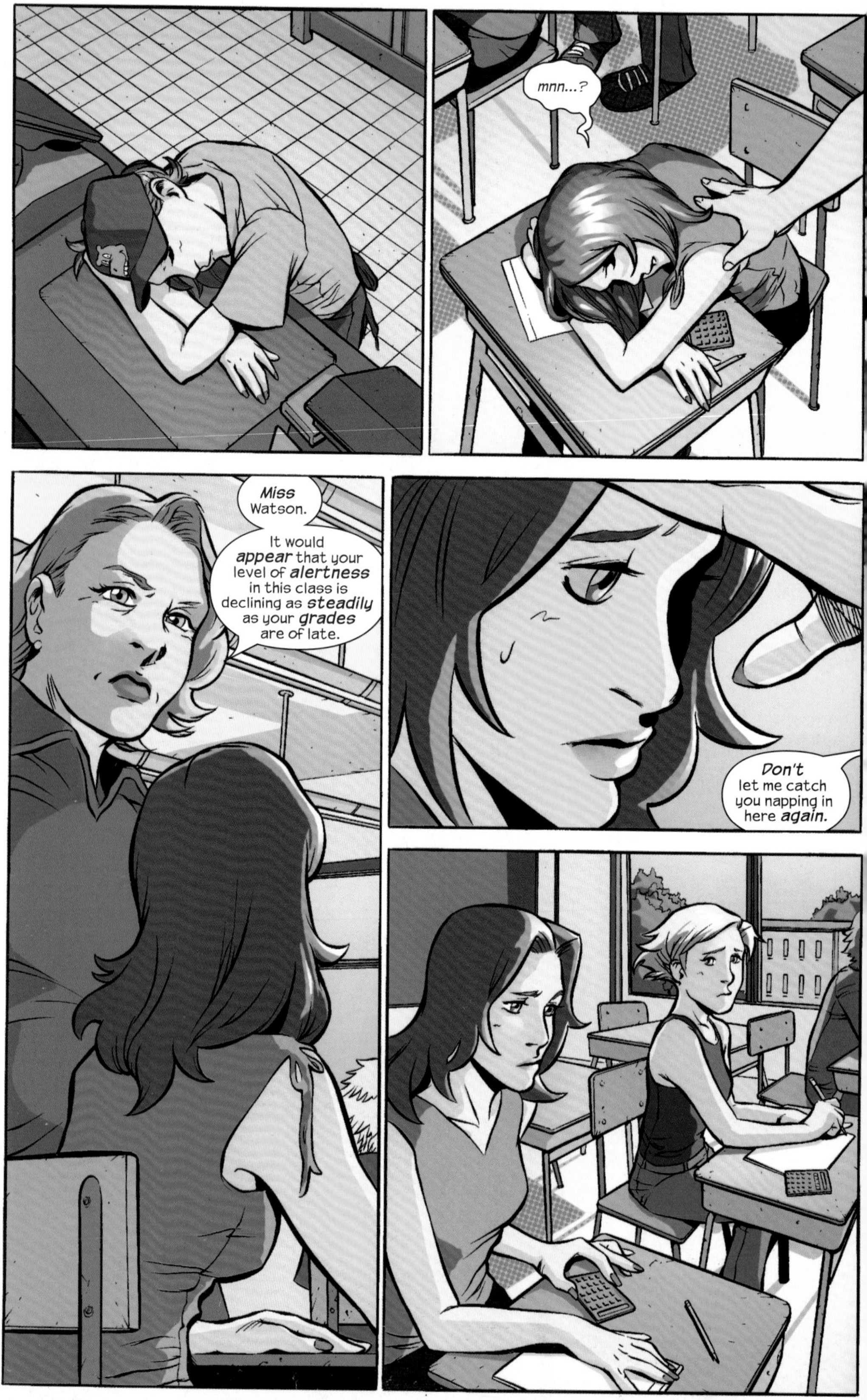
mnn...?
Miss Watson.
It would appear that your level of alertness in this class is declining as steadily as your grades are of late.
Don't let me catch you napping in here again.

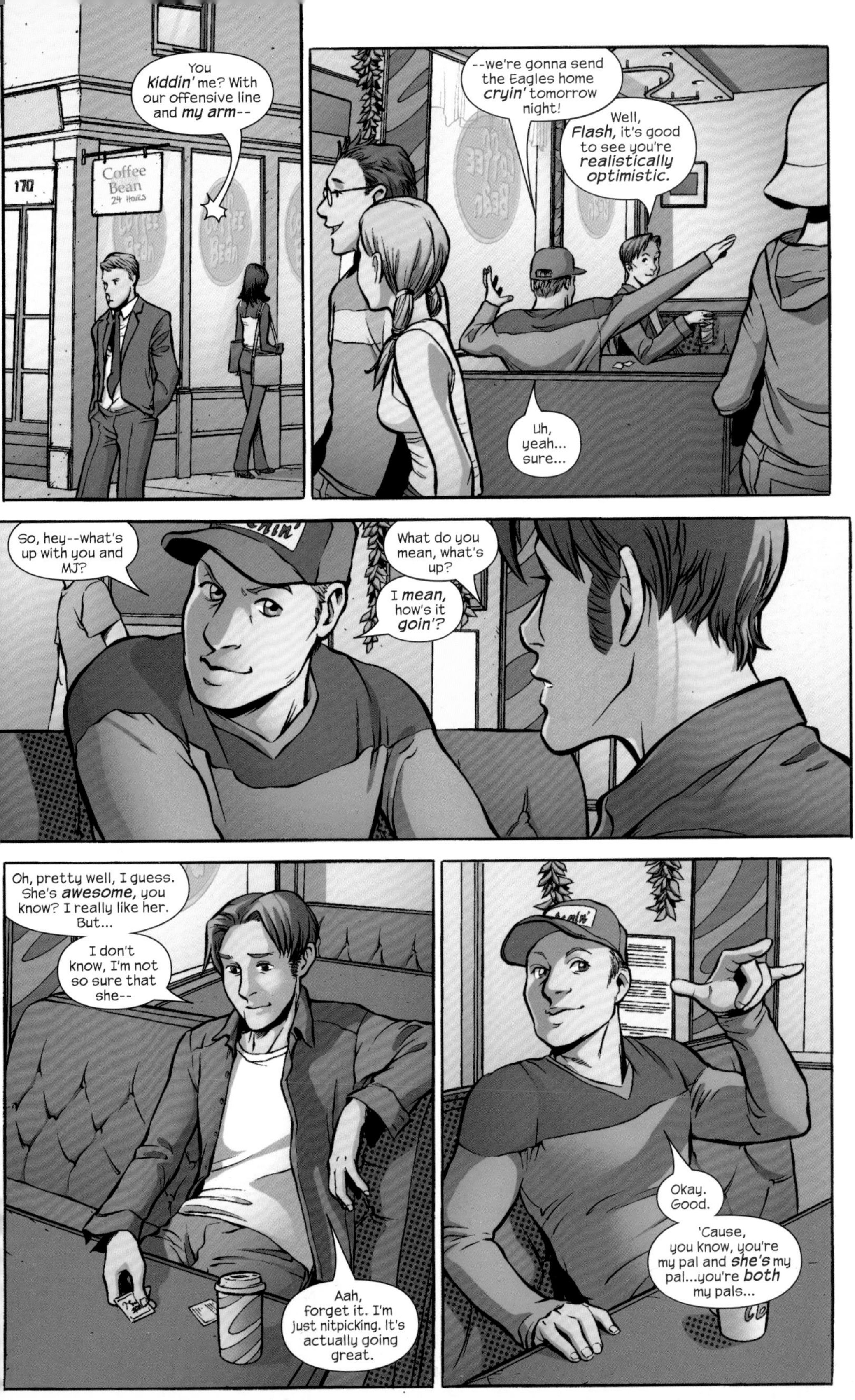
You kiddin' me? With our offensive line and my arm--
170
Coffee Bean 24 Hours
--we're gonna send the Eagles home cryin' tomorrow night!
Well, Flash, it's good to see you're realistically optimistic.
Uh, yeah... sure...
So, hey--what's up with you and MJ?
What do you mean, what's up?
I mean, how's it goin'?
Oh, pretty well, I guess. She's awesome, you know? I really like her. But...
I don't know, I'm not so sure that she--
Aah, forget it. I'm just nitpicking. It's actually going great.
Okay. Good.
'Cause, you know, you're my pal and she's my pal...you're both my pals...

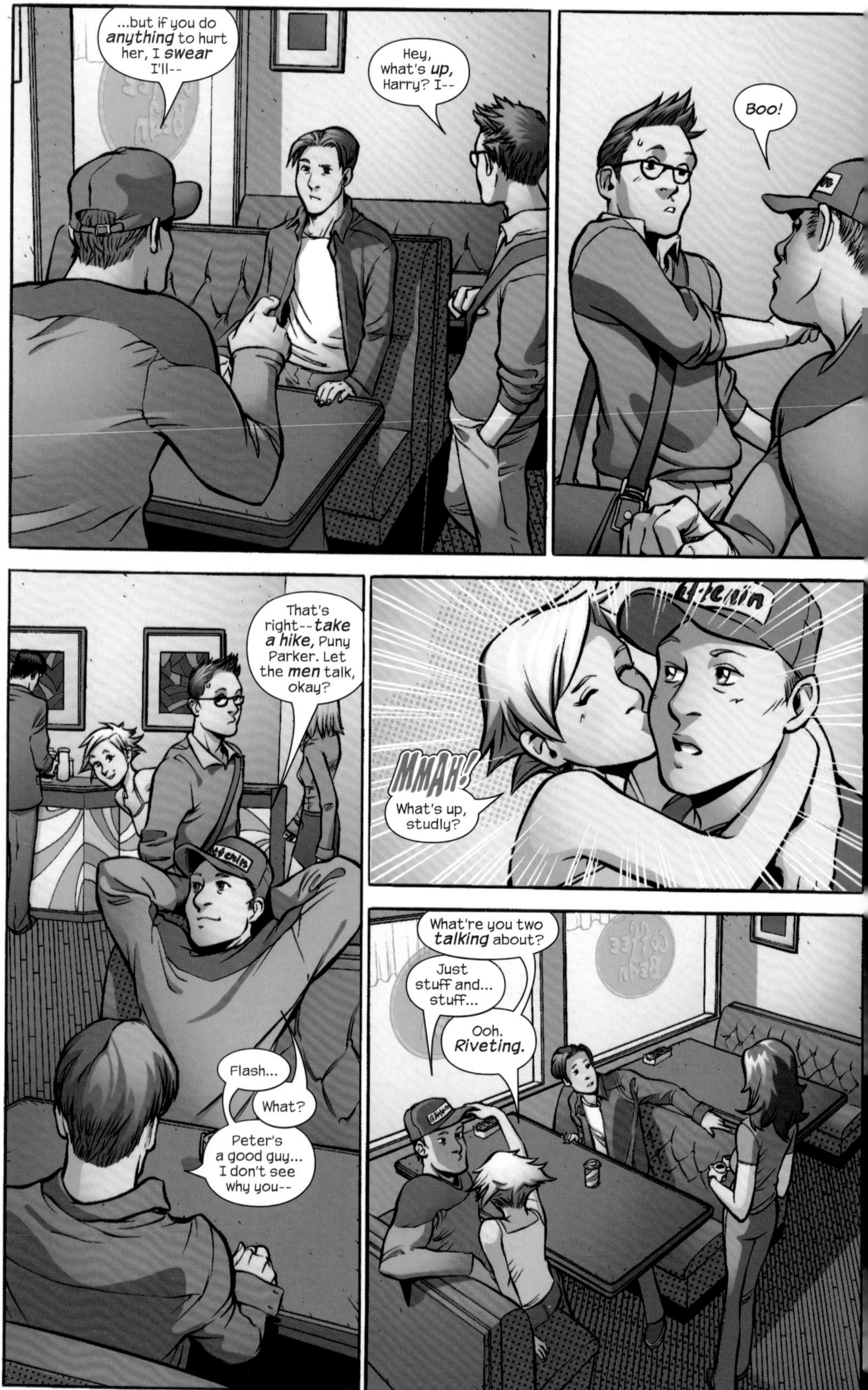

...but if you do anything to hurt her, I swear I'll--
Hey, what's up, Harry? I--
Boo!
That's right--take a hike, Puny Parker. Let the men talk, okay?
Flash...
What?
Peter's a good guy... I don't see why you--
MMAH!
What's up, studly?
What're you two talking about?
Just stuff and... stuff...
Ooh. Riveting.

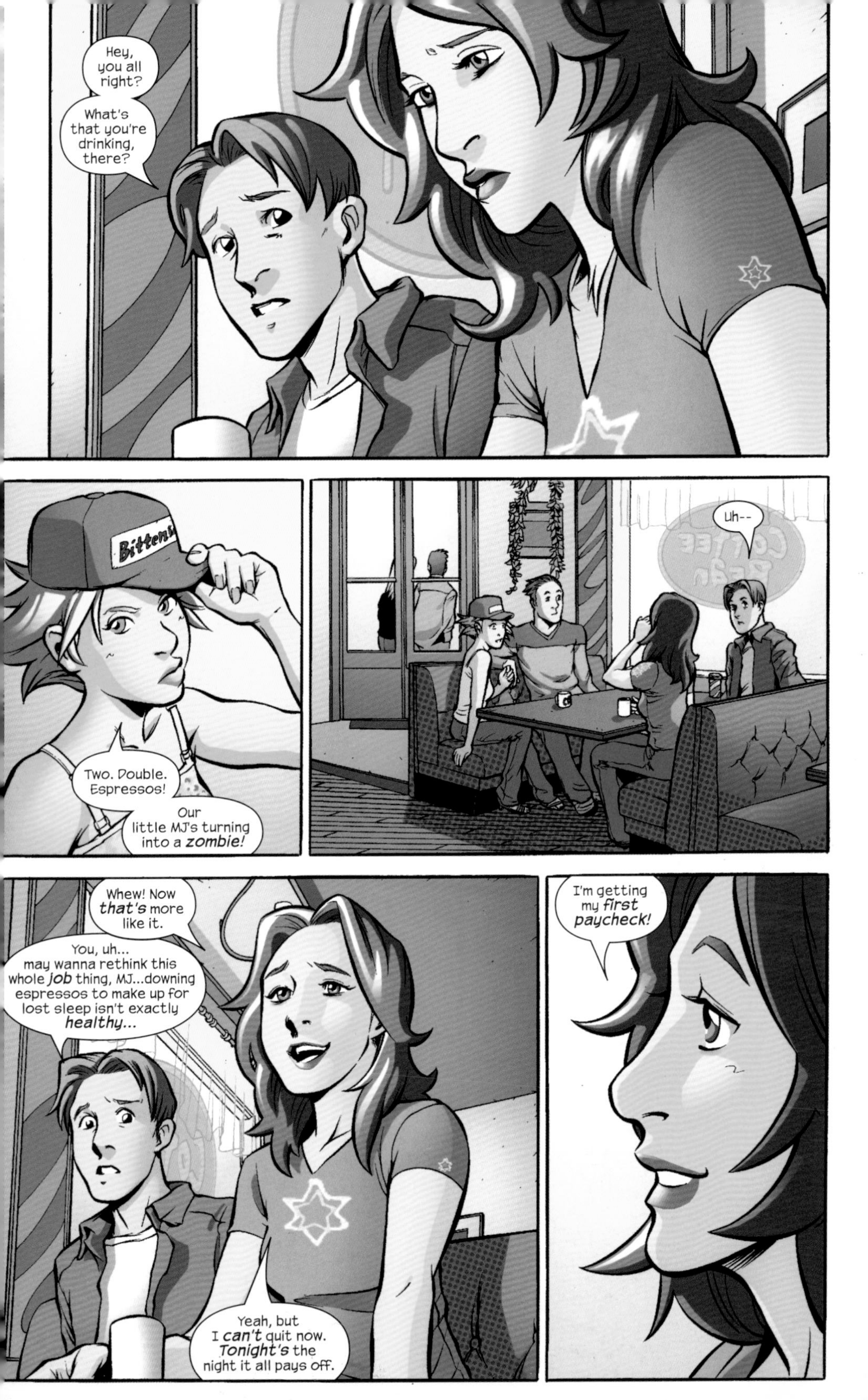
Hey, you all right?
What's that you're drinking, there?
Two. Double. Espressos!
Our little MJ's turning into a *zombie!*
Uh--
Whew! Now *that's* more like it.
You, uh... may wanna rethink this whole *job* thing, MJ...downing espressos to make up for lost sleep isn't exactly *healthy...*
Yeah, but I *can't* quit now. *Tonight's* the night it all pays off.
I'm getting my *first paycheck!*

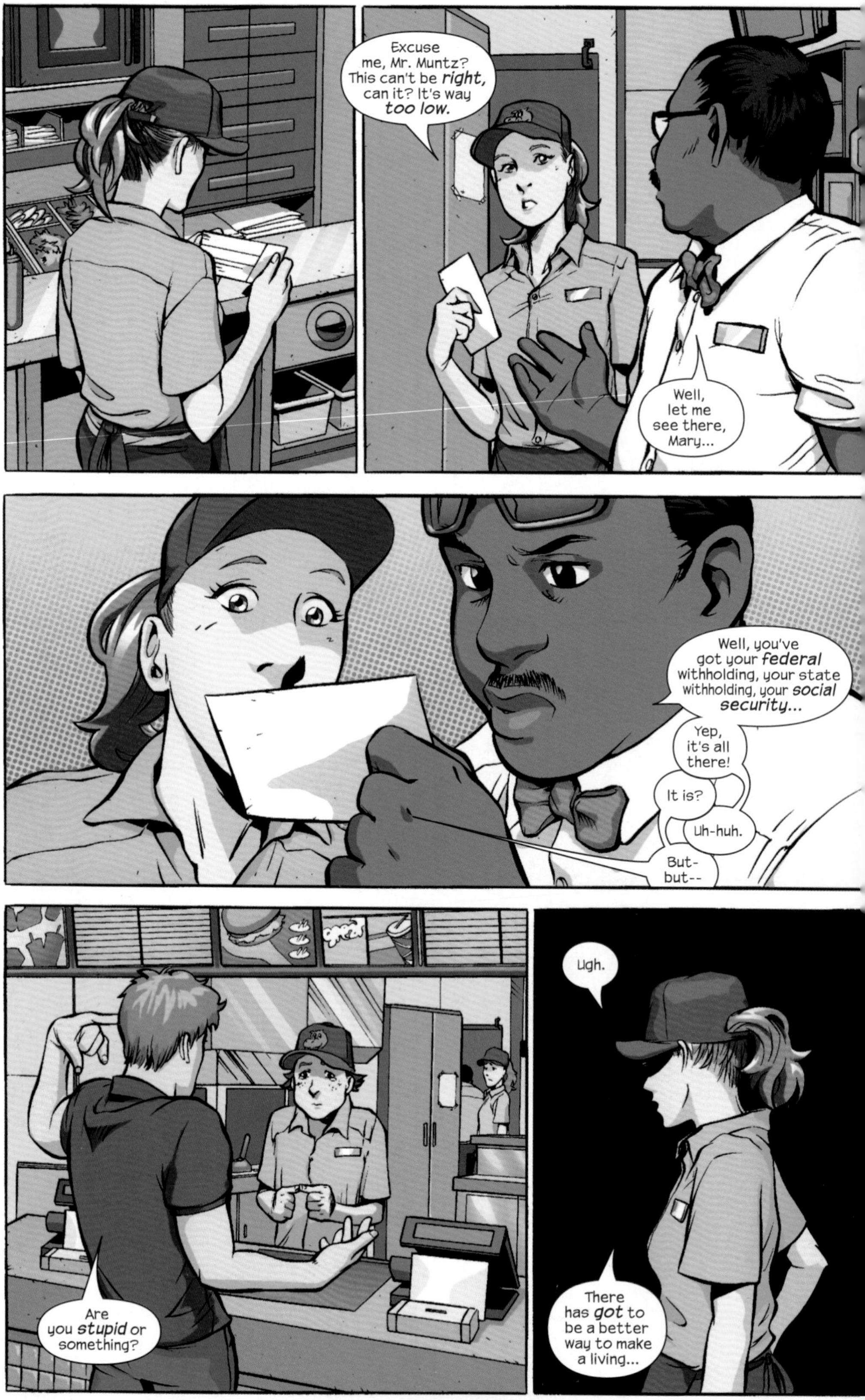

Excuse me, Mr. Muntz? This can't be *right,* can it? It's way *too low.*
Well, let me see there, Mary...
Well, you've got your *federal* withholding, your state withholding, your *social security...*
Yep, it's all there!
It is?
Uh-huh.
But- but--
Are you *stupid* or something?
Ugh.
There has *got* to be a better way to make a living...

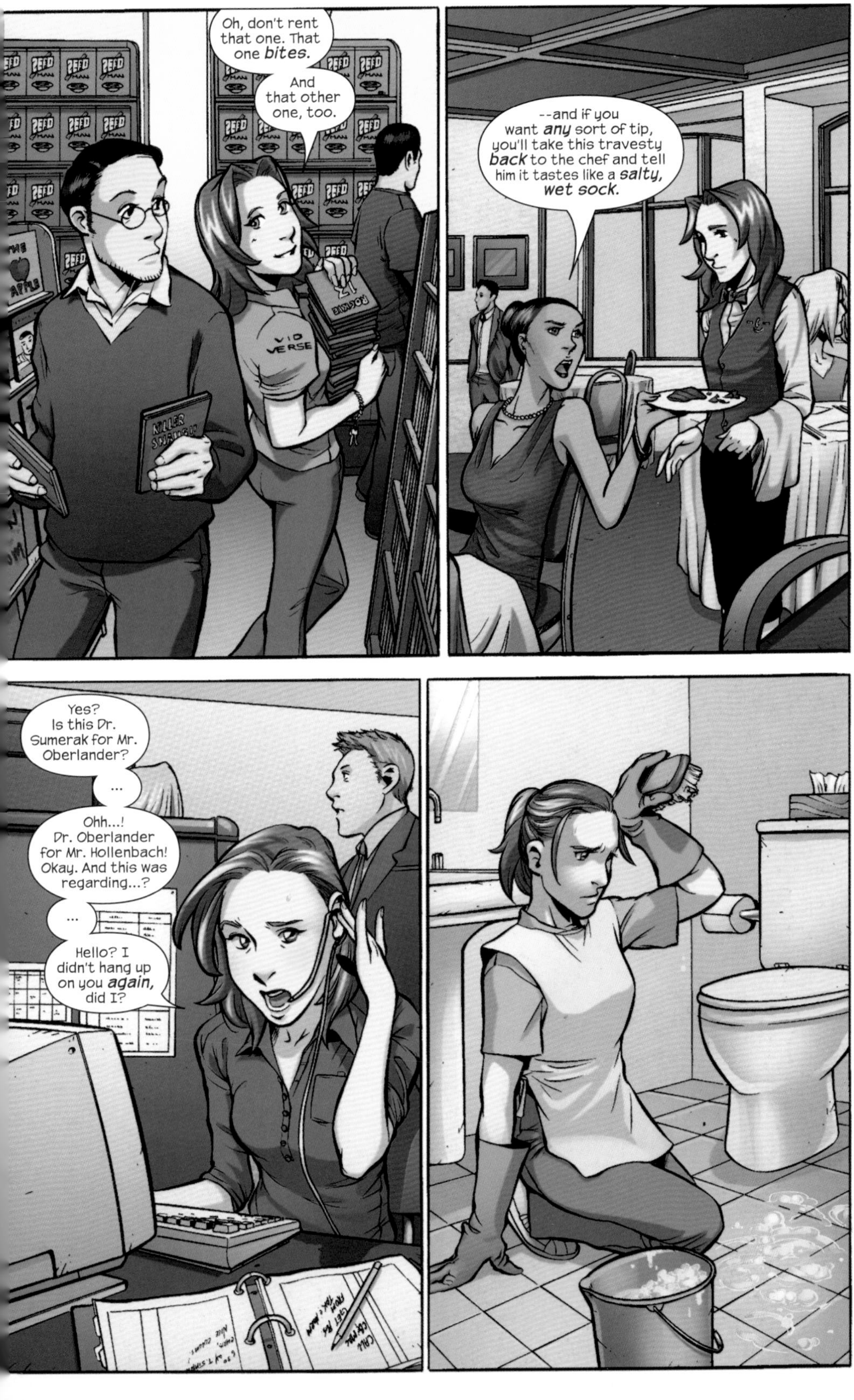
Oh, don't rent that one. That one *bites.*
And that other one, too.
VID VERSE
--and if you want ***any*** sort of tip, you'll take this travesty ***back*** to the chef and tell him it tastes like a ***salty, wet sock.***
Yes? Is this Dr. Sumerak for Mr. Oberlander?
...
Ohh...! Dr. Oberlander for Mr. Hollenbach! Okay. And this was regarding...?
...
Hello? I didn't hang up on you *again,* did I?

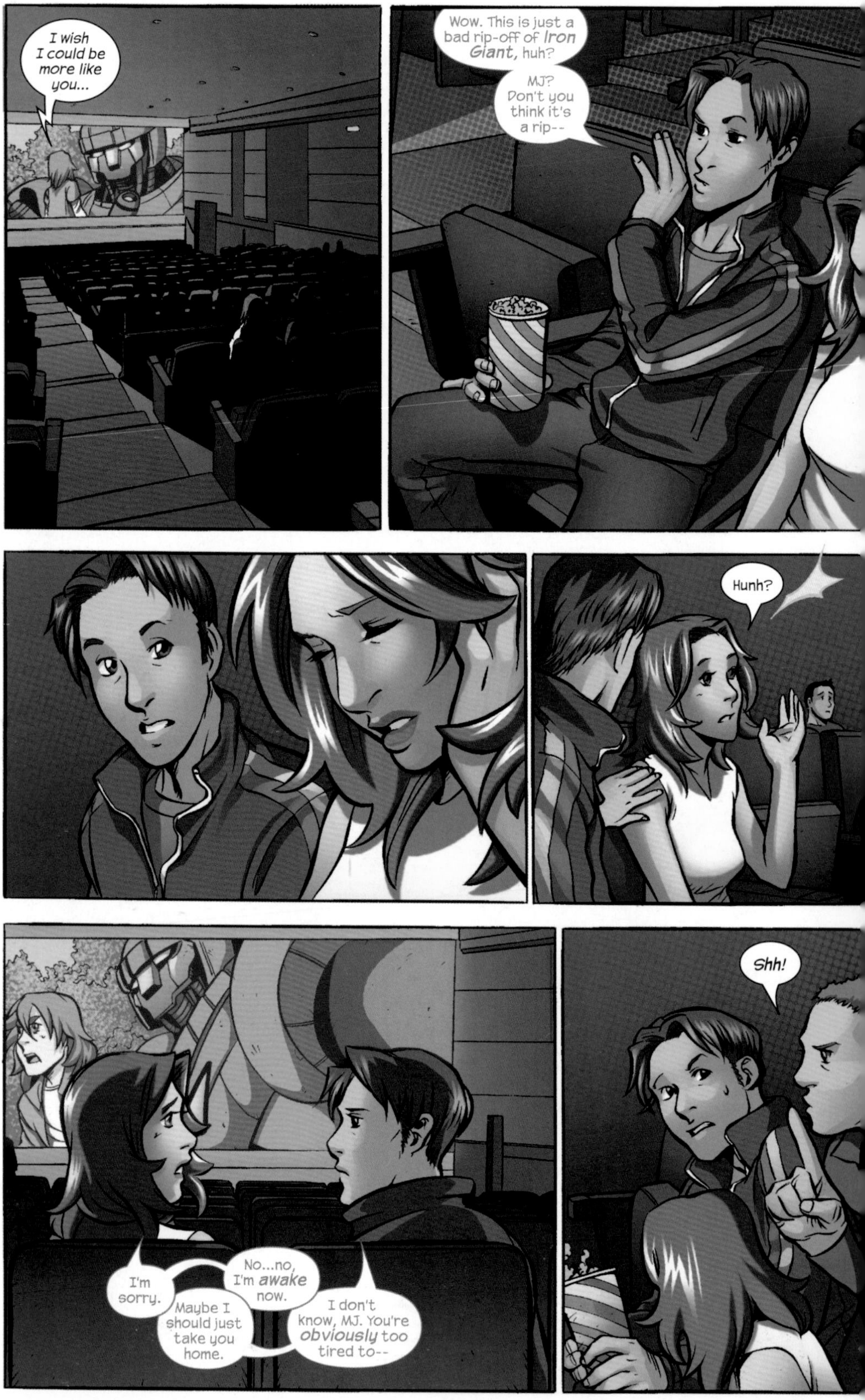
I wish I could be more like you...
Wow. This is just a bad rip-off of *Iron Giant*, huh?
MJ? Don't you think it's a rip--
Hunh?
I'm sorry.
No...no, I'm *awake* now.
Maybe I should just take you home.
I don't know, MJ. You're *obviously* too tired to--
Shh!

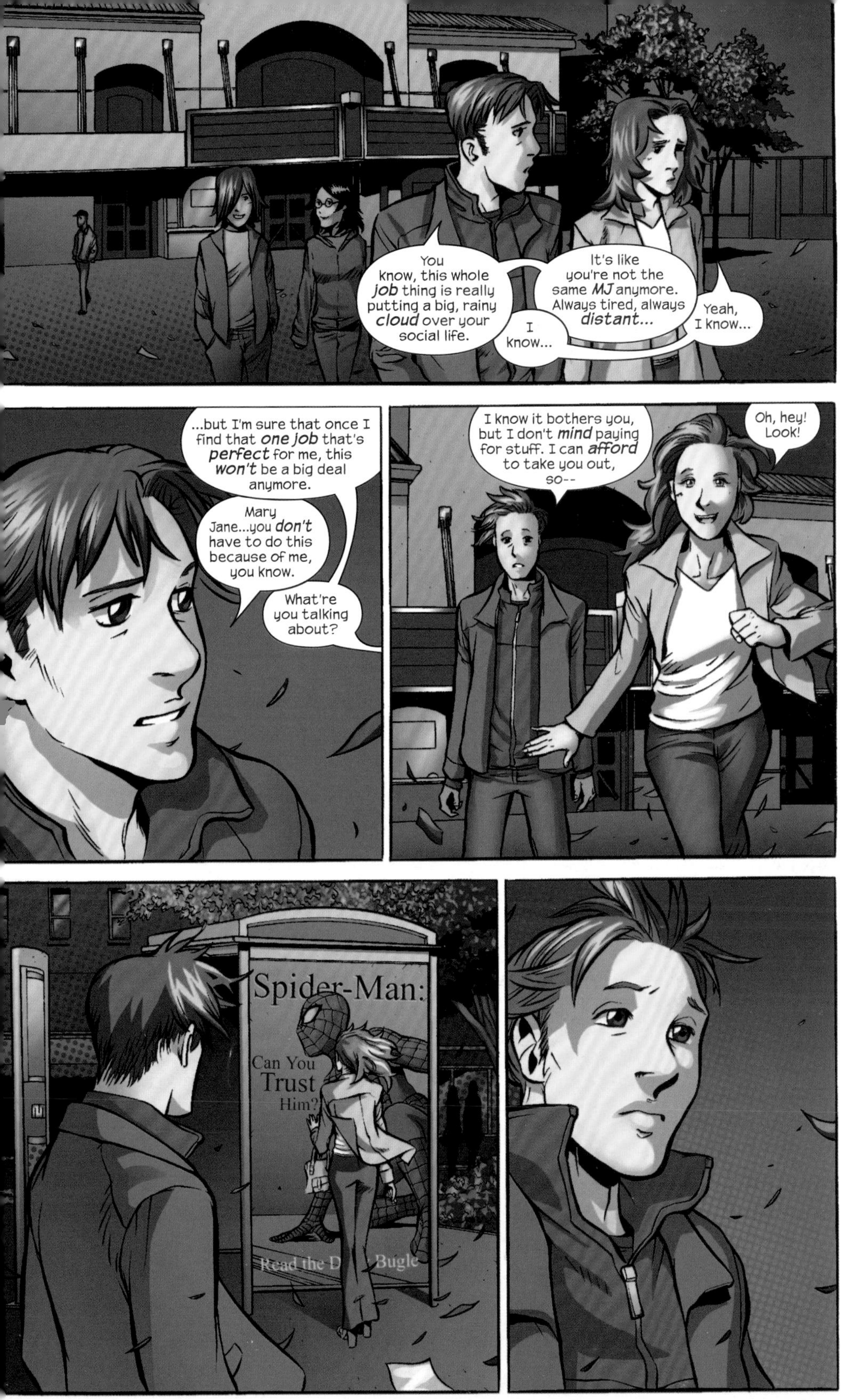
You know, this whole job thing is really putting a big, rainy cloud over your social life.
I know...
It's like you're not the same MJ anymore. Always tired, always distant...
Yeah, I know...
...but I'm sure that once I find that one job that's perfect for me, this won't be a big deal anymore.
Mary Jane...you don't have to do this because of me, you know.
What're you talking about?
I know it bothers you, but I don't mind paying for stuff. I can afford to take you out, so--
Oh, hey! Look!
Spider-Man:
Can You Trust Him?

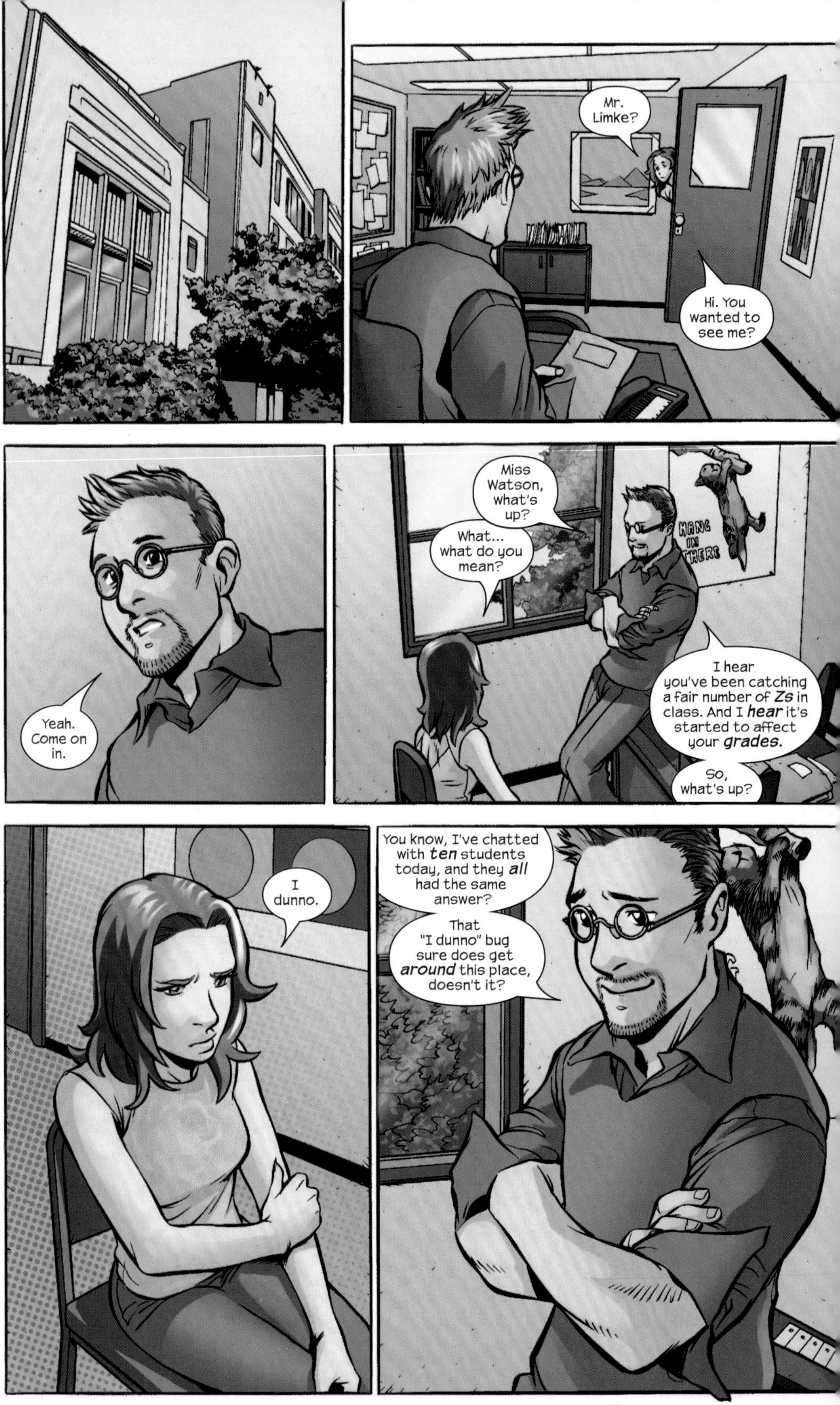
Mr. Limke?
Hi. You wanted to see me?
Yeah. Come on in.
Miss Watson, what's up?
What... what do you mean?
I hear you've been catching a fair number of Zs in class. And I hear it's started to affect your grades.
So, what's up?
HANG IN THERE
I dunno.
You know, I've chatted with ten students today, and they all had the same answer?
That "I dunno" bug sure does get around this place, doesn't it?

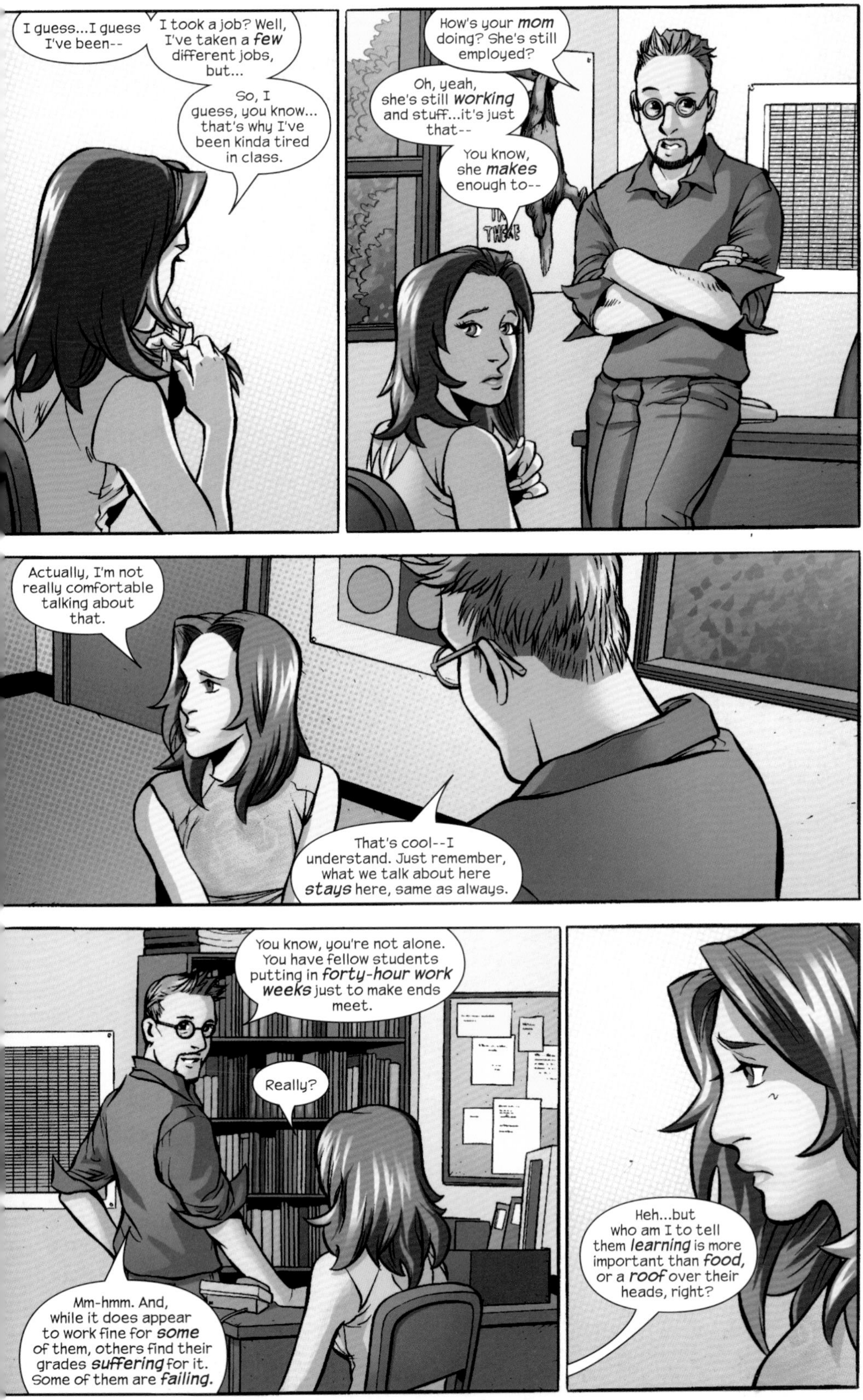
I guess...I guess I've been--
I took a job? Well, I've taken a few different jobs, but...
So, I guess, you know... that's why I've been kinda tired in class.
How's your mom doing? She's still employed?
Oh, yeah, she's still working and stuff...it's just that--
You know, she makes enough to--
Actually, I'm not really comfortable talking about that.
That's cool--I understand. Just remember, what we talk about here stays here, same as always.
You know, you're not alone. You have fellow students putting in forty-hour work weeks just to make ends meet.
Really?
Mm-hmm. And, while it does appear to work fine for some of them, others find their grades suffering for it. Some of them are failing.
Heh...but who am I to tell them learning is more important than food, or a roof over their heads, right?

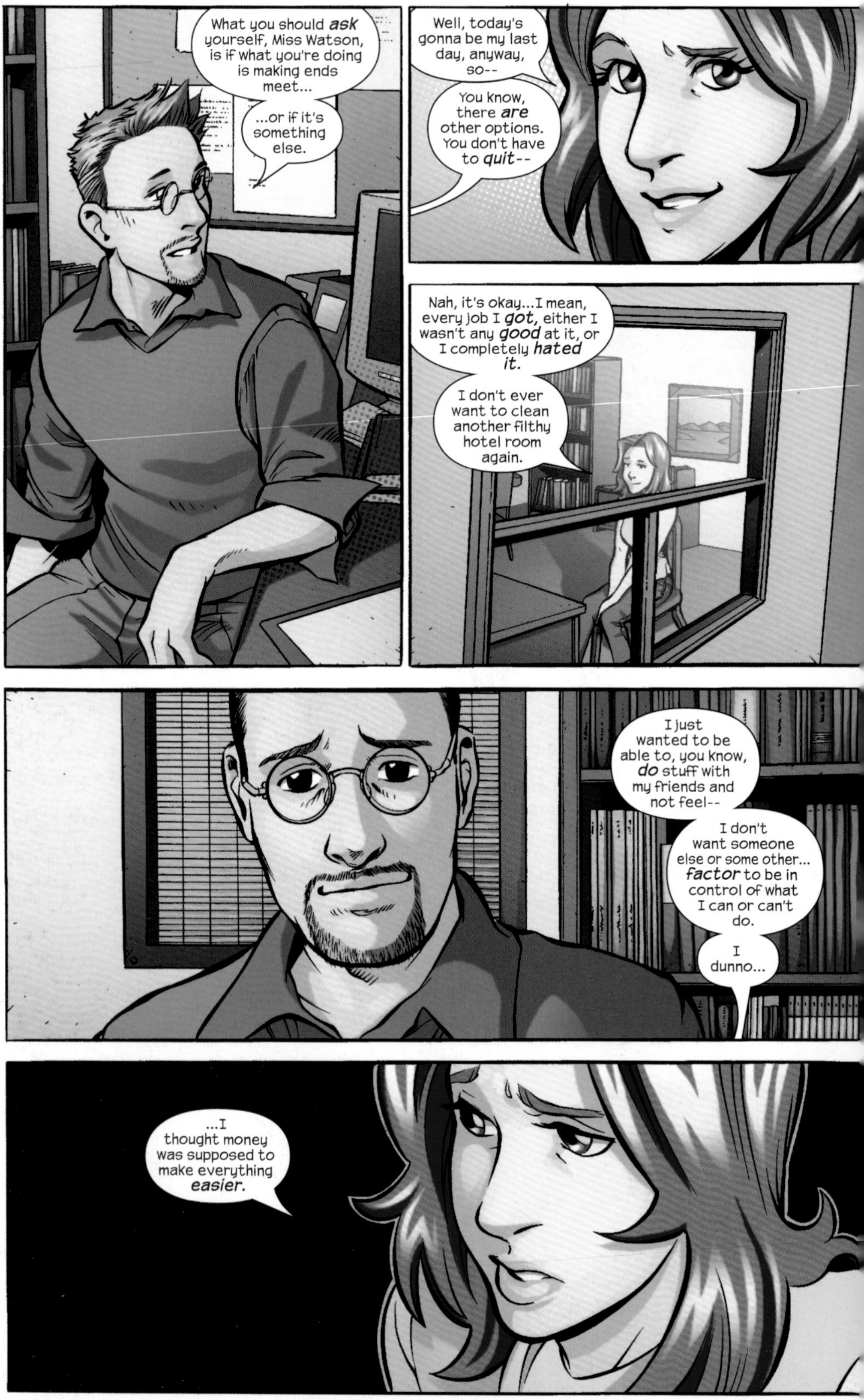
What you should *ask* yourself, Miss Watson, is if what you're doing is making ends meet...
...or if it's something else.
Well, today's gonna be my last day, anyway, so--
You know, there *are* other options. You don't have to *quit*--
Nah, it's okay...I mean, every job I *got,* either I wasn't any *good* at it, or I completely *hated it.*
I don't ever want to clean another filthy hotel room again.
I just wanted to be able to, you know, *do* stuff with my friends and not feel--
I don't want someone else or some other... *factor* to be in control of what I can or can't do.
I dunno...
...I thought money was supposed to make everything *easier.*

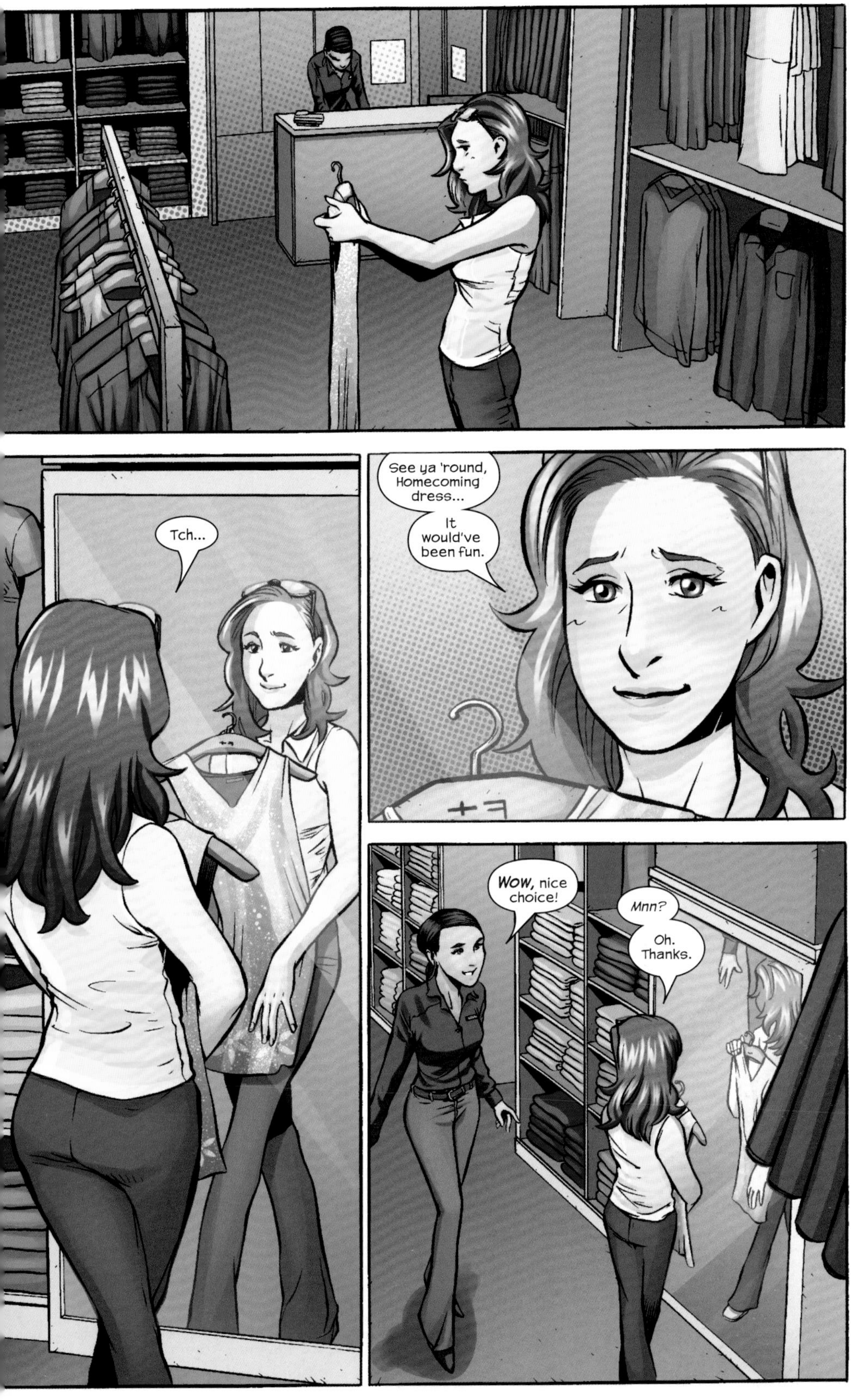
Tch...
See ya 'round, Homecoming dress...
It would've been fun.
WOW, nice choice!
Mnn?
Oh. Thanks.

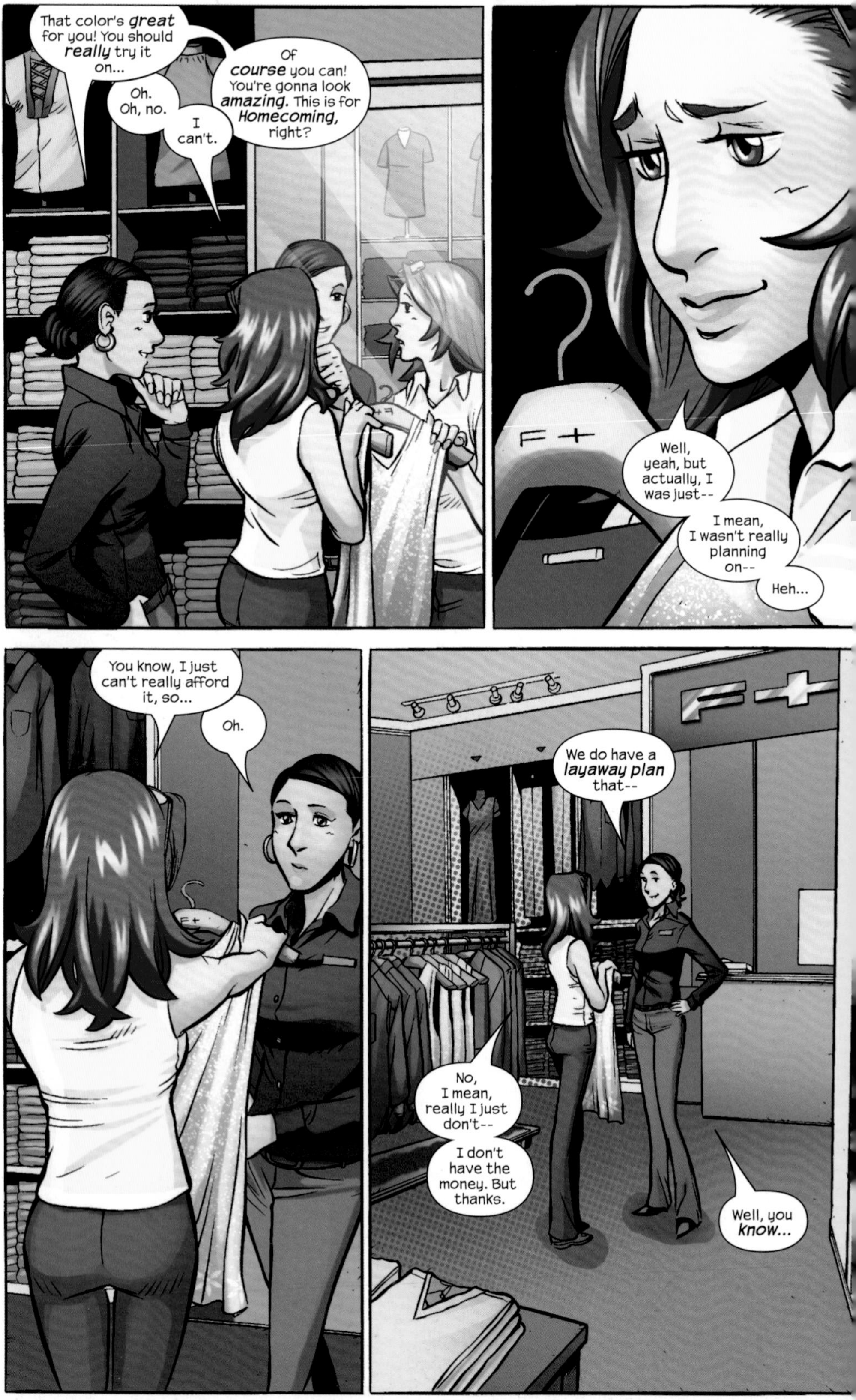

That color's great for you! You should really try it on...
Oh. Oh, no.
I can't.
Of course you can! You're gonna look amazing. This is for Homecoming, right?
F+
Well, yeah, but actually, I was just--
I mean, I wasn't really planning on--
Heh...
You know, I just can't really afford it, so...
Oh.
We do have a layaway plan that--
No, I mean, really I just don't--
I don't have the money. But thanks.
Well, you know...

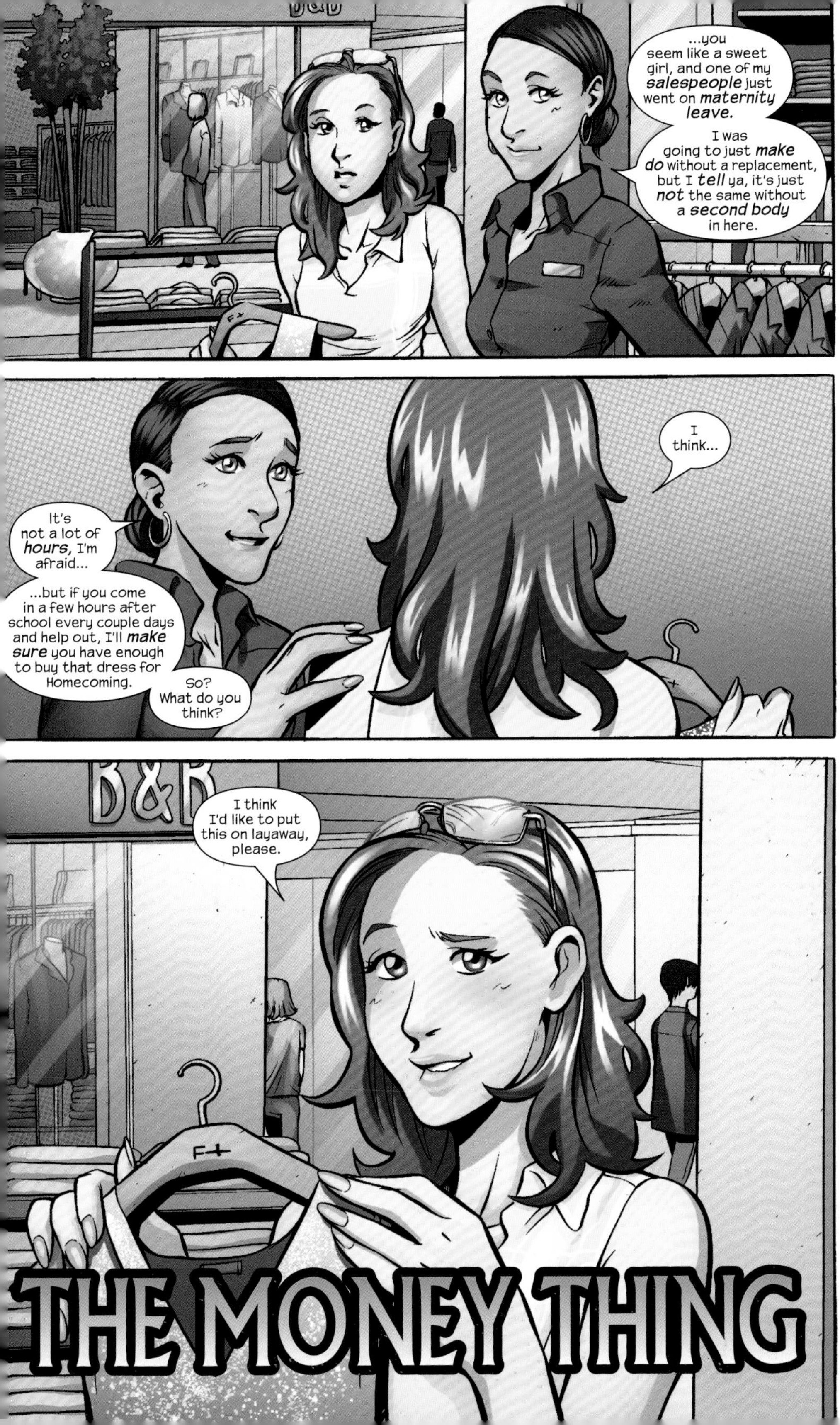

...you seem like a sweet girl, and one of my *salespeople* just went on *maternity leave.*
I was going to just *make do* without a replacement, but I *tell* ya, it's just *not* the same without a *second body* in here.
I think...
It's not a lot of *hours,* I'm afraid...
...but if you come in a few hours after school every couple days and help out, I'll *make sure* you have enough to buy that dress for Homecoming.
So? What do you think?
B&R
I think I'd like to put this on layaway, please.
THE MONEY THING

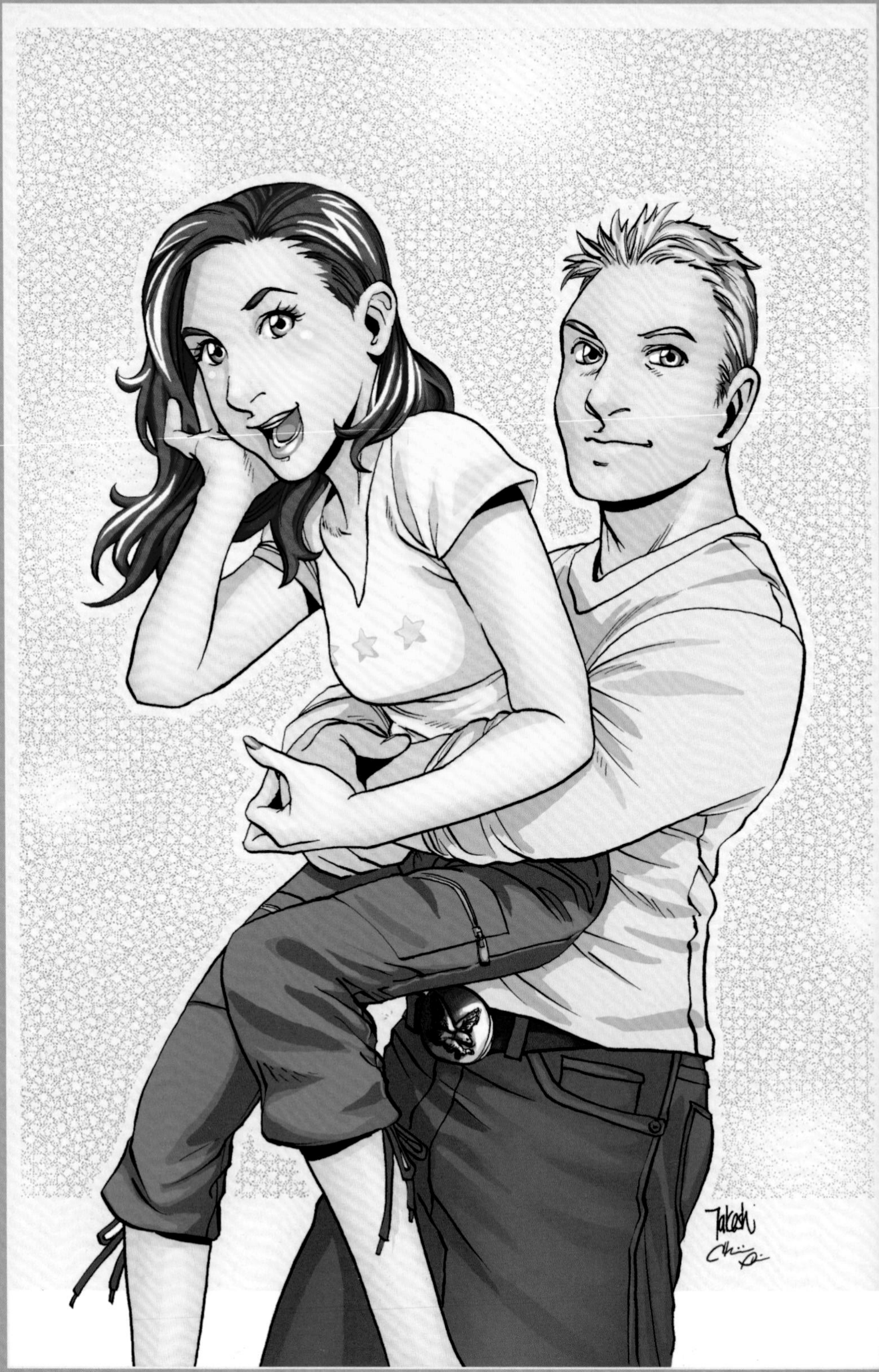
Takeshi

Mary Jane #3

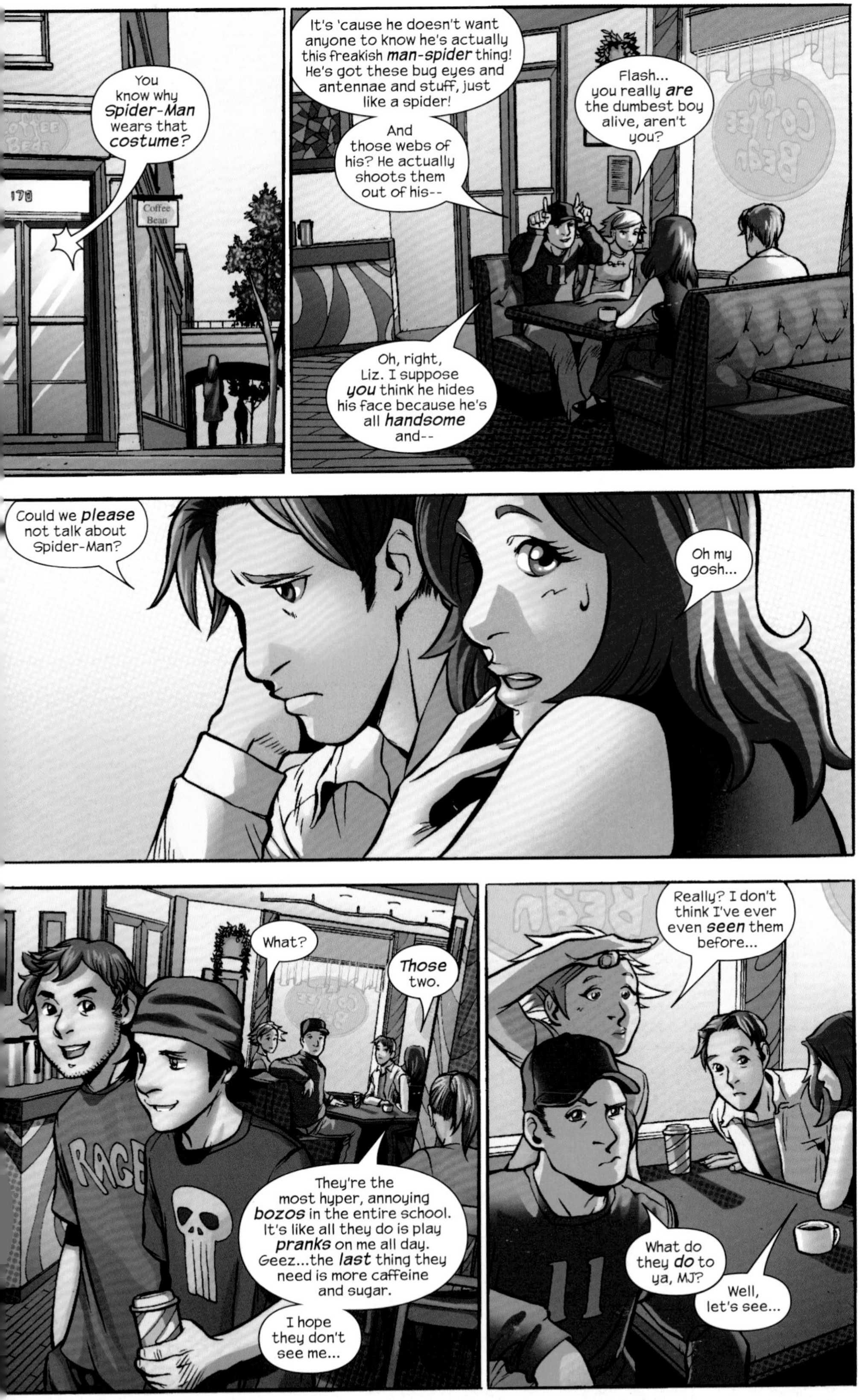
You know why Spider-Man wears that costume?
It's 'cause he doesn't want anyone to know he's actually this freakish man-spider thing! He's got these bug eyes and antennae and stuff, just like a spider!
And those webs of his? He actually shoots them out of his--
Flash... you really are the dumbest boy alive, aren't you?
Oh, right, Liz. I suppose you think he hides his face because he's all handsome and--
Coffee Bean
170
Could we please not talk about Spider-Man?
Oh my gosh...
What?
Those two.
They're the most hyper, annoying bozos in the entire school. It's like all they do is play pranks on me all day. Geez...the last thing they need is more caffeine and sugar.
I hope they don't see me...
Really? I don't think I've ever even seen them before...
What do they do to ya, MJ?
Well, let's see...
RAGE
11

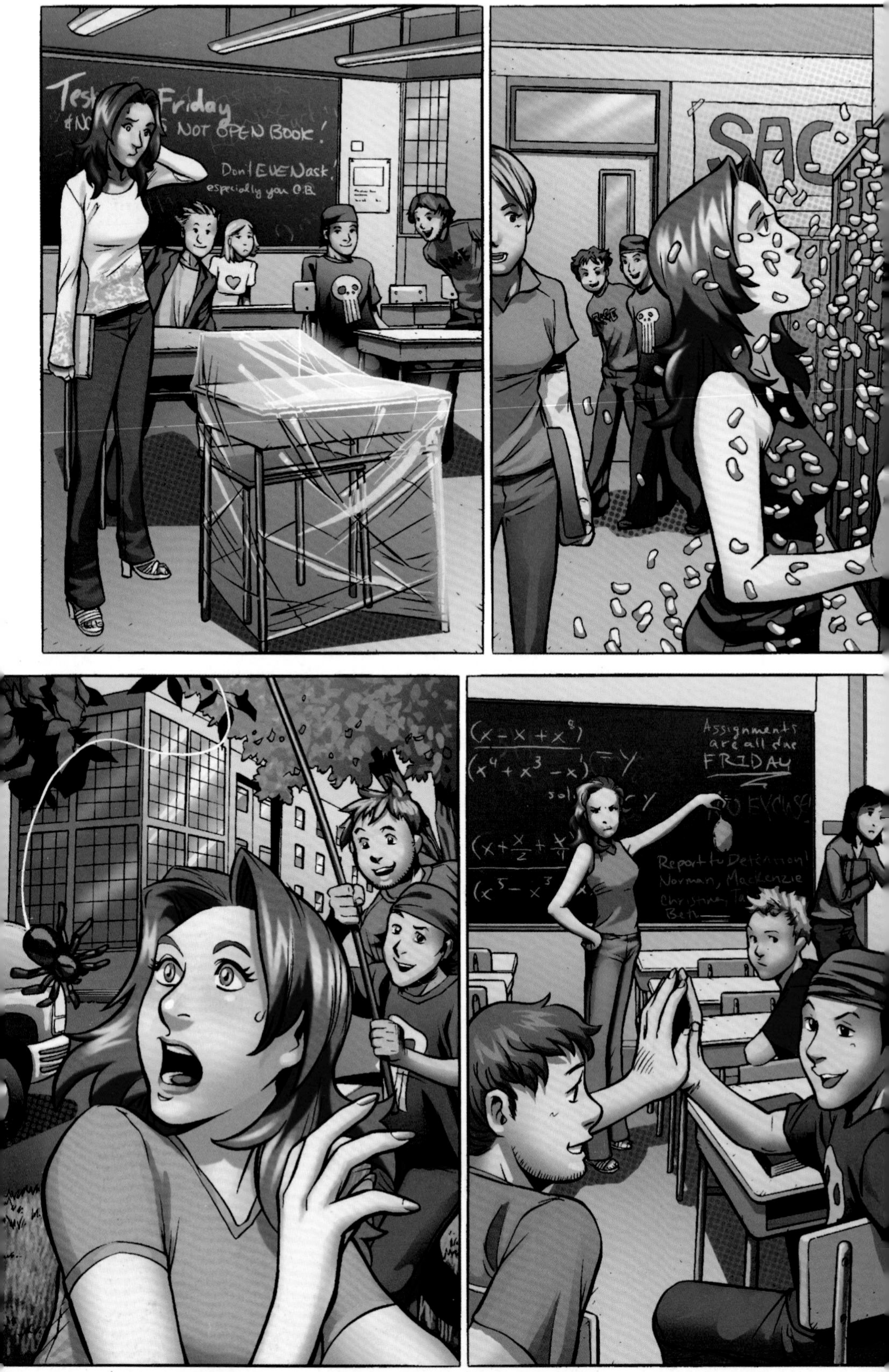

Friday
NOT OPEN BOOK!
Don't EVEN ask!
especially you C.B.
Assignments are all due FRIDAY
Report to Detention!
Norman, MacKenzie
Beth

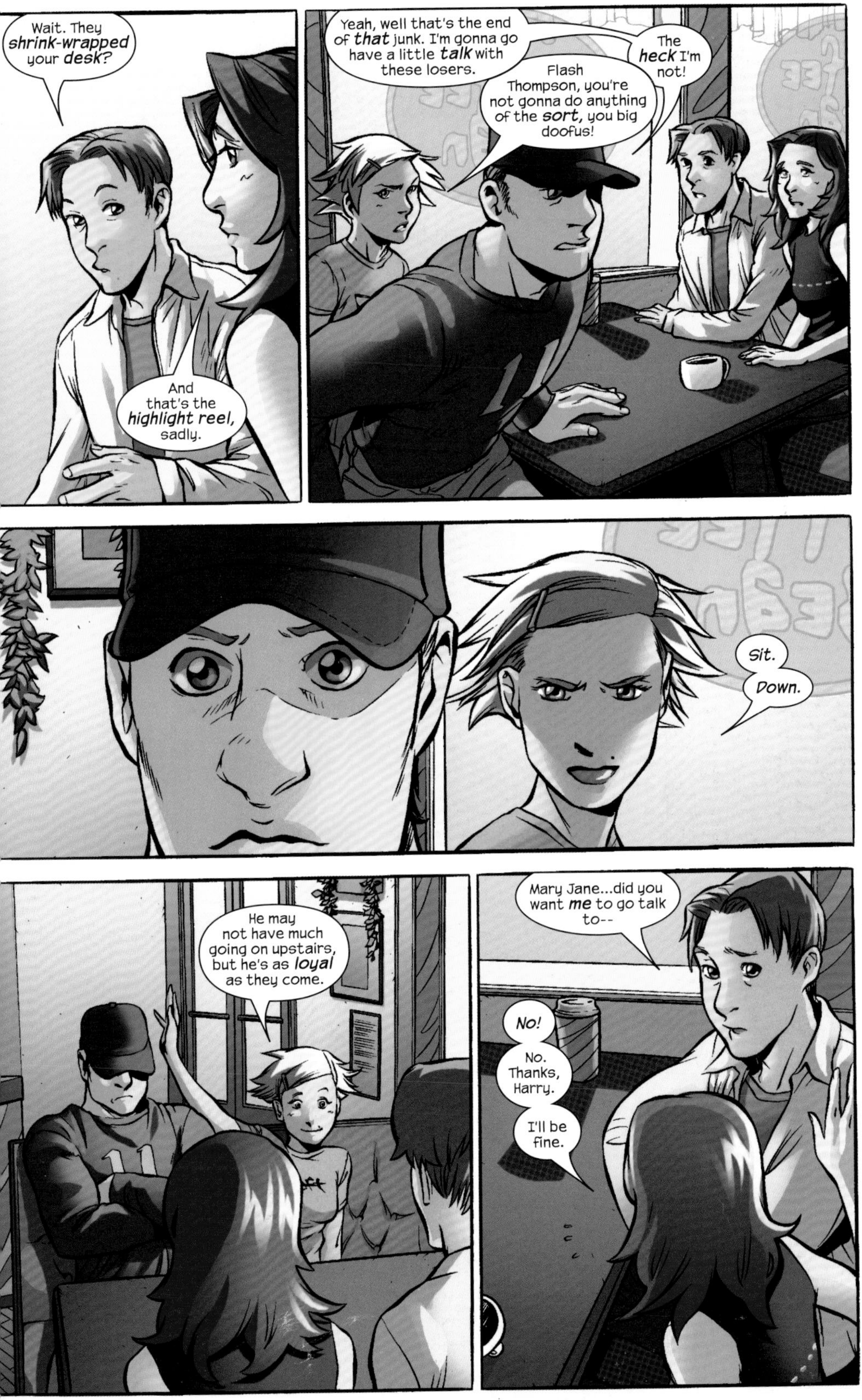
Wait. They shrink-wrapped your desk?
And that's the highlight reel, sadly.
Yeah, well that's the end of that junk. I'm gonna go have a little talk with these losers.
The heck I'm not!
Flash Thompson, you're not gonna do anything of the sort, you big doofus!
Sit.
Down.
He may not have much going on upstairs, but he's as loyal as they come.
Mary Jane...did you want me to go talk to--
No!
No. Thanks, Harry.
I'll be fine.

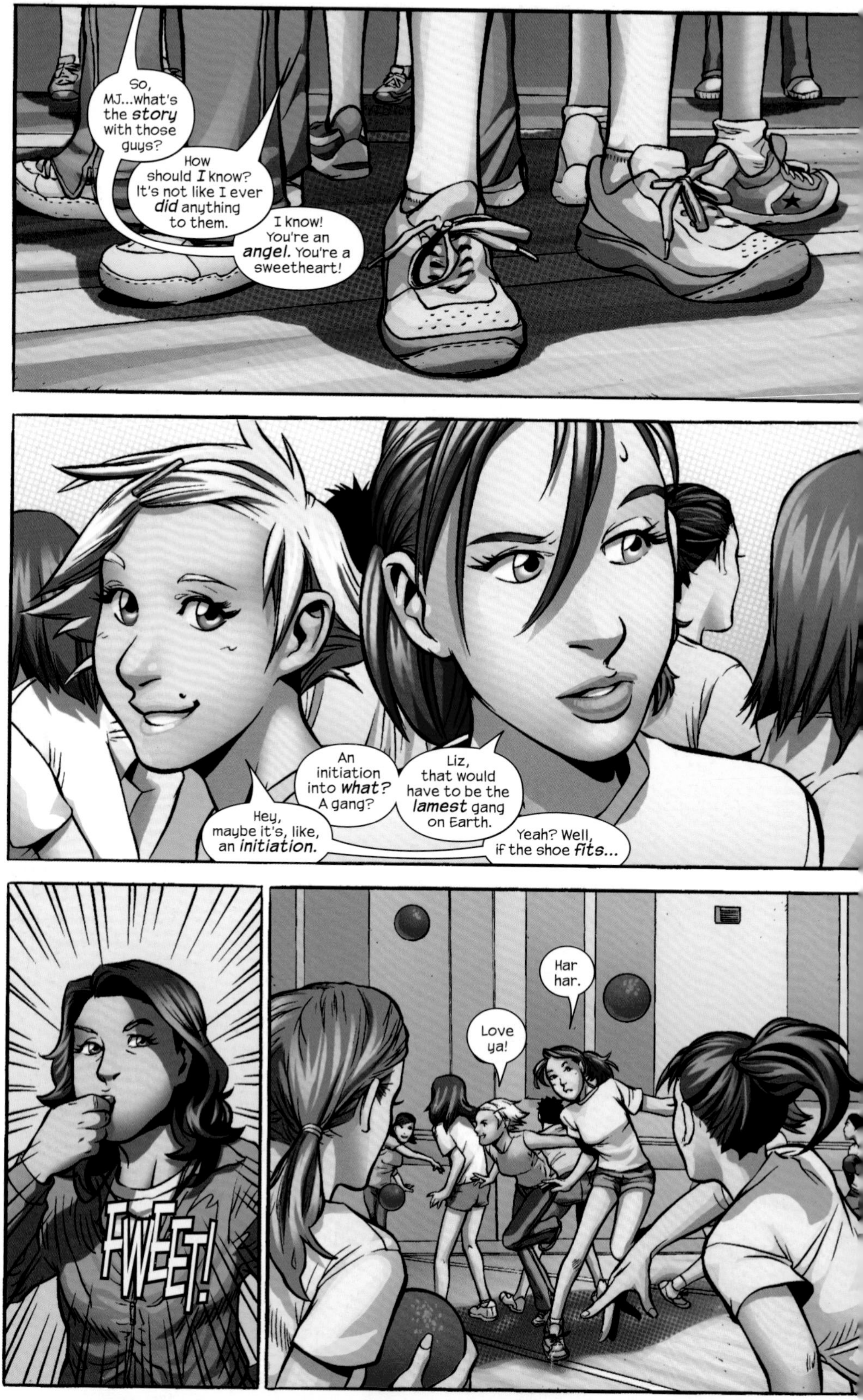
So, MJ...what's the story with those guys?
How should I know? It's not like I ever did anything to them.
I know! You're an angel. You're a sweetheart!
Hey, maybe it's, like, an initiation.
An initiation into what? A gang?
Liz, that would have to be the lamest gang on Earth.
Yeah? Well, if the shoe fits...
FWEET!
Love ya!
Har har.

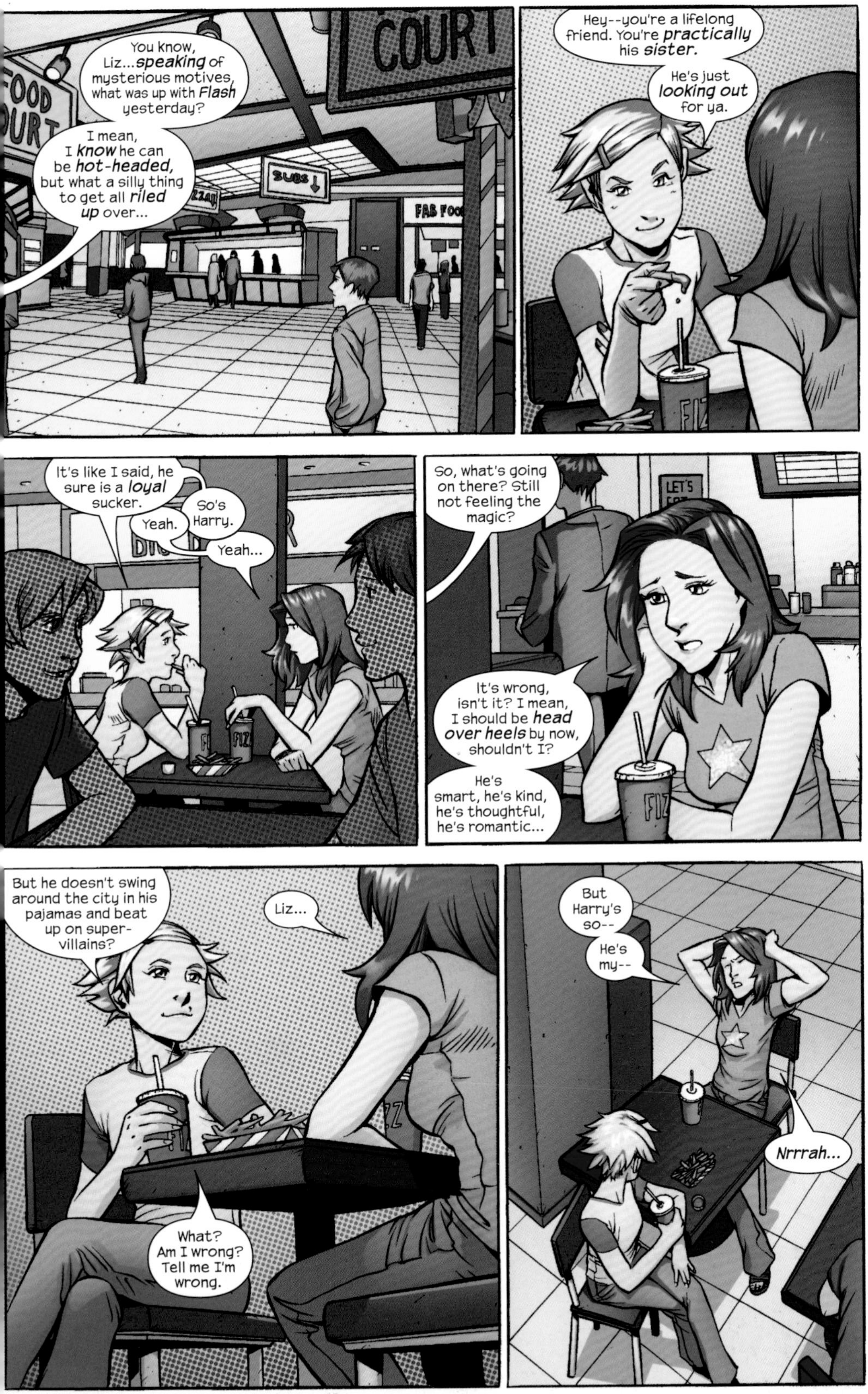
FOOD COURT
COURT
You know, Liz...speaking of mysterious motives, what was up with Flash yesterday?
I mean, I know he can be hot-headed, but what a silly thing to get all riled up over...
SUBS
FAB FOO
Hey--you're a lifelong friend. You're practically his sister.
He's just looking out for ya.
It's like I said, he sure is a loyal sucker.
So's Harry.
Yeah.
Yeah...
So, what's going on there? Still not feeling the magic?
It's wrong, isn't it? I mean, I should be head over heels by now, shouldn't I?
He's smart, he's kind, he's thoughtful, he's romantic...
But he doesn't swing around the city in his pajamas and beat up on super-villains?
Liz...
What? Am I wrong? Tell me I'm wrong.
But Harry's so--
He's my--
Nrrrah...

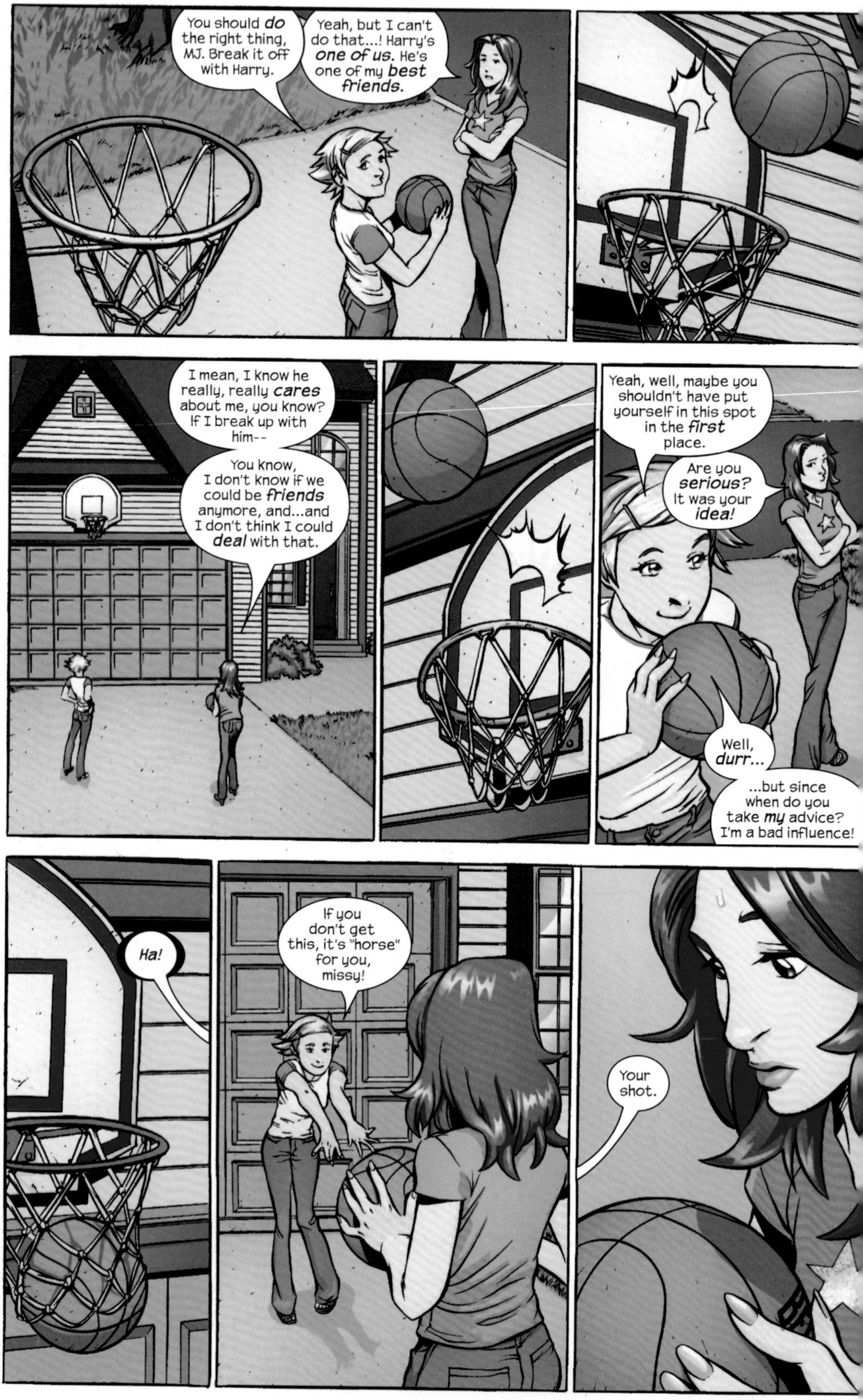
You should *do* the right thing, MJ. Break it off with Harry.
Yeah, but I can't do that...! Harry's *one of us*. He's one of my *best friends*.
I mean, I know he really, really *cares* about me, you know? If I break up with him--
You know, I don't know if we could be *friends* anymore, and...and I don't think I could *deal* with that.
Yeah, well, maybe you shouldn't have put yourself in this spot in the *first* place.
Are you *serious?* It was your *idea!*
Well, *durr...*
...but since when do you take *my* advice? I'm a bad influence!
Ha!
If you don't get this, it's "horse" for you, missy!
Your shot.

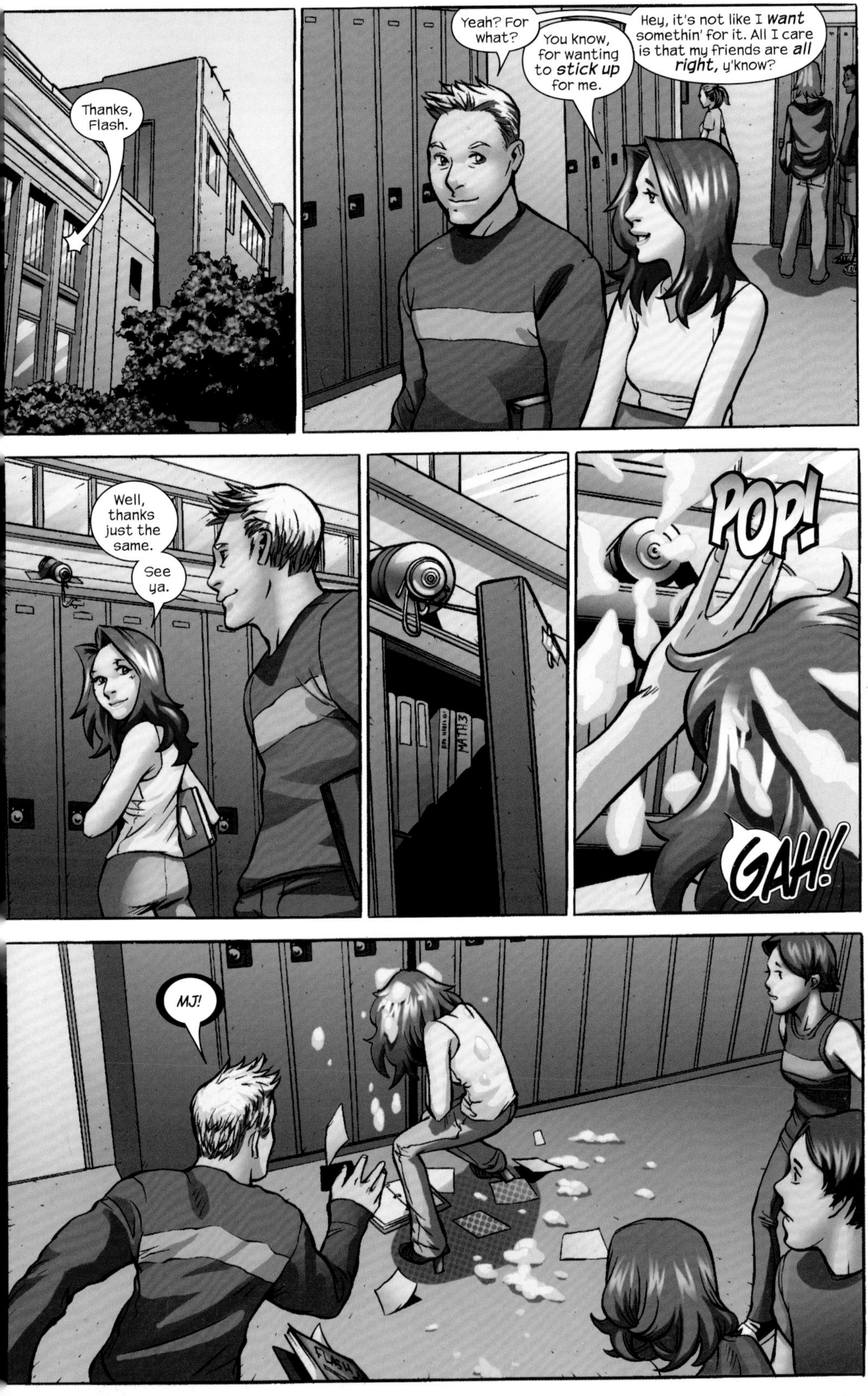
Thanks, Flash.
Yeah? For what?
You know, for wanting to **stick up** for me.
Hey, it's not like I *want* somethin' for it. All I care is that my friends are ***all right,*** y'know?
Well, thanks just the same.
See ya.
MATH 3
POP!
GAH!
MJ!
FLASH

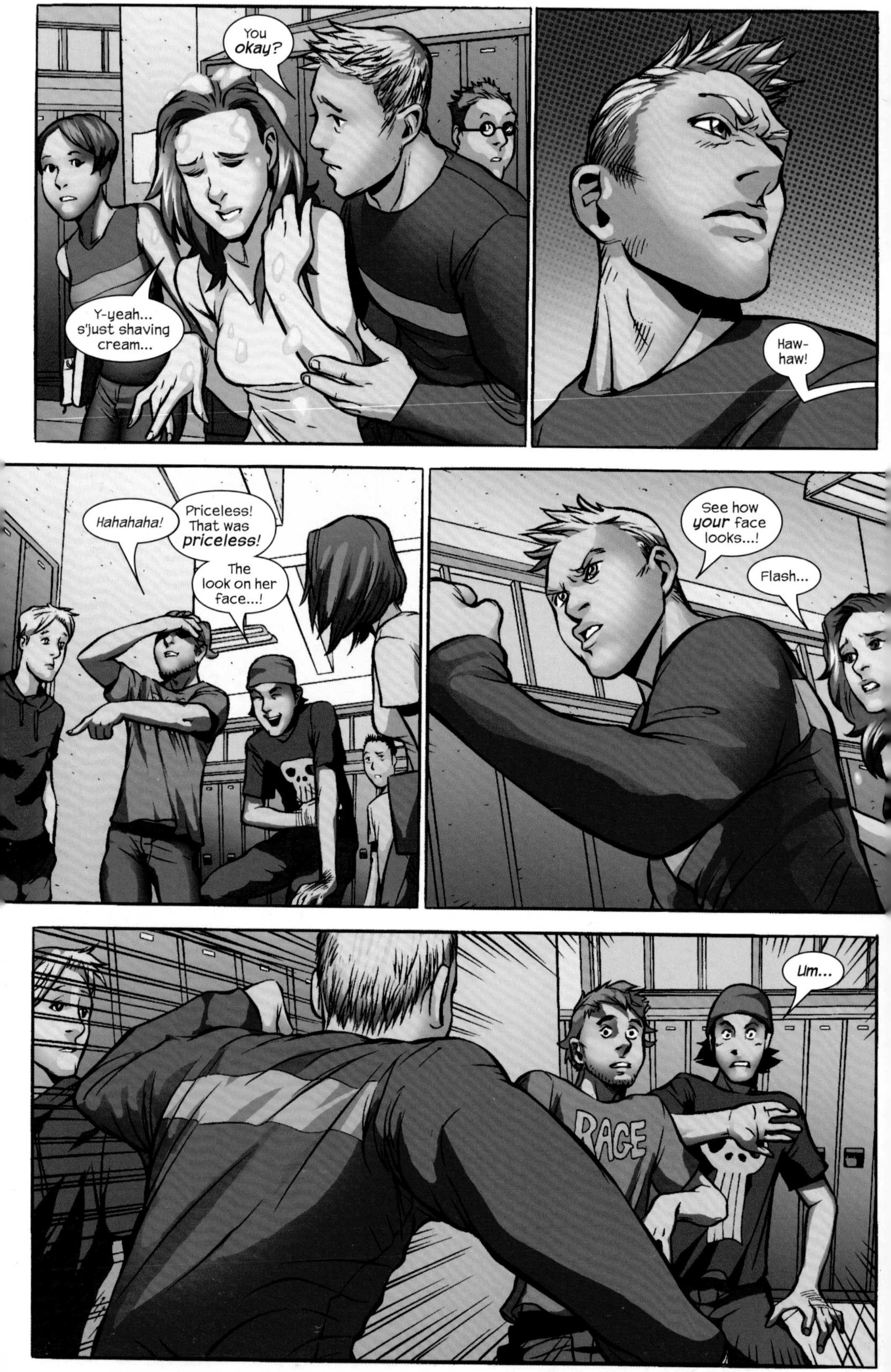
You okay?
Y-yeah... s'just shaving cream...
Haw-haw!
Hahahaha!
Priceless! That was priceless!
The look on her face...!
See how your face looks...!
Flash...
RAGE
Um...

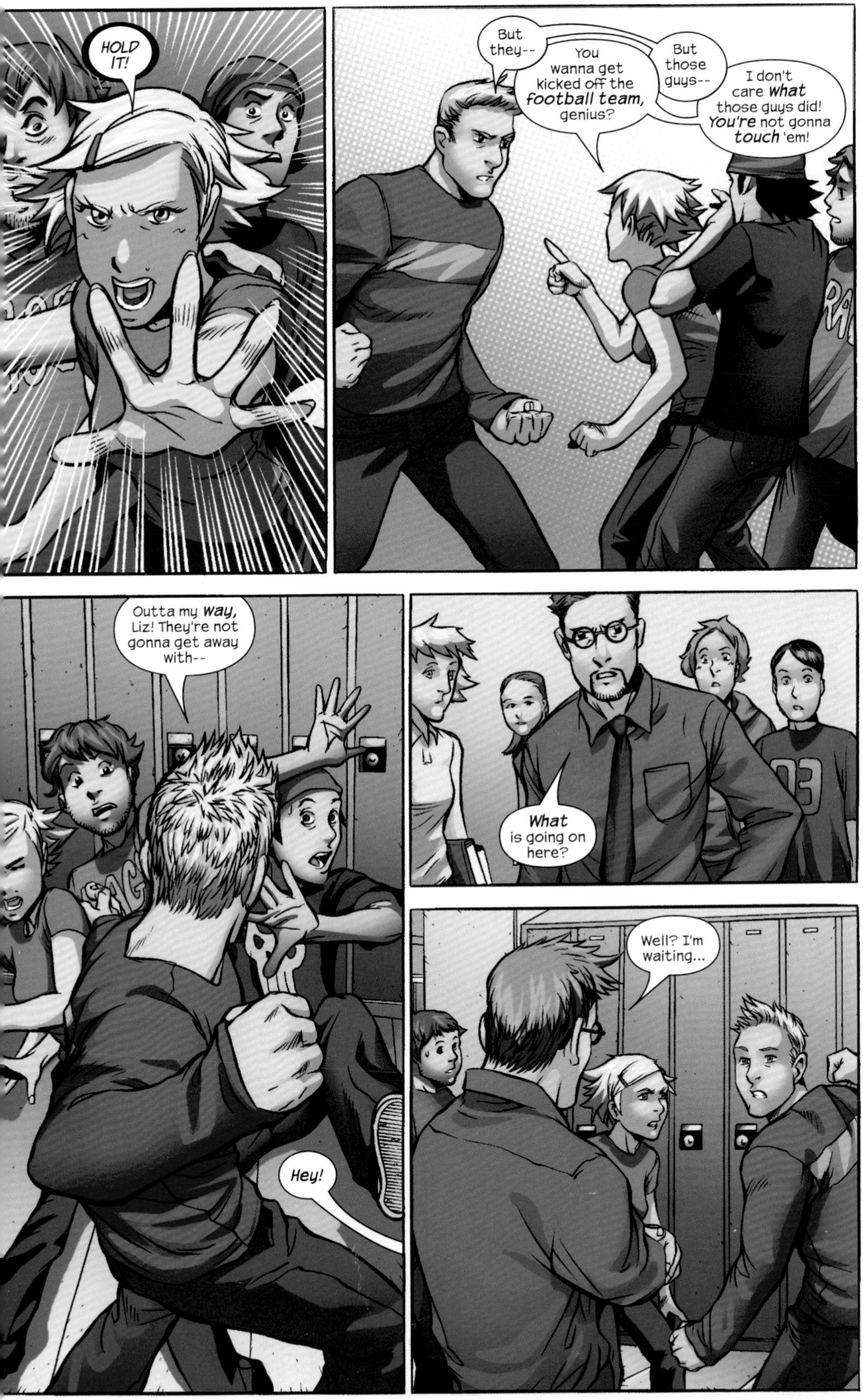
HOLD IT!
But they--
You wanna get kicked off the football team, genius?
But those guys--
I don't care what those guys did! You're not gonna touch 'em!
Outta my way, Liz! They're not gonna get away with--
Hey!
What is going on here?
Well? I'm waiting...

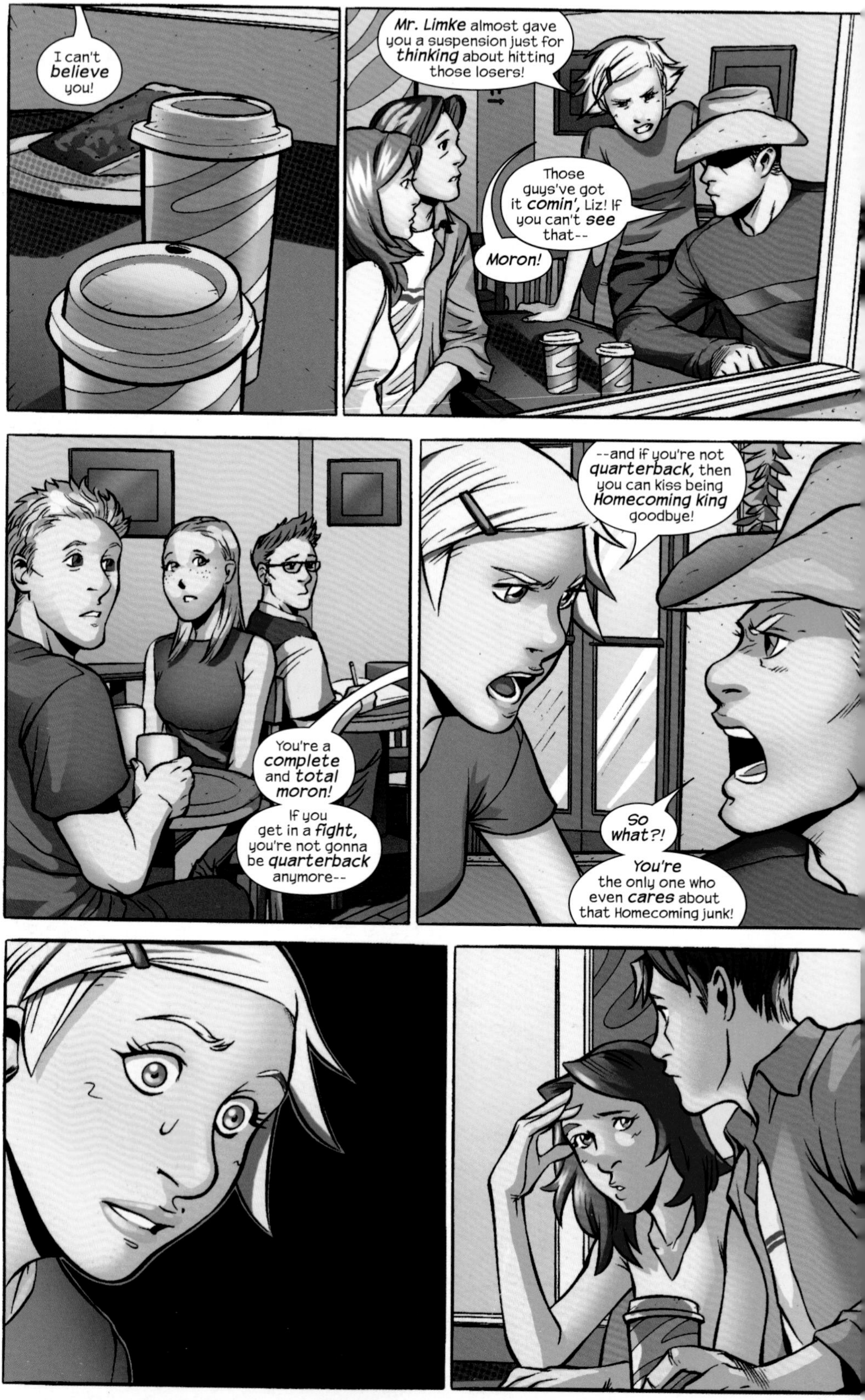
I can't believe you!
Mr. Limke almost gave you a suspension just for thinking about hitting those losers!
Those guys've got it comin', Liz! If you can't see that--
Moron!
You're a complete and total moron!
If you get in a fight, you're not gonna be quarterback anymore--
--and if you're not quarterback, then you can kiss being Homecoming king goodbye!
So what?!
You're the only one who even cares about that Homecoming junk!

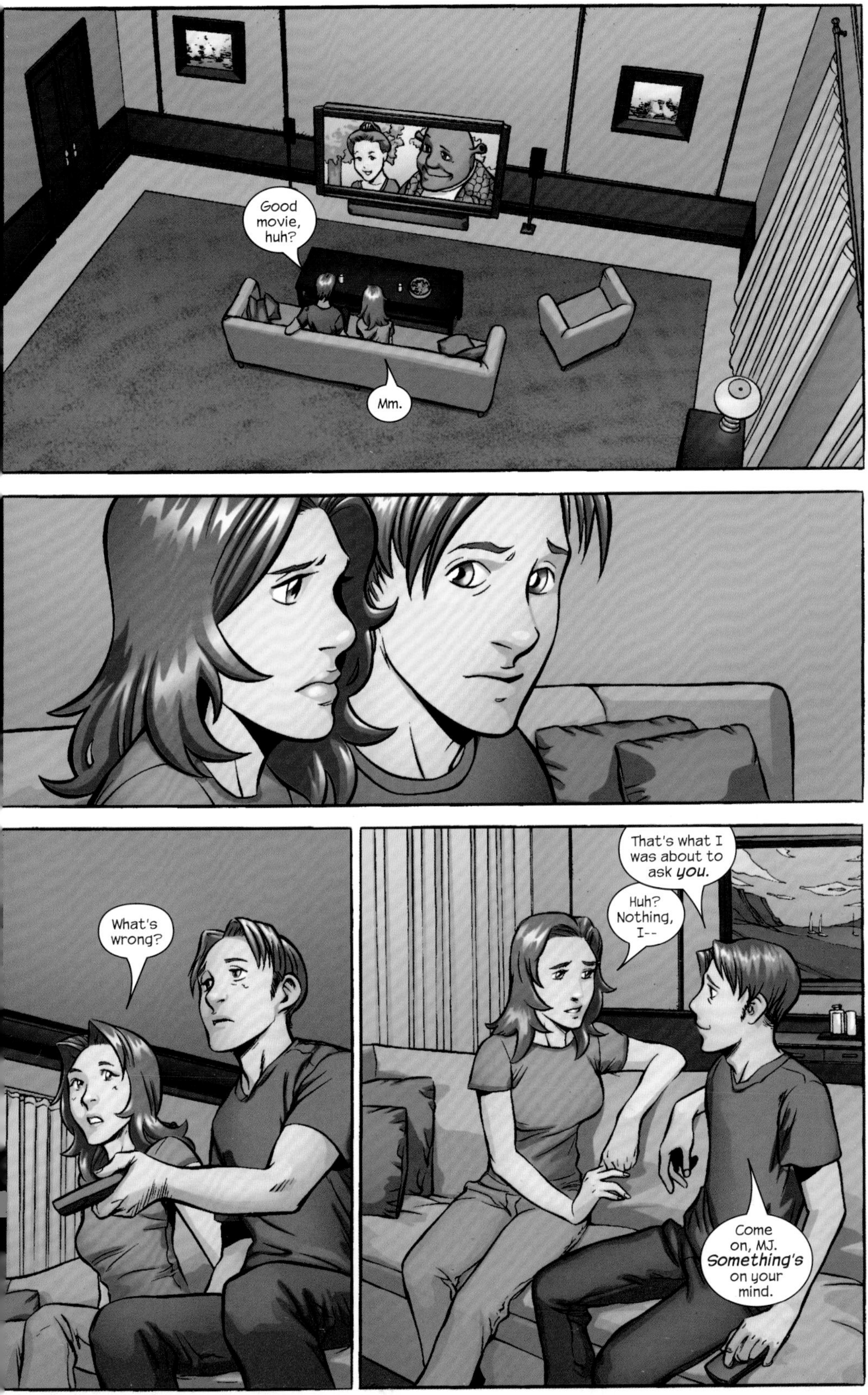
Good movie, huh?
Mm.
What's wrong?
Huh? Nothing, I--
That's what I was about to ask *you.*
Come on, MJ. *Something's* on your mind.

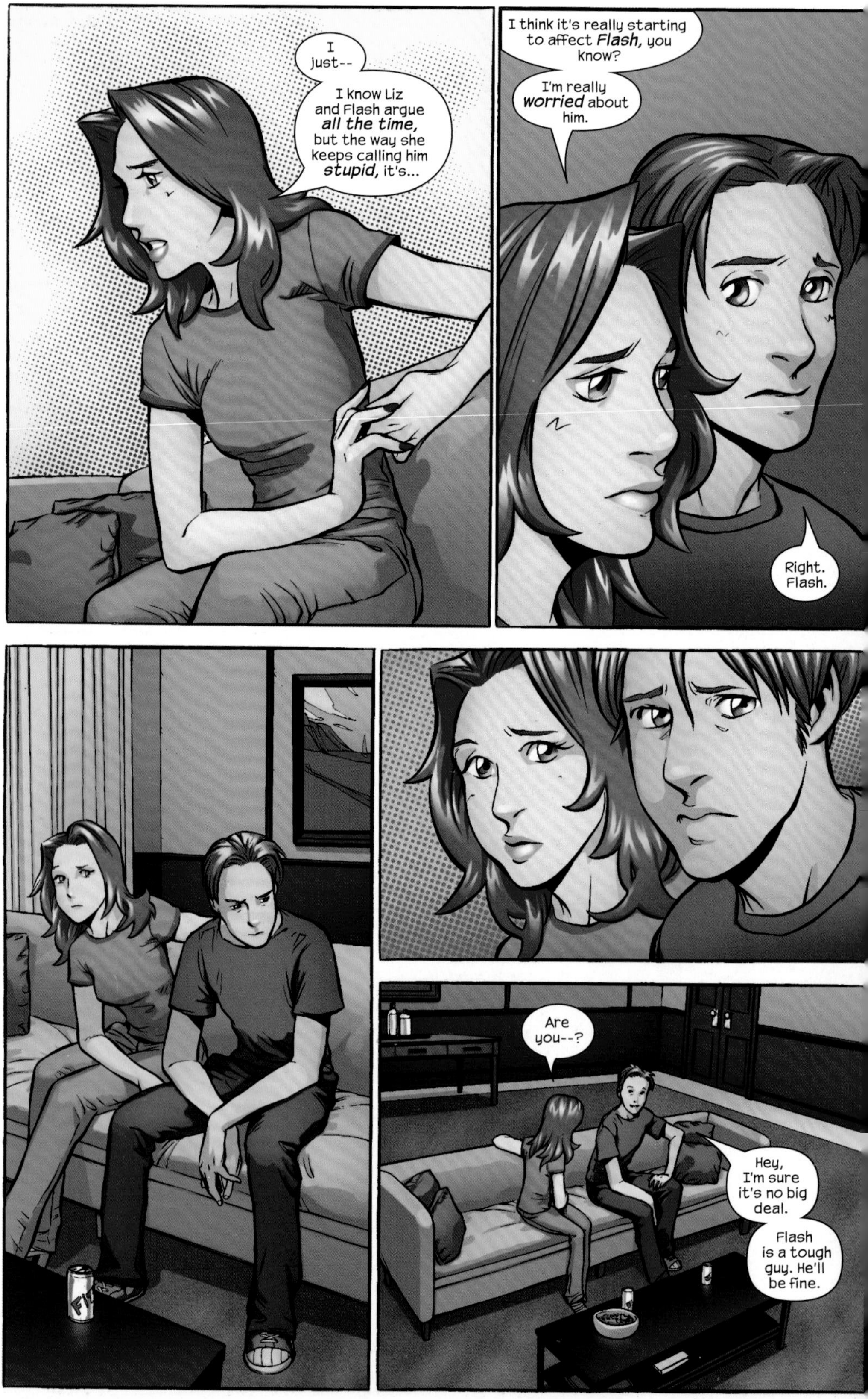
I just--
I know Liz and Flash argue **all the time,** but the way she keeps calling him **stupid,** it's...
I think it's really starting to affect **Flash,** you know?
I'm really **worried** about him.
Right. Flash.
Are you--?
Hey, I'm sure it's no big deal.
Flash is a tough guy. He'll be fine.

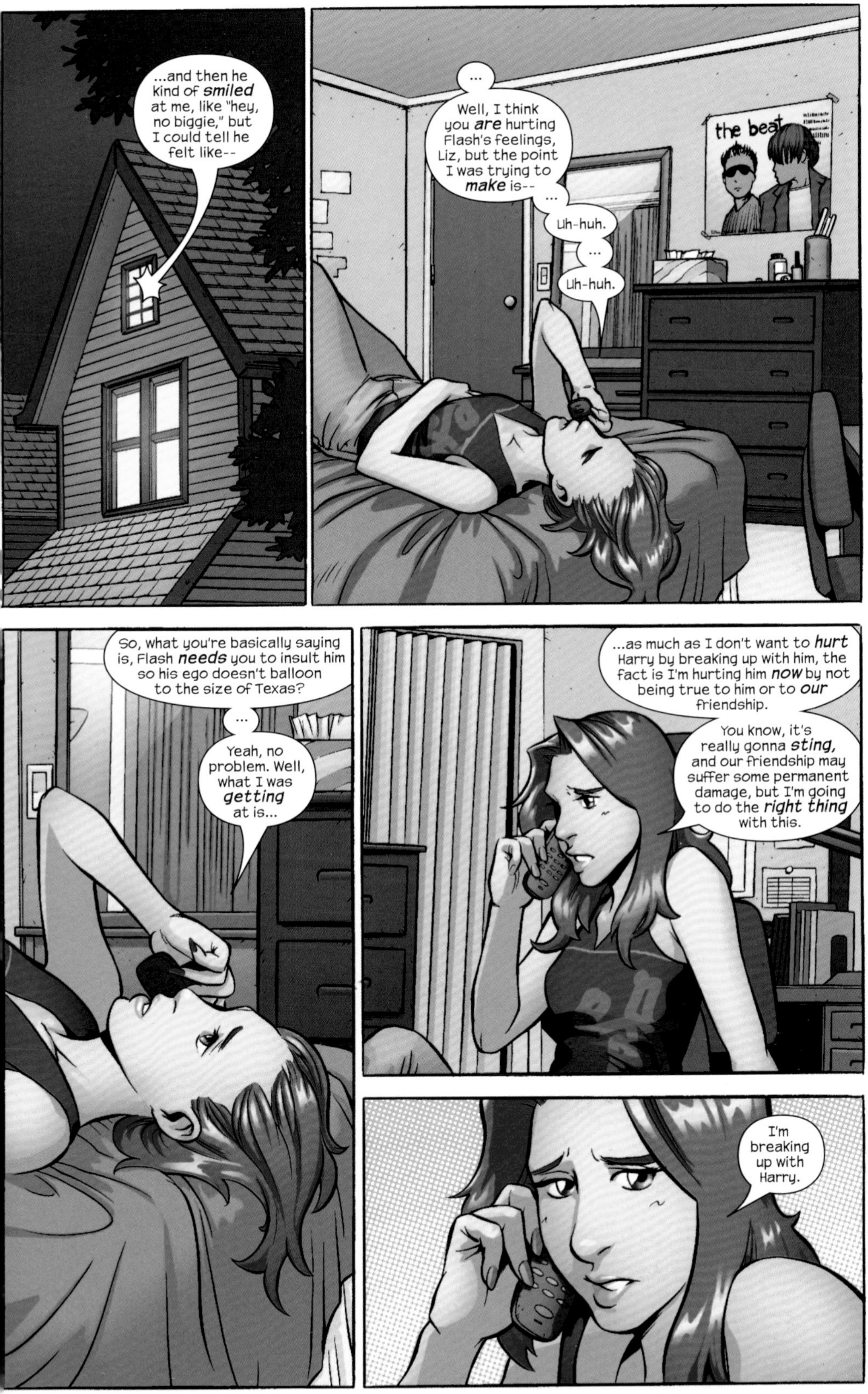
...and then he kind of smiled at me, like "hey, no biggie," but I could tell he felt like--
...
Well, I think you are hurting Flash's feelings, Liz, but the point I was trying to make is--
...
Uh-huh.
...
Uh-huh.
So, what you're basically saying is, Flash needs you to insult him so his ego doesn't balloon to the size of Texas?
...
Yeah, no problem. Well, what I was getting at is...
...as much as I don't want to hurt Harry by breaking up with him, the fact is I'm hurting him now by not being true to him or to our friendship.
You know, it's really gonna sting, and our friendship may suffer some permanent damage, but I'm going to do the right thing with this.
I'm breaking up with Harry.
the beat

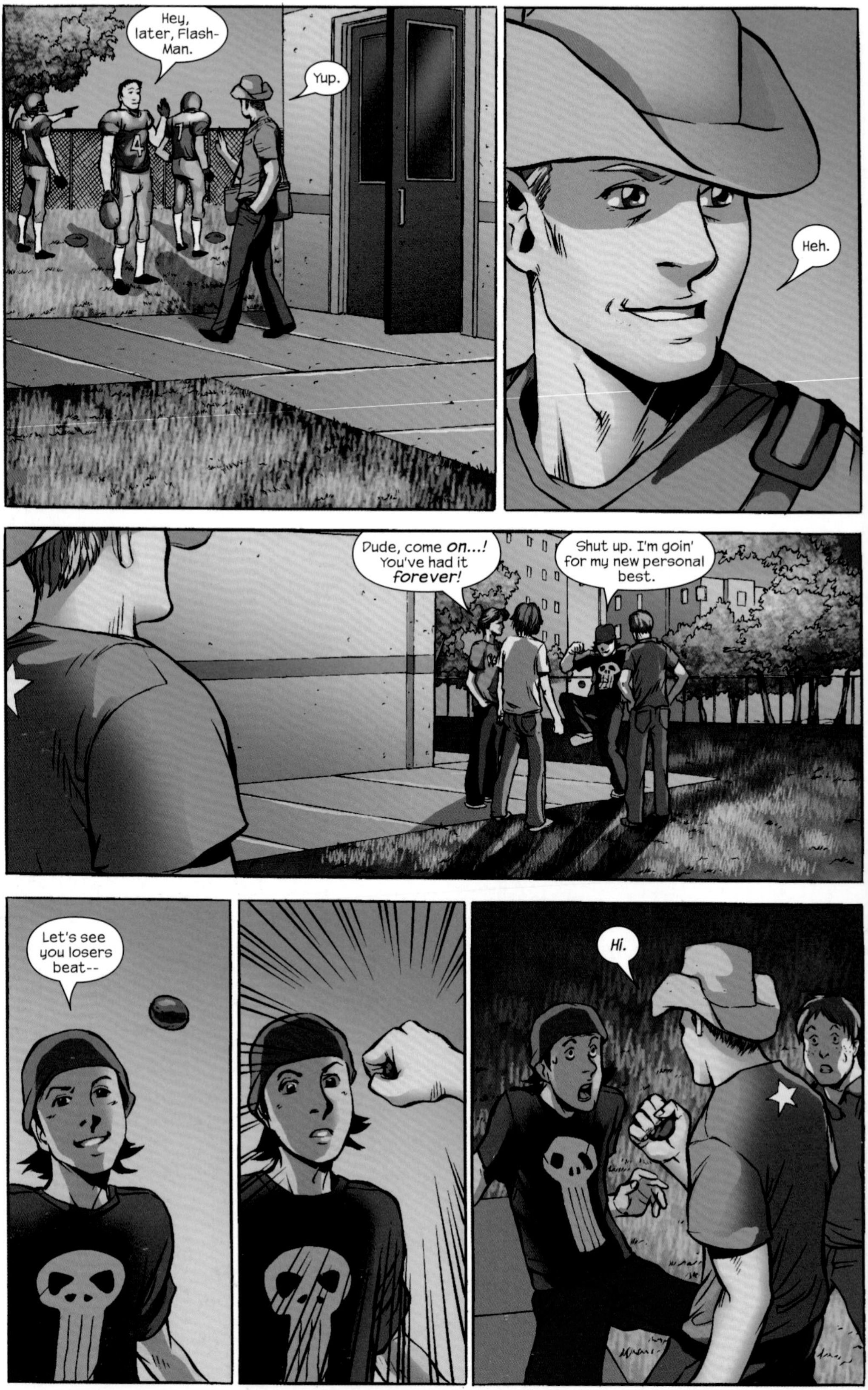
Hey, later, Flash-Man.
Yup.
Heh.
Dude, come on...! You've had it forever!
Shut up. I'm goin' for my new personal best.
Let's see you losers beat--
Hi.

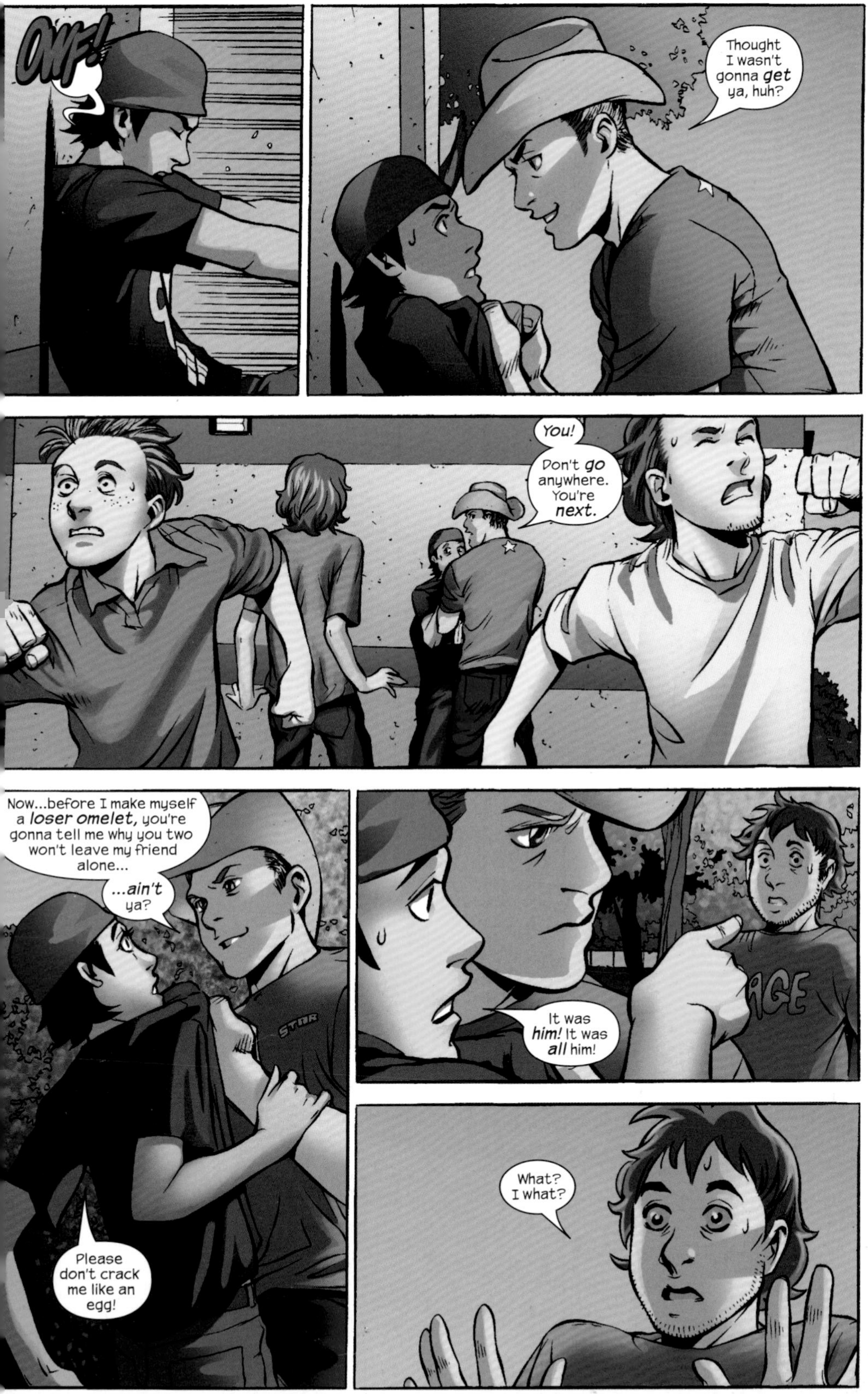
OWF!
Thought I wasn't gonna get ya, huh?
You!
Don't go anywhere. You're next.
Now...before I make myself a loser omelet, you're gonna tell me why you two won't leave my friend alone...
...ain't ya?
Please don't crack me like an egg!
It was him! It was all him!
What? I what?

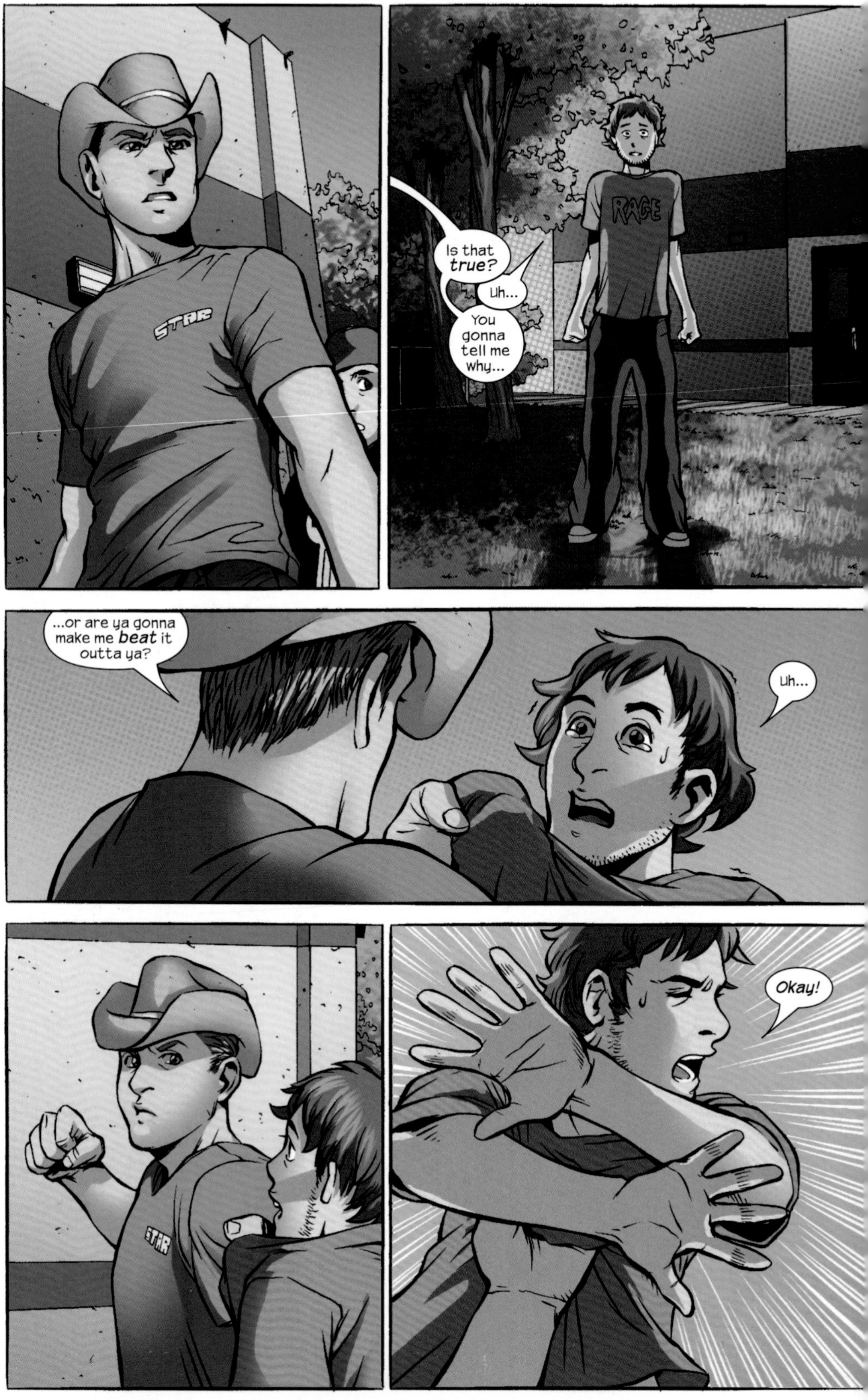
STAR
RAGE
Is that *true*?
Uh...
You gonna tell me why...
...or are ya gonna make me *beat* it outta ya?
Uh...
STAR
Okay!

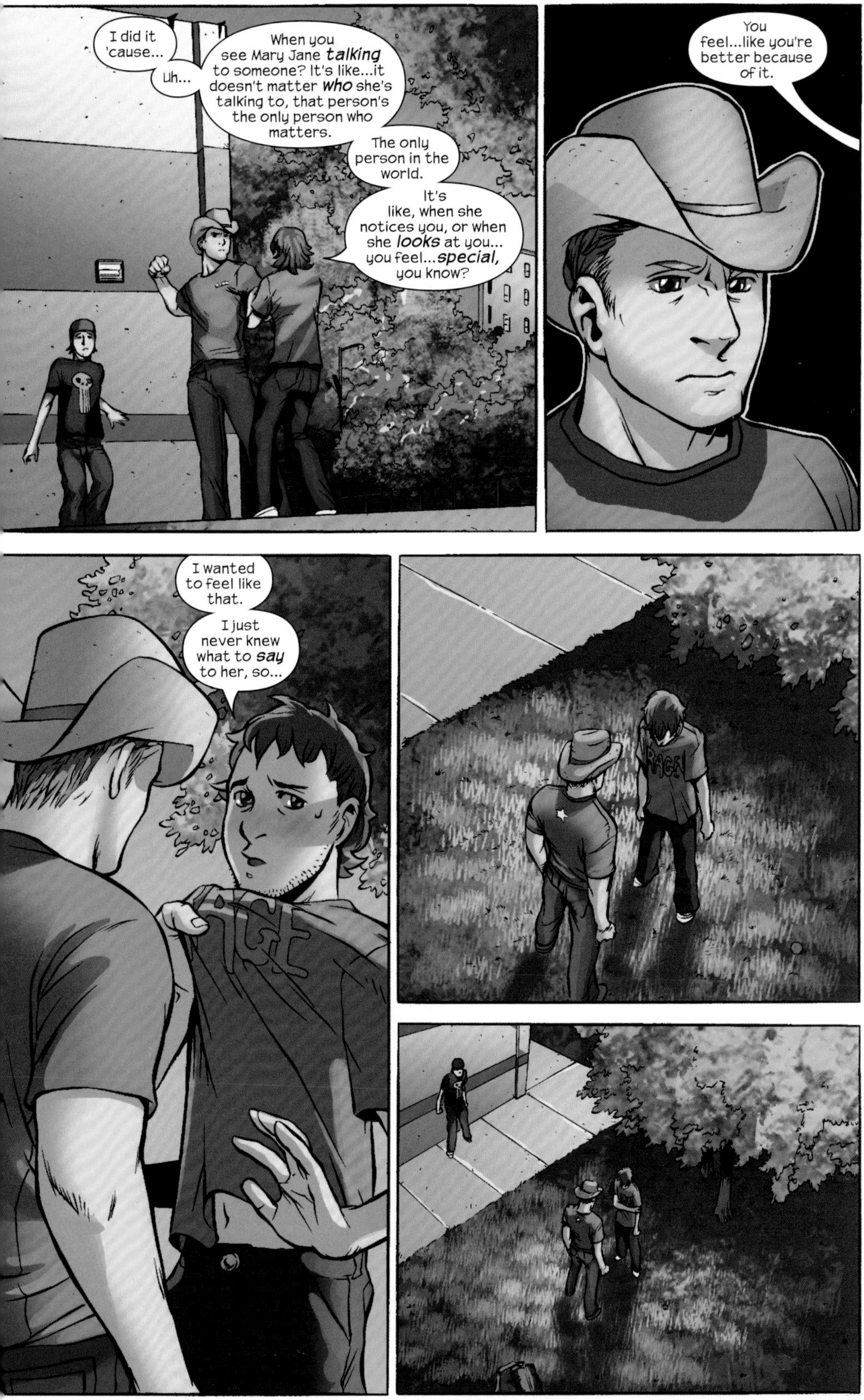
I did it 'cause...
Uh...
When you see Mary Jane *talking* to someone? It's like...it doesn't matter *who* she's talking to, that person's the only person who matters.
The only person in the world.
It's like, when she notices you, or when she *looks* at you... you feel...*special,* you know?
You feel...like you're better because of it.
I wanted to feel like that.
I just never knew what to *say* to her, so...

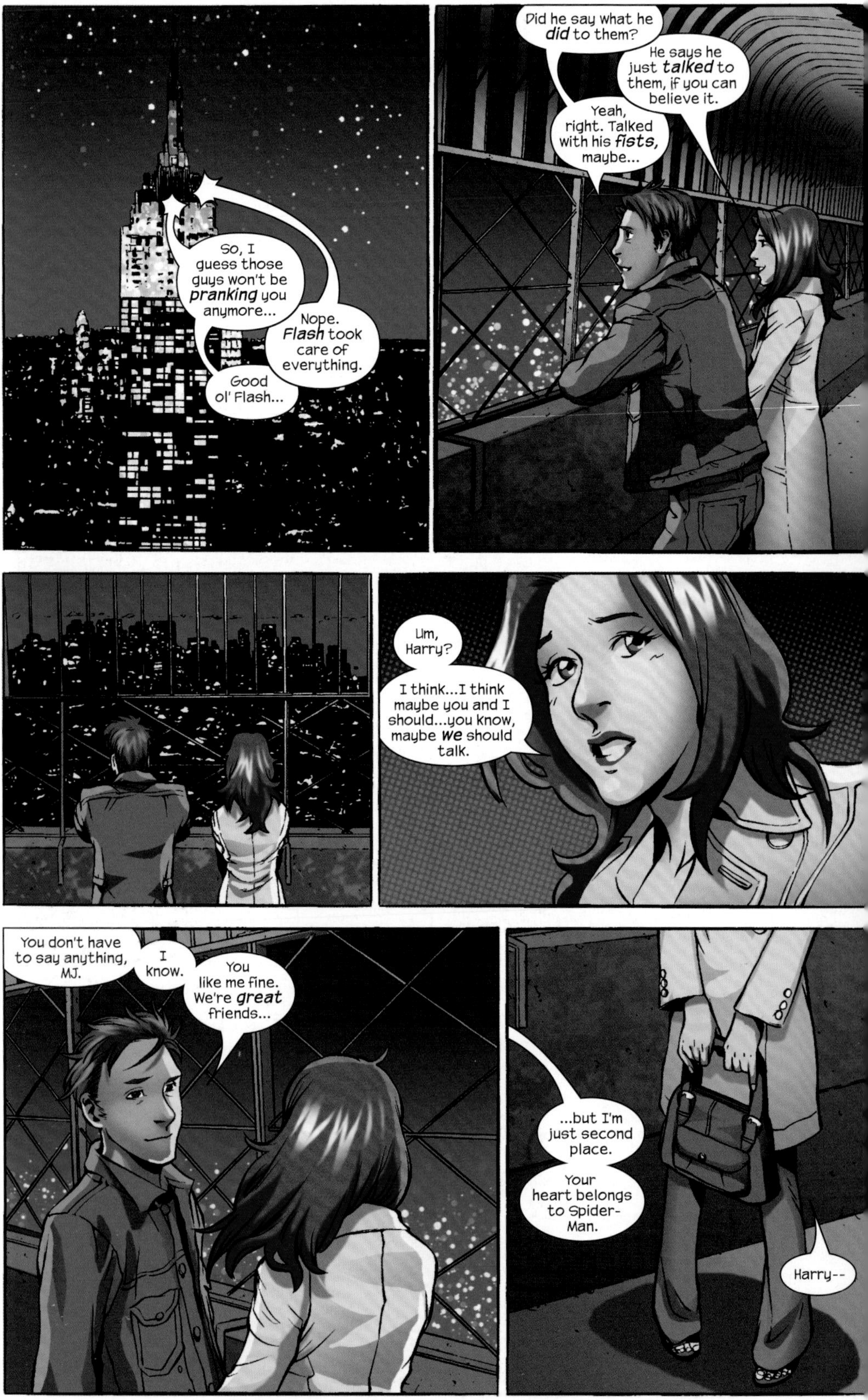
So, I guess those guys won't be **pranking** you anymore...
Nope. **Flash** took care of everything.
Good ol' Flash...
Did he say what he **did** to them?
He says he just **talked** to them, if you can believe it.
Yeah, right. Talked with his **fists,** maybe...
Um, Harry?
I think...I think maybe you and I should...you know, maybe **we** should talk.
You don't have to say anything, MJ.
I know.
You like me fine. We're **great** friends...
...but I'm just second place.
Your heart belongs to Spider-Man.
Harry--

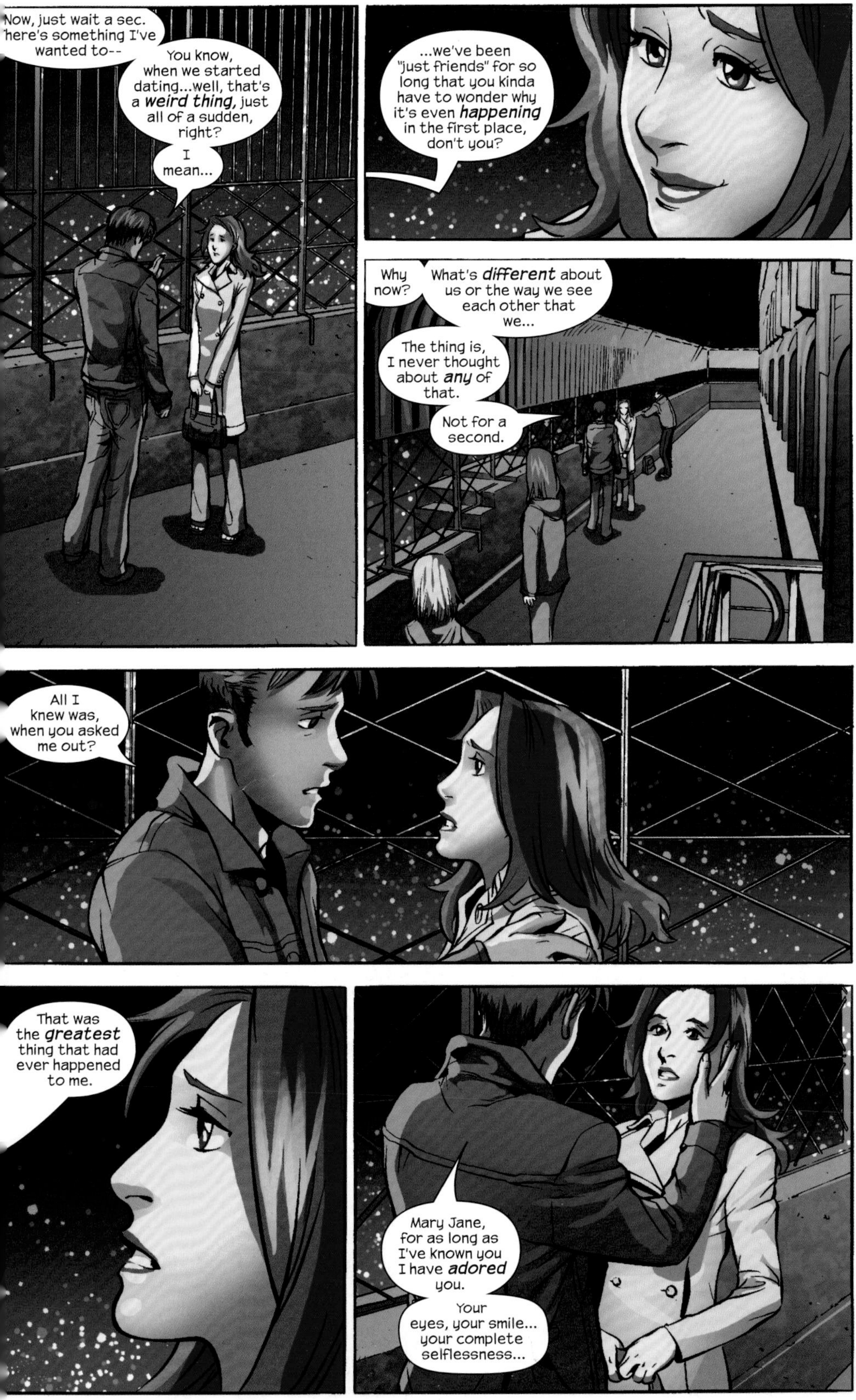

Now, just wait a sec. here's something I've wanted to--
You know, when we started dating...well, that's a weird thing, just all of a sudden, right?
I mean...
...we've been "just friends" for so long that you kinda have to wonder why it's even happening in the first place, don't you?
Why now?
What's different about us or the way we see each other that we...
The thing is, I never thought about any of that.
Not for a second.
All I knew was, when you asked me out?
That was the greatest thing that had ever happened to me.
Mary Jane, for as long as I've known you I have adored you.
Your eyes, your smile... your complete selflessness...

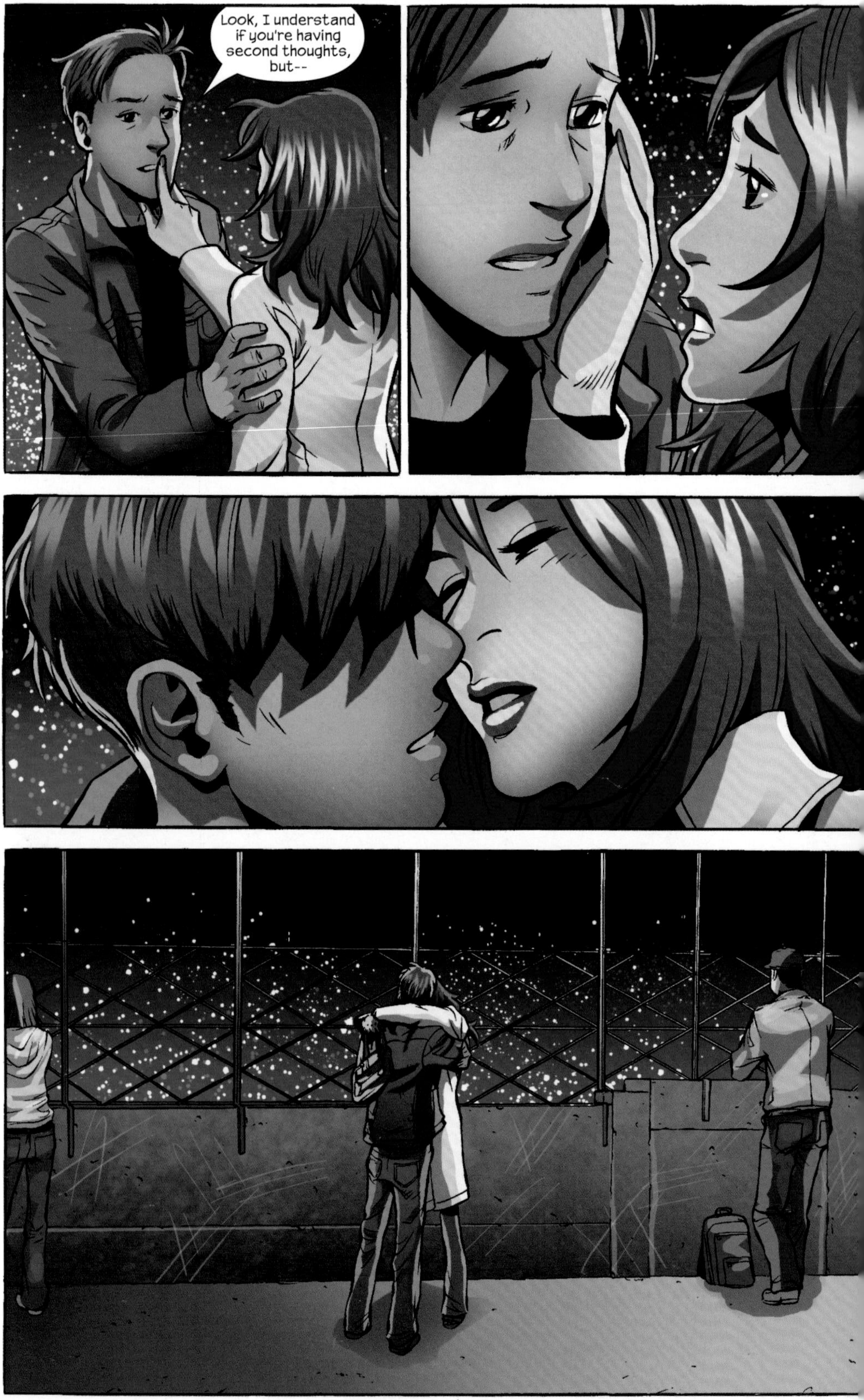
Look, I understand if you're having second thoughts, but--

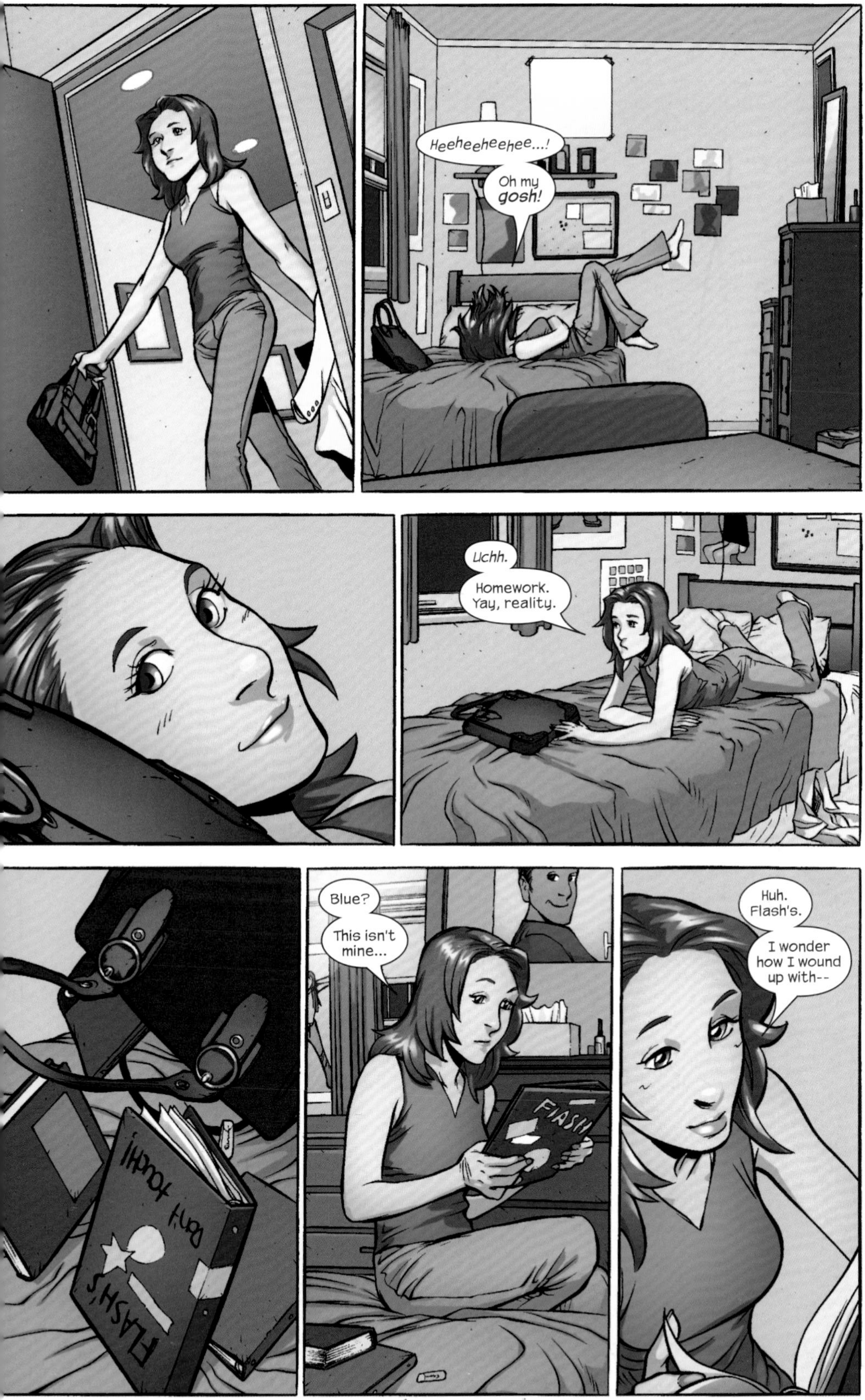
Heeheeheehee...!
Oh my gosh!
Uchh.
Homework. Yay, reality.
Blue?
This isn't mine...
FLASH
Huh. Flash's.
I wonder how I wound up with--

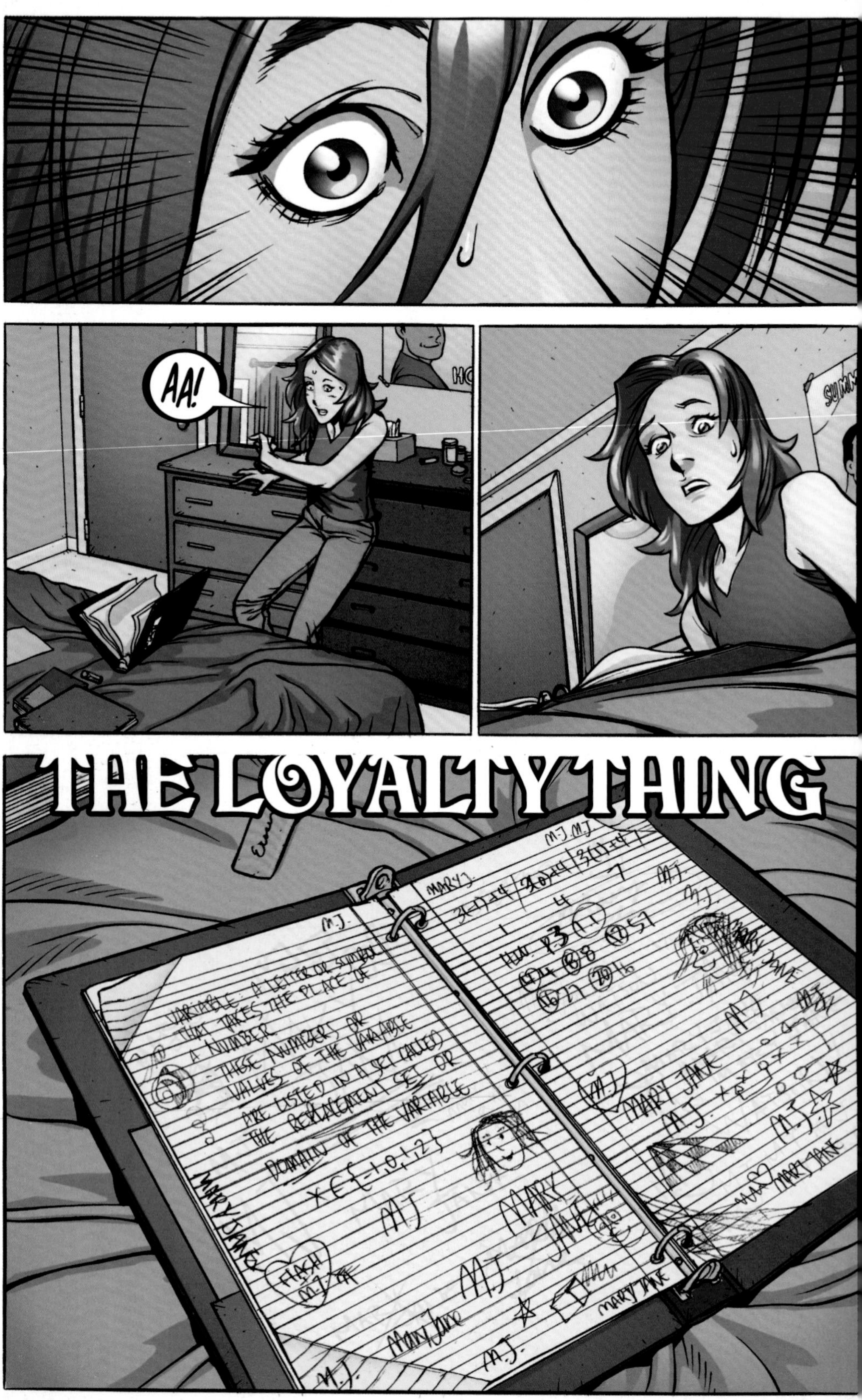
AA!
THE LOYALTY THING

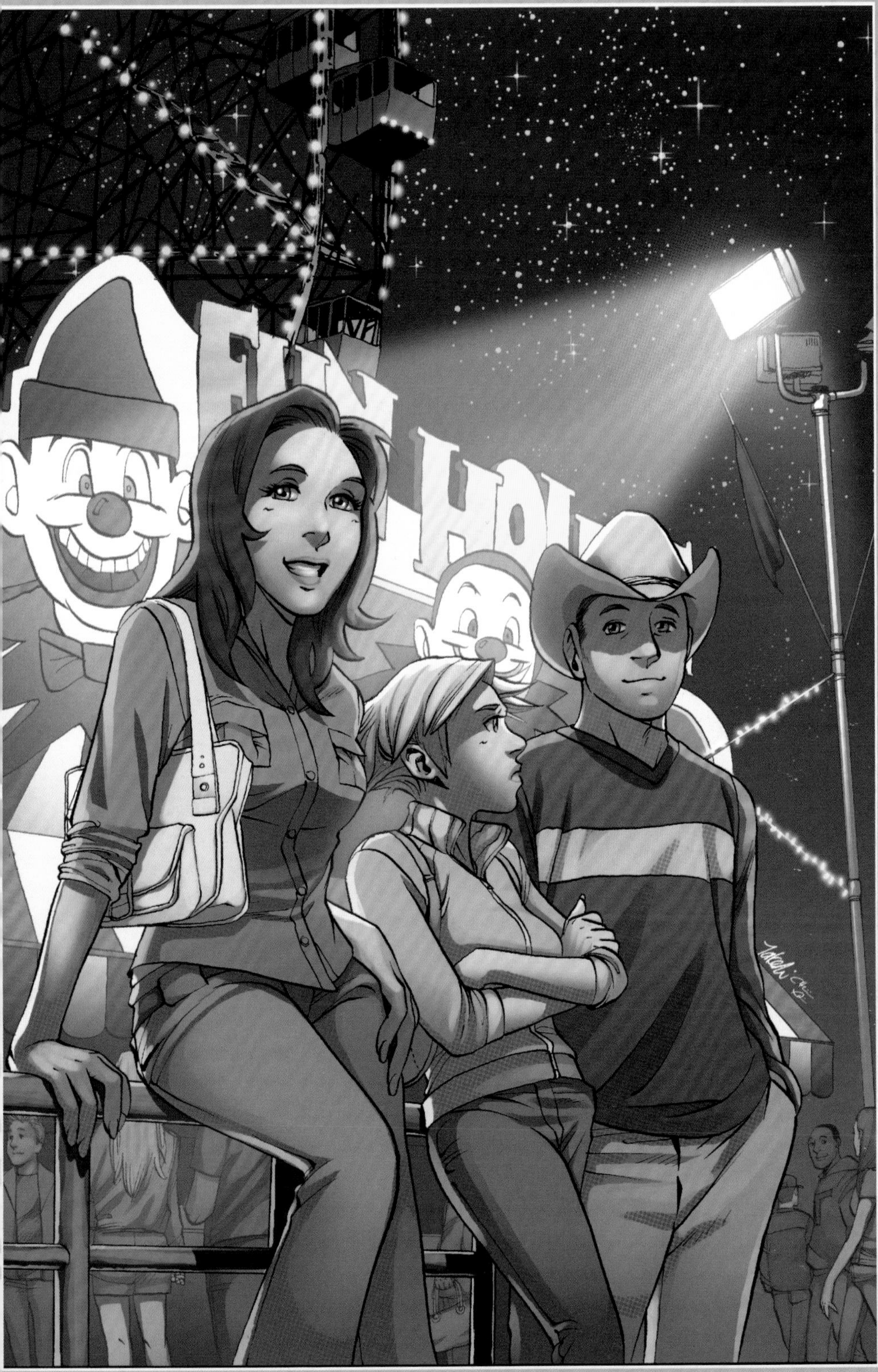

Mary Jane #4

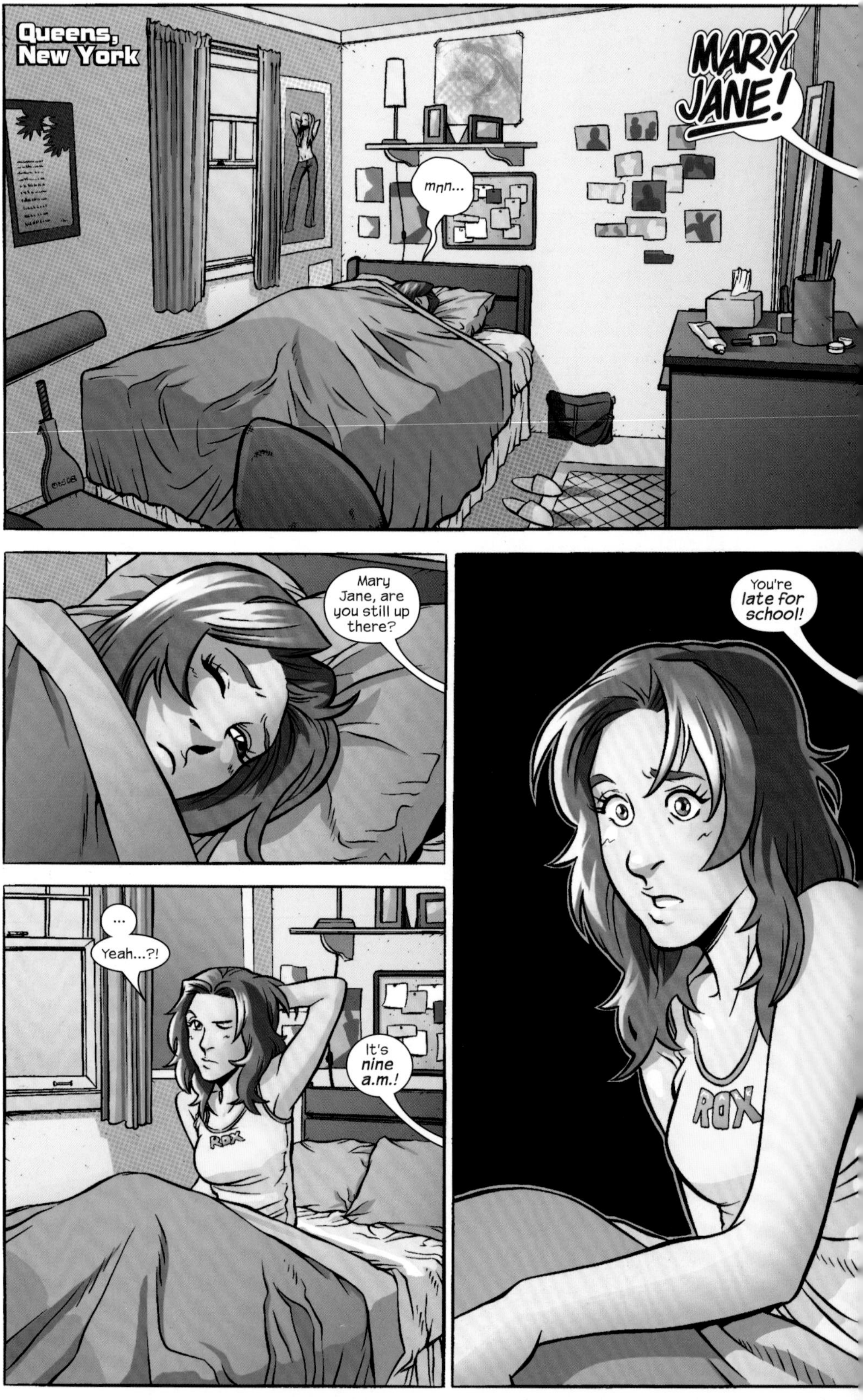
Queens, New York
mnn...
MARY JANE!
Mary Jane, are you still up there?
...
Yeah...?!
It's nine a.m.!
You're late for school!

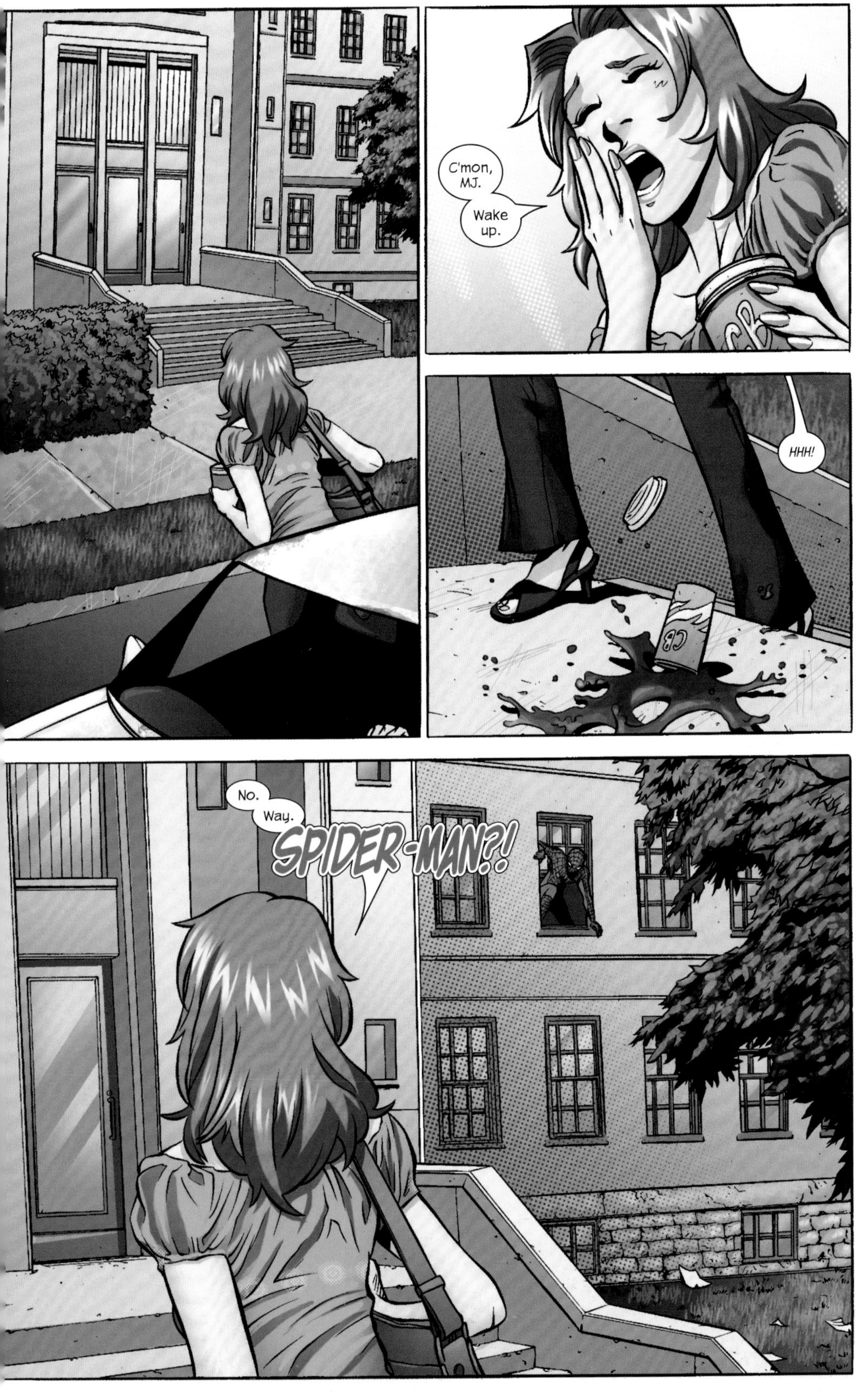
C'mon, MJ.
Wake up.
CB
HHH!
CB
No.
Way.
SPIDER-MAN?!

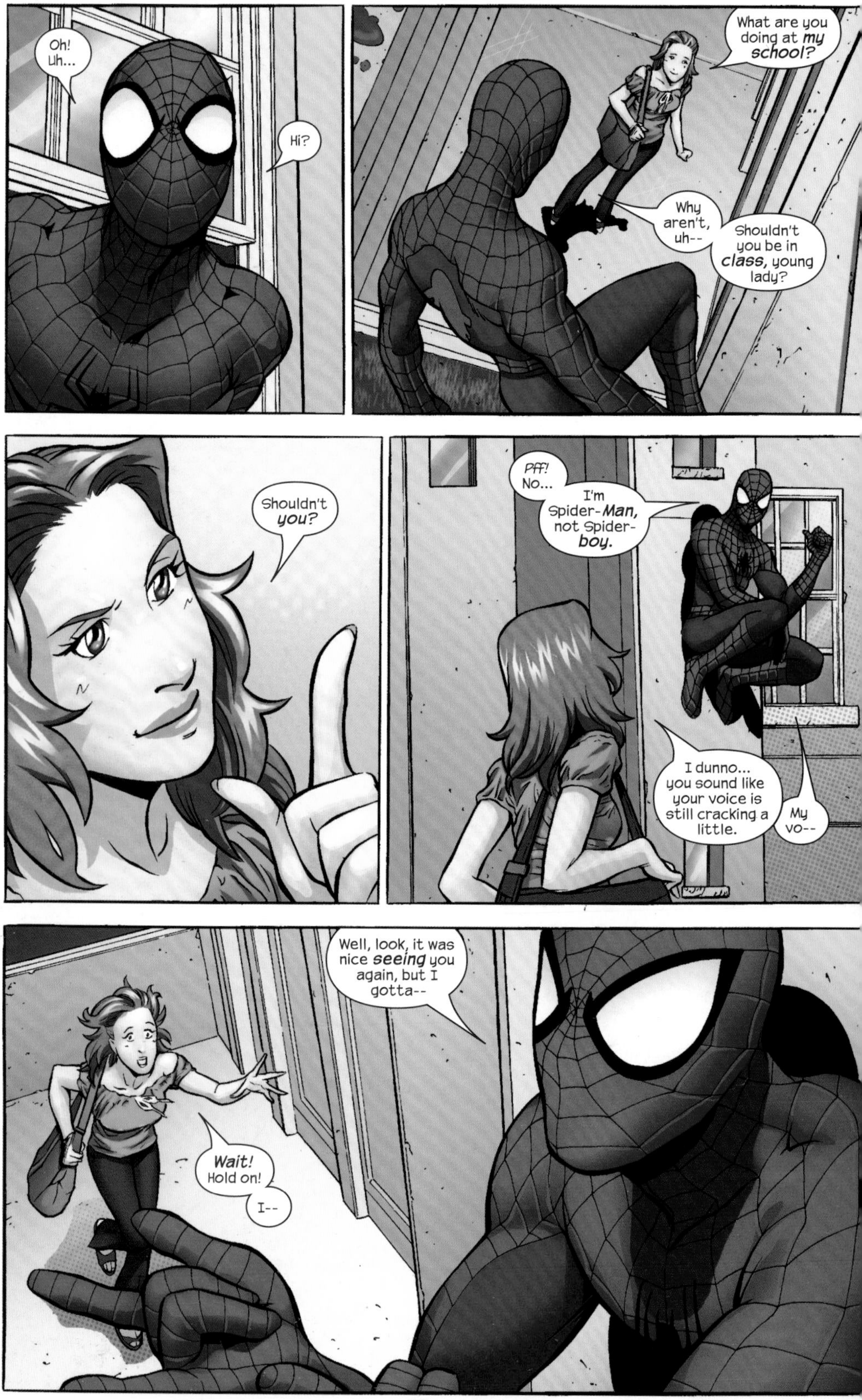
Oh! Uh...
Hi?
What are you doing at my school?
Why aren't, uh--
Shouldn't you be in class, young lady?
Shouldn't you?
Pff! No...
I'm Spider-Man, not Spider-boy.
I dunno... you sound like your voice is still cracking a little.
My vo--
Well, look, it was nice seeing you again, but I gotta--
Wait! Hold on!
I--

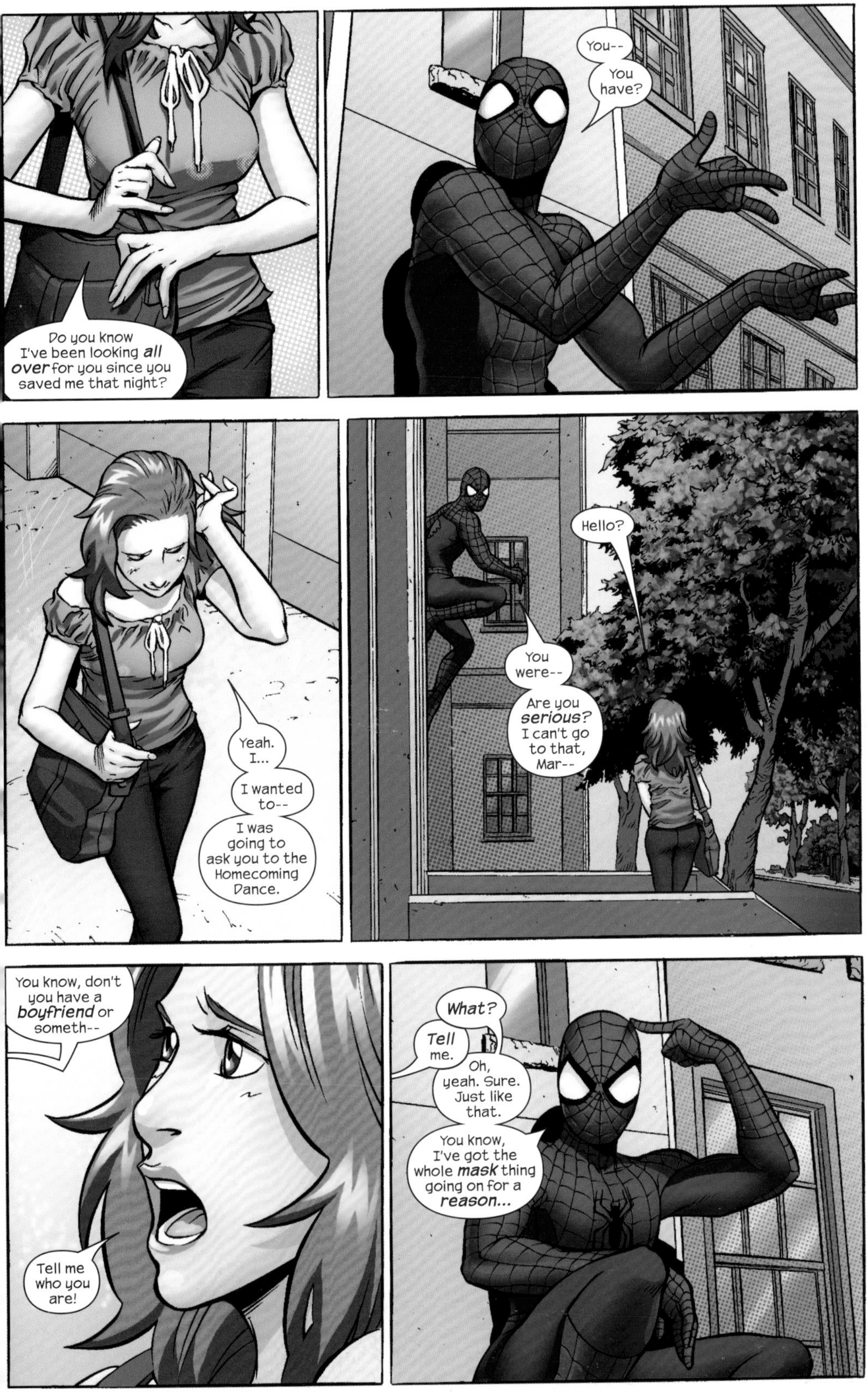
Do you know
I've been looking ***all over*** for you since you saved me that night?
You--
You have?
Yeah. I...
I wanted to--
I was going to ask you to the Homecoming Dance.
Hello?
You were--
Are you ***serious?*** I can't go to that, Mar--
You know, don't you have a ***boyfriend*** or someth--
Tell me who you are!
What?
Tell me.
Oh, yeah. Sure. Just like that.
You know, I've got the whole ***mask*** thing going on for a ***reason...***

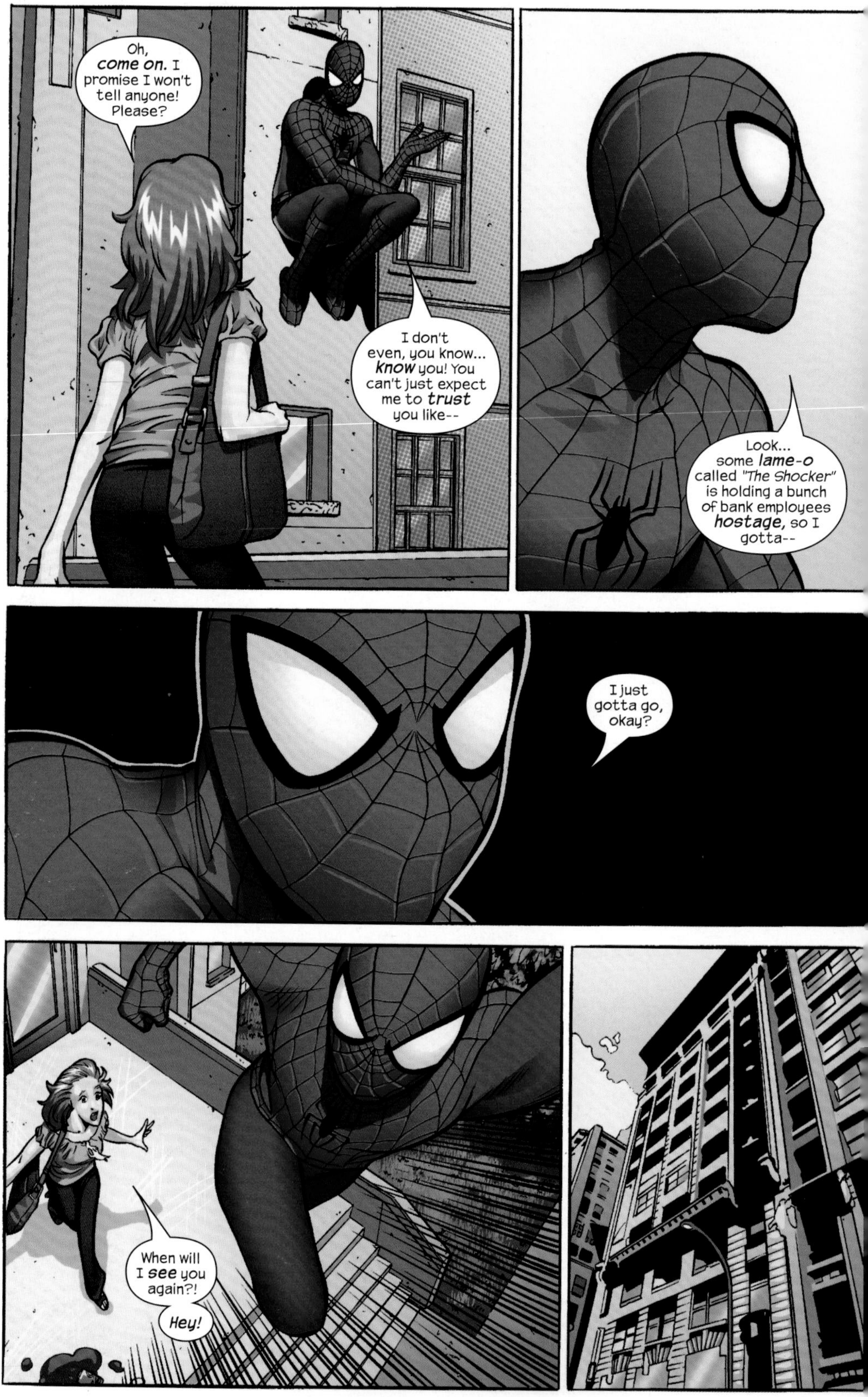

Oh, *come on.* I promise I won't tell anyone! Please?
I don't even, you know... *know* you! You can't just expect me to *trust* you like--
Look... some *lame-o* called *"The Shocker"* is holding a bunch of bank employees *hostage,* so I gotta--
I just gotta go, okay?
When will I *see* you again?!
Hey!

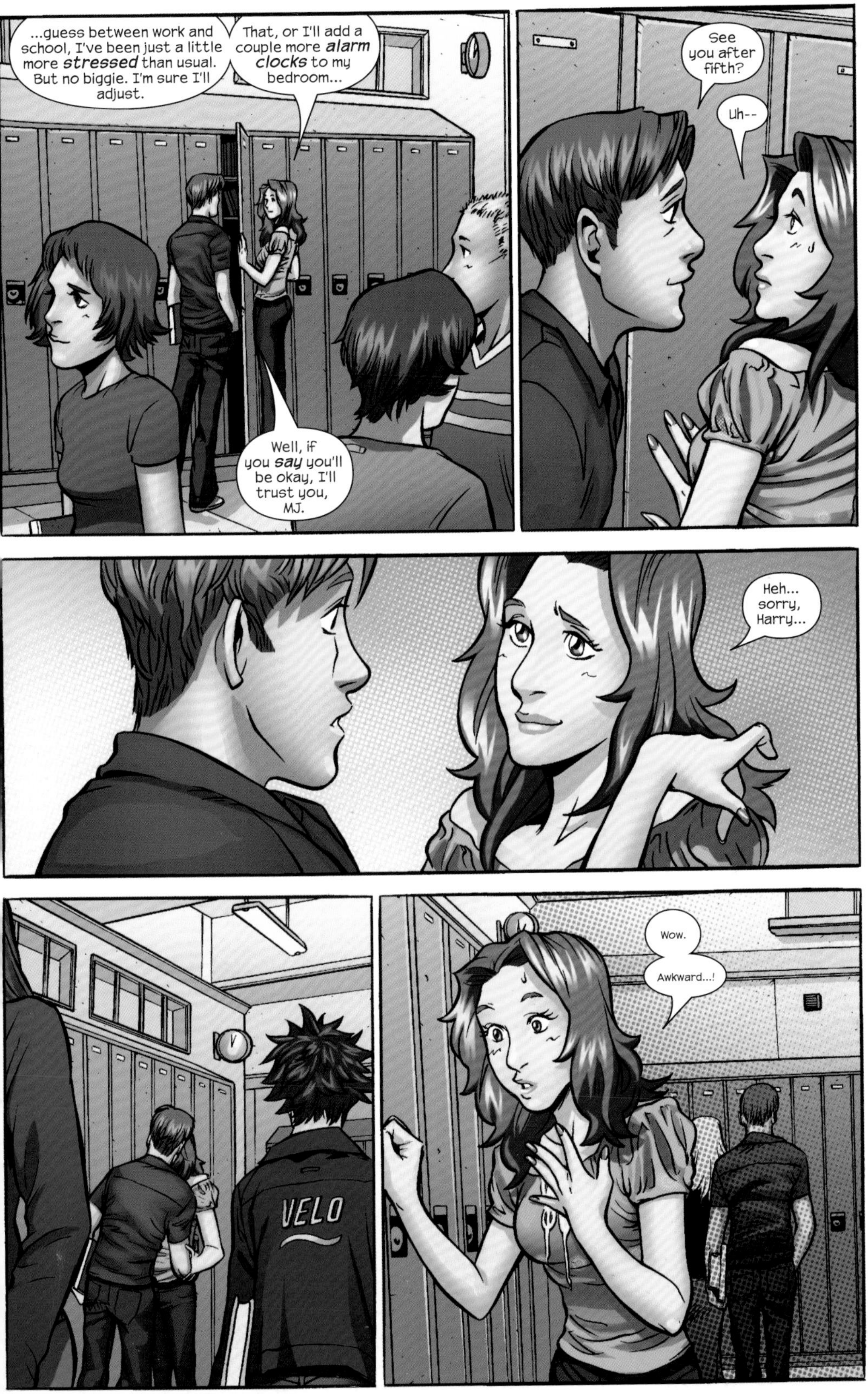
...guess between work and school, I've been just a little more stressed than usual. But no biggie. I'm sure I'll adjust.
That, or I'll add a couple more alarm clocks to my bedroom...
Well, if you say you'll be okay, I'll trust you, MJ.
See you after fifth?
Uh--
Heh... sorry, Harry...
VELO
Wow.
Awkward...!

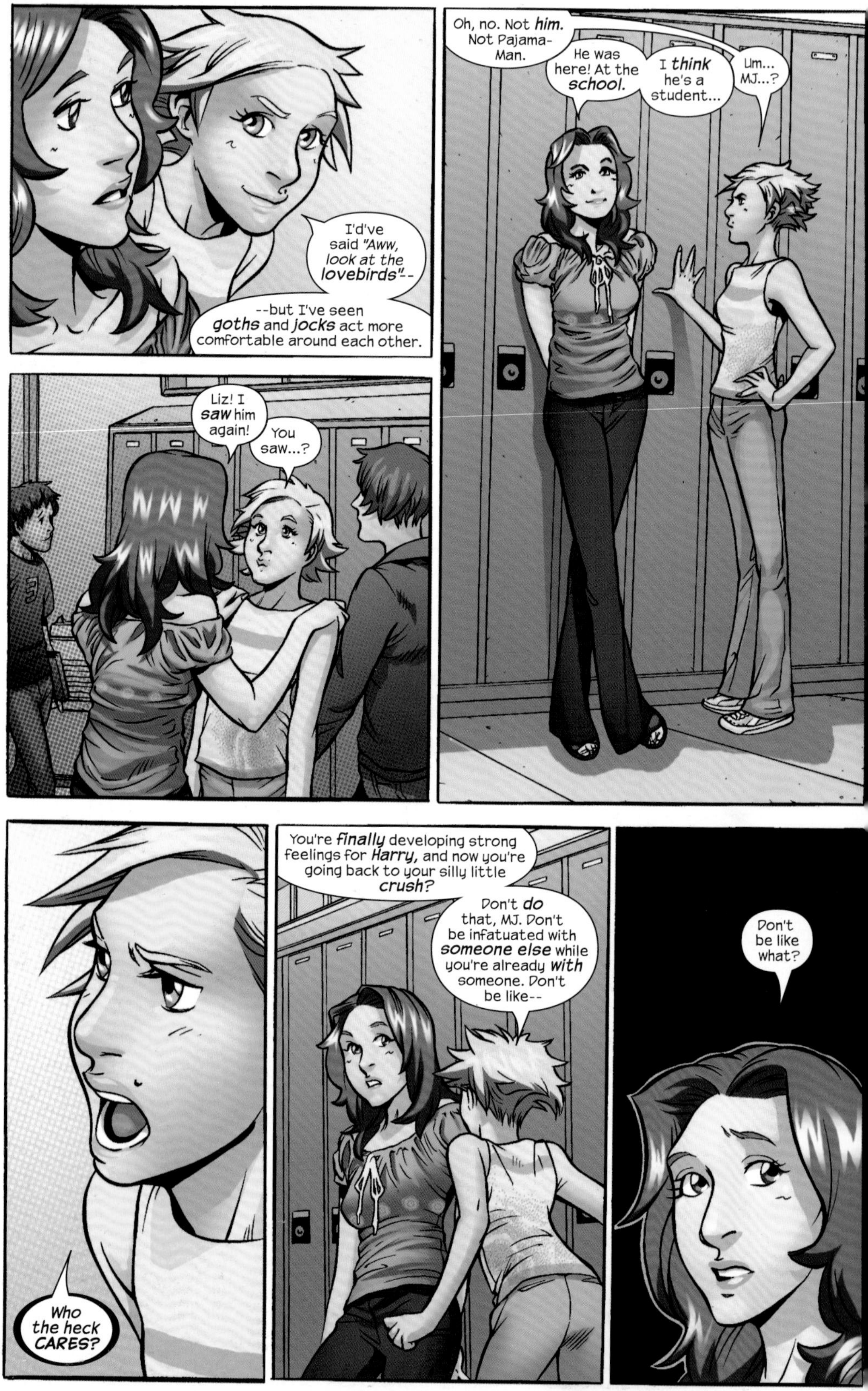

I'd've said "Aww, look at the lovebirds"--
--but I've seen goths and jocks act more comfortable around each other.
Liz! I saw him again!
You saw...?
Oh, no. Not him. Not Pajama-Man.
He was here! At the school.
I think he's a student...
Um... MJ...?
Who the heck CARES?
You're finally developing strong feelings for Harry, and now you're going back to your silly little crush?
Don't do that, MJ. Don't be infatuated with someone else while you're already with someone. Don't be like--
Don't be like what?

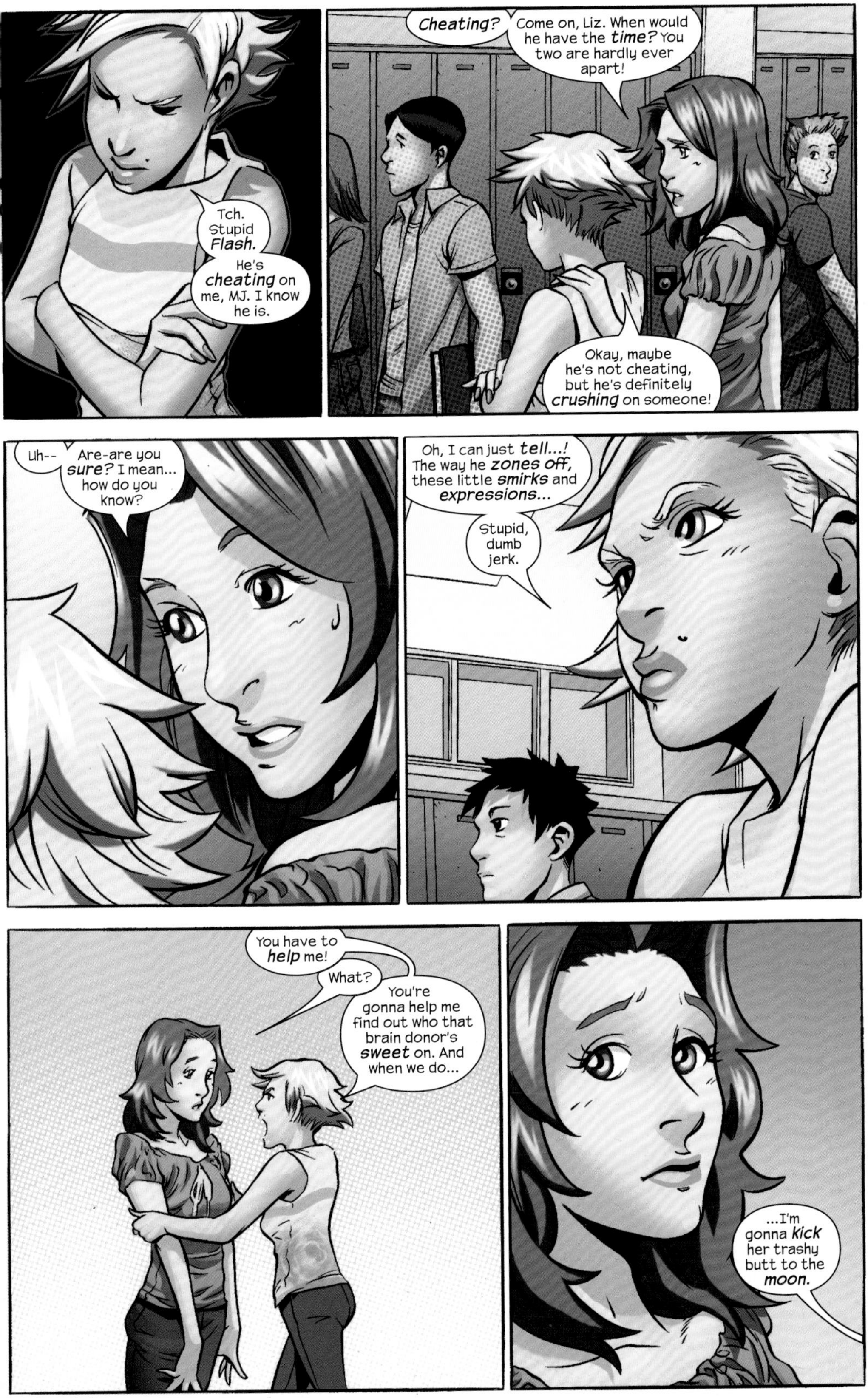
Tch. Stupid Flash.
He's cheating on me, MJ. I know he is.
Cheating?
Come on, Liz. When would he have the time? You two are hardly ever apart!
Okay, maybe he's not cheating, but he's definitely crushing on someone!
Uh--
Are-are you sure? I mean... how do you know?
Oh, I can just tell...! The way he zones off, these little smirks and expressions...
Stupid, dumb jerk.
You have to help me!
What?
You're gonna help me find out who that brain donor's sweet on. And when we do...
...I'm gonna kick her trashy butt to the moon.

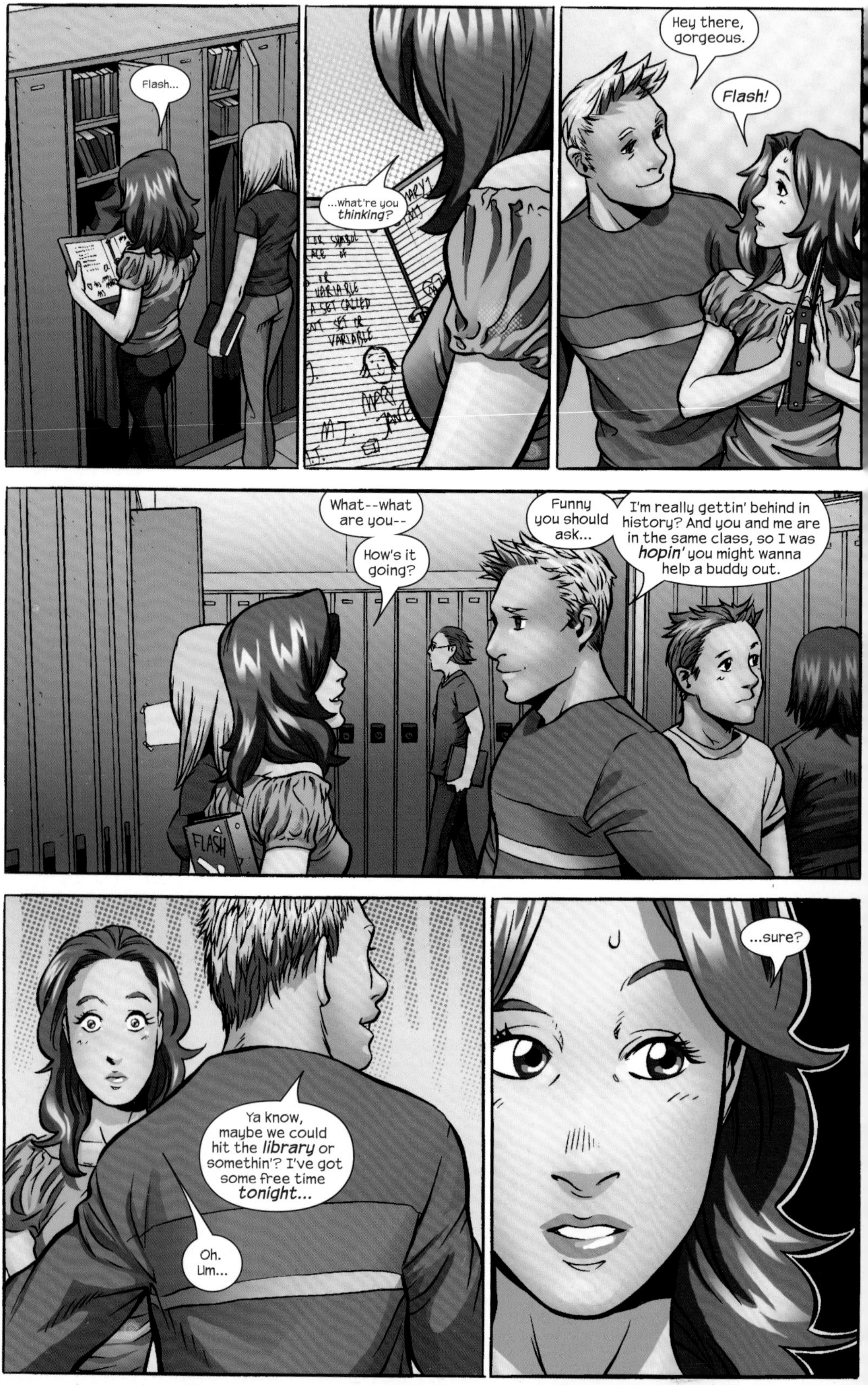

Flash...
...what're you thinking?
Hey there, gorgeous.
Flash!
What--what are you--
How's it going?
Funny you should ask...
I'm really gettin' behind in history? And you and me are in the same class, so I was hopin' you might wanna help a buddy out.
FLASH
Ya know, maybe we could hit the library or somethin'? I've got some free time tonight...
Oh. Um...
...sure?

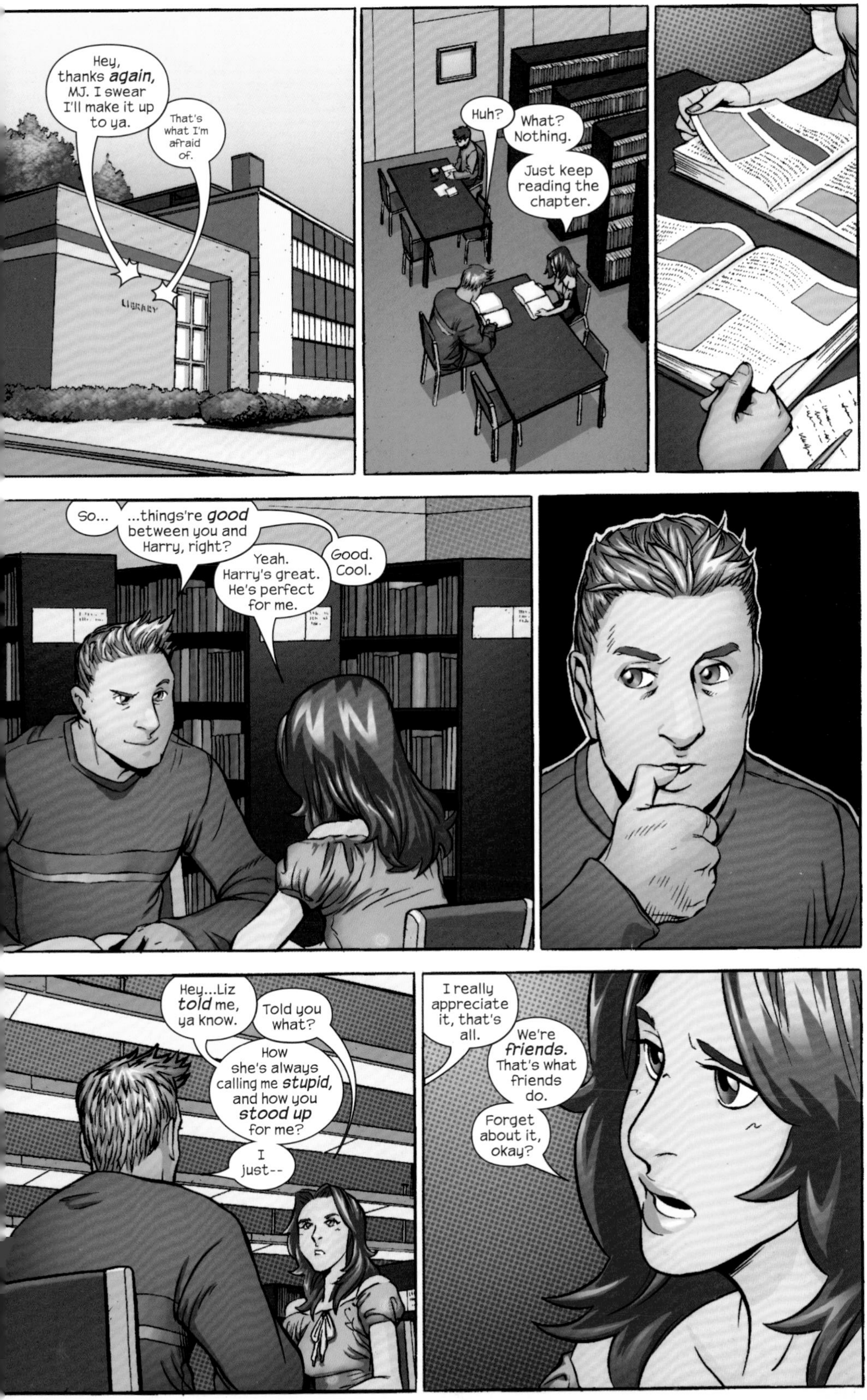

Hey, thanks *again,* MJ. I swear I'll make it up to ya.
That's what I'm afraid of.
LIBRARY
Huh?
What? Nothing.
Just keep reading the chapter.
So...
...things're *good* between you and Harry, right?
Yeah. Harry's great. He's perfect for me.
Good. Cool.
Hey...Liz *told* me, ya know.
Told you what?
How she's always calling me *stupid,* and how you *stood up* for me?
I just--
I really appreciate it, that's all.
We're *friends.* That's what friends do.
Forget about it, okay?

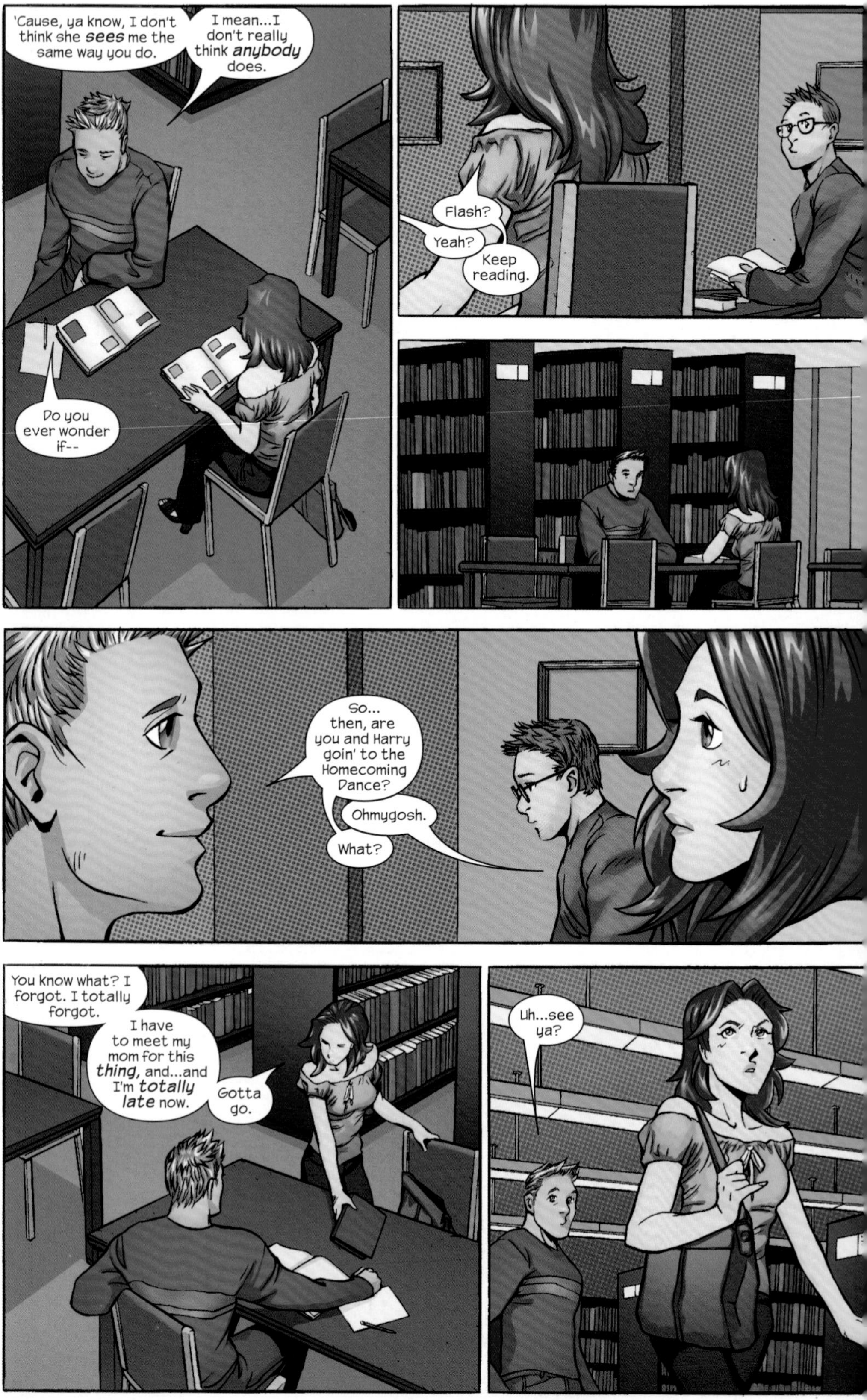
'Cause, ya know, I don't think she *sees* me the same way you do.
I mean...I don't really think *anybody* does.
Do you ever wonder if--
Flash?
Yeah?
Keep reading.
So... then, are you and Harry goin' to the Homecoming Dance?
Ohmygosh.
What?
You know what? I forgot. I totally forgot.
I have to meet my mom for this *thing,* and...and I'm *totally late* now.
Gotta go.
Uh...see ya?

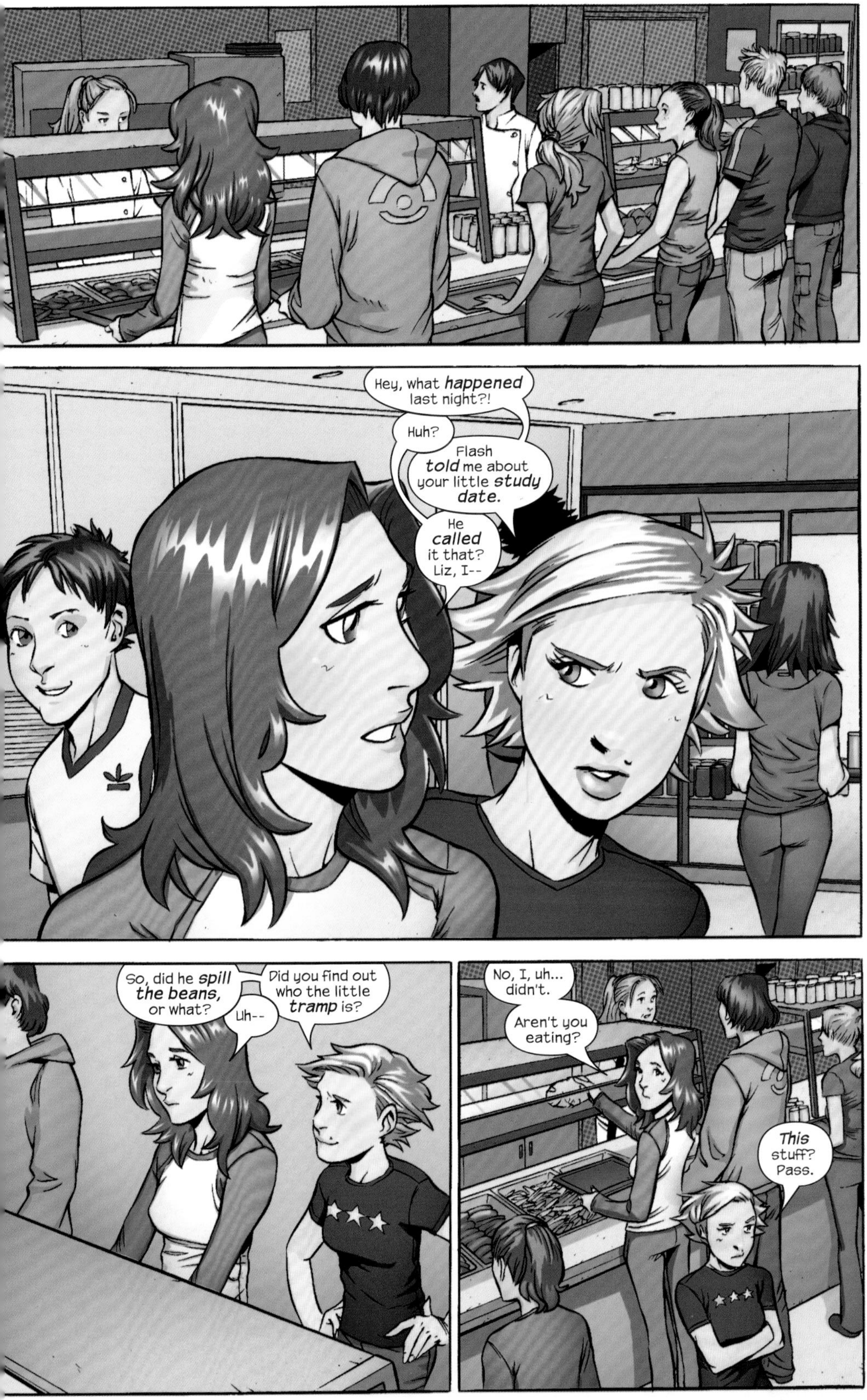
Hey, what happened last night?!
Huh?
Flash told me about your little study date.
He called it that? Liz, I--
So, did he spill the beans, or what?
Did you find out who the little tramp is?
Uh--
No, I, uh... didn't.
Aren't you eating?
This stuff? Pass.

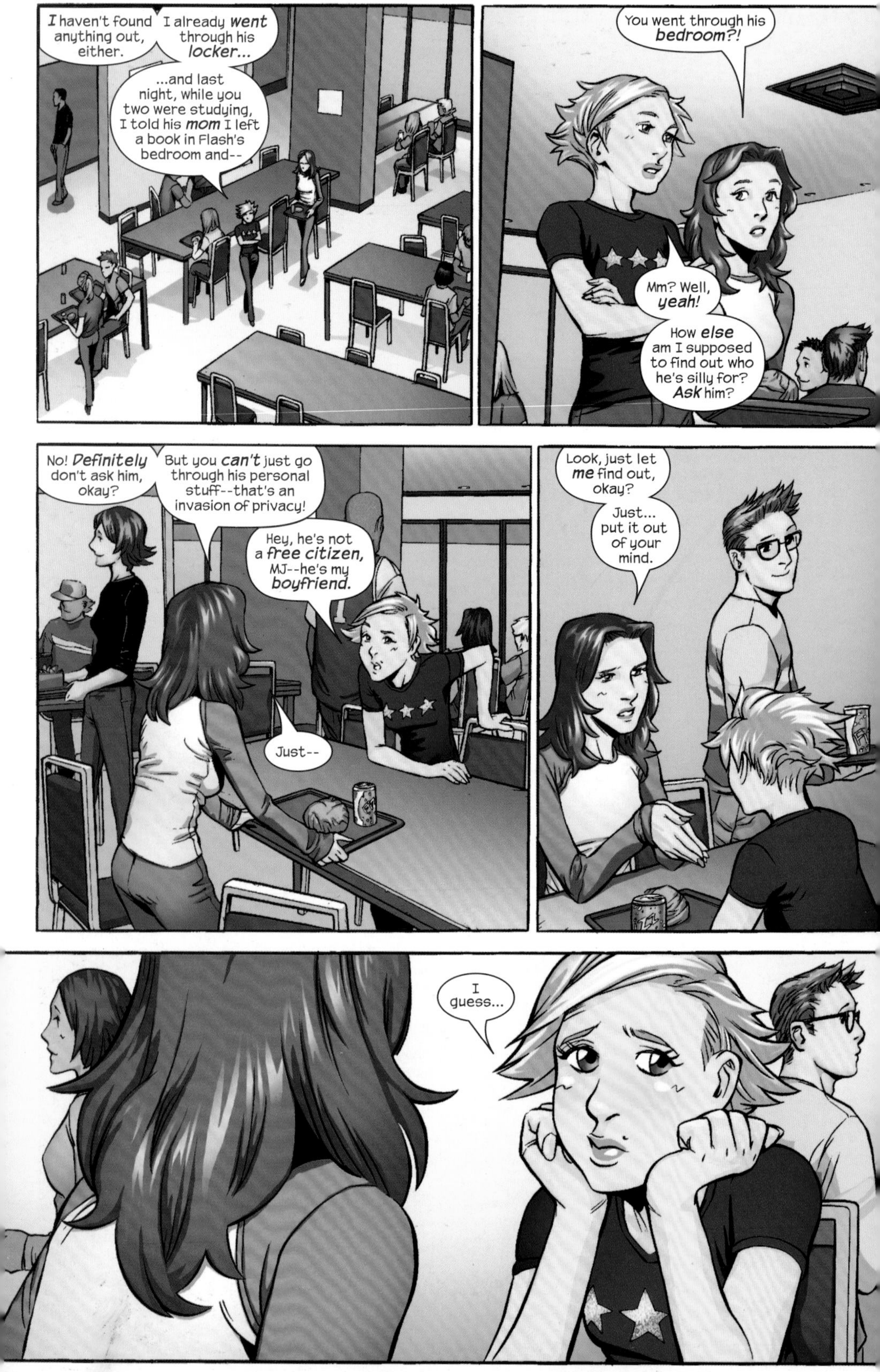
I haven't found anything out, either.
I already went through his locker...
...and last night, while you two were studying, I told his mom I left a book in Flash's bedroom and--
You went through his bedroom?!
Mm? Well, yeah!
How else am I supposed to find out who he's silly for? Ask him?
No! Definitely don't ask him, okay?
But you can't just go through his personal stuff--that's an invasion of privacy!
Hey, he's not a free citizen, MJ--he's my boyfriend.
Just--
Look, just let me find out, okay?
Just... put it out of your mind.
I guess...

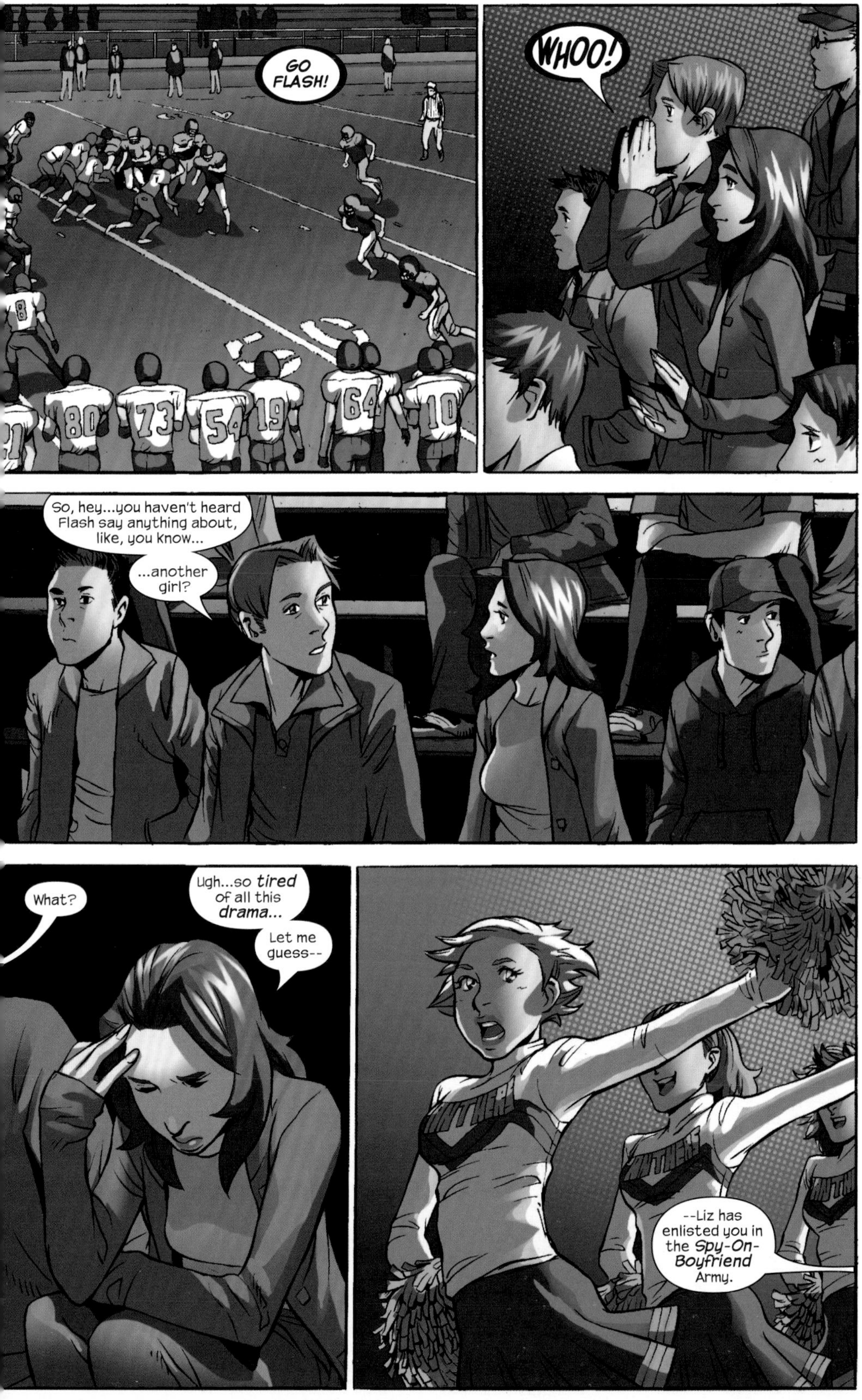
GO FLASH!
WHOO!
So, hey...you haven't heard Flash say anything about, like, you know...
...another girl?
What?
Ugh...so tired of all this drama...
Let me guess--
--Liz has enlisted you in the Spy-On-Boyfriend Army.

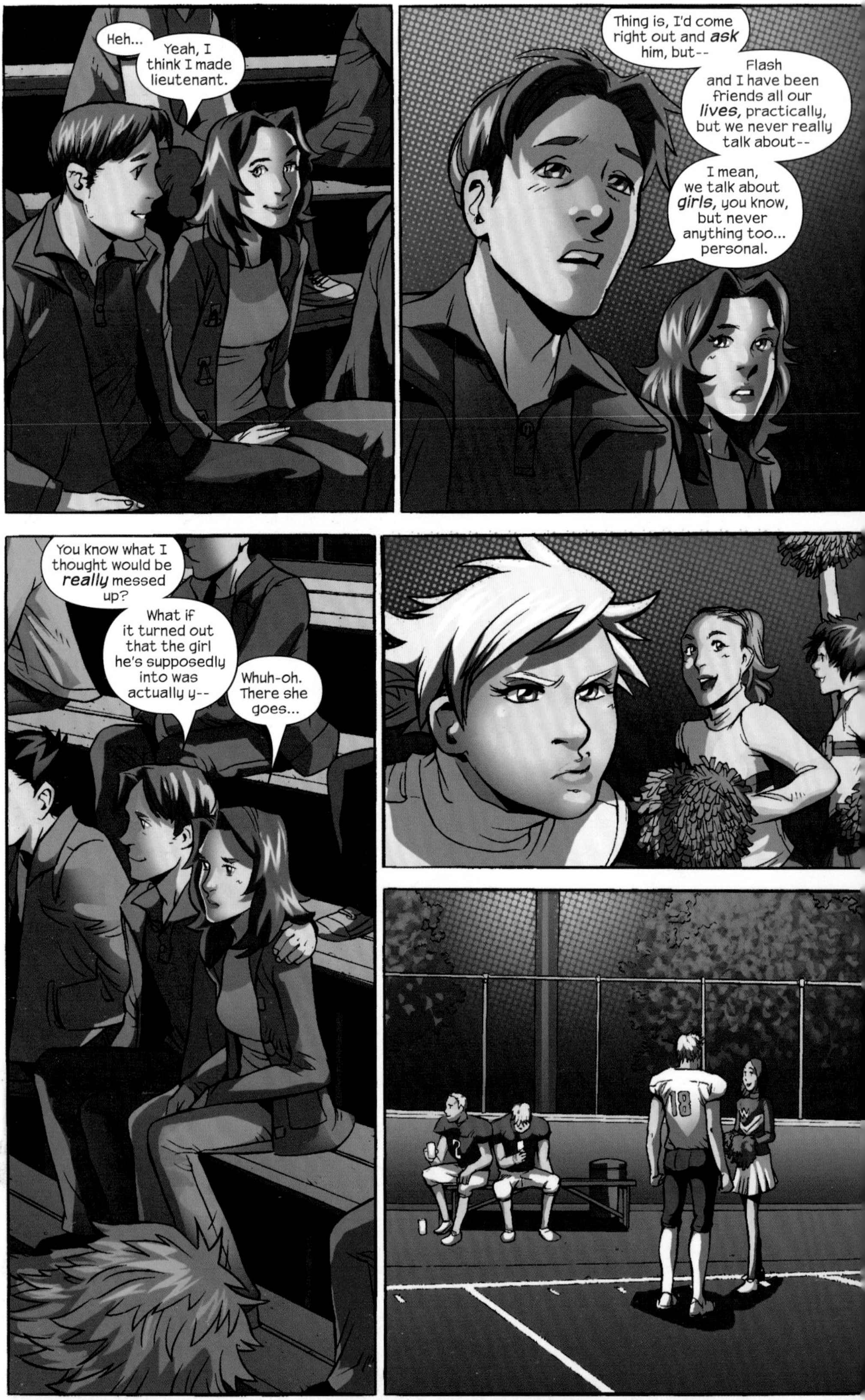
Heh...
Yeah, I think I made lieutenant.
Thing is, I'd come right out and *ask* him, but--
Flash and I have been friends all our *lives,* practically, but we never really talk about--
I mean, we talk about *girls,* you know, but never anything too... personal.
You know what I thought would be *really* messed up?
What if it turned out that the girl he's supposedly into was actually y--
Whuh-oh. There she goes...
18

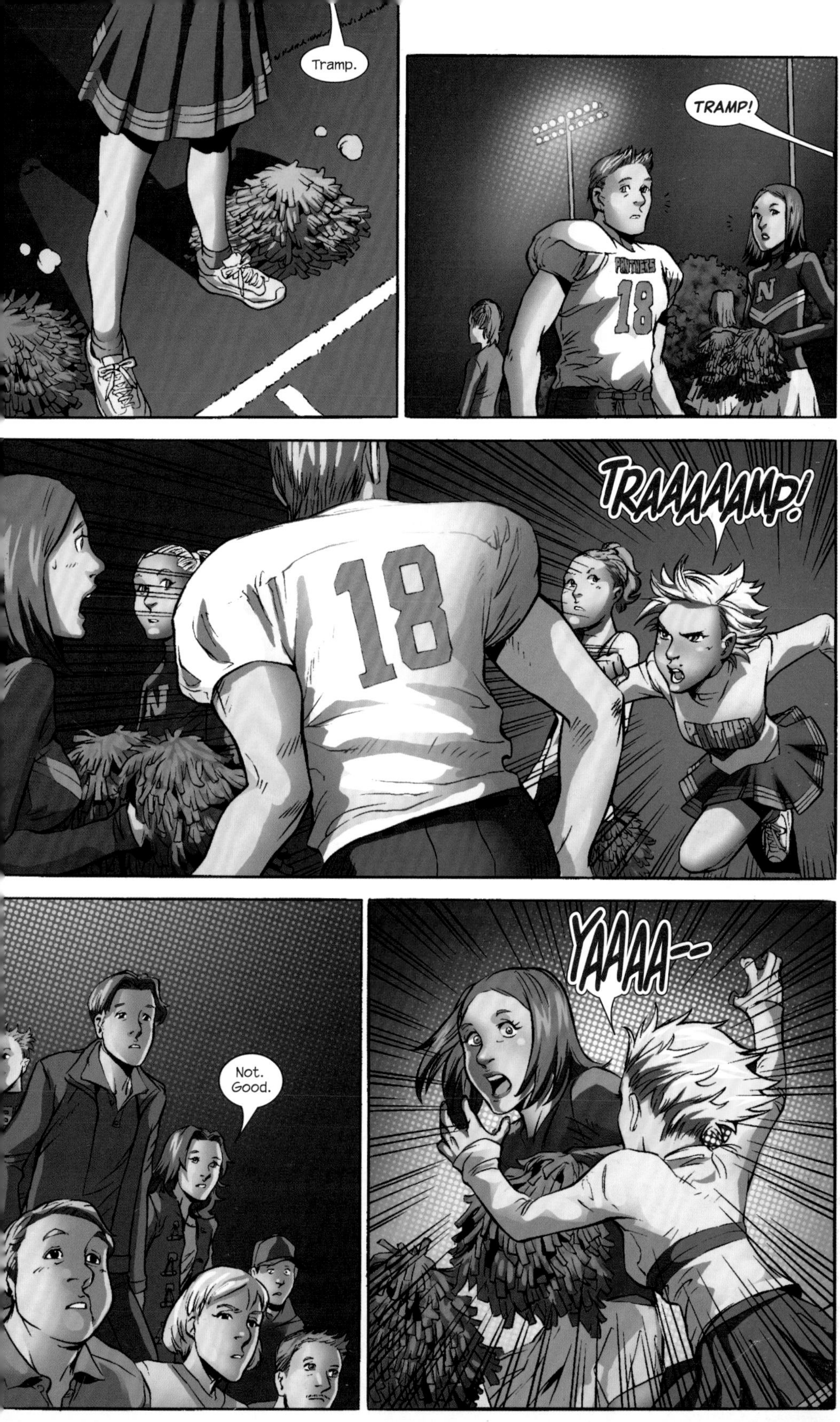
Tramp.
TRAMP!
TRAAAAAAMP!
Not.
Good.
YAAAA--

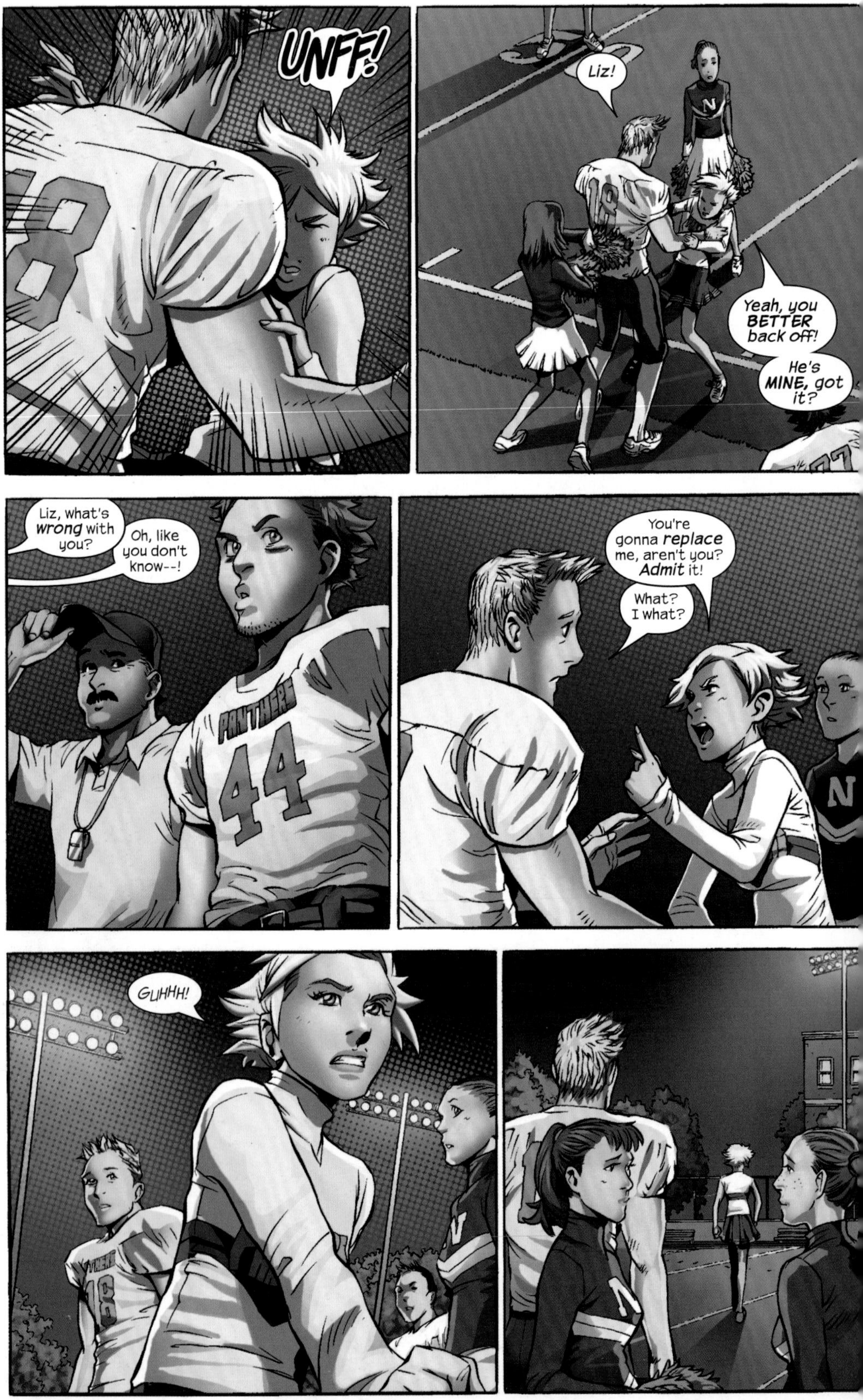
UNFF!
Liz!
Yeah, you BETTER back off!
He's MINE, got it?
Liz, what's wrong with you?
Oh, like you don't know--!
You're gonna replace me, aren't you? Admit it!
What? I what?
GUHHH!

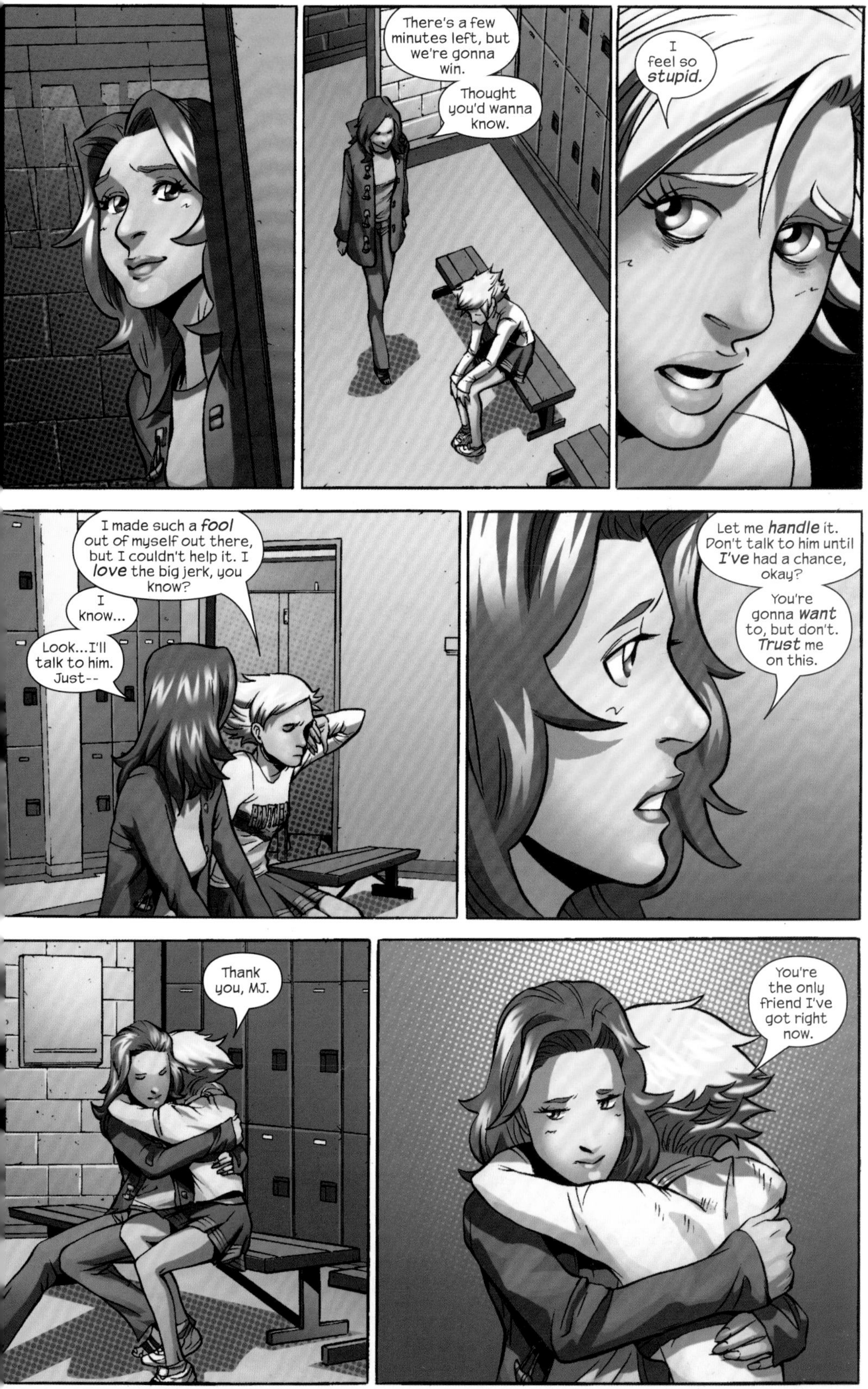
There's a few minutes left, but we're gonna win.
Thought you'd wanna know.
I feel so *stupid.*
I made such a *fool* out of myself out there, but I couldn't help it. I *love* the big jerk, you know?
I know...
Look...I'll talk to him. Just--
Let me *handle* it. Don't talk to him until *I've* had a chance, okay?
You're gonna *want* to, but don't. *Trust* me on this.
Thank you, MJ.
You're the only friend I've got right now.

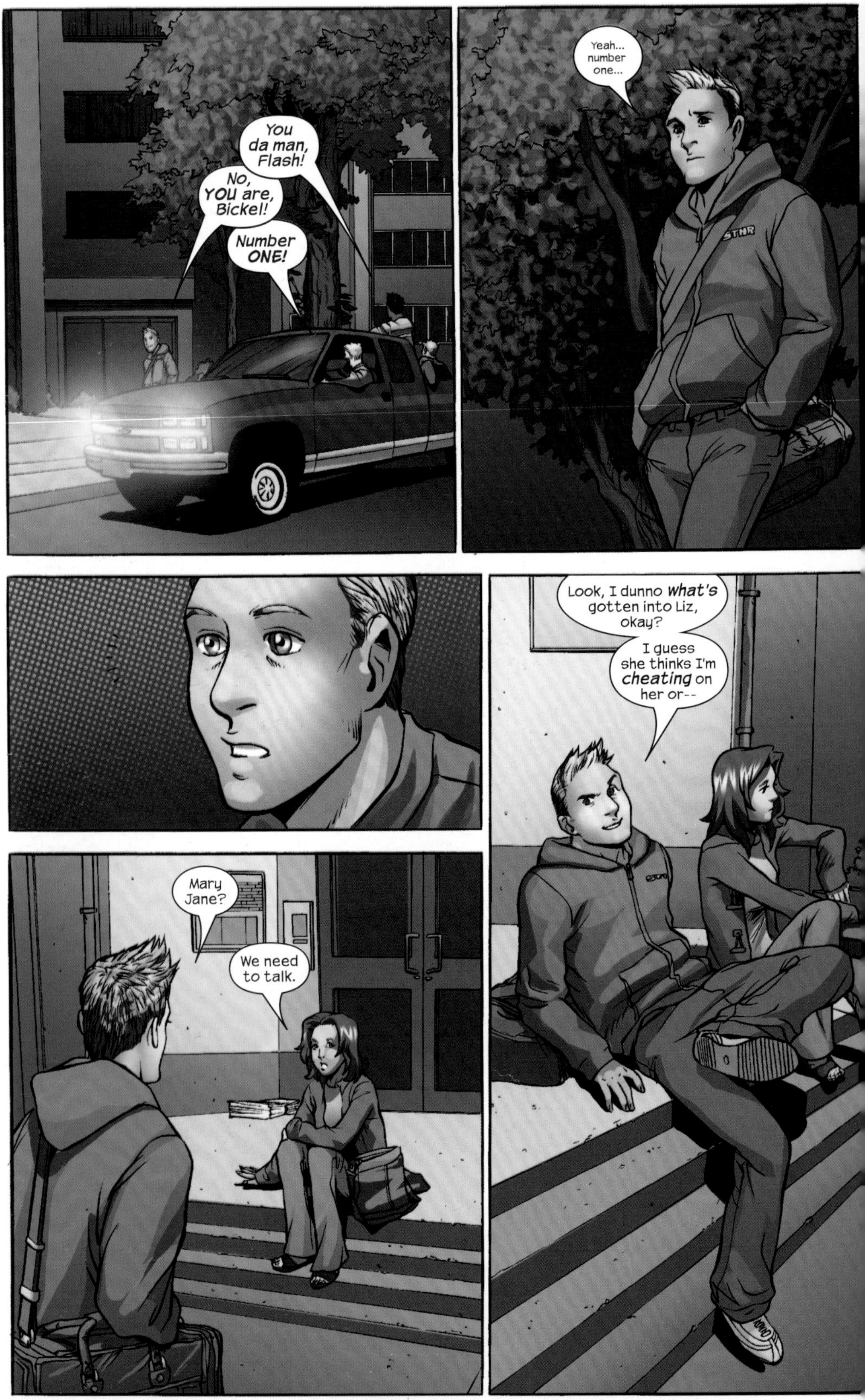
You da man, Flash!
No, YOU are, Bickel!
Number ONE!
Yeah... number one...
Look, I dunno what's gotten into Liz, okay?
I guess she thinks I'm cheating on her or--
Mary Jane?
We need to talk.

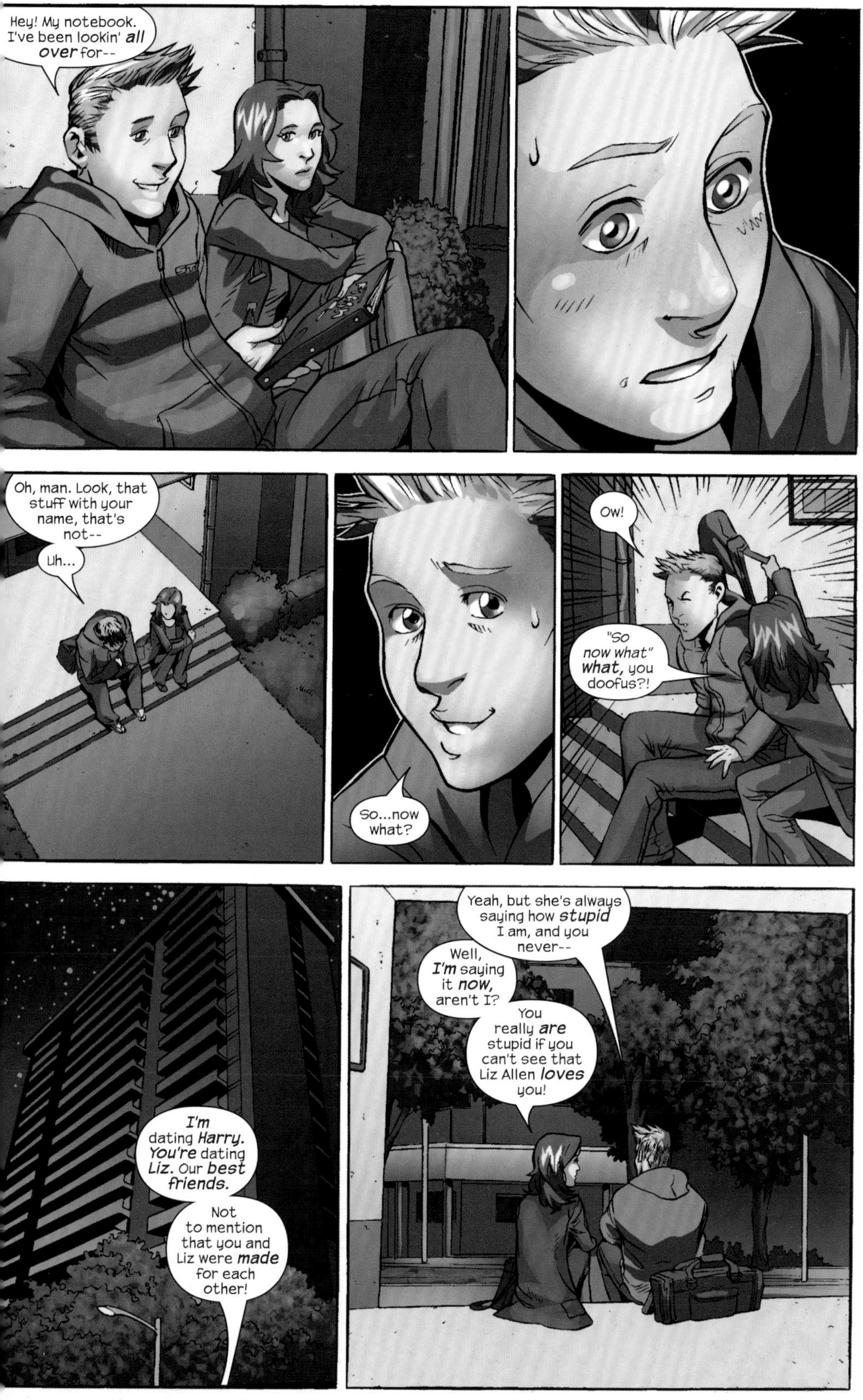
Hey! My notebook. I've been lookin' *all over* for--
Oh, man. Look, that stuff with your name, that's not--
Uh...
So...now what?
Ow!
"So now what" *what,* you doofus?!
I'm dating *Harry. You're* dating *Liz.* Our *best friends.*
Not to mention that you and Liz were *made* for each other!
Yeah, but she's always saying how *stupid* I am, and you never--
Well, *I'm* saying it *now,* aren't I?
You really *are* stupid if you can't see that Liz Allen *loves* you!

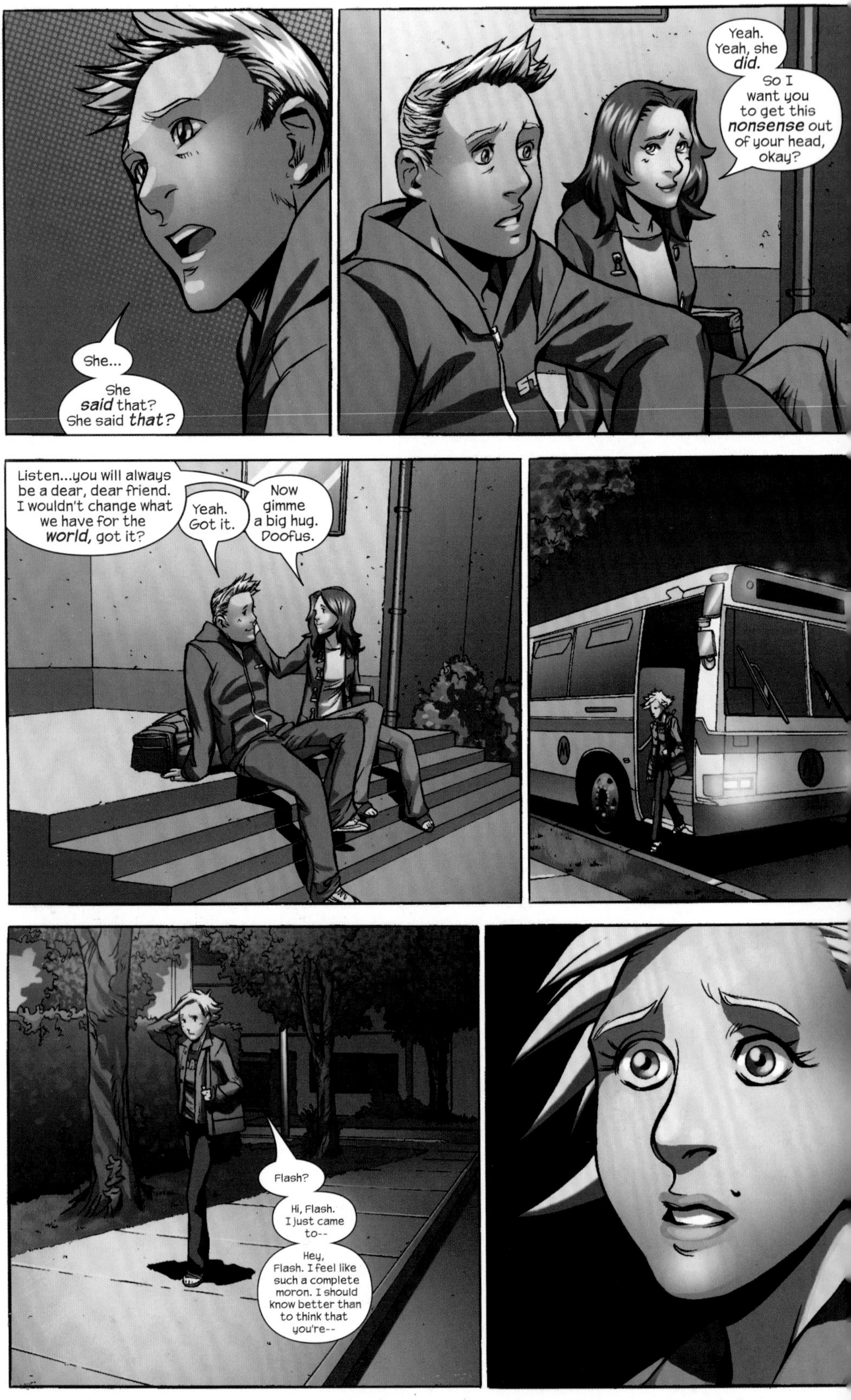
She...
She said that? She said that?
Yeah. Yeah, she did.
So I want you to get this nonsense out of your head, okay?
Listen...you will always be a dear, dear friend. I wouldn't change what we have for the world, got it?
Yeah. Got it.
Now gimme a big hug. Doofus.
Flash?
Hi, Flash. I just came to--
Hey, Flash. I feel like such a complete moron. I should know better than to think that you're--

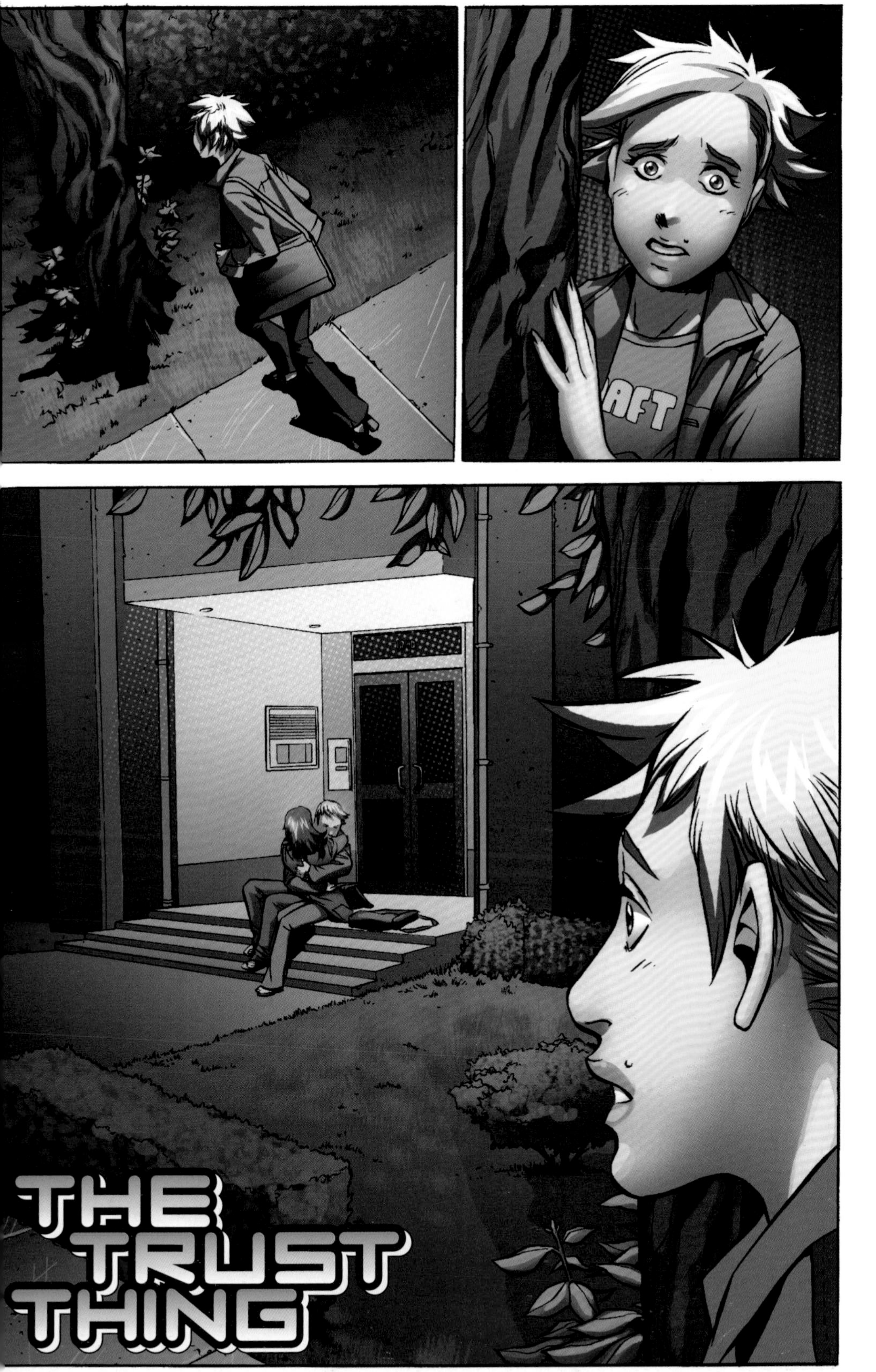
AFT
THE TRUST THING

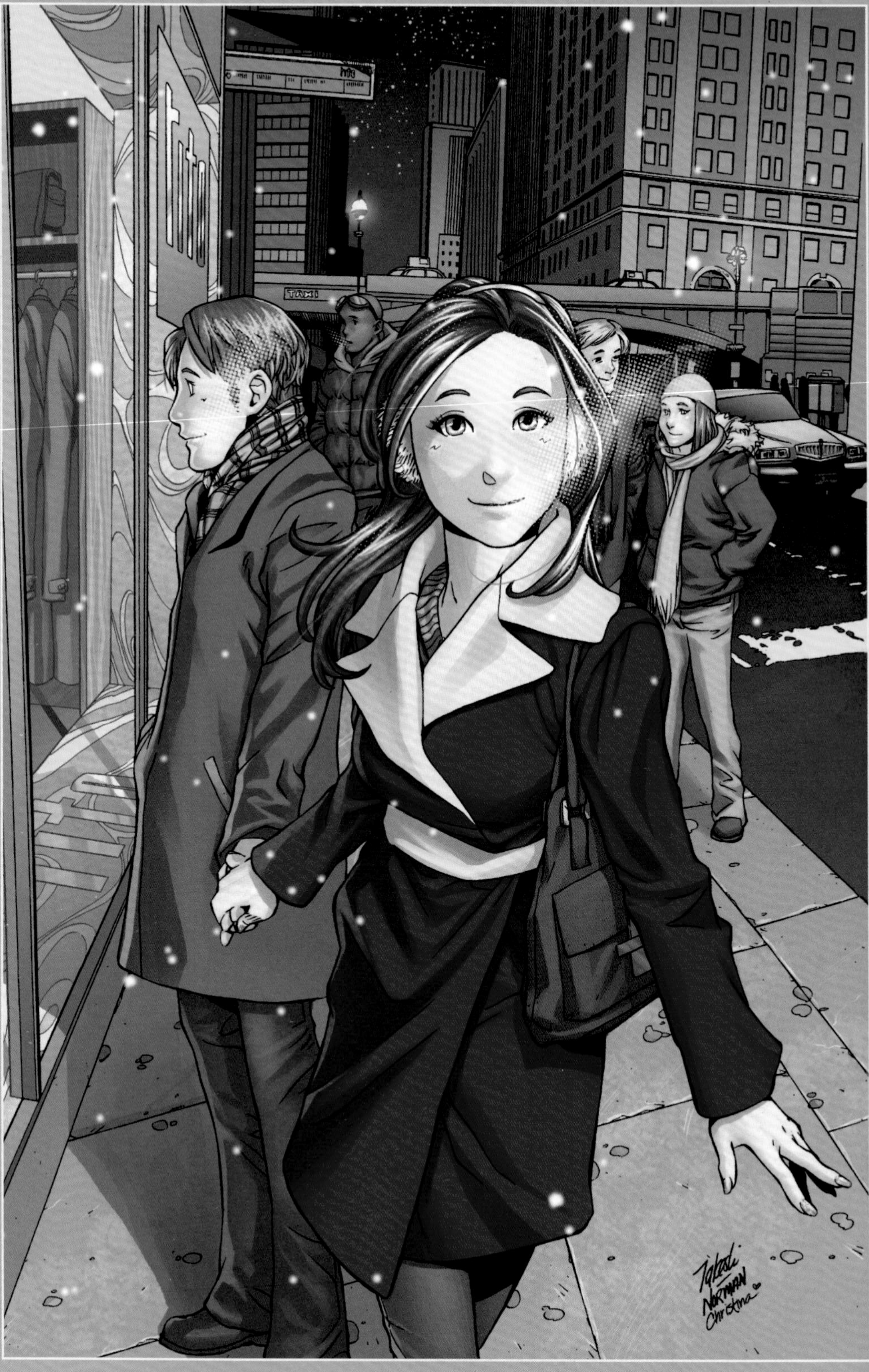
TAXI

Mary Jane: Homecoming #1

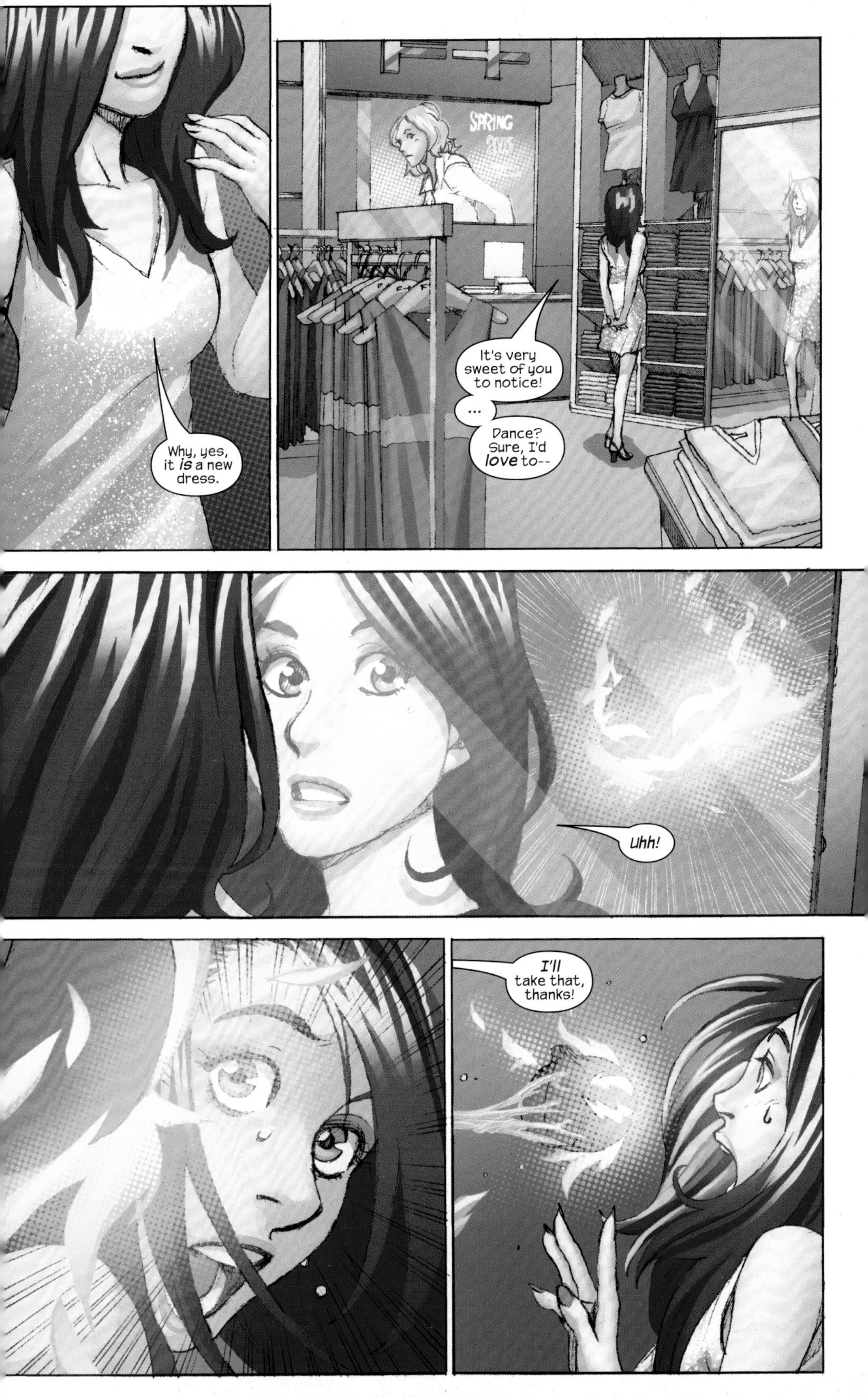
Why, yes, it *is* a new dress.
It's very sweet of you to notice!
...
Dance? Sure, I'd *love* to--
Uhh!
I'll take that, thanks!

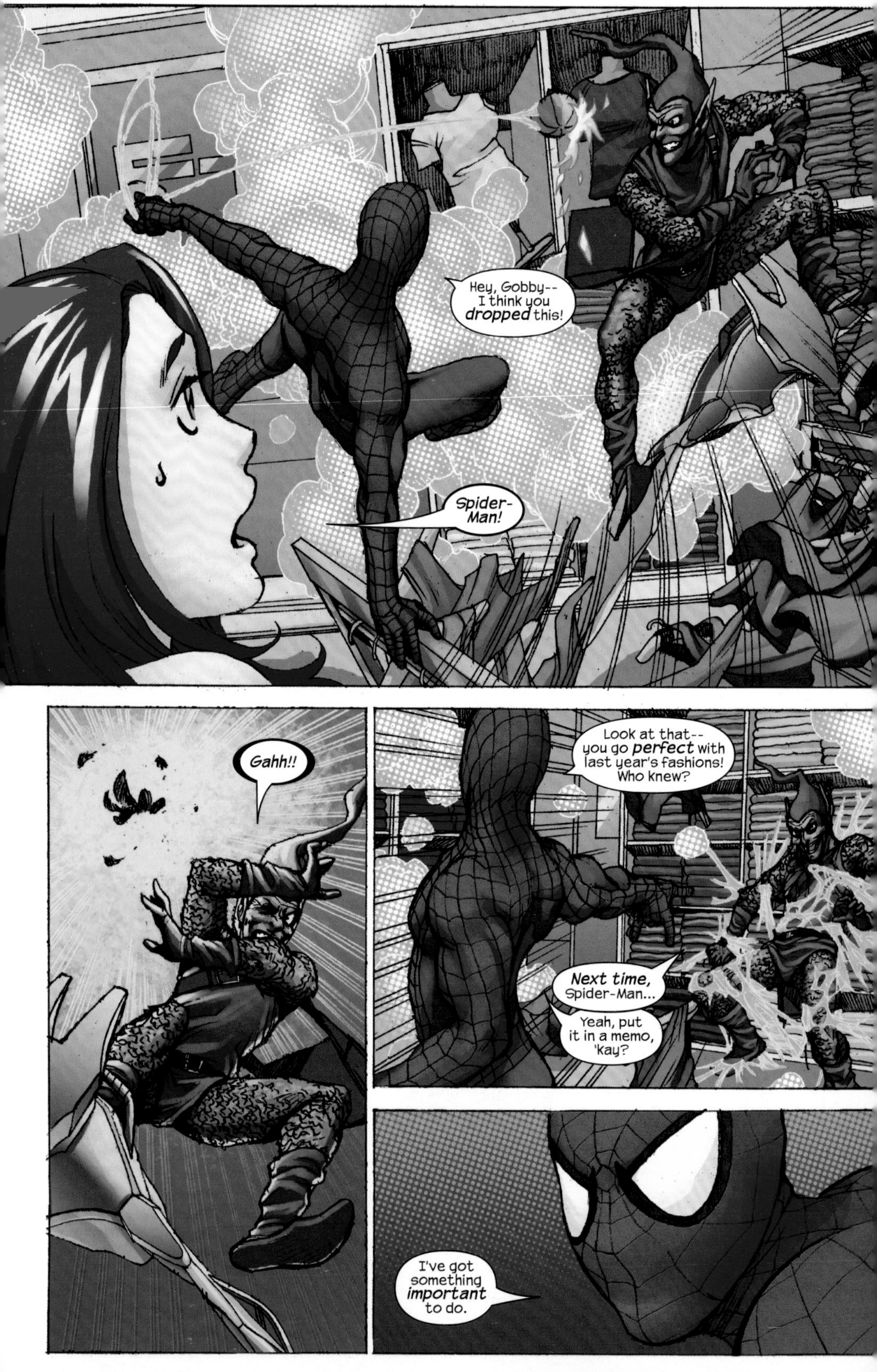
Hey, Gobby-- I think you dropped this!
Spider-Man!
Gahh!!
Look at that-- you go perfect with last year's fashions! Who knew?
Next time, Spider-Man...
Yeah, put it in a memo, 'kay?
I've got something important to do.

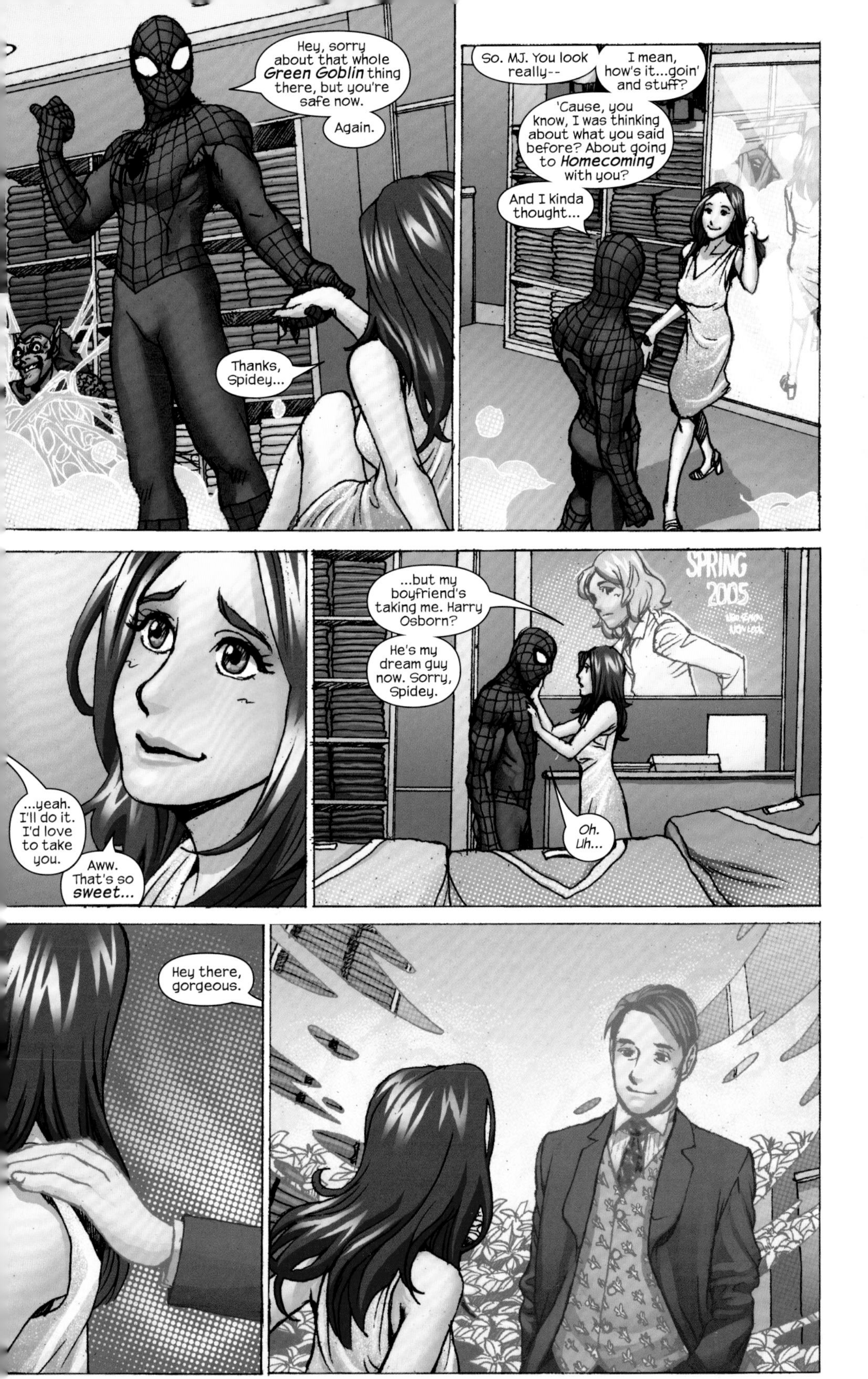
Hey, sorry about that whole Green Goblin thing there, but you're safe now.
Again.
Thanks, Spidey...
So. MJ. You look really--
I mean, how's it...goin' and stuff?
'Cause, you know, I was thinking about what you said before? About going to Homecoming with you?
And I kinda thought...
...yeah. I'll do it. I'd love to take you.
Aww. That's so sweet...
SPRING 2005
...but my boyfriend's taking me. Harry Osborn?
He's my dream guy now. Sorry, Spidey.
Oh. Uh...
Hey there, gorgeous.

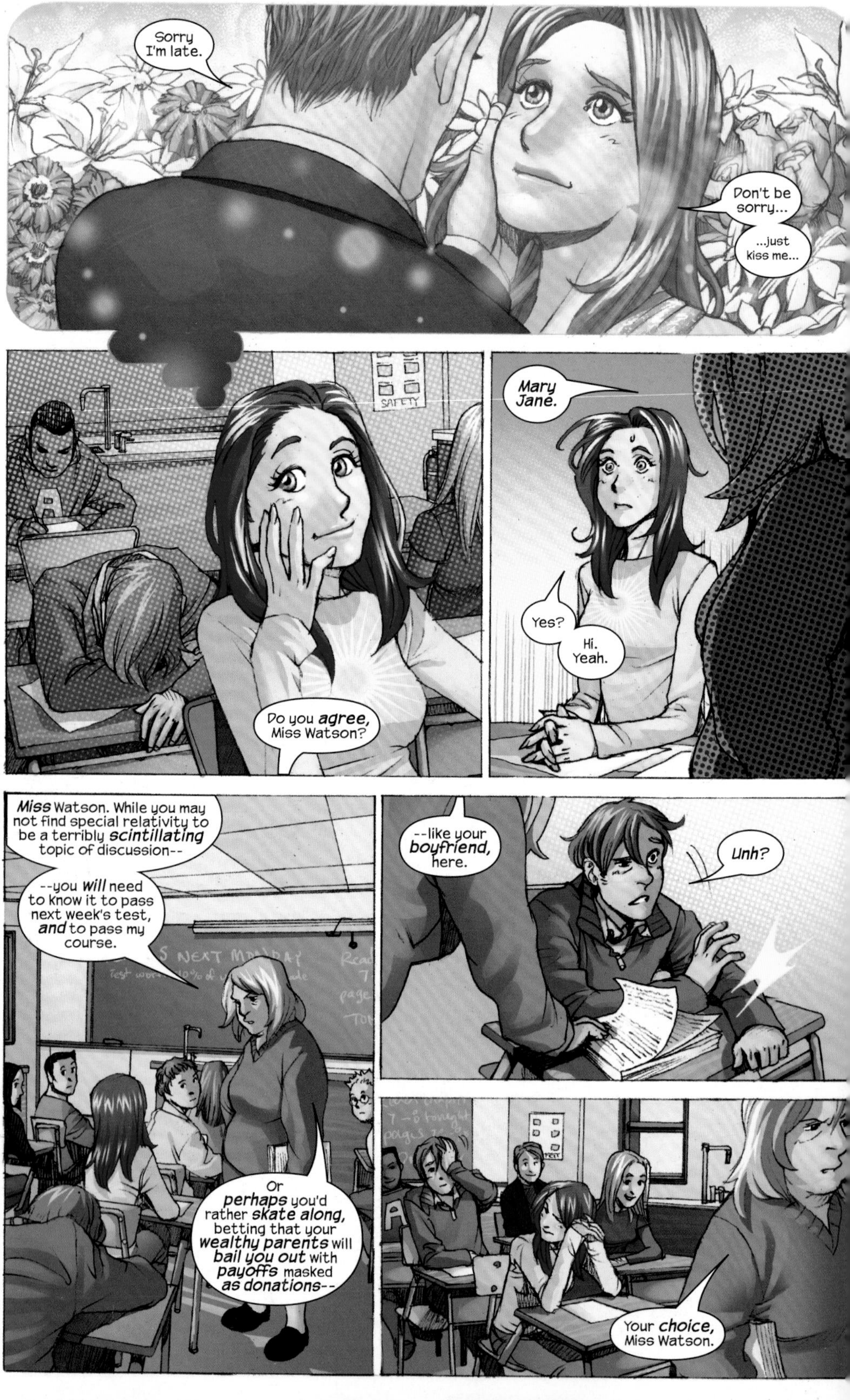
Sorry I'm late.
Don't be sorry...
...just kiss me...
Do you agree, Miss Watson?
Mary Jane.
Yes?
Hi. Yeah.
Miss Watson. While you may not find special relativity to be a terribly scintillating topic of discussion--
--you will need to know it to pass next week's test, and to pass my course.
Or perhaps you'd rather skate along, betting that your wealthy parents will bail you out with payoffs masked as donations--
--like your boyfriend, here.
Unh?
Your choice, Miss Watson.

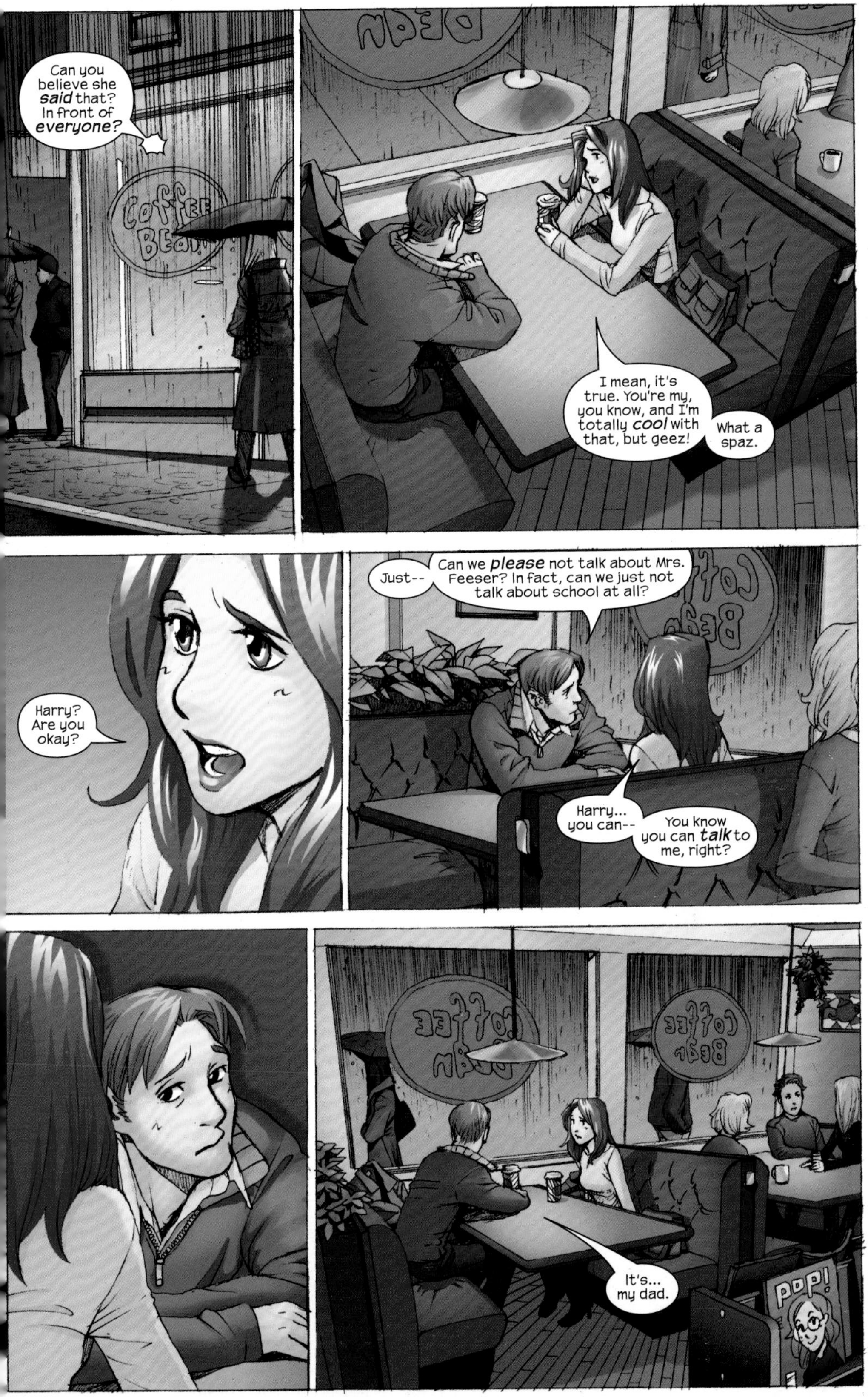
Can you believe she said that? In front of everyone?
I mean, it's true. You're my, you know, and I'm totally cool with that, but geez!
What a spaz.
Harry? Are you okay?
Just--
Can we please not talk about Mrs. Feeser? In fact, can we just not talk about school at all?
Harry... you can--
You know you can talk to me, right?
It's... my dad.
pop!

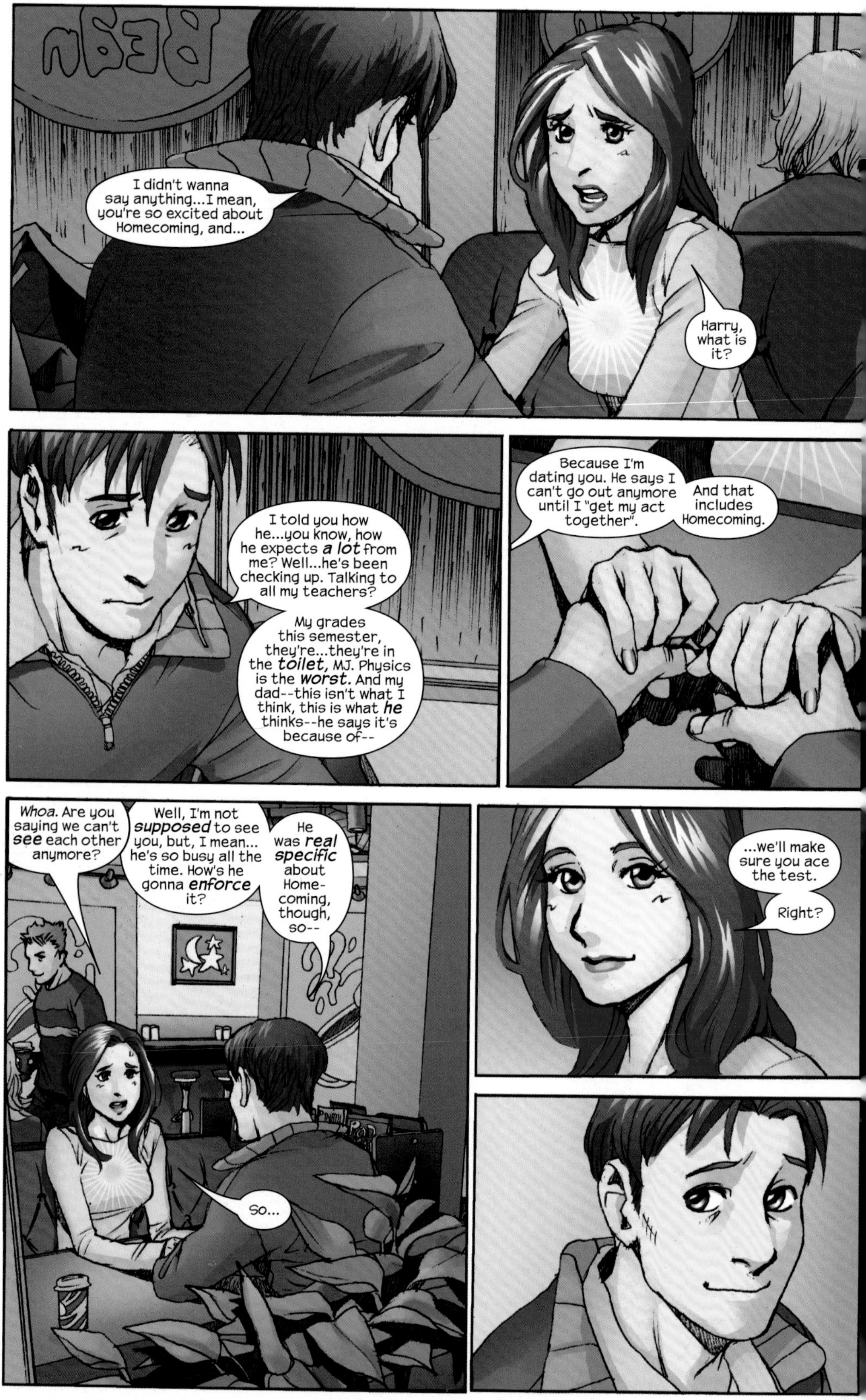
I didn't wanna say anything...I mean, you're so excited about Homecoming, and...
Harry, what is it?
I told you how he...you know, how he expects *a lot* from me? Well...he's been checking up. Talking to all my teachers?
My grades this semester, they're...they're in the *toilet*, MJ. Physics is the *worst.* And my dad--this isn't what I think, this is what *he* thinks--he says it's because of--
Because I'm dating you. He says I can't go out anymore until I "get my act together".
And that includes Homecoming.
Whoa. Are you saying we can't *see* each other anymore?
Well, I'm not *supposed* to see you, but, I mean... he's so busy all the time. How's he gonna *enforce* it?
He was *real specific* about Home-coming, though, so--
So...
...we'll make sure you ace the test.
Right?

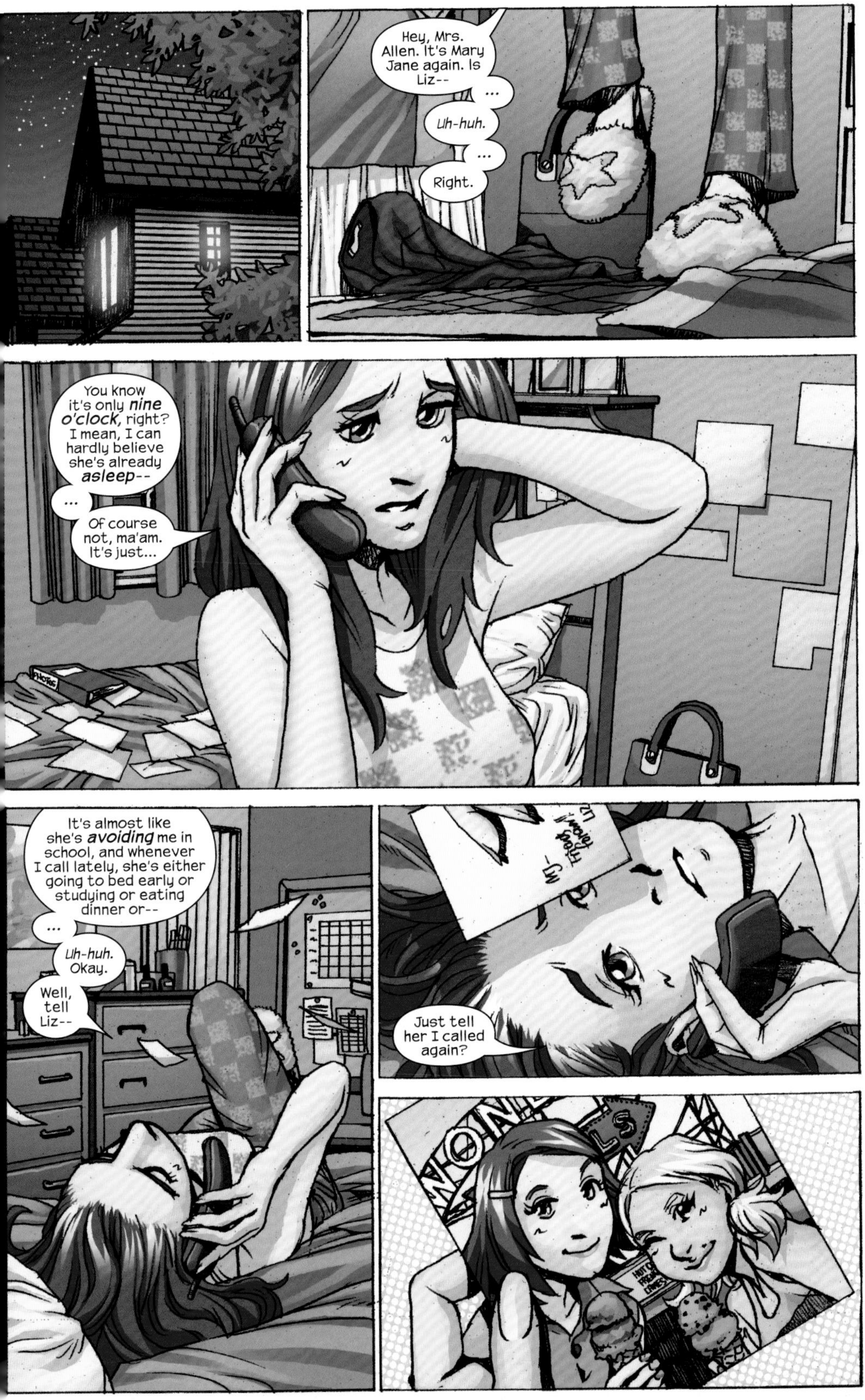
Hey, Mrs. Allen. It's Mary Jane again. Is Liz--
...
Uh-huh.
...
Right.
You know it's only *nine o'clock,* right? I mean, I can hardly believe she's already *asleep*--
...
Of course not, ma'am. It's just...
It's almost like she's *avoiding* me in school, and whenever I call lately, she's either going to bed early or studying or eating dinner or--
...
Uh-huh. Okay.
Well, tell Liz--
Just tell her I called again?

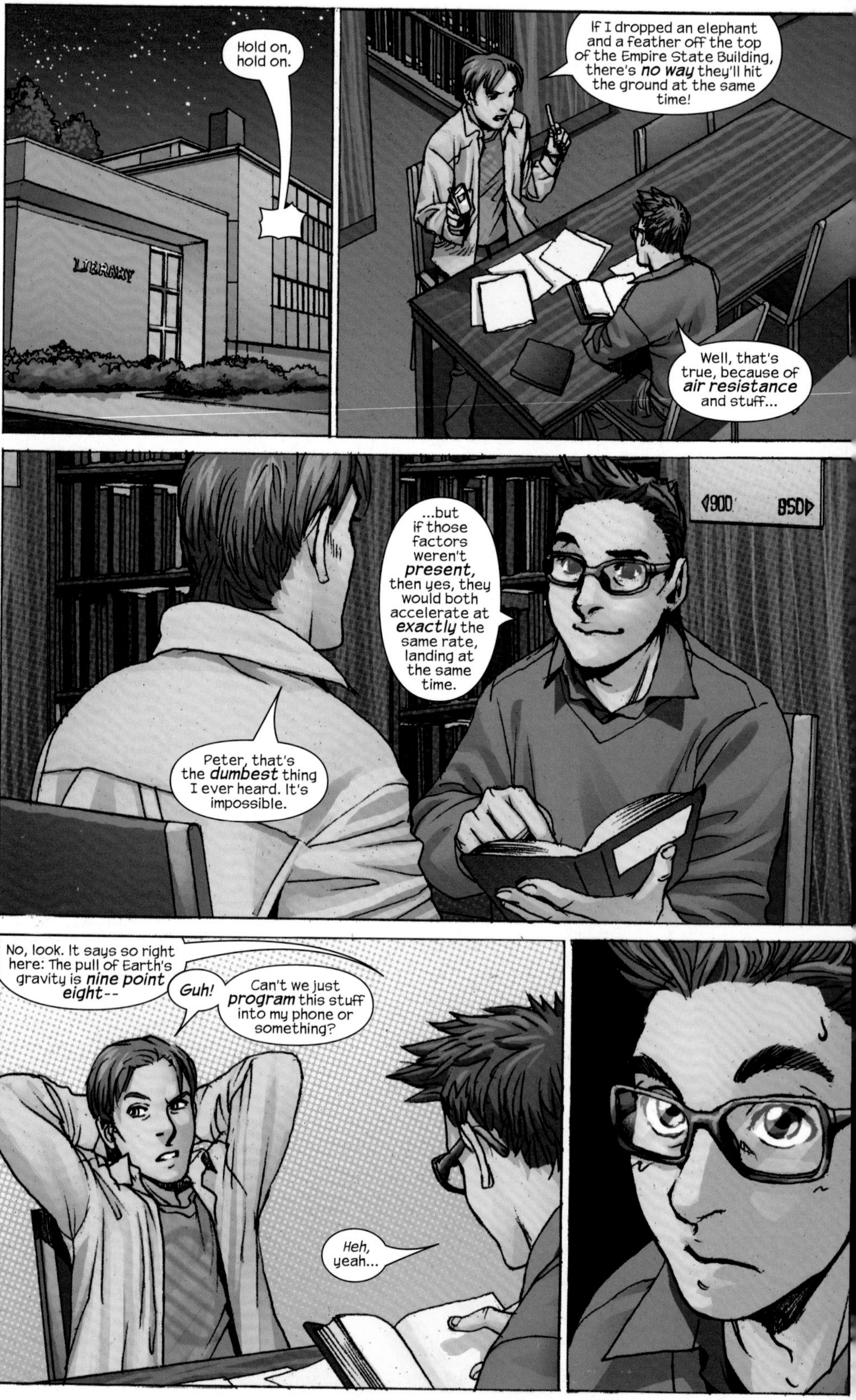
Hold on, hold on.
LIBRARY
If I dropped an elephant and a feather off the top of the Empire State Building, there's no way they'll hit the ground at the same time!
Well, that's true, because of air resistance and stuff...
◁900 950▷
...but if those factors weren't present, then yes, they would both accelerate at exactly the same rate, landing at the same time.
Peter, that's the dumbest thing I ever heard. It's impossible.
No, look. It says so right here: The pull of Earth's gravity is nine point eight--
Guh!
Can't we just program this stuff into my phone or something?
Heh, yeah...

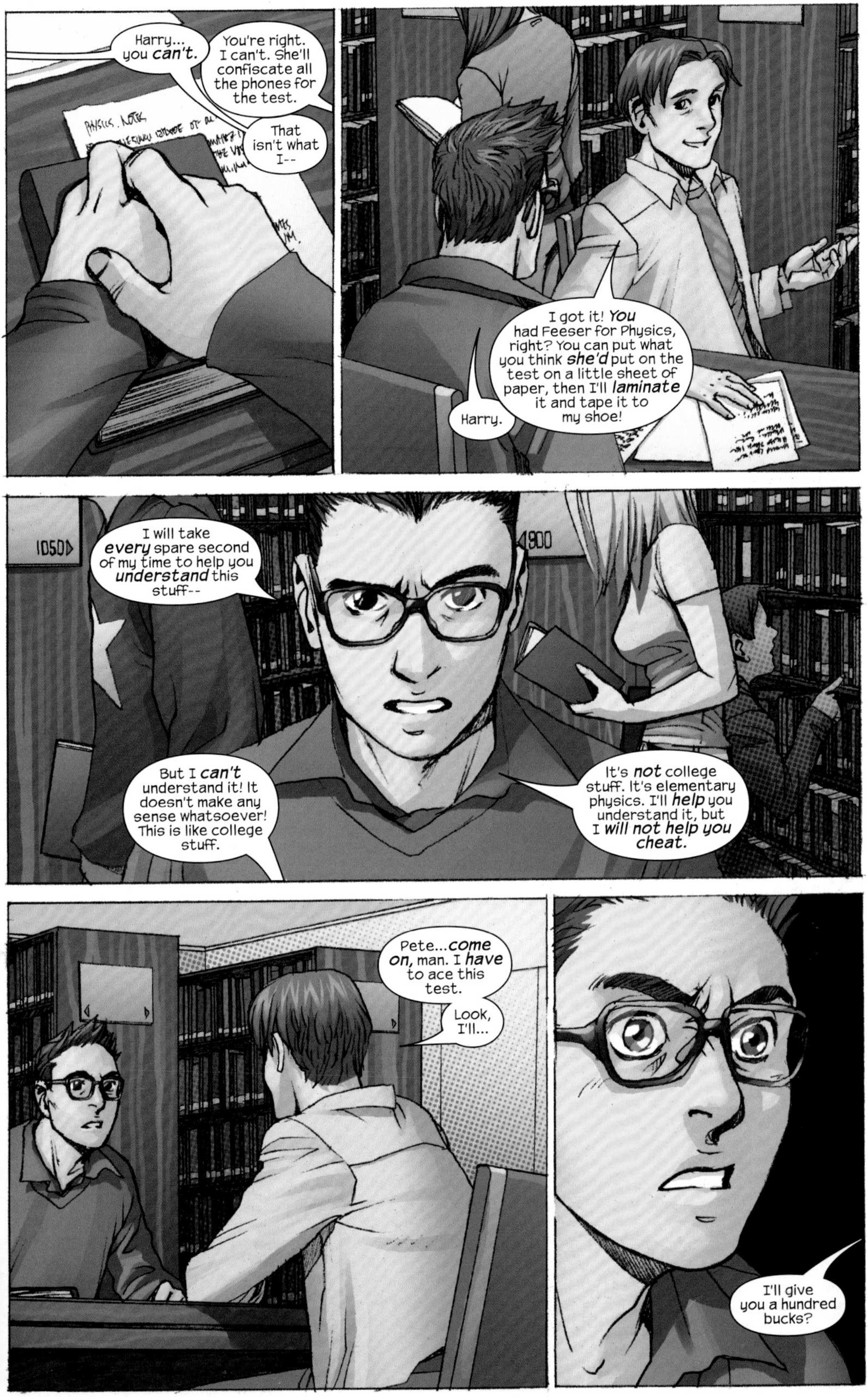
Harry... you can't.
You're right. I can't. She'll confiscate all the phones for the test.
That isn't what I--
I got it! You had Feeser for Physics, right? You can put what you think she'd put on the test on a little sheet of paper, then I'll laminate it and tape it to my shoe!
Harry.
1050
1900
I will take every spare second of my time to help you understand this stuff--
But I can't understand it! It doesn't make any sense whatsoever! This is like college stuff.
It's not college stuff. It's elementary physics. I'll help you understand it, but I will not help you cheat.
Pete...come on, man. I have to ace this test.
Look, I'll...
I'll give you a hundred bucks?

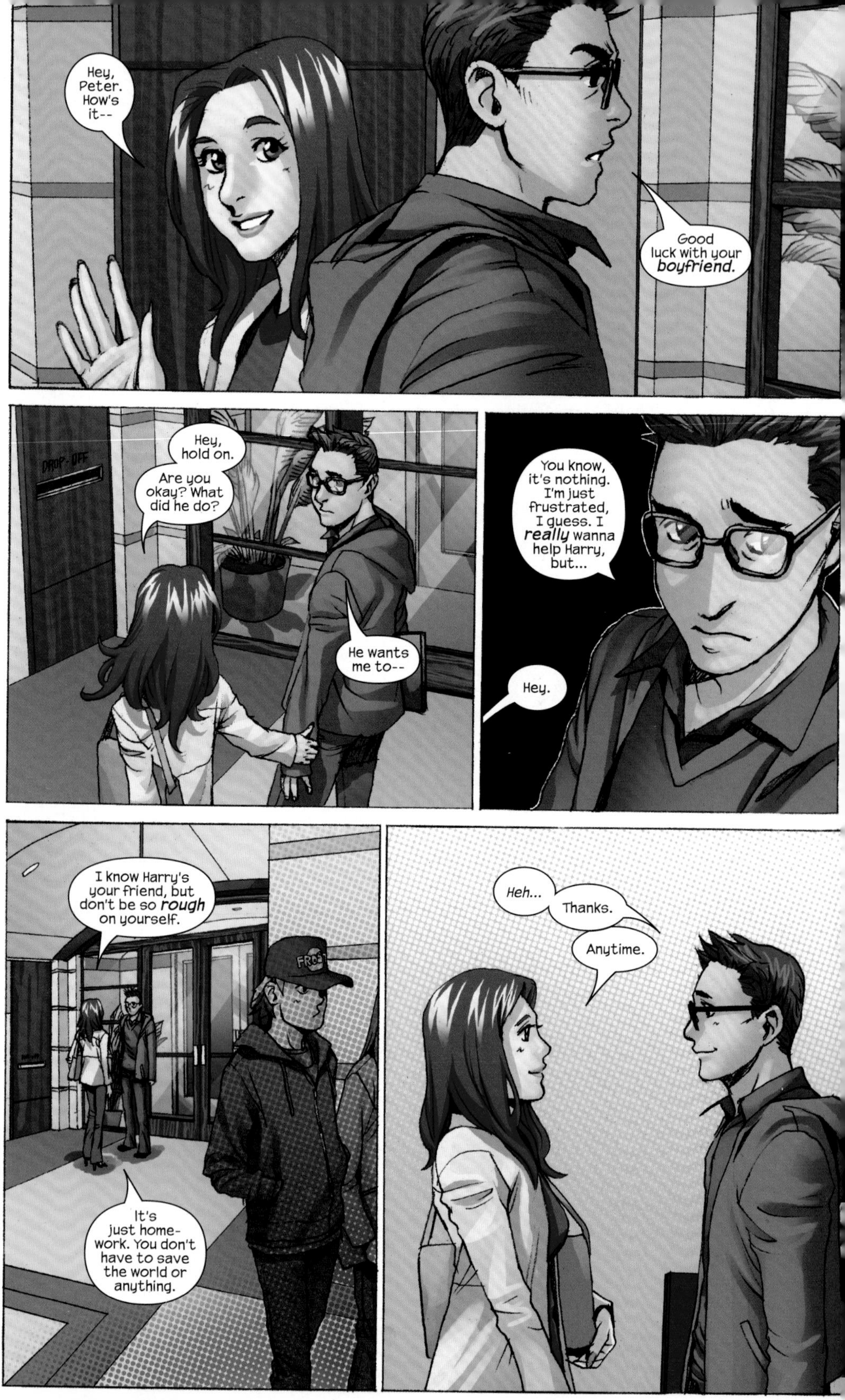
Hey, Peter. How's it--
Good luck with your *boyfriend.*
DROP-OFF
Hey, hold on.
Are you okay? What did he do?
He wants me to--
You know, it's nothing. I'm just frustrated, I guess. I *really* wanna help Harry, but...
Hey.
I know Harry's your friend, but don't be so *rough* on yourself.
It's just home-work. You don't have to save the world or anything.
Heh...
Thanks.
Anytime.

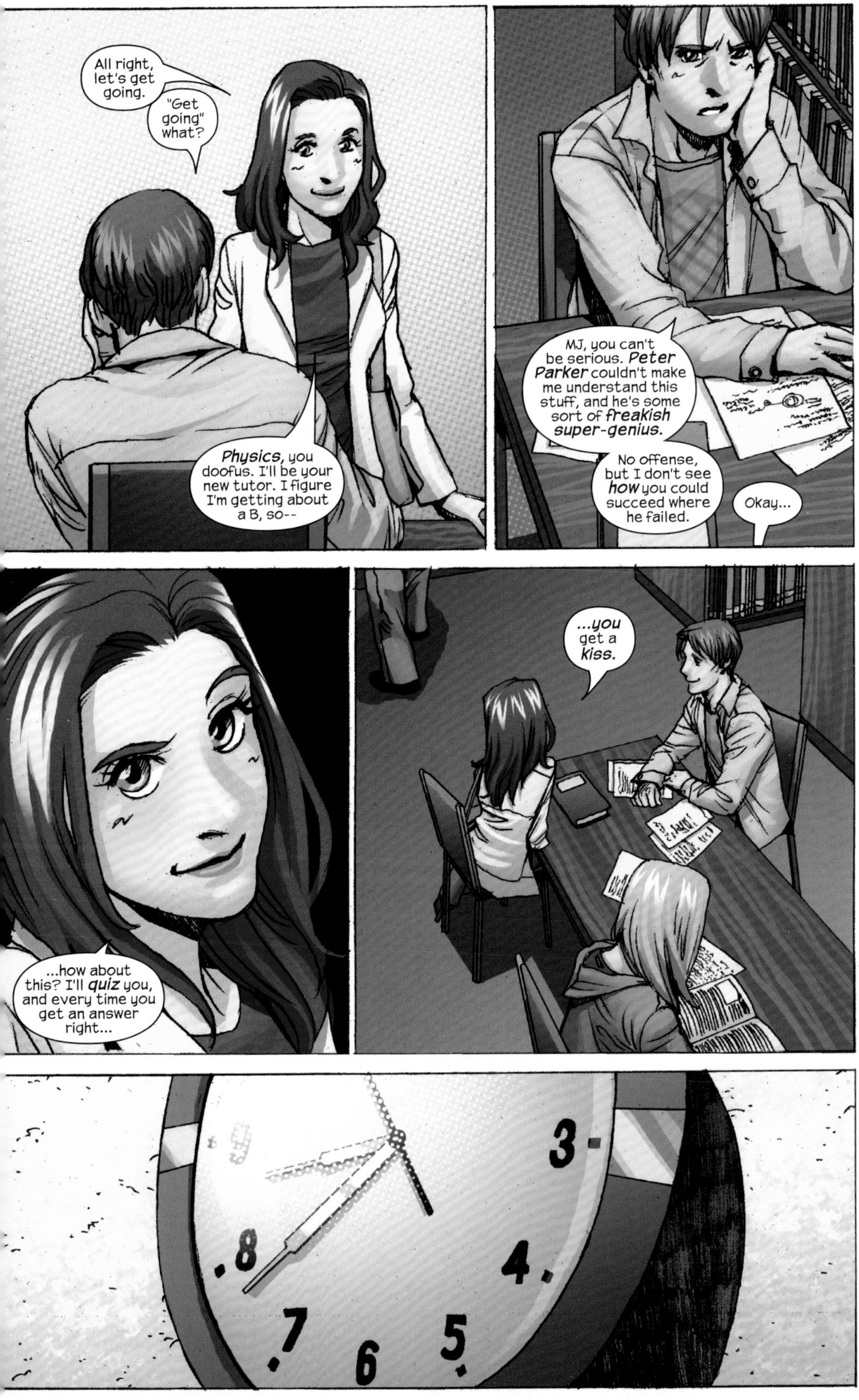
All right, let's get going.
"Get going" what?
Physics, you doofus. I'll be your new tutor. I figure I'm getting about a B, so--
MJ, you can't be serious. Peter Parker couldn't make me understand this stuff, and he's some sort of freakish super-genius.
No offense, but I don't see how you could succeed where he failed.
Okay...
...how about this? I'll quiz you, and every time you get an answer right...
...you get a kiss.
3
4
5
6
7
8

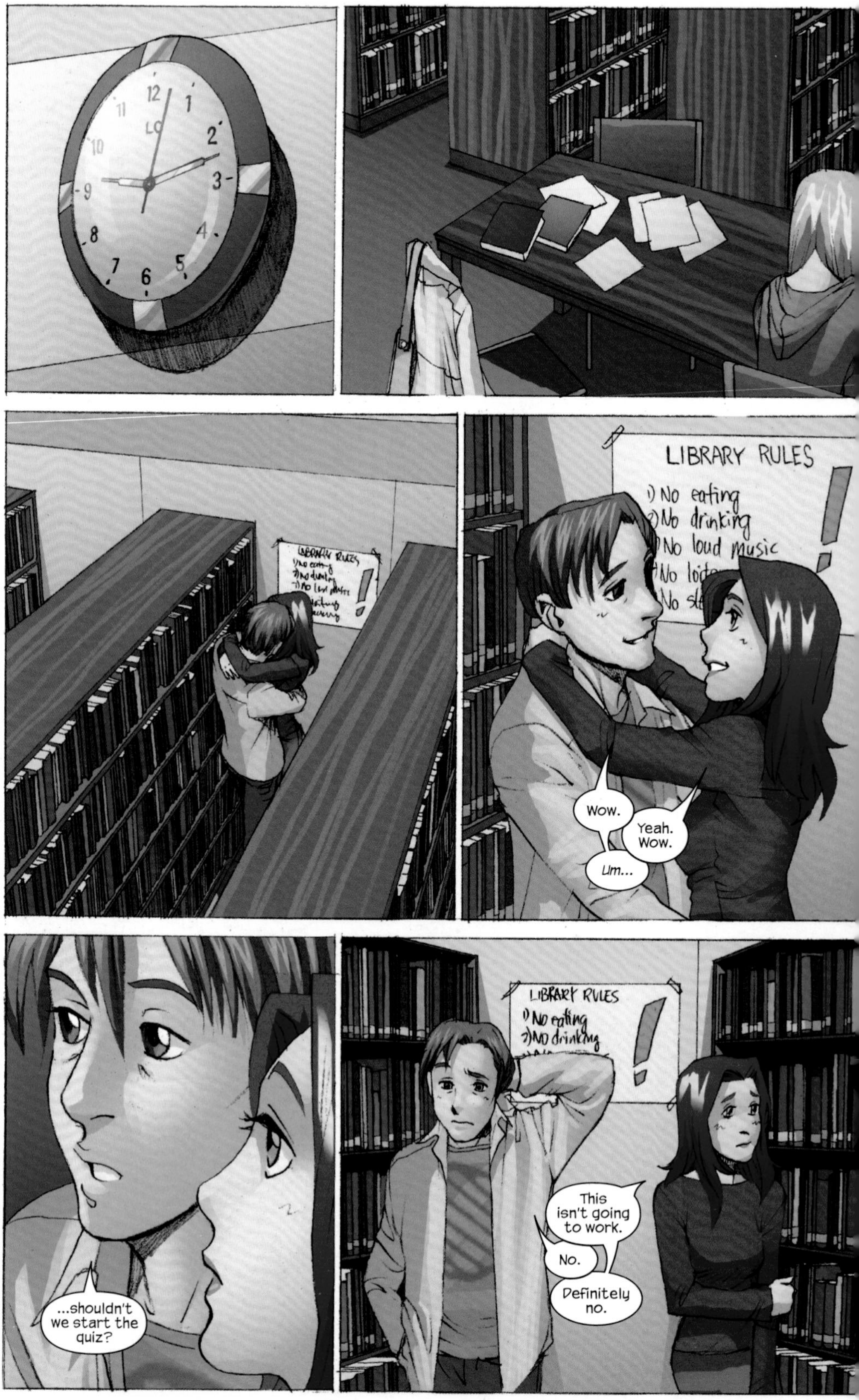

LIBRARY RULES
1) No eating
2) No drinking
3) No loud music
Wow.
Yeah. Wow.
Um...
...shouldn't we start the quiz?
This isn't going to work.
No.
Definitely no.

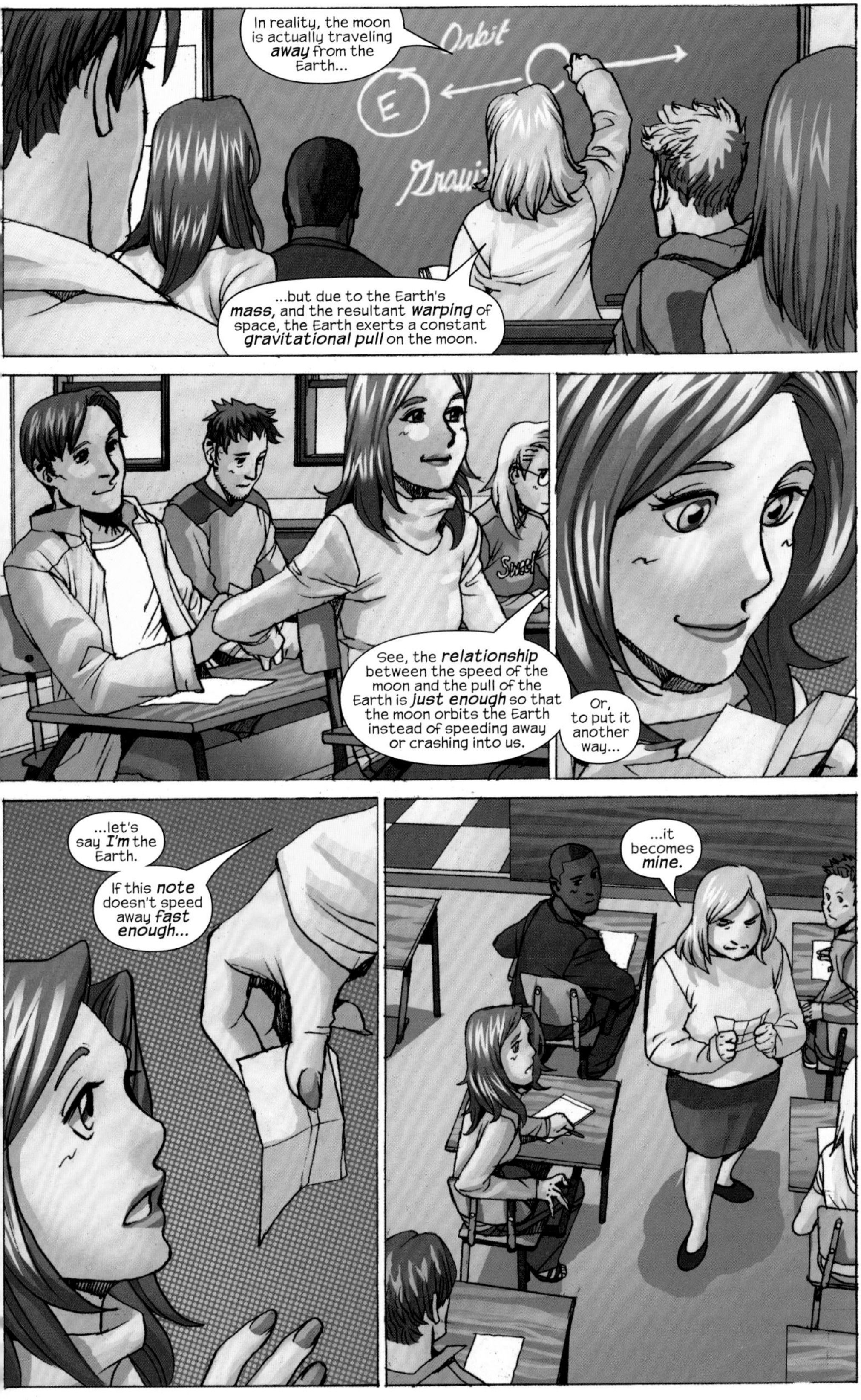
In reality, the moon is actually traveling *away* from the Earth...
Orbit
E
...but due to the Earth's *mass,* and the resultant *warping* of space, the Earth exerts a constant *gravitational pull* on the moon.
See, the *relationship* between the speed of the moon and the pull of the Earth is *just enough* so that the moon orbits the Earth instead of speeding away or crashing into us.
Or, to put it another way...
...let's say *I'm* the Earth.
If this *note* doesn't speed away *fast enough...*
...it becomes *mine.*

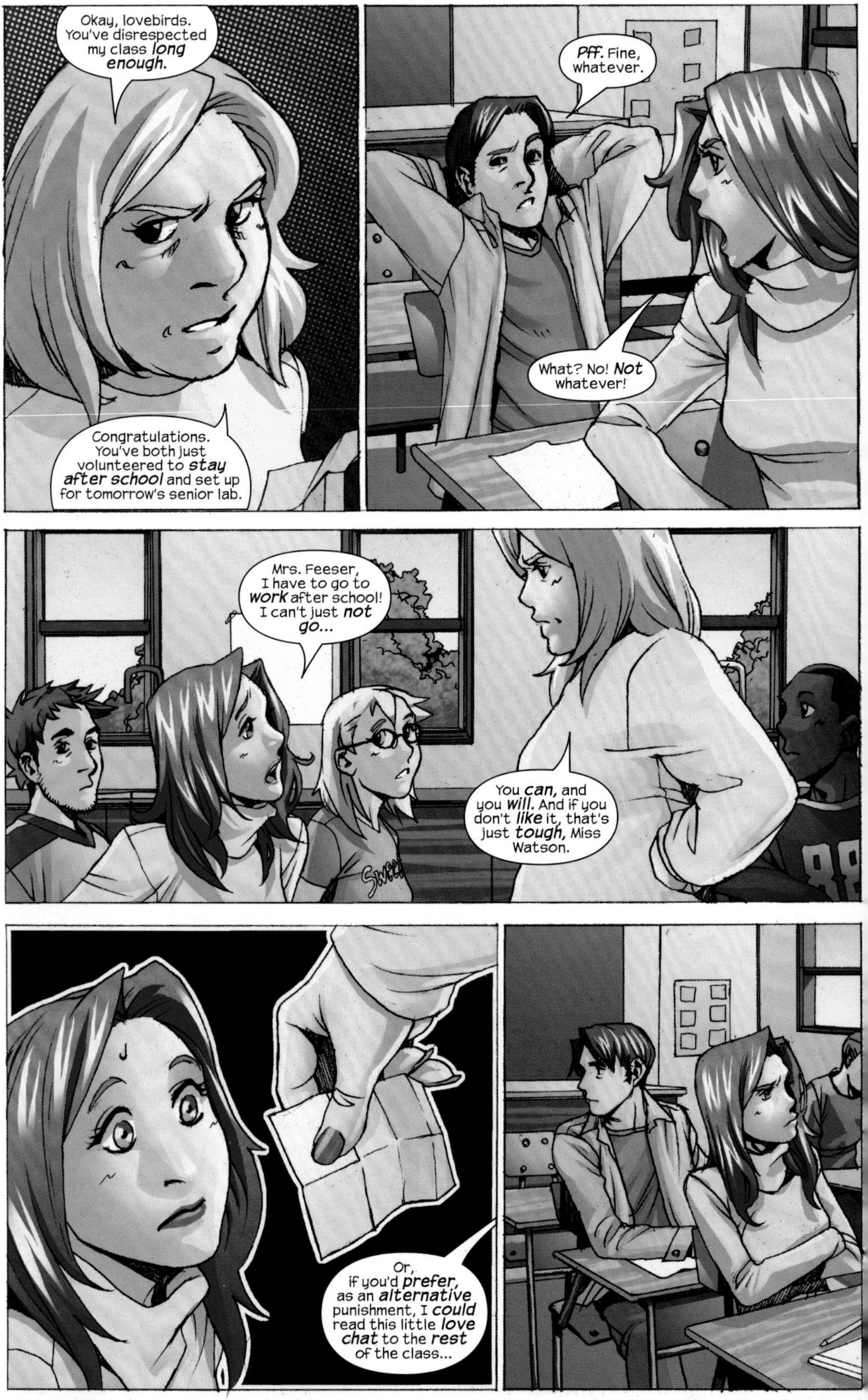

Okay, lovebirds. You've disrespected my class long enough.
Congratulations. You've both just volunteered to stay after school and set up for tomorrow's senior lab.
Pff. Fine, whatever.
What? No! Not whatever!
Mrs. Feeser, I have to go to work after school! I can't just not go...
You can, and you will. And if you don't like it, that's just tough, Miss Watson.
Or, if you'd prefer, as an alternative punishment, I could read this little love chat to the rest of the class...

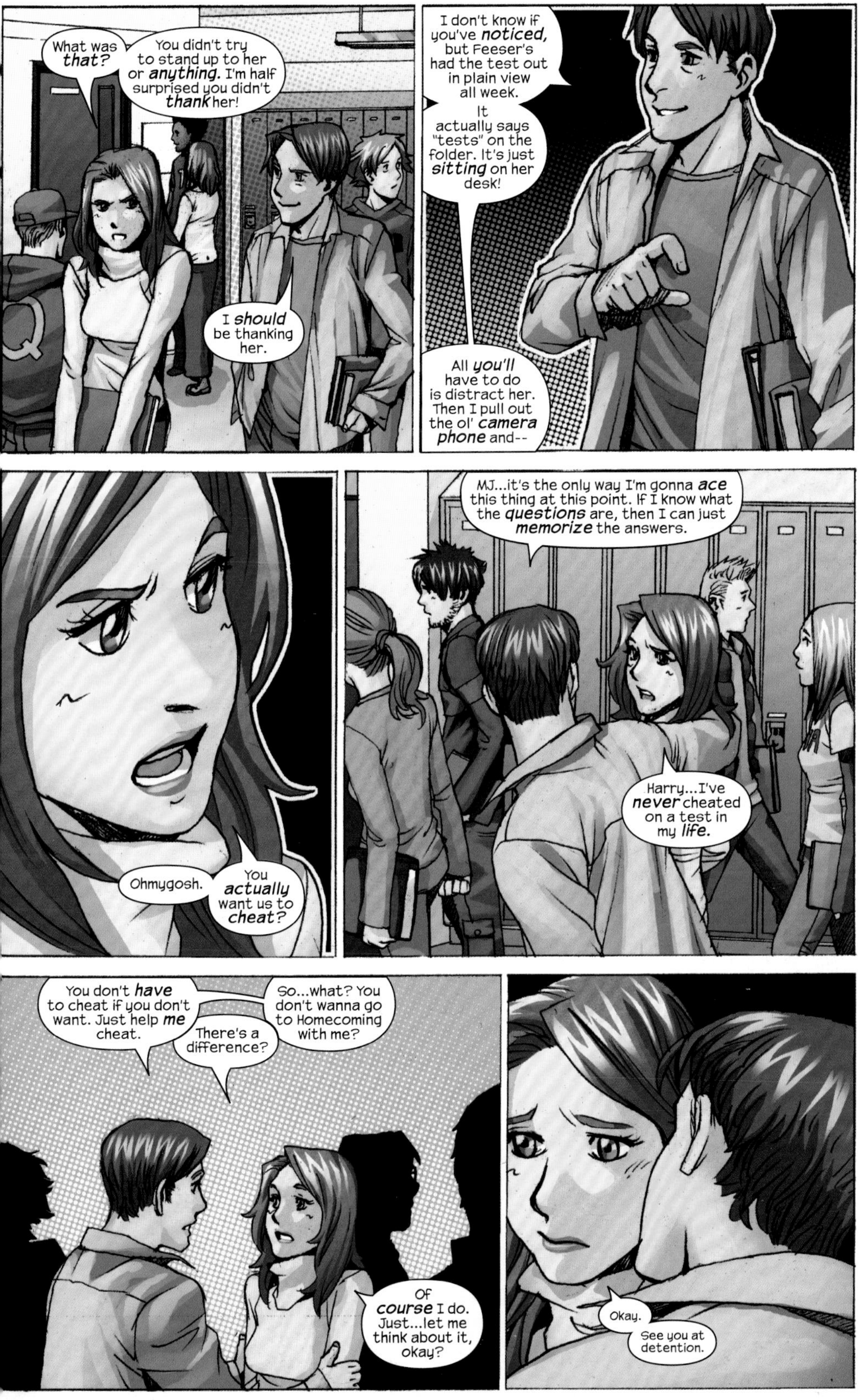

What was that?
You didn't try to stand up to her or anything. I'm half surprised you didn't thank her!
I should be thanking her.
I don't know if you've noticed, but Feeser's had the test out in plain view all week.
It actually says "tests" on the folder. It's just sitting on her desk!
All you'll have to do is distract her. Then I pull out the ol' camera phone and--
Ohmygosh.
You actually want us to cheat?
MJ...it's the only way I'm gonna ace this thing at this point. If I know what the questions are, then I can just memorize the answers.
Harry...I've never cheated on a test in my life.
You don't have to cheat if you don't want. Just help me cheat.
There's a difference?
So...what? You don't wanna go to Homecoming with me?
Of course I do. Just...let me think about it, okay?
Okay.
See you at detention.

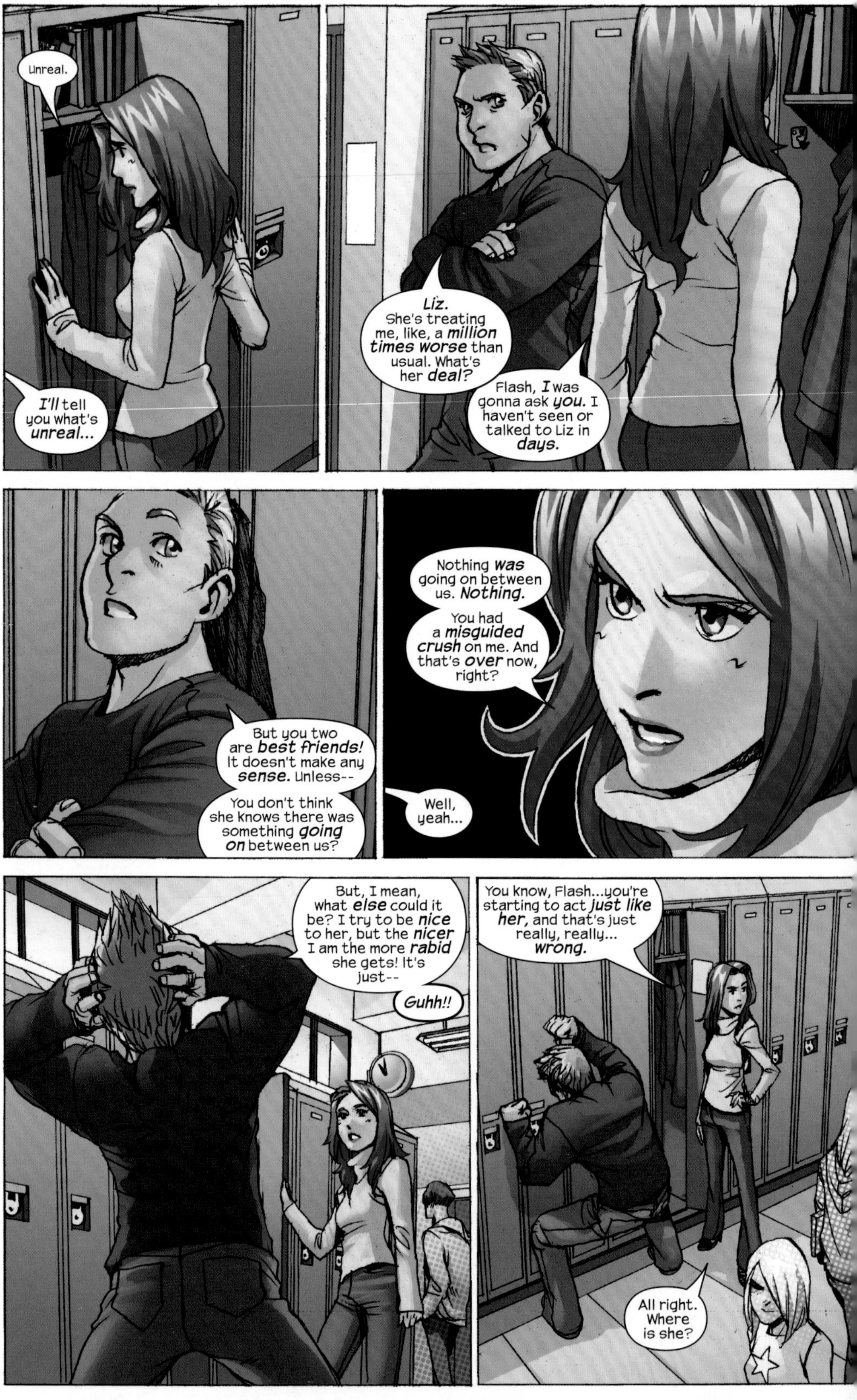
Unreal.
I'll tell you what's unreal...
Liz. She's treating me, like, a million times worse than usual. What's her deal?
Flash, I was gonna ask you. I haven't seen or talked to Liz in days.
But you two are best friends! It doesn't make any sense. Unless--
You don't think she knows there was something going on between us?
Nothing was going on between us. Nothing.
You had a misguided crush on me. And that's over now, right?
Well, yeah...
But, I mean, what else could it be? I try to be nice to her, but the nicer I am the more rabid she gets! It's just--
Guhh!!
You know, Flash...you're starting to act just like her, and that's just really, really... wrong.
All right. Where is she?

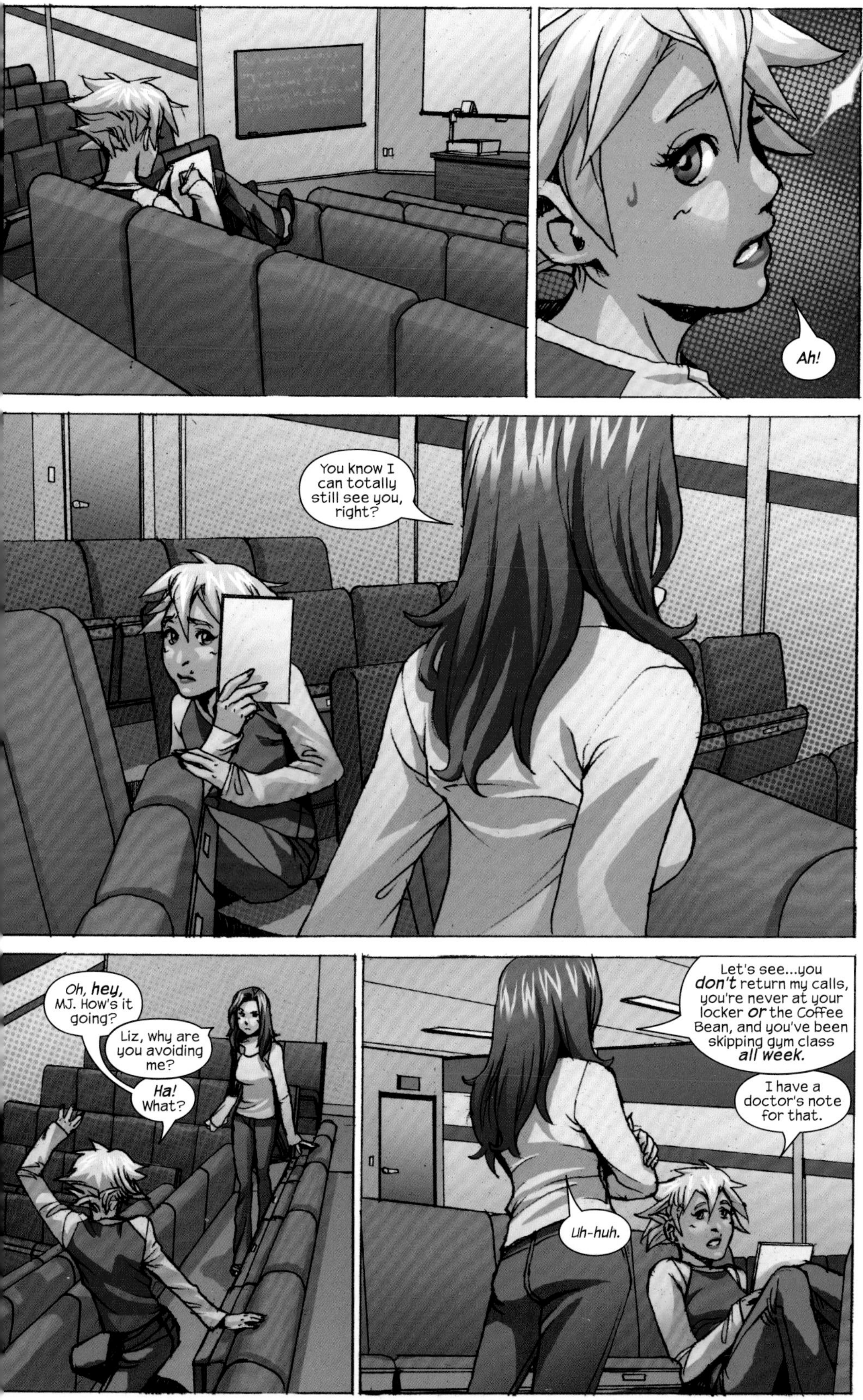
Ah!
You know I can totally still see you, right?
Oh, hey, MJ. How's it going?
Liz, why are you avoiding me?
Ha! What?
Let's see...you don't return my calls, you're never at your locker or the Coffee Bean, and you've been skipping gym class all week.
I have a doctor's note for that.
Uh-huh.

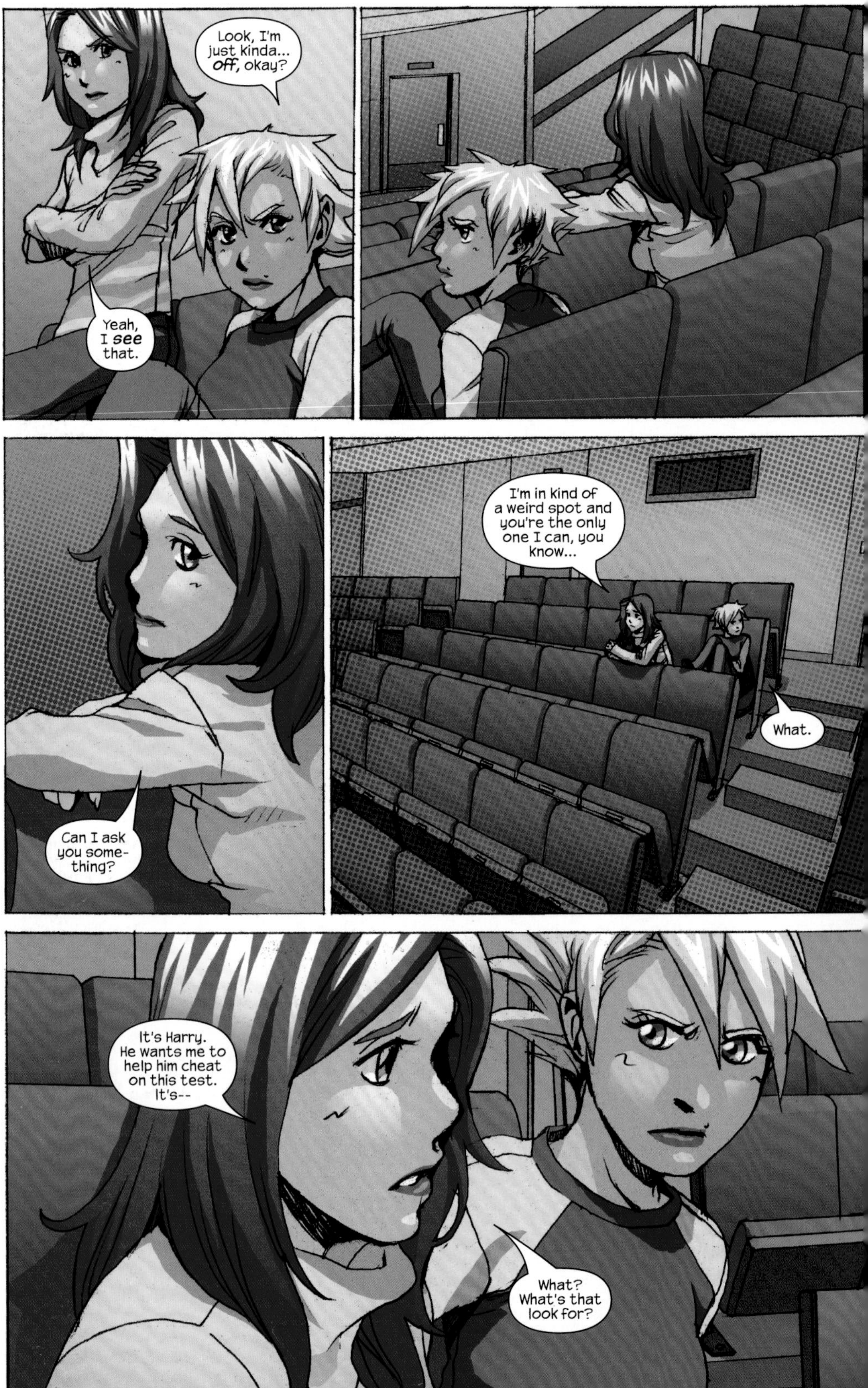
Look, I'm just kinda... *off*, okay?
Yeah, I **see** that.
Can I ask you some-thing?
I'm in kind of a weird spot and you're the only one I can, you know...
What.
It's Harry. He wants me to help him cheat on this test. It's--
What? What's that look for?

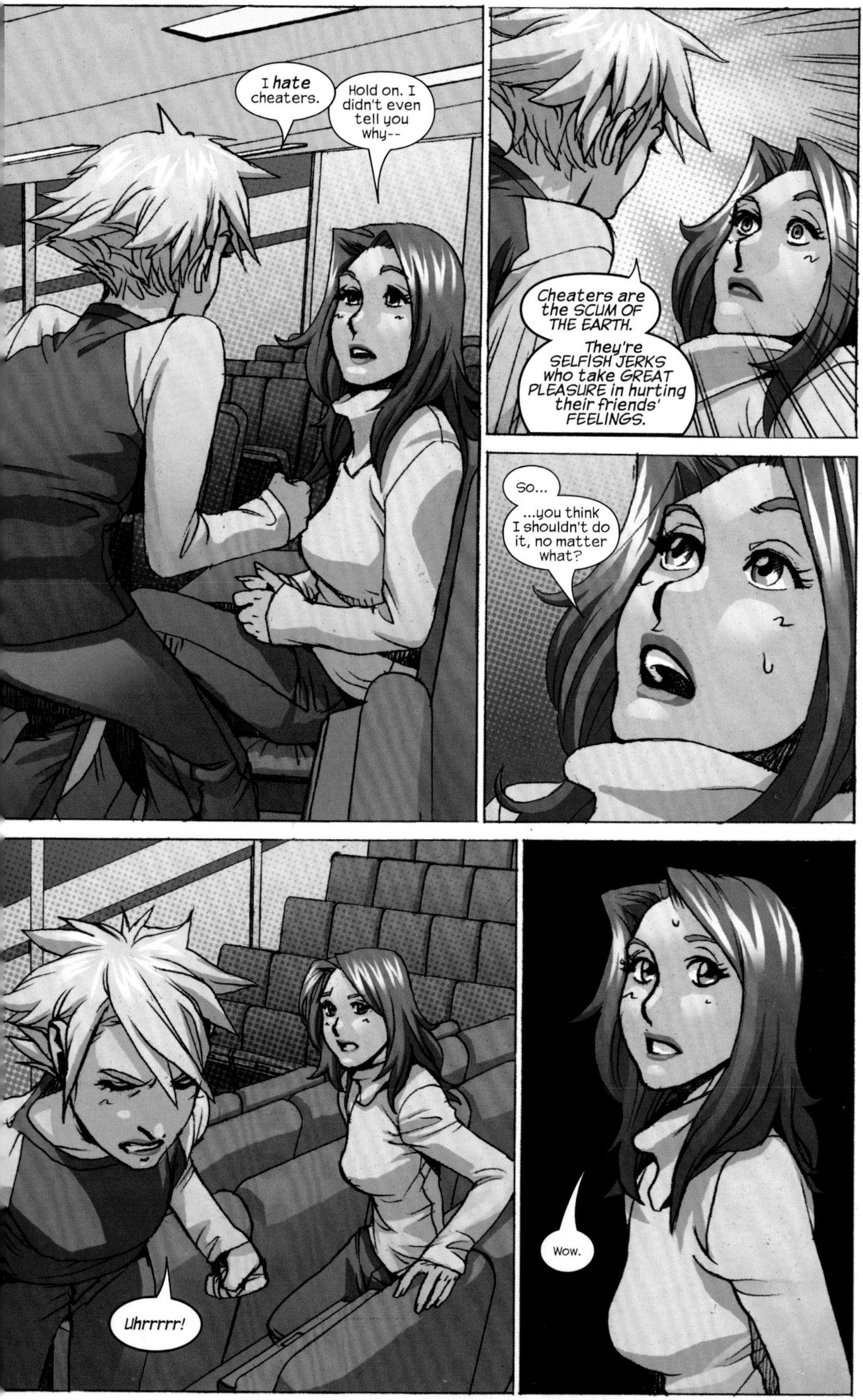
I hate cheaters.
Hold on. I didn't even tell you why--
Cheaters are the SCUM OF THE EARTH.
They're SELFISH JERKS who take GREAT PLEASURE in hurting their friends' FEELINGS.
So...
...you think I shouldn't do it, no matter what?
Uhrrrrr!
Wow.

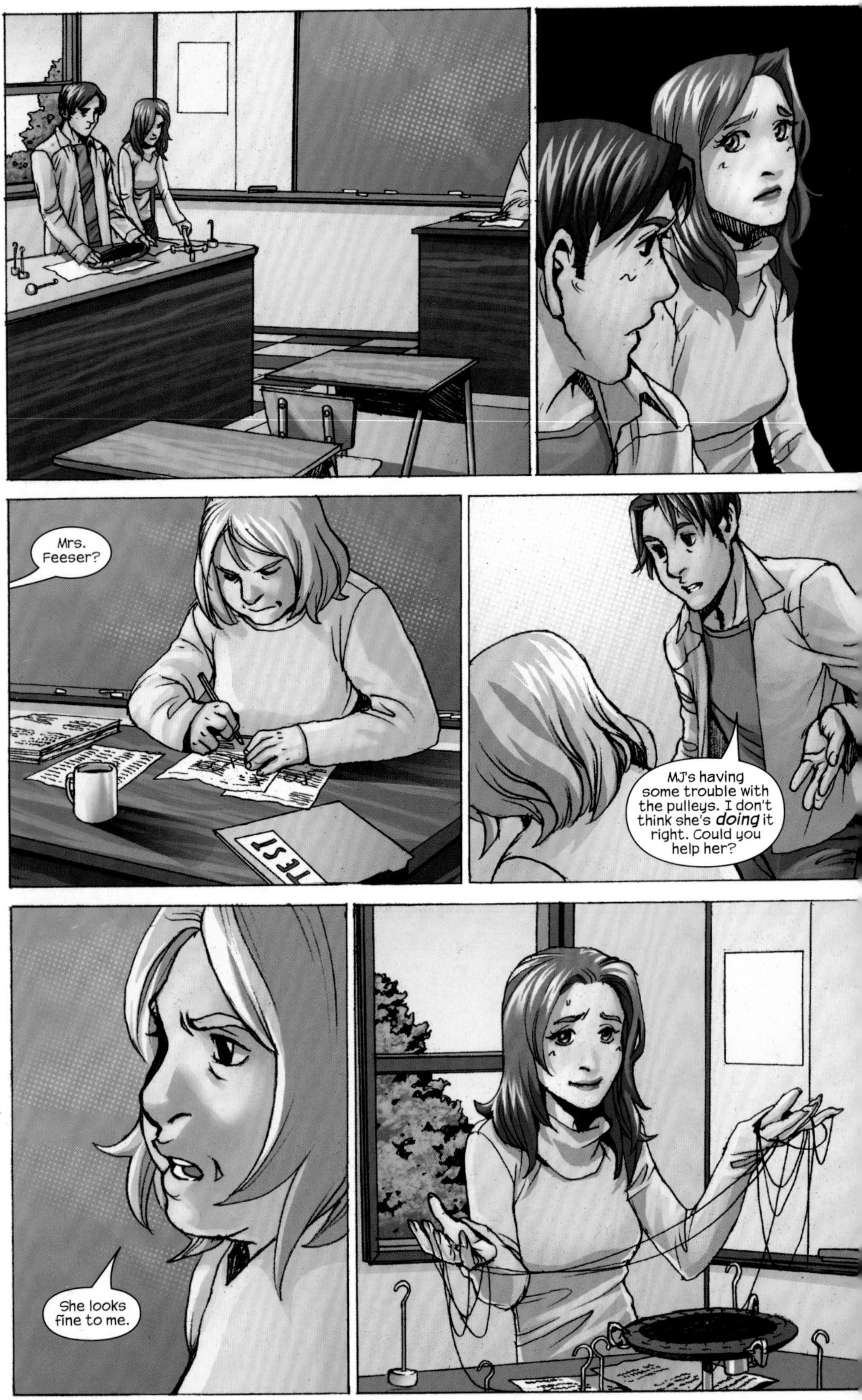
Mrs. Feeser?
TEST
MJ's having some trouble with the pulleys. I don't think she's *doing* it right. Could you help her?
She looks fine to me.

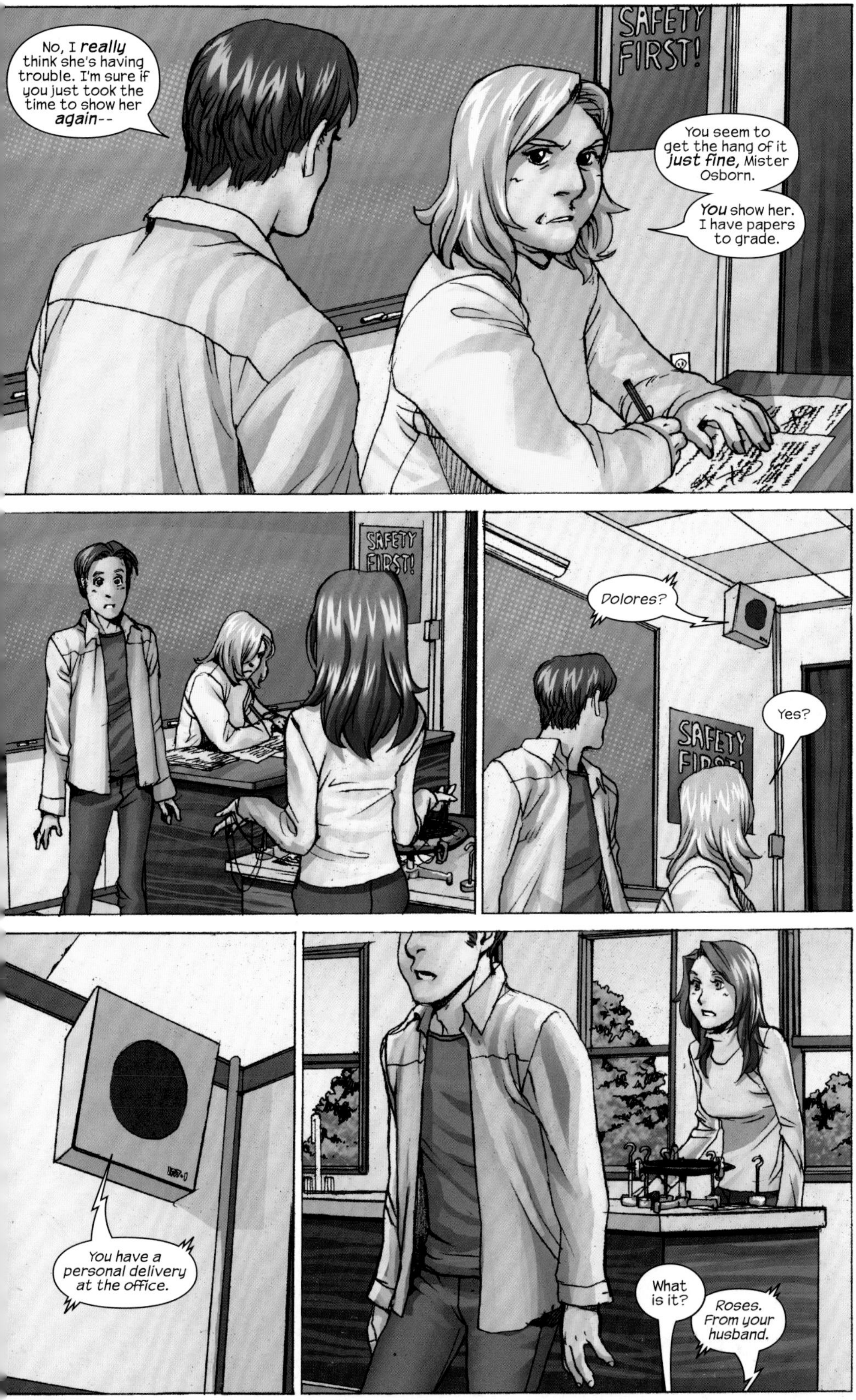
No, I really think she's having trouble. I'm sure if you just took the time to show her again--
SAFETY FIRST!
You seem to get the hang of it just fine, Mister Osborn.
You show her. I have papers to grade.
SAFETY FIRST!
Dolores?
Yes?
You have a personal delivery at the office.
What is it?
Roses. From your husband.

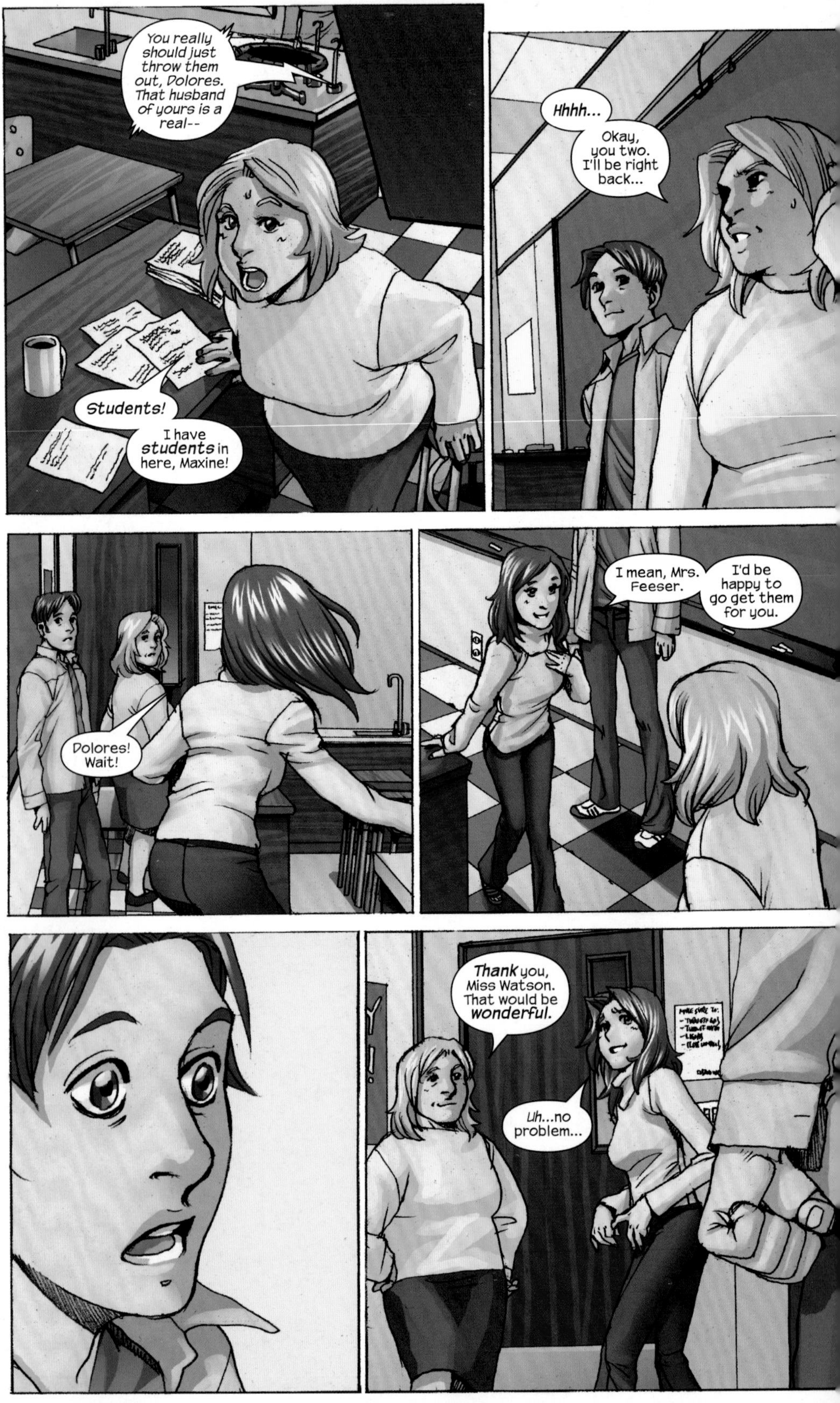
You really should just throw them out, Dolores. That husband of yours is a real--
Students!
I have students in here, Maxine!
Hhhh...
Okay, you two. I'll be right back...
Dolores! Wait!
I mean, Mrs. Feeser.
I'd be happy to go get them for you.
Thank you, Miss Watson. That would be wonderful.
Uh...no problem...

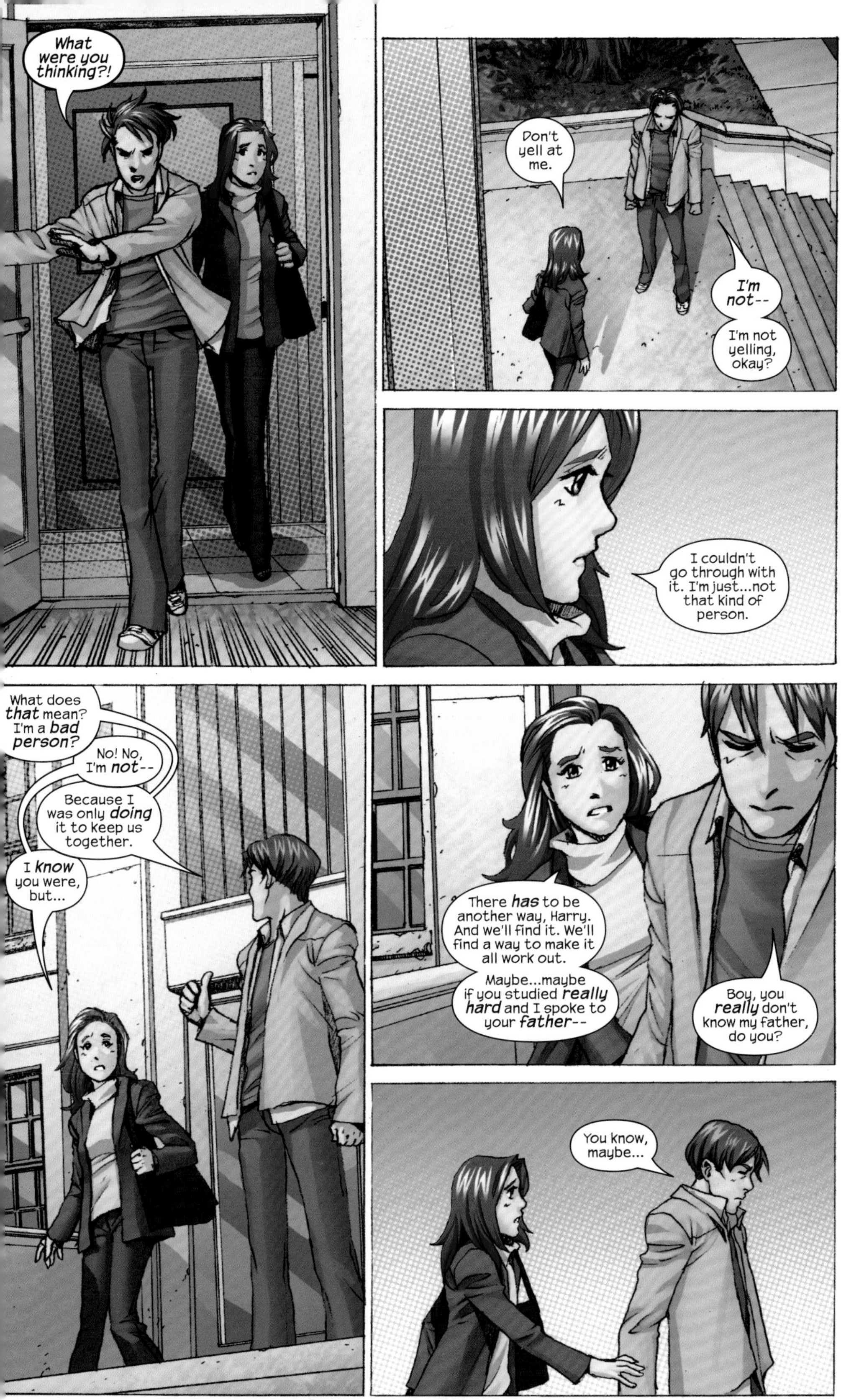
What were you thinking?!
Don't yell at me.
I'm not--
I'm not yelling, okay?
I couldn't go through with it. I'm just...not that kind of person.
What does that mean? I'm a bad person?
No! No, I'm not--
Because I was only doing it to keep us together.
I know you were, but...
There has to be another way, Harry. And we'll find it. We'll find a way to make it all work out.
Maybe...maybe if you studied really hard and I spoke to your father--
Boy, you really don't know my father, do you?
You know, maybe...

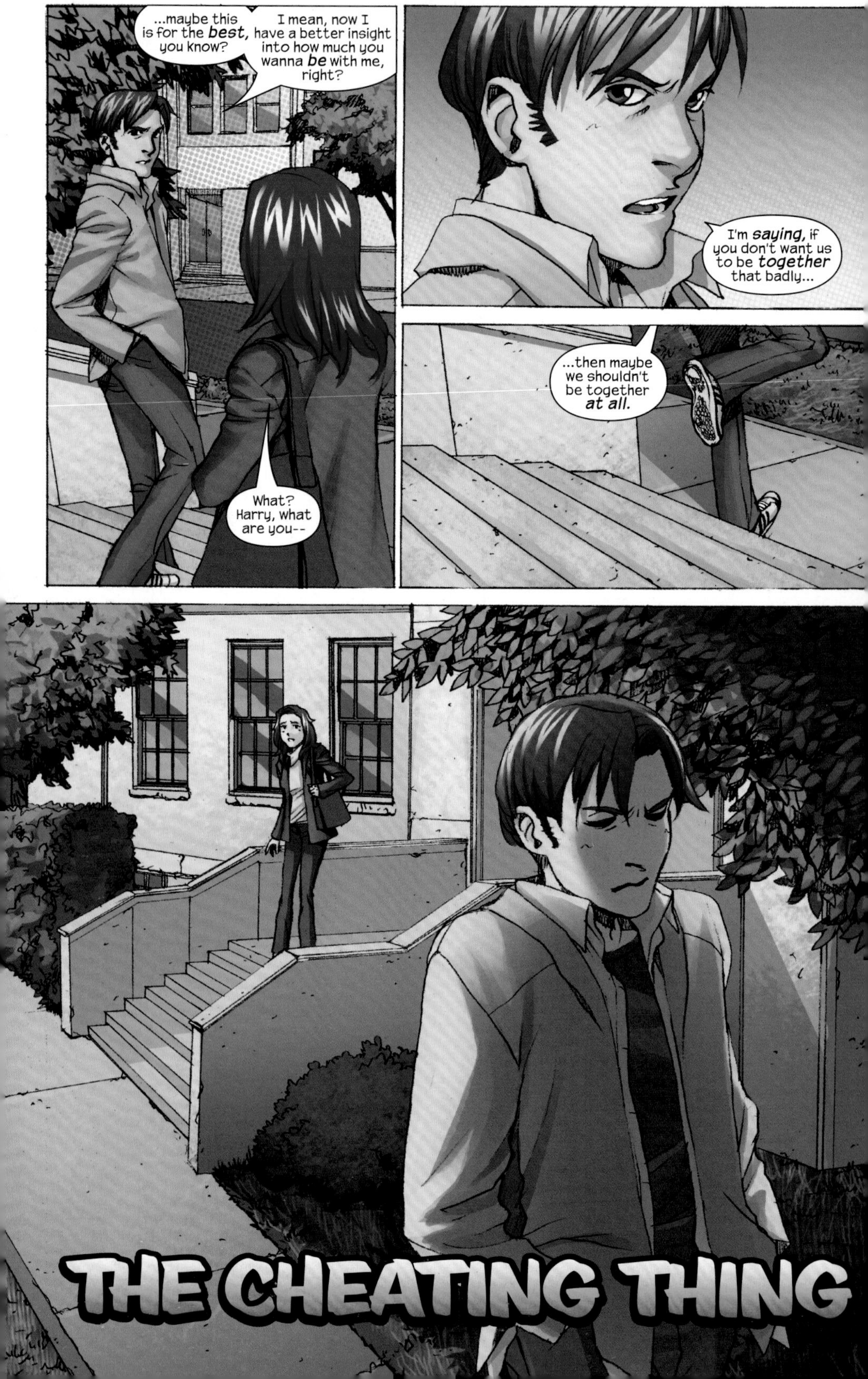
...maybe this is for the best, you know?
I mean, now I have a better insight into how much you wanna be with me, right?
What? Harry, what are you--
I'm saying, if you don't want us to be together that badly...
...then maybe we shouldn't be together at all.
THE CHEATING THING

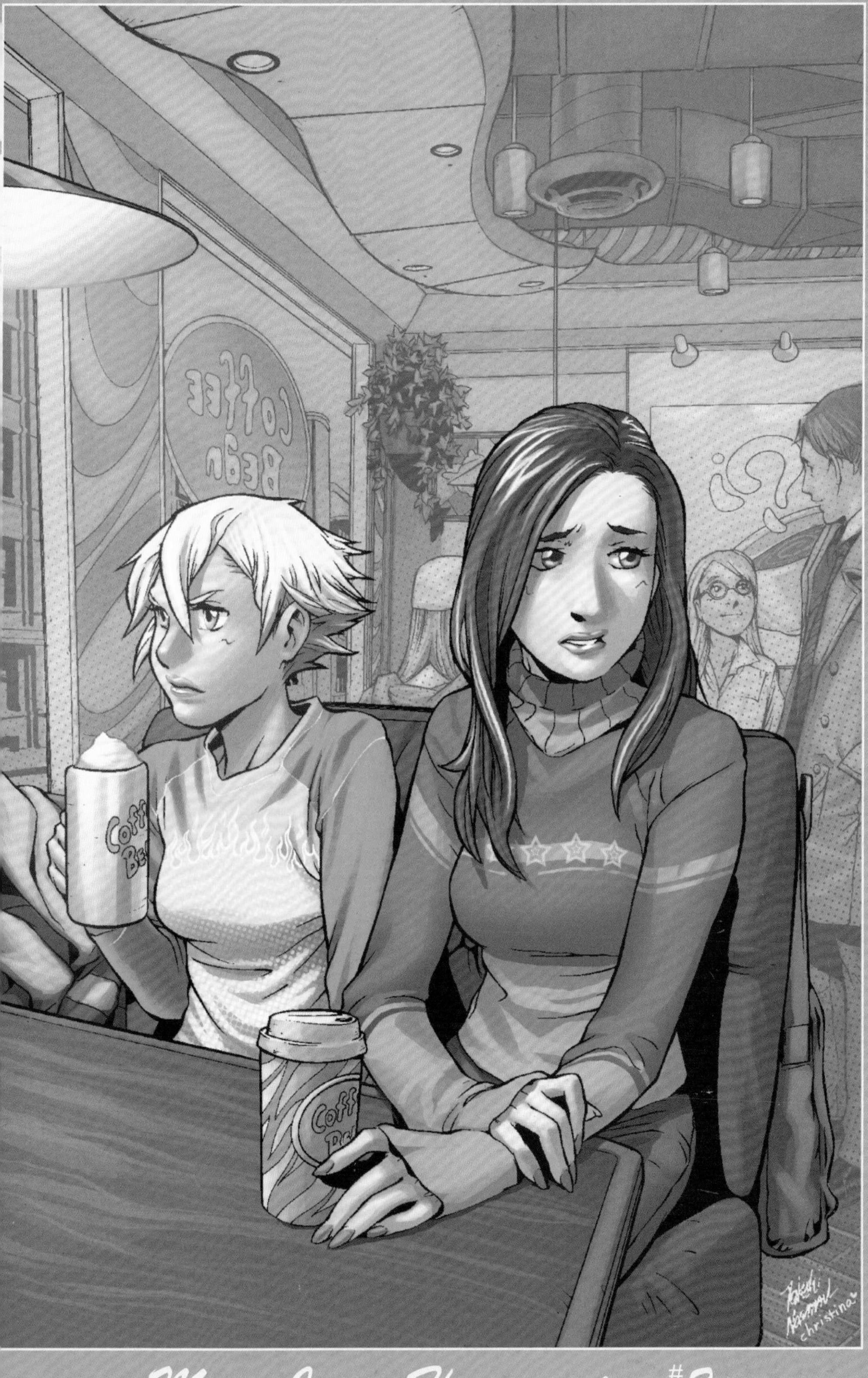

Mary Jane: Homecoming #2

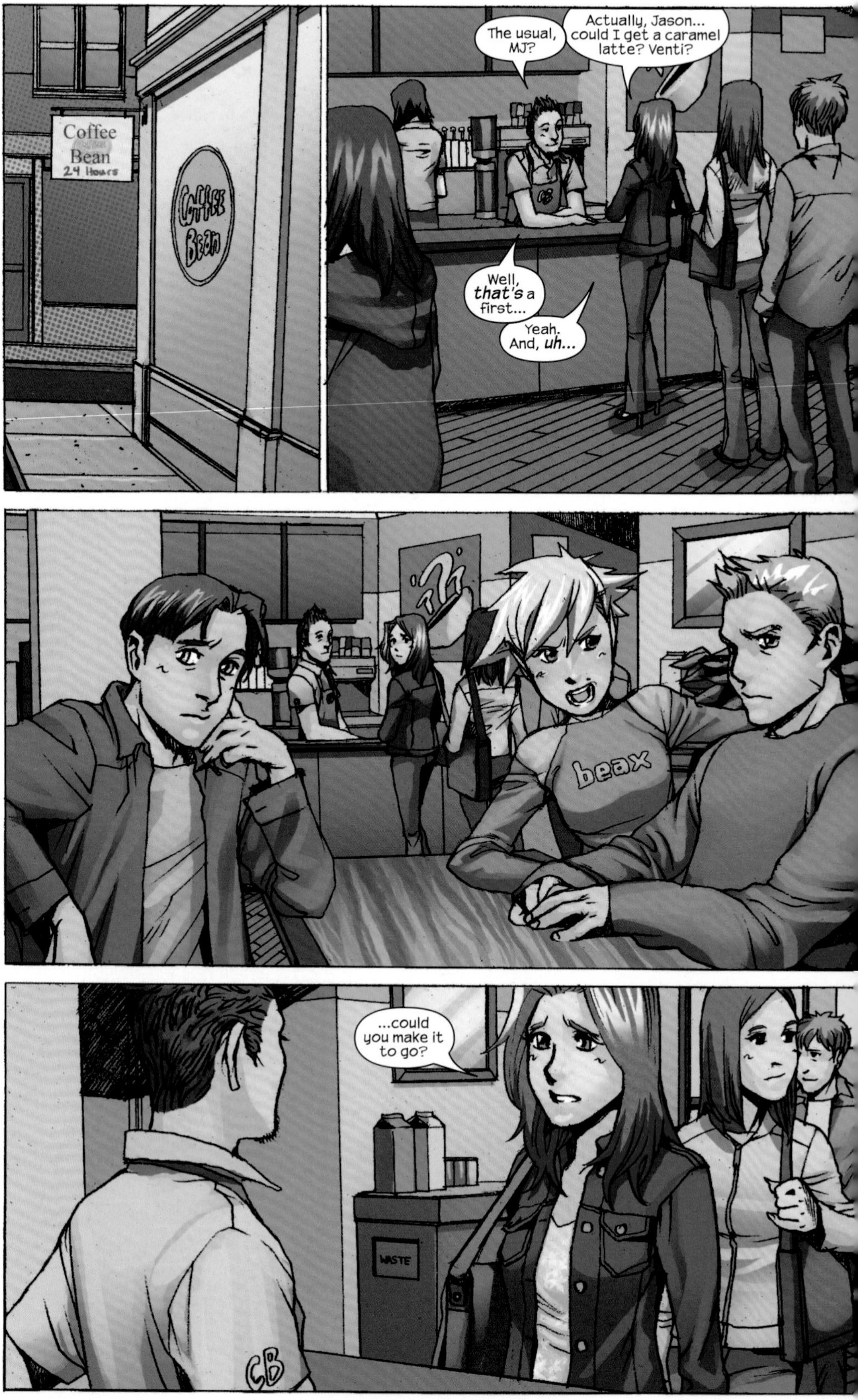
Coffee Bean 24 Hours
Coffee Bean
The usual, MJ?
Actually, Jason... could I get a caramel latte? Venti?
Well, *that's* a first...
Yeah. And, *uh...*
beax
...could you make it to go?
WASTE
CB

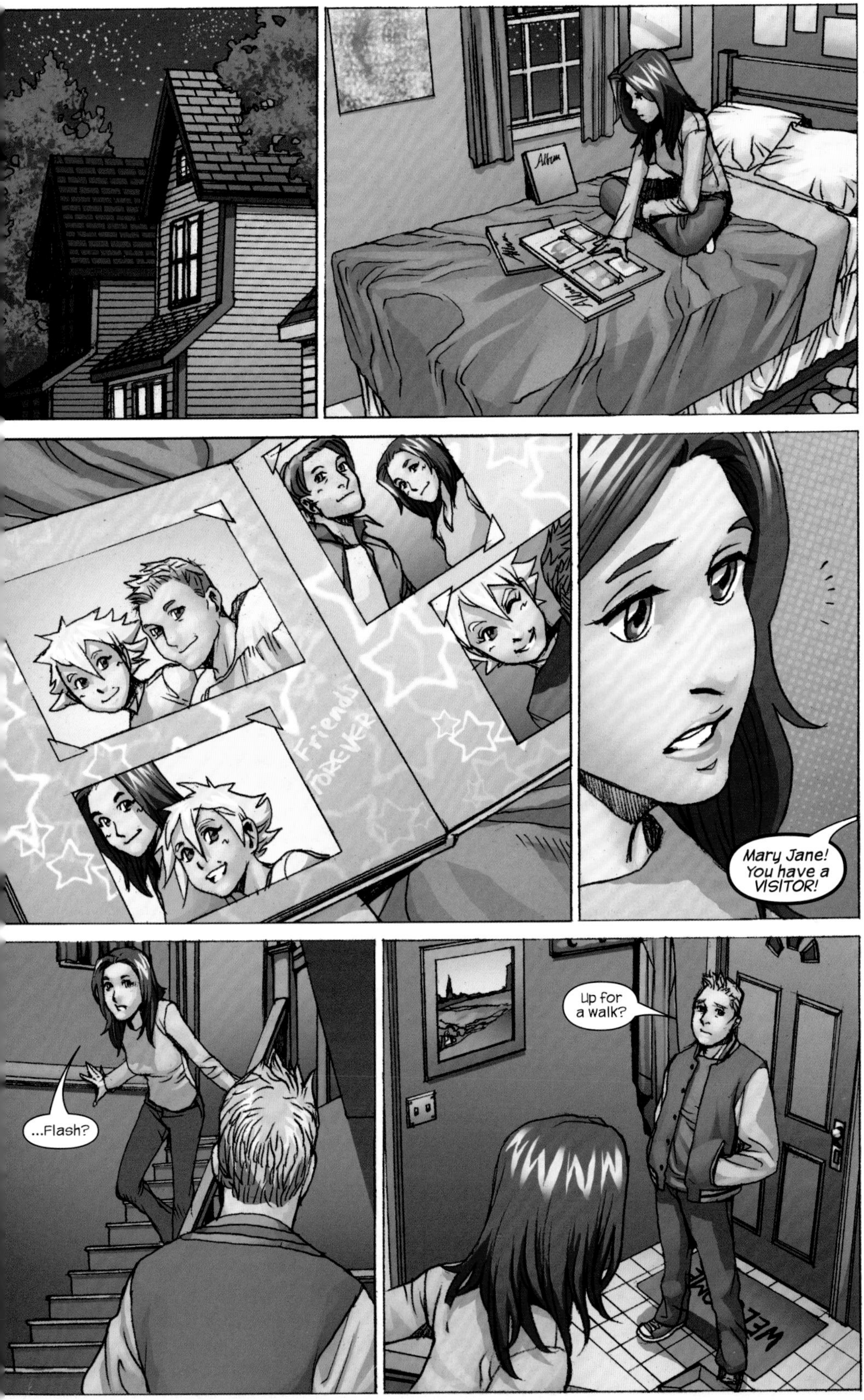
Album
Friends FOREVER
Mary Jane! You have a VISITOR!
...Flash?
Up for a walk?
WELCOME

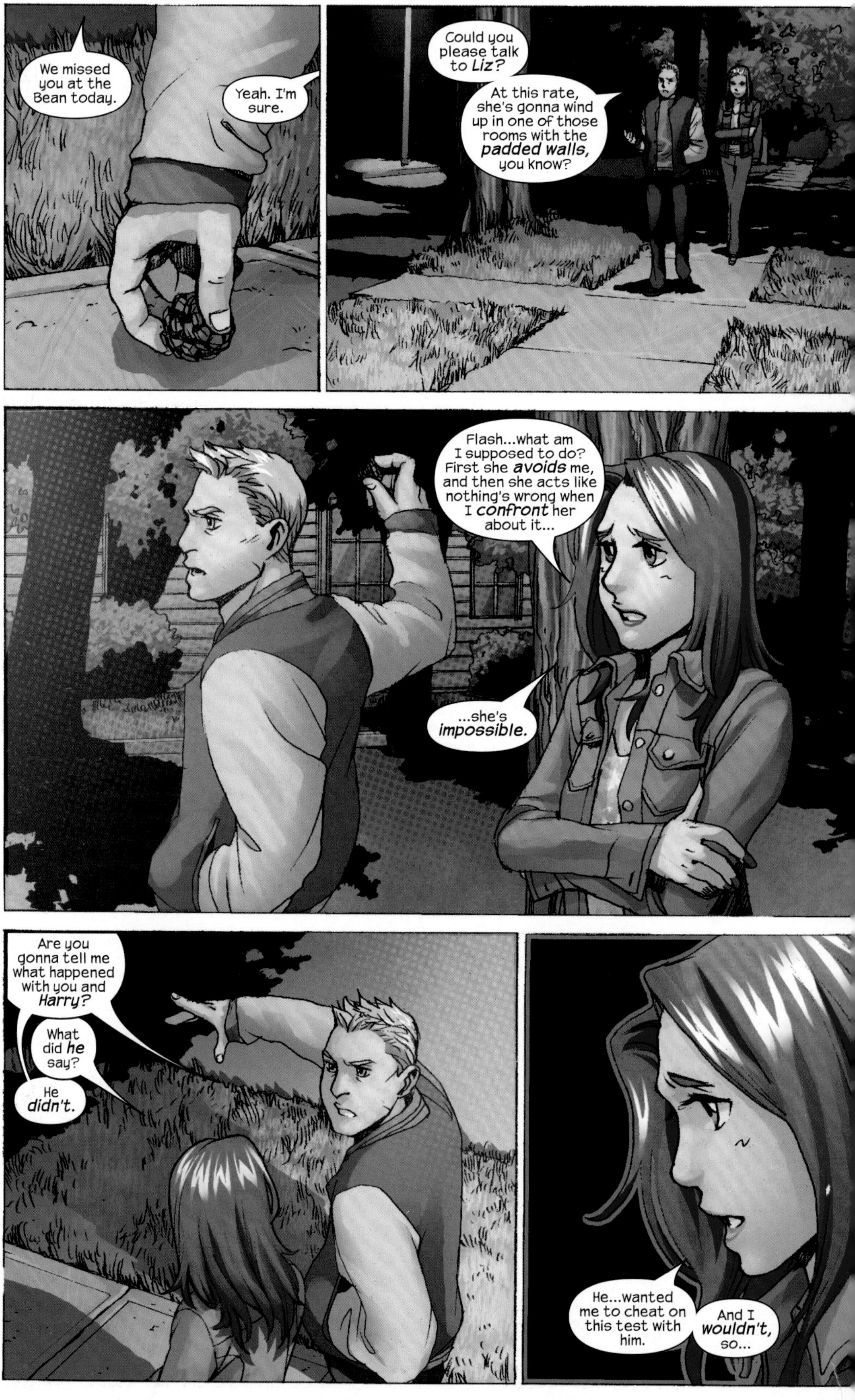

We missed you at the Bean today.
Yeah. I'm sure.
Could you please talk to Liz?
At this rate, she's gonna wind up in one of those rooms with the padded walls, you know?
Flash...what am I supposed to do? First she avoids me, and then she acts like nothing's wrong when I confront her about it...
...she's impossible.
Are you gonna tell me what happened with you and Harry?
What did he say?
He didn't.
He...wanted me to cheat on this test with him.
And I wouldn't, so...

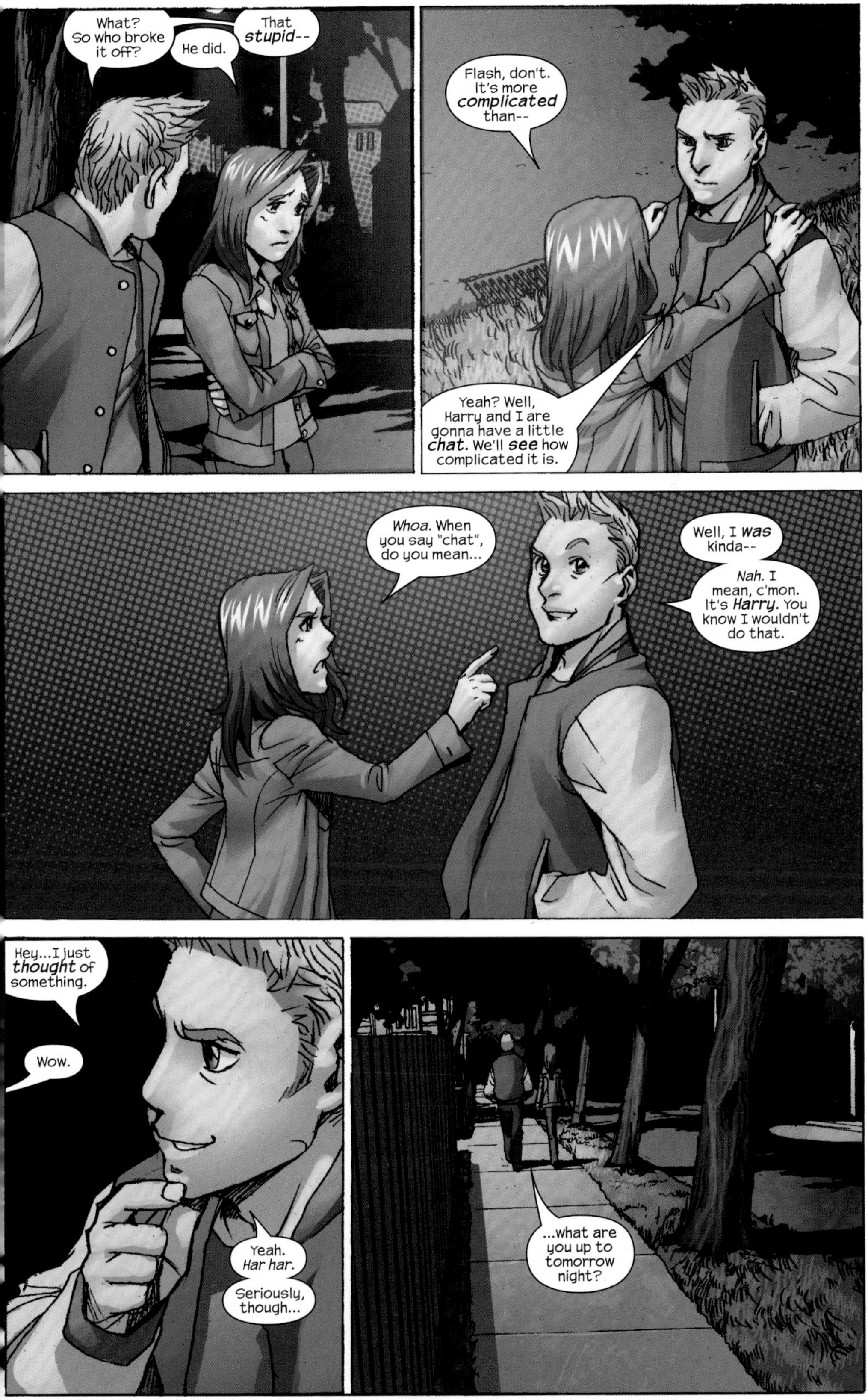
What? So who broke it off?
That stupid--
He did.
Flash, don't. It's more complicated than--
Yeah? Well, Harry and I are gonna have a little chat. We'll see how complicated it is.
Whoa. When you say "chat", do you mean...
Well, I was kinda--
Nah. I mean, c'mon. It's Harry. You know I wouldn't do that.
Hey...I just thought of something.
Wow.
Yeah. Har har.
Seriously, though...
...what are you up to tomorrow night?

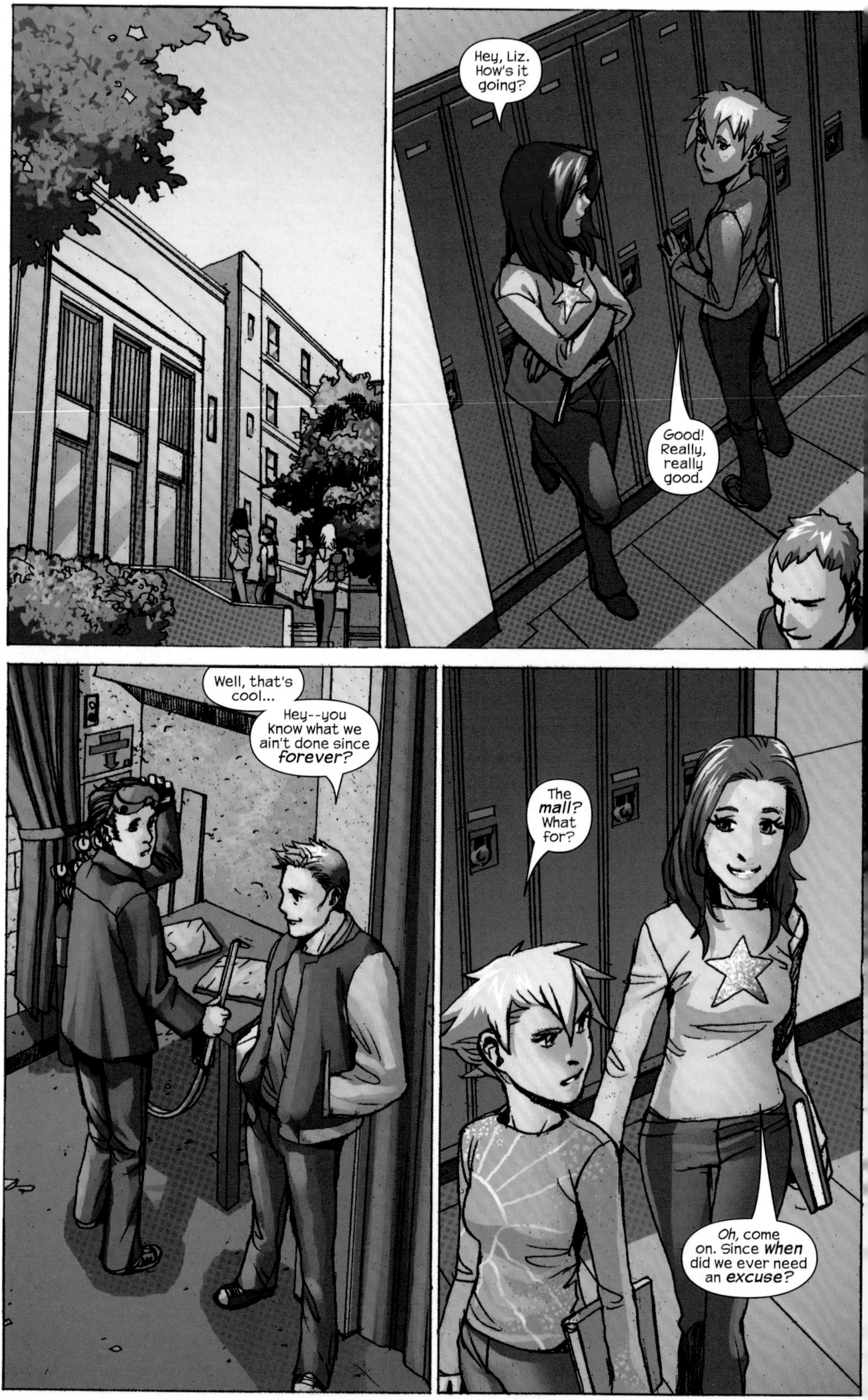

Hey, Liz. How's it going?
Good! Really, really good.
Well, that's cool...
Hey--you know what we ain't done since *forever?*
The *mall?* What for?
Oh, come on. Since ***when*** did we ever need an *excuse?*

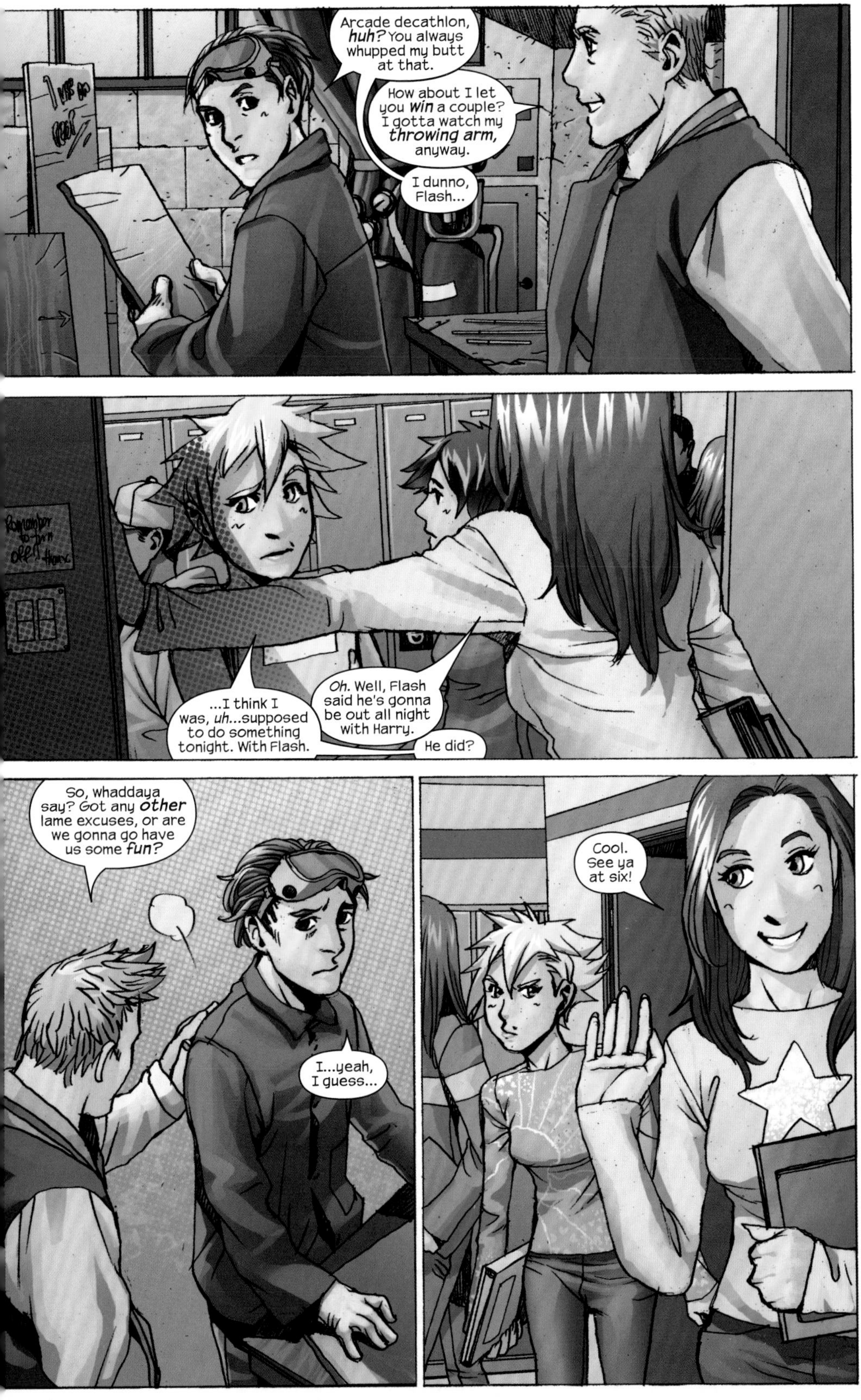
Arcade decathlon, *huh?* You always whupped my butt at that.
How about I let you *win* a couple? I gotta watch my *throwing arm,* anyway.
I dunno, Flash...
...I think I was, *uh*...supposed to do something tonight. With Flash.
Oh. Well, Flash said he's gonna be out all night with Harry.
He did?
So, whaddaya say? Got any *other* lame excuses, or are we gonna go have us some *fun?*
I...yeah, I guess...
Cool. See ya at six!

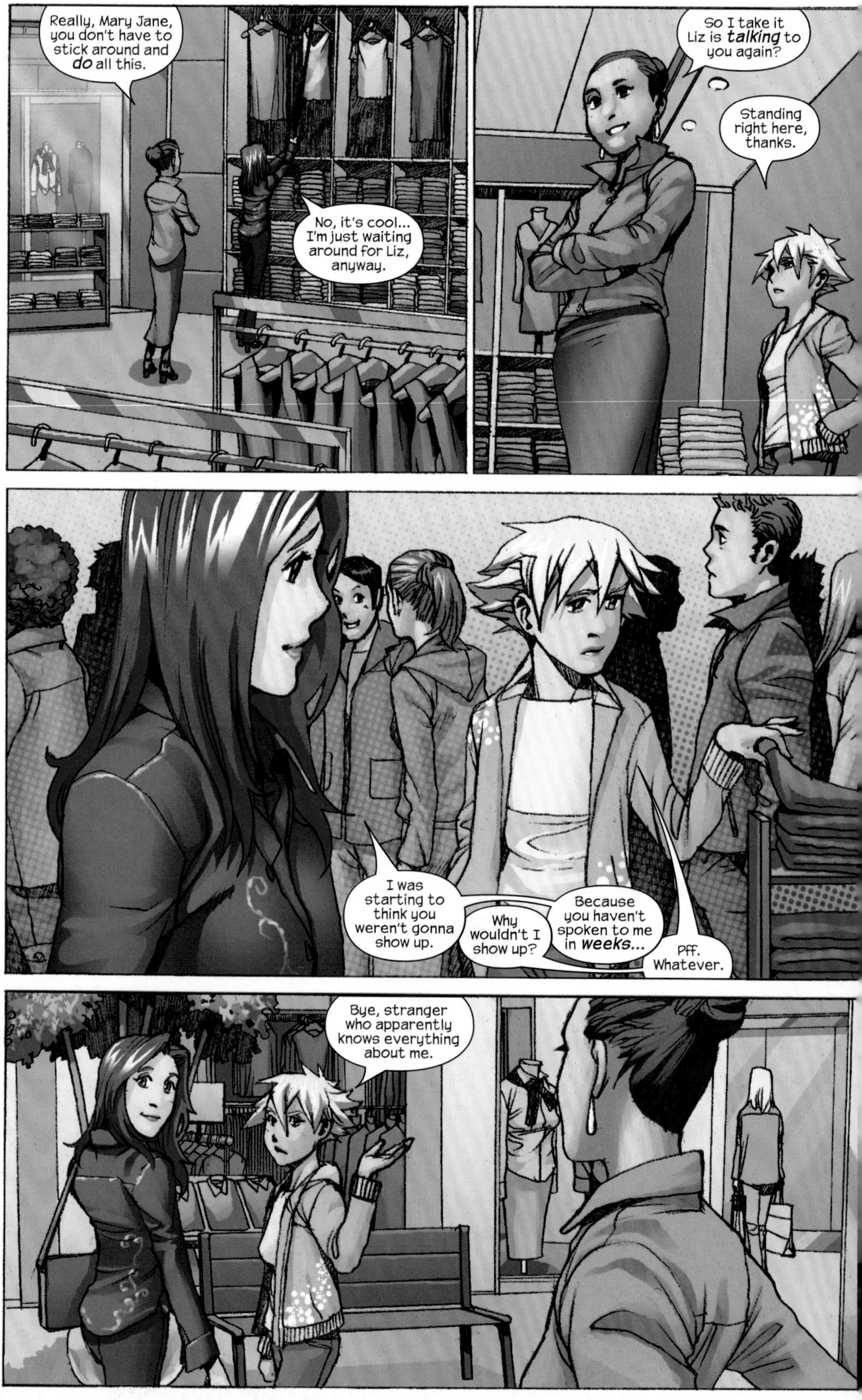
Really, Mary Jane, you don't have to stick around and *do* all this.
No, it's cool... I'm just waiting around for Liz, anyway.
So I take it Liz is *talking* to you again?
Standing right here, thanks.
I was starting to think you weren't gonna show up.
Why wouldn't I show up?
Because you haven't spoken to me in *weeks...*
Pff. Whatever.
Bye, stranger who apparently knows everything about me.

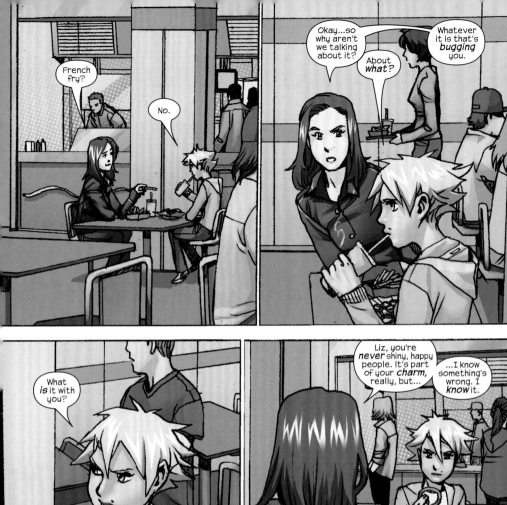

French fry?

No.

Okay...so why aren't we talking about it?

About *what*?

Whatever it is that's *bugging* you.

What *is* it with you?

You know, just because I'm not shiny, happy people all the time *doesn't* mean anything's wrong.

Liz, you're *never* shiny, happy people. It's part of your *charm*, really, but...

...I know something's wrong. I *know* it.

These onion rings suck.

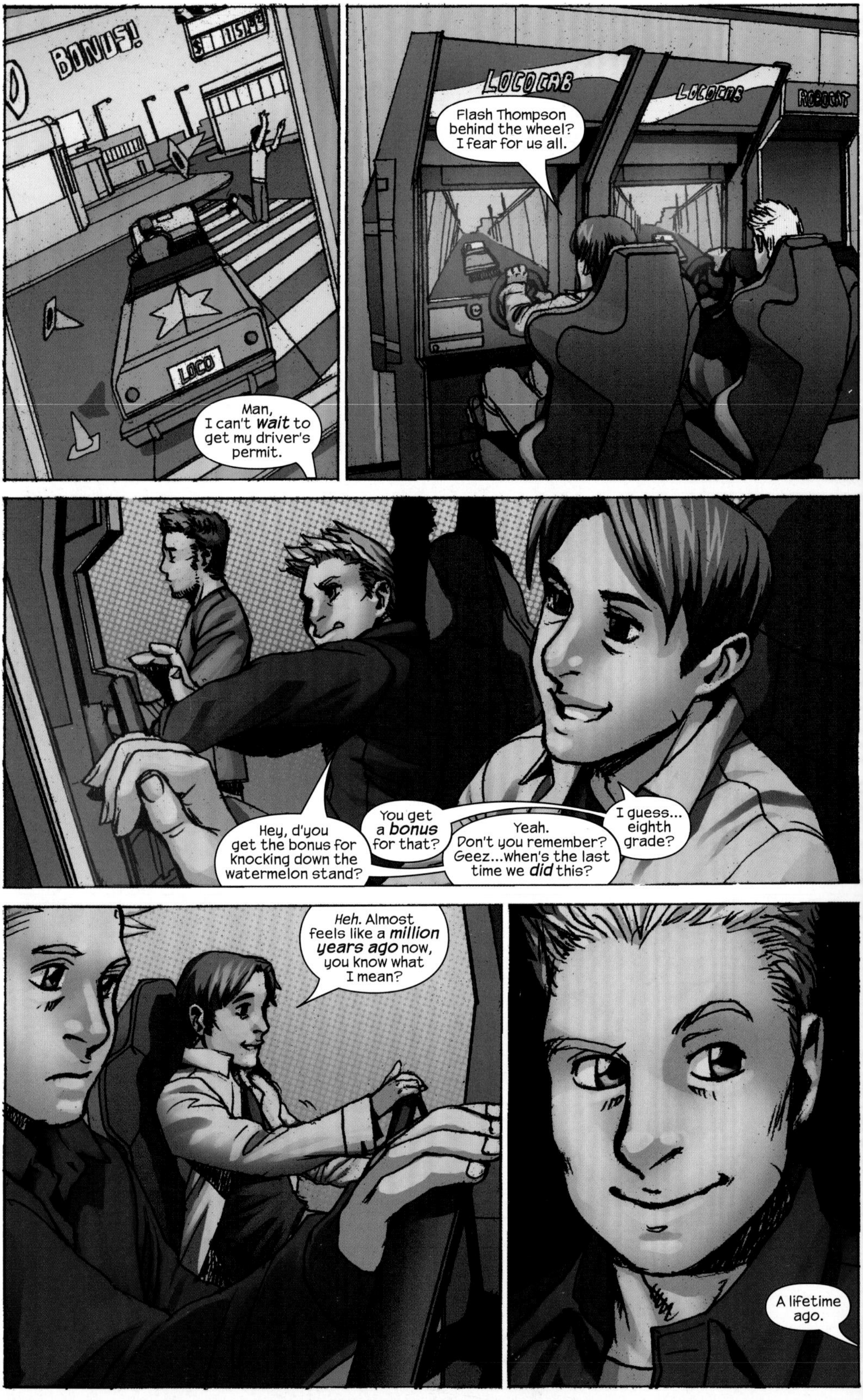
BONUS!
LOCO
Man, I can't *wait* to get my driver's permit.
LOCOCAB
Flash Thompson behind the wheel? I fear for us all.
Hey, d'you get the bonus for knocking down the watermelon stand?
You get a ***bonus*** for that?
Yeah. Don't you remember? Geez...when's the last time we ***did*** this?
I guess... eighth grade?
Heh. Almost feels like a ***million years ago*** now, you know what I mean?
A lifetime ago.

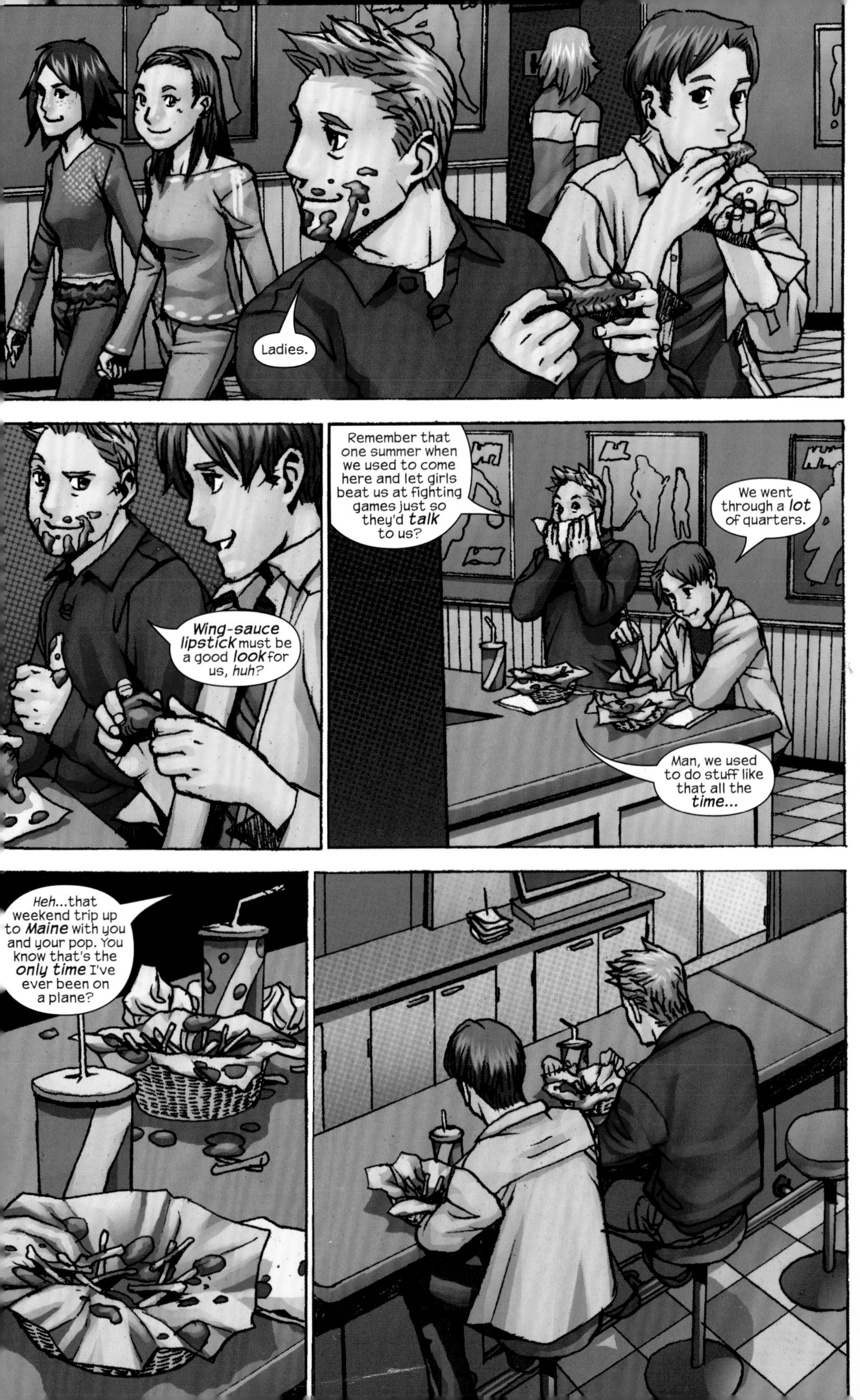
Ladies.
Wing-sauce lipstick must be a good look for us, huh?
Remember that one summer when we used to come here and let girls beat us at fighting games just so they'd talk to us?
We went through a lot of quarters.
Man, we used to do stuff like that all the time...
Heh...that weekend trip up to Maine with you and your pop. You know that's the only time I've ever been on a plane?

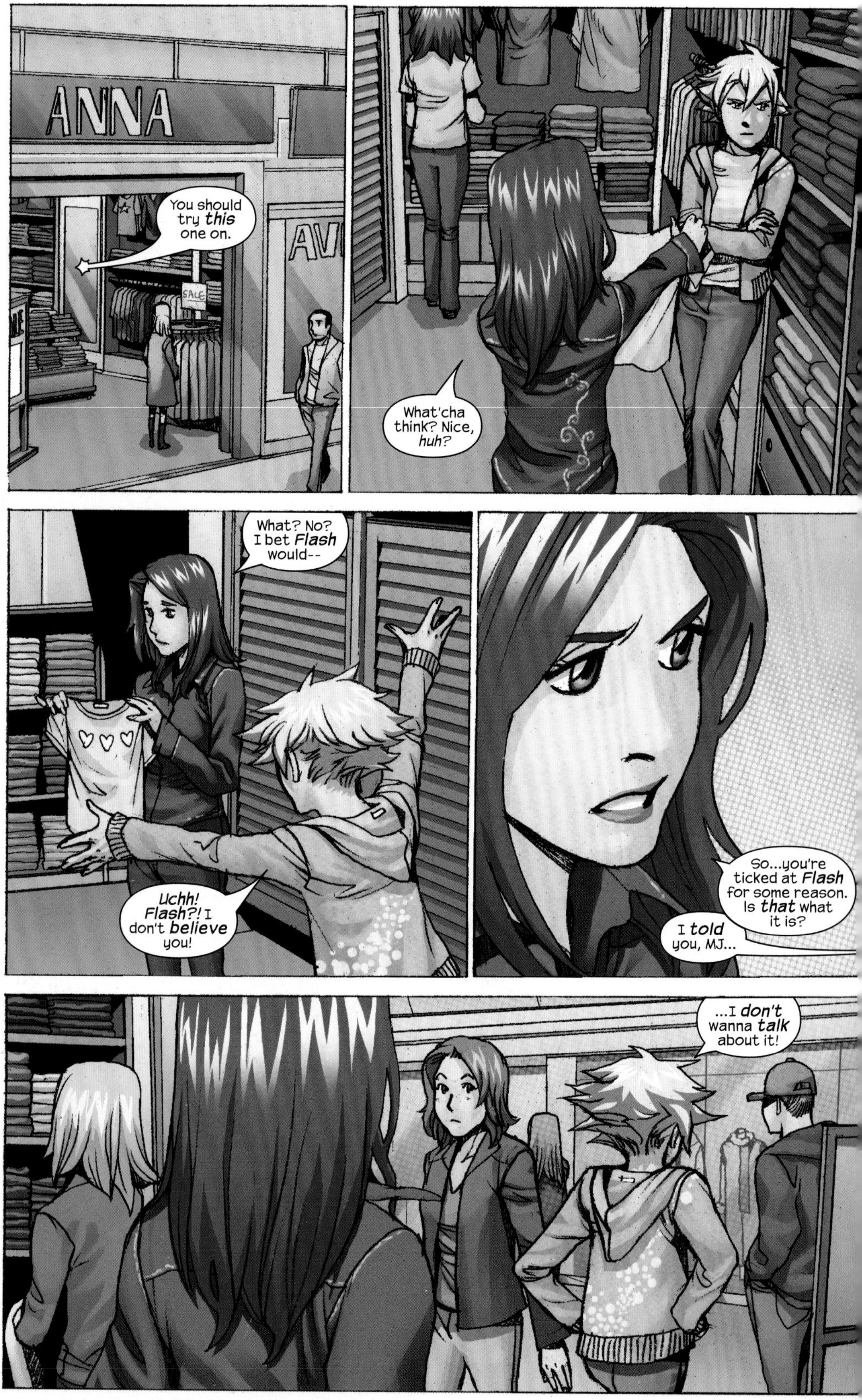
ANNA
SALE
You should try *this* one on.
What'cha think? Nice, *huh*?
What? No? I bet *Flash* would--
Uchh! Flash?! I don't *believe* you!
So...you're ticked at *Flash* for some reason. Is *that* what it is?
I *told* you, MJ...
...I *don't* wanna *talk* about it!

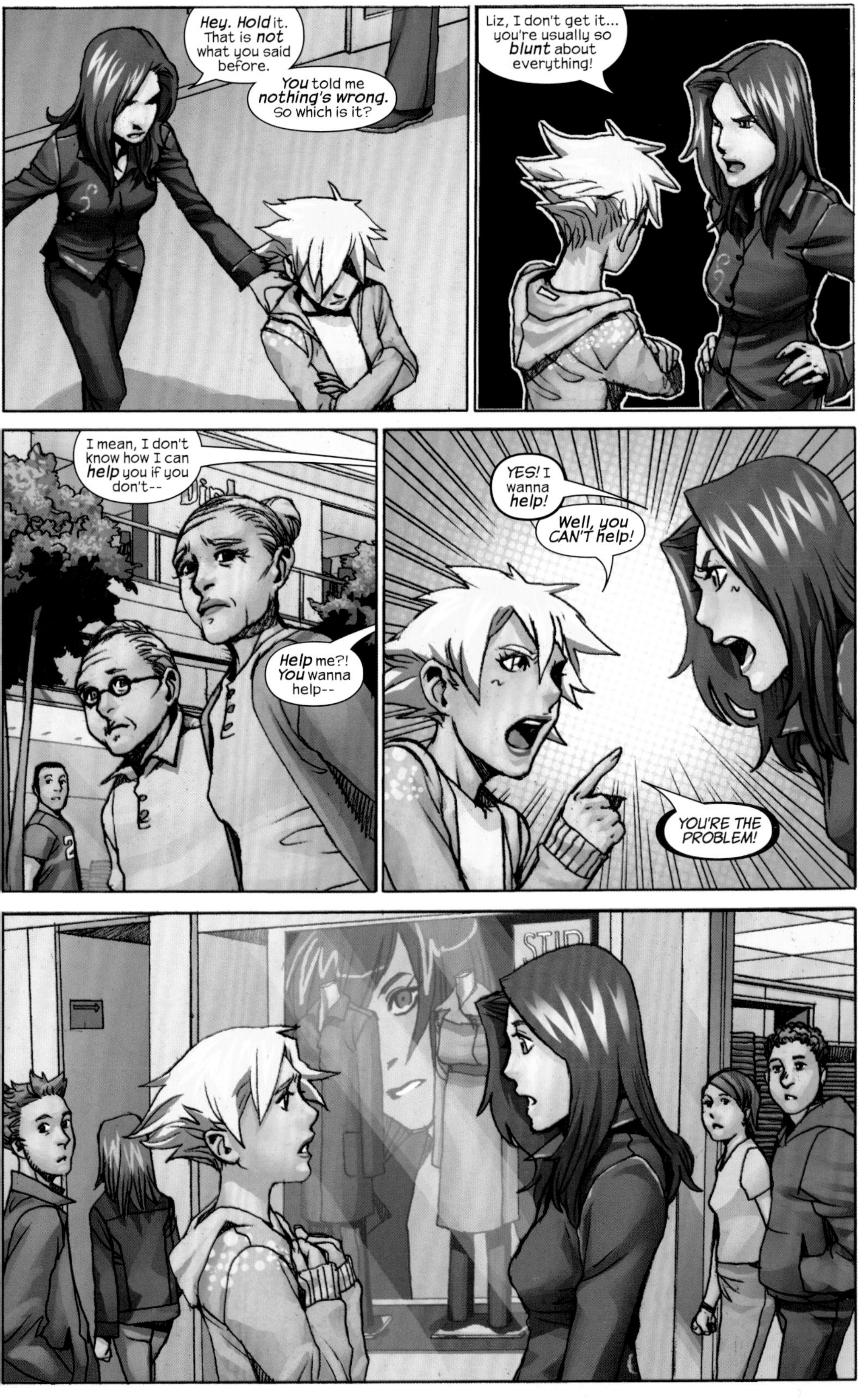

Hey. Hold it. That is not what you said before.
You told me nothing's wrong. So which is it?
Liz, I don't get it... you're usually so blunt about everything!
I mean, I don't know how I can help you if you don't--
Help me?! You wanna help--
YES! I wanna help!
Well, you CAN'T help!
YOU'RE THE PROBLEM!

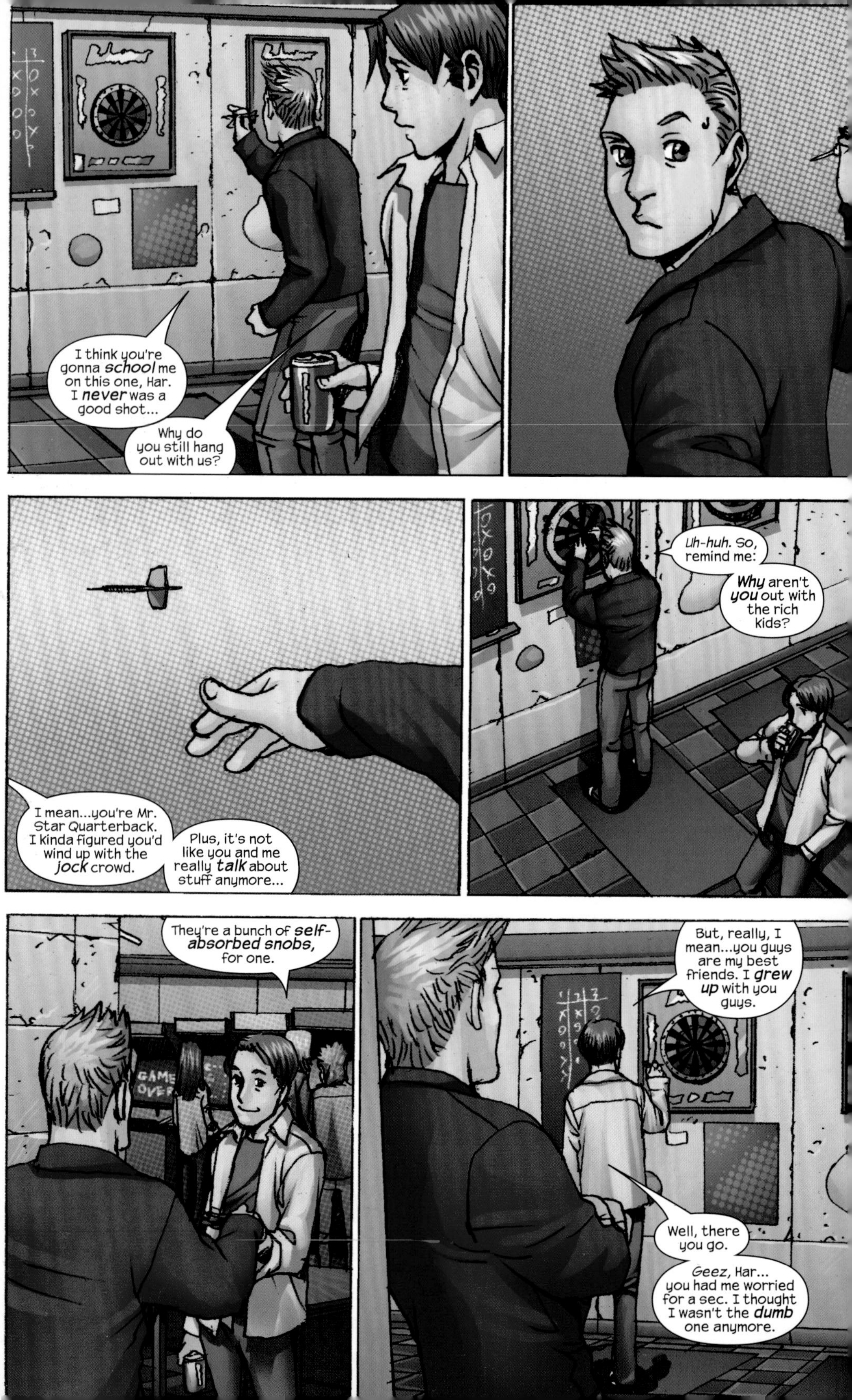
I think you're gonna *school* me on this one, Har. I *never* was a good shot...
Why do you still hang out with us?
Uh-huh. So, remind me:
Why aren't *you* out with the rich kids?
I mean...you're Mr. Star Quarterback. I kinda figured you'd wind up with the *jock* crowd.
Plus, it's not like you and me really *talk* about stuff anymore...
They're a bunch of *self-absorbed snobs,* for one.
GAME OVER
But, really, I mean...you guys are my best friends. I *grew up* with you guys.
Well, there you go.
Geez, Har... you had me worried for a sec. I thought I wasn't the *dumb* one anymore.

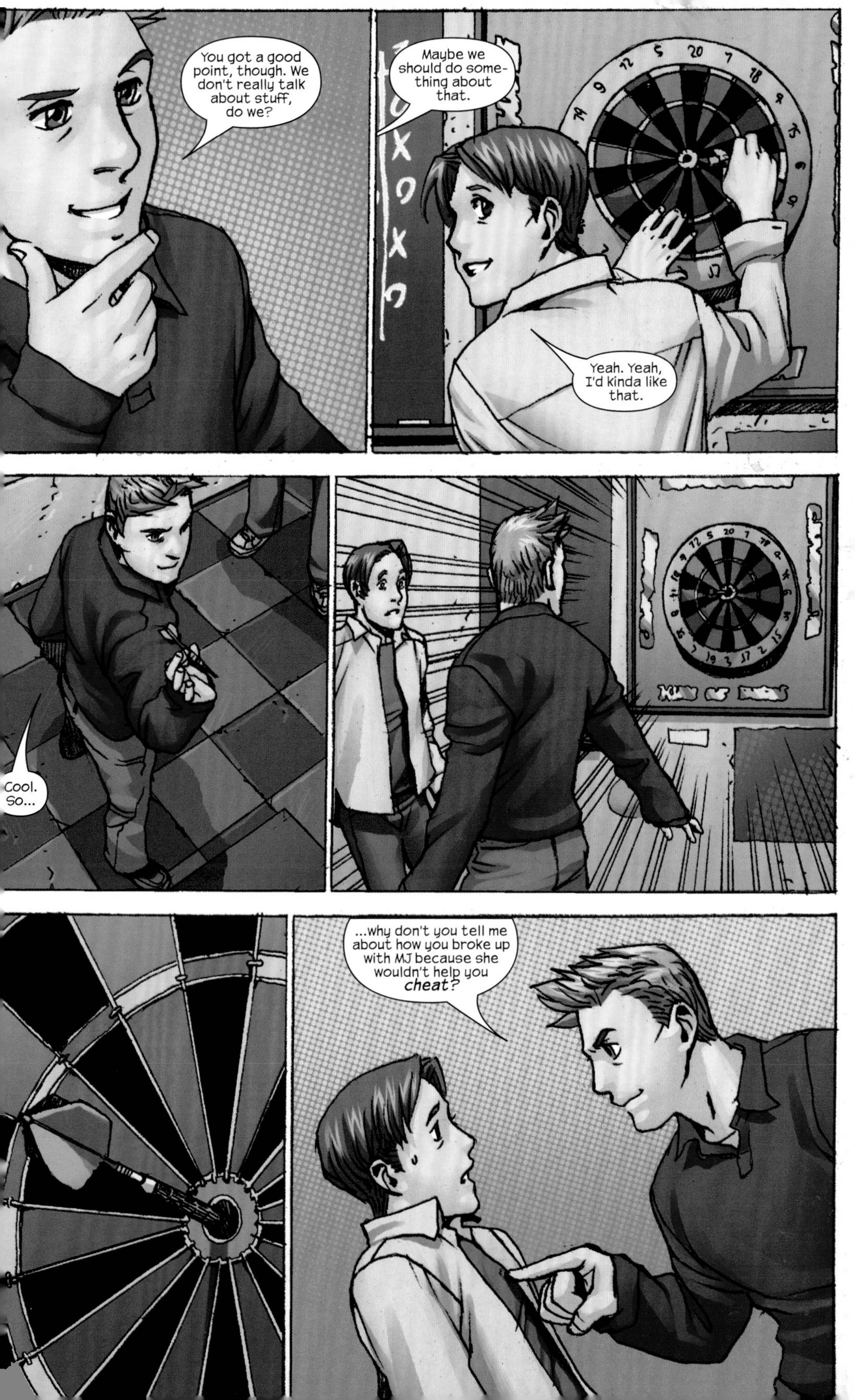
You got a good point, though. We don't really talk about stuff, do we?
Maybe we should do something about that.
Yeah. Yeah, I'd kinda like that.
Cool. So...
...why don't you tell me about how you broke up with MJ because she wouldn't help you *cheat*?

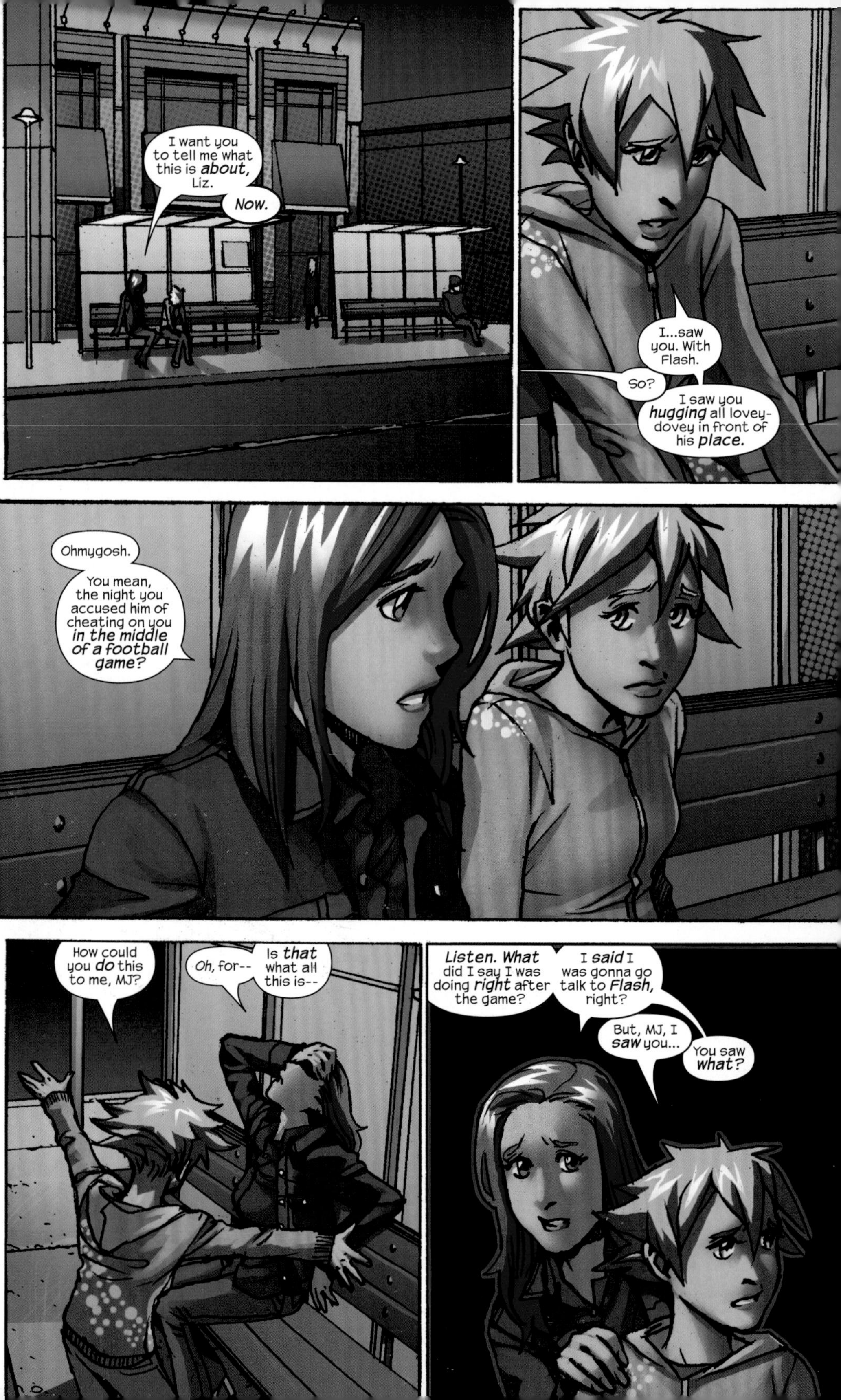
I want you to tell me what this is about, Liz.
Now.
I...saw you. With Flash.
So?
I saw you hugging all lovey-dovey in front of his place.
Ohmygosh.
You mean, the night you accused him of cheating on you in the middle of a football game?
How could you do this to me, MJ?
Oh, for--
Is that what all this is--
Listen. What did I say I was doing right after the game?
I said I was gonna go talk to Flash, right?
But, MJ, I saw you...
You saw what?

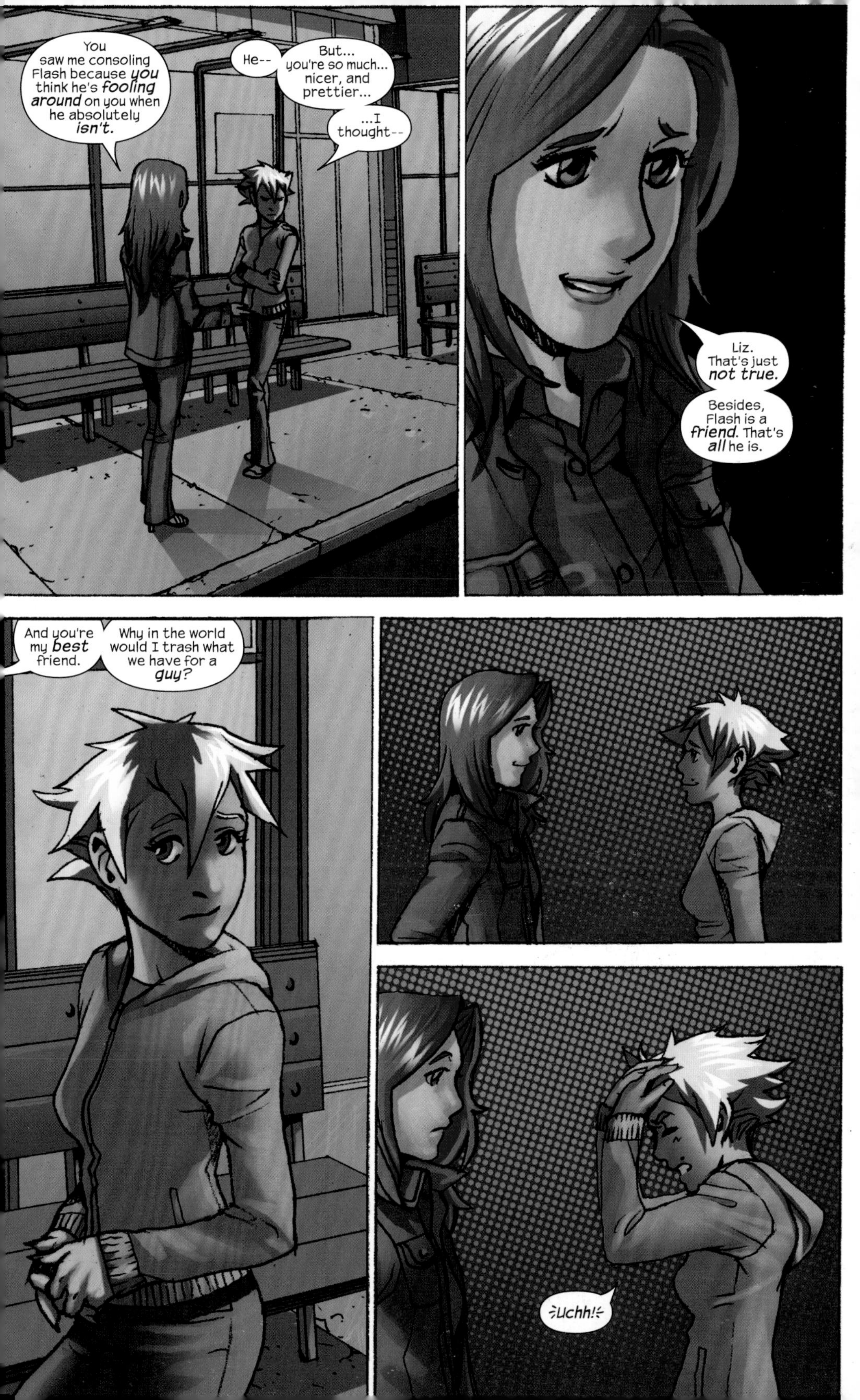

You saw me consoling Flash because *you* think he's *fooling around* on you when he absolutely *isn't.*
He--
But... you're so much... nicer, and prettier...
...I thought--
Liz. That's just *not true.*
Besides, Flash is a *friend*. That's *all* he is.
And you're my *best* friend.
Why in the world would I trash what we have for a *guy*?
Uchh!

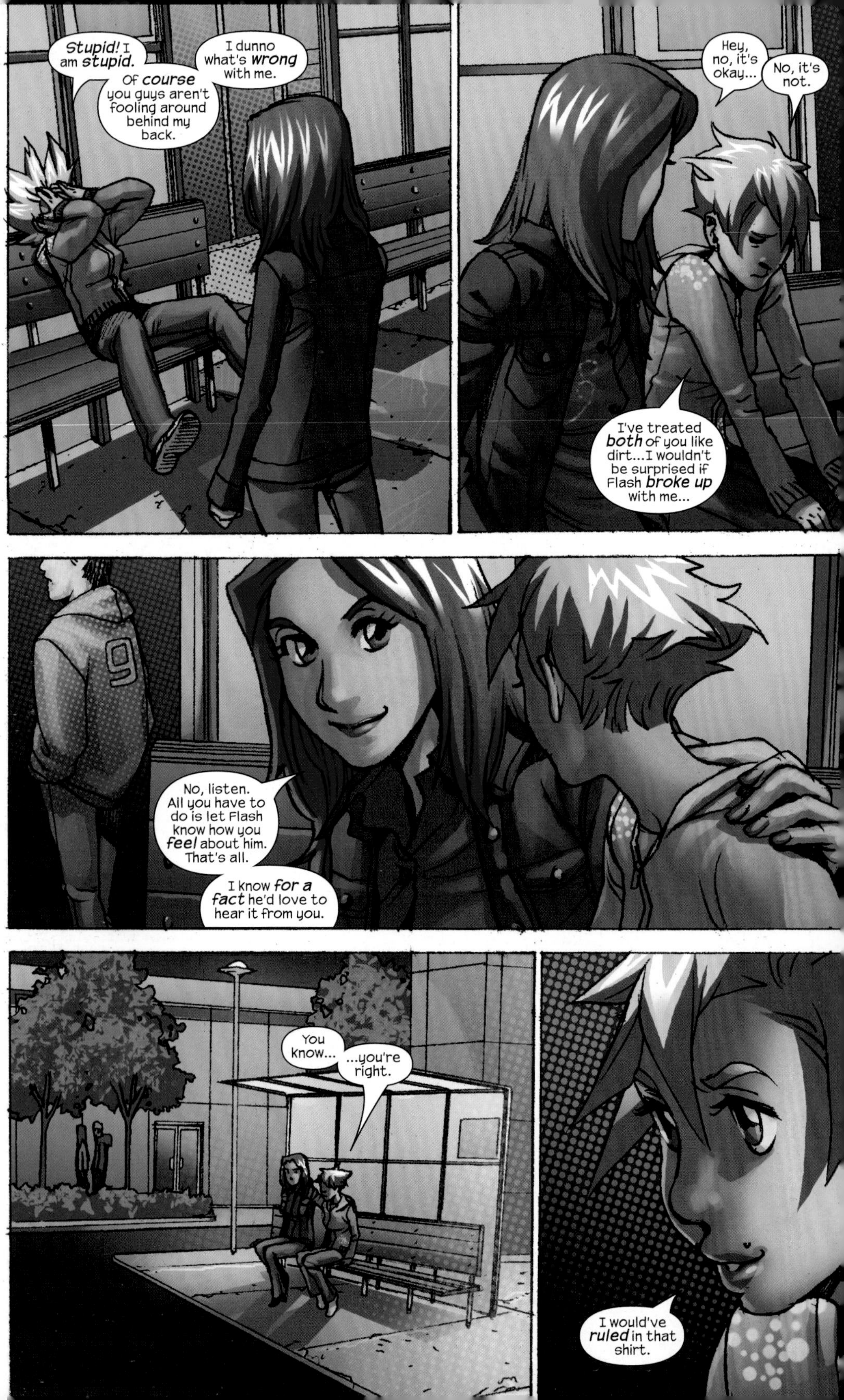
Stupid! I am stupid.
Of course you guys aren't fooling around behind my back.
I dunno what's wrong with me.
Hey, no, it's okay...
No, it's not.
I've treated both of you like dirt...I wouldn't be surprised if Flash broke up with me...
No, listen. All you have to do is let Flash know how you feel about him. That's all.
I know for a fact he'd love to hear it from you.
You know...
...you're right.
I would've ruled in that shirt.

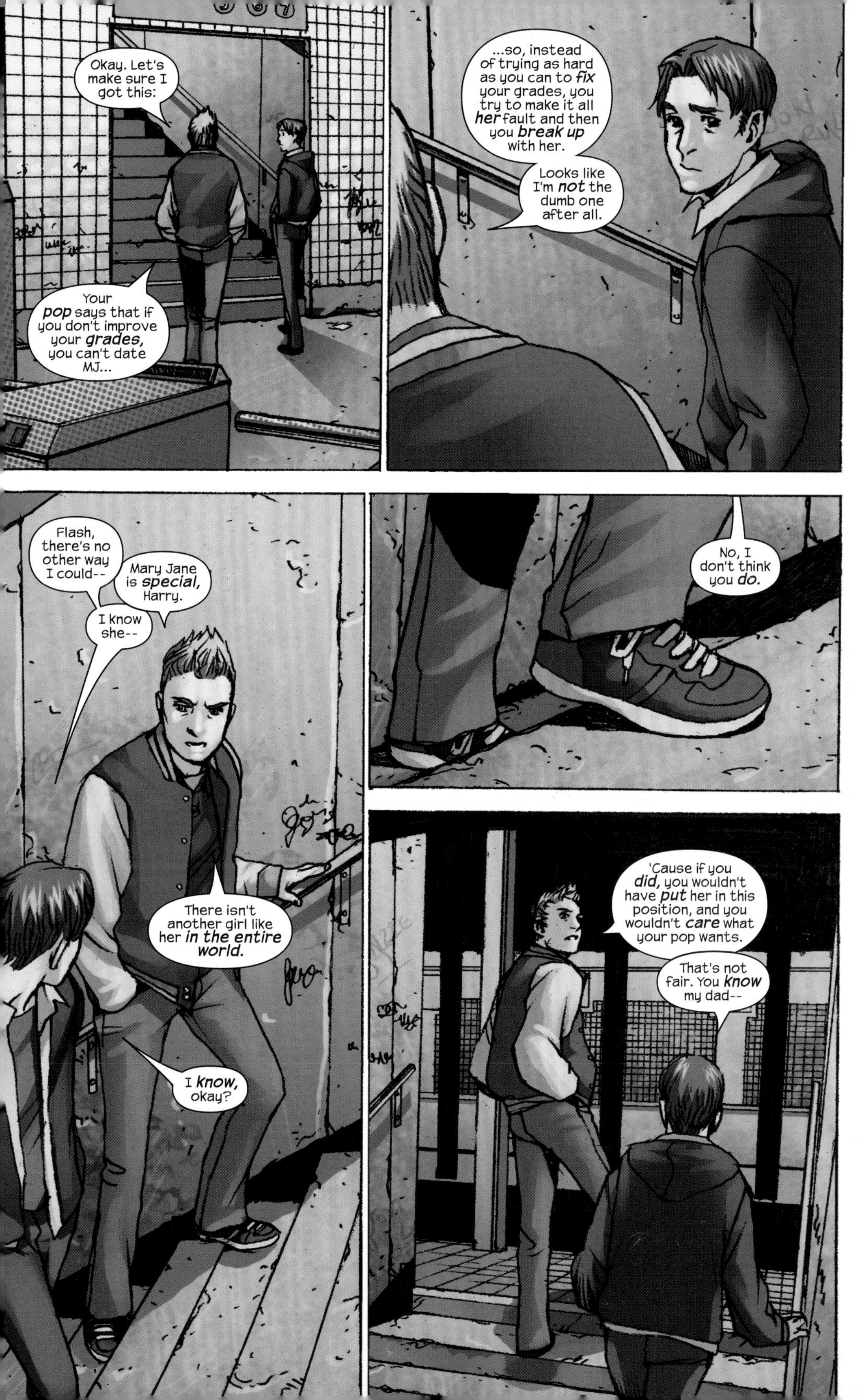

Okay. Let's make sure I got this:
Your *pop* says that if you don't improve your *grades,* you can't date MJ...
...so, instead of trying as hard as you can to *fix* your grades, you try to make it all *her* fault and then you *break up* with her.
Looks like I'm *not* the dumb one after all.
Flash, there's no other way I could--
Mary Jane is *special,* Harry.
I know she--
There isn't another girl like her *in the entire world.*
I *know,* okay?
No, I don't think you *do.*
'Cause if you *did,* you wouldn't have *put* her in this position, and you wouldn't *care* what your pop wants.
That's not fair. You *know* my dad--

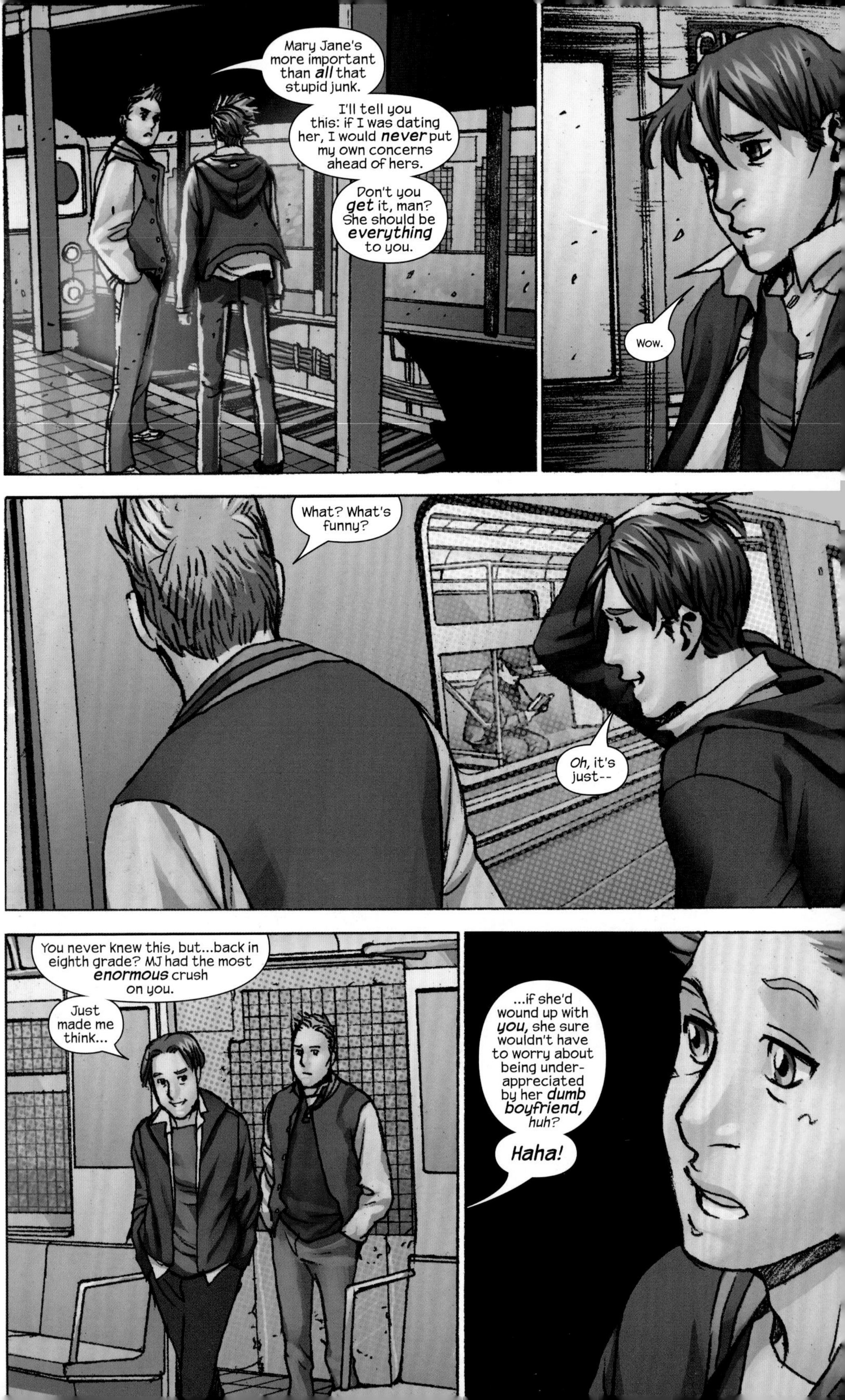
Mary Jane's more important than *all* that stupid junk.
I'll tell you this: if I was dating her, I would *never* put my own concerns ahead of hers.
Don't you *get* it, man? She should be *everything* to you.
Wow.
What? What's funny?
Oh, it's just--
You never knew this, but...back in eighth grade? MJ had the most *enormous* crush on you.
Just made me think...
...if she'd wound up with *you,* she sure wouldn't have to worry about being under-appreciated by her *dumb boyfriend,* huh?
Haha!

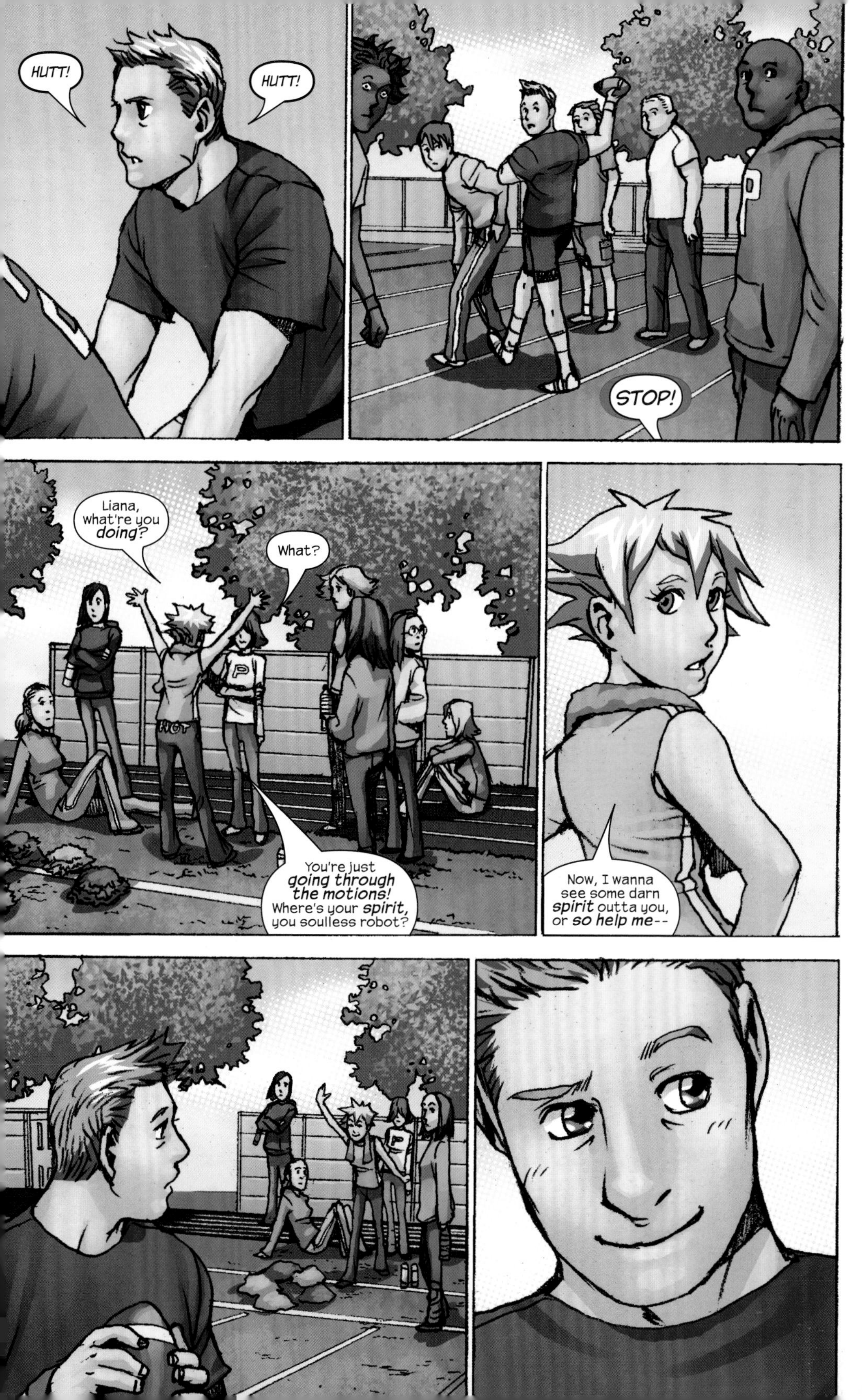

HUTT!
HUTT!
STOP!
Liana, what're you doing?
What?
You're just going through the motions! Where's your spirit, you soulless robot?
Now, I wanna see some darn spirit outta you, or so help me--

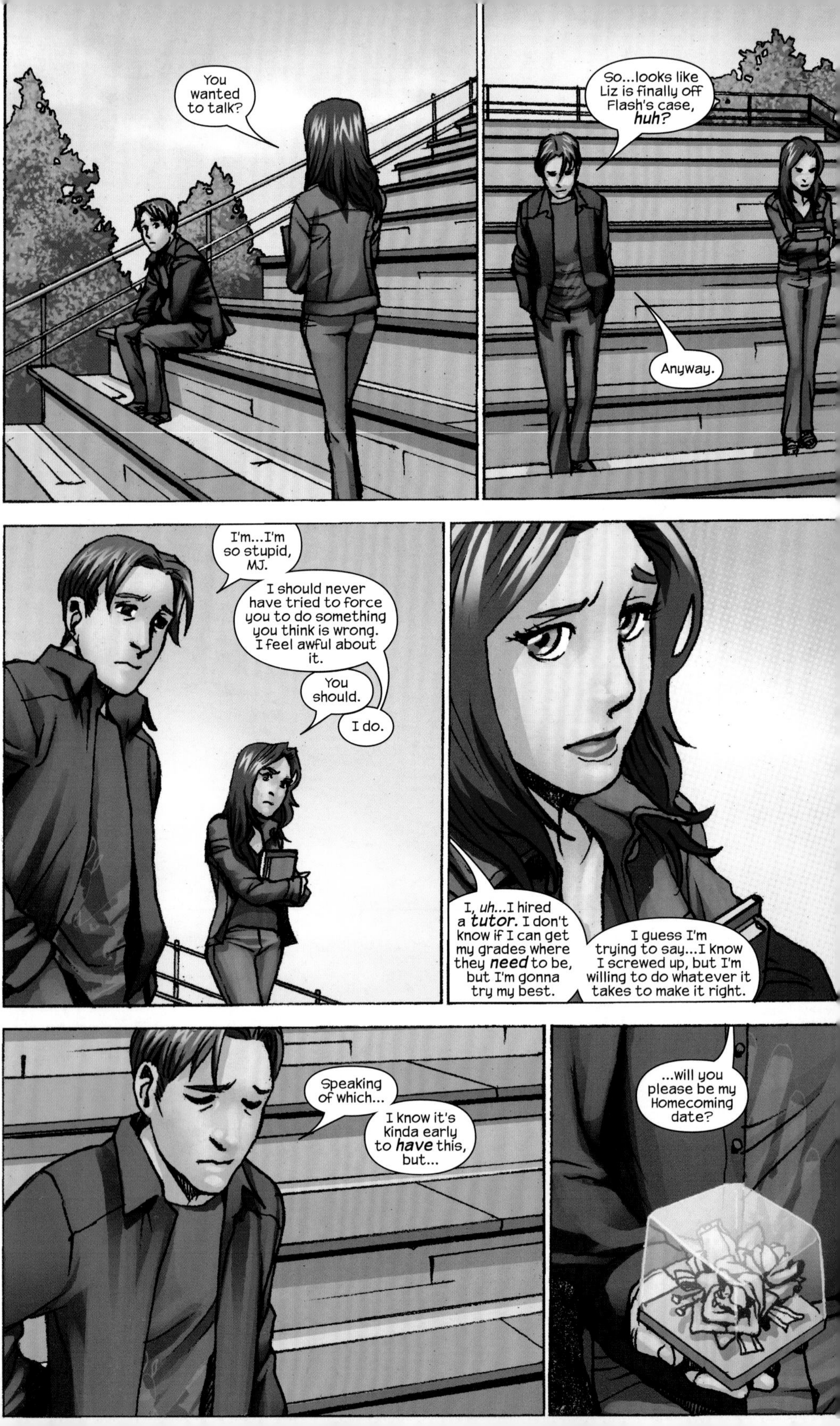
You wanted to talk?
So...looks like Liz is finally off Flash's case, *huh?*
Anyway.
I'm...I'm so stupid, MJ.
I should never have tried to force you to do something you think is wrong. I feel awful about it.
You should.
I do.
I, *uh*...I hired a *tutor.* I don't know if I can get my grades where they *need* to be, but I'm gonna try my best.
I guess I'm trying to say...I know I screwed up, but I'm willing to do whatever it takes to make it right.
Speaking of which...
I know it's kinda early to *have* this, but...
...will you please be my Homecoming date?

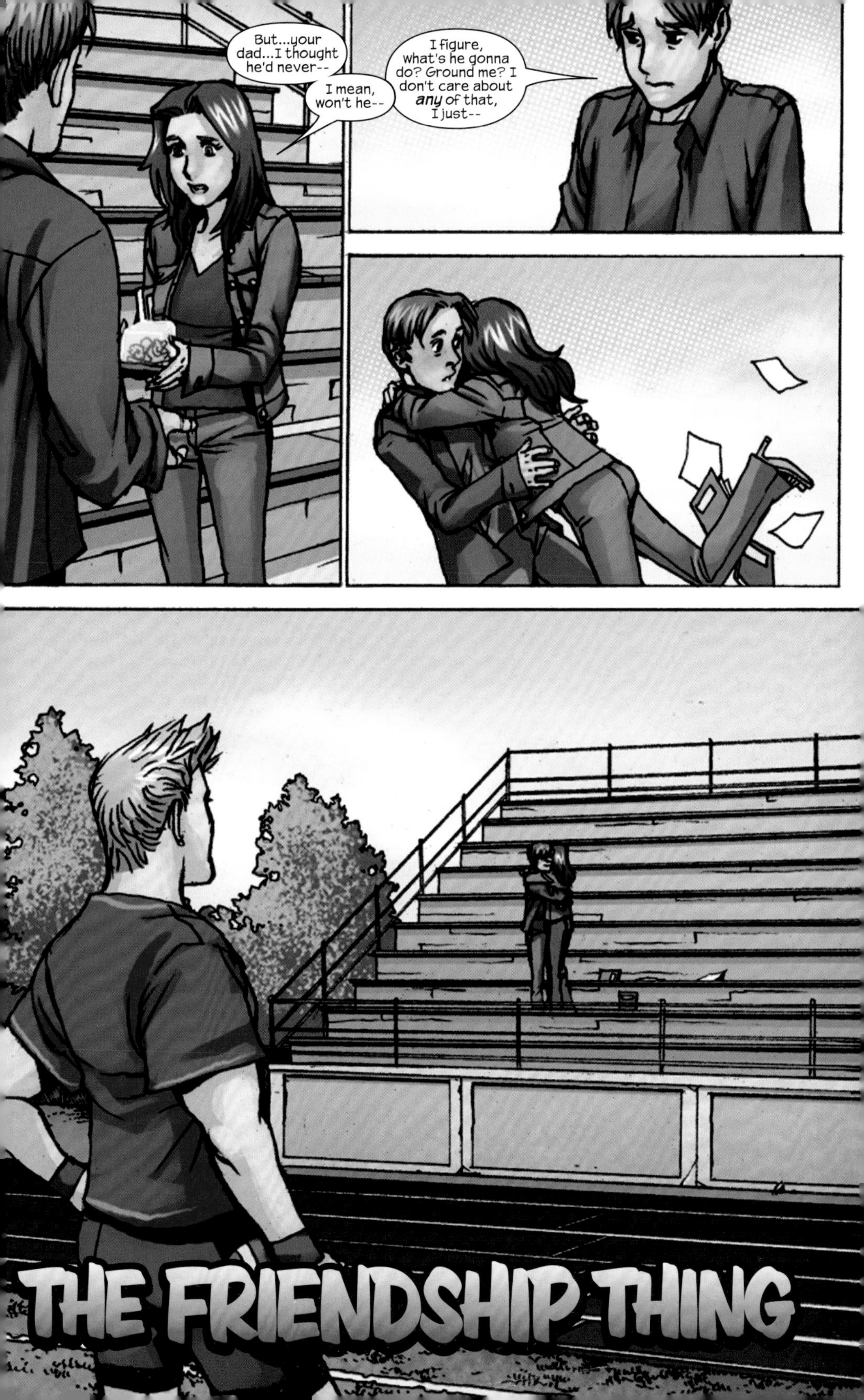
But...your dad...I thought he'd never--
I mean, won't he--
I figure, what's he gonna do? Ground me? I don't care about *any* of that, I just--
THE FRIENDSHIP THING

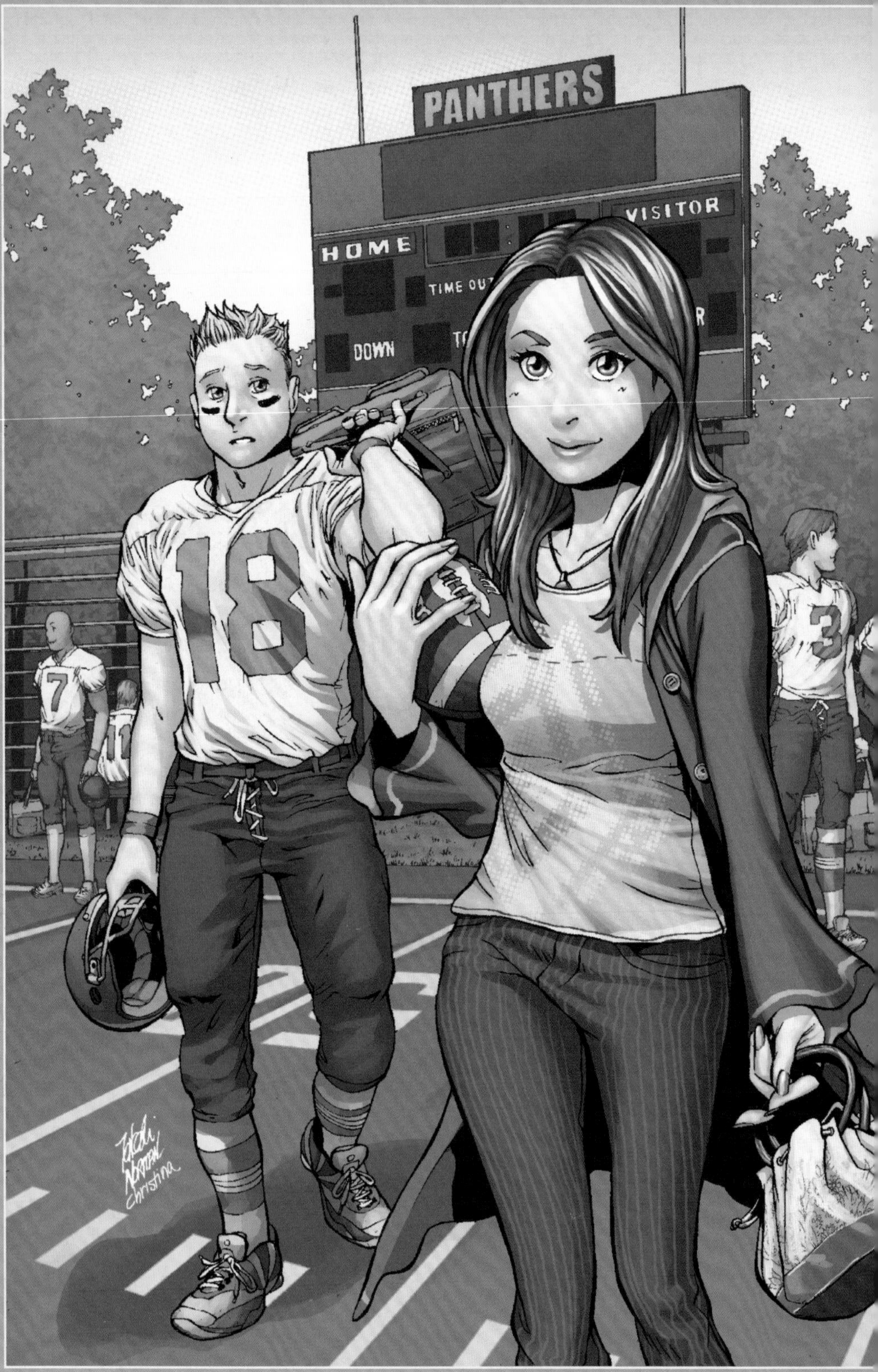
PANTHERS
VISITOR
HOME
TIME OUT
DOWN
18
7
3

Mary Jane: Homecoming #3

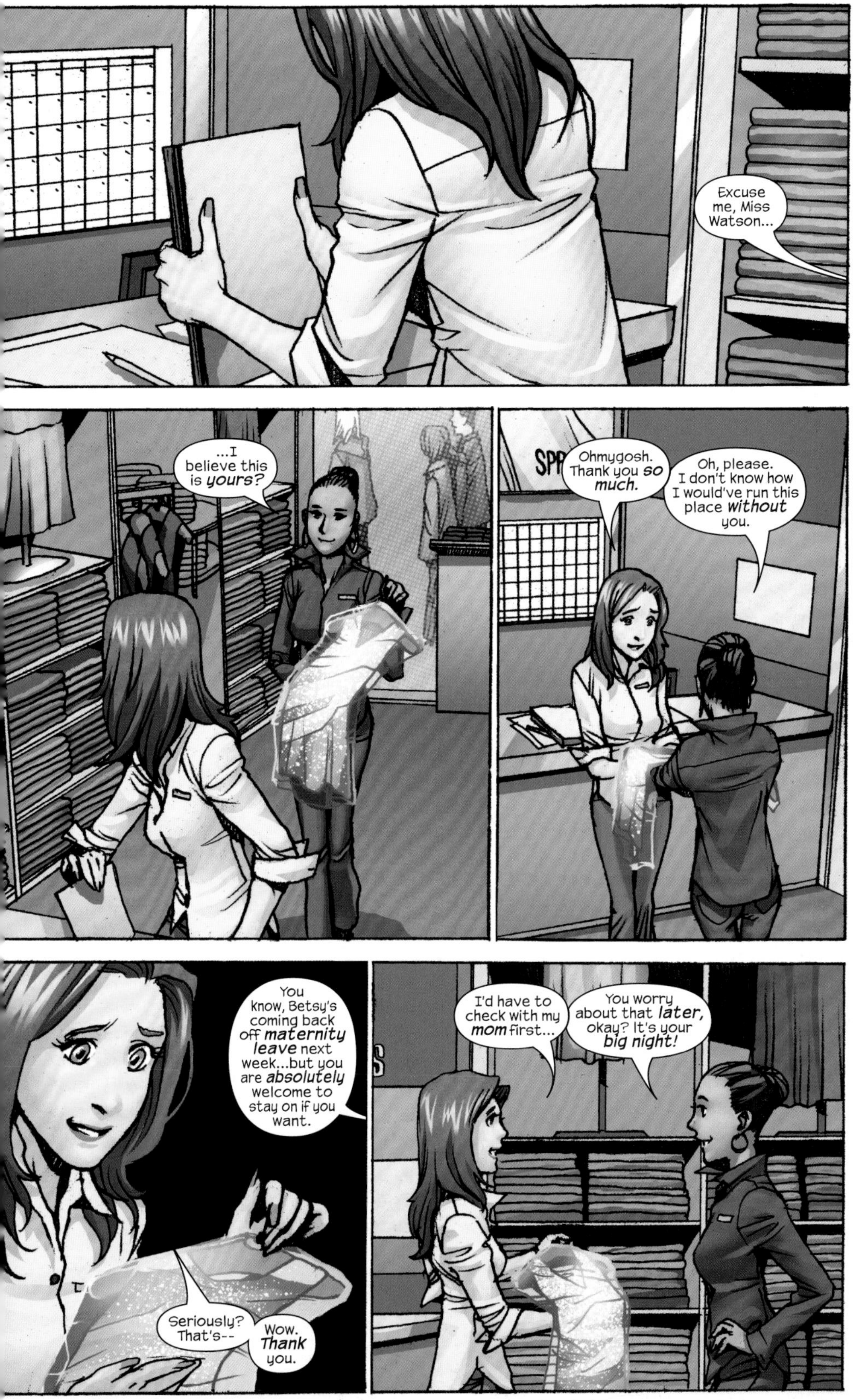
Excuse me, Miss Watson...
...I believe this is *yours?*
SPR
Ohmygosh. Thank you *so much.*
Oh, please. I don't know how I would've run this place *without* you.
You know, Betsy's coming back off *maternity leave* next week...but you are *absolutely* welcome to stay on if you want.
Seriously? That's--
Wow. *Thank* you.
I'd have to check with my *mom* first...
You worry about that *later,* okay? It's your *big night!*

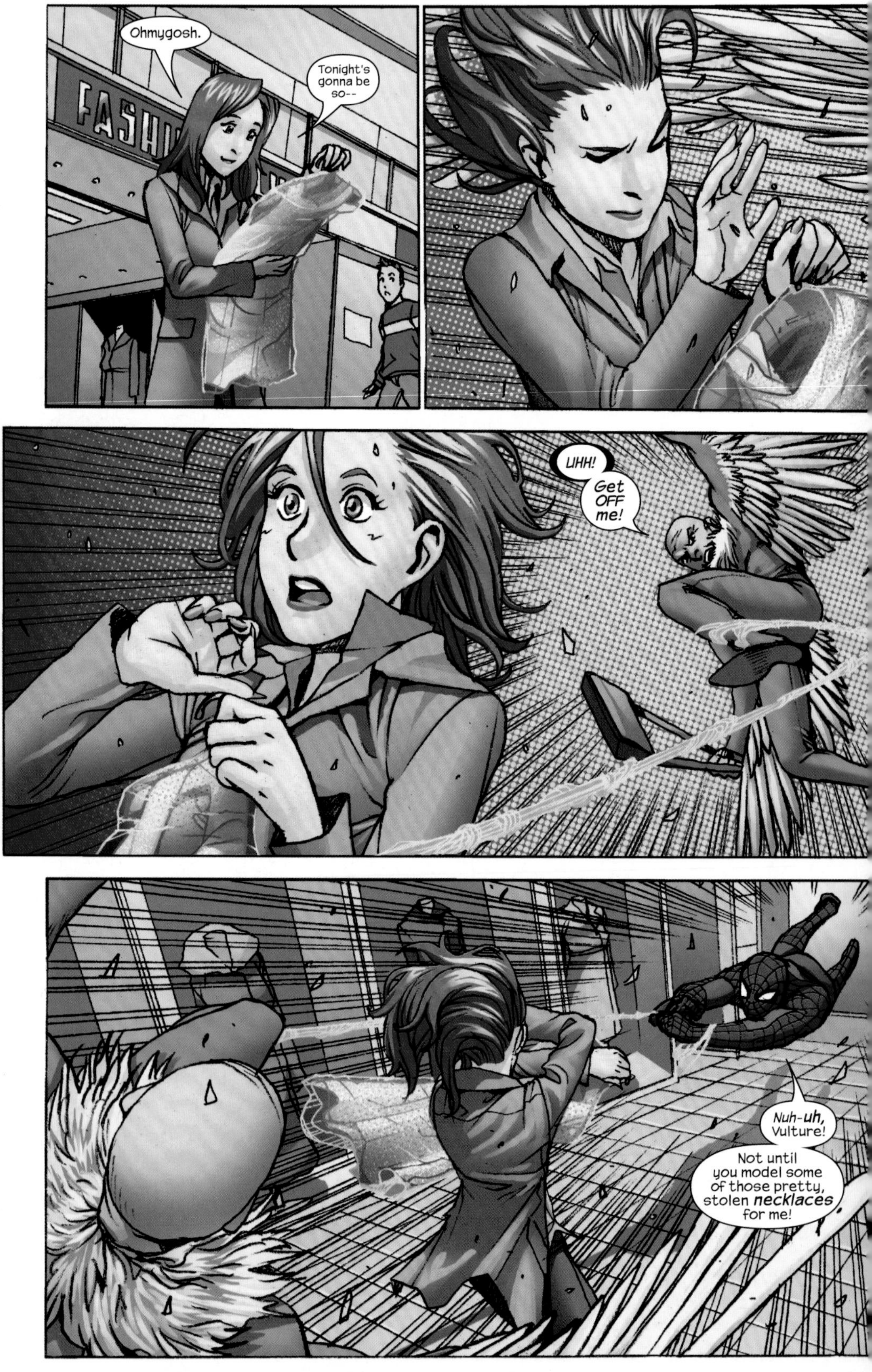
Ohmygosh.
Tonight's gonna be so--
UHH!
Get OFF me!
Nuh-uh, Vulture!
Not until you model some of those pretty, stolen necklaces for me!

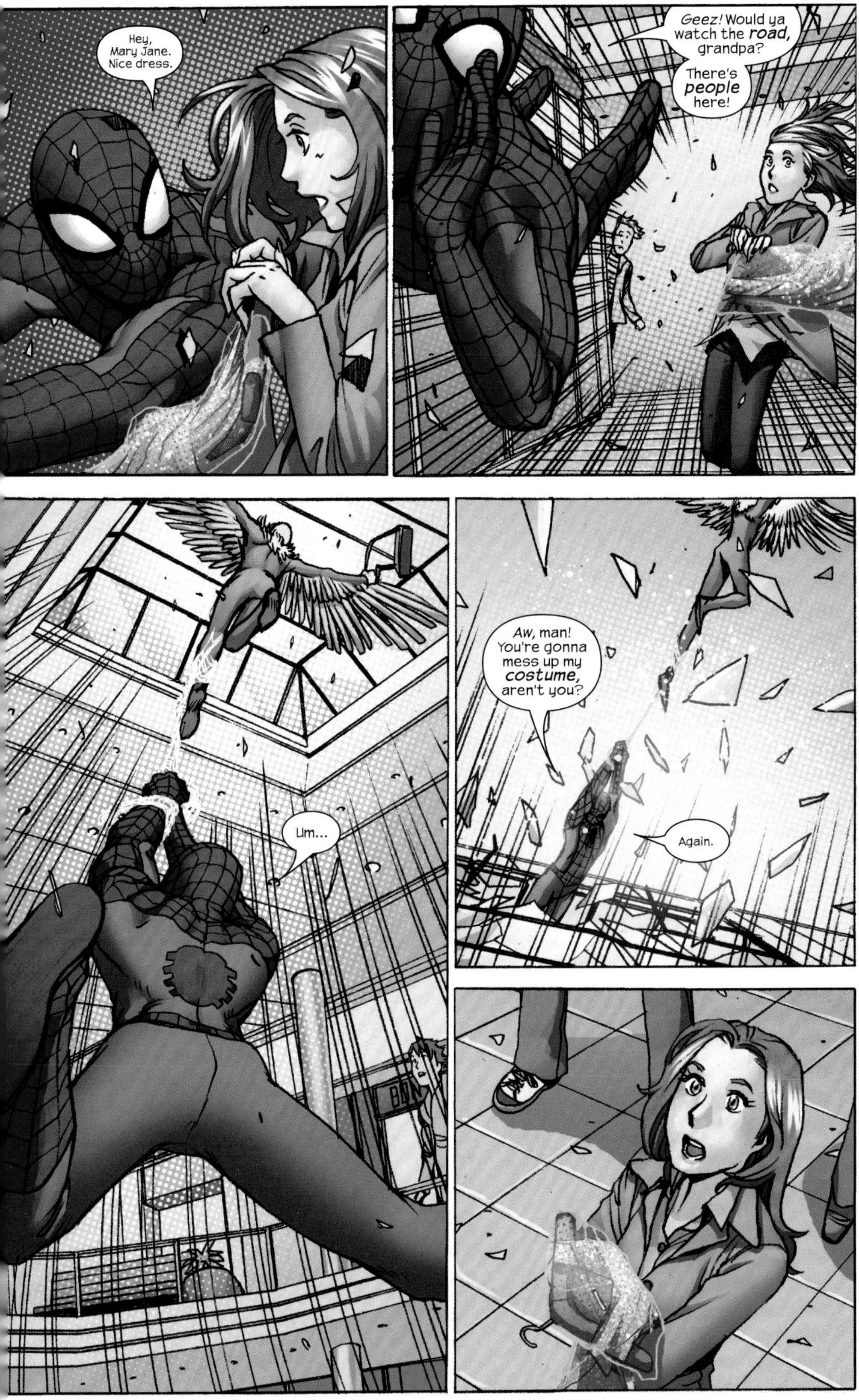
Hey, Mary Jane. Nice dress.
Geez! Would ya watch the road, grandpa?
There's people here!
Um...
Aw, man! You're gonna mess up my costume, aren't you?
Again.

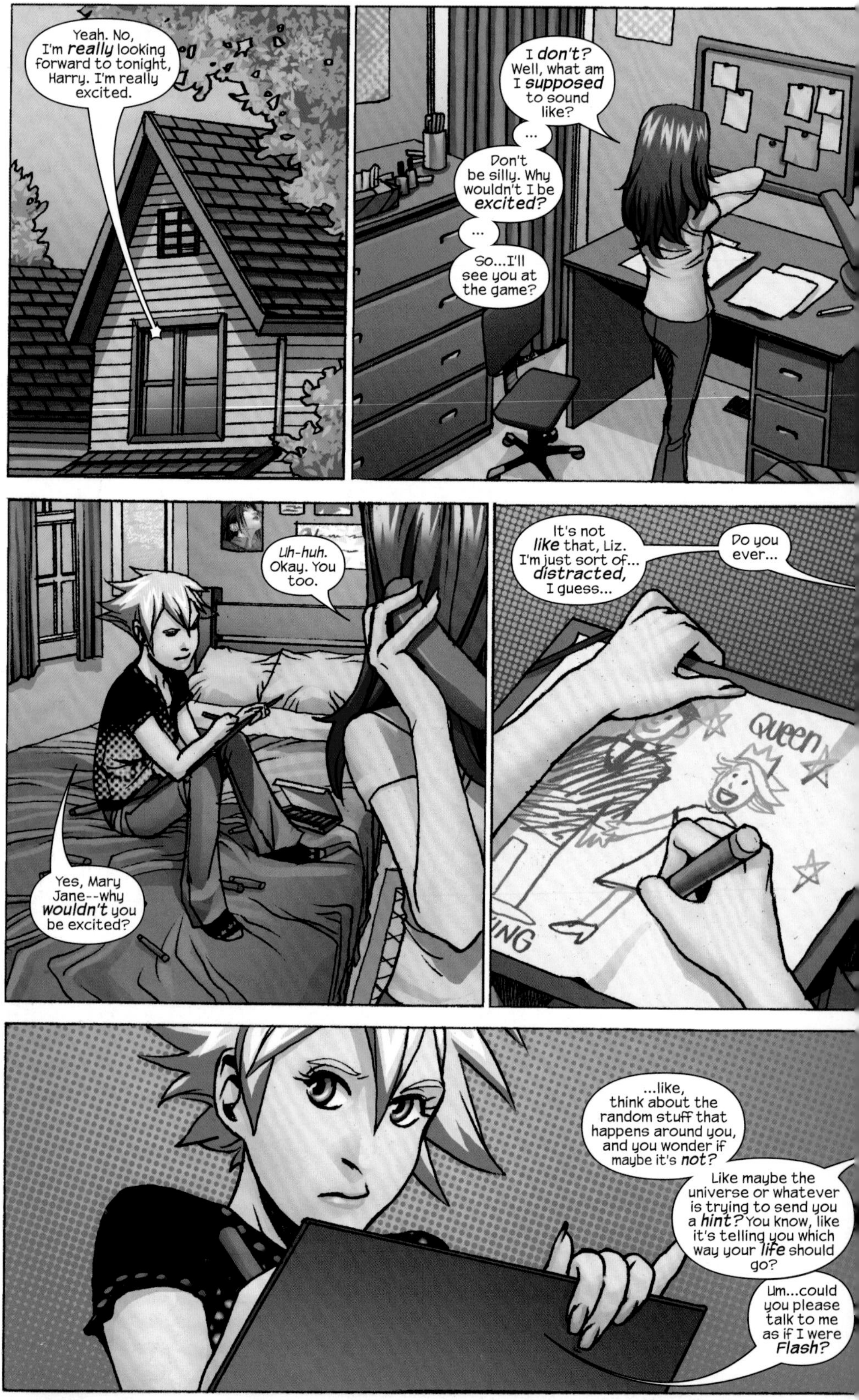

Yeah. No, I'm *really* looking forward to tonight, Harry. I'm really excited.
I *don't*? Well, what am I *supposed* to sound like?
...
Don't be silly. Why wouldn't I be *excited*?
...
So...I'll see you at the game?
Uh-huh. Okay. You too.
Yes, Mary Jane--why *wouldn't* you be excited?
It's not *like* that, Liz. I'm just sort of... *distracted,* I guess...
Do you ever...
Queen
ING
...like, think about the random stuff that happens around you, and you wonder if maybe it's *not?*
Like maybe the universe or whatever is trying to send you a *hint?* You know, like it's telling you which way your *life* should go?
Um...could you please talk to me as if I were *Flash?*

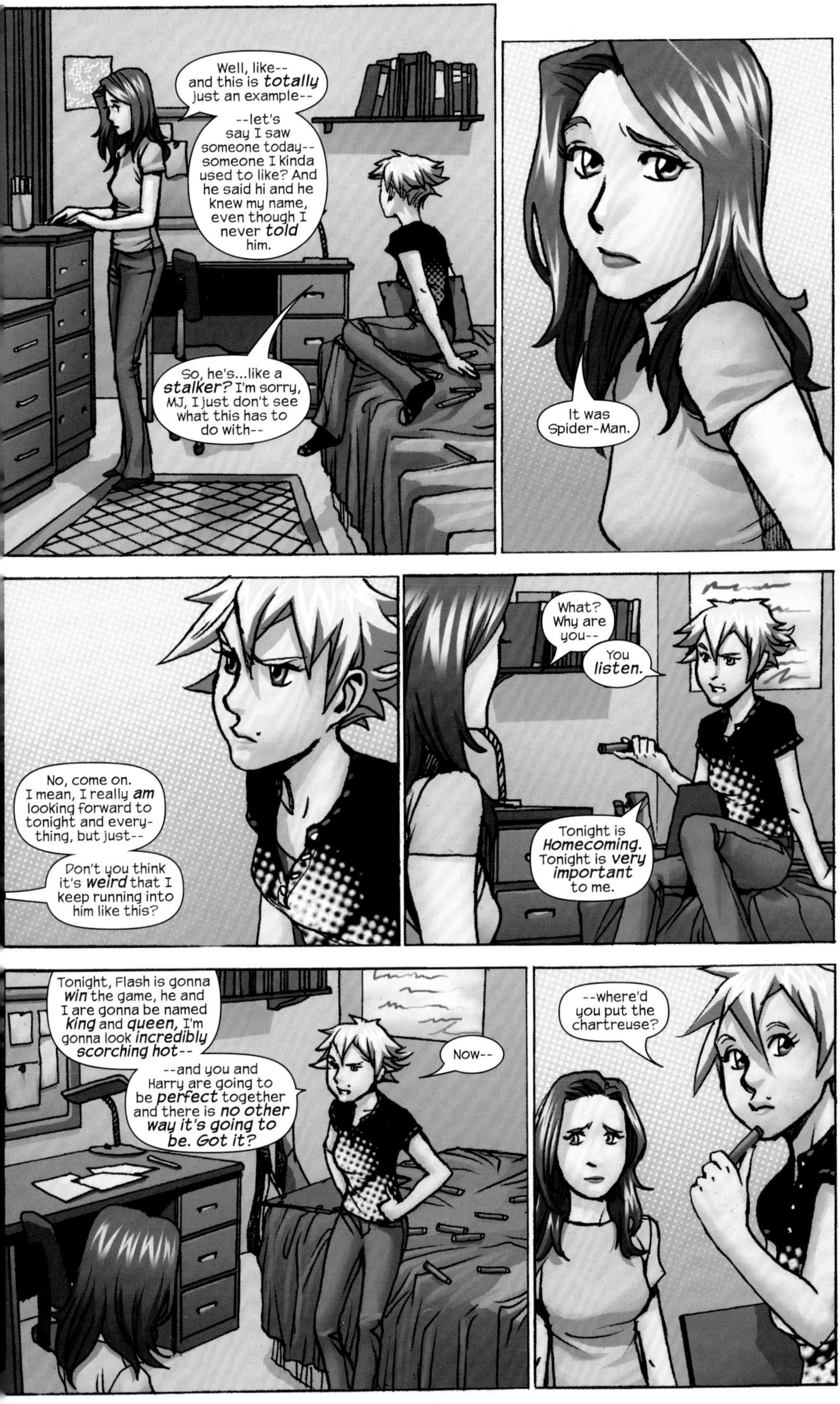

Well, like-- and this is *totally* just an example--
--let's say I saw someone today--someone I kinda used to like? And he said hi and he knew my name, even though I never *told* him.
So, he's...like a *stalker?* I'm sorry, MJ, I just don't see what this has to do with--
It was Spider-Man.
No, come on. I mean, I really *am* looking forward to tonight and everything, but just--
Don't you think it's *weird* that I keep running into him like this?
What? Why are you--
You *listen.*
Tonight is *Homecoming.* Tonight is *very important* to me.
Tonight, Flash is gonna *win* the game, he and I are gonna be named *king* and *queen,* I'm gonna look *incredibly scorching hot*--
--and you and Harry are going to be *perfect* together and there is *no other way it's going to be. Got it?*
Now--
--where'd you put the chartreuse?

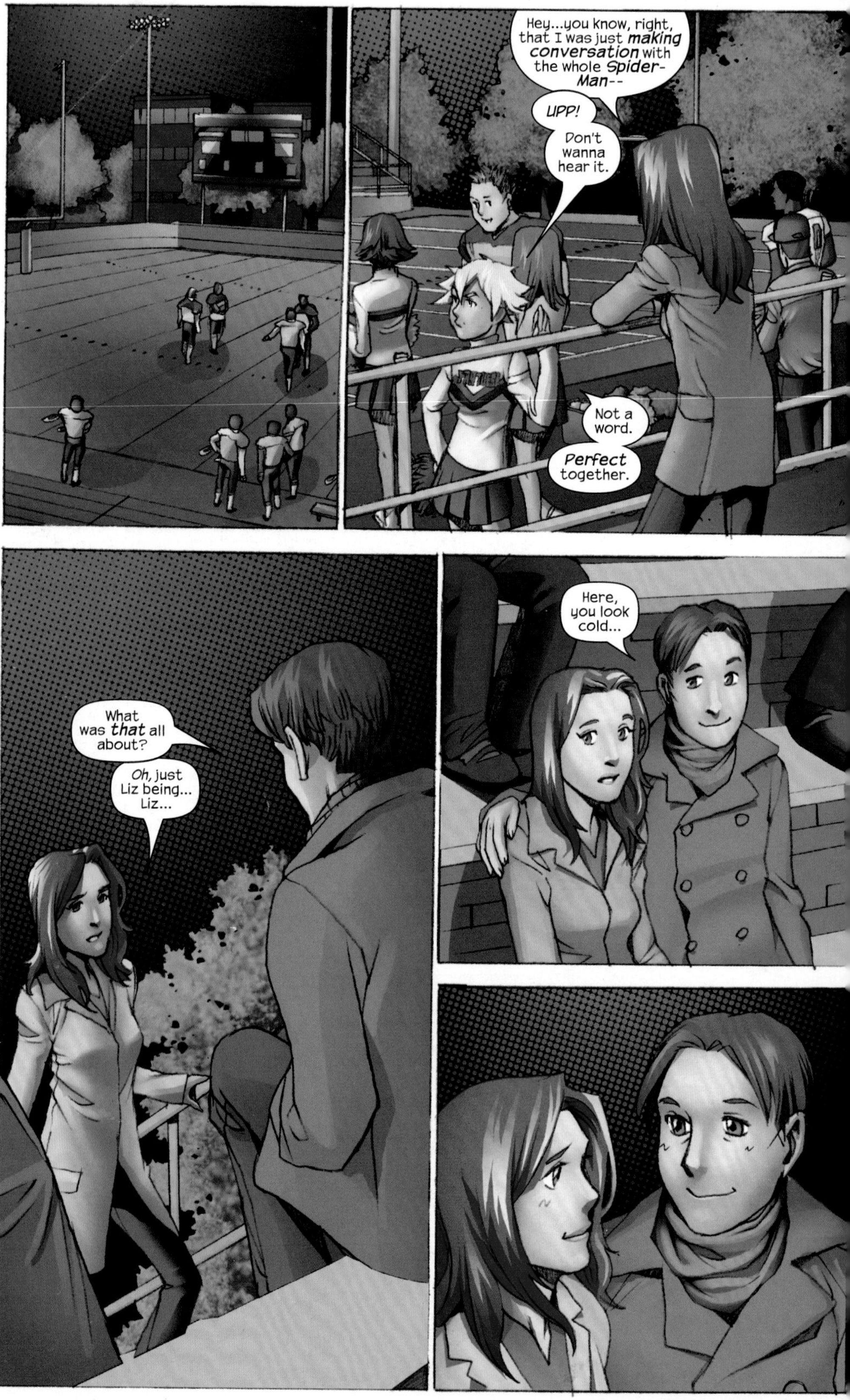
Hey...you know, right, that I was just *making conversation* with the whole *Spider-Man*--
UPP!
Don't wanna hear it.
Not a word.
Perfect together.
What was ***that*** all about?
Oh, just Liz being... Liz...
Here, you look cold...

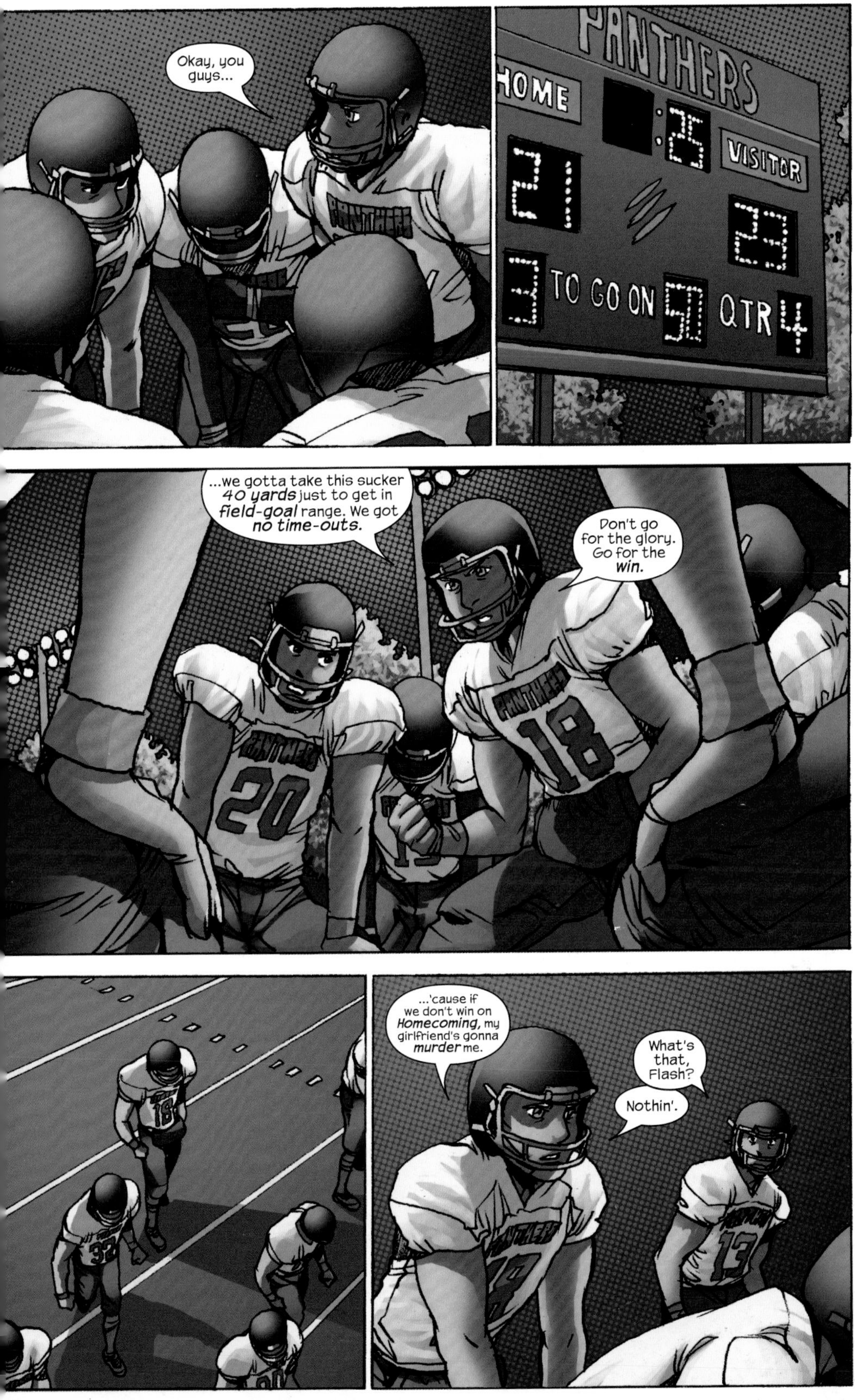

Okay, you guys...
PANTHERS
HOME
:25
VISITOR
21
23
3 TO GO ON 50 QTR 4
...we gotta take this sucker *40 yards* just to get in *field-goal* range. We got *no time-outs.*
Don't go for the glory. Go for the *win.*
...'cause if we don't win on *Homecoming,* my girlfriend's gonna *murder* me.
What's that, Flash?
Nothin'.

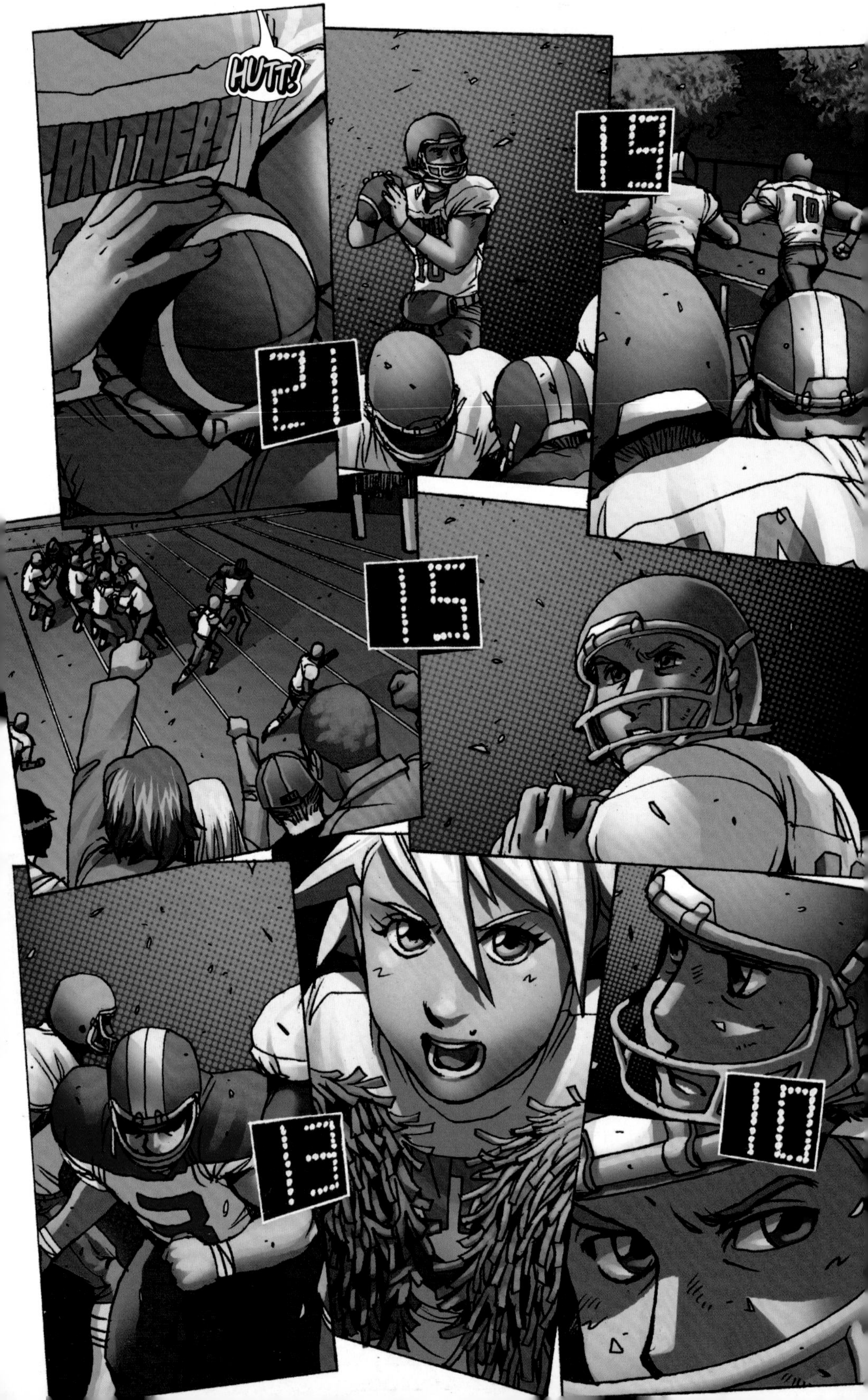
HUTT!
21
19
15
13
10

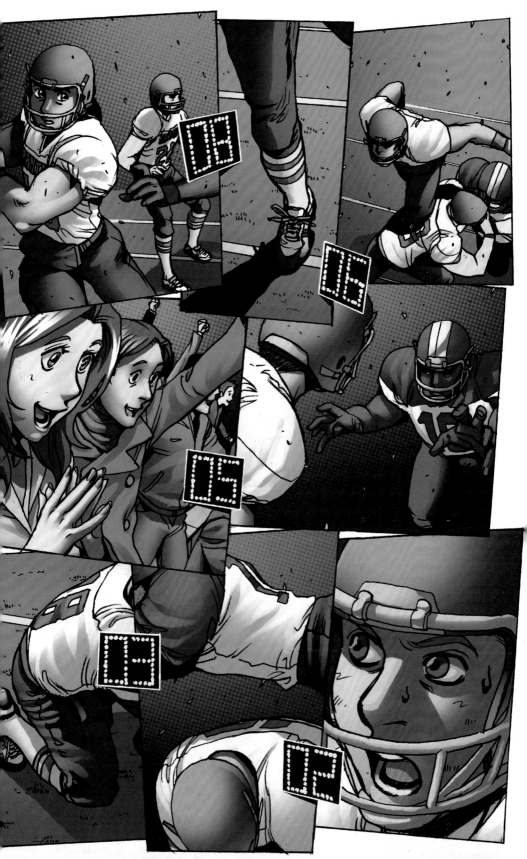

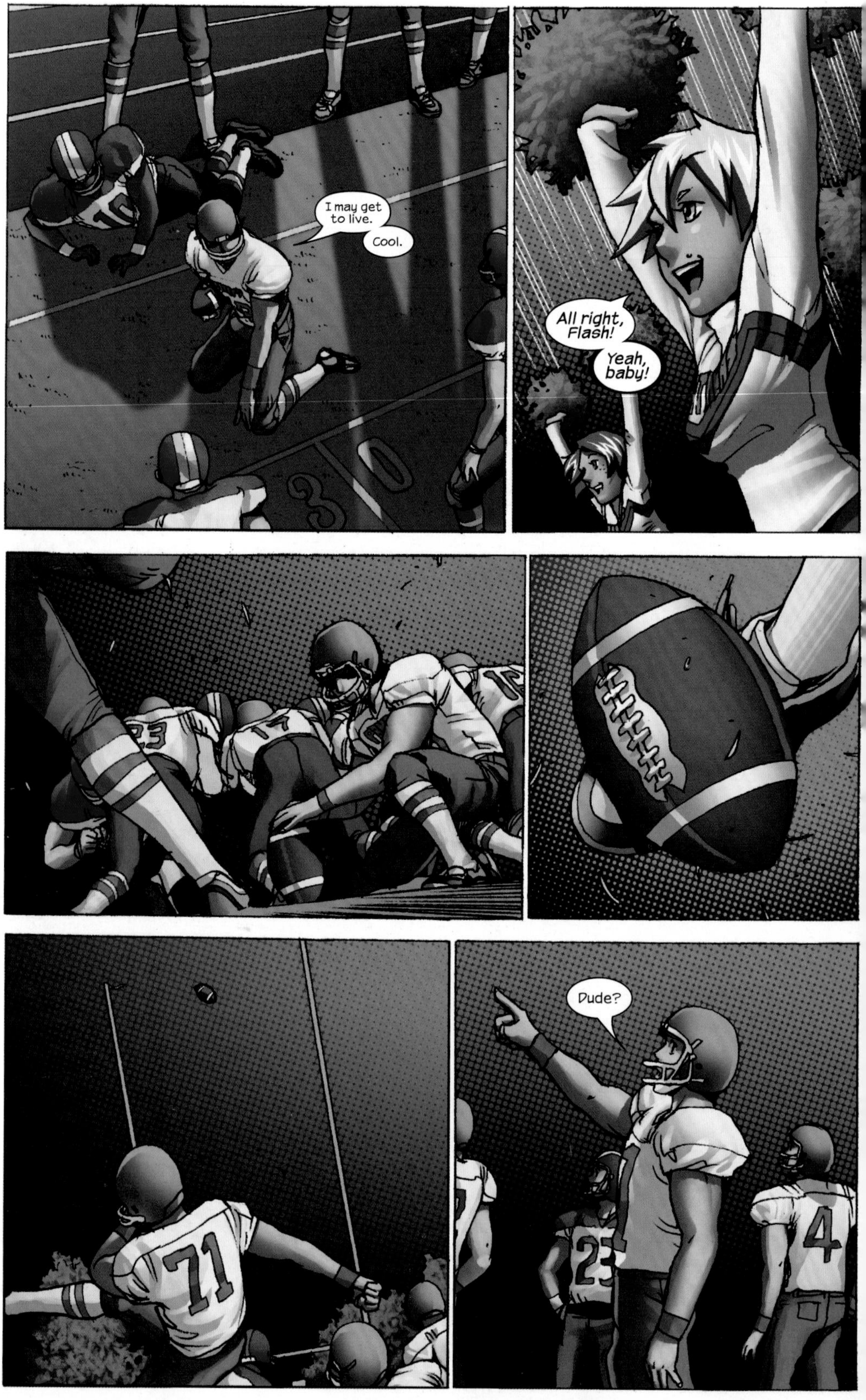
I may get to live.
Cool.
All right, Flash!
Yeah, baby!
Dude?

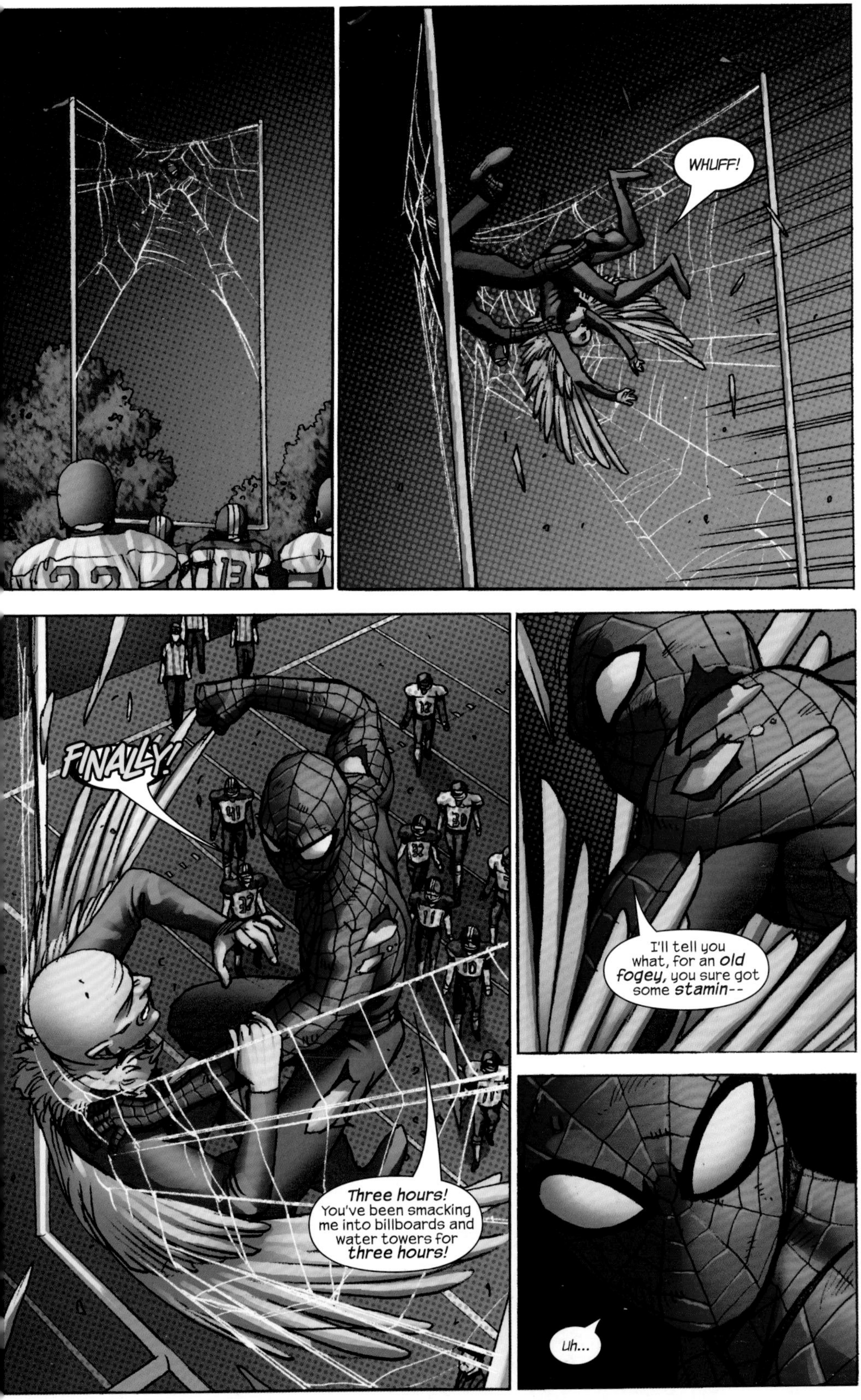
WHUFF!
FINALLY!
Three hours! You've been smacking me into billboards and water towers for three hours!
I'll tell you what, for an old fogey, you sure got some stamin--
Uh...

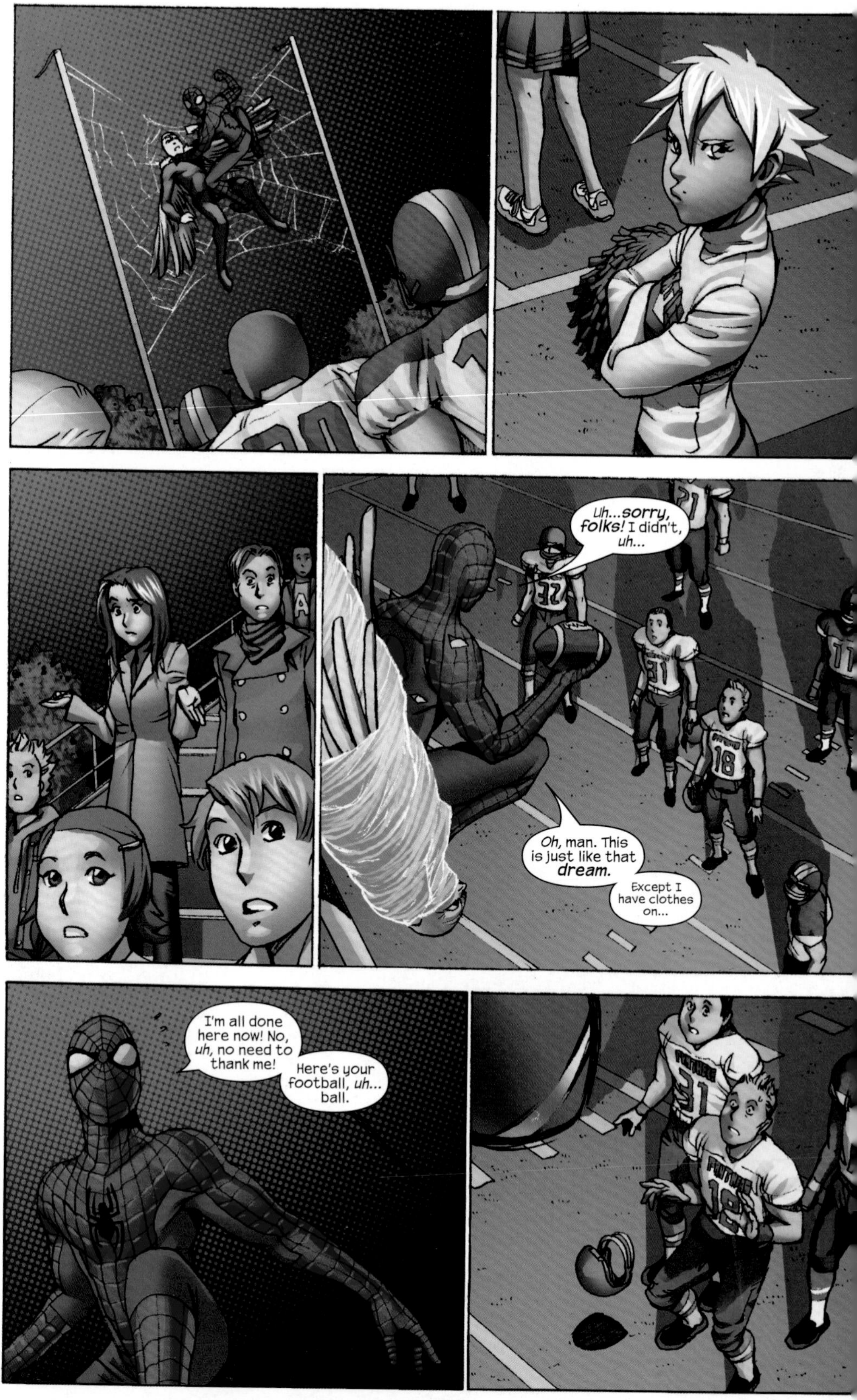
Uh...sorry, folks! I didn't, uh...
Oh, man. This is just like that dream.
Except I have clothes on...
I'm all done here now! No, uh, no need to thank me!
Here's your football, uh... ball.

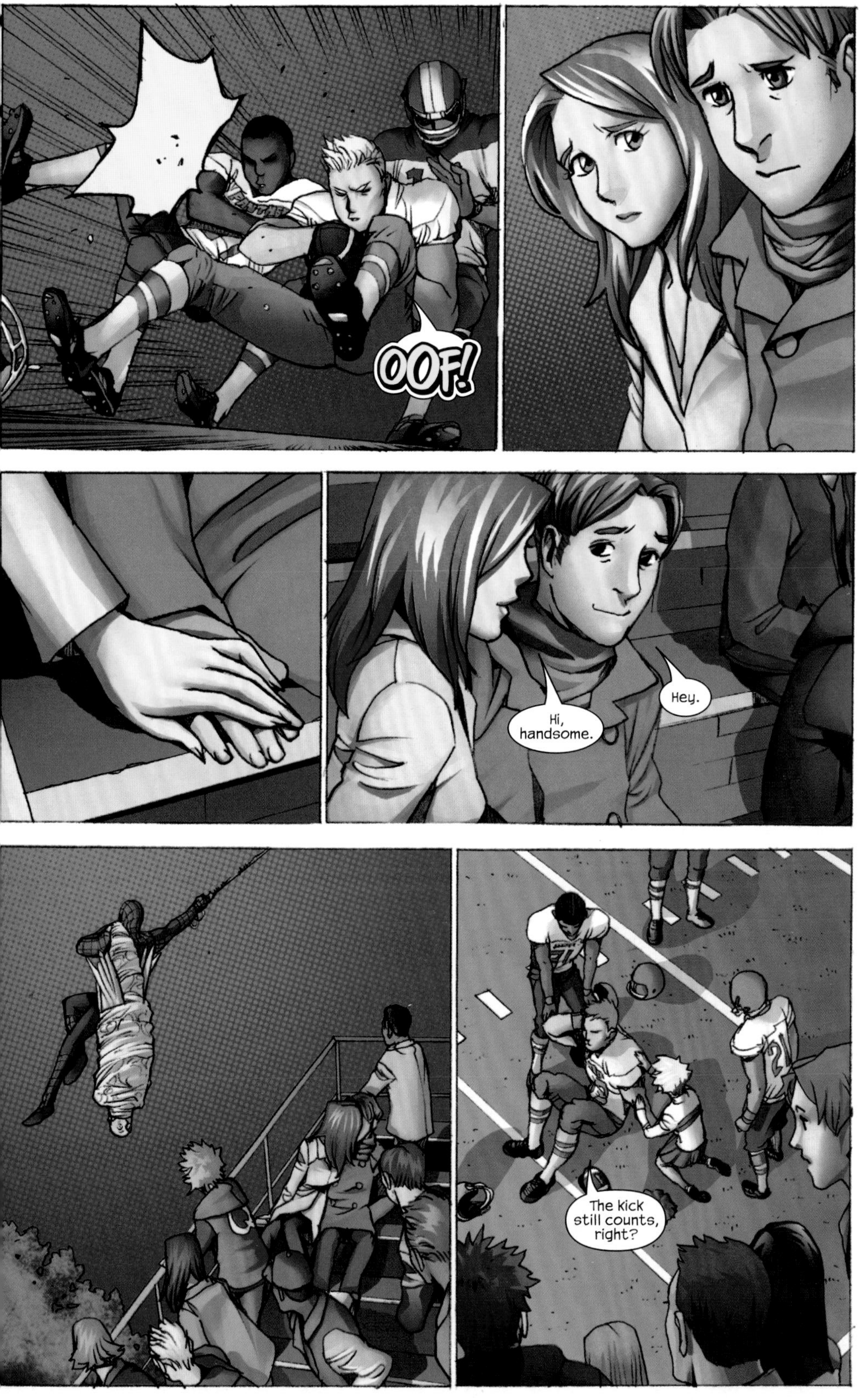
OOF!
Hi, handsome.
Hey.
The kick still counts, right?

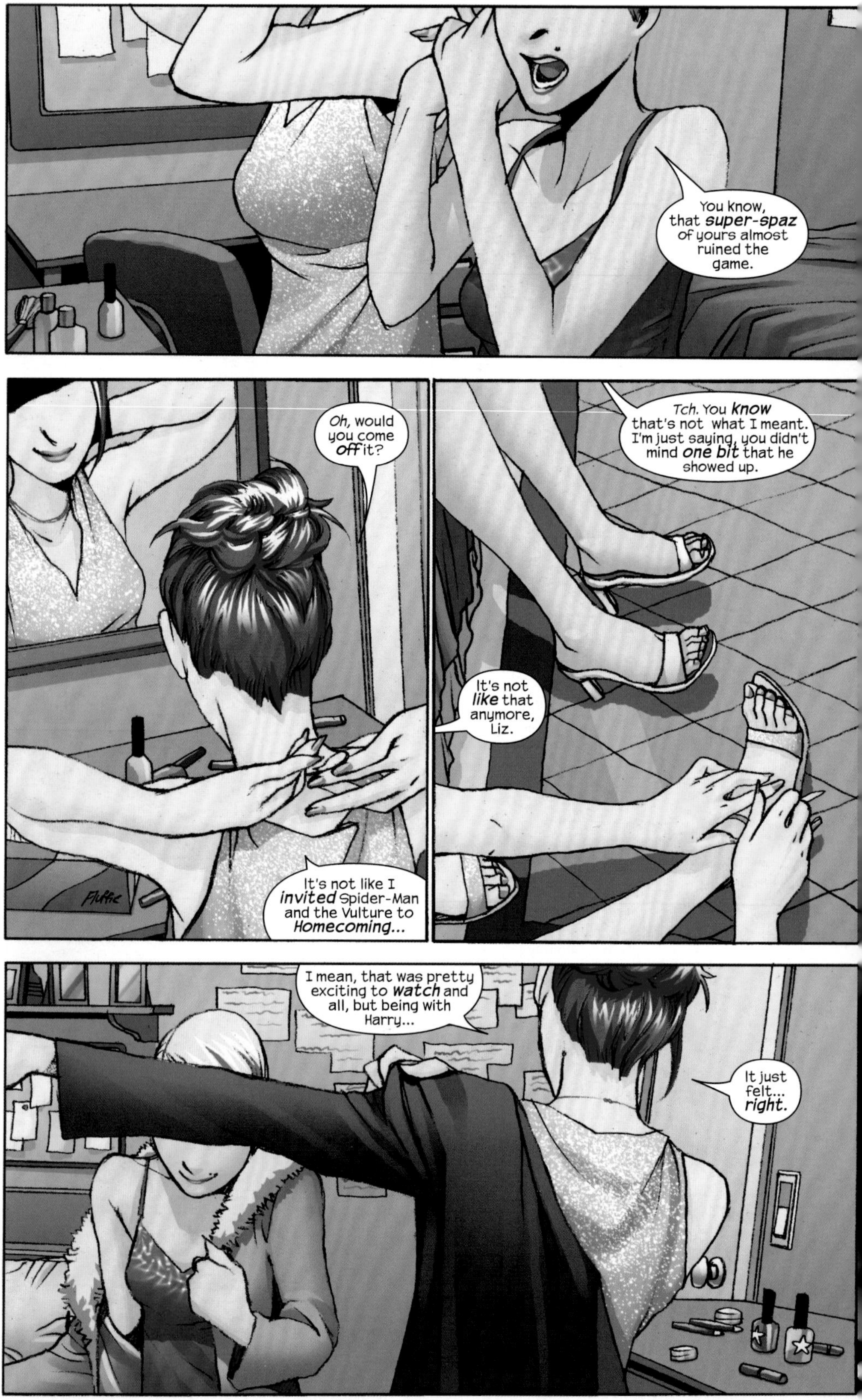
You know, that *super-spaz* of yours almost ruined the game.
Oh, would you come *off* it?
Tch. You *know* that's not what I meant. I'm just saying, you didn't mind *one bit* that he showed up.
It's not *like* that anymore, Liz.
It's not like I *invited* Spider-Man and the Vulture to *Homecoming...*
Fluffie
I mean, that was pretty exciting to *watch* and all, but being with Harry...
It just felt... *right.*

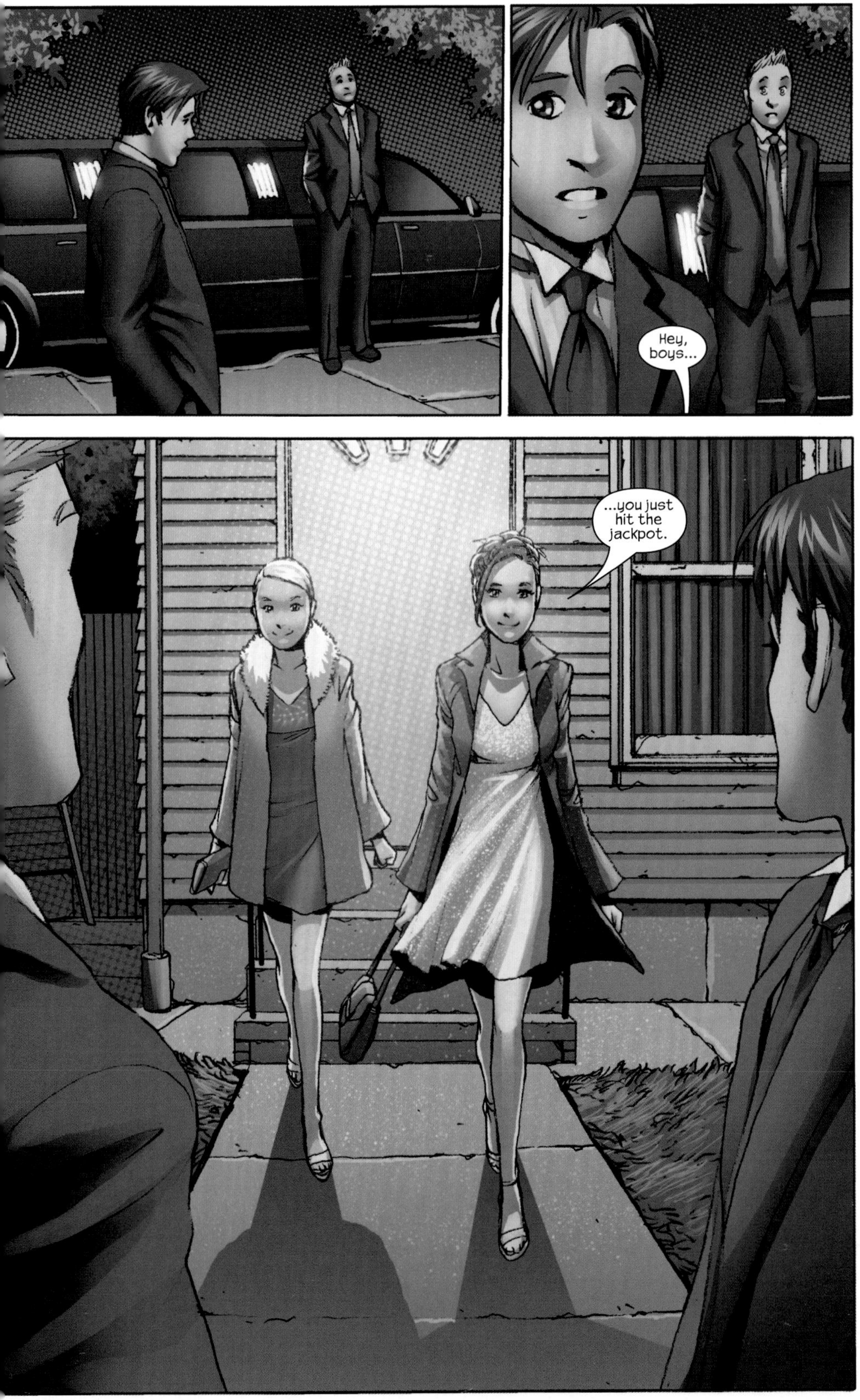
Hey, boys...
...you just hit the jackpot.

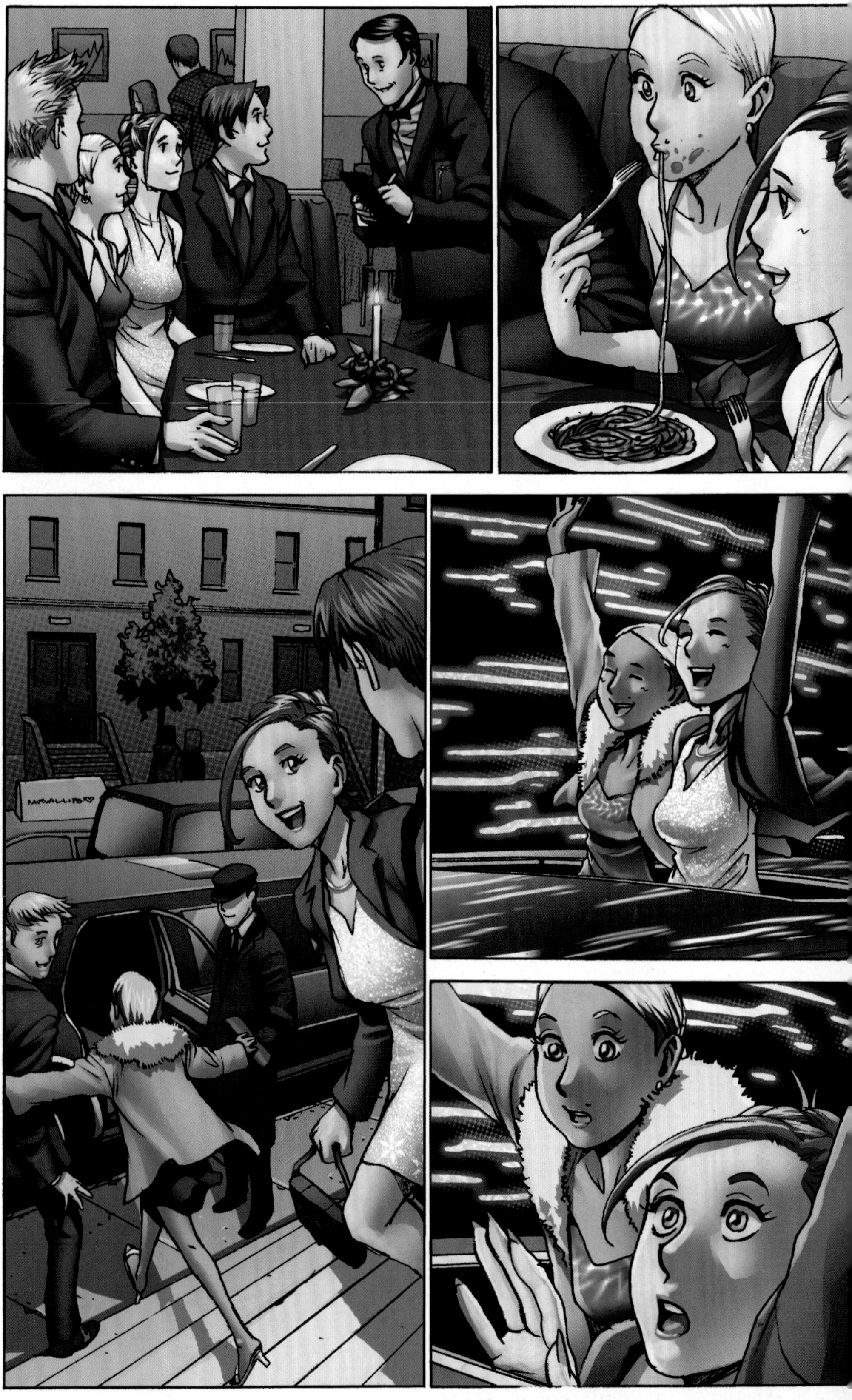

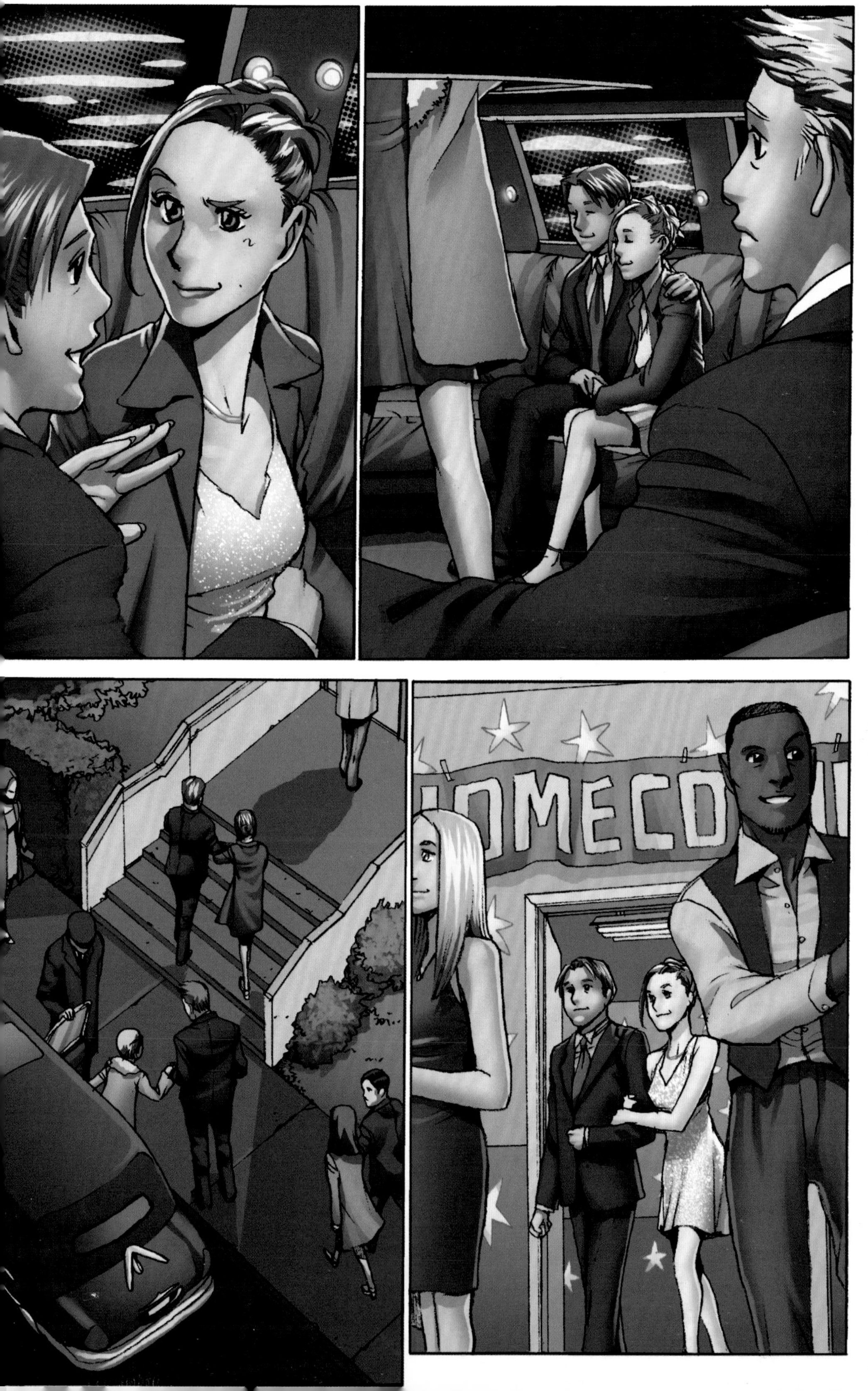

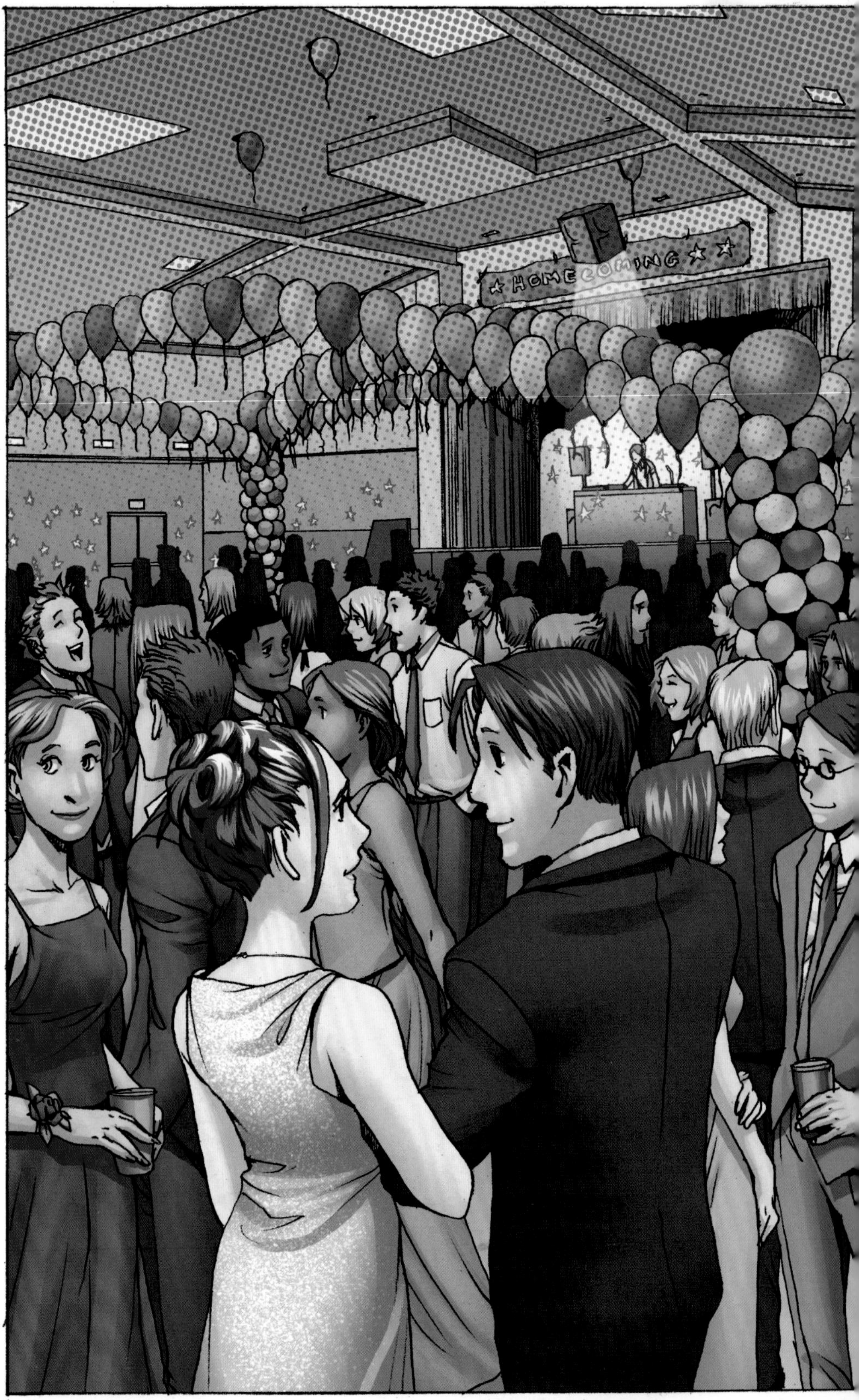
HOMECOMING

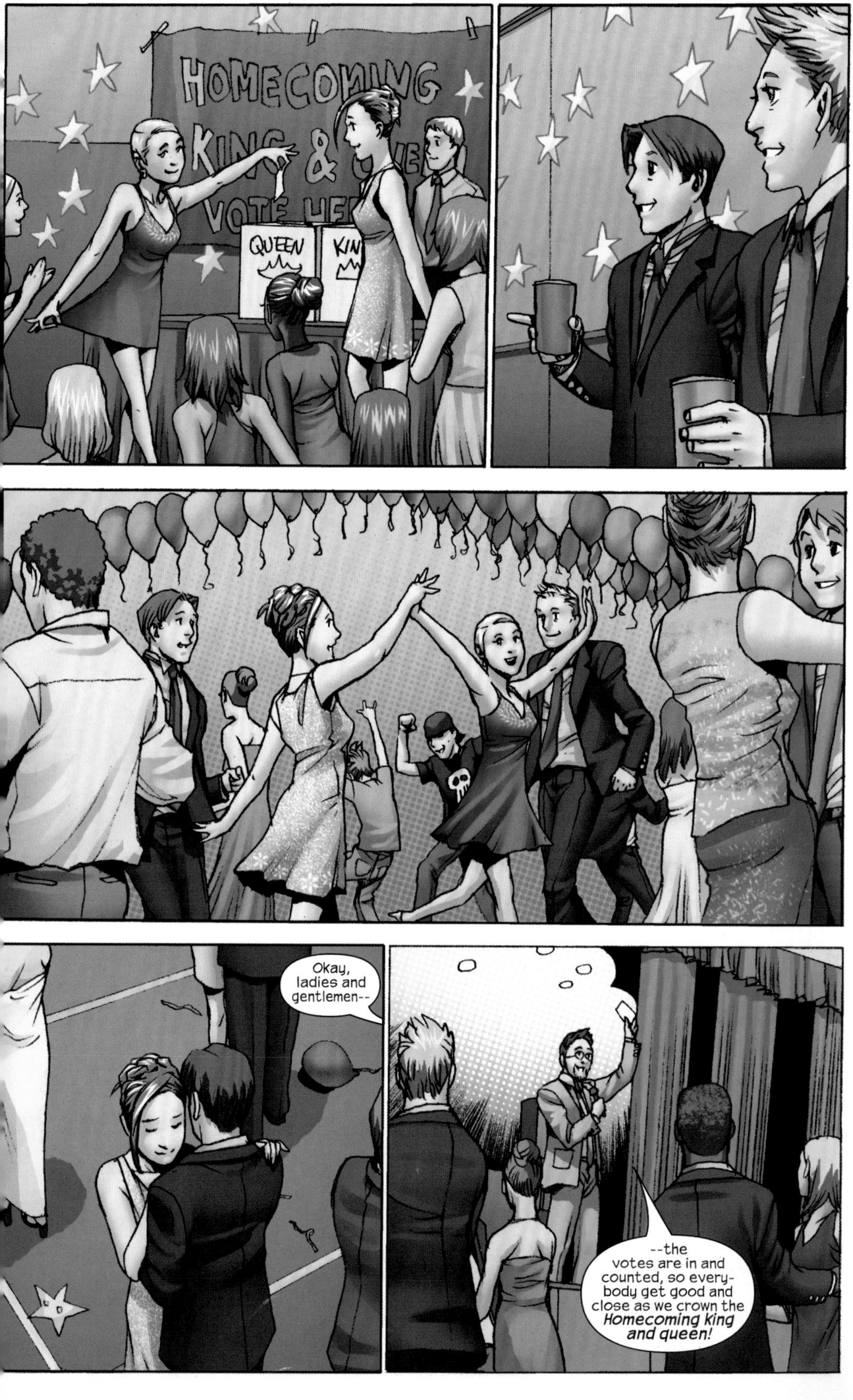
HOMECOMING
QUEEN
Okay, ladies and gentlemen--
--the votes are in and counted, so every-body get good and close as we crown the *Homecoming king and queen!*

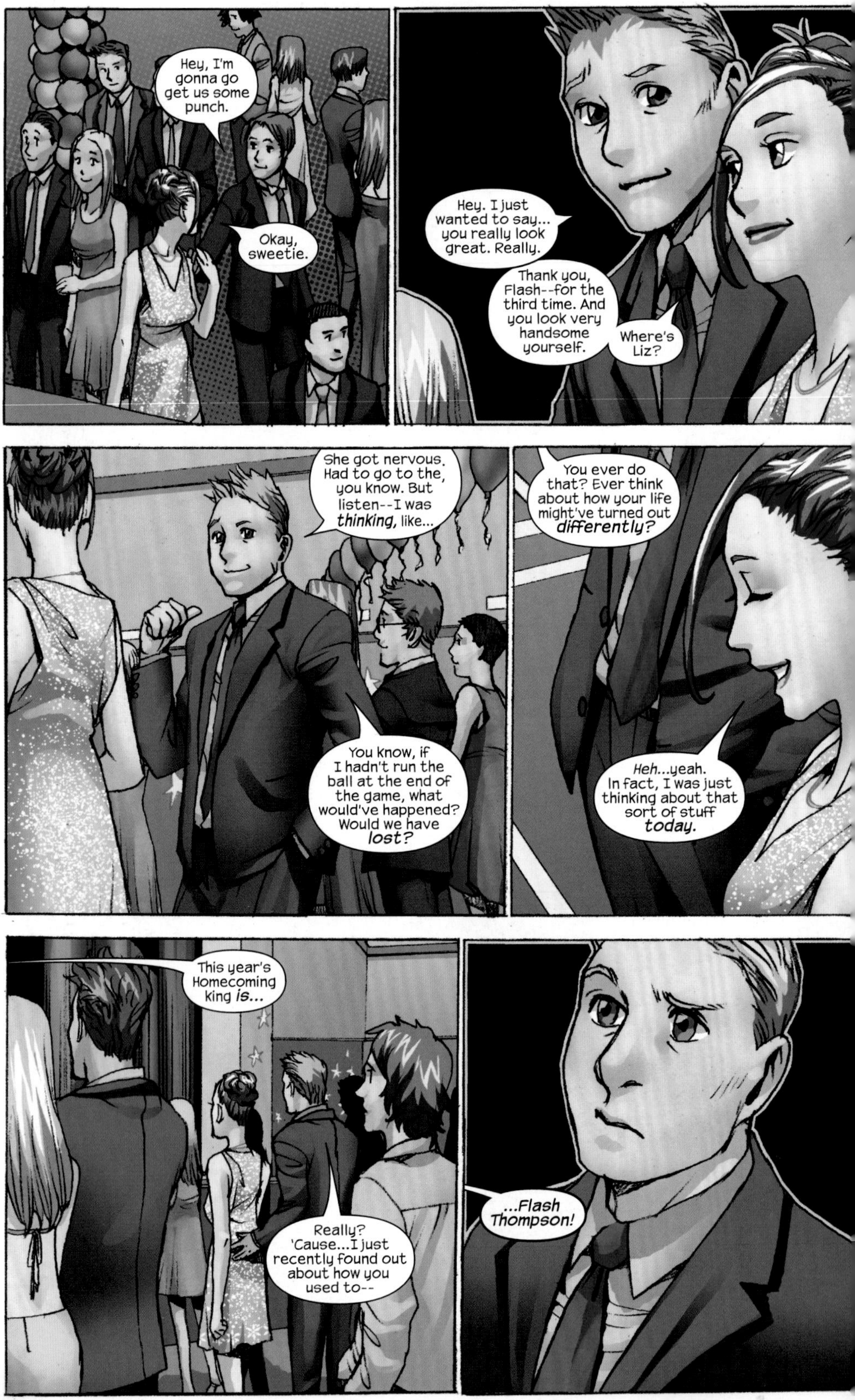
Hey, I'm gonna go get us some punch.
Okay, sweetie.
Hey. I just wanted to say... you really look great. Really.
Thank you, Flash--for the third time. And you look very handsome yourself.
Where's Liz?
She got nervous. Had to go to the, you know. But listen--I was *thinking,* like...
You know, if I hadn't run the ball at the end of the game, what would've happened? Would we have *lost?*
You ever do that? Ever think about how your life might've turned out *differently?*
Heh...yeah. In fact, I was just thinking about that sort of stuff *today.*
This year's Homecoming King *is...*
Really? 'Cause...I just recently found out about how you used to--
...Flash Thompson!

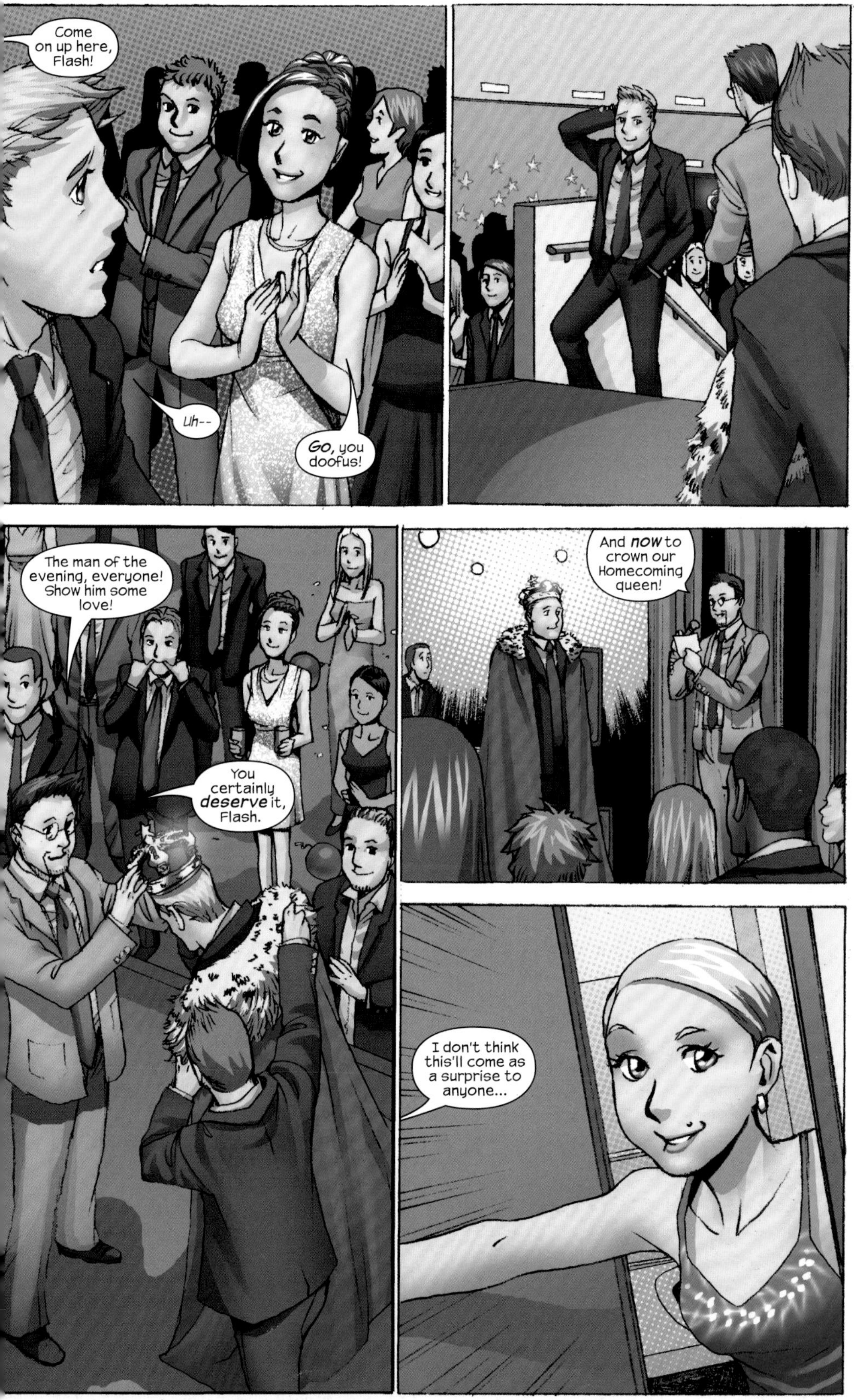
Come on up here, Flash!
Uh--
Go, you doofus!
The man of the evening, everyone! Show him some love!
You certainly deserve it, Flash.
And now to crown our Homecoming queen!
I don't think this'll come as a surprise to anyone...

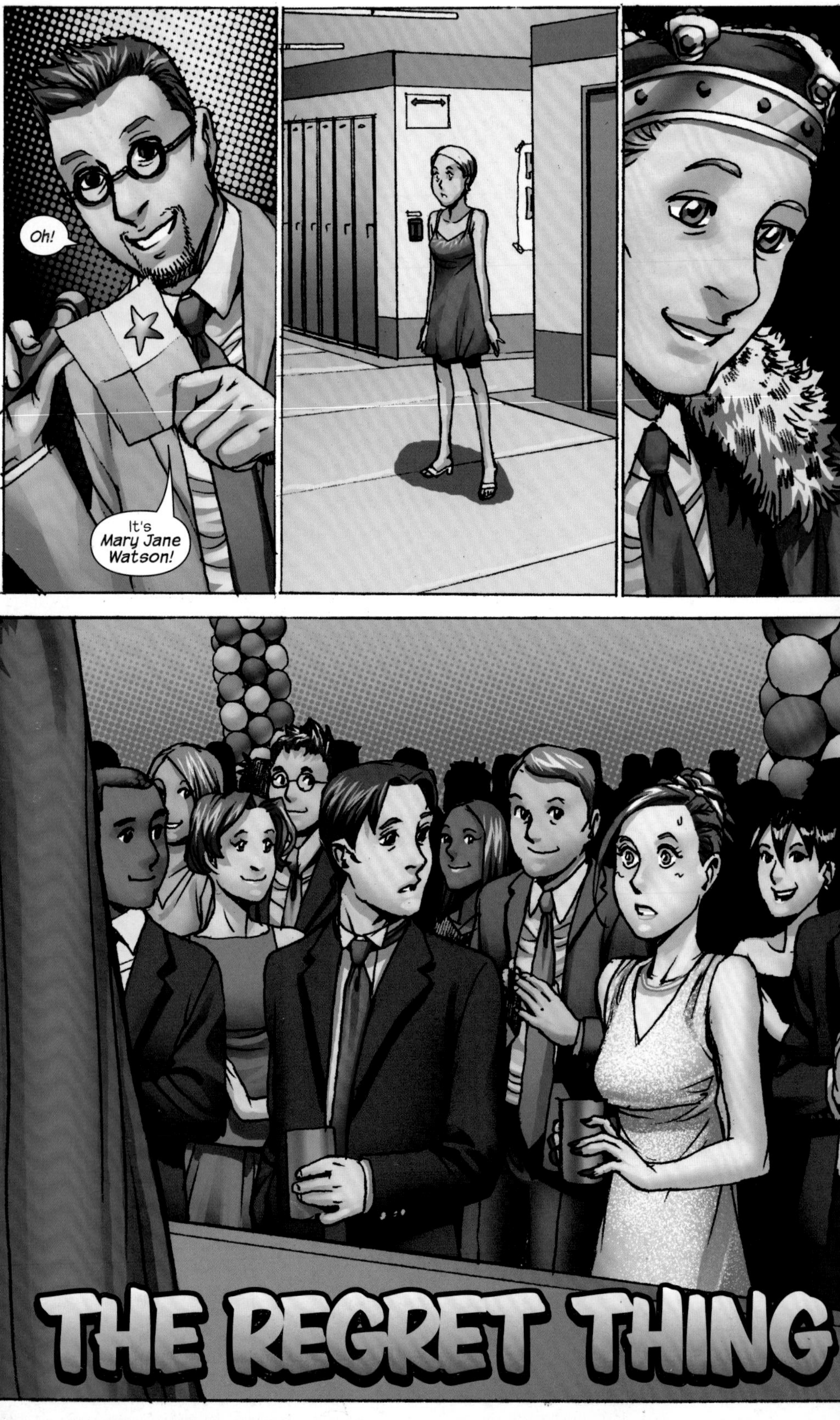
Oh!
It's Mary Jane Watson!
THE REGRET THING

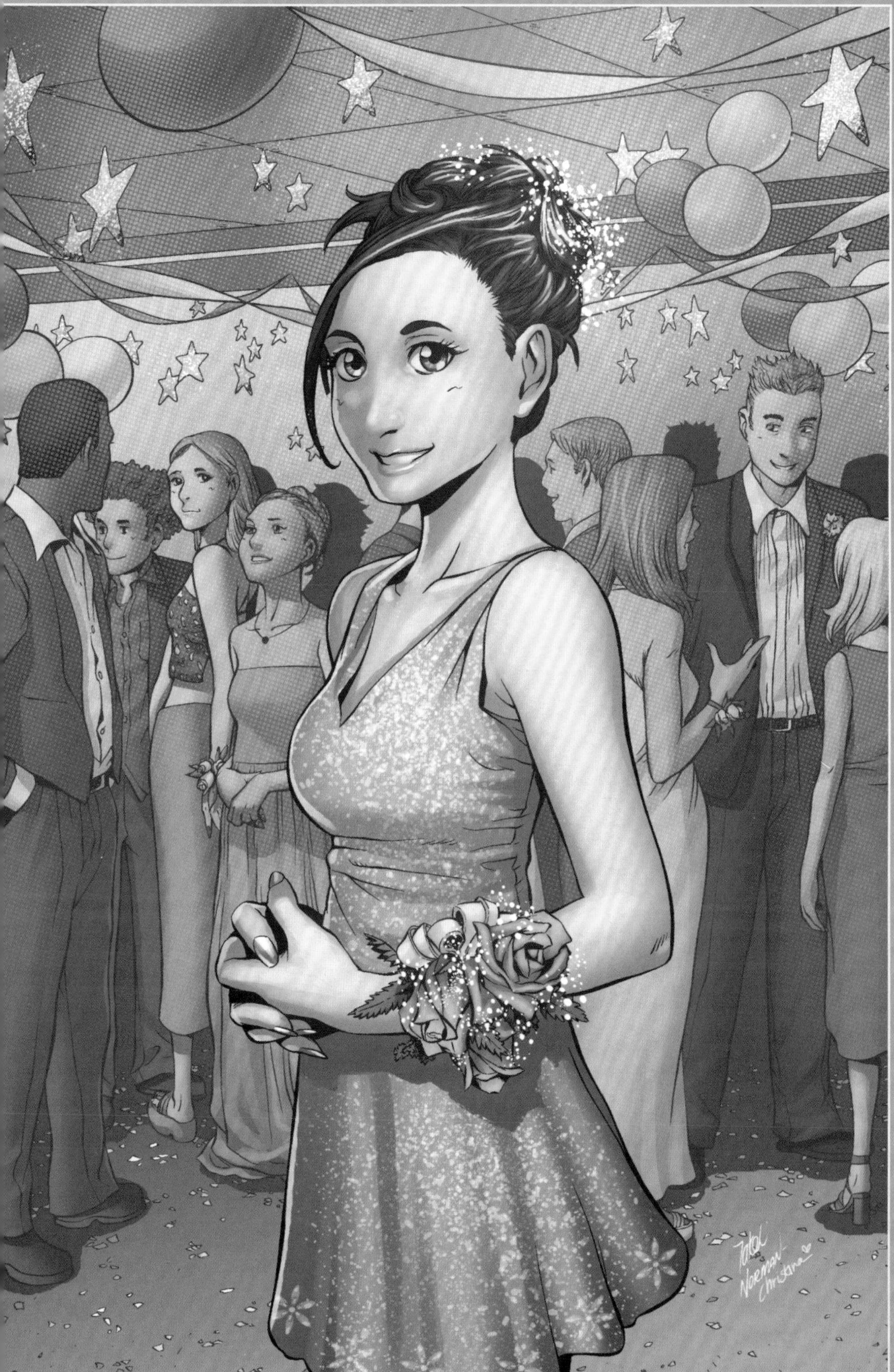

Mary Jane: Homecoming #4

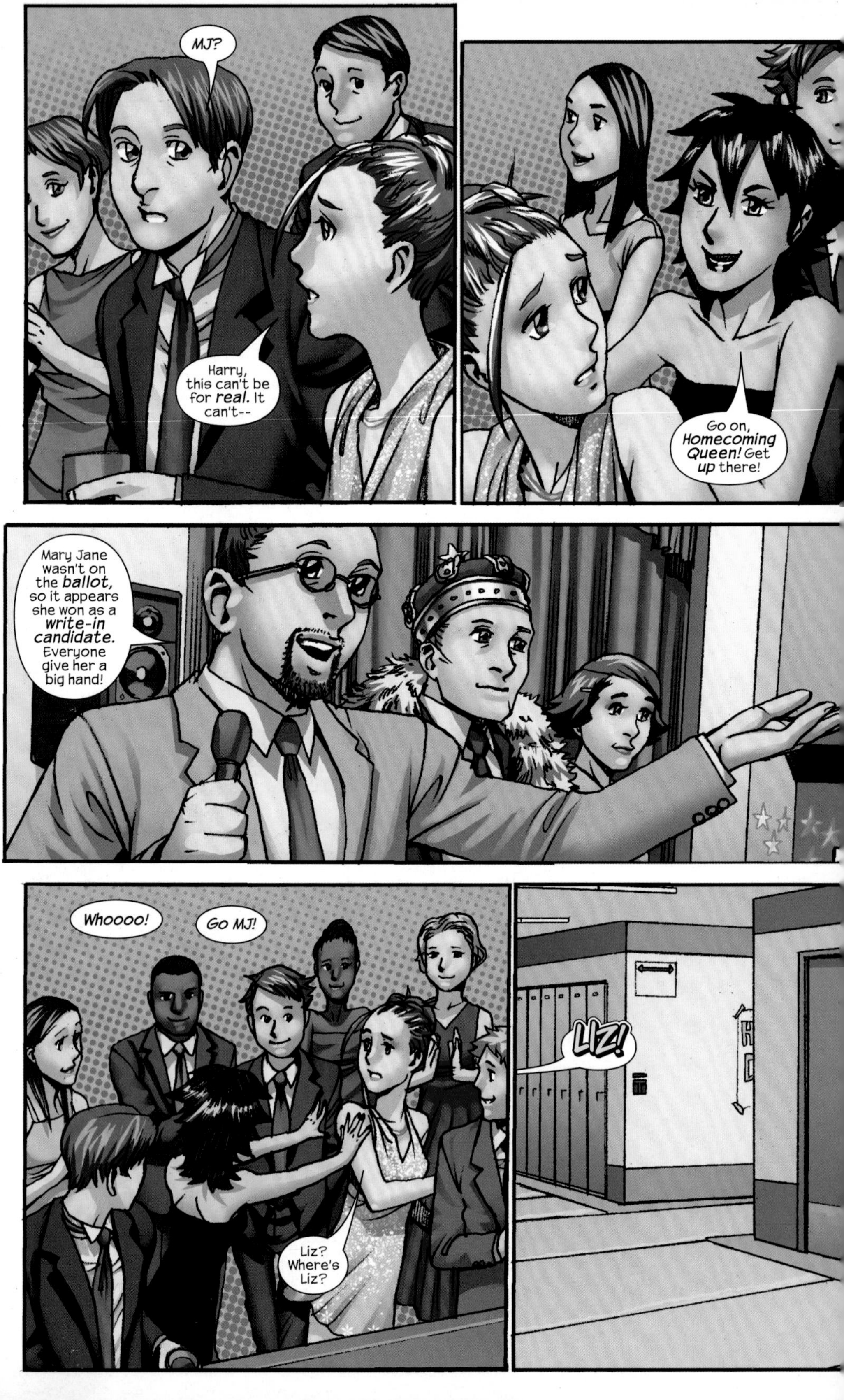
MJ?
Harry, this can't be for real. It can't--
Go on, Homecoming Queen! Get up there!
Mary Jane wasn't on the ballot, so it appears she won as a write-in candidate. Everyone give her a big hand!
Whoooo!
Go MJ!
Liz? Where's Liz?
LIZ!

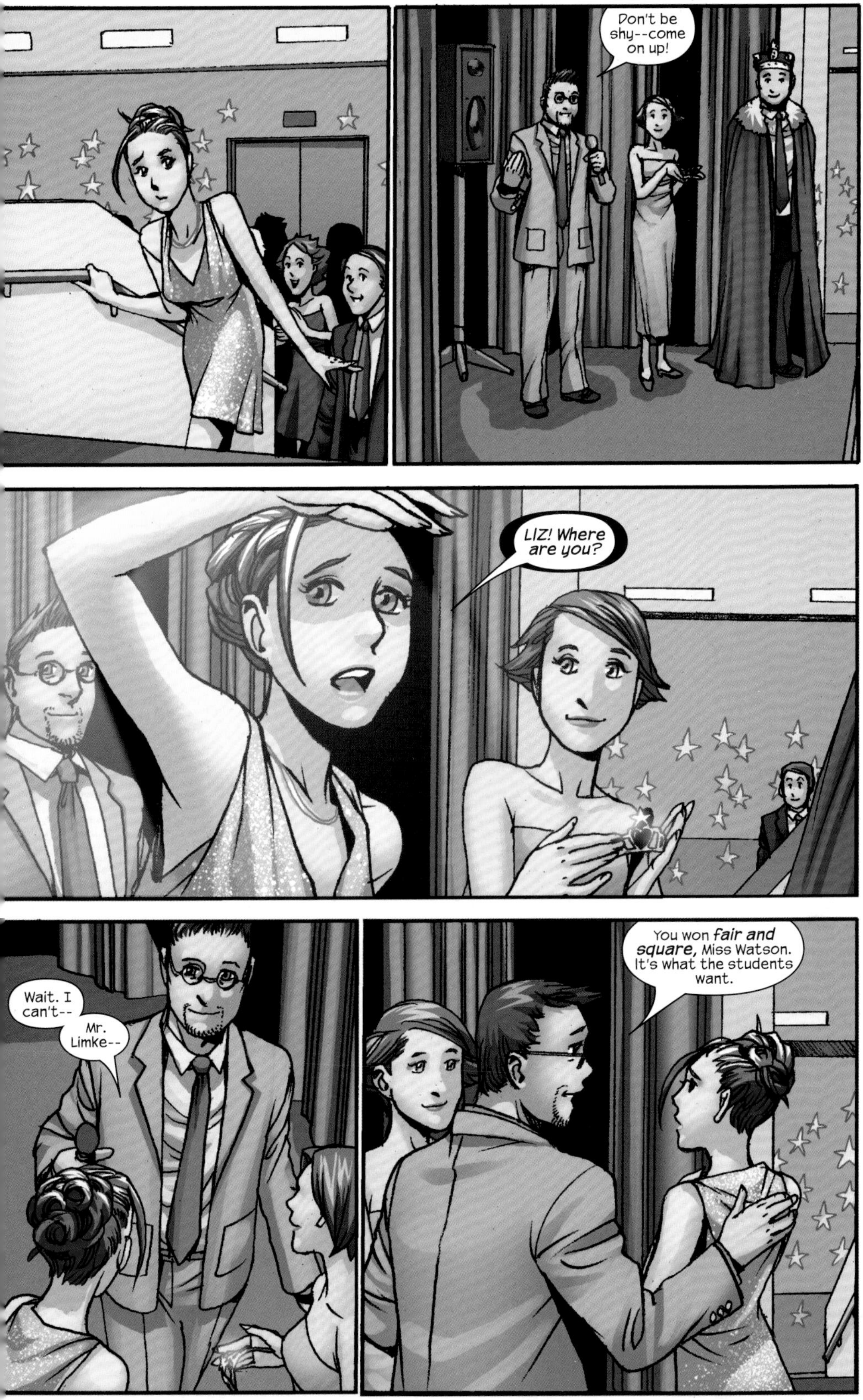

Don't be shy--come on up!
LIZ! Where are you?
Wait. I can't--
Mr. Limke--
You won fair and square, Miss Watson. It's what the students want.

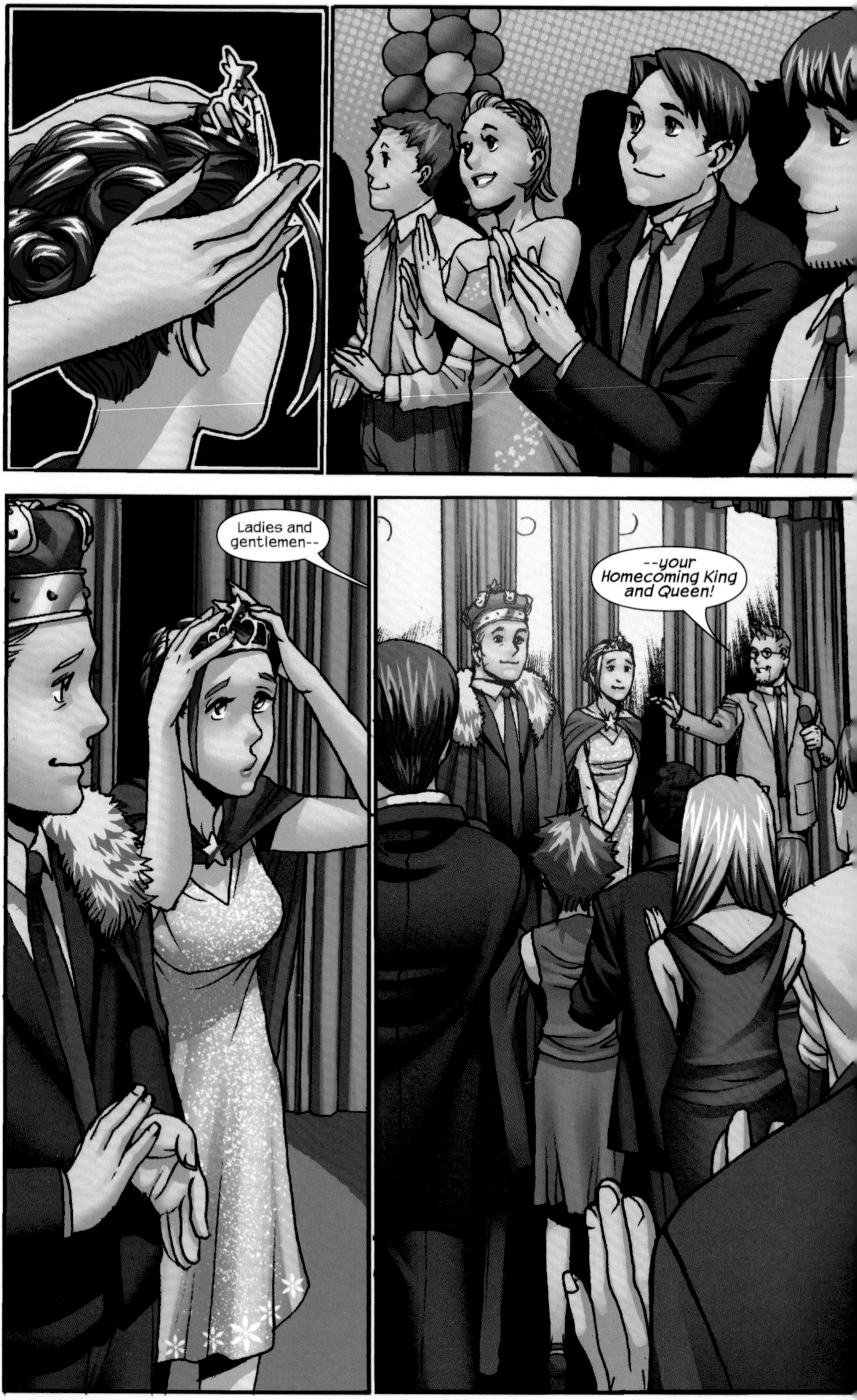
Ladies and gentlemen--
--your Homecoming King and Queen!

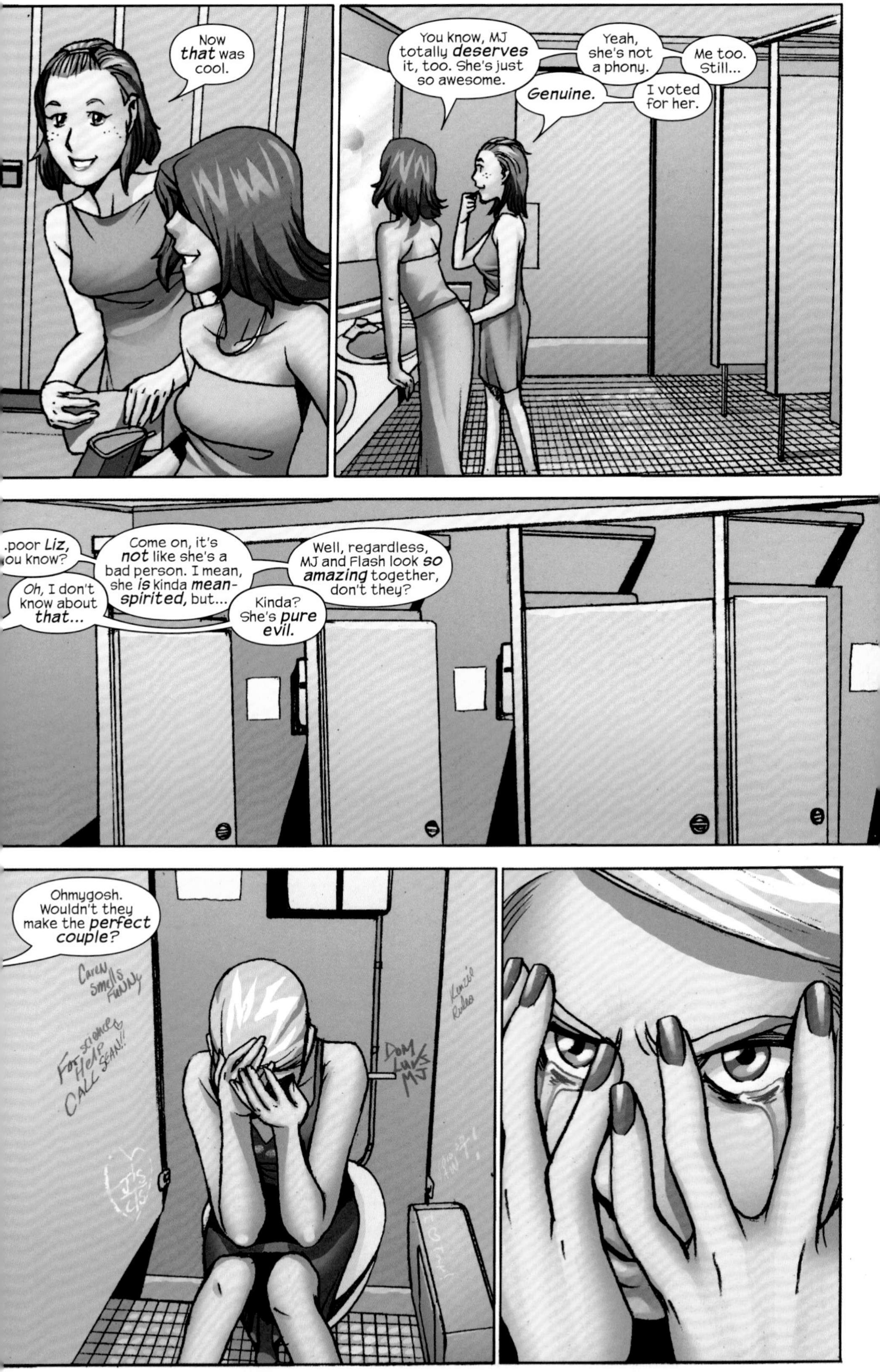
Now that was cool.
You know, MJ totally deserves it, too. She's just so awesome.
Yeah, she's not a phony.
Genuine.
Me too. Still...
I voted for her.
.poor Liz, ou know?
Oh, I don't know about that...
Come on, it's not like she's a bad person. I mean, she is kinda mean-spirited, but...
Kinda? She's pure evil.
Well, regardless, MJ and Flash look so amazing together, don't they?
Ohmygosh. Wouldn't they make the perfect couple?
Caren smells funny
For science help CALL SEAN!!
DOM LUVS MJ

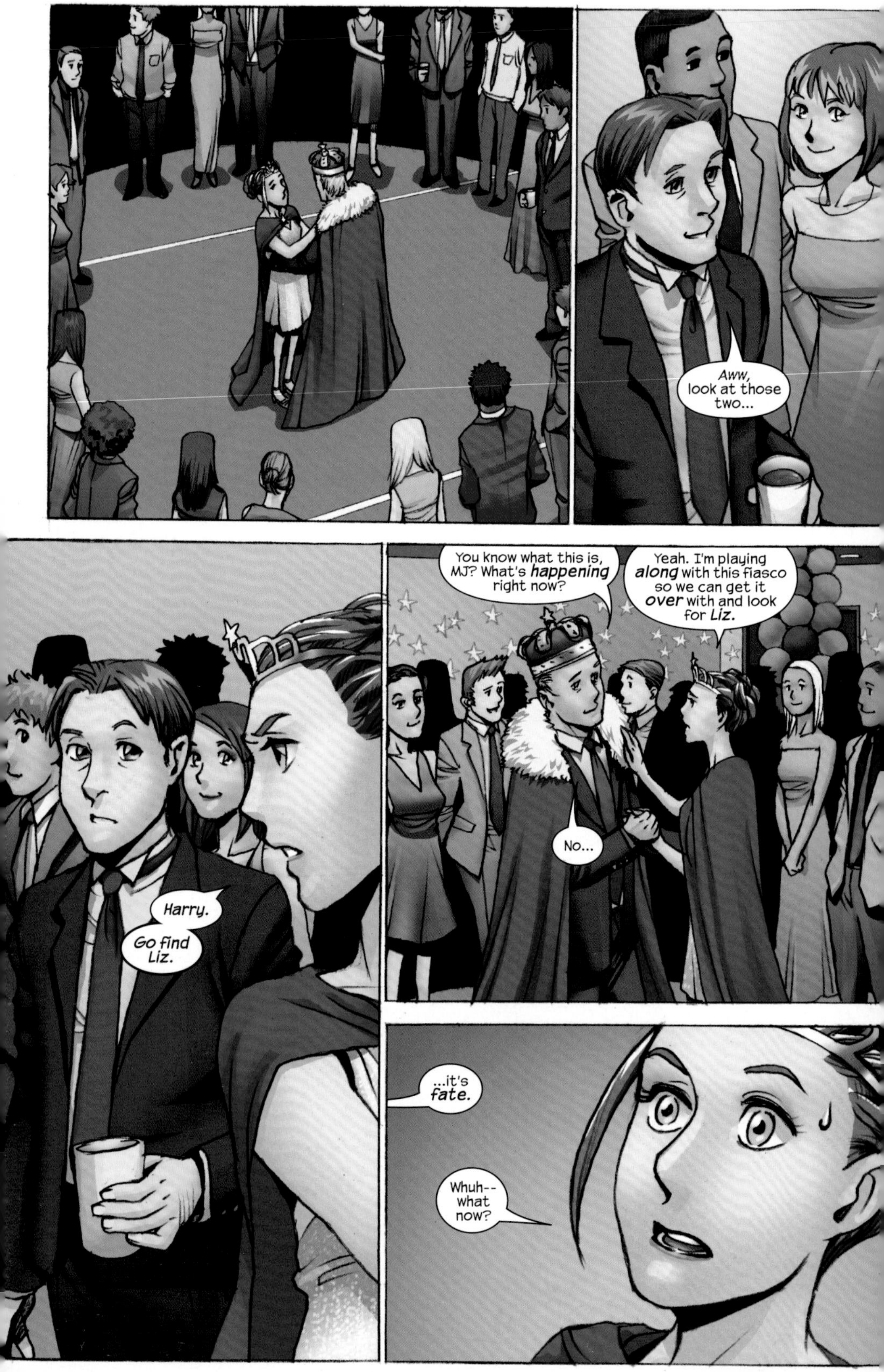
Aww, look at those two...
Harry.
Go find Liz.
You know what this is, MJ? What's happening right now?
Yeah. I'm playing along with this fiasco so we can get it over with and look for Liz.
No...
...it's fate.
Whuh-- what now?

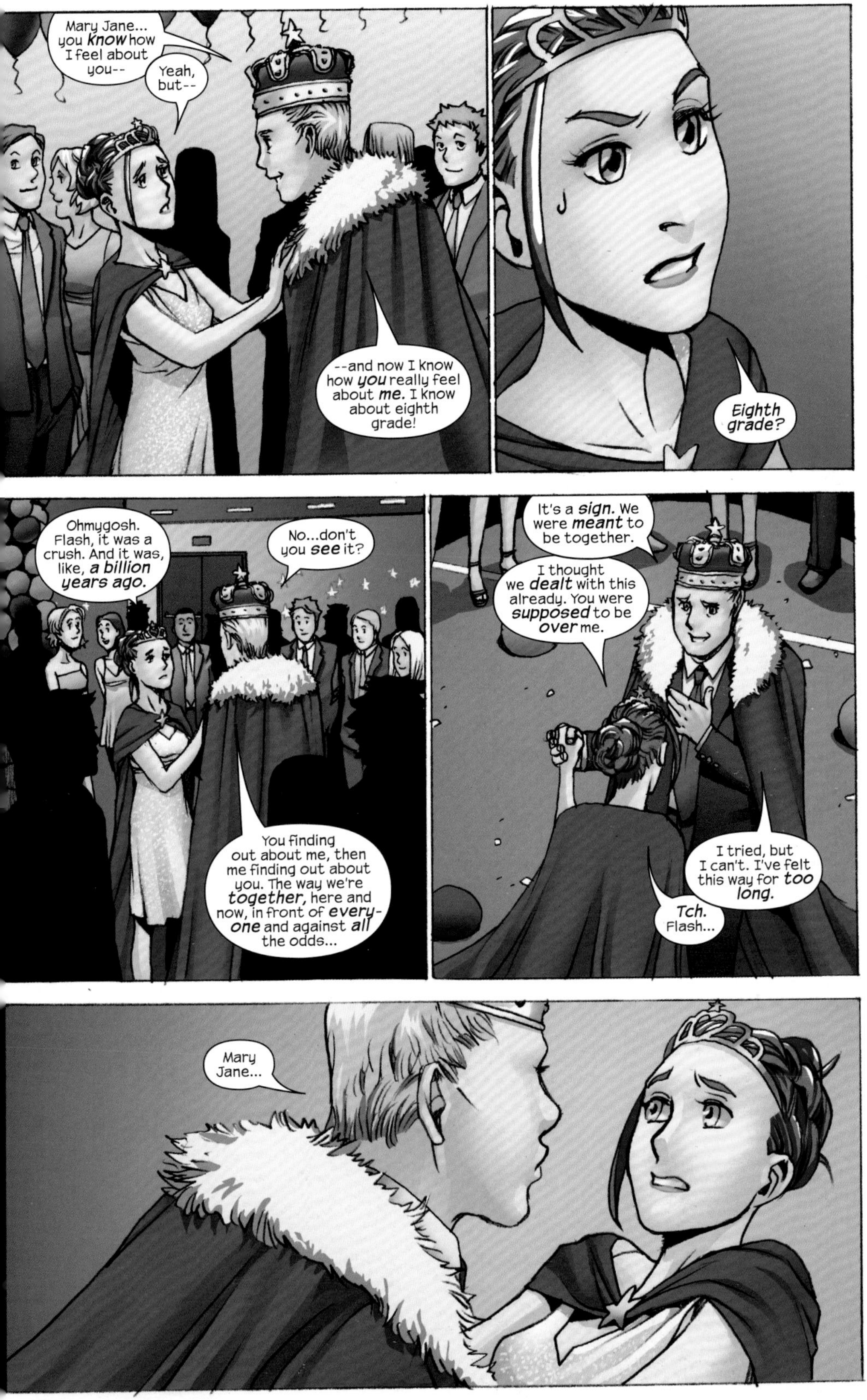
Mary Jane... you know how I feel about you--
Yeah, but--
--and now I know how you really feel about me. I know about eighth grade!
Eighth grade?
Ohmygosh. Flash, it was a crush. And it was, like, a billion years ago.
No...don't you see it?
You finding out about me, then me finding out about you. The way we're together, here and now, in front of every-one and against all the odds...
It's a sign. We were meant to be together.
I thought we dealt with this already. You were supposed to be over me.
I tried, but I can't. I've felt this way for too long.
Tch. Flash...
Mary Jane...

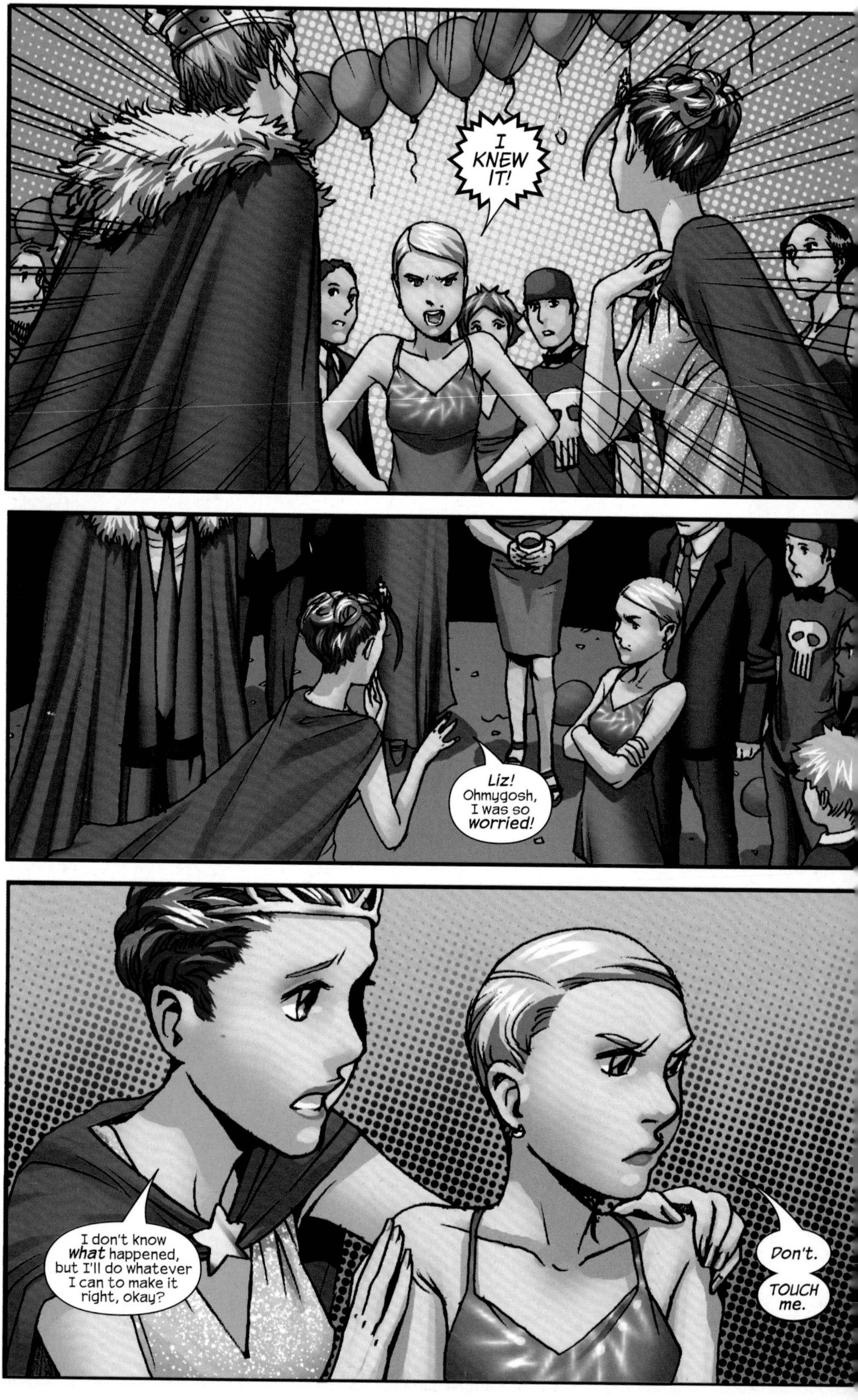

I KNEW IT!
Liz! Ohmygosh, I was so worried!
I don't know what happened, but I'll do whatever I can to make it right, okay?
Don't.
TOUCH me.

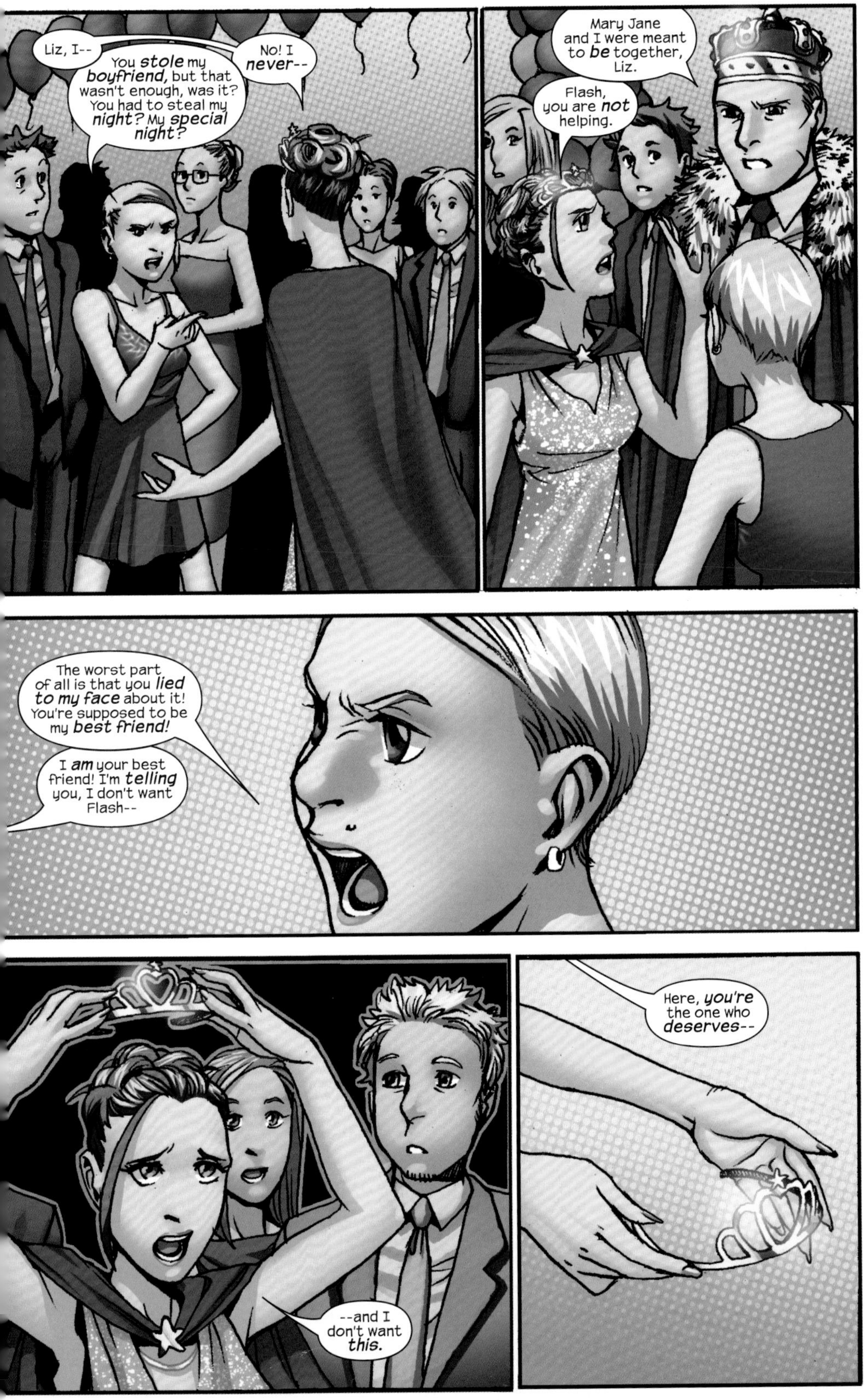
Liz, I--
You stole my boyfriend, but that wasn't enough, was it? You had to steal my night? My special night?
No! I never--
Mary Jane and I were meant to be together, Liz.
Flash, you are not helping.
The worst part of all is that you lied to my face about it! You're supposed to be my best friend!
I am your best friend! I'm telling you, I don't want Flash--
--and I don't want this.
Here, you're the one who deserves--

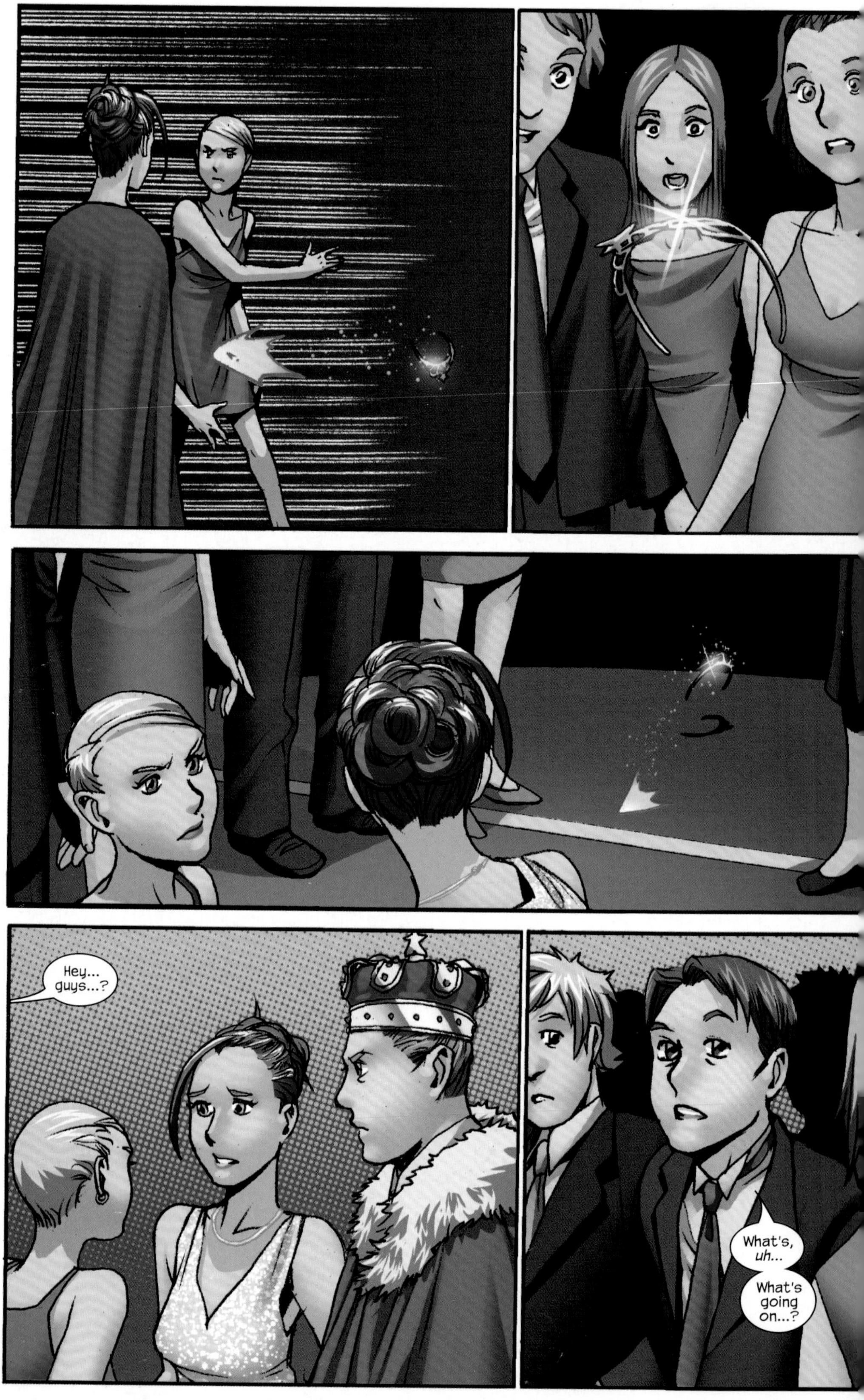
Hey... guys...?
What's, *uh...*
What's going on...?

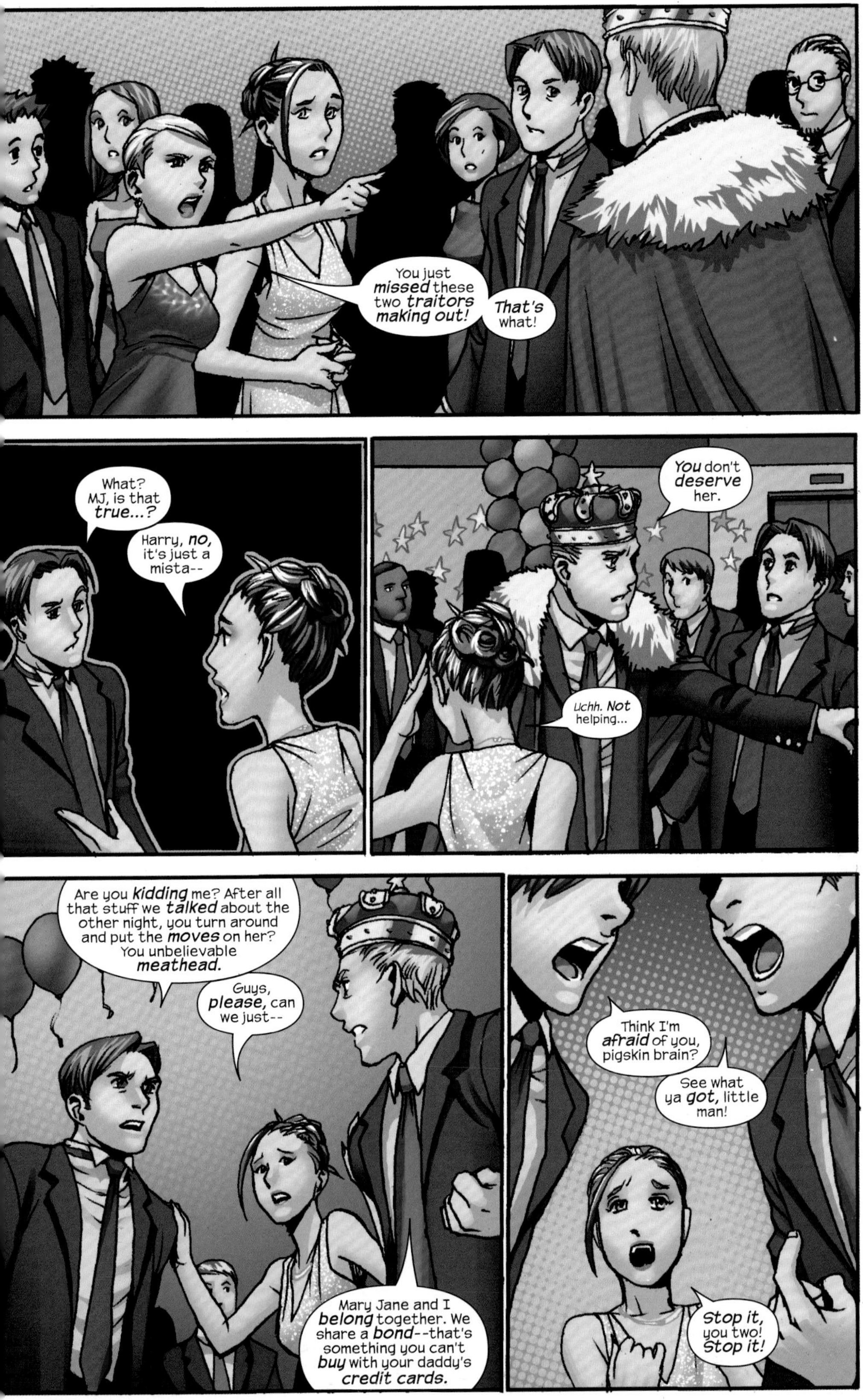
You just missed these two traitors making out!
That's what!
What? MJ, is that true...?
Harry, no, it's just a mista--
You don't deserve her.
Uchh. Not helping...
Are you kidding me? After all that stuff we talked about the other night, you turn around and put the moves on her? You unbelievable meathead.
Guys, please, can we just--
Mary Jane and I belong together. We share a bond--that's something you can't buy with your daddy's credit cards.
Think I'm afraid of you, pigskin brain?
See what ya got, little man!
Stop it, you two! Stop it!

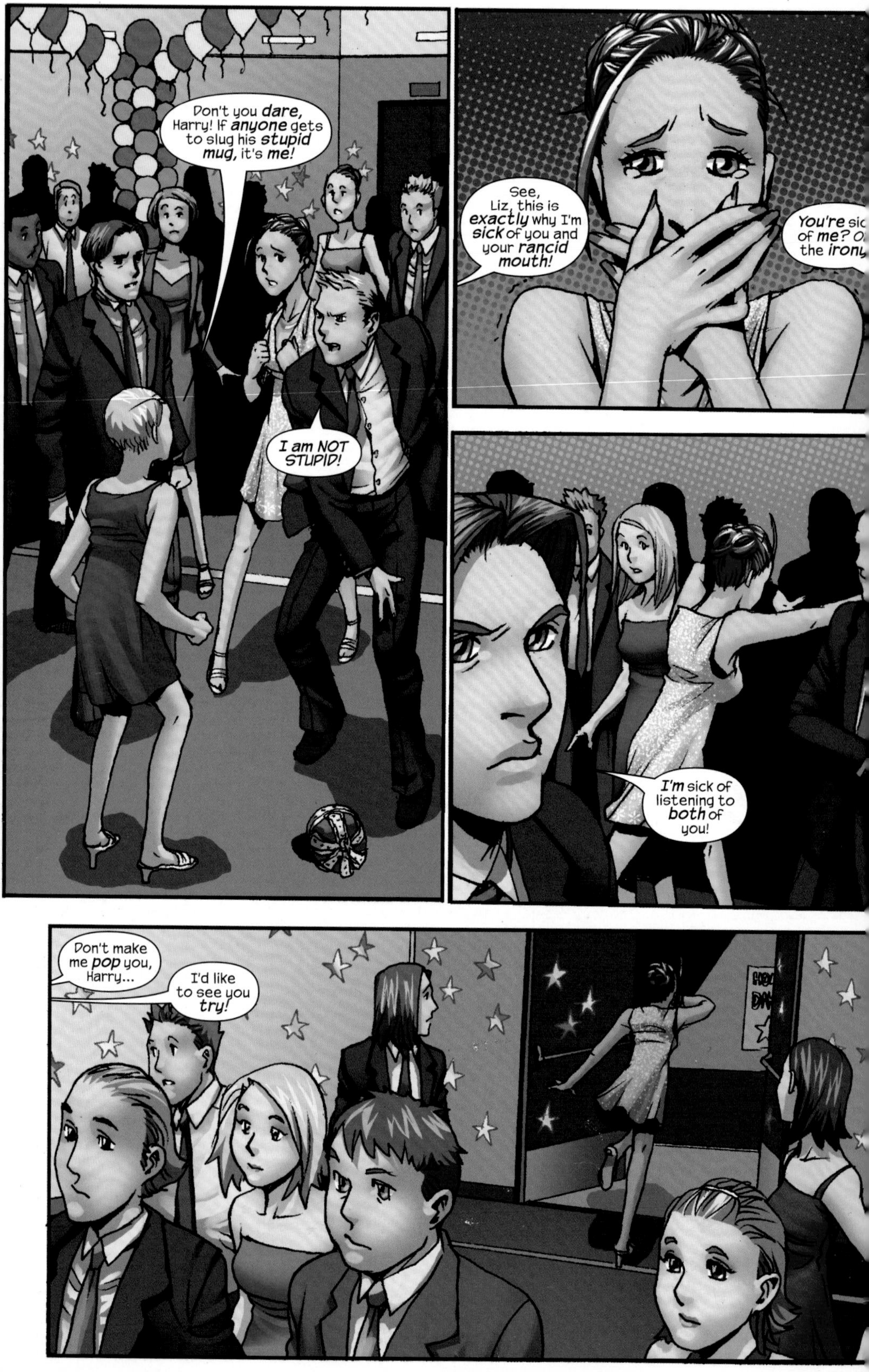
Don't you dare, Harry! If anyone gets to slug his stupid mug, it's me!
I am NOT STUPID!
See, Liz, this is exactly why I'm sick of you and your rancid mouth!
You're sic of me? O the iron
I'm sick of listening to both of you!
Don't make me pop you, Harry...
I'd like to see you try!

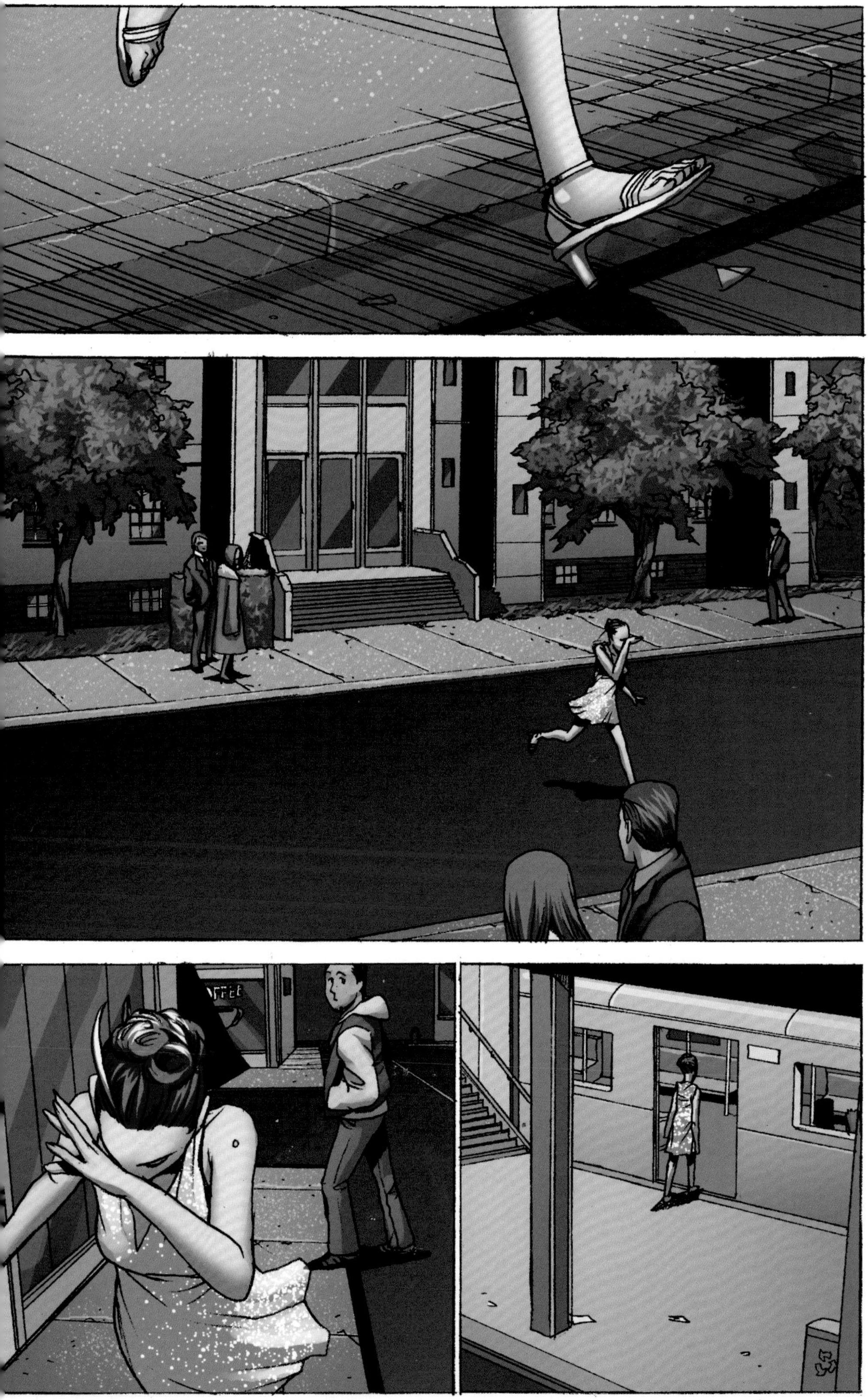

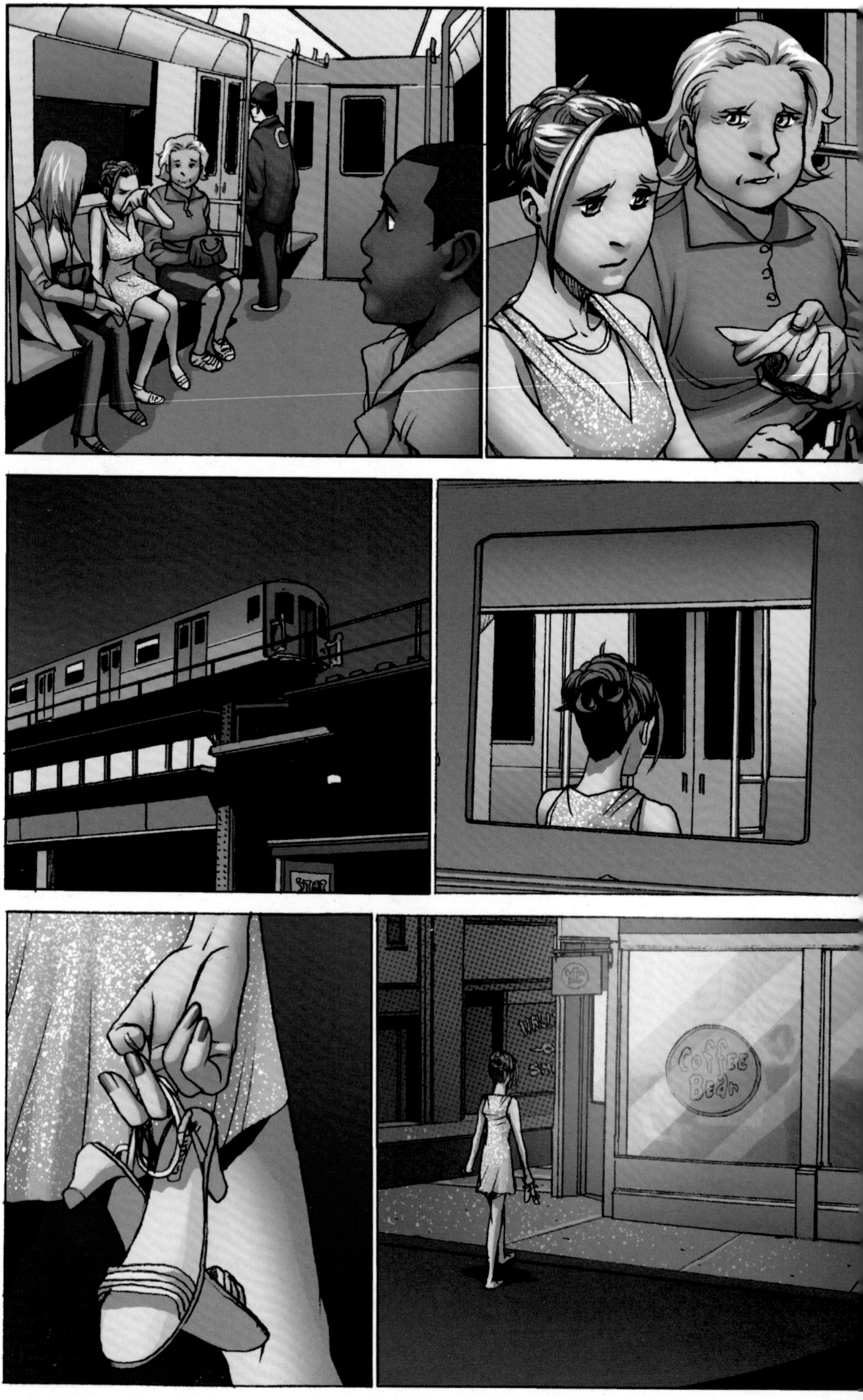
Coffee Bear

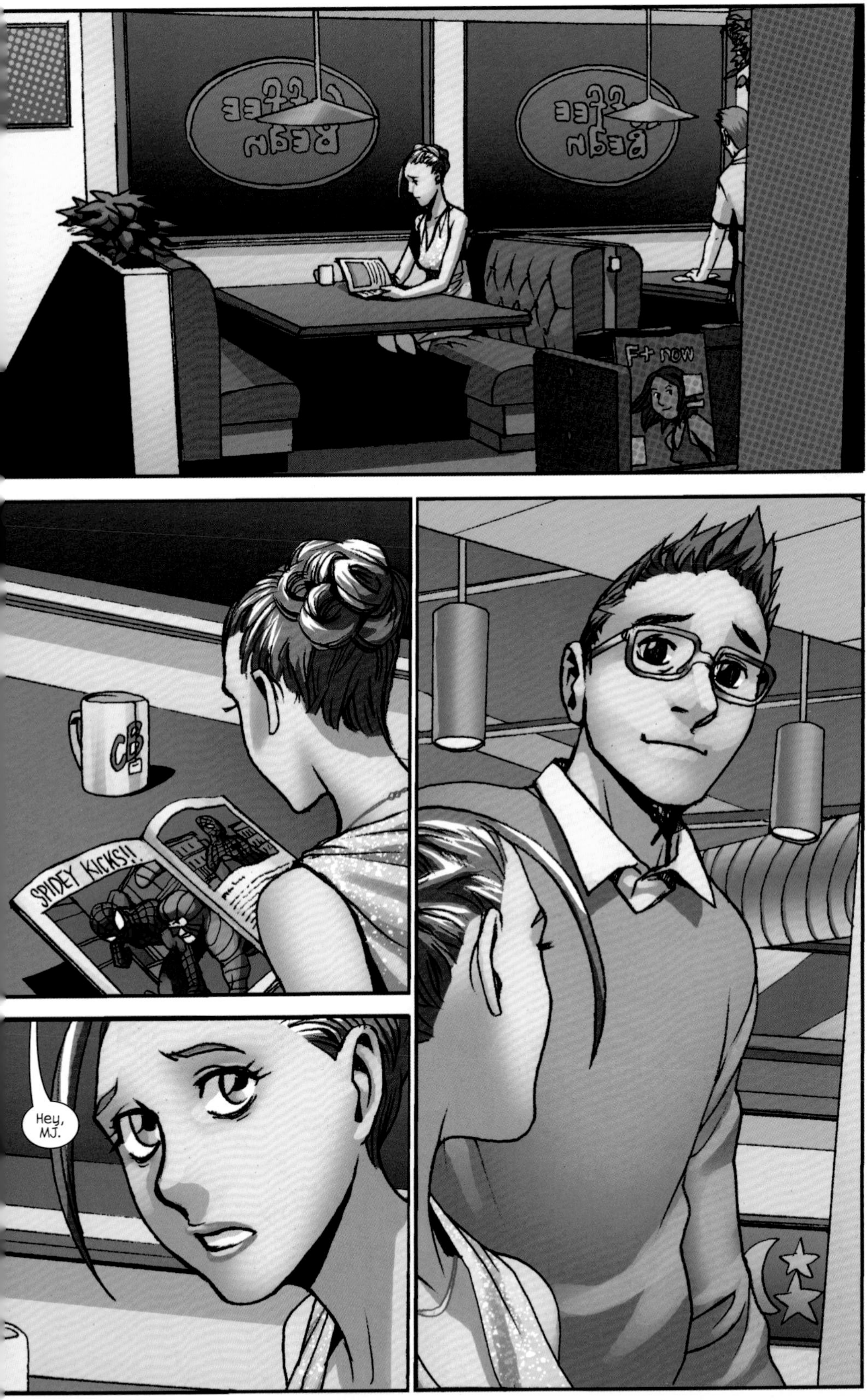

F+ now
SPIDEY KICKS!!
Hey, MJ.

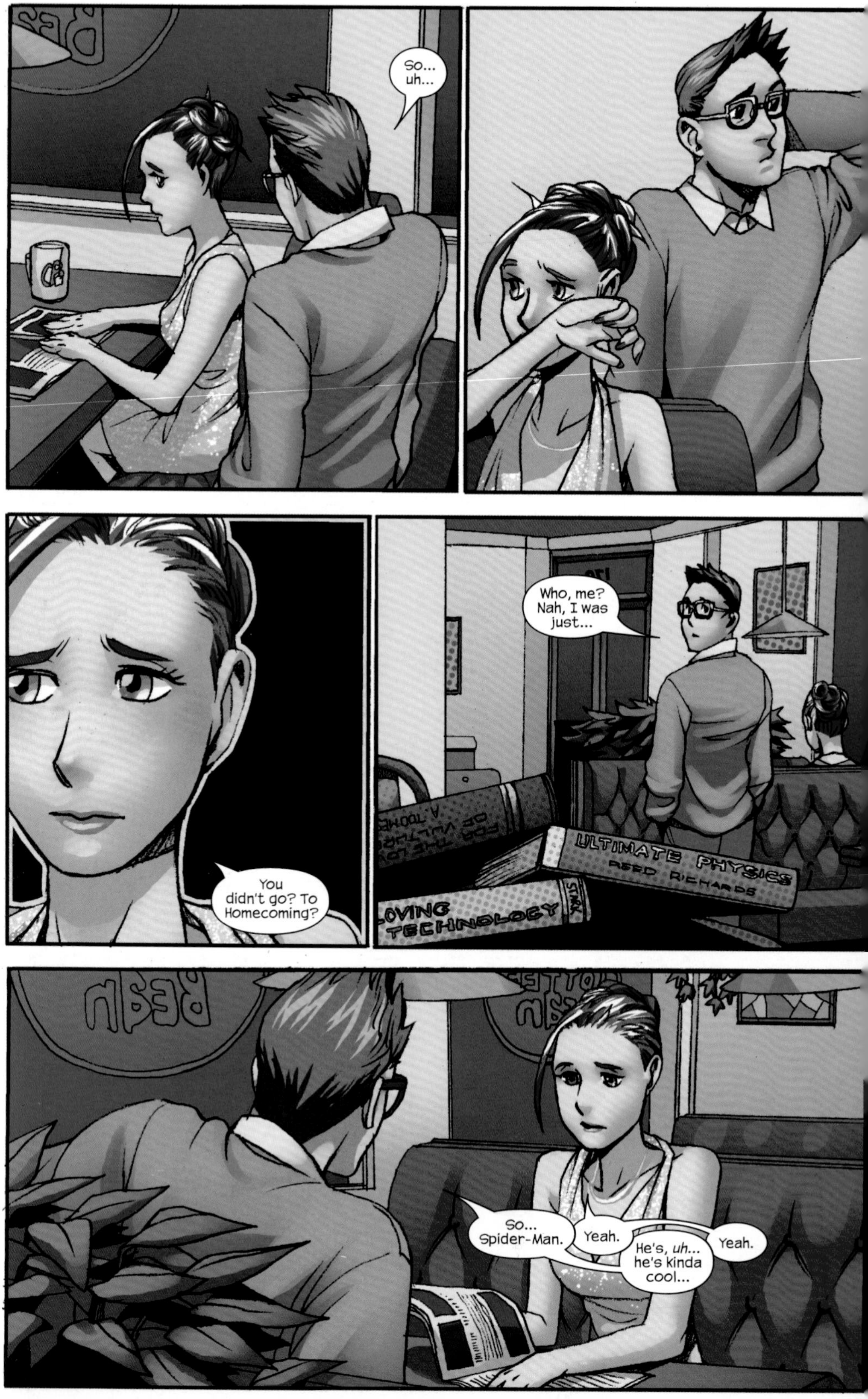
So... uh...
You didn't go? To Homecoming?
Who, me? Nah, I was just...
ULTIMATE PHYSICS
REED RICHARDS
STARK
So... Spider-Man.
Yeah.
He's, *uh*... he's kinda cool...
Yeah.

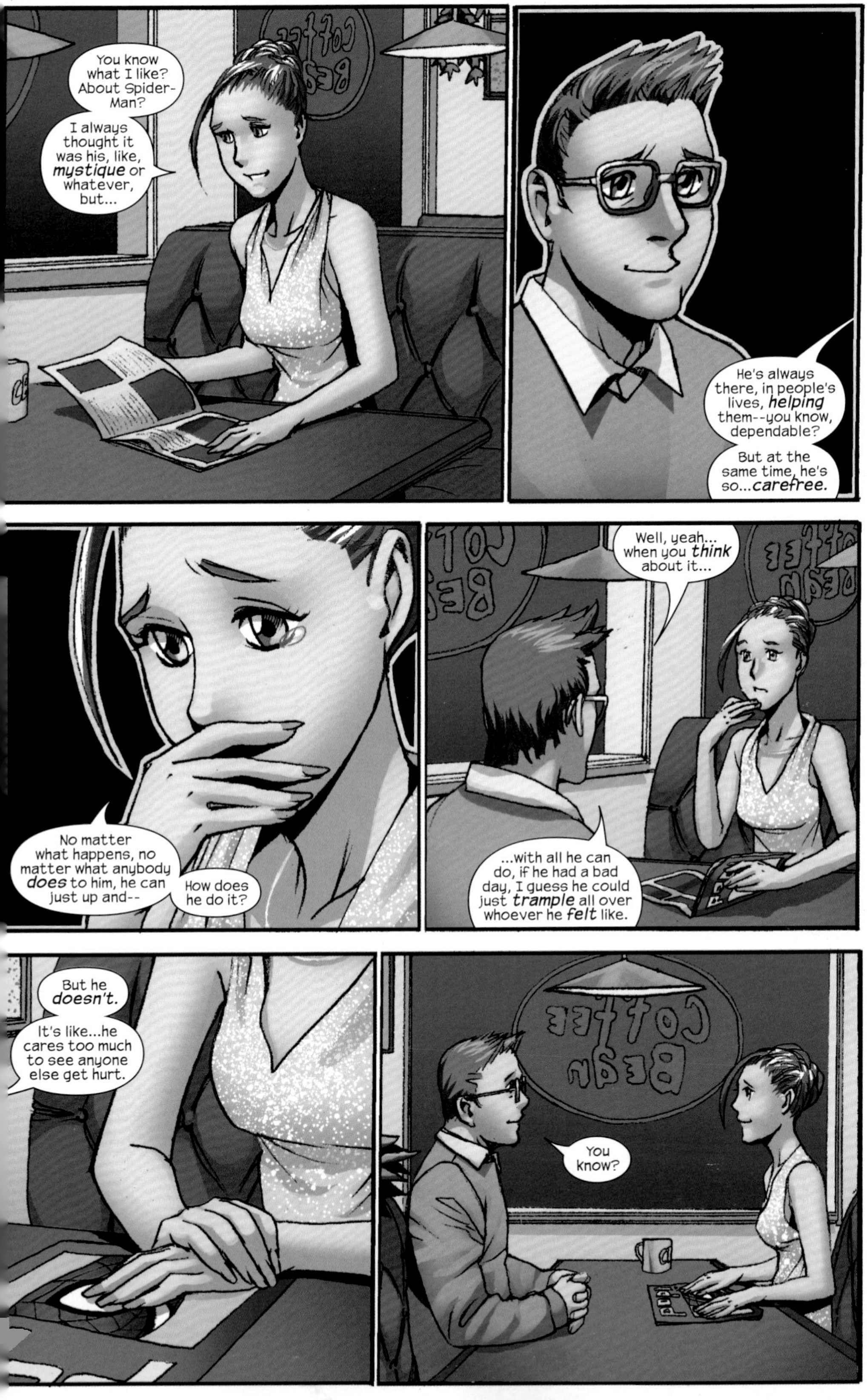
You know what I like? About Spider-Man?
I always thought it was his, like, mystique or whatever, but...
He's always there, in people's lives, helping them--you know, dependable?
But at the same time, he's so...carefree.
No matter what happens, no matter what anybody does to him, he can just up and--
How does he do it?
Well, yeah... when you think about it...
...with all he can do, if he had a bad day, I guess he could just trample all over whoever he felt like.
But he doesn't.
It's like...he cares too much to see anyone else get hurt.
You know?

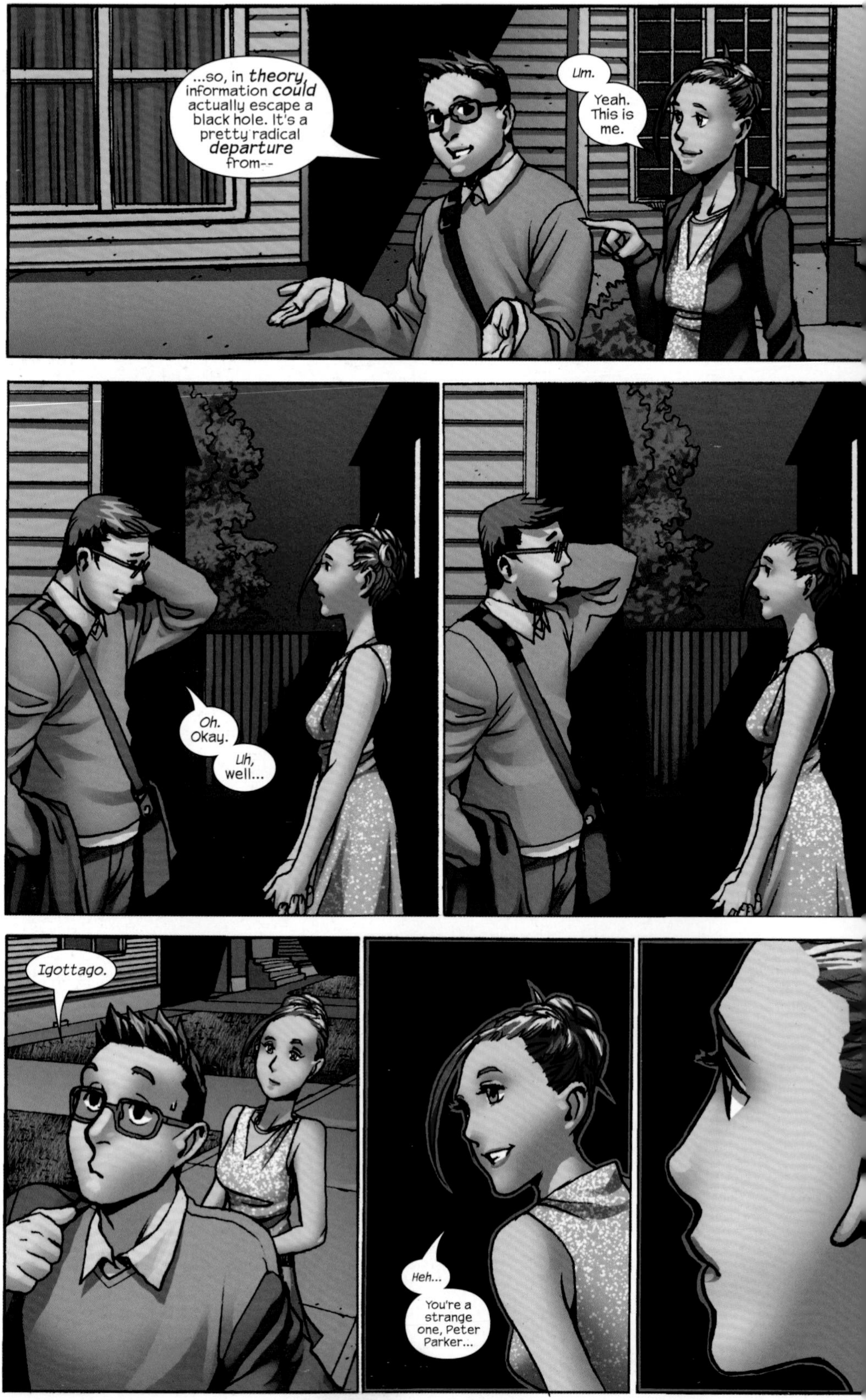
...so, in theory, information could actually escape a black hole. It's a pretty radical departure from--
Um.
Yeah. This is me.
Oh. Okay.
Uh, well...
Igottago.
Heh...
You're a strange one, Peter Parker...

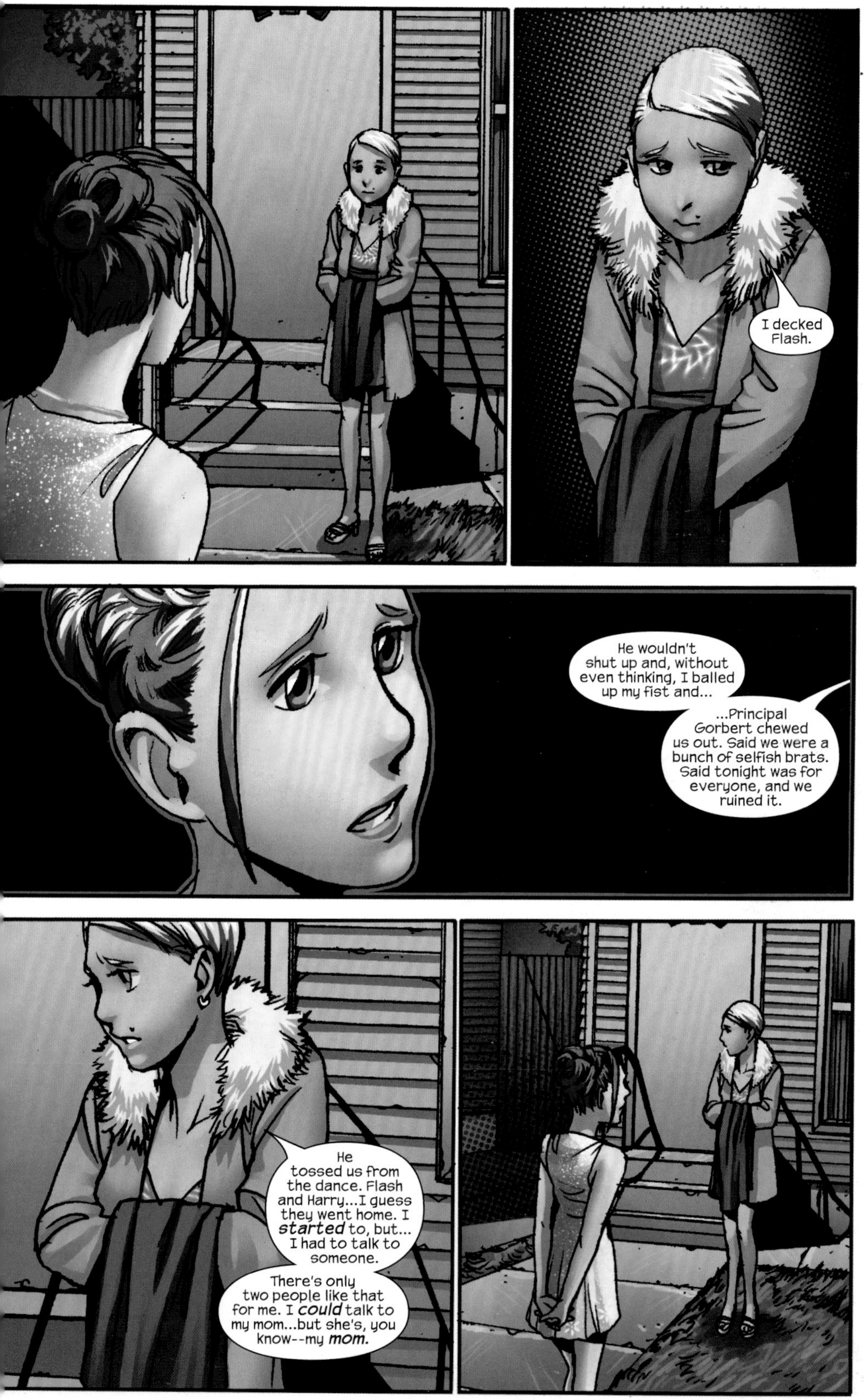

I decked Flash.
He wouldn't shut up and, without even thinking, I balled up my fist and...
...Principal Gorbert chewed us out. Said we were a bunch of selfish brats. Said tonight was for everyone, and we ruined it.
He tossed us from the dance. Flash and Harry...I guess they went home. I *started* to, but... I had to talk to someone.
There's only two people like that for me. I *could* talk to my mom...but she's, you know--my *mom.*

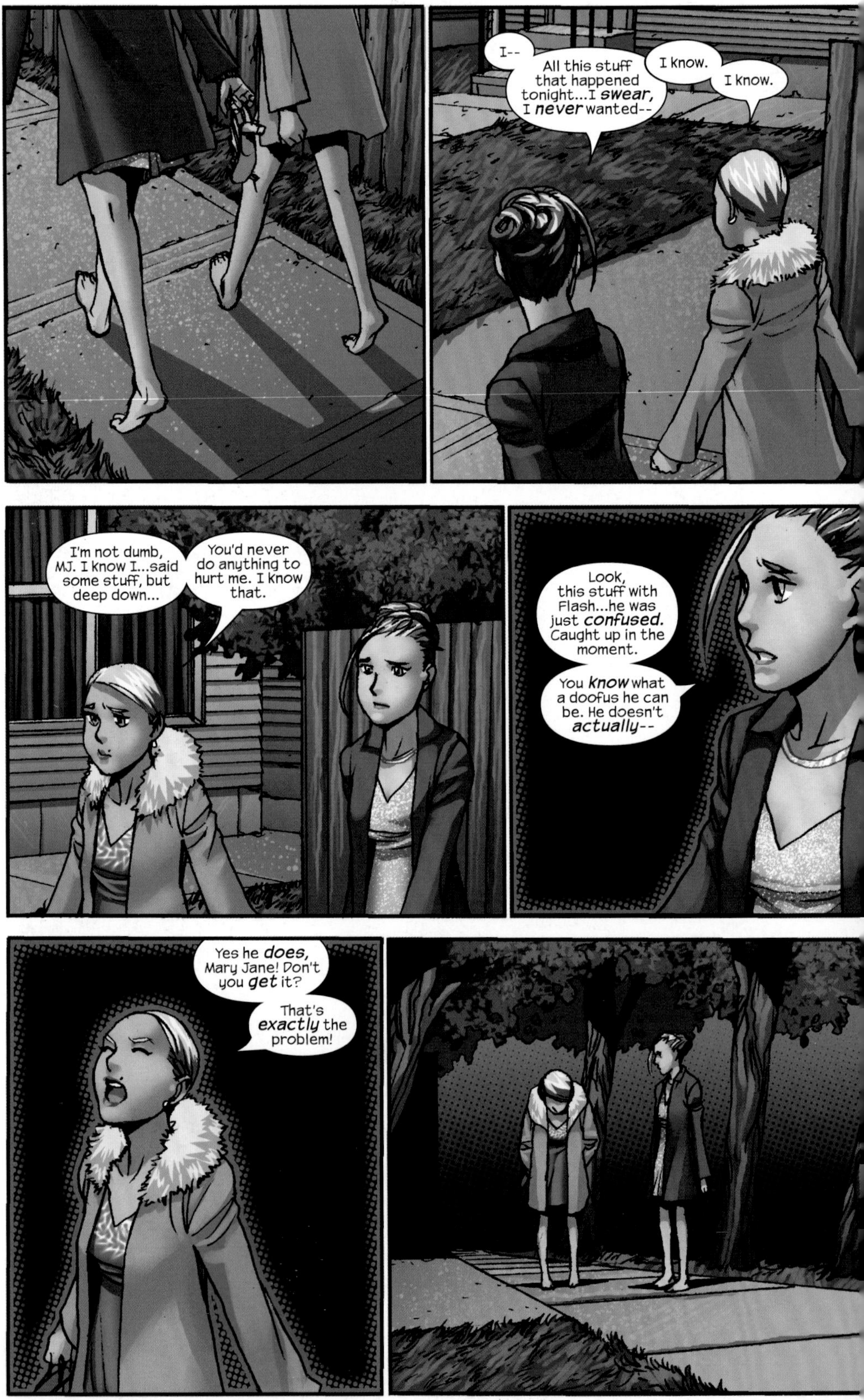
I--
All this stuff that happened tonight...I swear, I never wanted--
I know.
I know.
I'm not dumb, MJ. I know I...said some stuff, but deep down...
You'd never do anything to hurt me. I know that.
Look, this stuff with Flash...he was just confused. Caught up in the moment.
You know what a doofus he can be. He doesn't actually--
Yes he does, Mary Jane! Don't you get it?
That's exactly the problem!

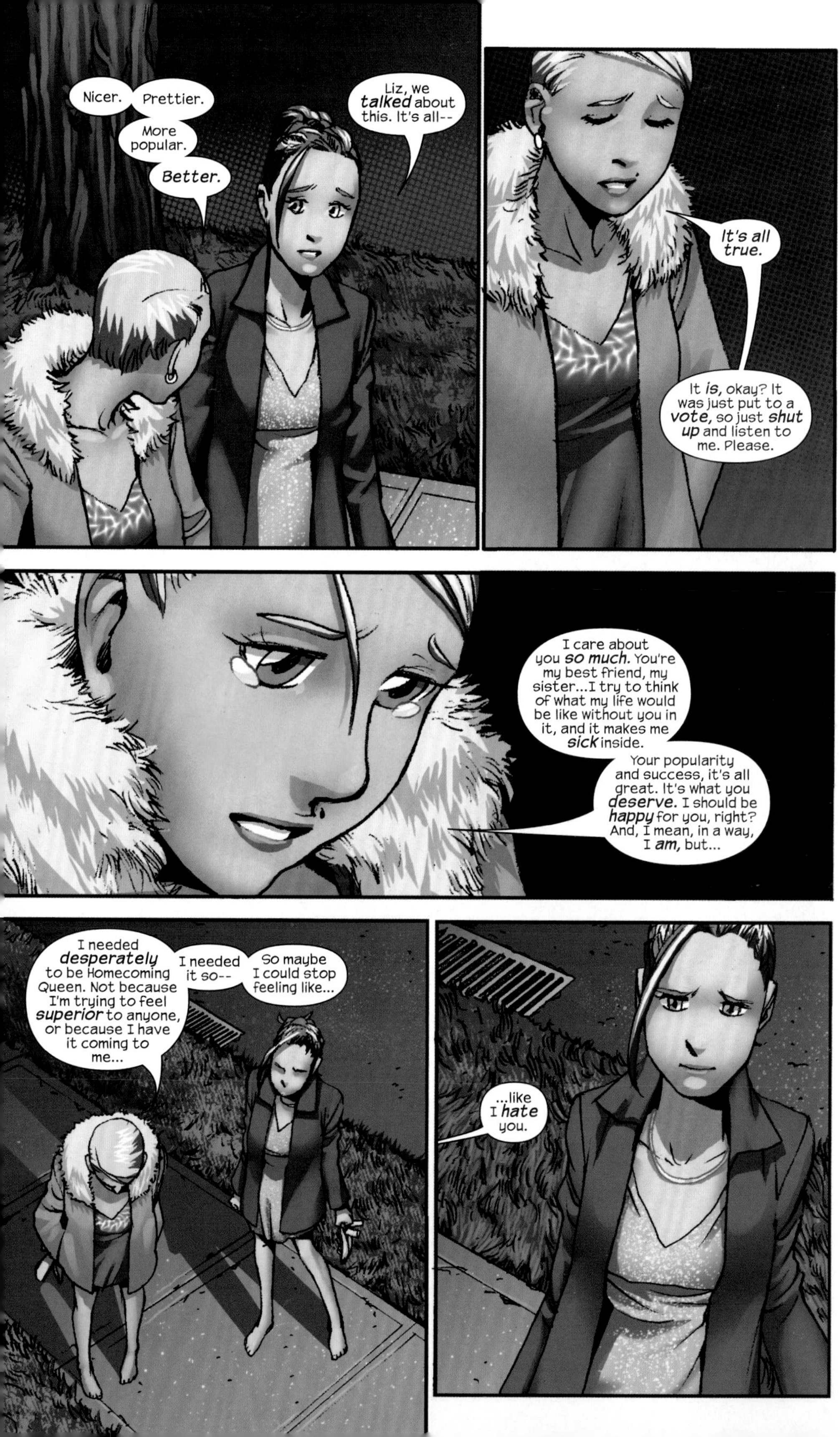
Nicer.
Prettier.
More popular.
Better.
Liz, we talked about this. It's all--
It's all true.
It is, okay? It was just put to a vote, so just shut up and listen to me. Please.
I care about you so much. You're my best friend, my sister...I try to think of what my life would be like without you in it, and it makes me sick inside.
Your popularity and success, it's all great. It's what you deserve. I should be happy for you, right? And, I mean, in a way, I am, but...
I needed desperately to be Homecoming Queen. Not because I'm trying to feel superior to anyone, or because I have it coming to me...
I needed it so--
So maybe I could stop feeling like...
...like I hate you.

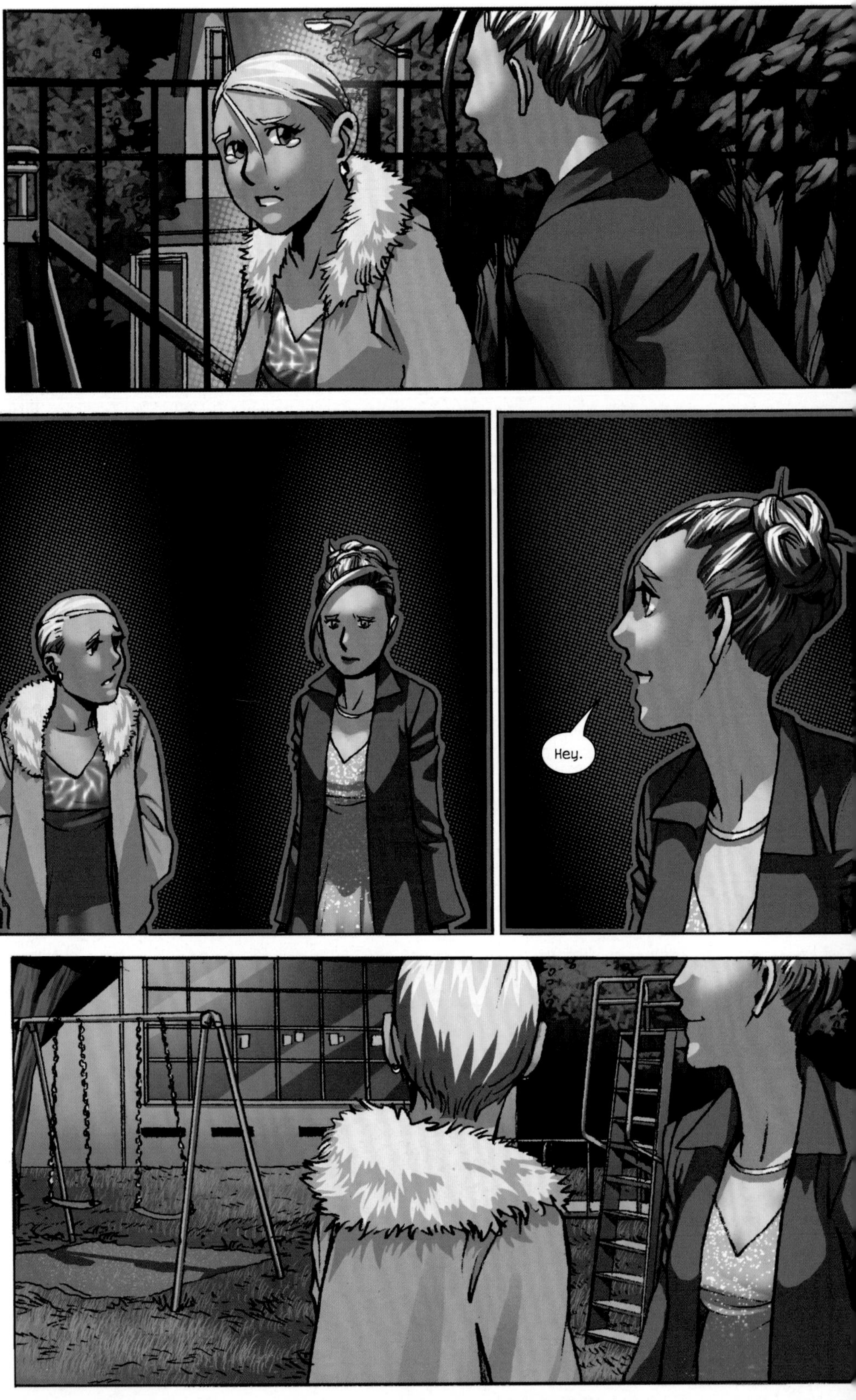
Hey.

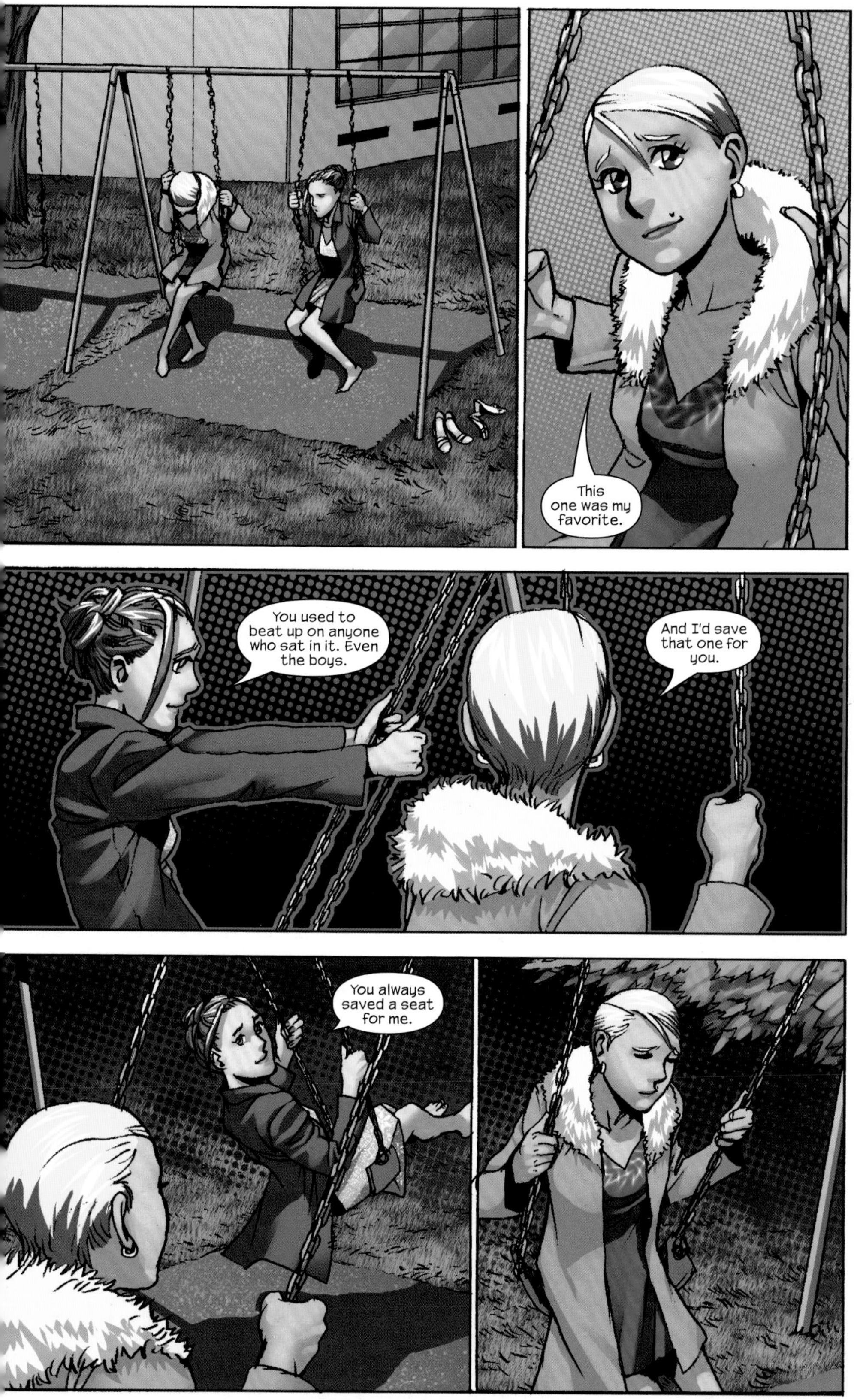
This one was my favorite.
You used to beat up on anyone who sat in it. Even the boys.
And I'd save that one for you.
You always saved a seat for me.

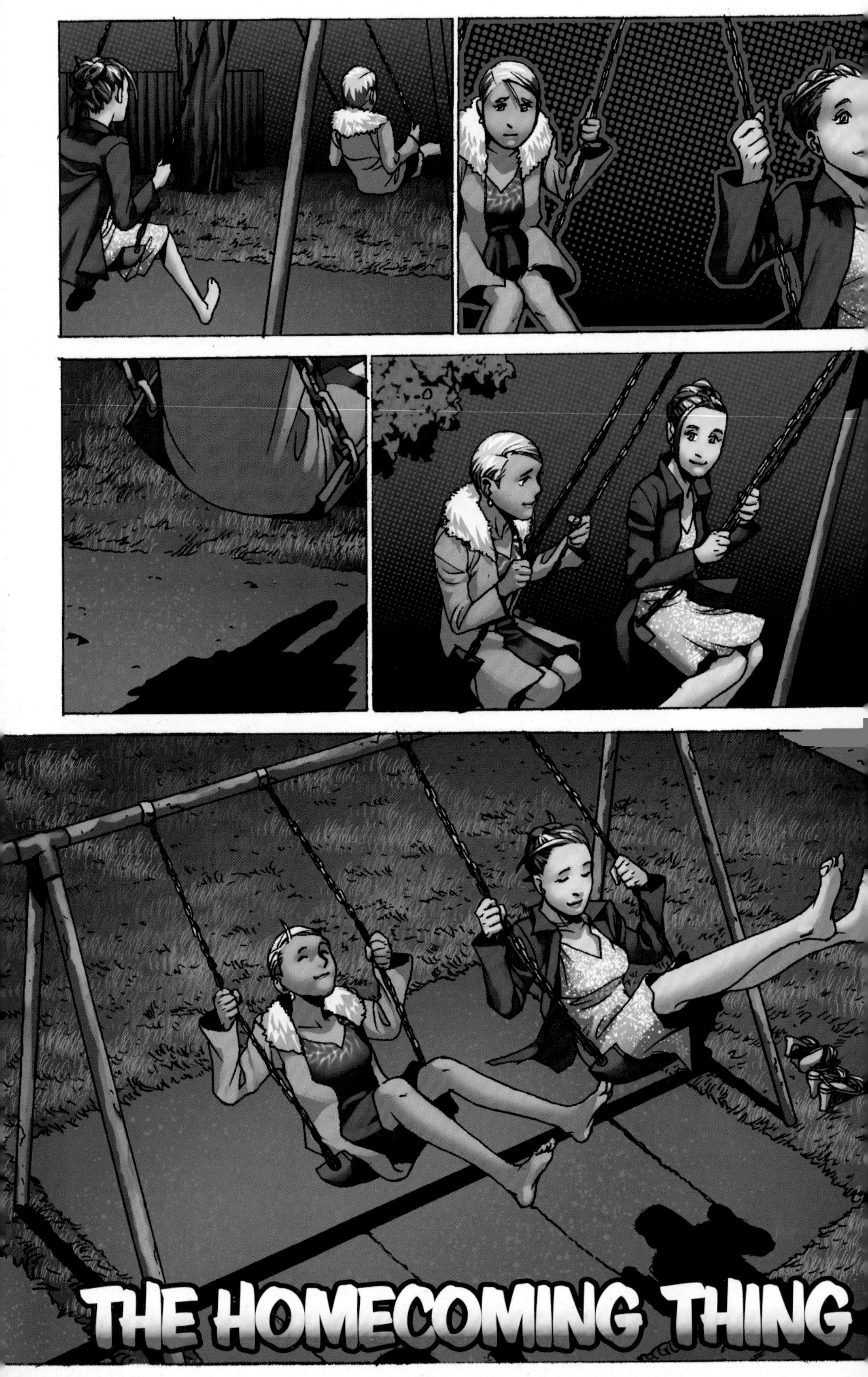
THE HOMECOMING THING

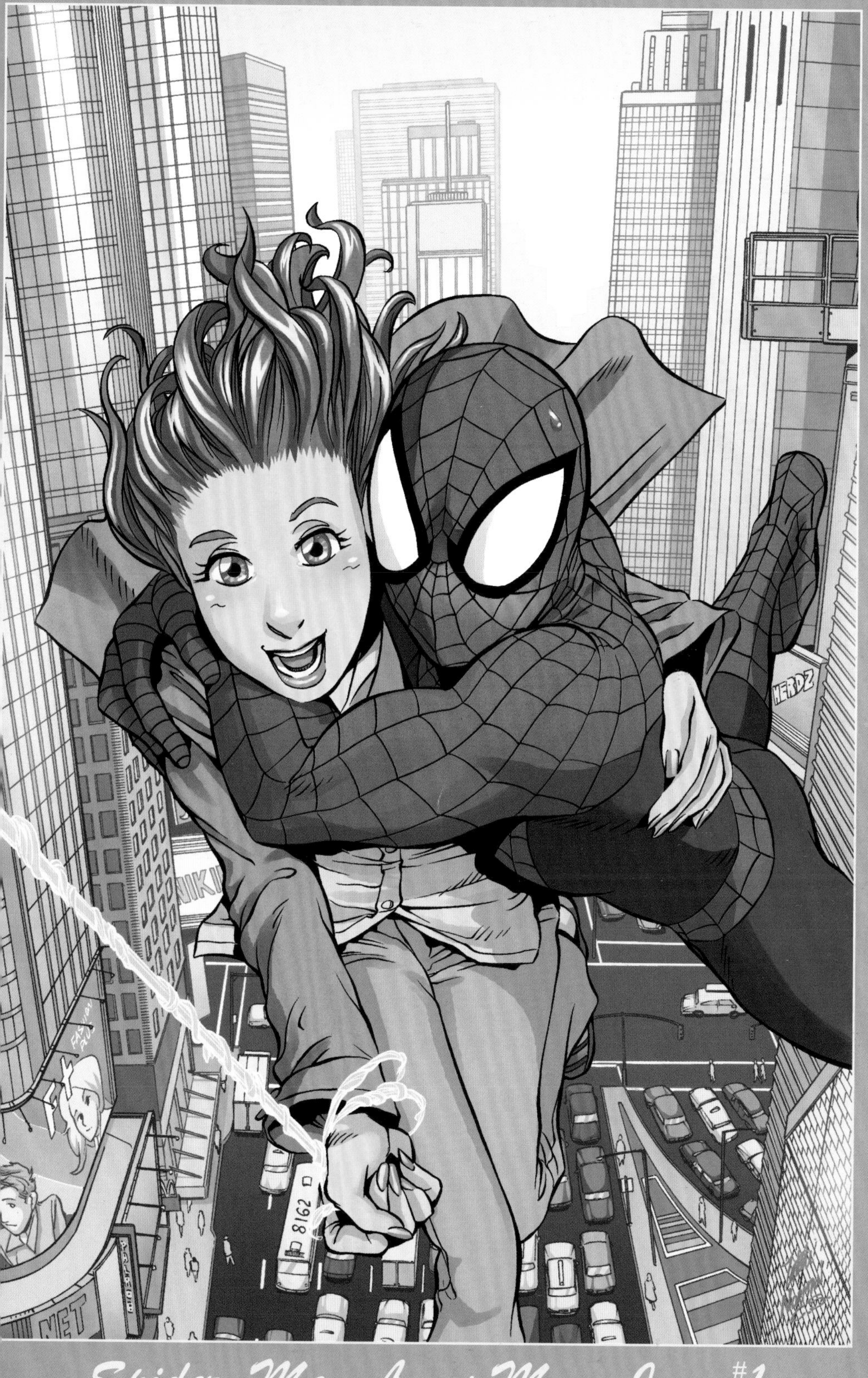
8162
NET

Spider-Man Loves Mary Jane #1

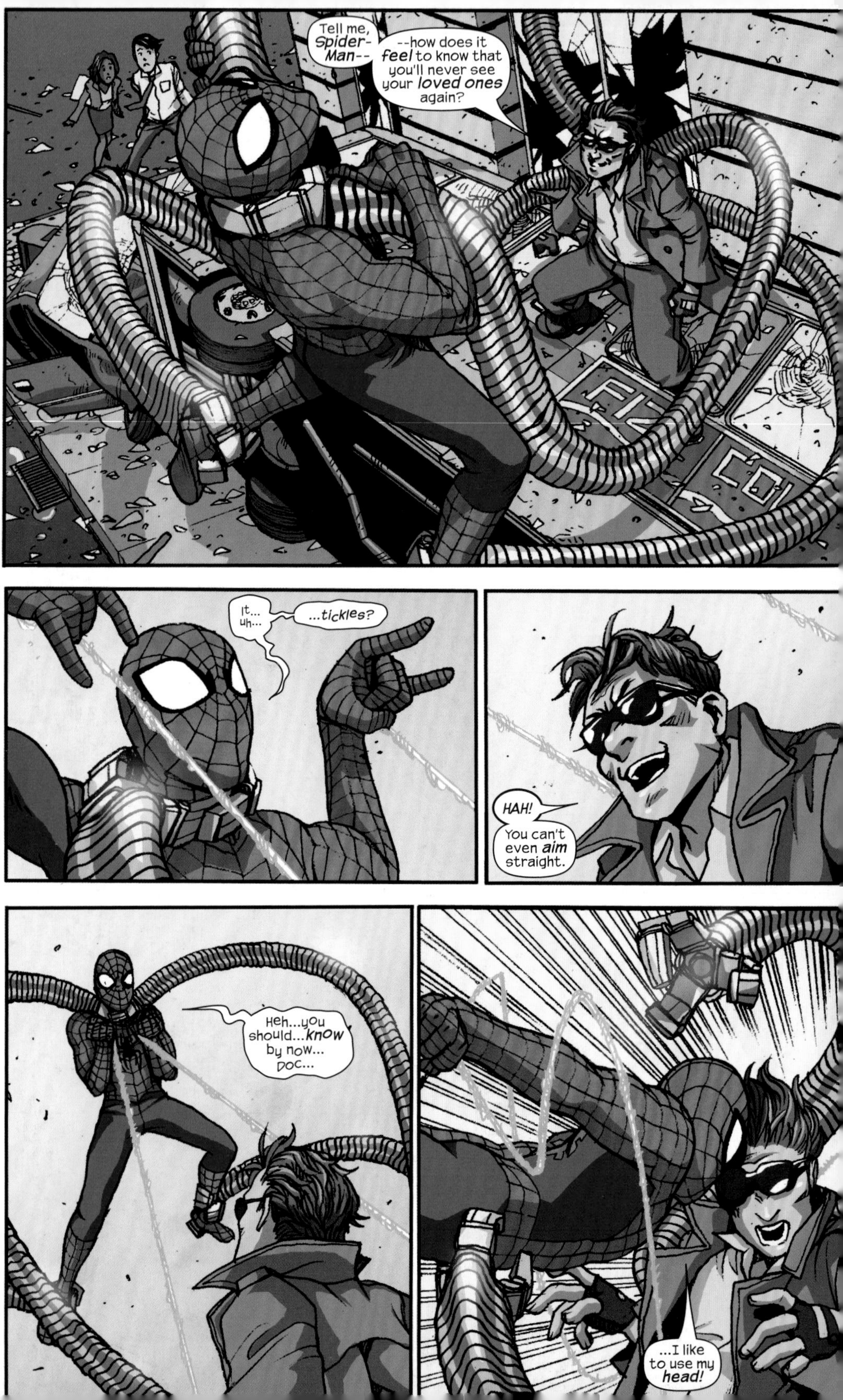
Tell me, Spider-Man--
--how does it feel to know that you'll never see your loved ones again?
It... uh...
...tickles?
HAH!
You can't even aim straight.
Heh...you should...know by now... Doc...
...I like to use my head!

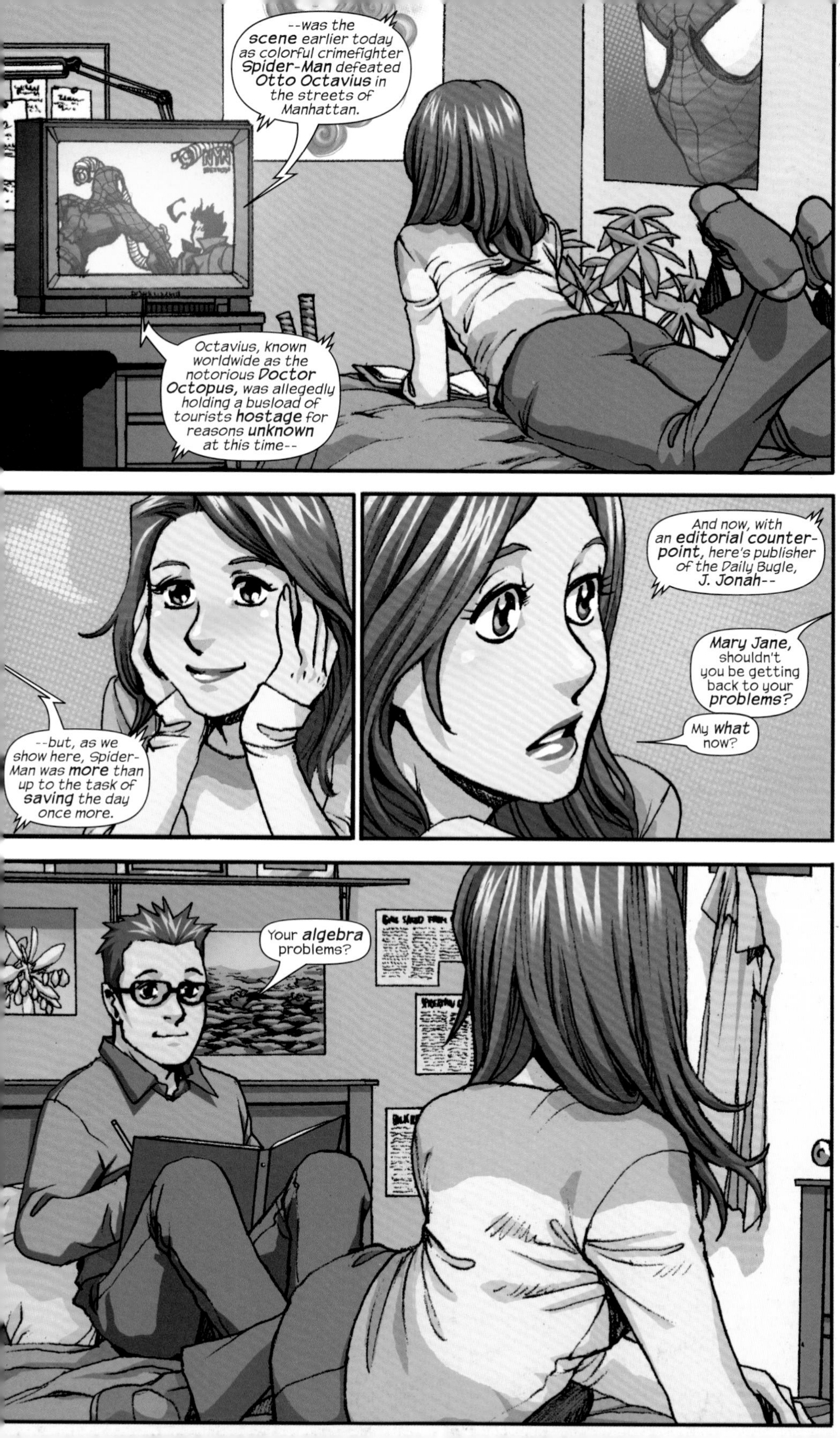
--was the scene earlier today as colorful crimefighter Spider-Man defeated Otto Octavius in the streets of Manhattan.
Octavius, known worldwide as the notorious Doctor Octopus, was allegedly holding a busload of tourists hostage for reasons unknown at this time--
--but, as we show here, Spider-Man was more than up to the task of saving the day once more.
And now, with an editorial counter-point, here's publisher of the Daily Bugle, J. Jonah--
Mary Jane, shouldn't you be getting back to your problems?
My what now?
Your algebra problems?

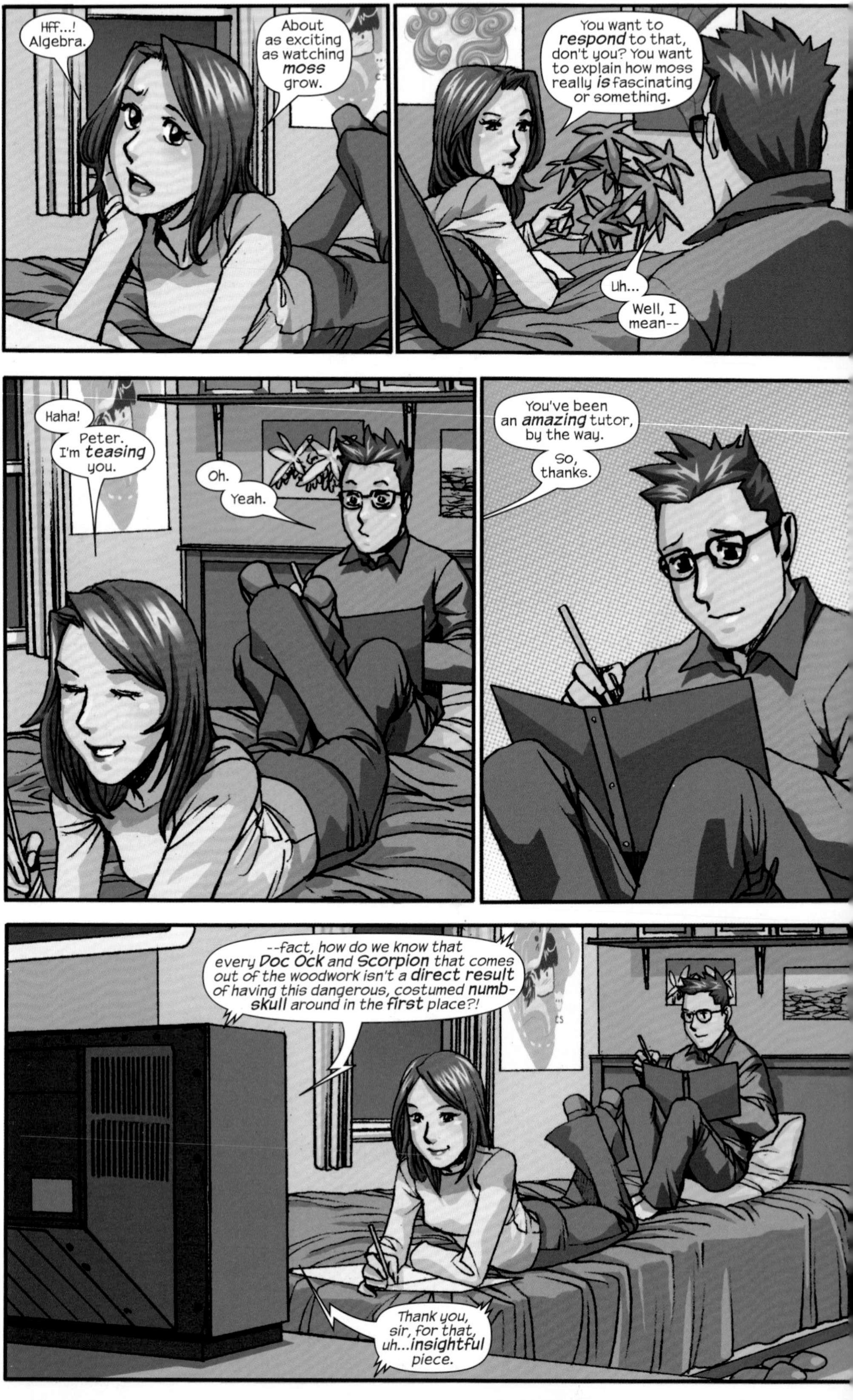
Hff...! Algebra.
About as exciting as watching moss grow.
You want to respond to that, don't you? You want to explain how moss really is fascinating or something.
Uh...
Well, I mean--
Haha!
Peter. I'm teasing you.
Oh.
Yeah.
You've been an amazing tutor, by the way.
So, thanks.
--fact, how do we know that every Doc Ock and Scorpion that comes out of the woodwork isn't a direct result of having this dangerous, costumed numb-skull around in the first place?!
Thank you, sir, for that, uh...insightful piece.

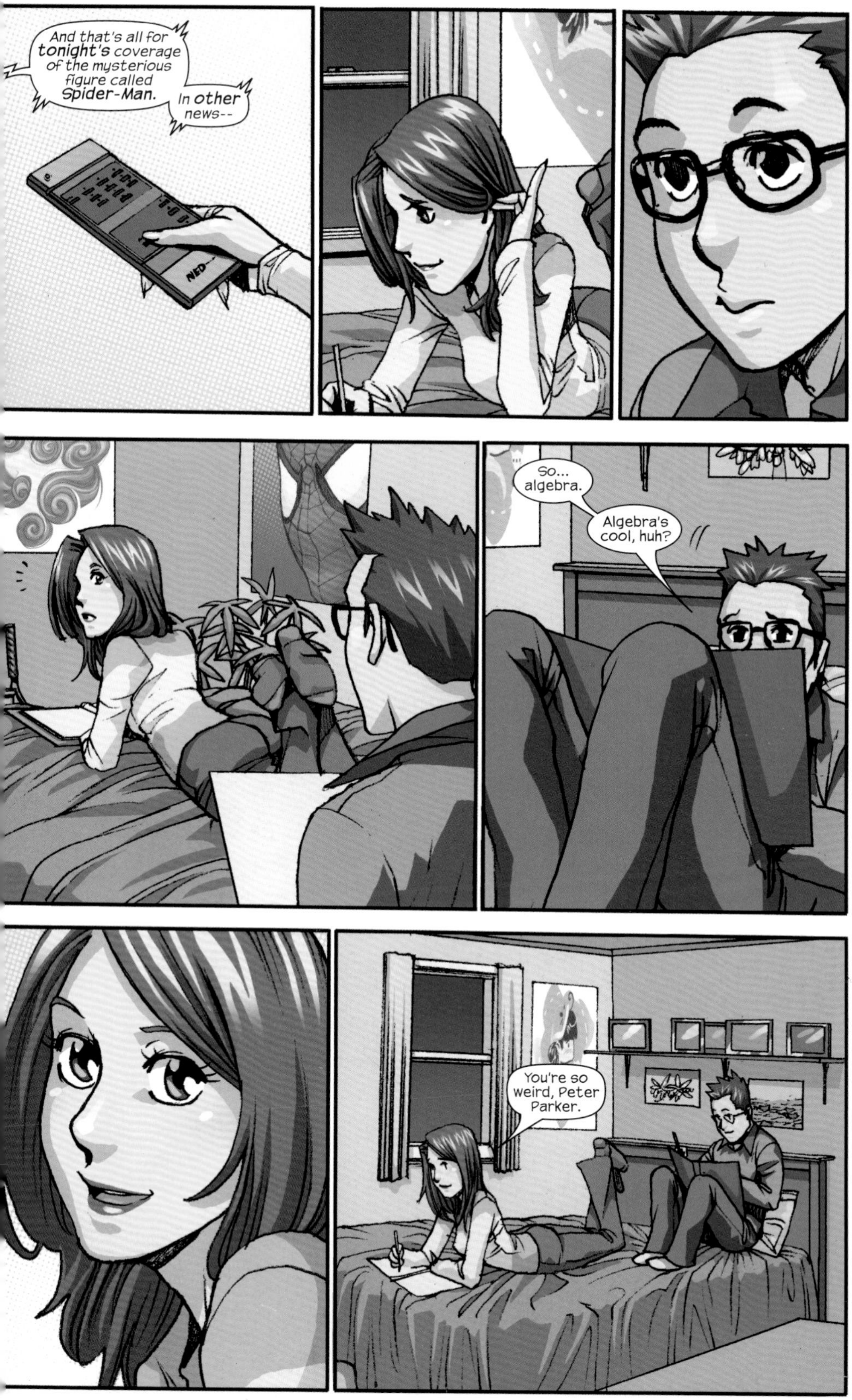

And that's all for tonight's coverage of the mysterious figure called Spider-Man.
In other news--
NED
So... algebra.
Algebra's cool, huh?
You're so weird, Peter Parker.

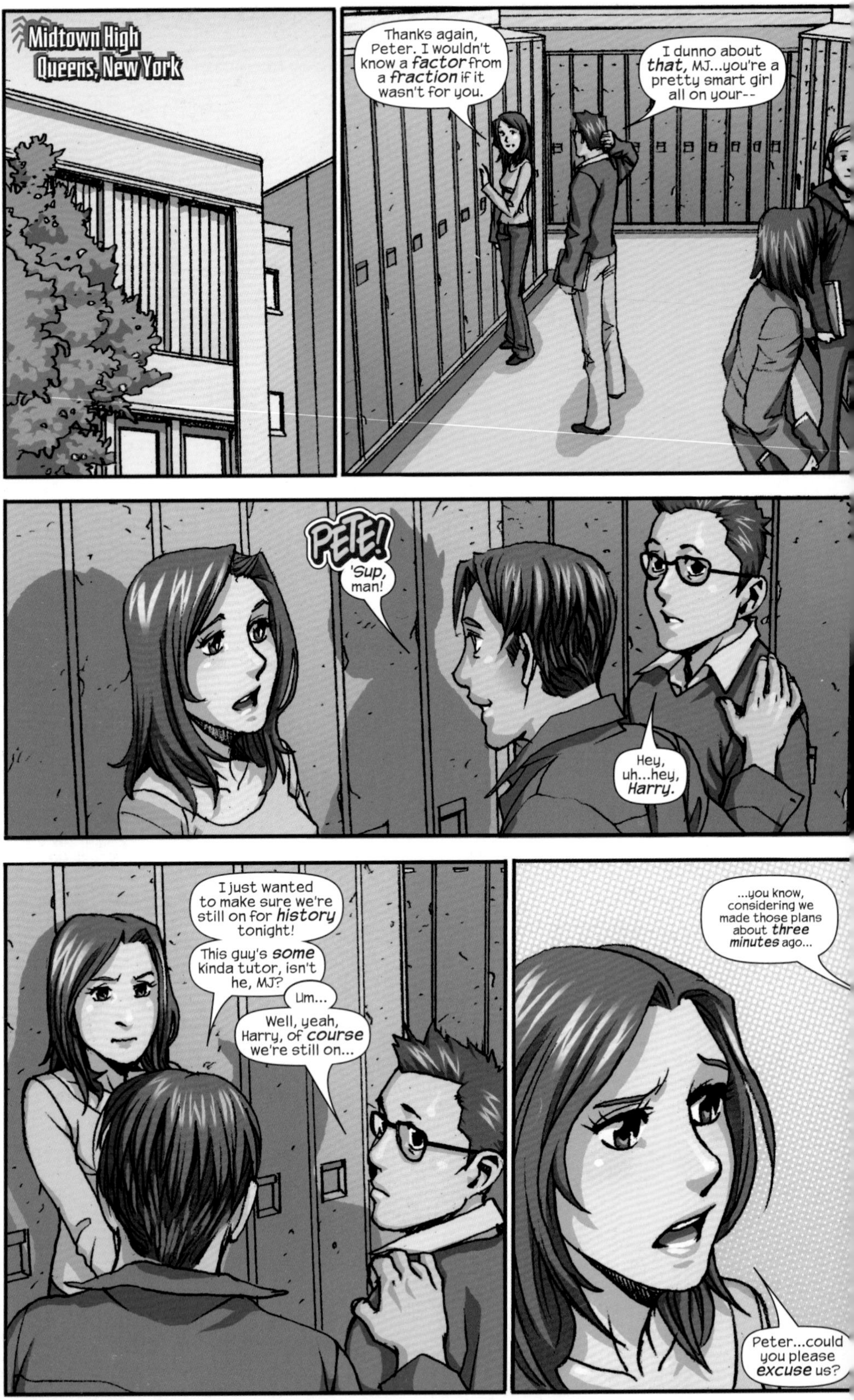
Midtown High
Queens, New York
Thanks again, Peter. I wouldn't know a *factor* from a *fraction* if it wasn't for you.
I dunno about *that*, MJ...you're a pretty smart girl all on your--
PETE!
'Sup, man!
Hey, uh...hey, *Harry*.
I just wanted to make sure we're still on for *history* tonight!
This guy's *some* kinda tutor, isn't he, MJ?
Um...
Well, yeah, Harry, of *course* we're still on...
...you know, considering we made those plans about *three minutes* ago...
Peter...could you please *excuse* us?

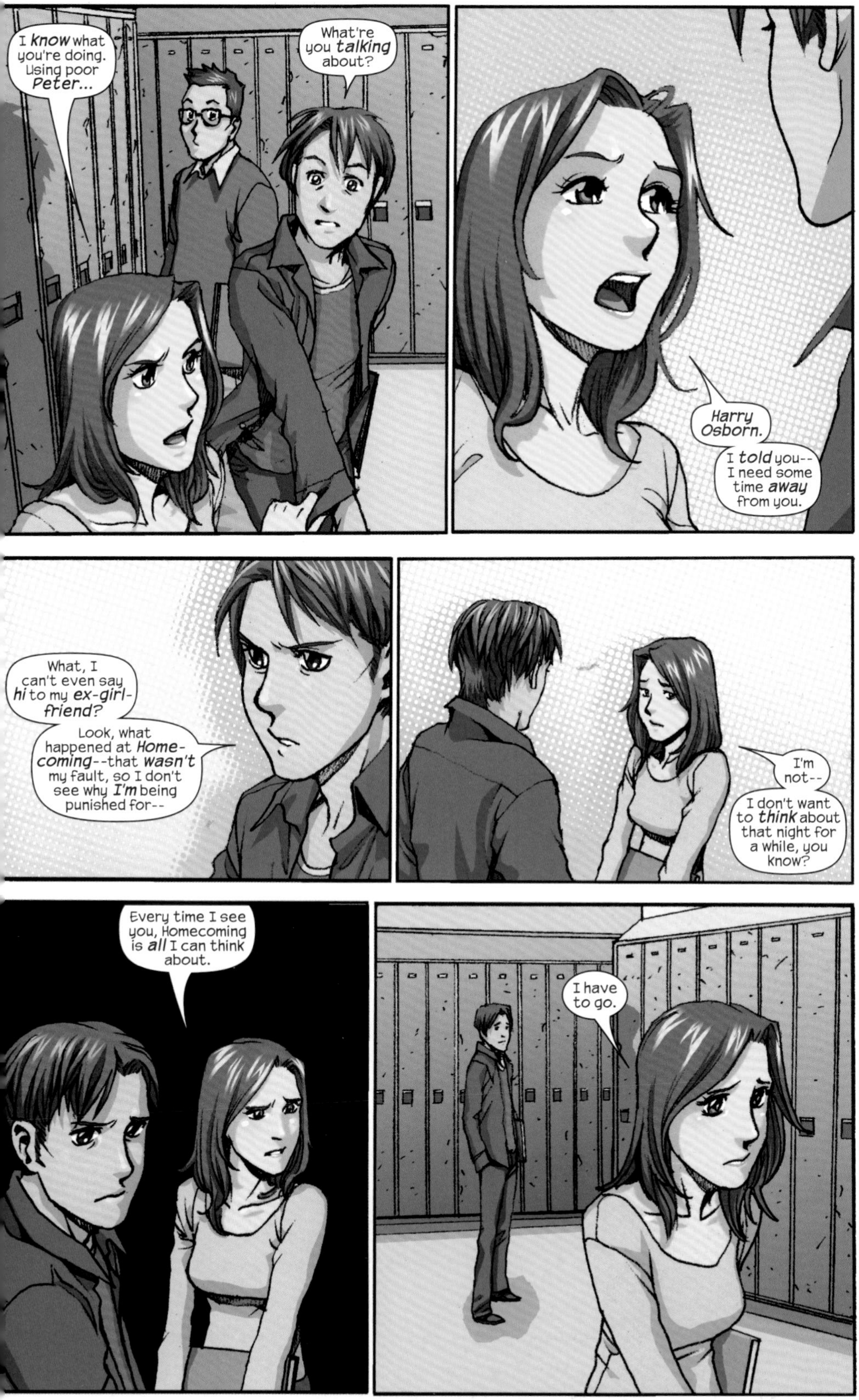
I know what you're doing. Using poor Peter...
What're you talking about?
Harry Osborn.
I told you-- I need some time away from you.
What, I can't even say hi to my ex-girl-friend?
Look, what happened at Home-coming--that wasn't my fault, so I don't see why I'm being punished for--
I'm not--
I don't want to think about that night for a while, you know?
Every time I see you, Homecoming is all I can think about.
I have to go.

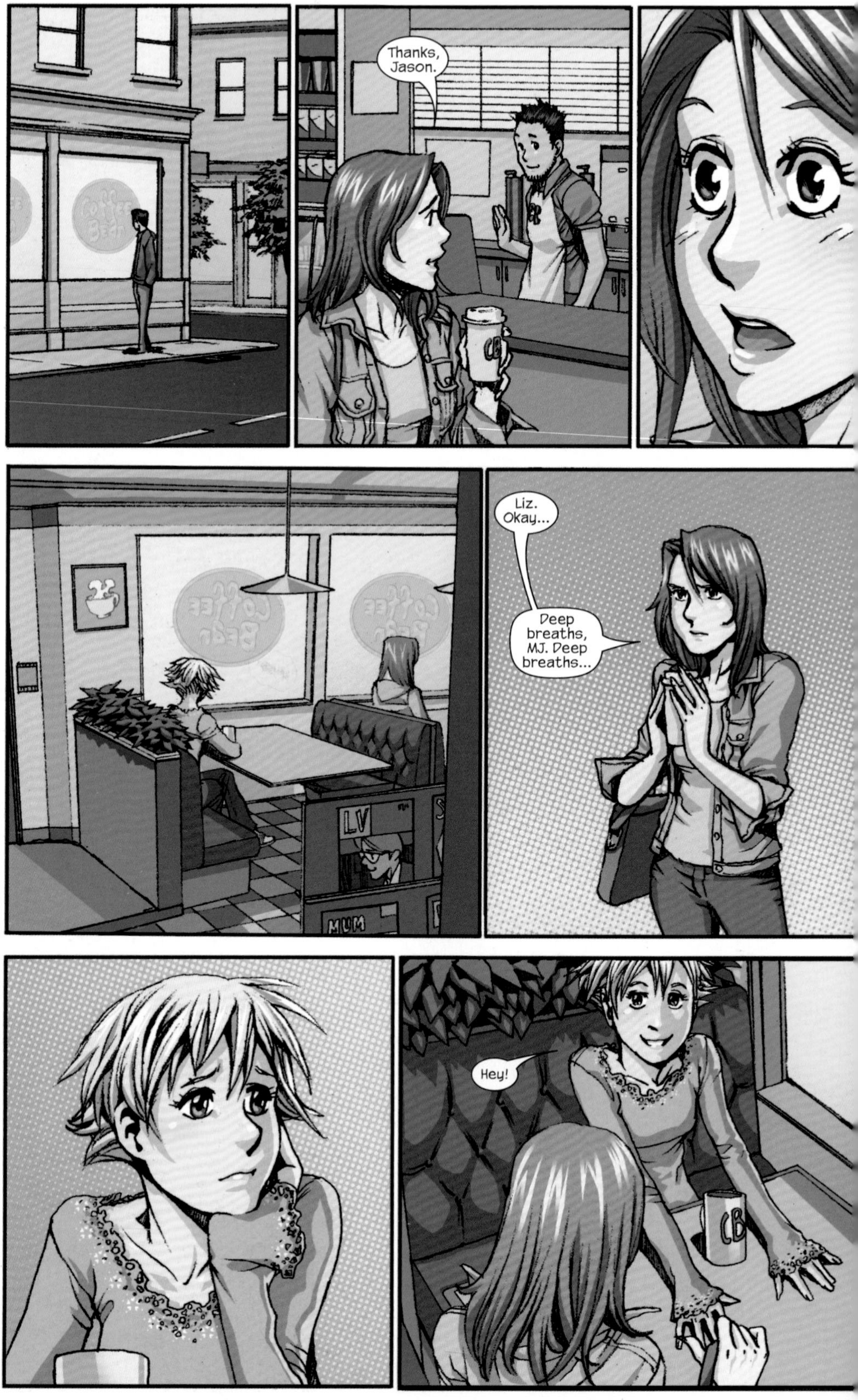
Thanks, Jason.
Liz. Okay...
Deep breaths, MJ. Deep breaths...
Hey!

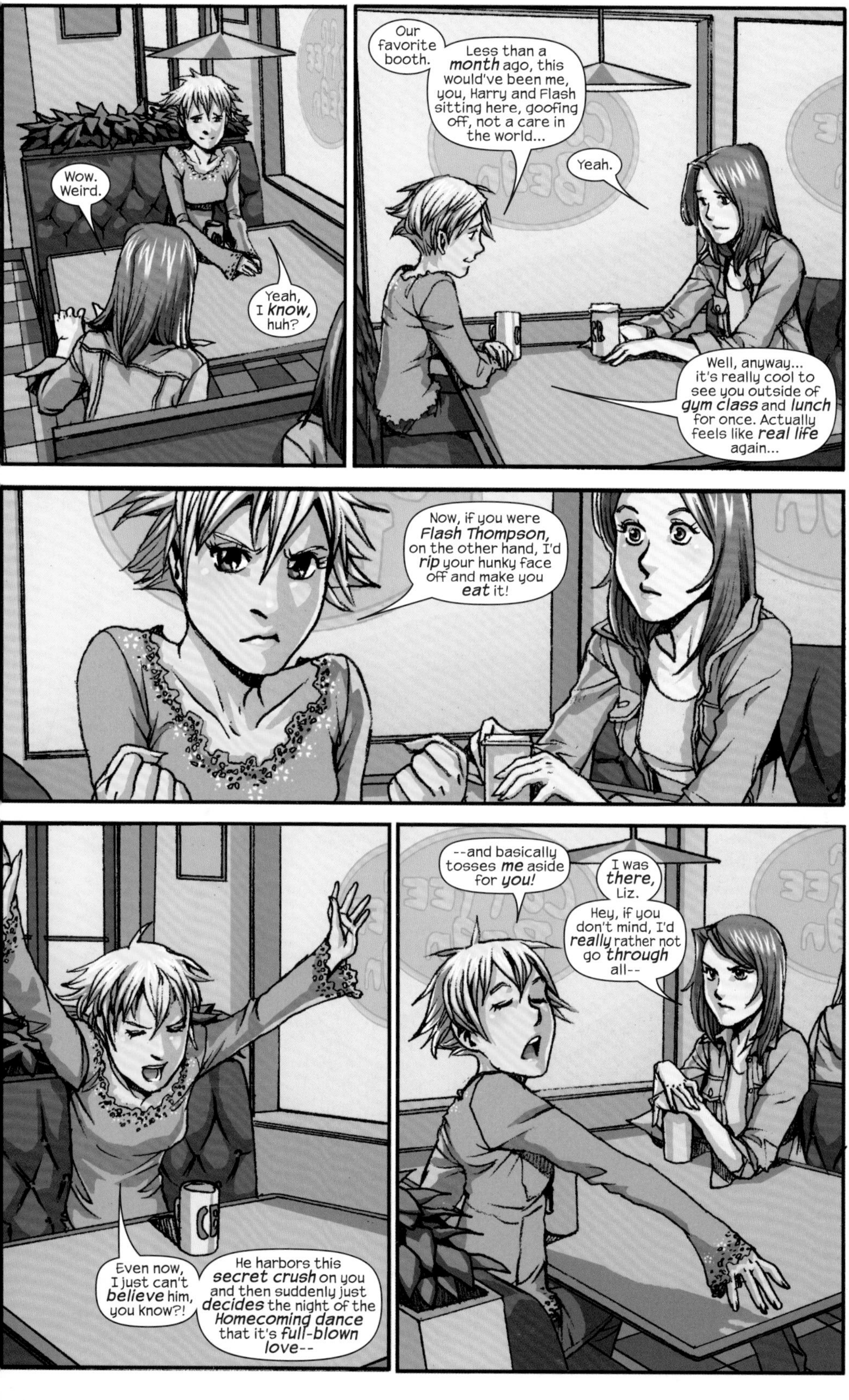
Wow. Weird.
Yeah, I know, huh?
Our favorite booth.
Less than a month ago, this would've been me, you, Harry and Flash sitting here, goofing off, not a care in the world...
Yeah.
Well, anyway... it's really cool to see you outside of gym class and lunch for once. Actually feels like real life again...
Now, if you were Flash Thompson, on the other hand, I'd rip your hunky face off and make you eat it!
Even now, I just can't believe him, you know?!
He harbors this secret crush on you and then suddenly just decides the night of the Homecoming dance that it's full-blown love--
--and basically tosses me aside for you!
I was there, Liz.
Hey, if you don't mind, I'd really rather not go through all--

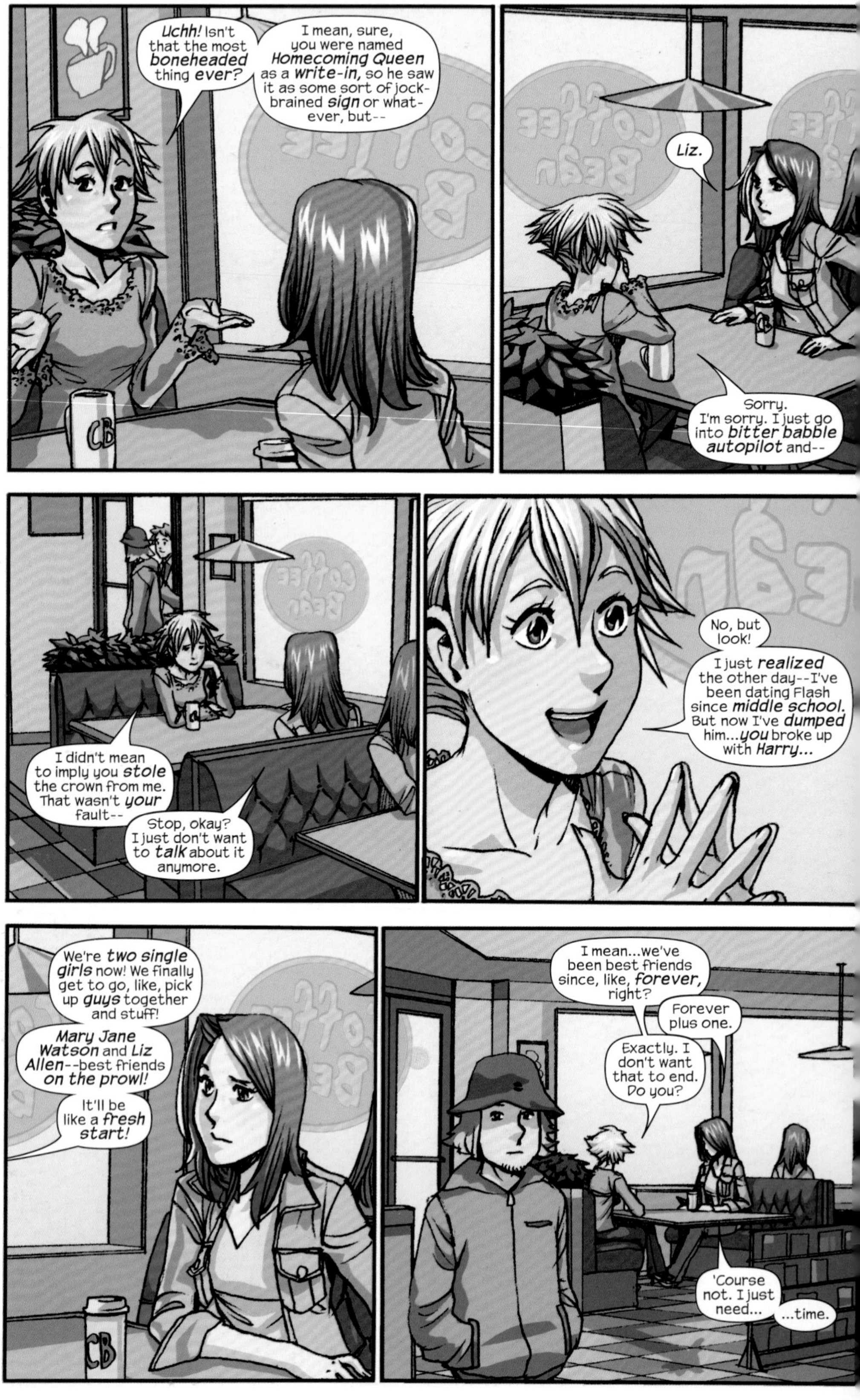
Uchh! Isn't that the most boneheaded thing ever?
I mean, sure, you were named Homecoming Queen as a write-in, so he saw it as some sort of jock-brained sign or whatever, but--
Liz.
Sorry. I'm sorry. I just go into bitter babble autopilot and--
I didn't mean to imply you stole the crown from me. That wasn't your fault--
Stop, okay? I just don't want to talk about it anymore.
No, but look!
I just realized the other day--I've been dating Flash since middle school. But now I've dumped him...you broke up with Harry...
We're two single girls now! We finally get to go, like, pick up guys together and stuff!
Mary Jane Watson and Liz Allen--best friends on the prowl!
It'll be like a fresh start!
I mean...we've been best friends since, like, forever, right?
Forever plus one.
Exactly. I don't want that to end. Do you?
'Course not. I just need...
...time.

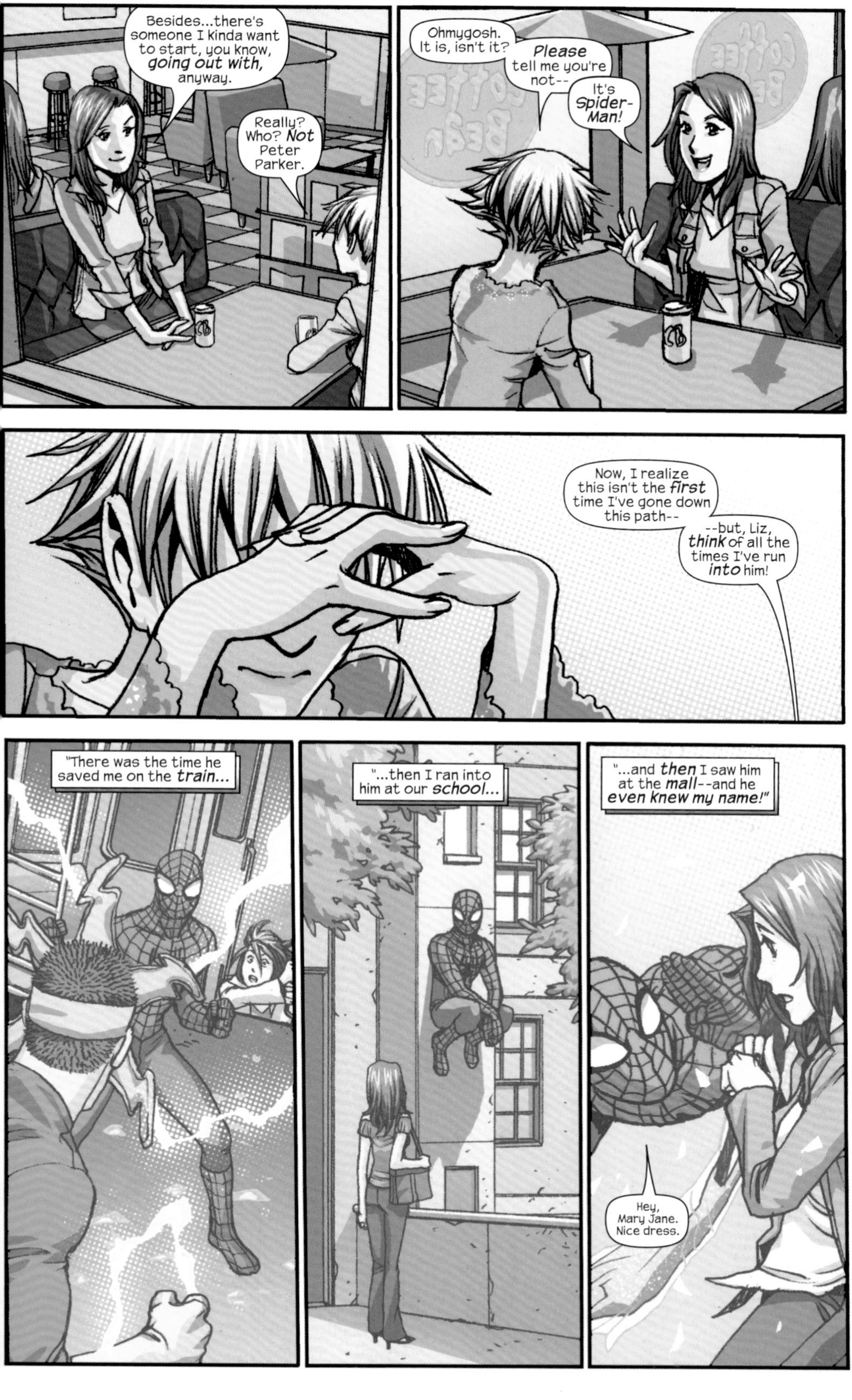

Besides...there's someone I kinda want to start, you know, going out with, anyway.
Really? Who? Not Peter Parker.
Ohmygosh. It is, isn't it?
Please tell me you're not--
It's Spider-Man!
Now, I realize this isn't the first time I've gone down this path--
--but, Liz, think of all the times I've run into him!
"There was the time he saved me on the train...
"...then I ran into him at our school...
"...and then I saw him at the mall--and he even knew my name!"
Hey, Mary Jane. Nice dress.

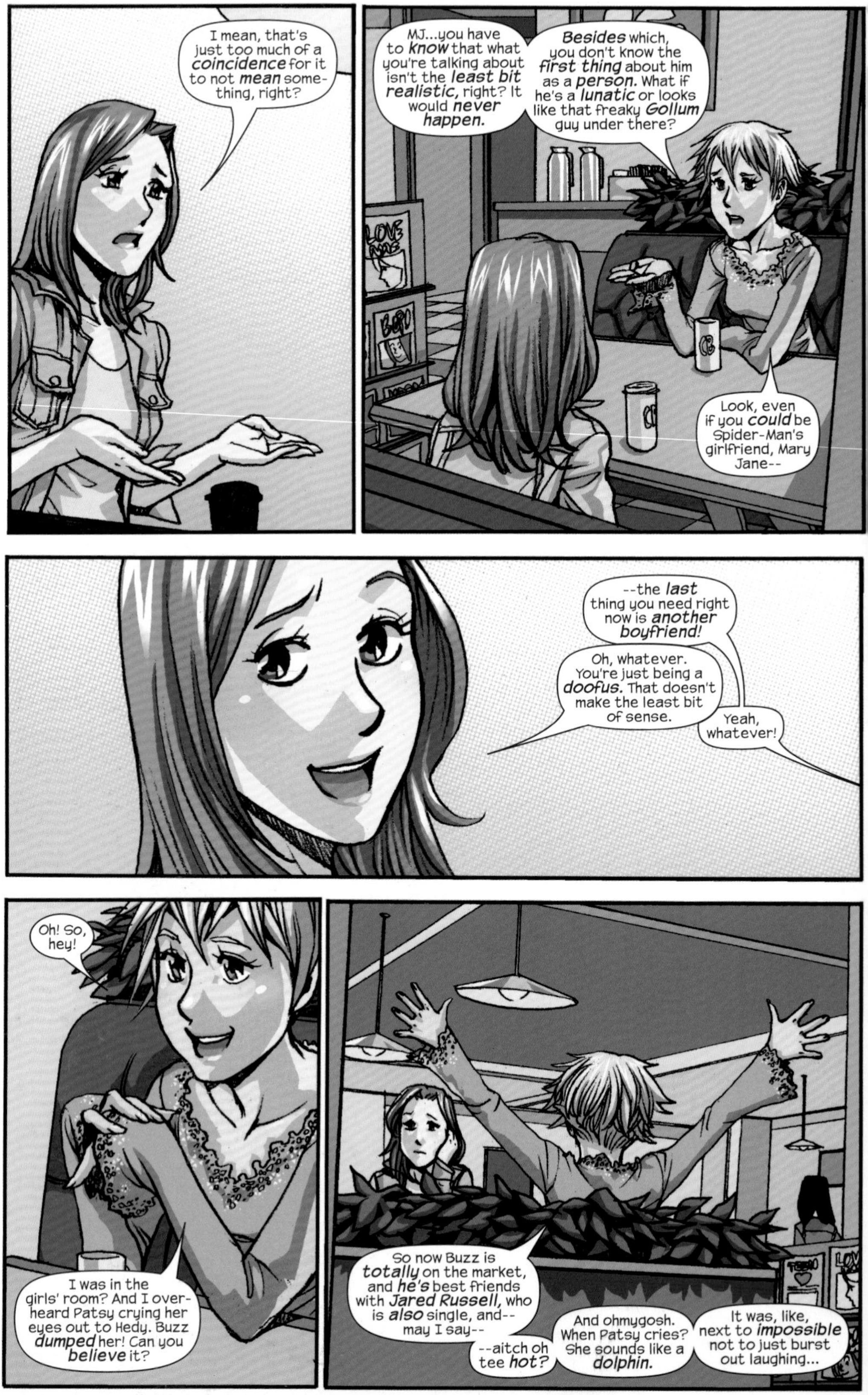

I mean, that's just too much of a coincidence for it to not mean something, right?
MJ...you have to know that what you're talking about isn't the least bit realistic, right? It would never happen.
Besides which, you don't know the first thing about him as a person. What if he's a lunatic or looks like that freaky Gollum guy under there?
Look, even if you could be Spider-Man's girlfriend, Mary Jane--
--the last thing you need right now is another boyfriend!
Oh, whatever. You're just being a doofus. That doesn't make the least bit of sense.
Yeah, whatever!
Oh! So, hey!
I was in the girls' room? And I overheard Patsy crying her eyes out to Hedy. Buzz dumped her! Can you believe it?
So now Buzz is totally on the market, and he's best friends with Jared Russell, who is also single, and--may I say--
--aitch oh tee hot?
And ohmygosh. When Patsy cries? She sounds like a dolphin.
It was, like, next to impossible not to just burst out laughing...

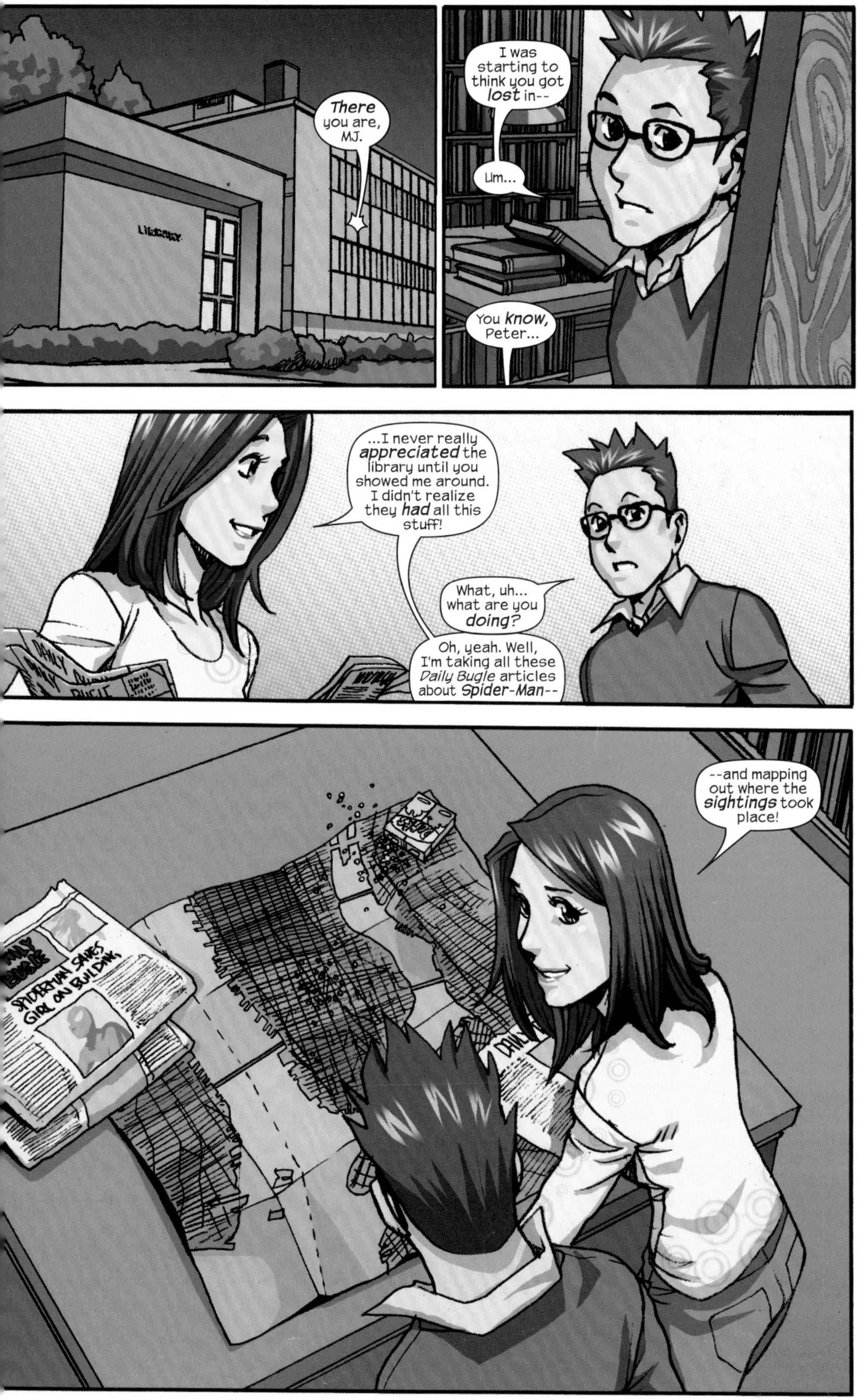

LIBRARY
There you are, MJ.
I was starting to think you got lost in--
Um...
You know, Peter...
...I never really appreciated the library until you showed me around. I didn't realize they had all this stuff!
What, uh... what are you doing?
Oh, yeah. Well, I'm taking all these Daily Bugle articles about Spider-Man--
--and mapping out where the sightings took place!
SPIDERMAN SAVES GIRL ON BUILDING

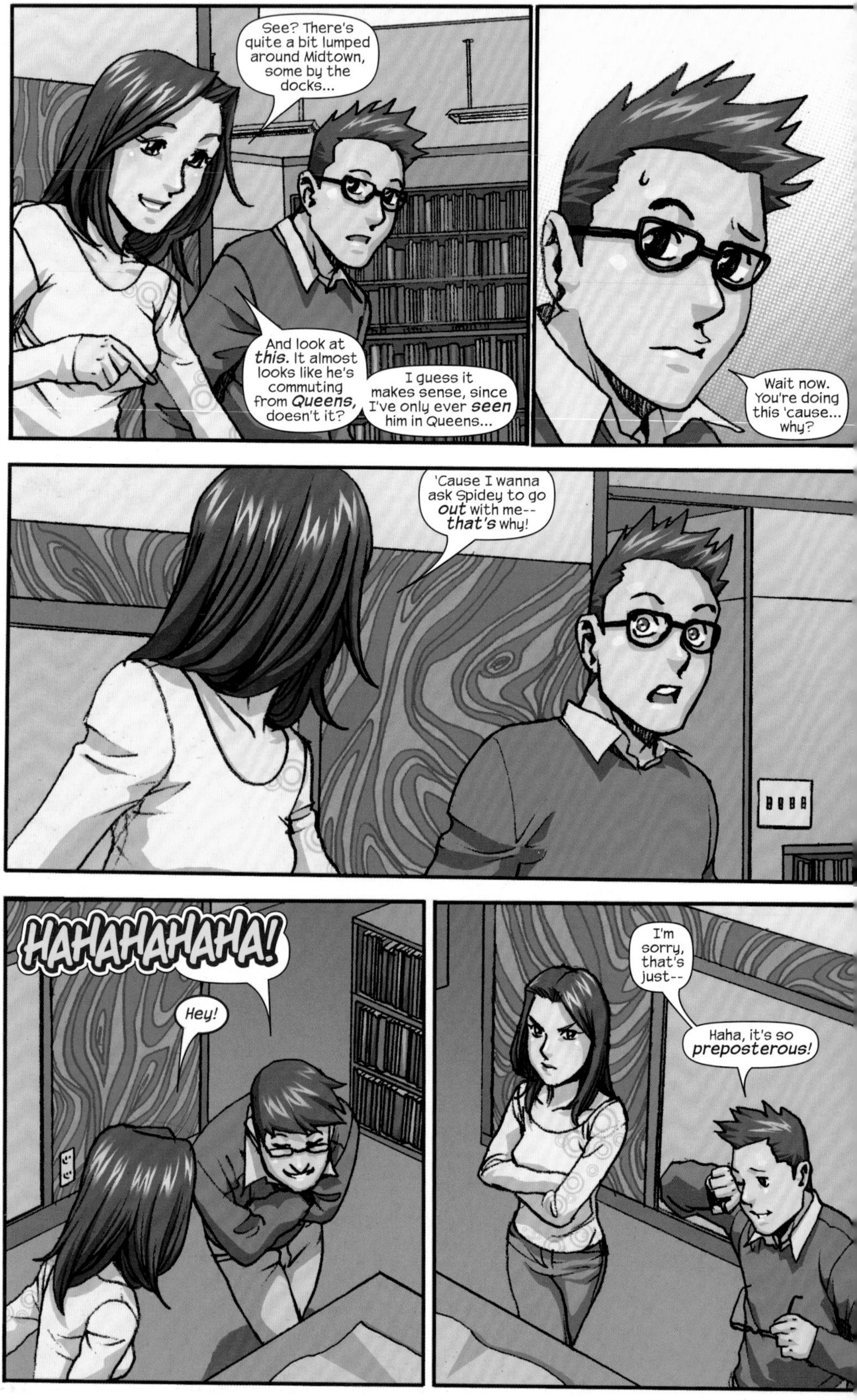
See? There's quite a bit lumped around Midtown, some by the docks...
And look at *this.* It almost looks like he's commuting from *Queens,* doesn't it?
I guess it makes sense, since I've only ever *seen* him in Queens...
Wait now. You're doing this 'cause... why?
'Cause I wanna ask Spidey to go *out* with me-- *that's* why!
HAHAHAHAHA!
Hey!
I'm sorry, that's just--
Haha, it's so *preposterous!*

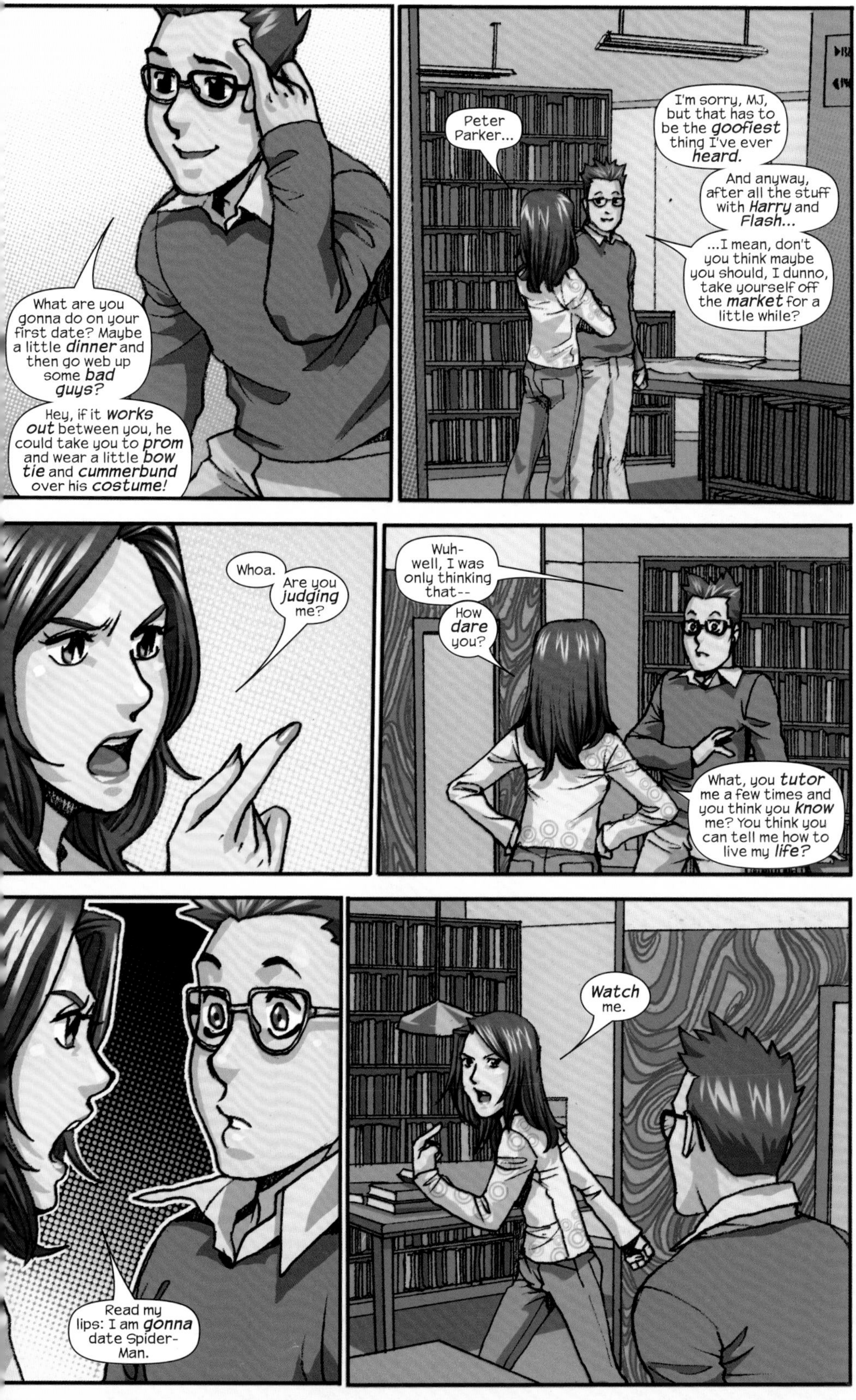
What are you gonna do on your first date? Maybe a little dinner and then go web up some bad guys?
Hey, if it works out between you, he could take you to prom and wear a little bow tie and cummerbund over his costume!
Peter Parker...
I'm sorry, MJ, but that has to be the goofiest thing I've ever heard.
And anyway, after all the stuff with Harry and Flash...
...I mean, don't you think maybe you should, I dunno, take yourself off the market for a little while?
Whoa.
Are you judging me?
Wuh-well, I was only thinking that--
How dare you?
What, you tutor me a few times and you think you know me? You think you can tell me how to live my life?
Read my lips: I am gonna date Spider-Man.
Watch me.

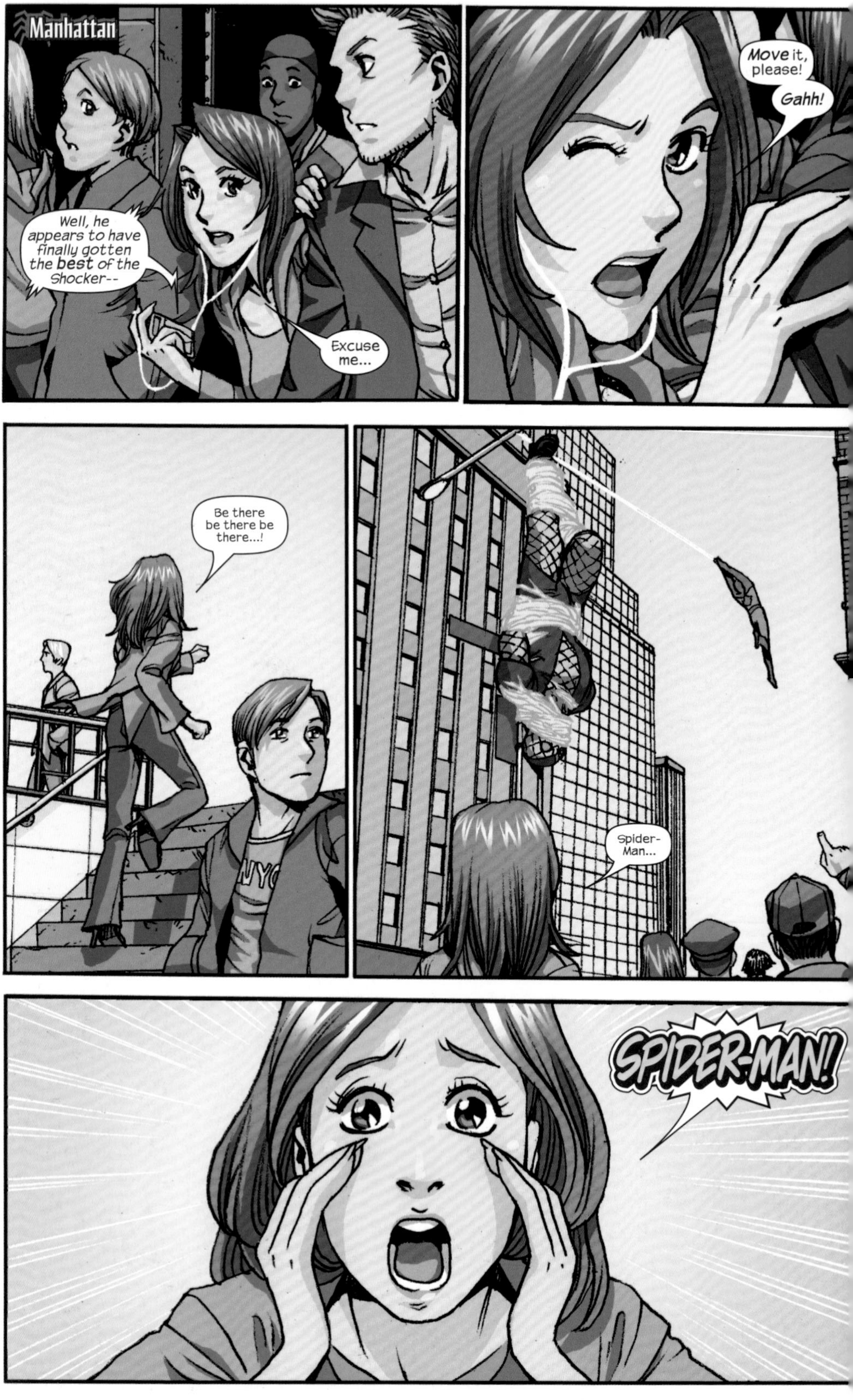
Manhattan
Well, he appears to have finally gotten the best of the Shocker--
Excuse me...
Move it, please!
Gahh!
Be there be there be there...!
Spider-Man...
SPIDER-MAN!

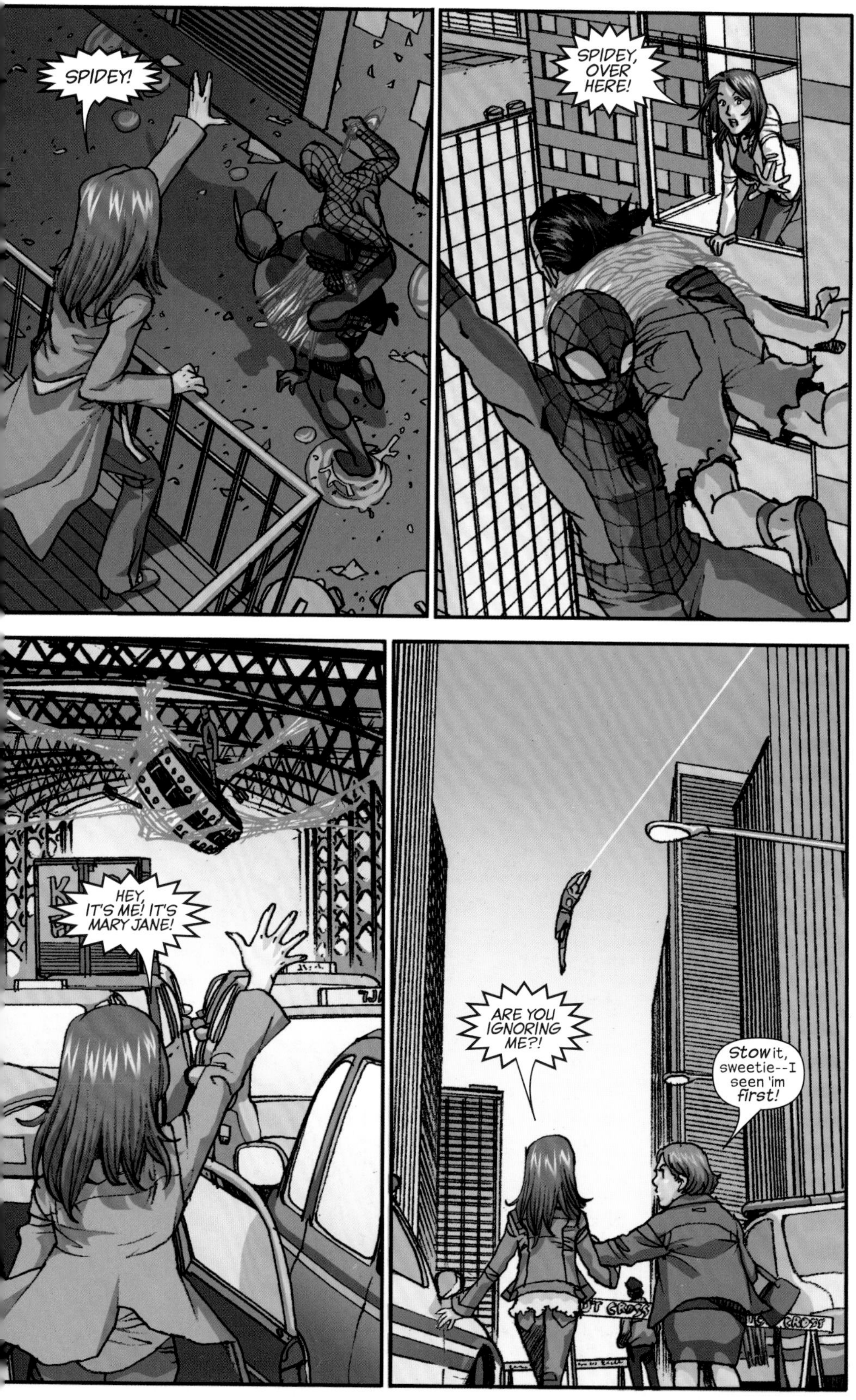
SPIDEY!
SPIDEY, OVER HERE!
HEY, IT'S ME! IT'S MARY JANE!
ARE YOU IGNORING ME?!
Stow it, sweetie--I seen 'im first!

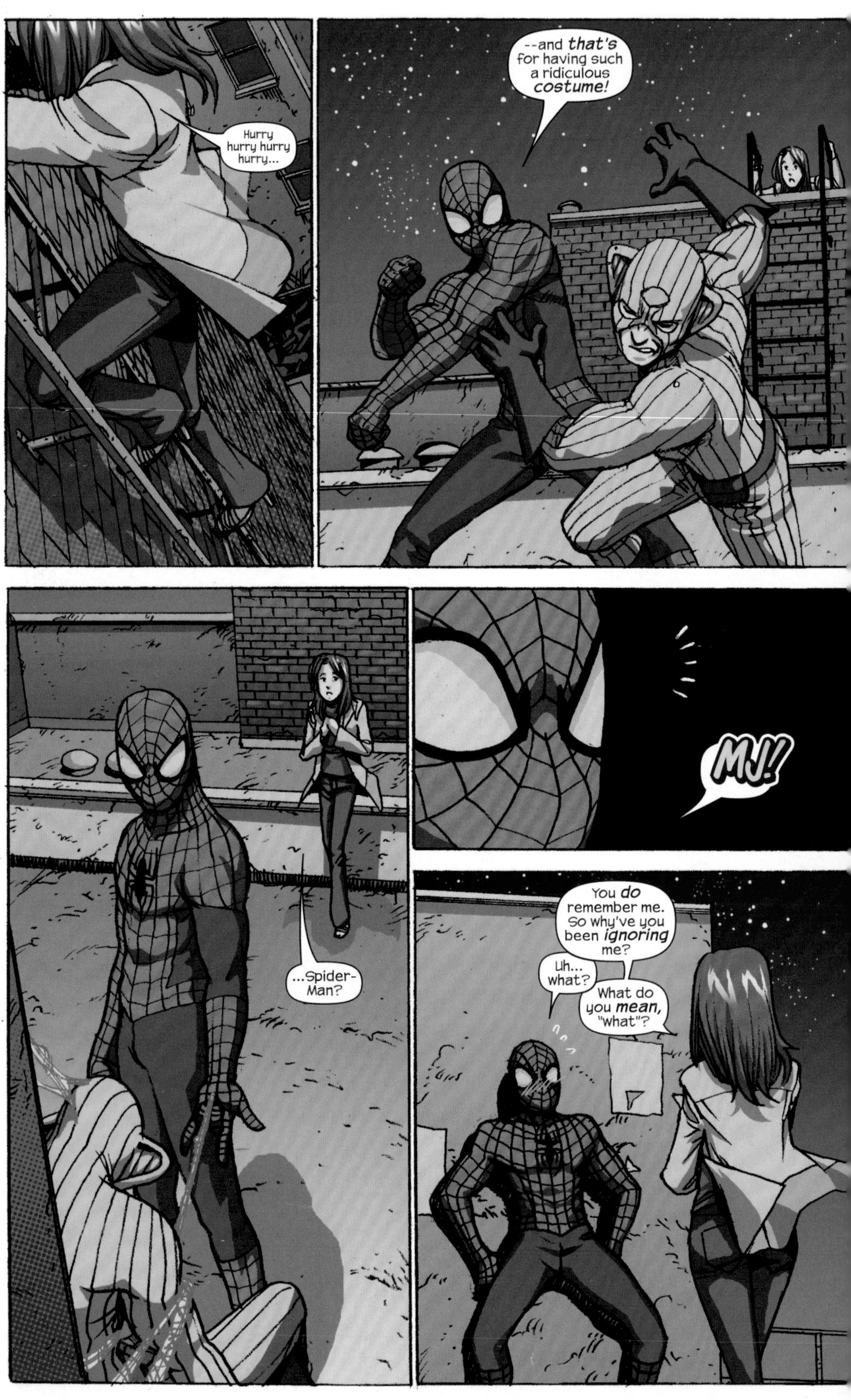
Hurry hurry hurry hurry...
--and that's for having such a ridiculous costume!
...Spider-Man?
MJ!
You do remember me. So why've you been ignoring me?
Uh... what?
What do you mean, "what"?

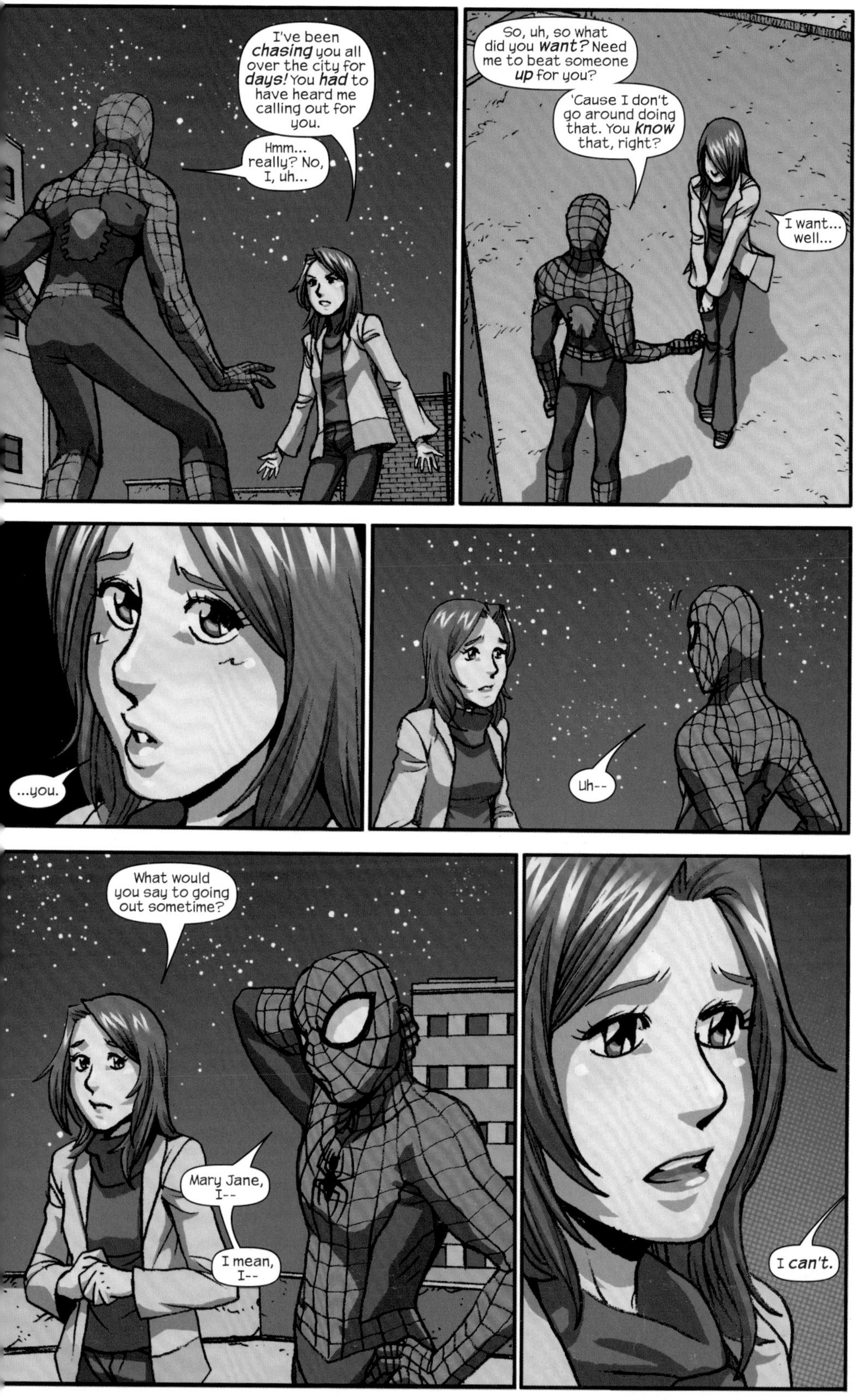
I've been chasing you all over the city for days! You had to have heard me calling out for you.
Hmm... really? No, I, uh...
So, uh, so what did you want? Need me to beat someone up for you?
'Cause I don't go around doing that. You know that, right?
I want... well...
...you.
Uh--
What would you say to going out sometime?
Mary Jane, I--
I mean, I--
I can't.

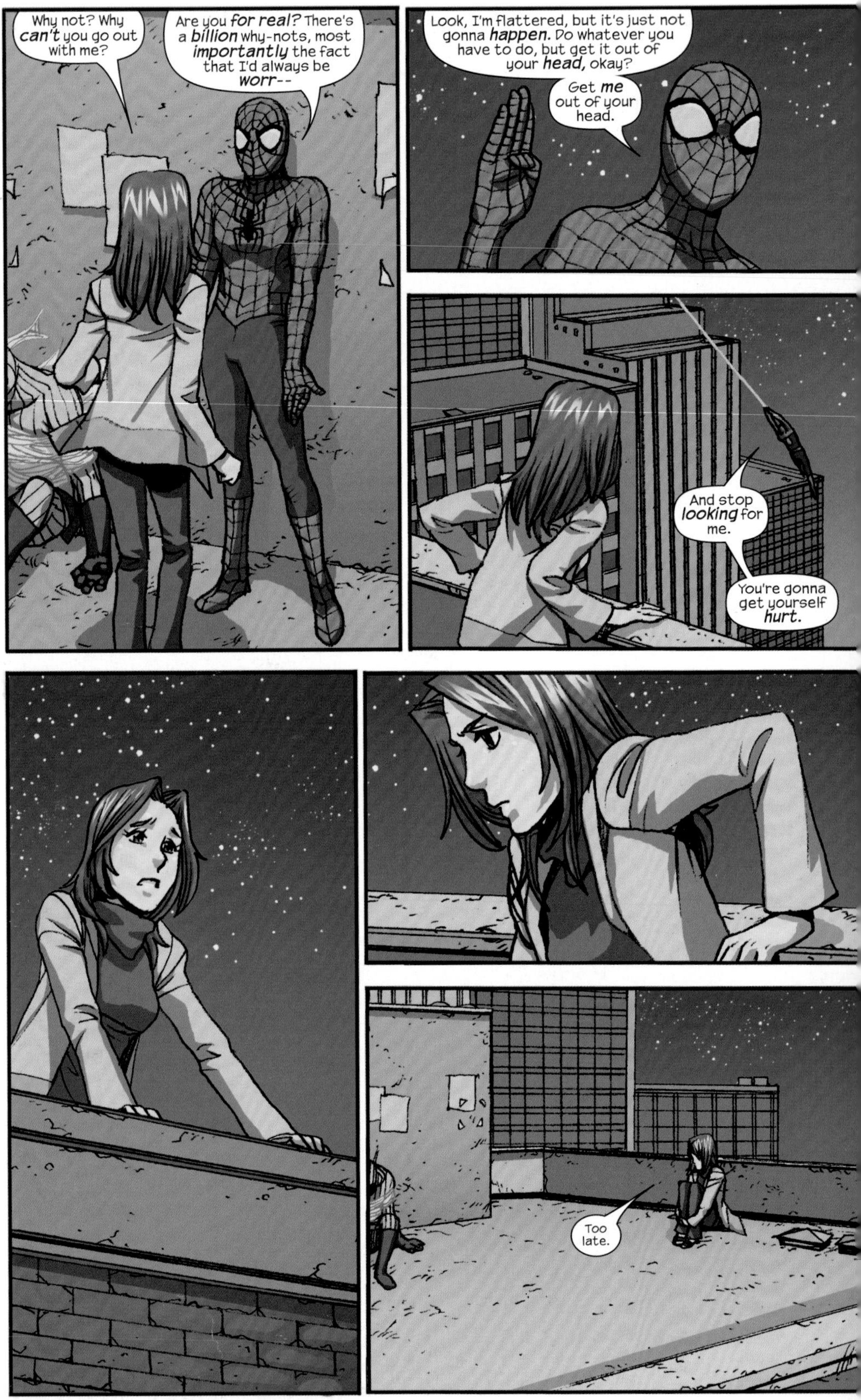

Why not? Why *can't* you go out with me?
Are you *for real?* There's a *billion* why-nots, most *importantly* the fact that I'd always be *worr*--
Look, I'm flattered, but it's just not gonna *happen.* Do whatever you have to do, but get it out of your *head,* okay?
Get *me* out of your head.
And stop *looking* for me.
You're gonna get yourself *hurt.*
Too late.

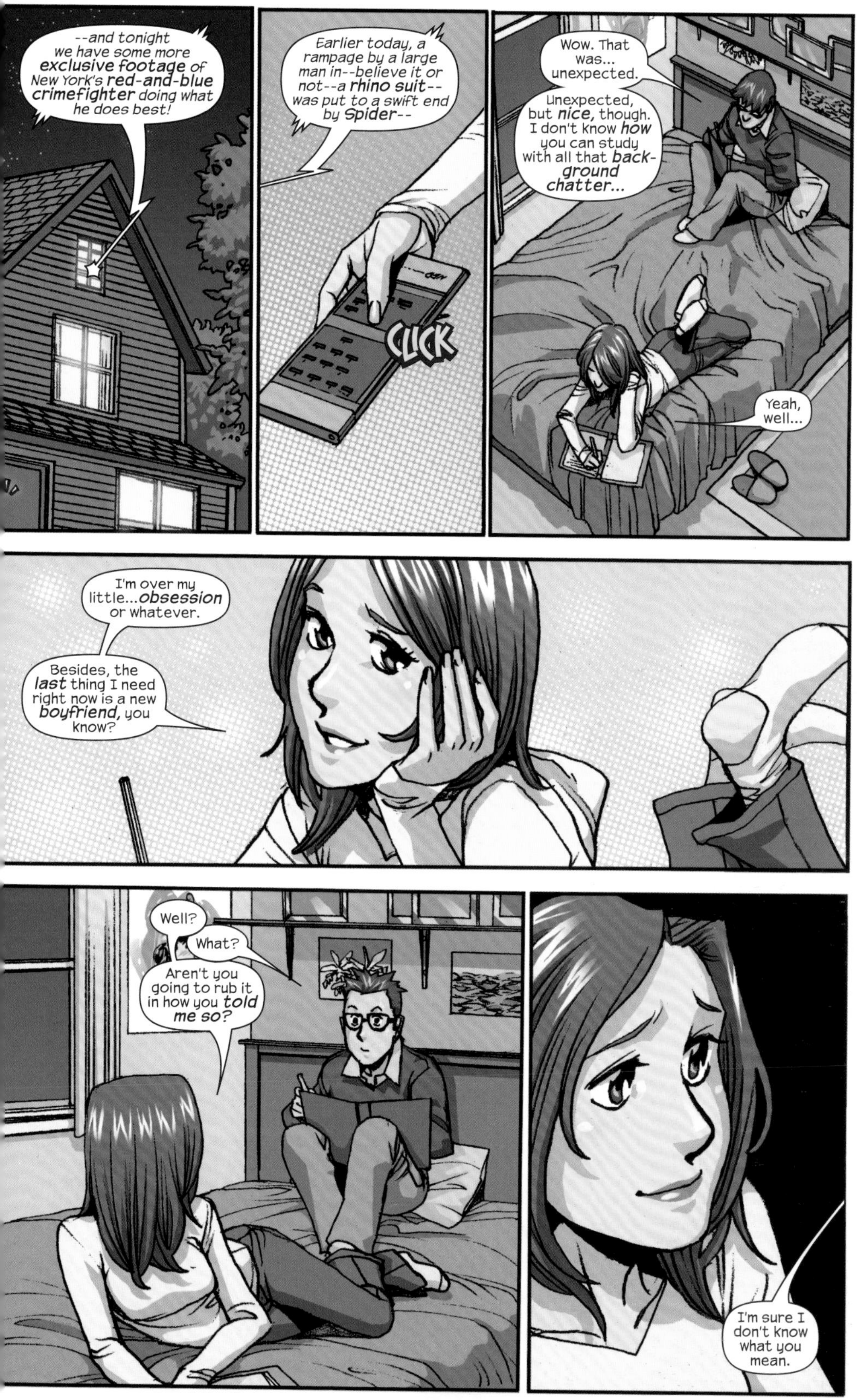
--and tonight we have some more exclusive footage of New York's red-and-blue crimefighter doing what he does best!
Earlier today, a rampage by a large man in--believe it or not--a rhino suit--was put to a swift end by Spider--
CLICK
Wow. That was... unexpected.
Unexpected, but nice, though. I don't know how you can study with all that back-ground chatter...
Yeah, well...
I'm over my little...obsession or whatever.
Besides, the last thing I need right now is a new boyfriend, you know?
Well?
What?
Aren't you going to rub it in how you told me so?
I'm sure I don't know what you mean.

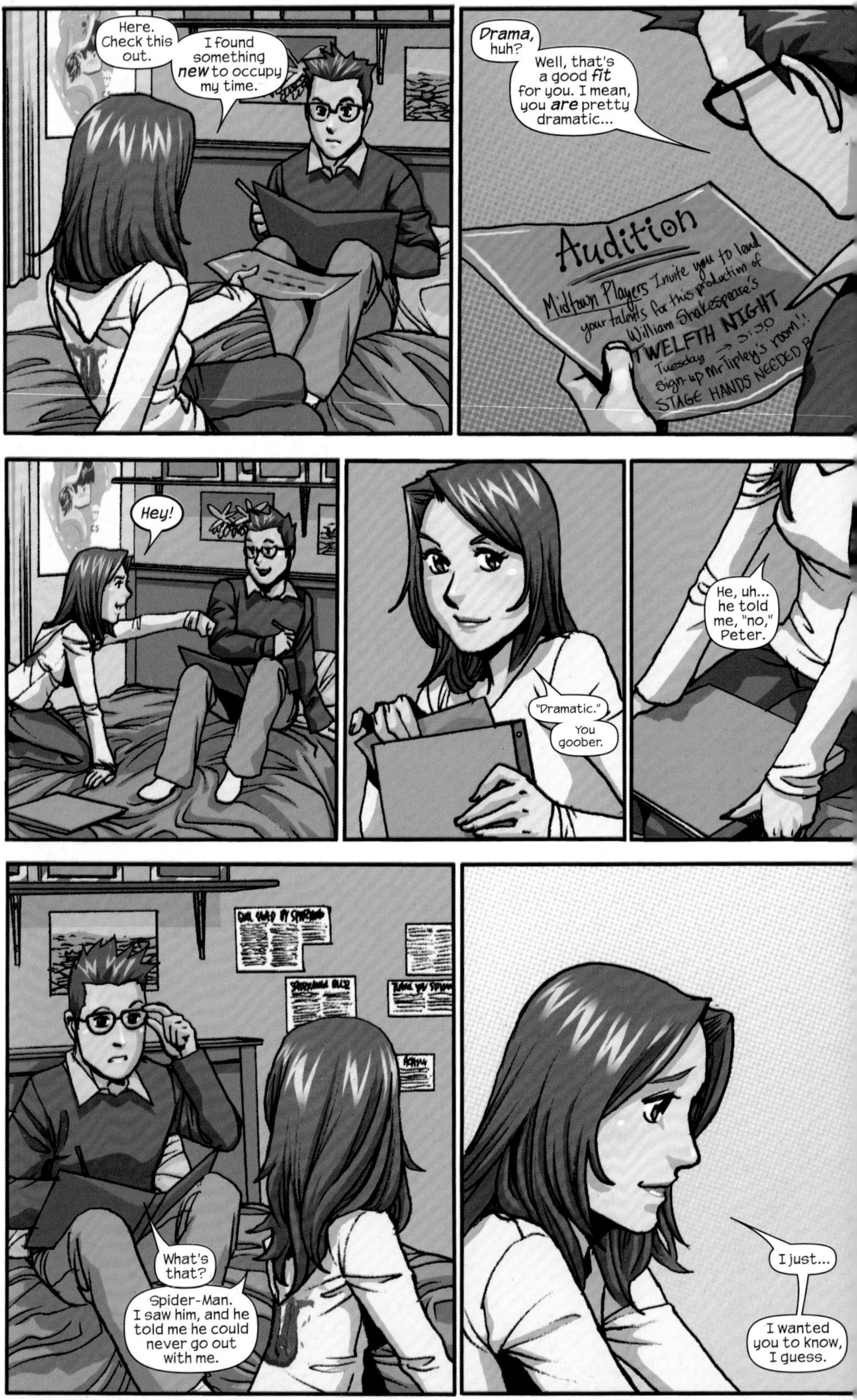
Here. Check this out.
I found something *new* to occupy my time.
Drama, huh?
Well, that's a good *fit* for you. I mean, you *are* pretty dramatic...
Audition
Midtown Players Invite you to lend your talents for this production of William Shakespeare's
TWELFTH NIGHT
Tuesday → 3:30
Sign-up Mr.Tipley's room!!
STAGE HANDS NEEDED
Hey!
"Dramatic." You goober.
He, uh... he told me, "no," Peter.
What's that?
Spider-Man. I saw him, and he told me he could never go out with me.
I just...
I wanted you to know, I guess.

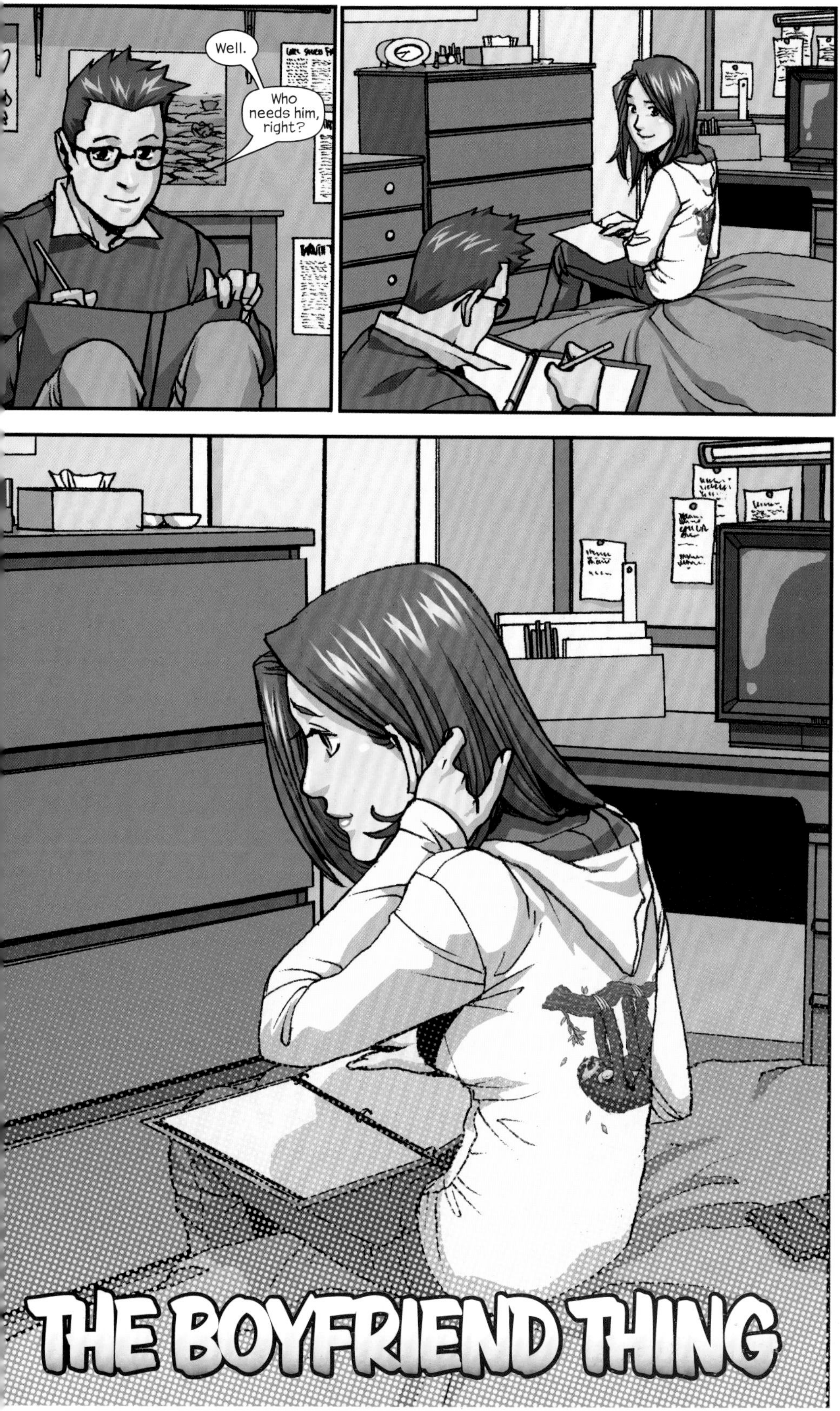

Well.
Who needs him, right?
THE BOYFRIEND THING

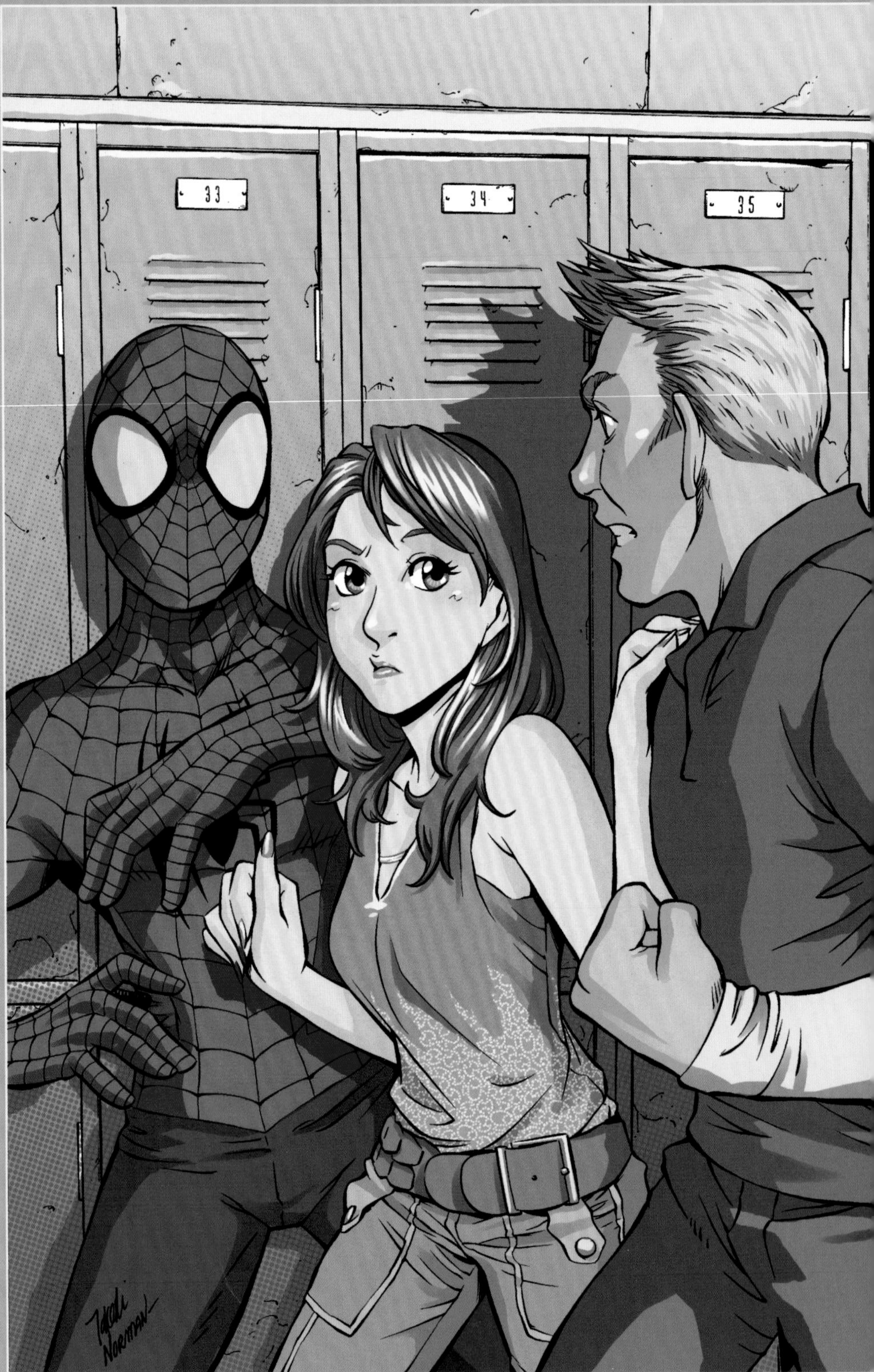
33
34
35

Spider-Man Loves Mary Jane #2

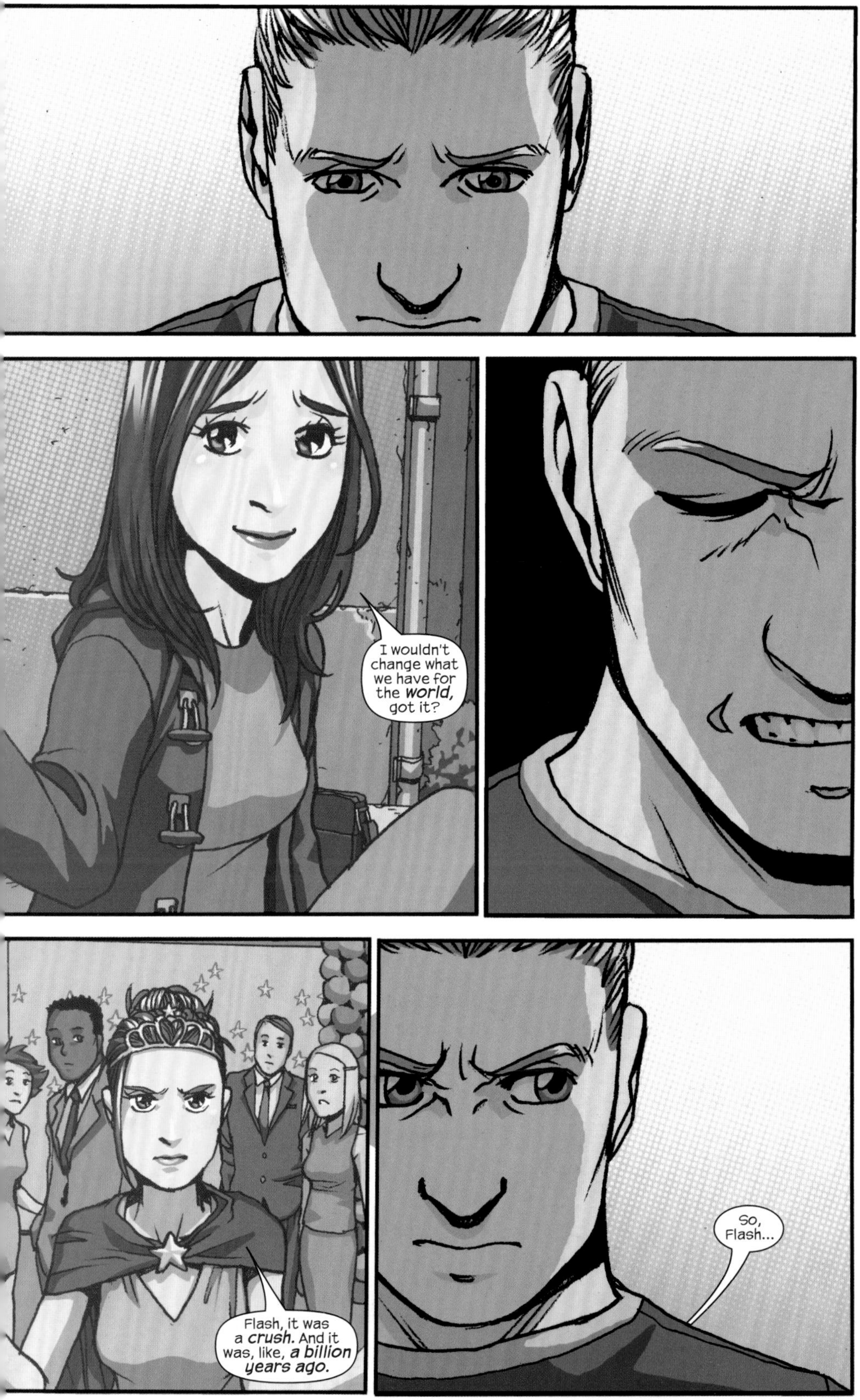
I wouldn't change what we have for the *world,* got it?
Flash, it was a *crush.* And it was, like, *a billion years ago.*
So, Flash...

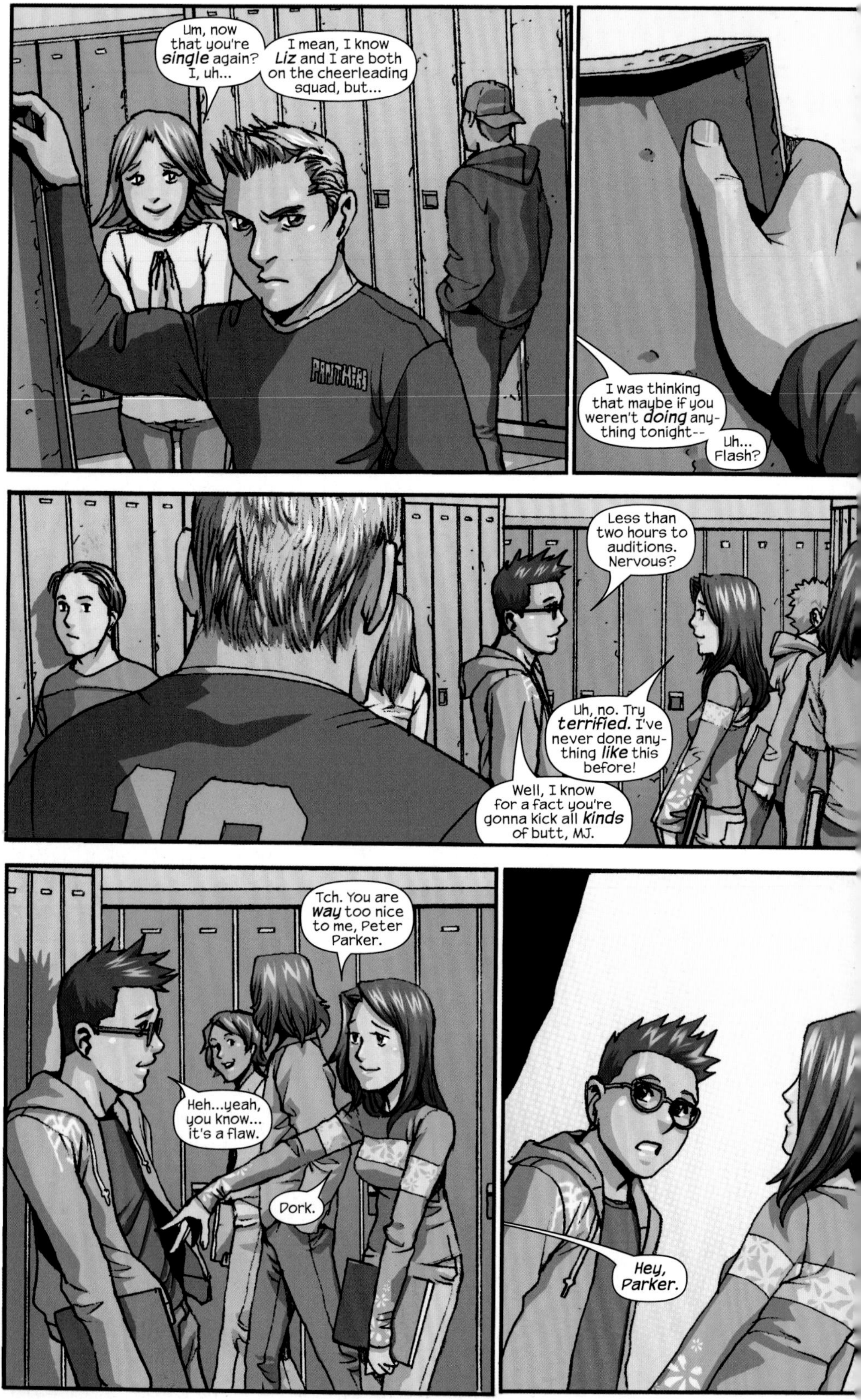
Um, now that you're *single* again? I, uh...
I mean, I know *Liz* and I are both on the cheerleading squad, but...
I was thinking that maybe if you weren't *doing* anything tonight--
Uh... Flash?
Less than two hours to auditions. Nervous?
Uh, no. Try *terrified.* I've never done anything *like* this before!
Well, I know for a fact you're gonna kick all *kinds* of butt, MJ.
Tch. You are *way* too nice to me, Peter Parker.
Heh...yeah, you know... it's a flaw.
Dork.
Hey, Parker.

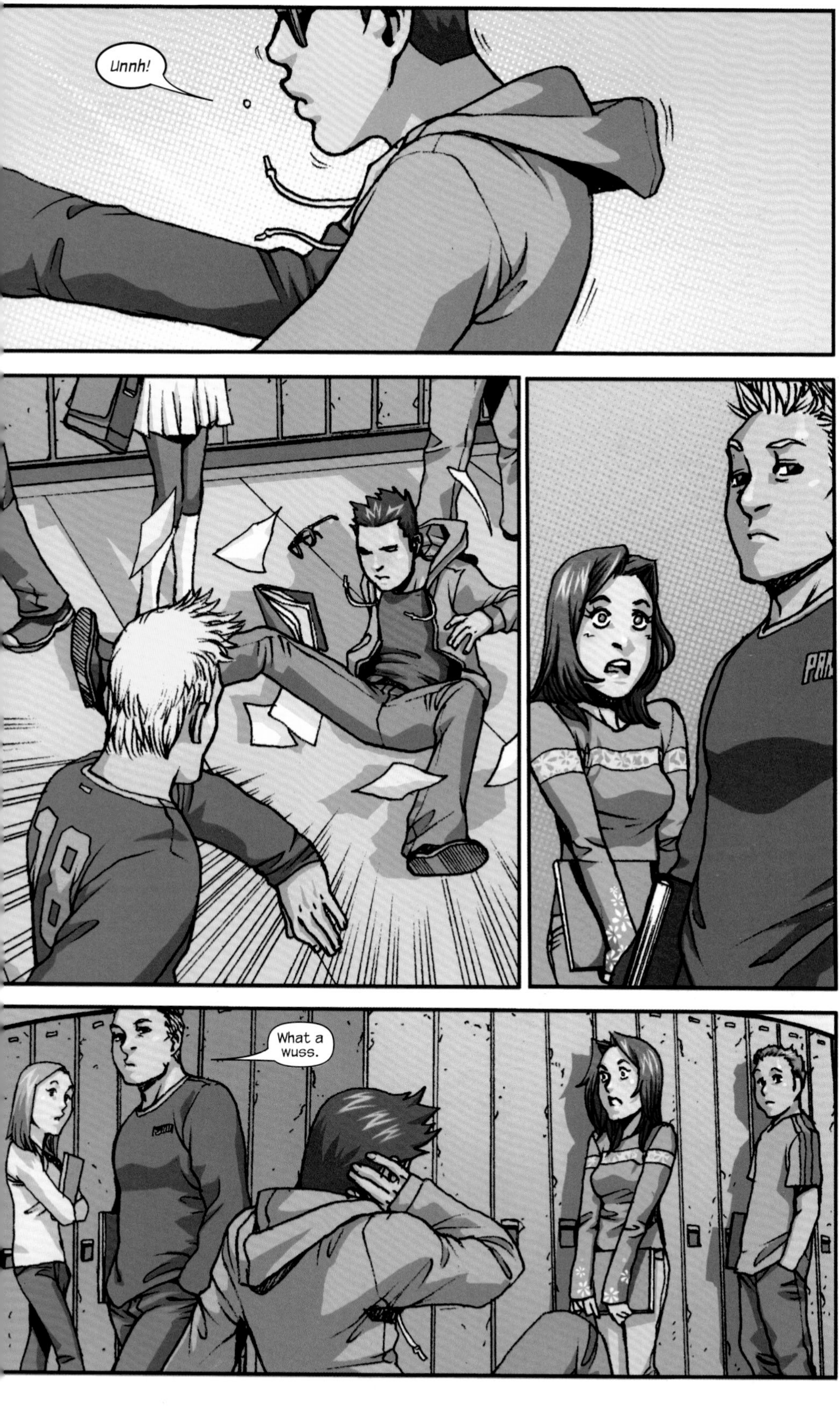
Unnh!
What a wuss.

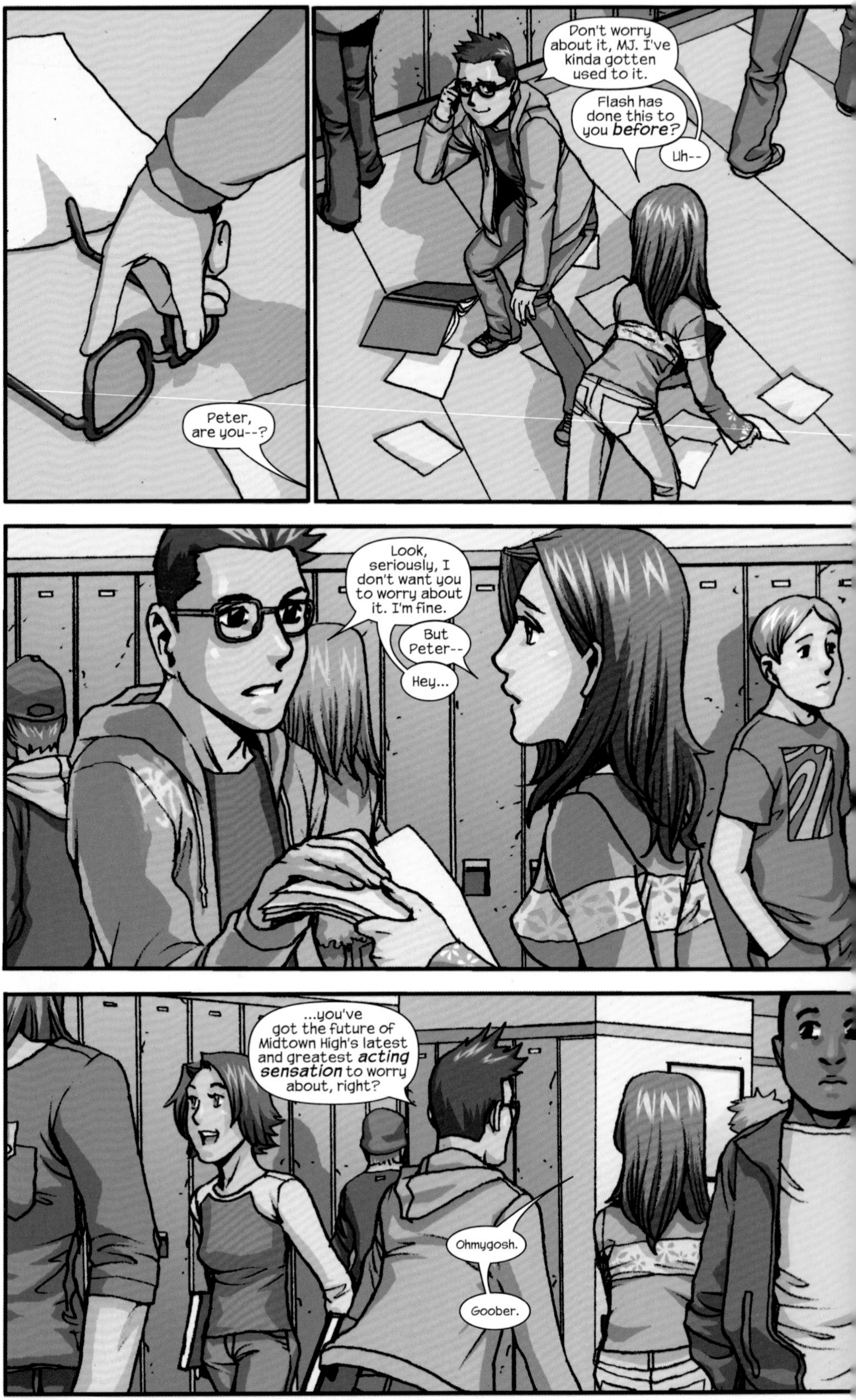
Peter, are you--?
Don't worry about it, MJ. I've kinda gotten used to it.
Flash has done this to you *before*?
Uh--
Look, seriously, I don't want you to worry about it. I'm fine.
But Peter--
Hey...
...you've got the future of Midtown High's latest and greatest *acting sensation* to worry about, right?
Ohmygosh.
Goober.

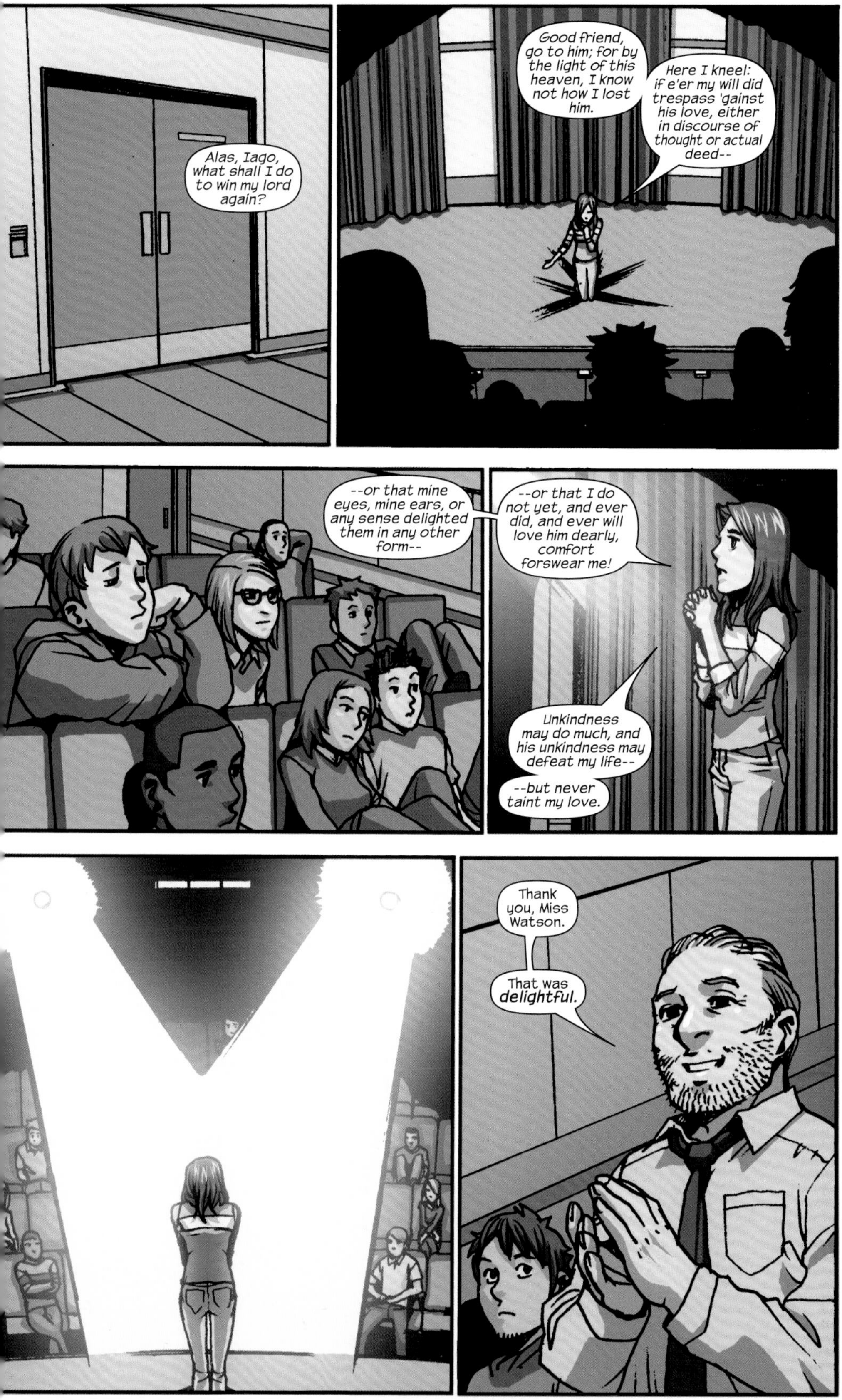
Alas, Iago, what shall I do to win my lord again?
Good friend, go to him; for by the light of this heaven, I know not how I lost him.
Here I kneel: if e'er my will did trespass 'gainst his love, either in discourse of thought or actual deed--
--or that mine eyes, mine ears, or any sense delighted them in any other form--
--or that I do not yet, and ever did, and ever will love him dearly, comfort forswear me!
Unkindness may do much, and his unkindness may defeat my life--
--but never taint my love.
Thank you, Miss Watson.
That was delightful.

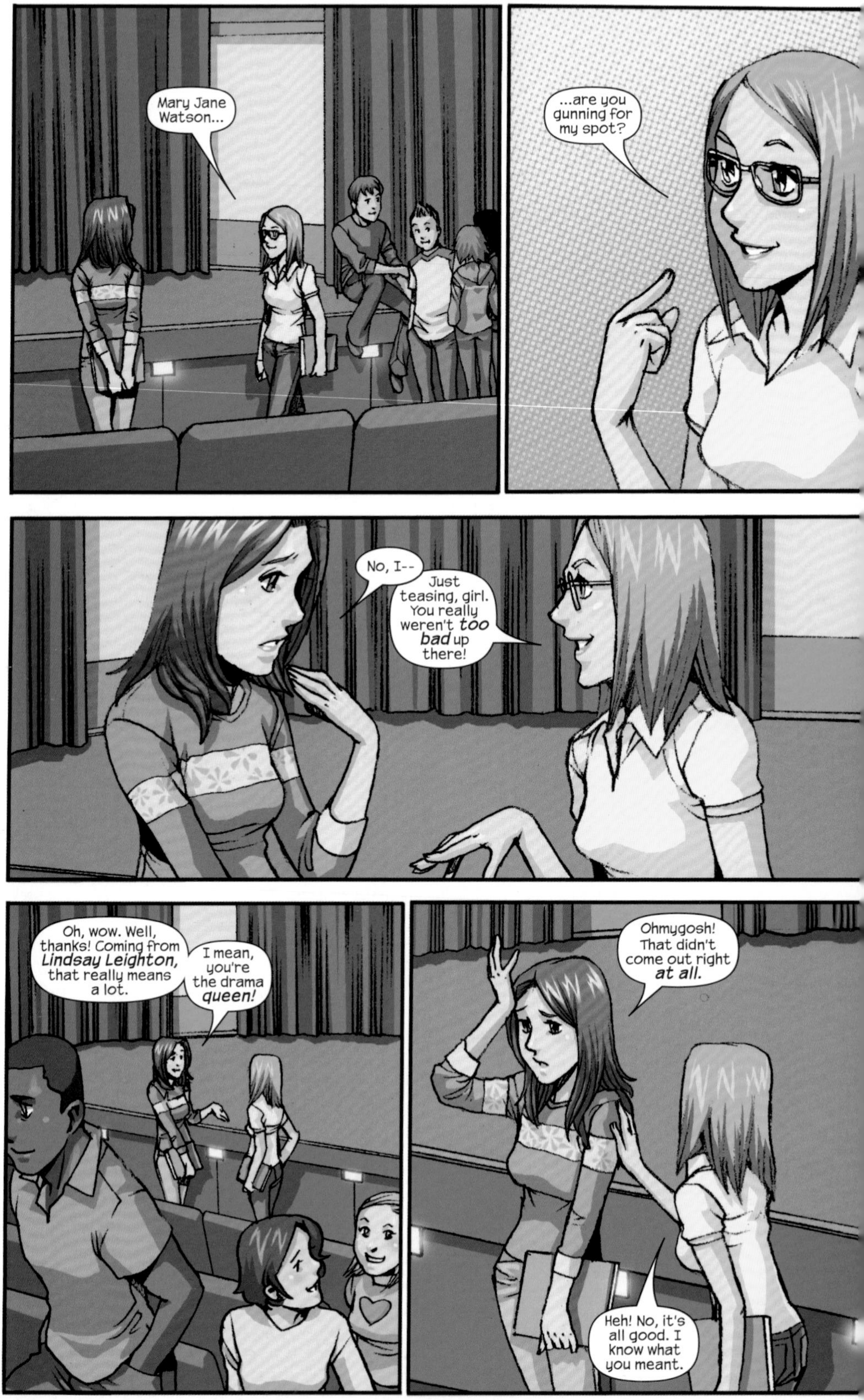
Mary Jane Watson...
...are you gunning for my spot?
No, I--
Just teasing, girl. You really weren't *too bad* up there!
Oh, wow. Well, thanks! Coming from *Lindsay Leighton,* that really means a lot.
I mean, you're the drama *queen!*
Ohmygosh! That didn't come out right *at all.*
Heh! No, it's all good. I know what you meant.

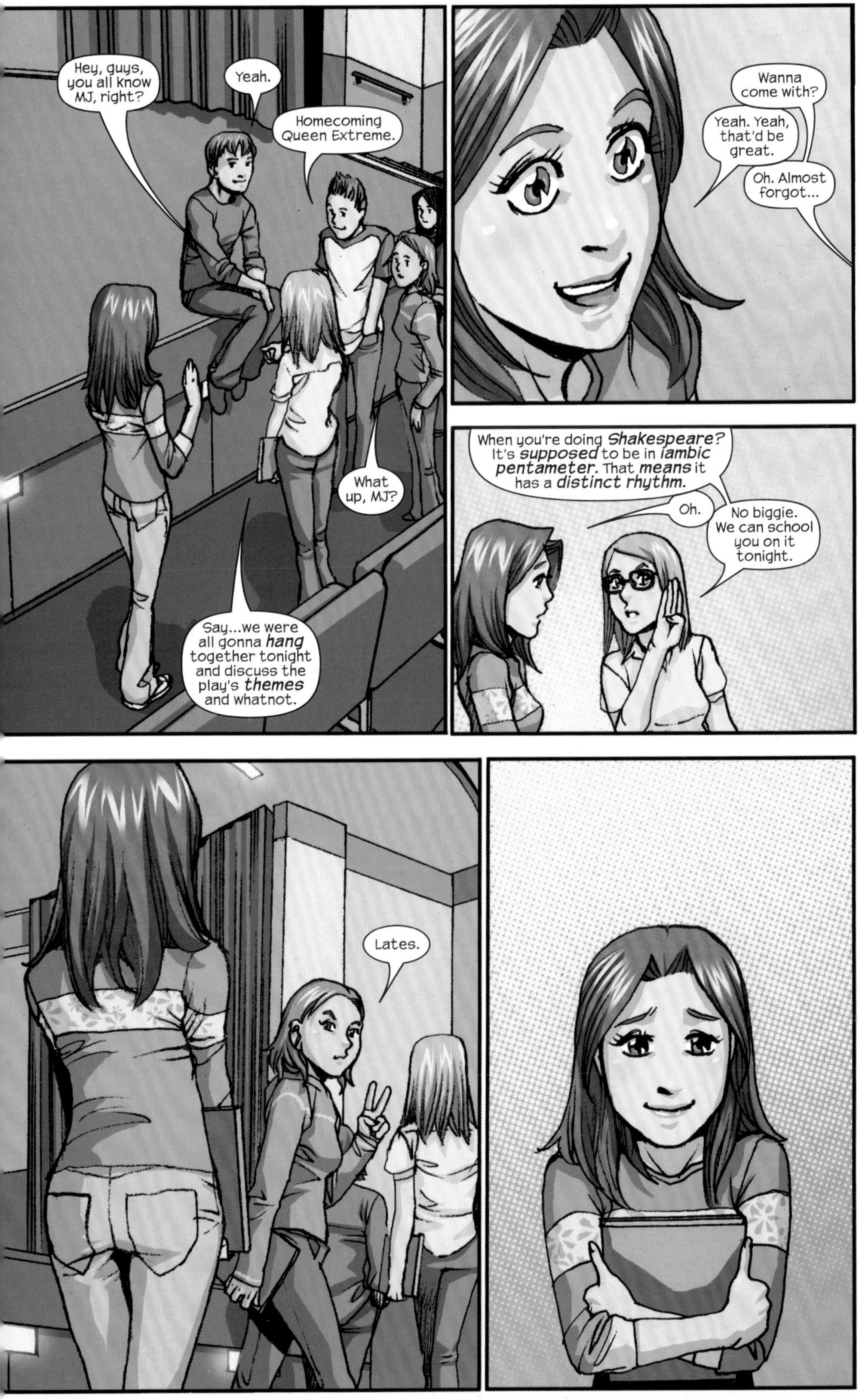
Hey, guys, you all know MJ, right?
Yeah.
Homecoming Queen Extreme.
What up, MJ?
Say...we were all gonna *hang* together tonight and discuss the play's *themes* and whatnot.
Wanna come with?
Yeah. Yeah, that'd be great.
Oh. Almost forgot...
When you're doing *Shakespeare?* It's *supposed* to be in *iambic pentameter.* That *means* it has a *distinct rhythm.*
Oh.
No biggie. We can school you on it tonight.
Lates.

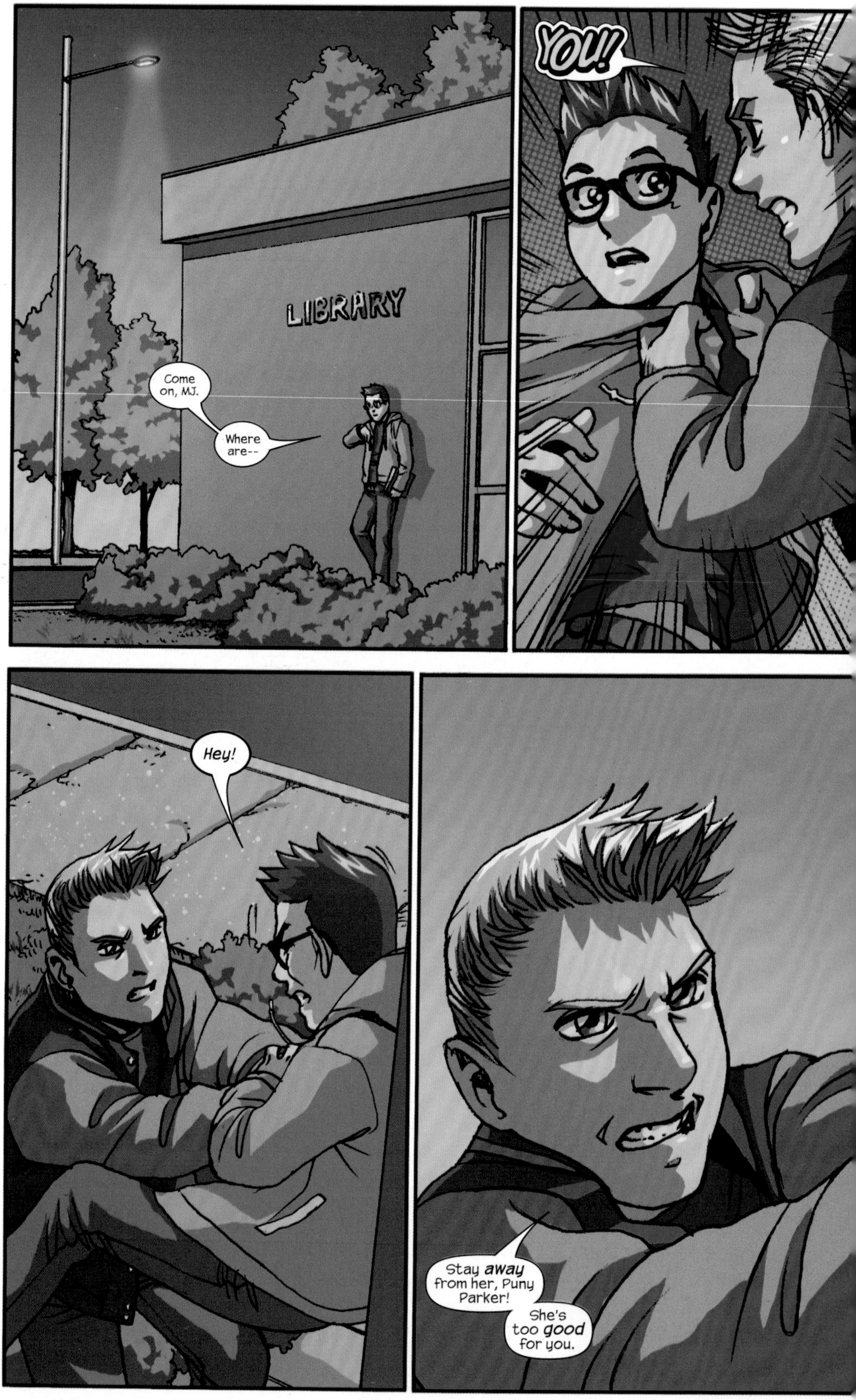

LIBRARY
Come on, MJ.
Where are--
YOU!
Hey!
Stay *away* from her, Puny Parker!
She's too *good* for you.

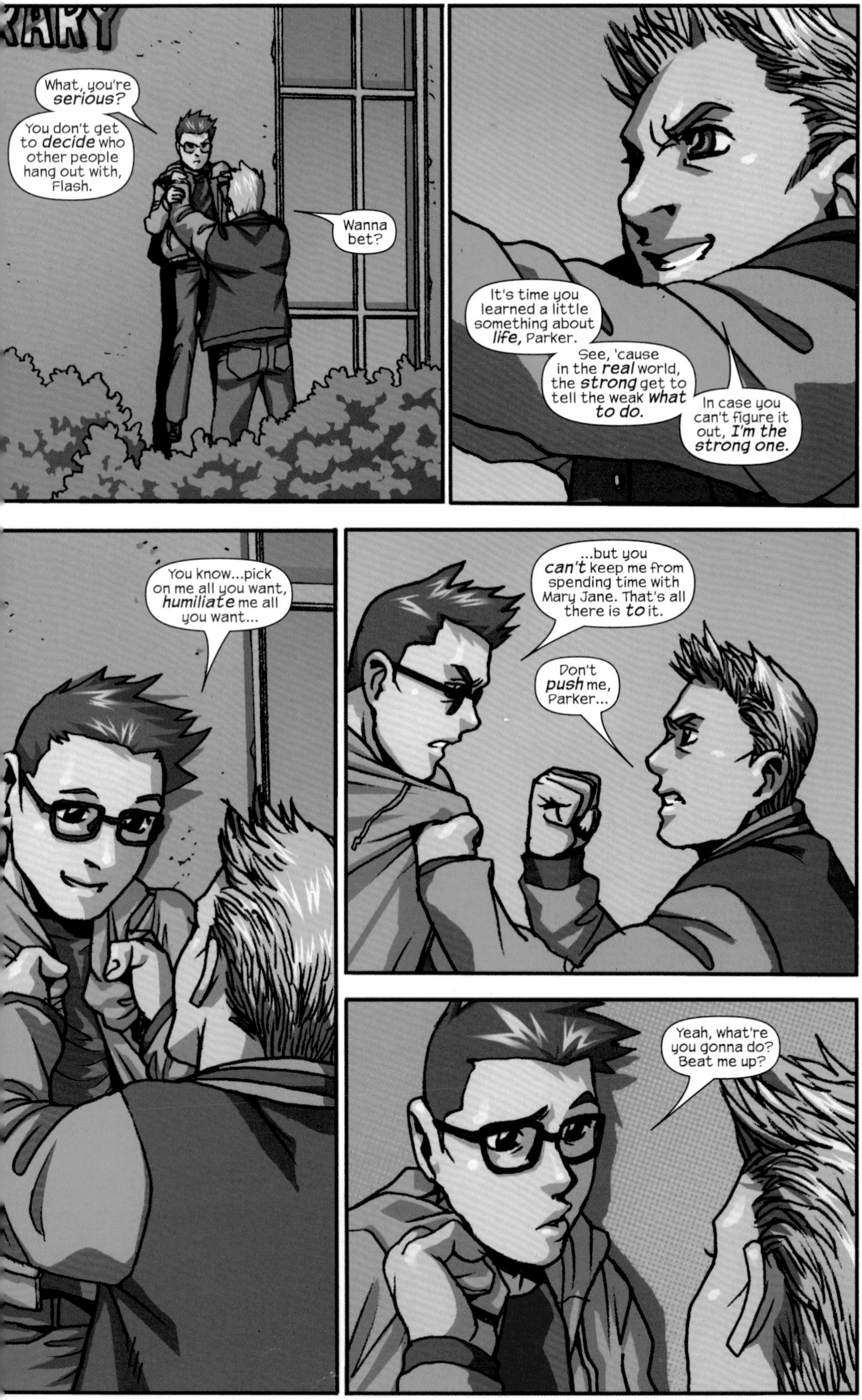
RARY
What, you're serious?
You don't get to decide who other people hang out with, Flash.
Wanna bet?
It's time you learned a little something about life, Parker.
See, 'cause in the real world, the strong get to tell the weak what to do.
In case you can't figure it out, I'm the strong one.
You know...pick on me all you want, humiliate me all you want...
...but you can't keep me from spending time with Mary Jane. That's all there is to it.
Don't push me, Parker...
Yeah, what're you gonna do? Beat me up?

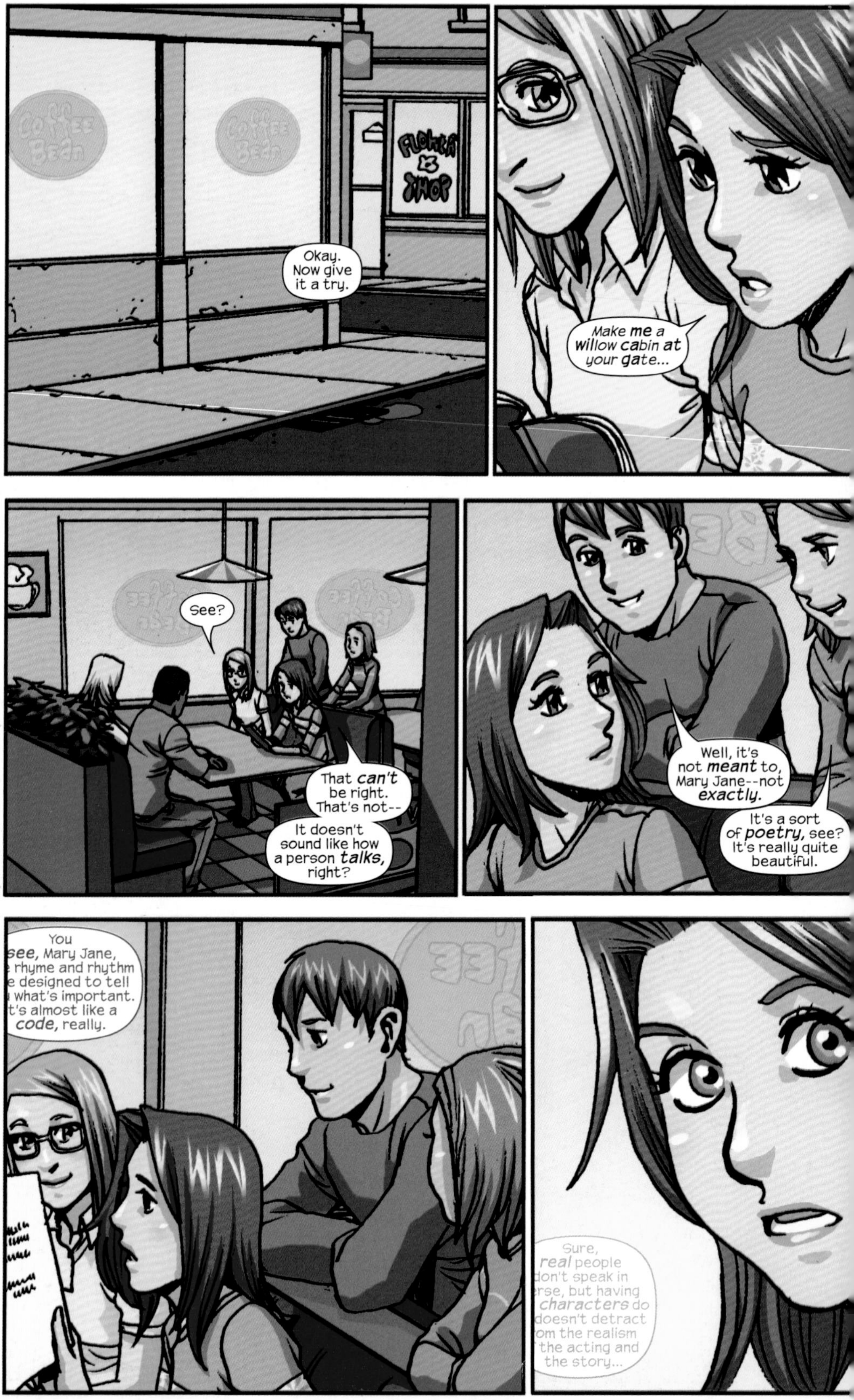
Okay. Now give it a try.
Make me a willow cabin at your gate...
See?
That can't be right. That's not--
It doesn't sound like how a person talks, right?
Well, it's not meant to, Mary Jane--not exactly.
It's a sort of poetry, see? It's really quite beautiful.
You see, Mary Jane, e rhyme and rhythm e designed to tell what's important. t's almost like a code, really.
Sure, real people don't speak in erse, but having characters do doesn't detract om the realism the acting and the story...

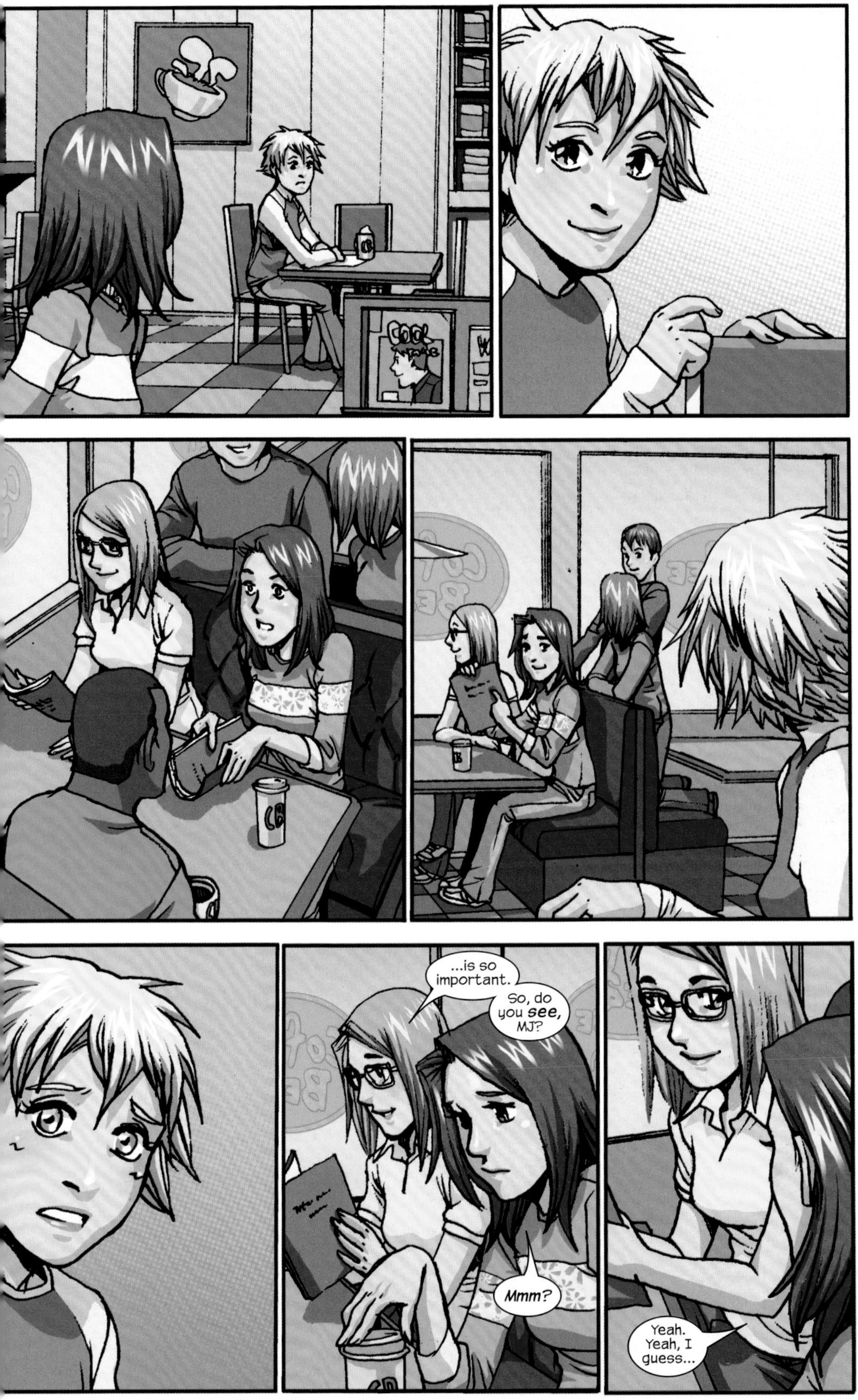

...is so important.
So, do you *see,* MJ?
Mmm?
Yeah. Yeah, I guess...

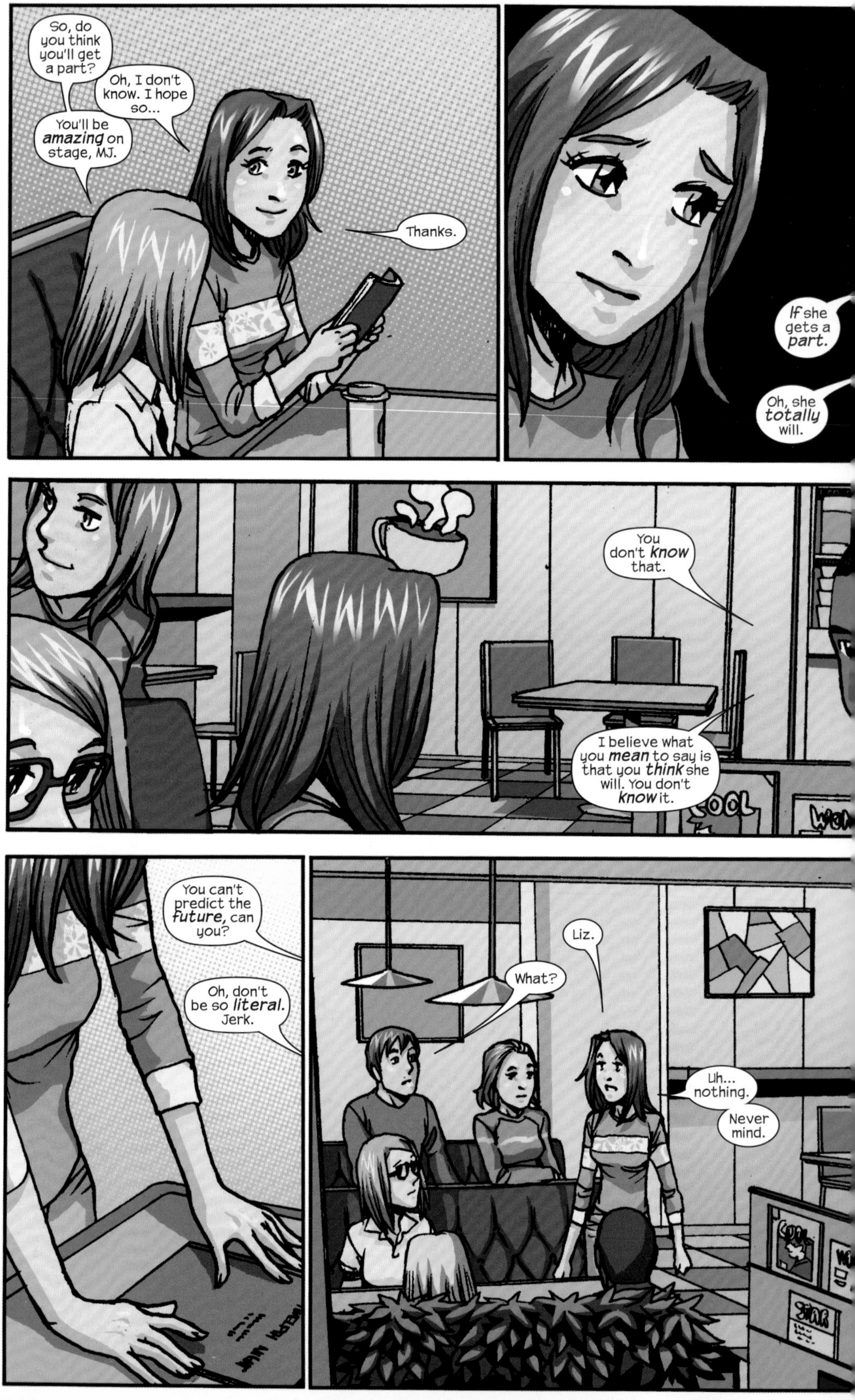
So, do you think you'll get a part?
Oh, I don't know. I hope so...
You'll be *amazing* on stage, MJ.
Thanks.
If she gets a *part.*
Oh, she *totally* will.
You don't *know* that.
I believe what you *mean* to say is that you *think* she will. You don't *know* it.
COOL
You can't predict the *future,* can you?
Oh, don't be so *literal.* Jerk.
Liz.
What?
Uh... nothing.
Never mind.

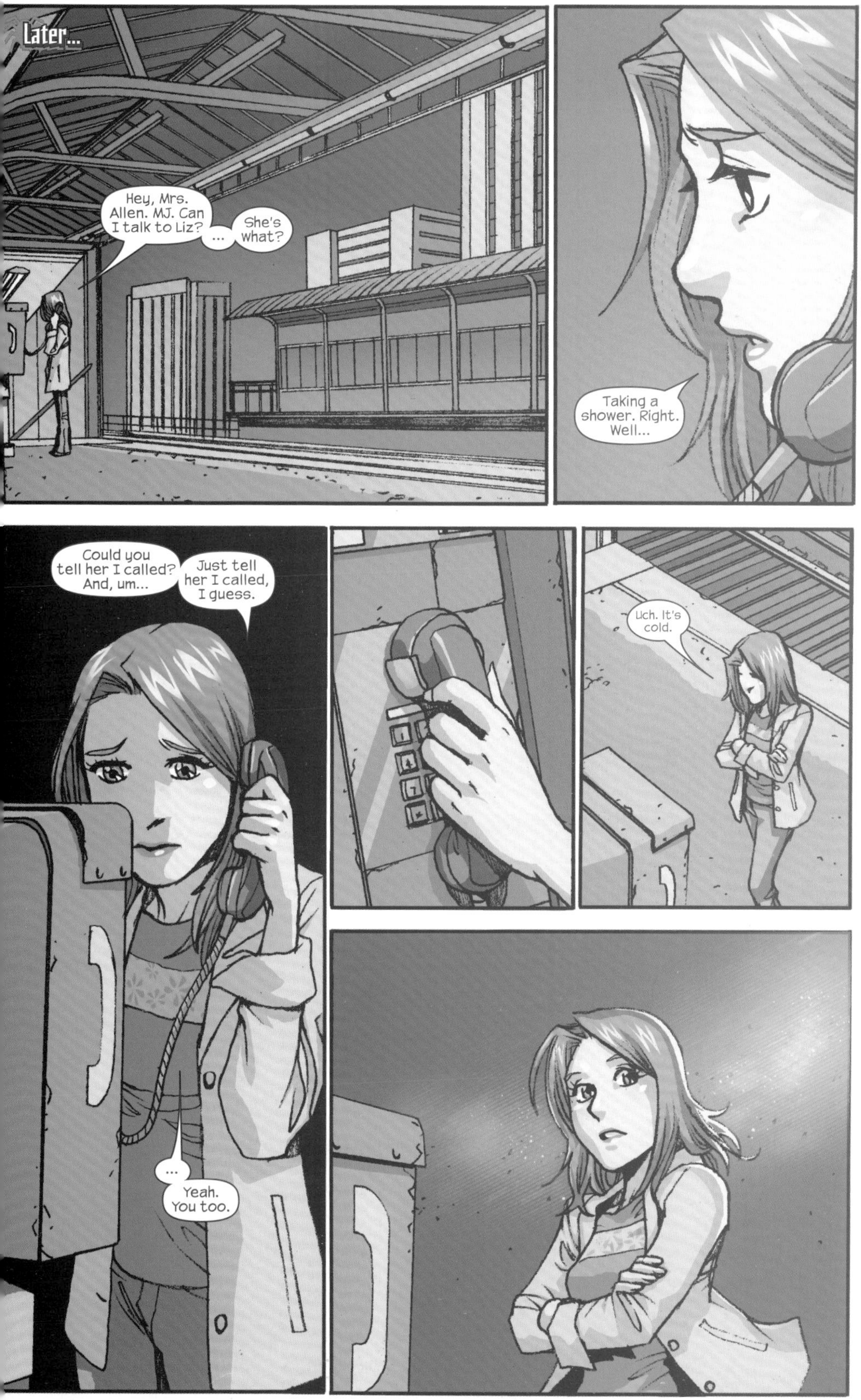
Later...
Hey, Mrs. Allen. MJ. Can I talk to Liz?
...
She's what?
Taking a shower. Right. Well...
Could you tell her I called? And, um...
Just tell her I called, I guess.
...
Yeah. You too.
Uch. It's cold.

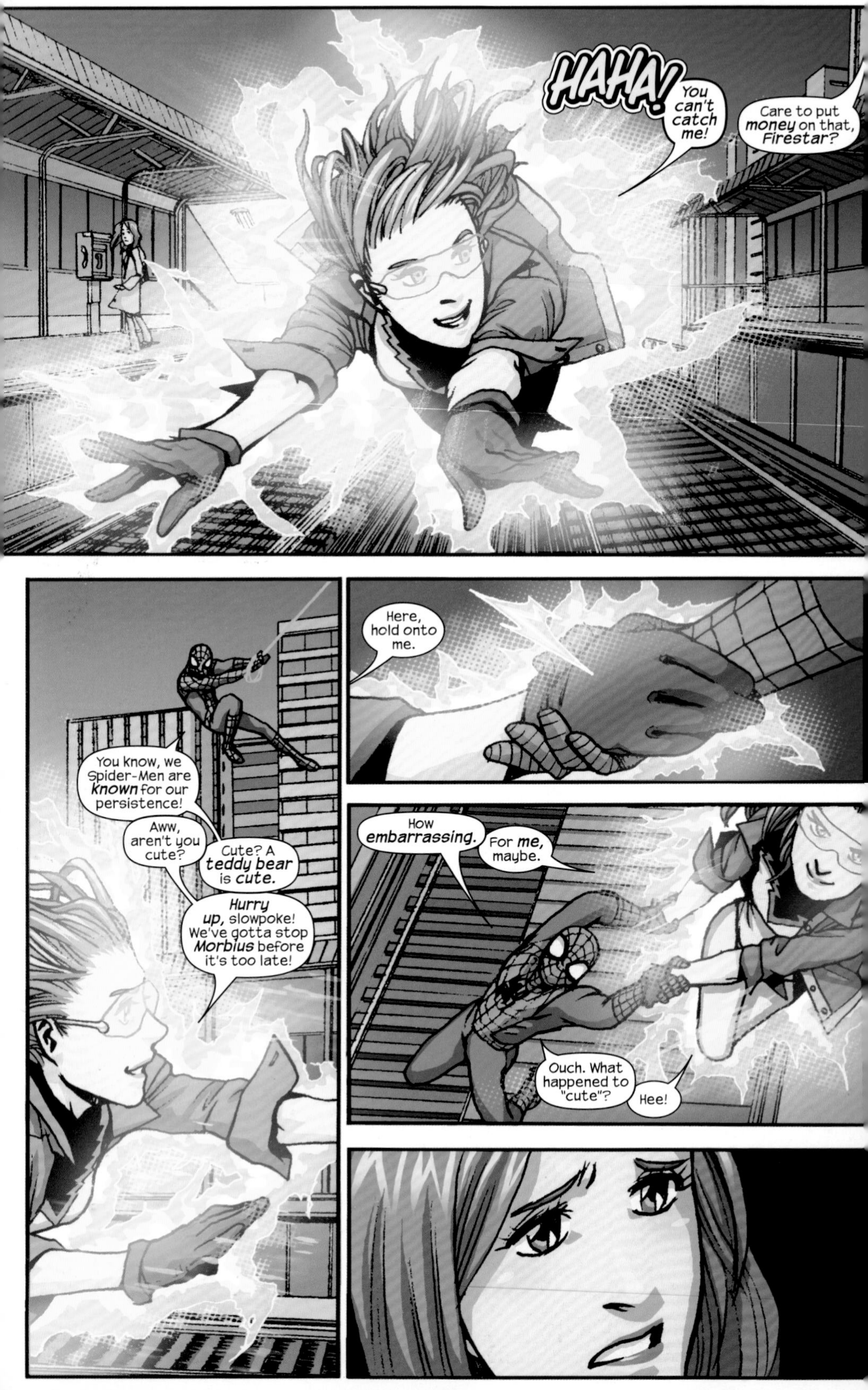
HAHA!
You can't catch me!
Care to put money on that, Firestar?
You know, we Spider-Men are known for our persistence!
Aww, aren't you cute?
Cute? A teddy bear is cute.
Hurry up, slowpoke! We've gotta stop Morbius before it's too late!
Here, hold onto me.
How embarrassing.
For me, maybe.
Ouch. What happened to "cute"?
Hee!

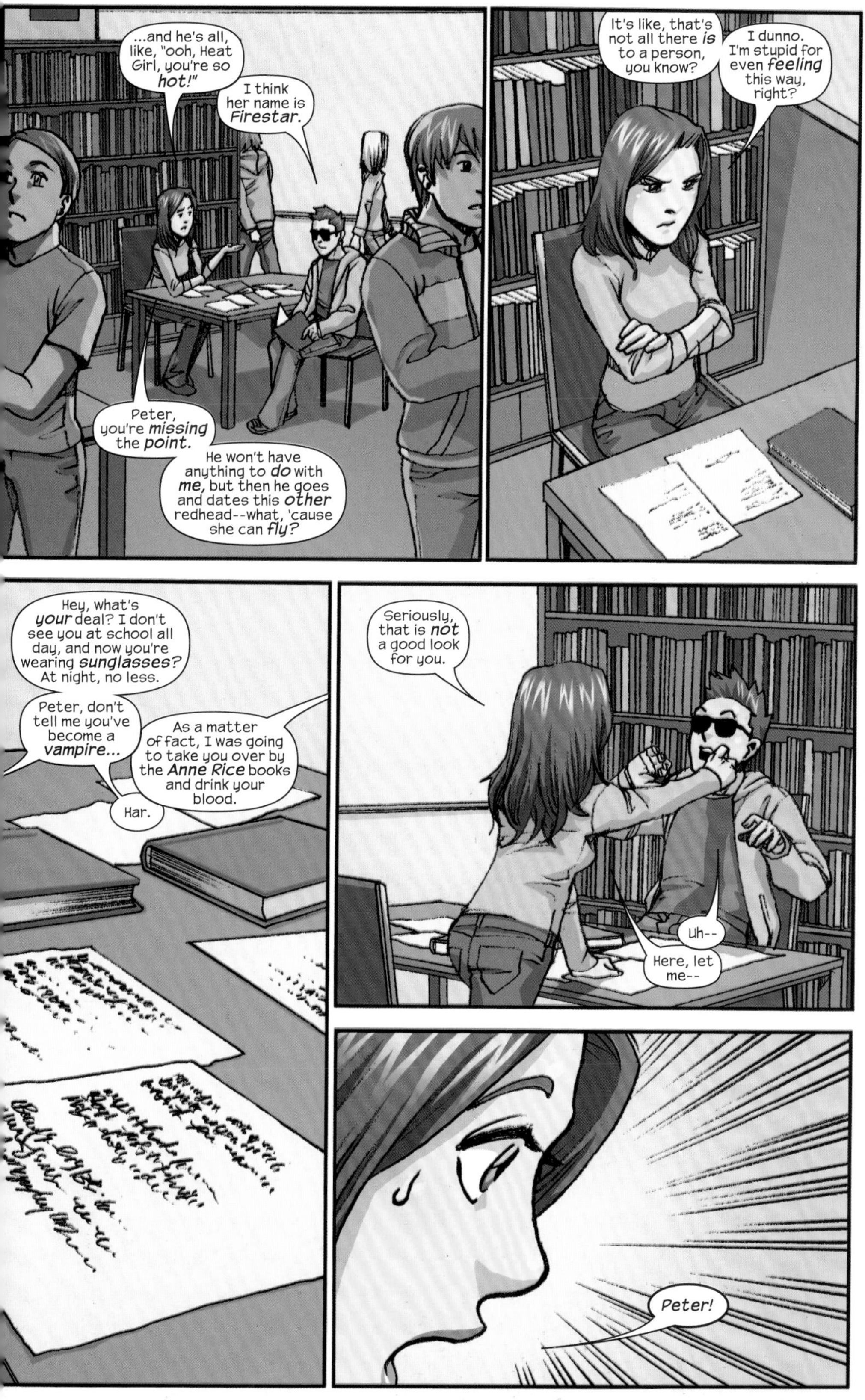
...and he's all, like, "ooh, Heat Girl, you're so *hot!*"
I think her name is *Firestar*.
Peter, you're *missing* the *point*.
He won't have anything to *do* with *me*, but then he goes and dates this *other* redhead--what, 'cause she can *fly?*
It's like, that's not all there *is* to a person, you know?
I dunno. I'm stupid for even *feeling* this way, right?
Hey, what's *your* deal? I don't see you at school all day, and now you're wearing *sunglasses?* At night, no less.
Peter, don't tell me you've become a *vampire...*
As a matter of fact, I was going to take you over by the *Anne Rice* books and drink your blood.
Har.
Seriously, that is *not* a good look for you.
Uh--
Here, let me--
Peter!

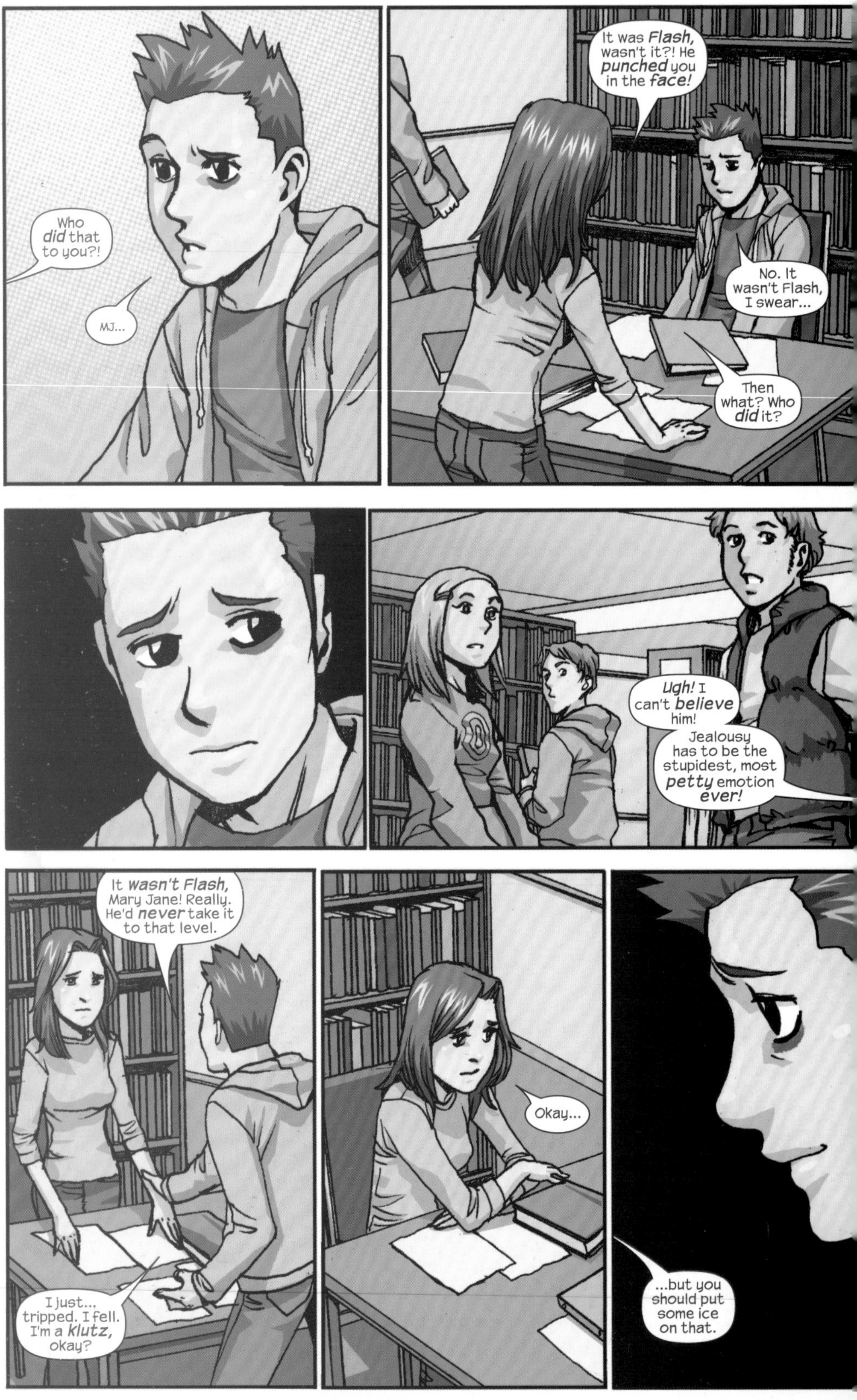
Who did that to you?!
MJ...
It was Flash, wasn't it?! He punched you in the face!
No. It wasn't Flash, I swear...
Then what? Who did it?
Ugh! I can't believe him!
Jealousy has to be the stupidest, most petty emotion ever!
It wasn't Flash, Mary Jane! Really. He'd never take it to that level.
I just... tripped. I fell. I'm a klutz, okay?
Okay...
...but you should put some ice on that.

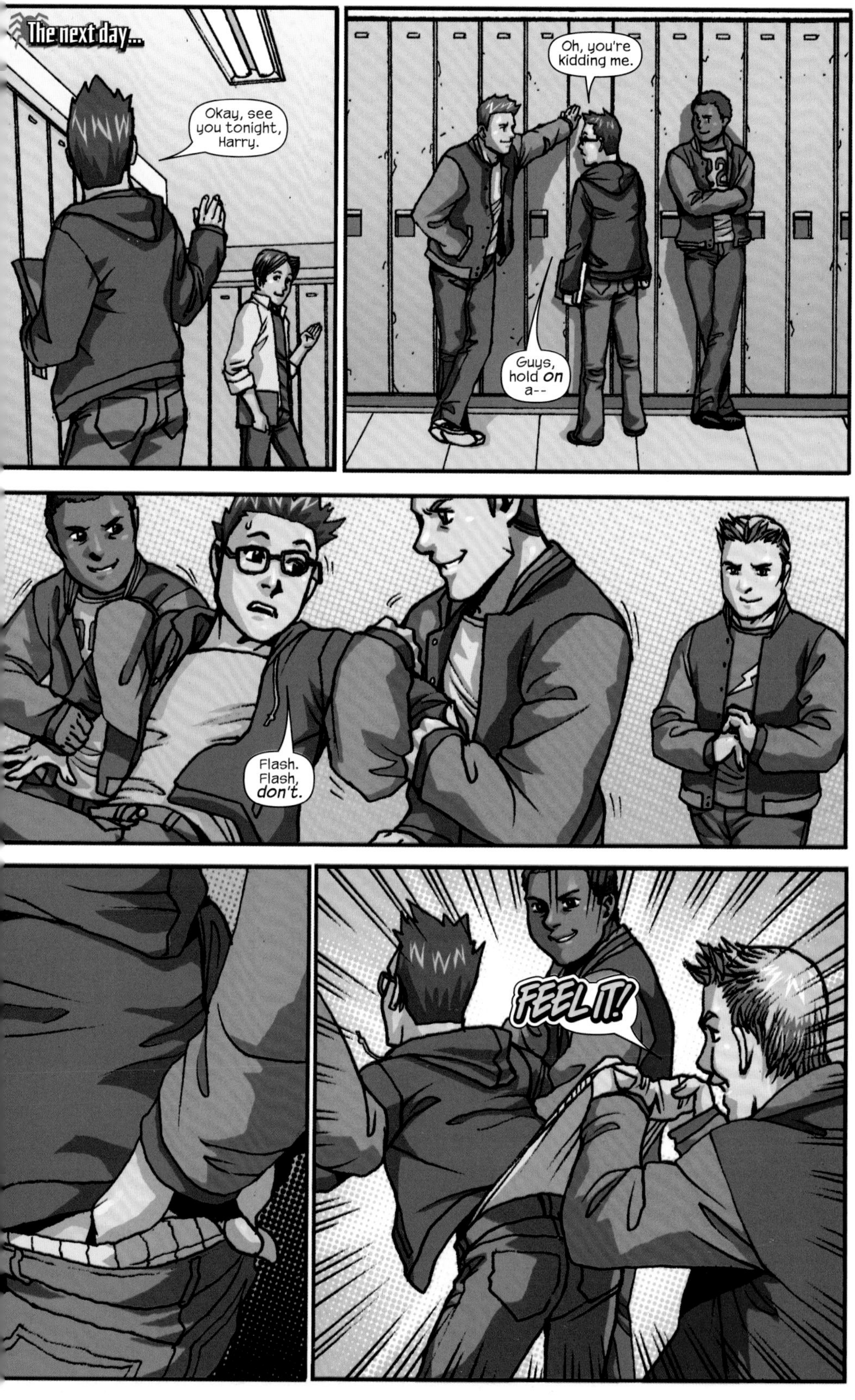
The next day...
Okay, see you tonight, Harry.
Oh, you're kidding me.
Guys, hold on a--
Flash. Flash, don't.
FEEL IT!

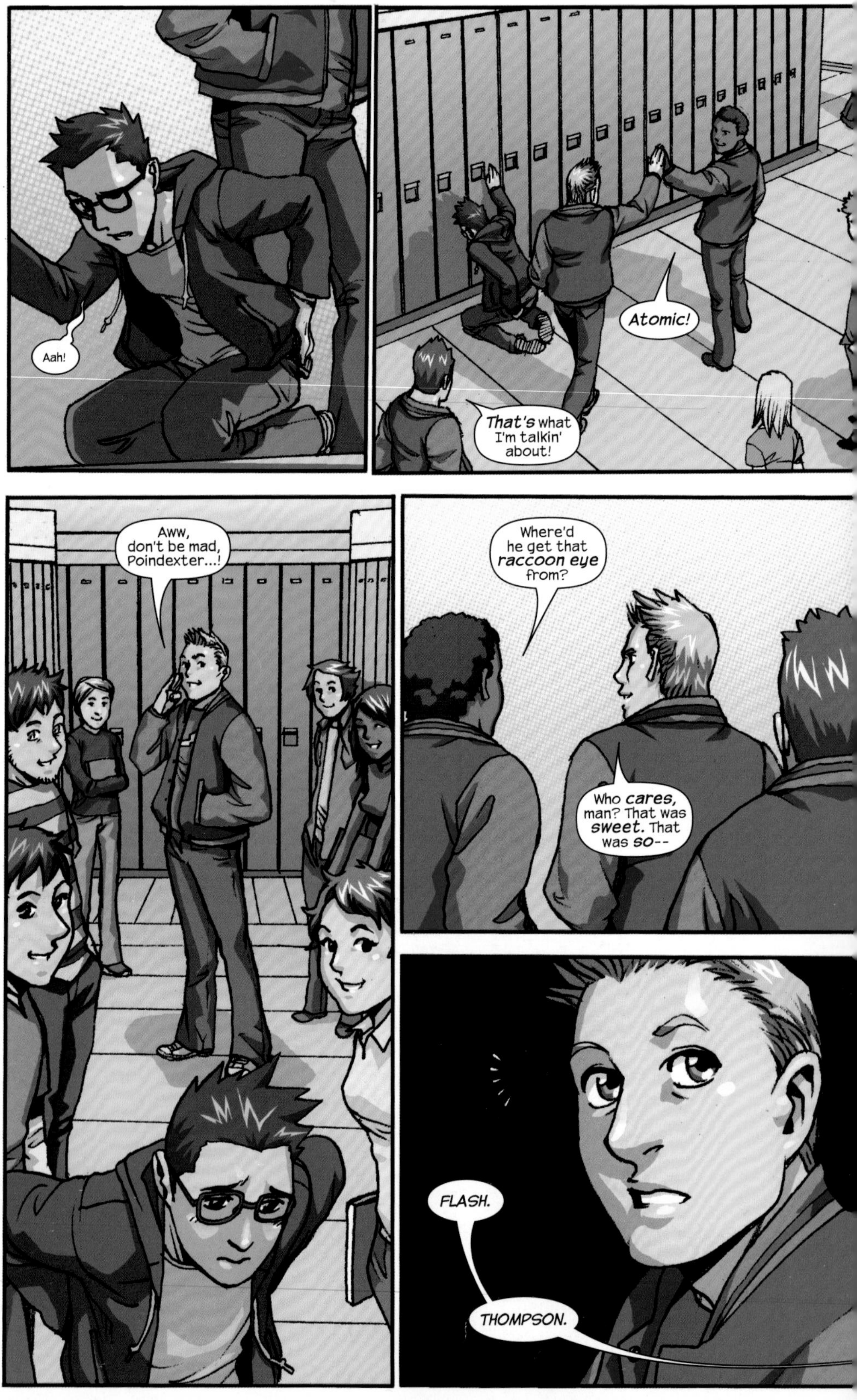
Aah!
Atomic!
That's what I'm talkin' about!
Aww, don't be mad, Poindexter...!
Where'd he get that raccoon eye from?
Who cares, man? That was sweet. That was so--
FLASH.
THOMPSON.

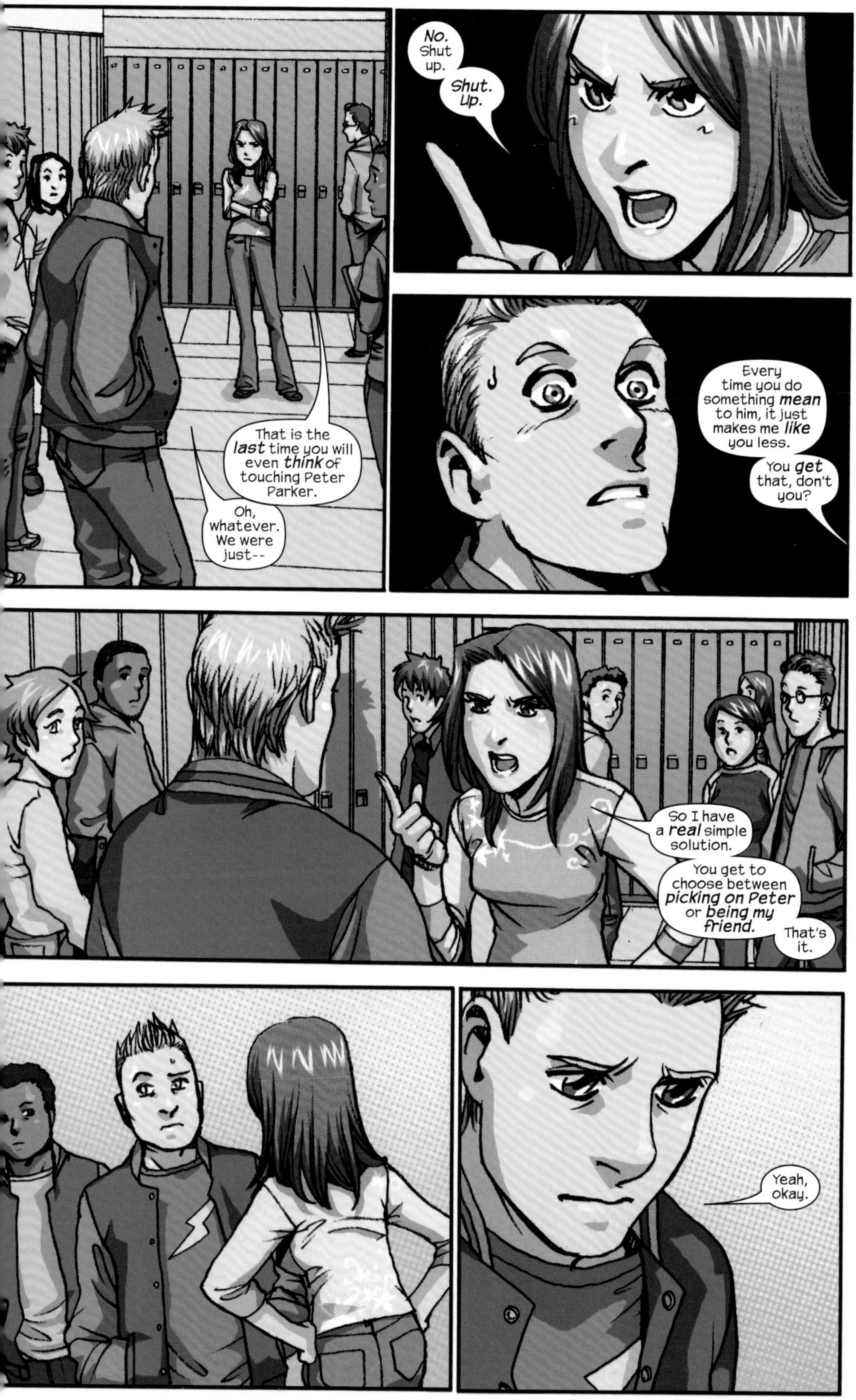
That is the last time you will even think of touching Peter Parker.
Oh, whatever. We were just--
No. Shut up.
Shut. Up.
Every time you do something mean to him, it just makes me like you less.
You get that, don't you?
So I have a real simple solution.
You get to choose between picking on Peter or being my friend.
That's it.
Yeah, okay.

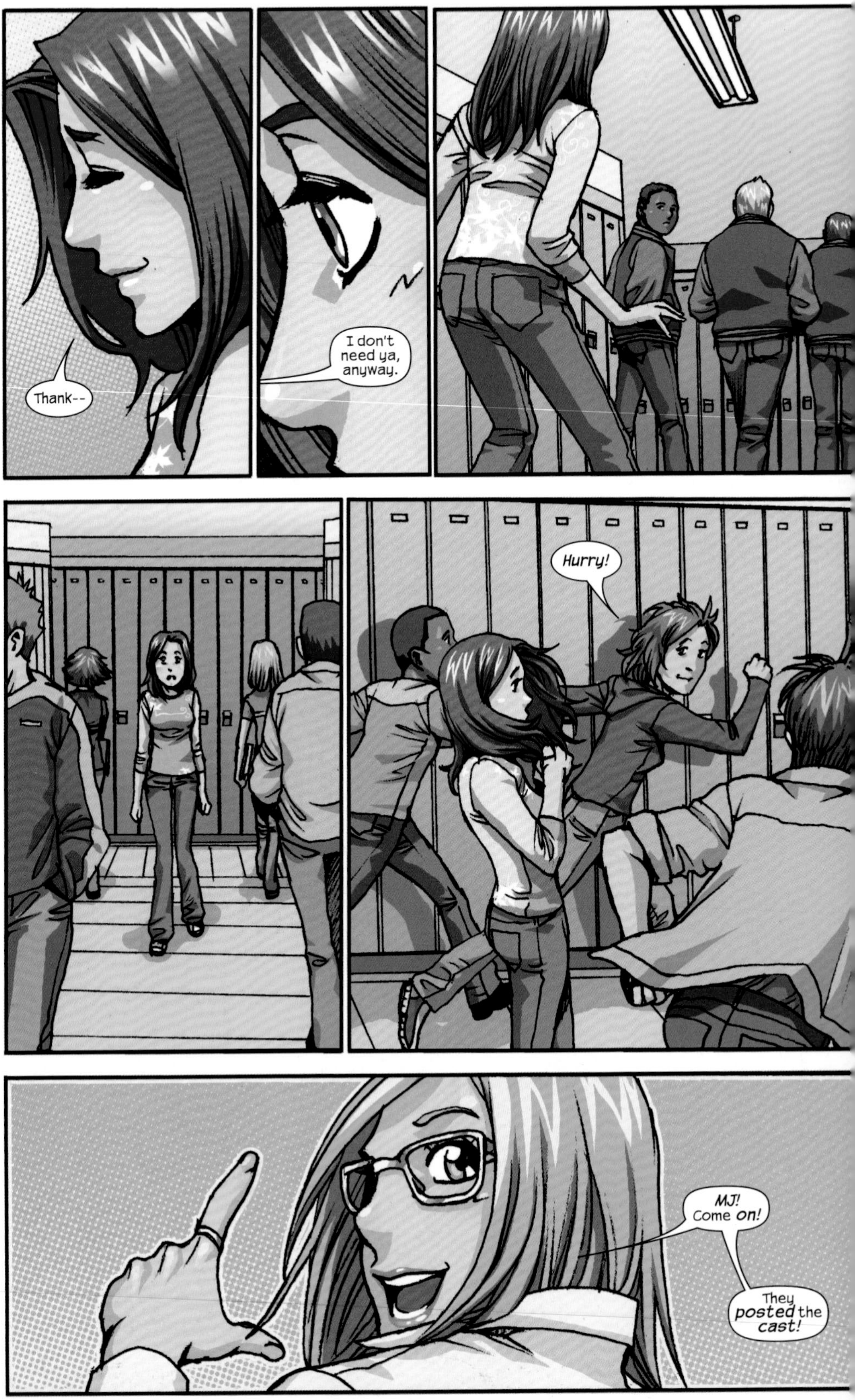

Thank--
I don't need ya, anyway.
Hurry!
MJ! Come on!
They posted the cast!

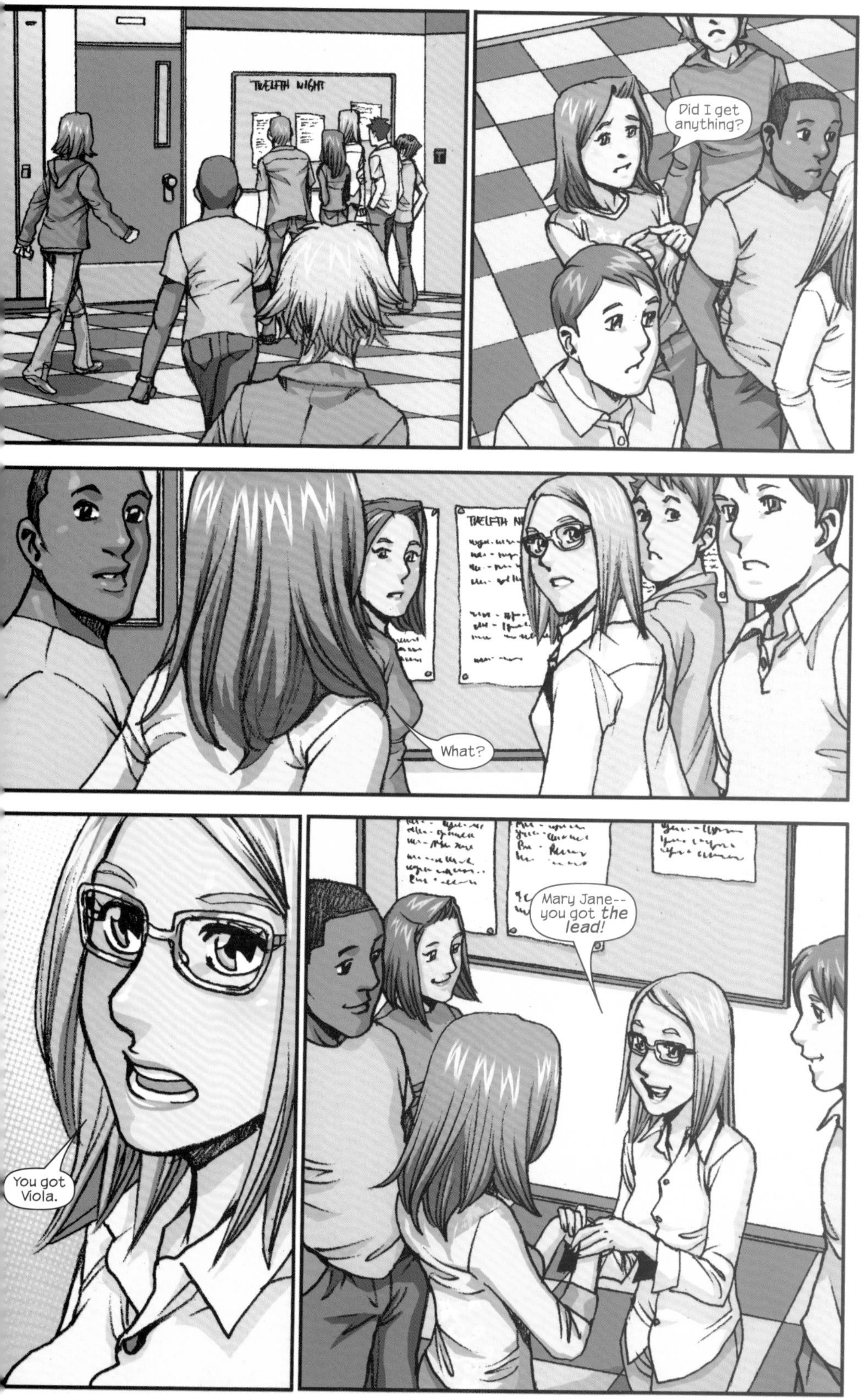
TWELFTH NIGHT
Did I get anything?
What?
You got Viola.
Mary Jane-- you got the lead!

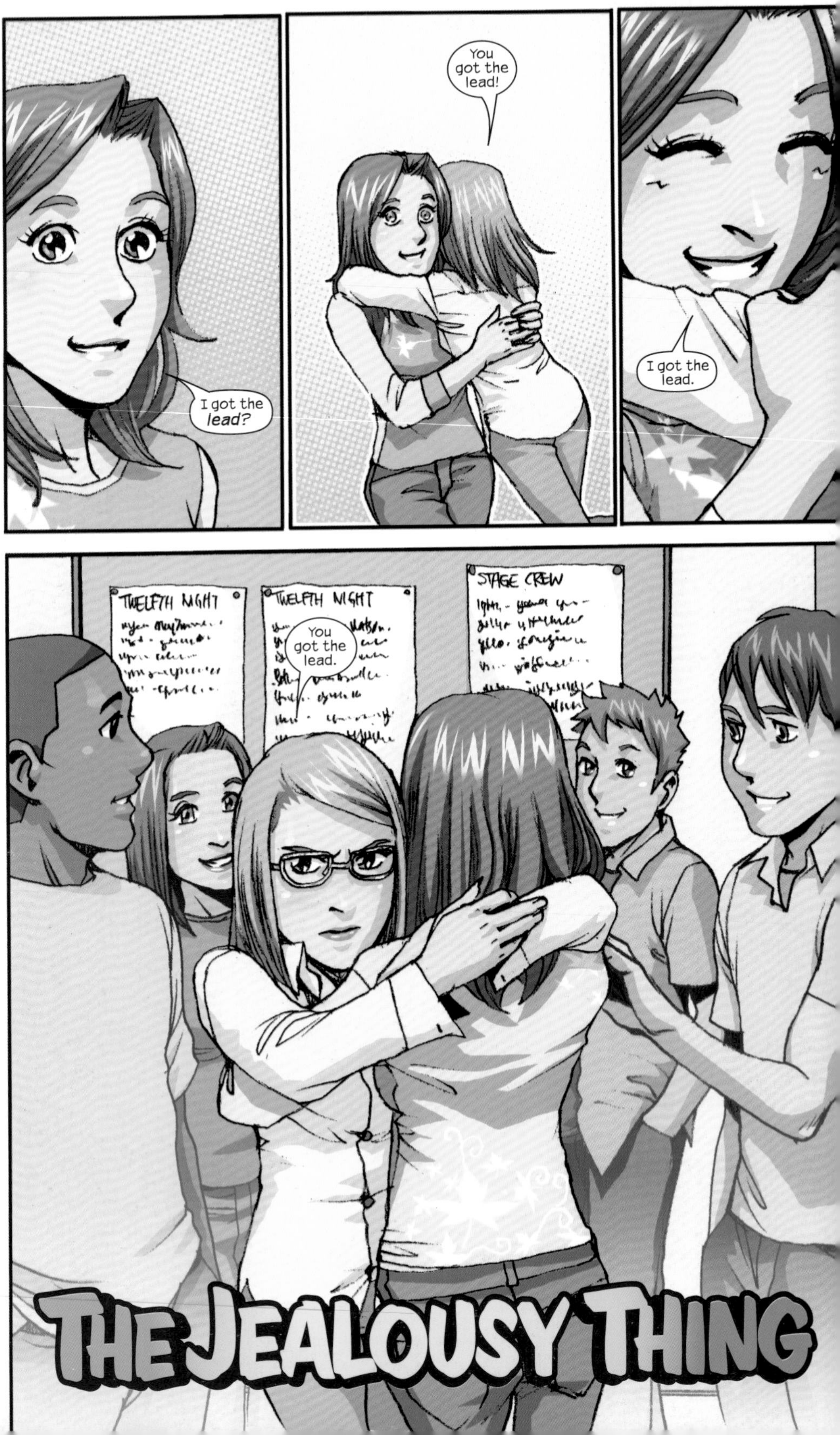
I got the lead?
You got the lead!
I got the lead.
TWELFTH NIGHT
TWELFTH NIGHT
STAGE CREW
You got the lead.
THE JEALOUSY THING

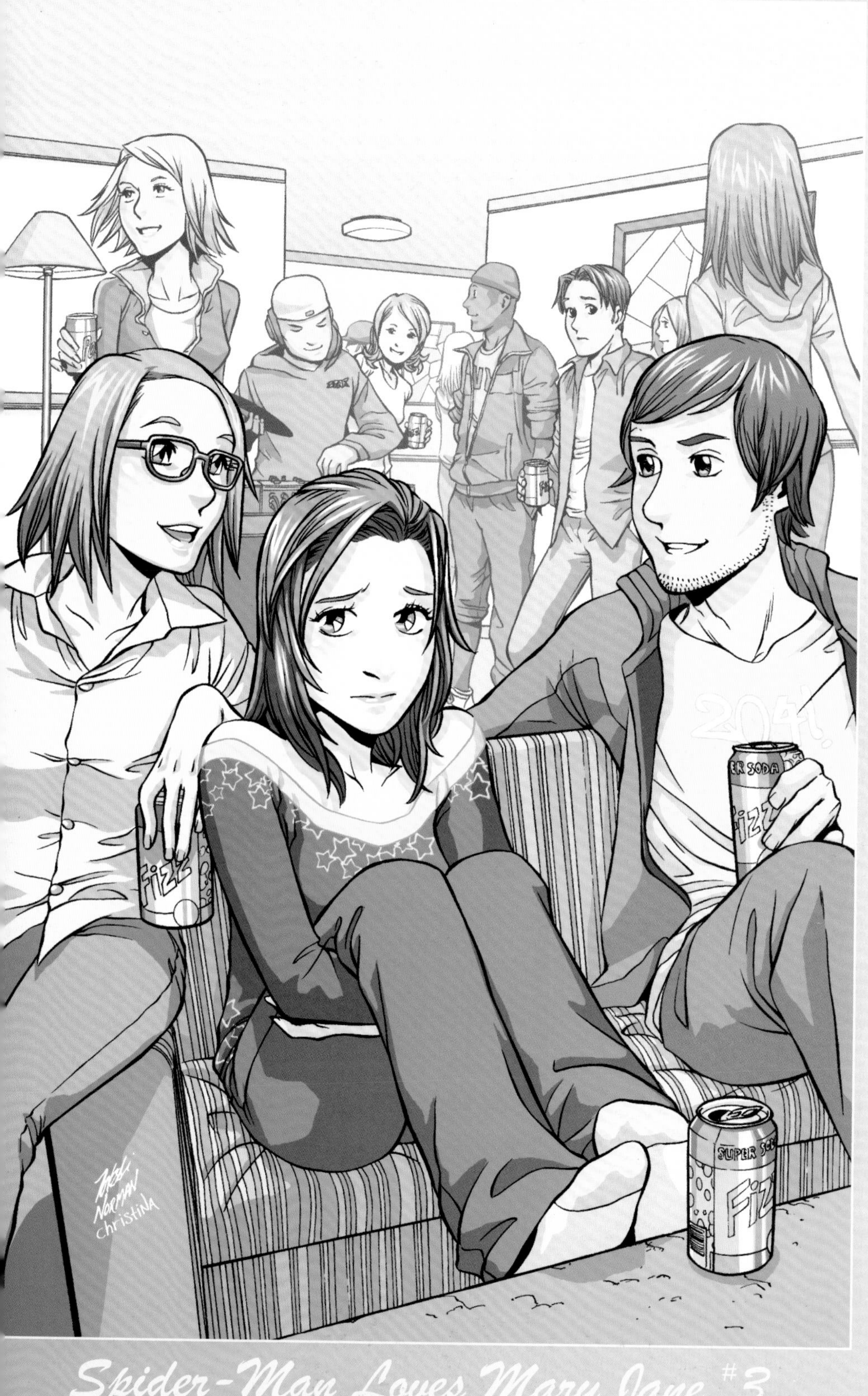
SUPER SODA
Fizz

Spider-Man Loves Mary Jane #3

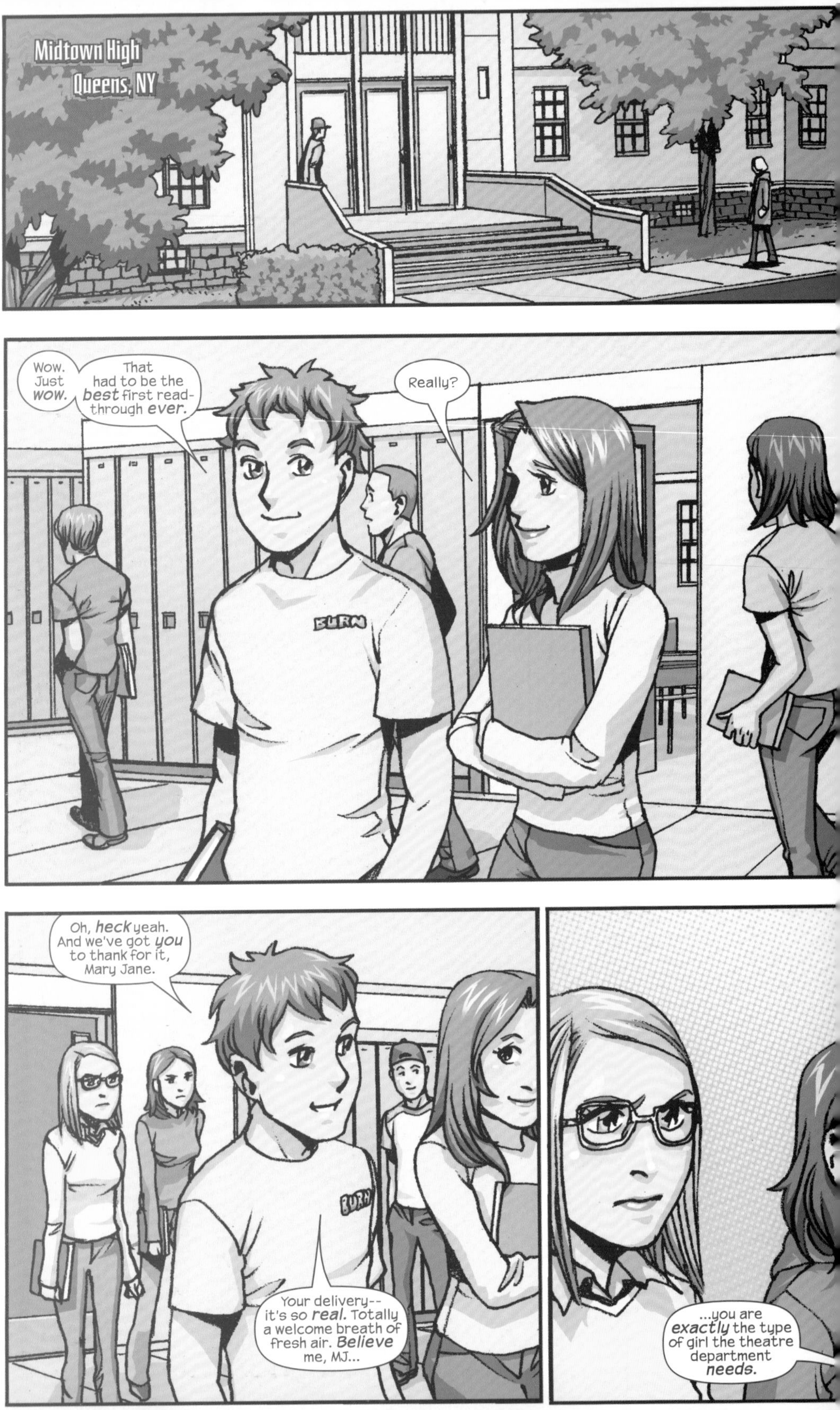
Midtown High
Queens, NY
Wow. Just *wow.*
That had to be the *best* first read-through *ever.*
Really?
Oh, *heck* yeah. And we've got *you* to thank for it, Mary Jane.
Your delivery-- it's so *real.* Totally a welcome breath of fresh air. *Believe* me, MJ...
...you are *exactly* the type of girl the theatre department *needs.*

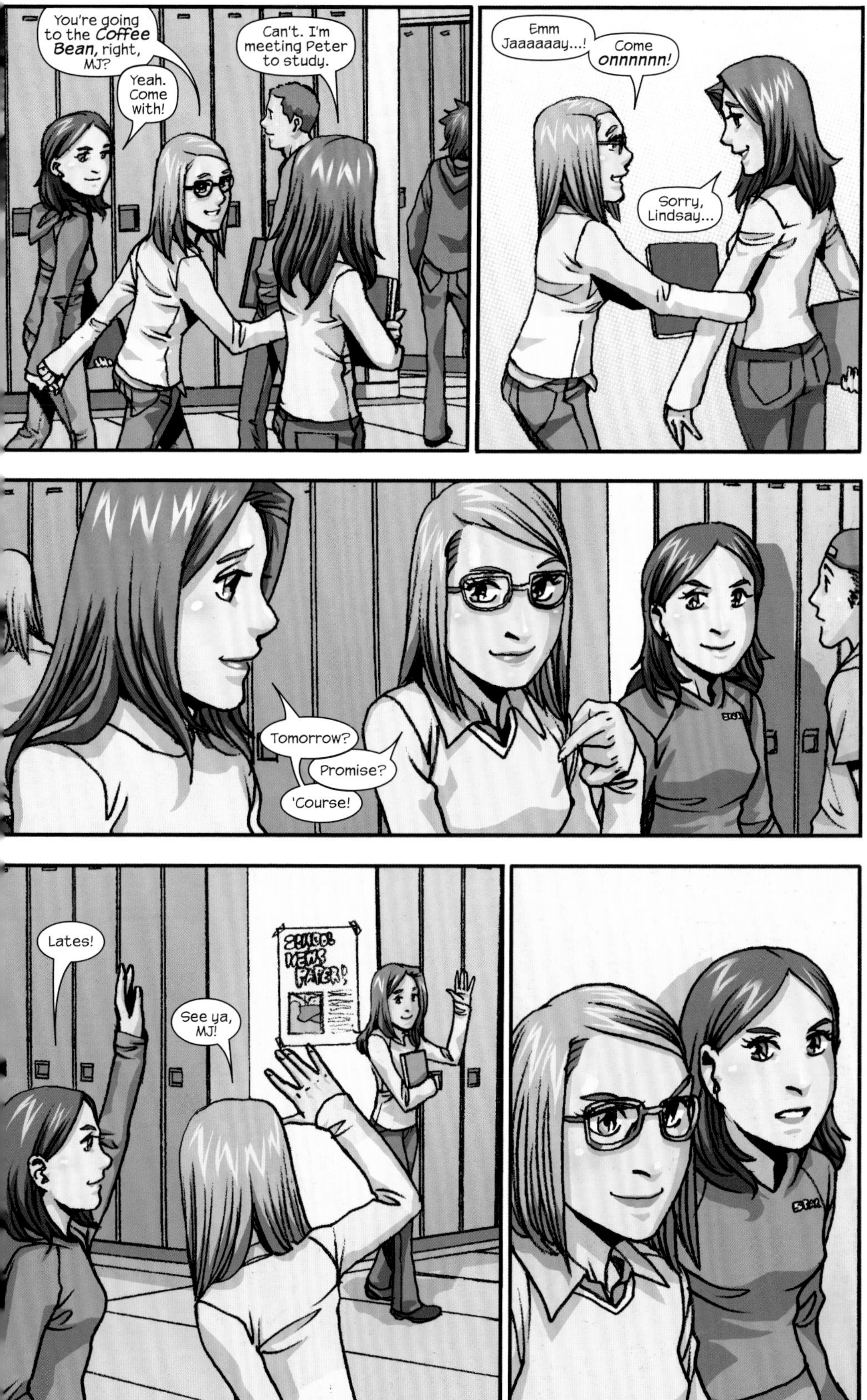
You're going to the *Coffee Bean,* right, MJ?
Yeah. Come with!
Can't. I'm meeting Peter to study.
Emm Jaaaaaay...!
Come *onnnnnn!*
Sorry, Lindsay...
Tomorrow?
Promise?
'Course!
Lates!
See ya, MJ!
SCHOOL NEWS PAPER!

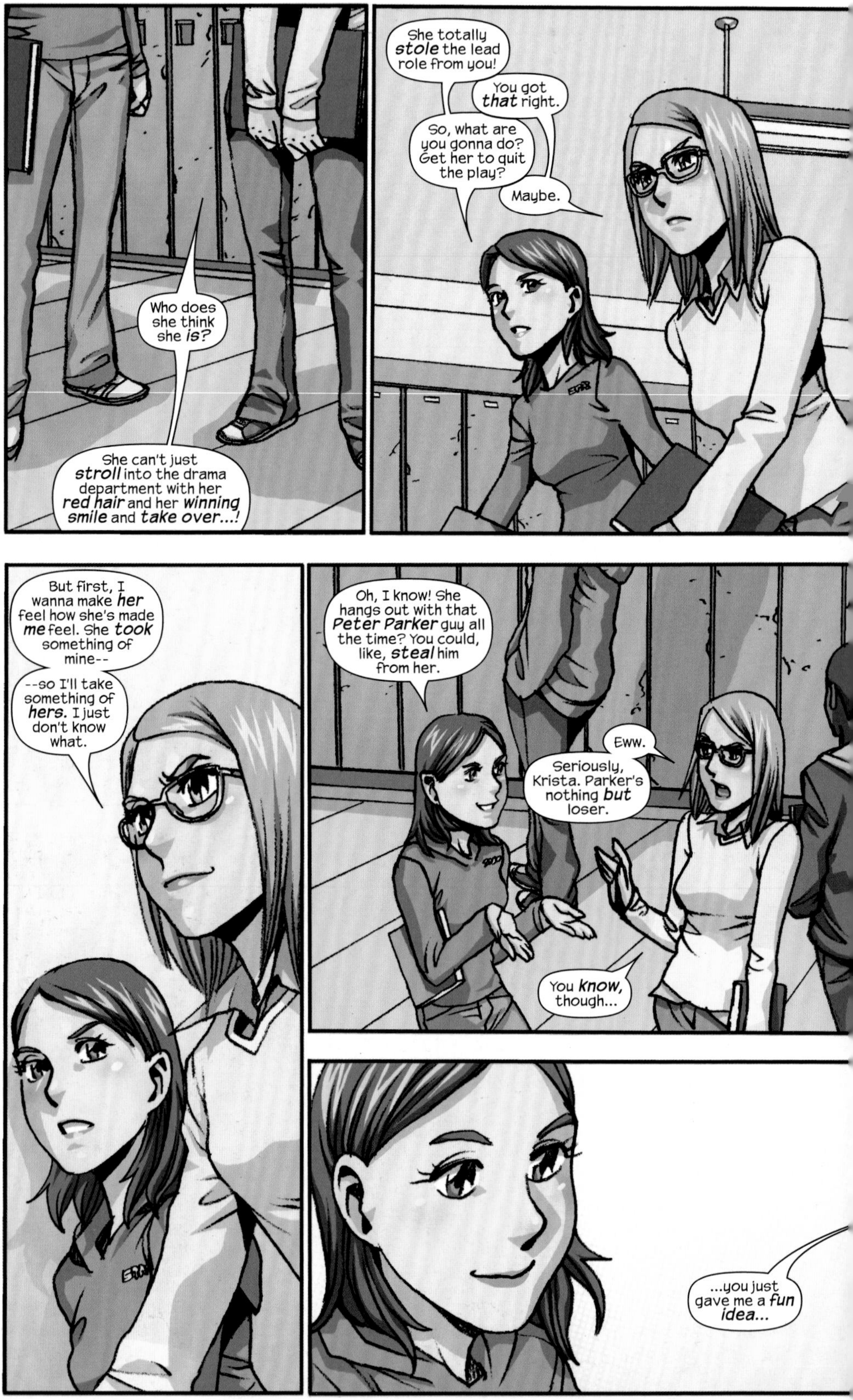
Who does she think she *is?*
She can't just *stroll* into the drama department with her *red hair* and her *winning smile* and *take over...!*
She totally *stole* the lead role from you!
You got *that* right.
So, what are you gonna do? Get her to quit the play?
Maybe.
But first, I wanna make *her* feel how she's made *me* feel. She *took* something of mine--
--so I'll take something of *hers.* I just don't know what.
Oh, I know! She hangs out with that *Peter Parker* guy all the time? You could, like, *steal* him from her.
Eww.
Seriously, Krista. Parker's nothing *but* loser.
You *know,* though...
...you just gave me a *fun idea...*

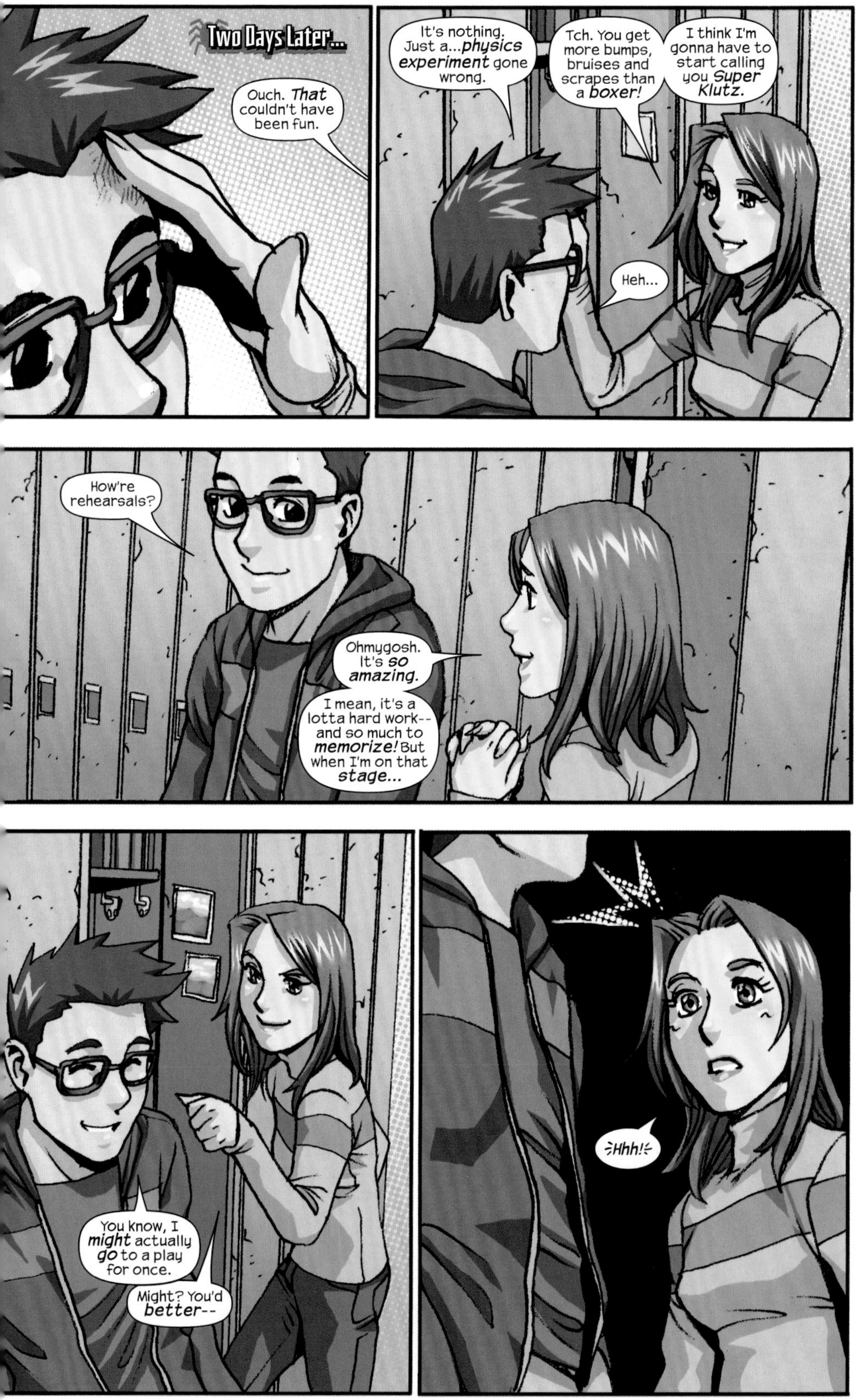

Two Days Later...
Ouch. That couldn't have been fun.
It's nothing. Just a...physics experiment gone wrong.
Tch. You get more bumps, bruises and scrapes than a boxer!
I think I'm gonna have to start calling you Super Klutz.
Heh...
How're rehearsals?
Ohmygosh. It's so amazing.
I mean, it's a lotta hard work--and so much to memorize! But when I'm on that stage...
You know, I might actually go to a play for once.
Might? You'd better--
Hhh!

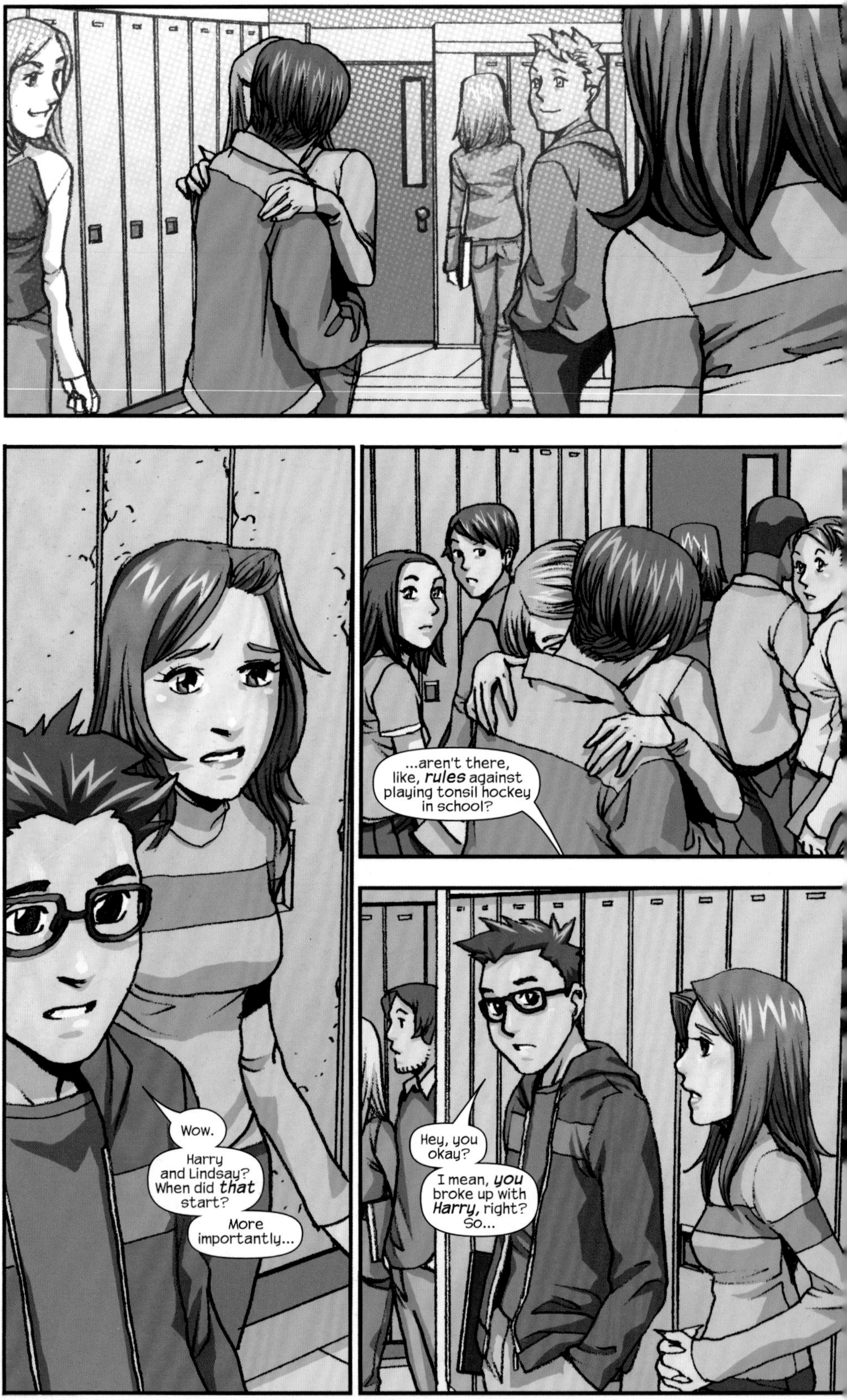
...aren't there, like, rules against playing tonsil hockey in school?
Wow.
Harry and Lindsay? When did that start?
More importantly...
Hey, you okay?
I mean, you broke up with Harry, right? So...

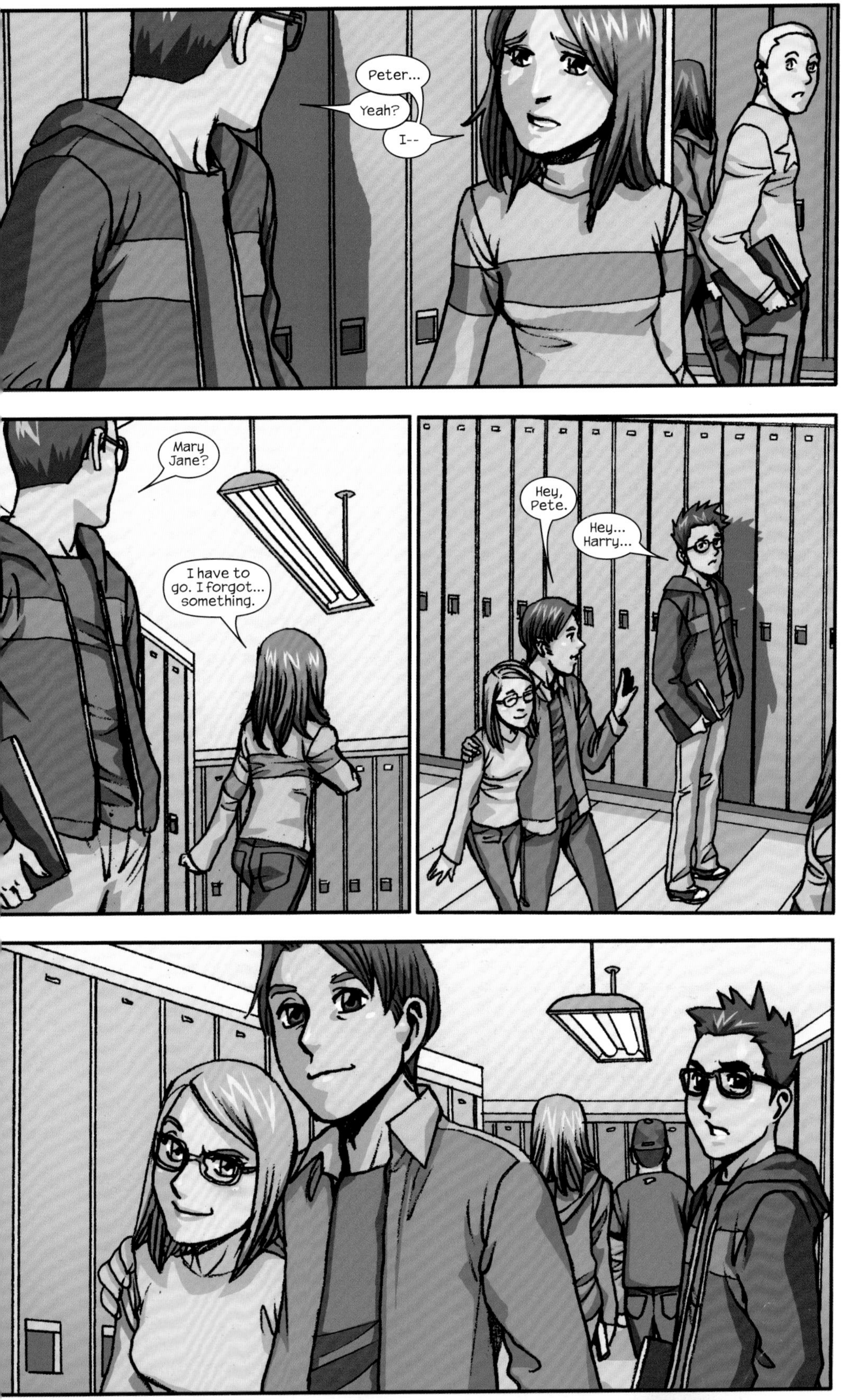
Peter...
Yeah?
I--
Mary Jane?
I have to go. I forgot... something.
Hey, Pete.
Hey... Harry...

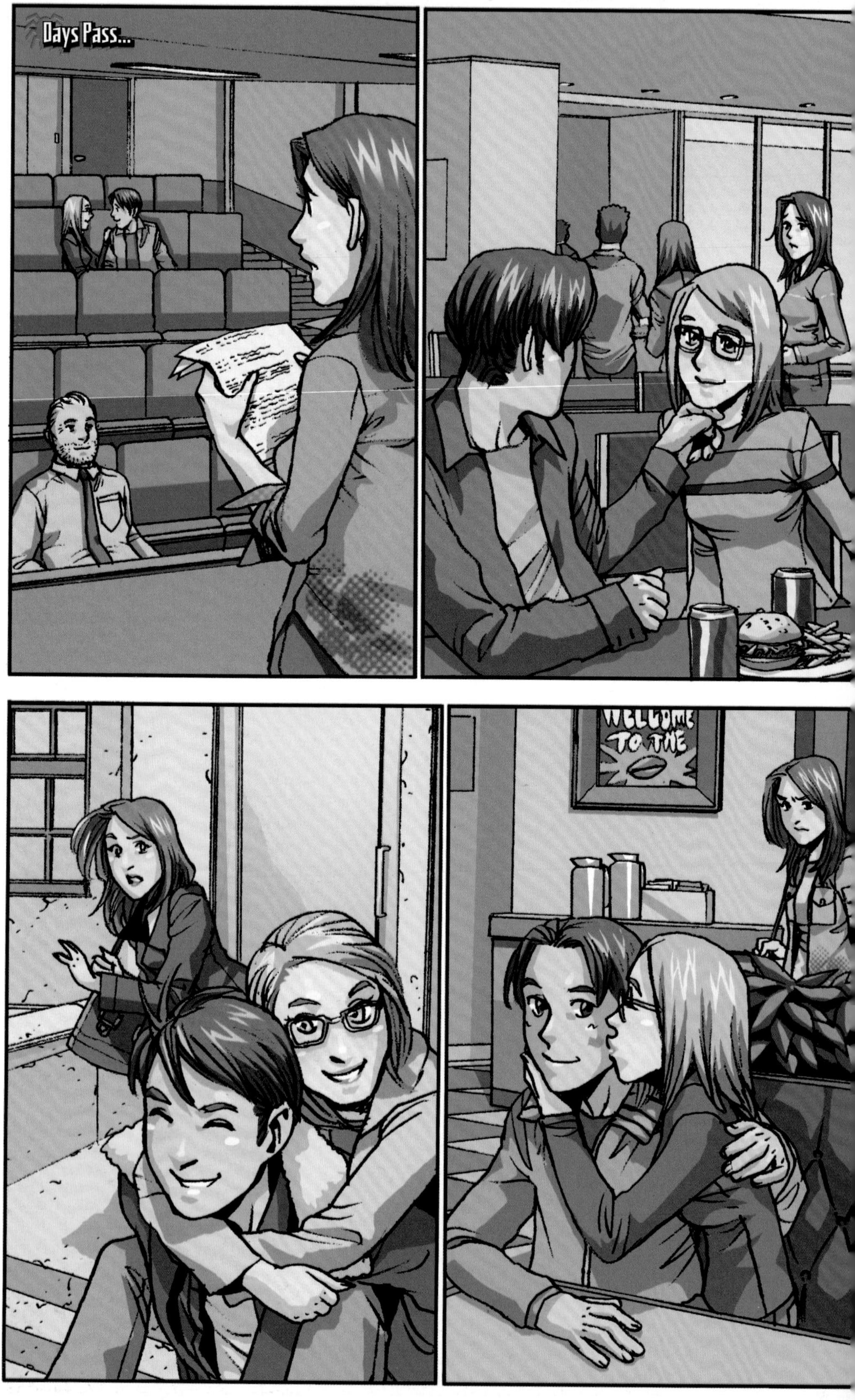
Days Pass...
WELCOME
TO THE

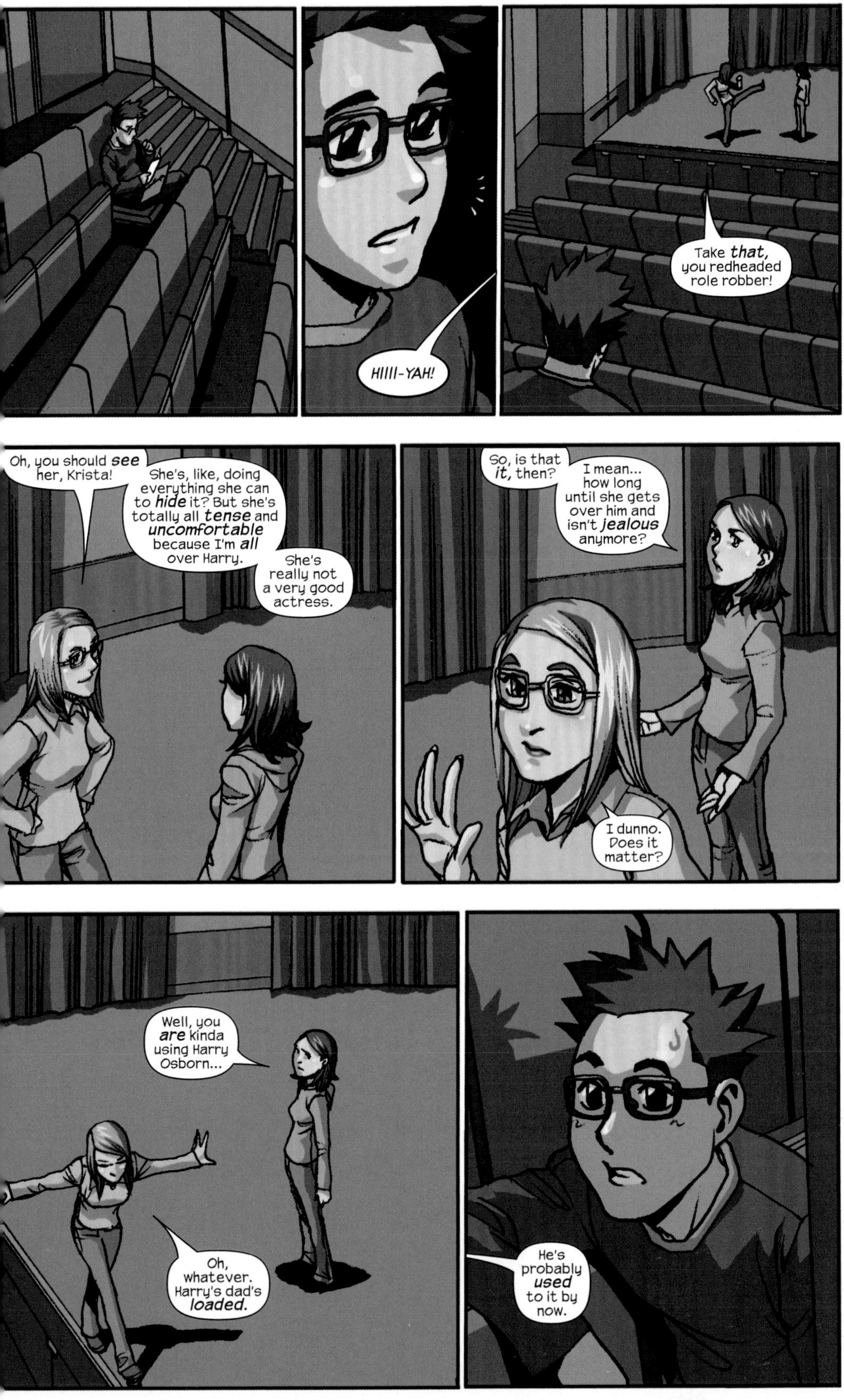
HIIII-YAH!
Take that, you redheaded role robber!
Oh, you should see her, Krista!
She's, like, doing everything she can to hide it? But she's totally all tense and uncomfortable because I'm all over Harry.
She's really not a very good actress.
So, is that it, then?
I mean... how long until she gets over him and isn't jealous anymore?
I dunno. Does it matter?
Well, you are kinda using Harry Osborn...
Oh, whatever. Harry's dad's loaded.
He's probably used to it by now.

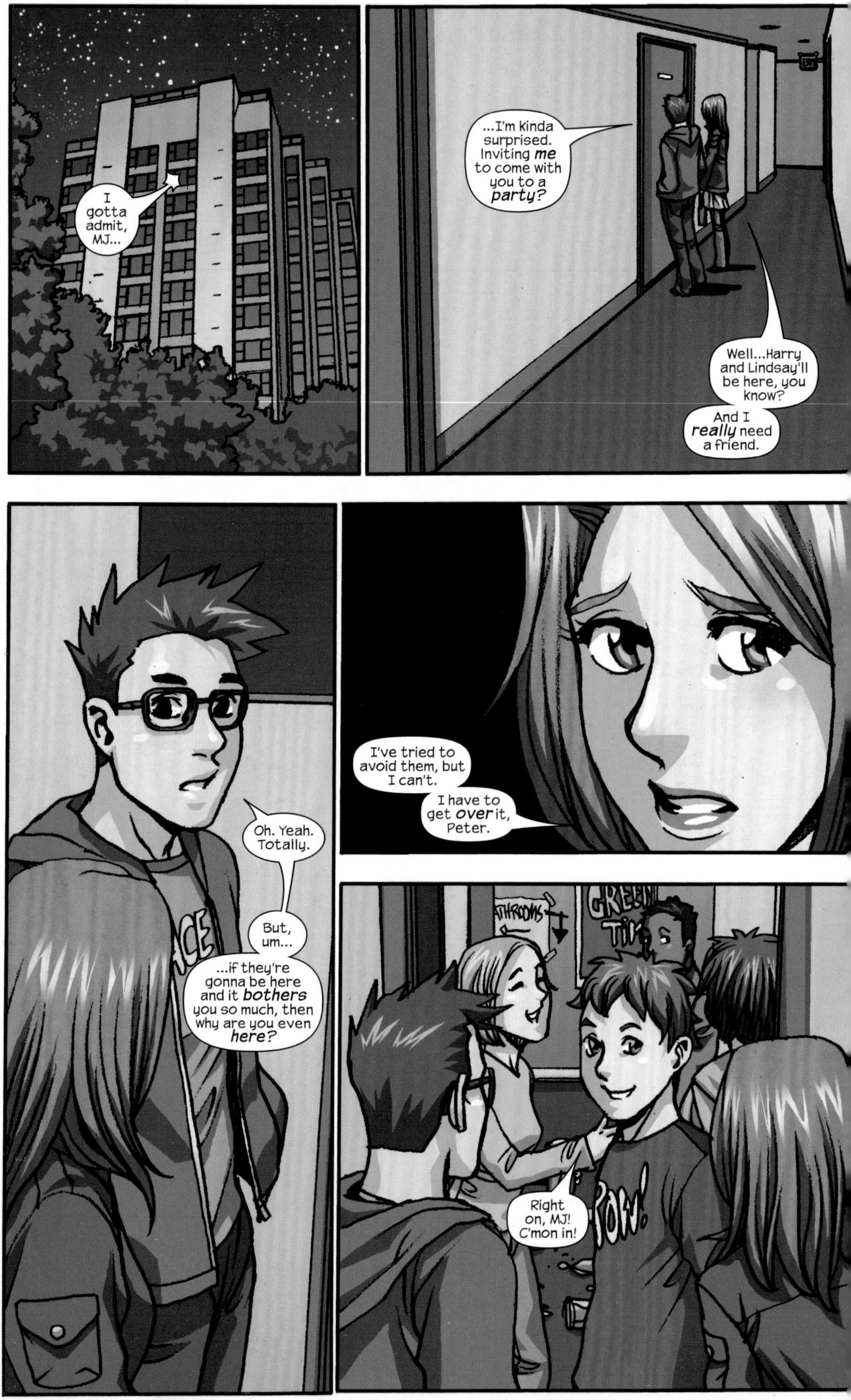

I gotta admit, MJ...
...I'm kinda surprised. Inviting *me* to come with you to a *party*?
Well...Harry and Lindsay'll be here, you know?
And I *really* need a friend.
Oh. Yeah. Totally.
But, um...
...if they're gonna be here and it *bothers* you so much, then why are you even *here*?
I've tried to avoid them, but I can't.
I have to get *over* it, Peter.
Right on, MJ! C'mon in!

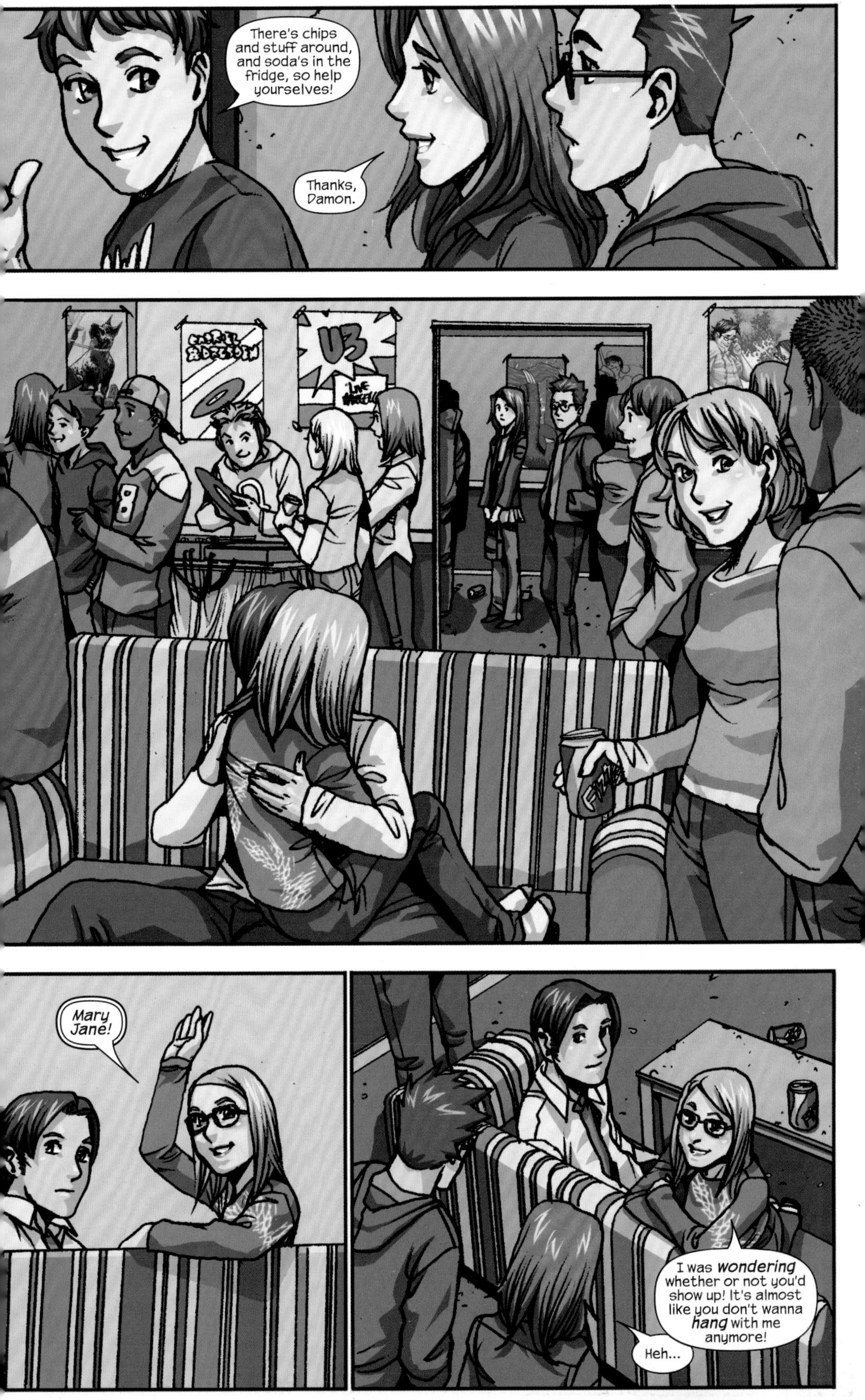
There's chips and stuff around, and soda's in the fridge, so help yourselves!
Thanks, Damon.
U3
Mary Jane!
I was *wondering* whether or not you'd show up! It's almost like you don't wanna *hang* with me anymore!
Heh...

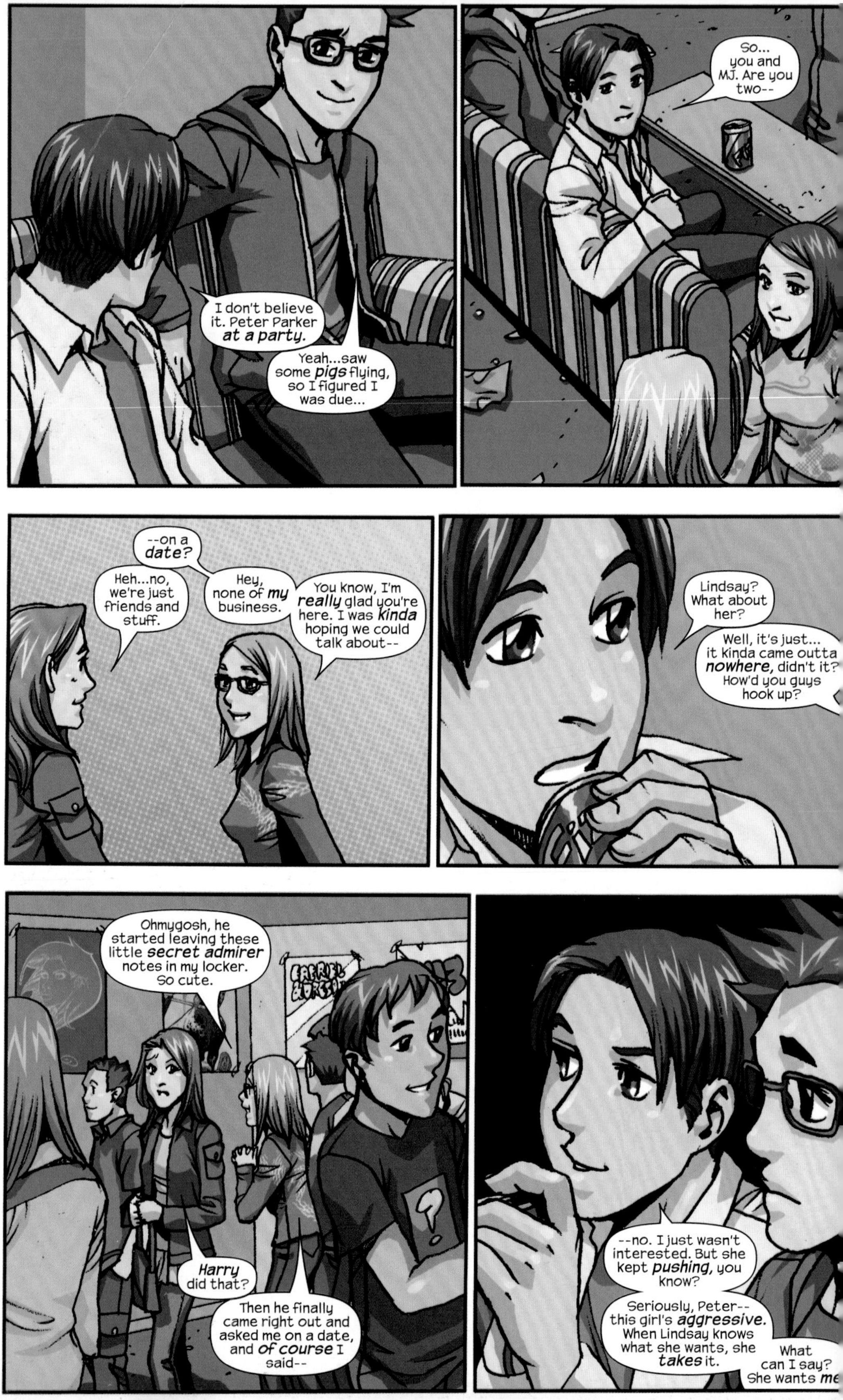
I don't believe it. Peter Parker *at a party.*
Yeah...saw some *pigs* flying, so I figured I was due...
So... you and MJ. Are you two--
--on a *date?*
Heh...no, we're just friends and stuff.
Hey, none of *my* business.
You know, I'm *really* glad you're here. I was *kinda* hoping we could talk about--
Lindsay? What about her?
Well, it's just... it kinda came outta *nowhere,* didn't it? How'd you guys hook up?
Ohmygosh, he started leaving these little *secret admirer* notes in my locker. So cute.
Harry did that?
Then he finally came right out and asked me on a date, and *of course* I said--
--no. I just wasn't interested. But she kept *pushing,* you know?
Seriously, Peter-- this girl's *aggressive.* When Lindsay knows what she wants, she *takes* it.
What can I say? She wants me

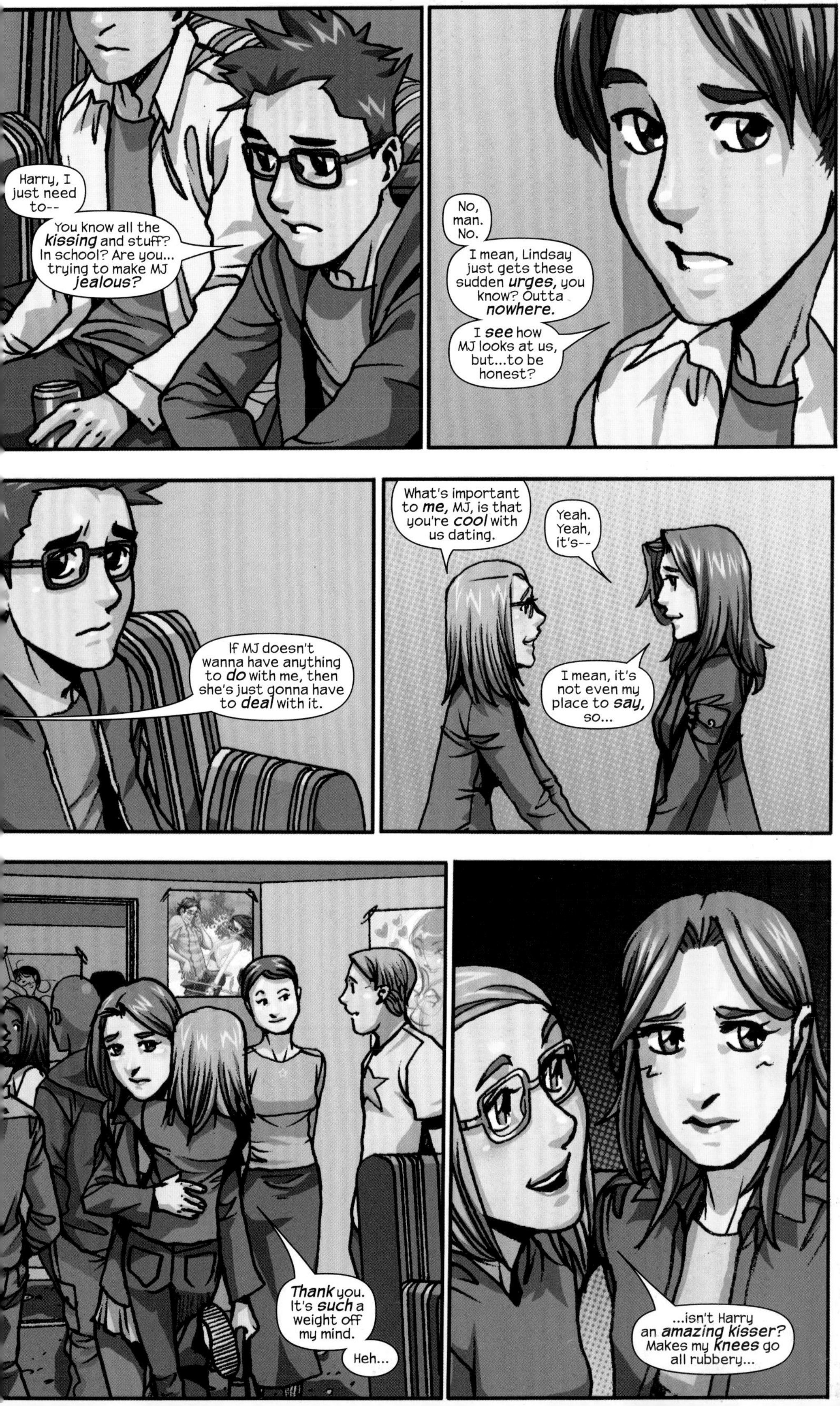
Harry, I just need to--
You know all the *kissing* and stuff? In school? Are you... trying to make MJ *jealous?*
No, man. No.
I mean, Lindsay just gets these sudden *urges*, you know? Outta *nowhere.*
I *see* how MJ looks at us, but...to be honest?
If MJ doesn't wanna have anything to *do* with me, then she's just gonna have to *deal* with it.
What's important to *me*, MJ, is that you're *cool* with us dating.
Yeah. Yeah, it's--
I mean, it's not even my place to *say*, so...
Thank you. It's *such* a weight off my mind.
Heh...
...isn't Harry an *amazing kisser?* Makes my *knees* go all rubbery...

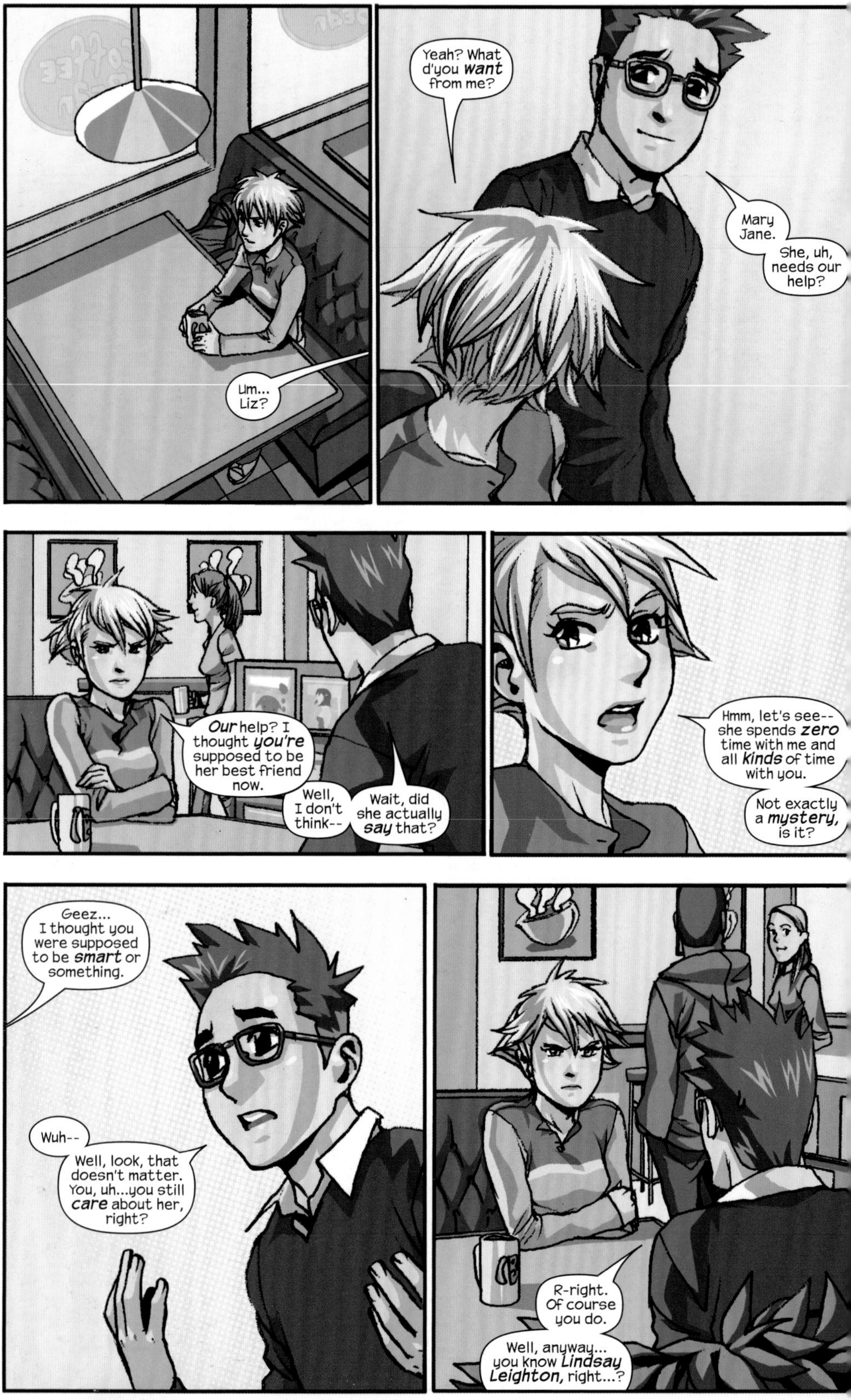
Um... Liz?
Yeah? What d'you *want* from me?
Mary Jane.
She, uh, needs our help?
Our help? I thought *you're* supposed to be her best friend now.
Well, I don't think--
Wait, did she actually *say* that?
Hmm, let's see-- she spends *zero* time with me and all *kinds* of time with you.
Not exactly a *mystery,* is it?
Geez... I thought you were supposed to be *smart* or something.
Wuh--
Well, look, that doesn't matter. You, uh...you still *care* about her, right?
R-right. Of course you do.
Well, anyway... you know *Lindsay Leighton,* right...?

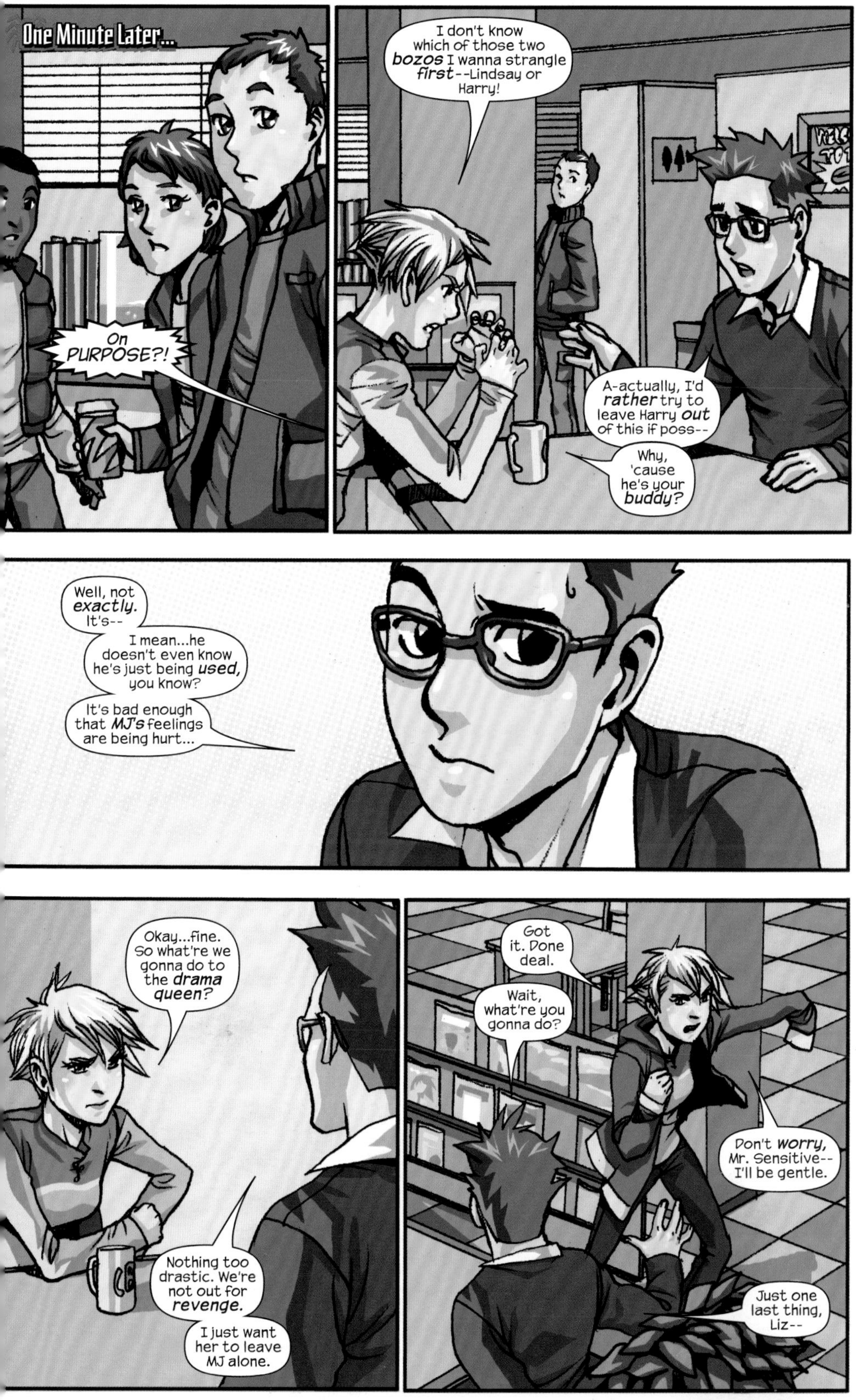
One Minute Later...
On PURPOSE?!
I don't know which of those two bozos I wanna strangle first--Lindsay or Harry!
A-actually, I'd rather try to leave Harry out of this if poss--
Why, 'cause he's your buddy?
Well, not exactly. It's--
I mean...he doesn't even know he's just being used, you know?
It's bad enough that MJ's feelings are being hurt...
Okay...fine. So what're we gonna do to the drama queen?
Nothing too drastic. We're not out for revenge.
I just want her to leave MJ alone.
Got it. Done deal.
Wait, what're you gonna do?
Don't worry, Mr. Sensitive-- I'll be gentle.
Just one last thing, Liz--

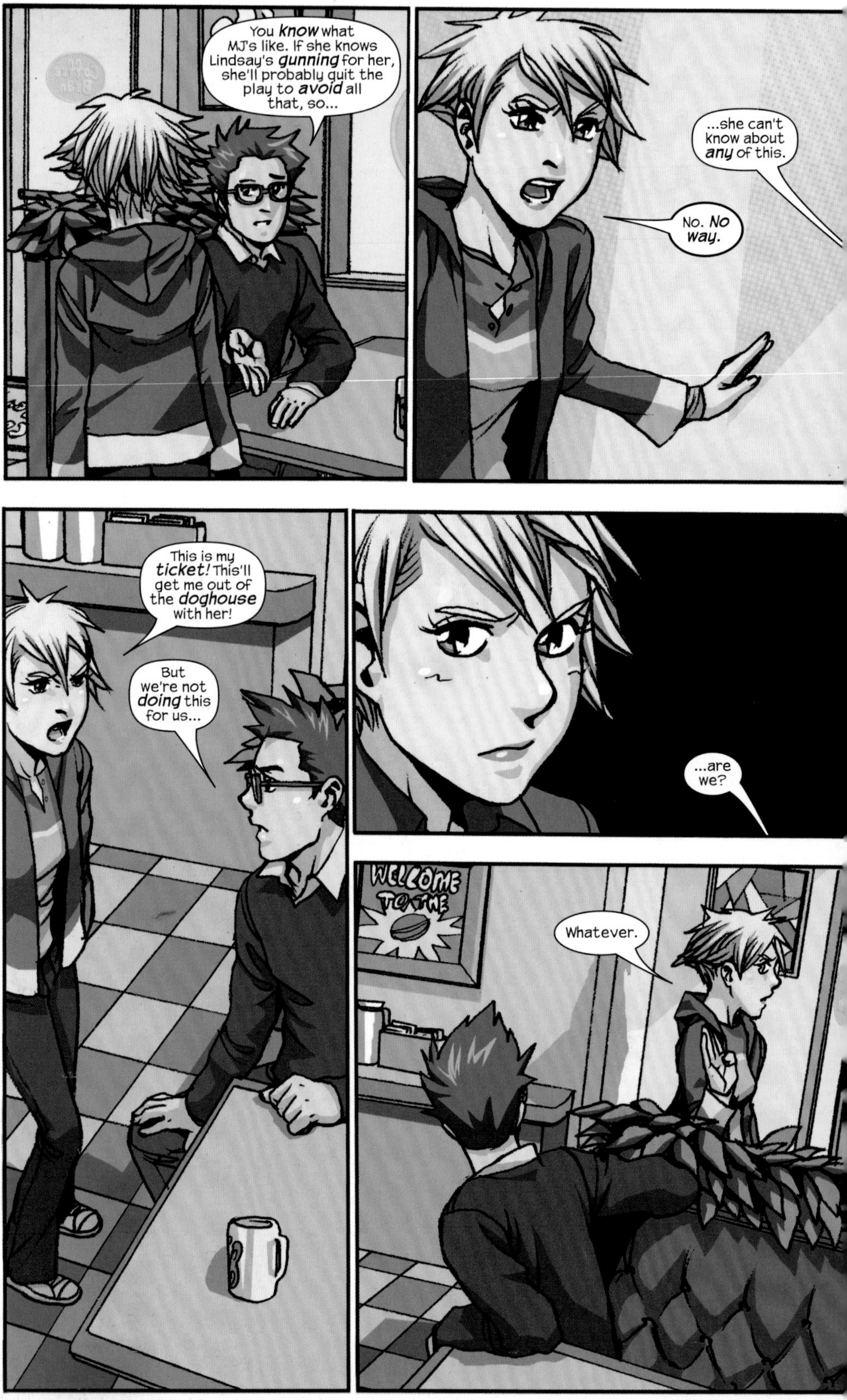
You know what MJ's like. If she knows Lindsay's gunning for her, she'll probably quit the play to avoid all that, so...
...she can't know about any of this.
No. No way.
This is my ticket! This'll get me out of the doghouse with her!
But we're not doing this for us...
...are we?
WELCOME TO THE
Whatever.

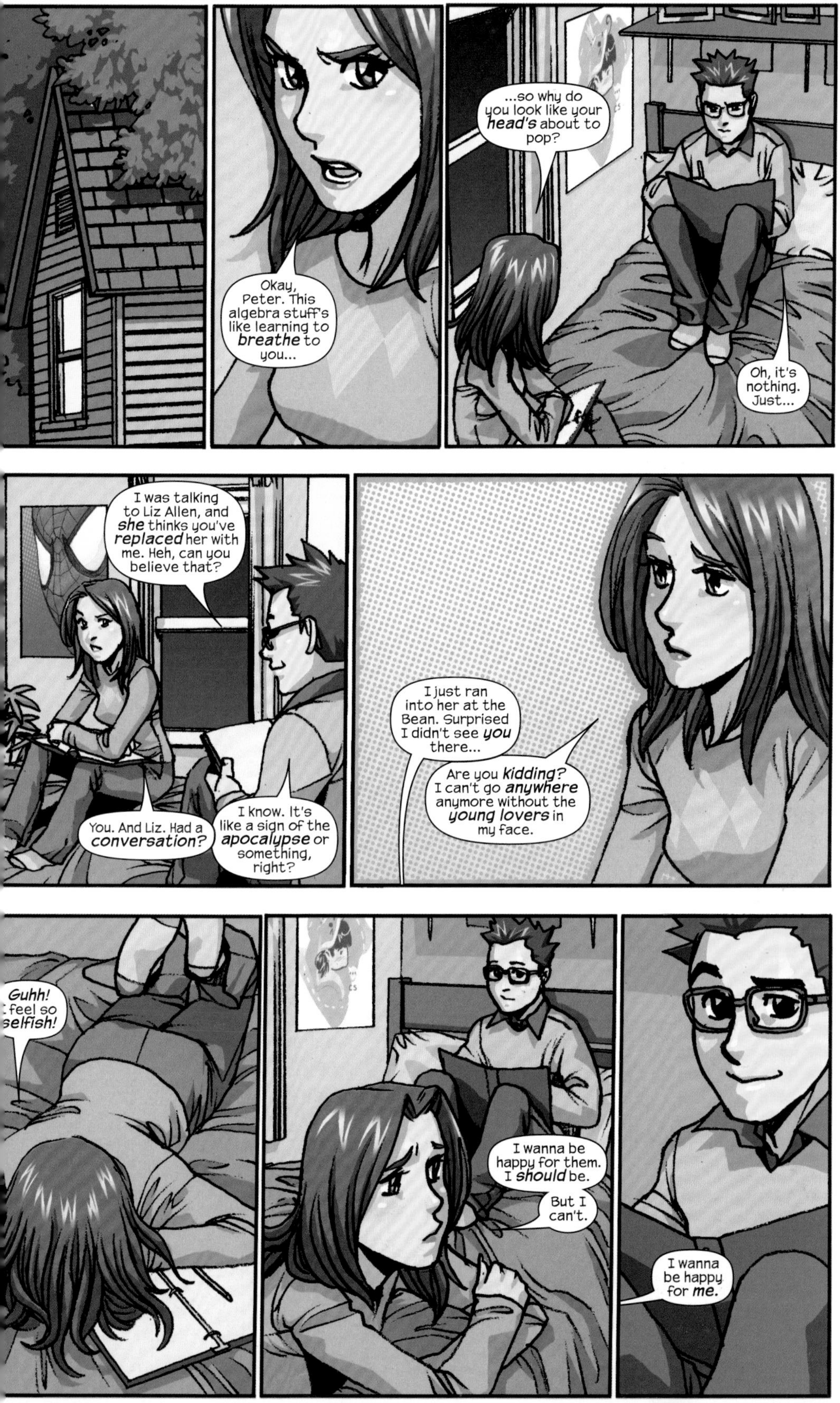
Okay, Peter. This algebra stuff's like learning to *breathe* to you...
...so why do you look like your *head's* about to pop?
Oh, it's nothing. Just...
I was talking to Liz Allen, and *she* thinks you've *replaced* her with me. Heh, can you believe that?
You. And Liz. Had a *conversation?*
I know. It's like a sign of the *apocalypse* or something, right?
I just ran into her at the Bean. Surprised I didn't see *you* there...
Are you *kidding?* I can't go *anywhere* anymore without the *young lovers* in my face.
Guhh! I feel so *selfish!*
I wanna be happy for them. I *should* be.
But I can't.
I wanna be happy for *me.*

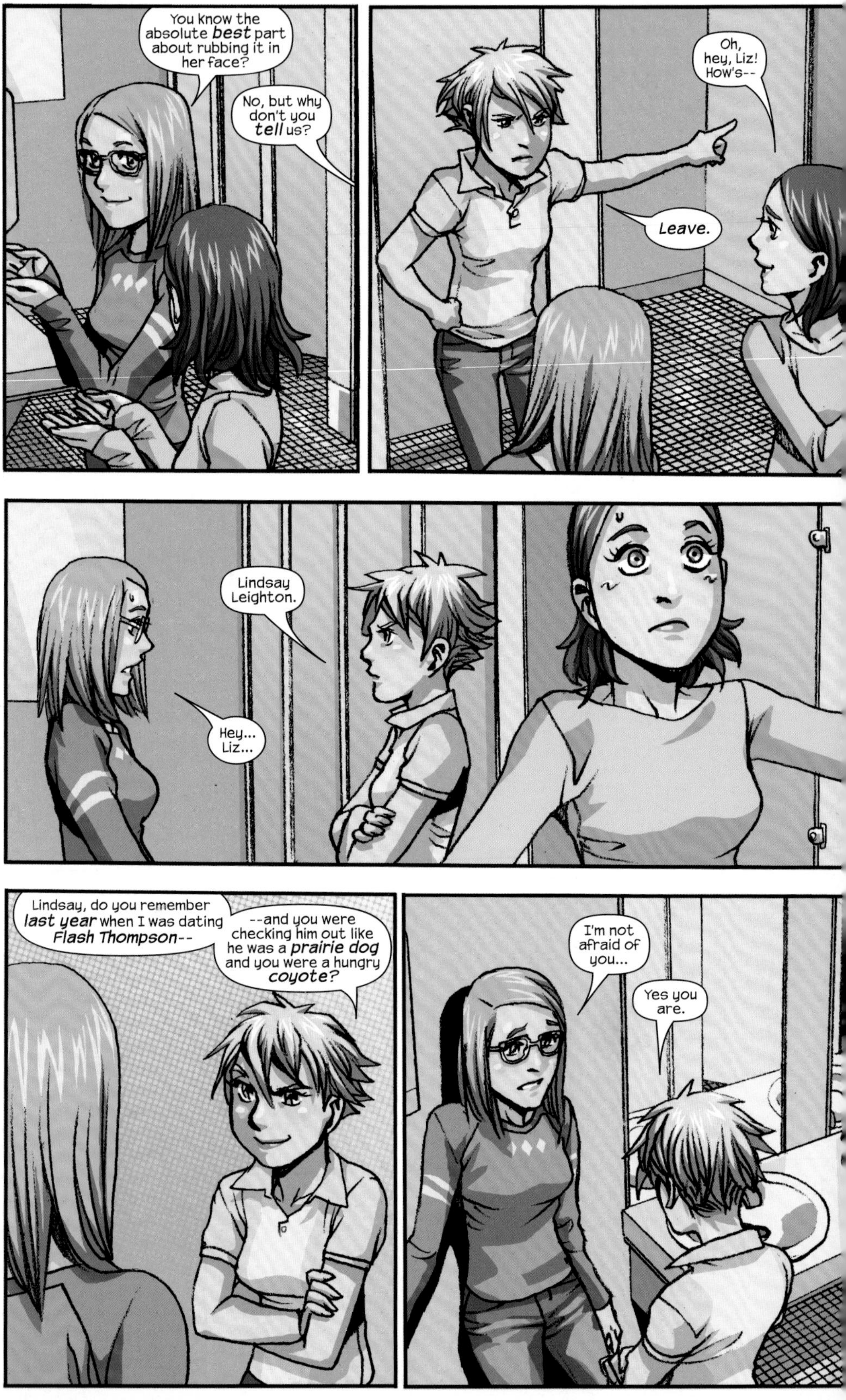

You know the absolute best part about rubbing it in her face?
No, but why don't you tell us?
Oh, hey, Liz! How's--
Leave.
Lindsay Leighton.
Hey... Liz...
Lindsay, do you remember last year when I was dating Flash Thompson--
--and you were checking him out like he was a prairie dog and you were a hungry coyote?
I'm not afraid of you...
Yes you are.

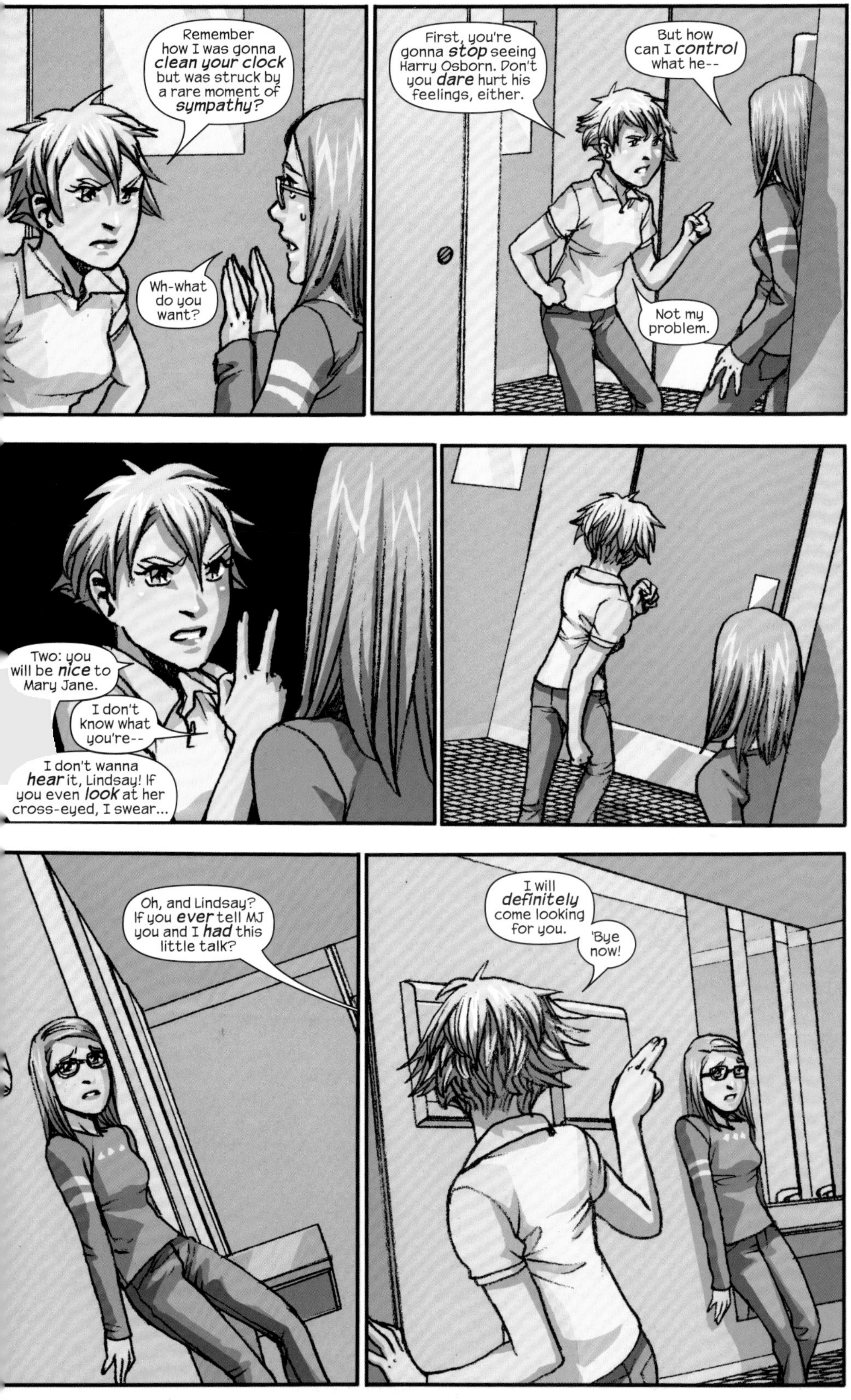
Remember how I was gonna clean your clock but was struck by a rare moment of sympathy?
Wh-what do you want?
First, you're gonna stop seeing Harry Osborn. Don't you dare hurt his feelings, either.
But how can I control what he--
Not my problem.
Two: you will be nice to Mary Jane.
I don't know what you're--
I don't wanna hear it, Lindsay! If you even look at her cross-eyed, I swear...
Oh, and Lindsay? If you ever tell MJ you and I had this little talk?
I will definitely come looking for you.
'Bye now!

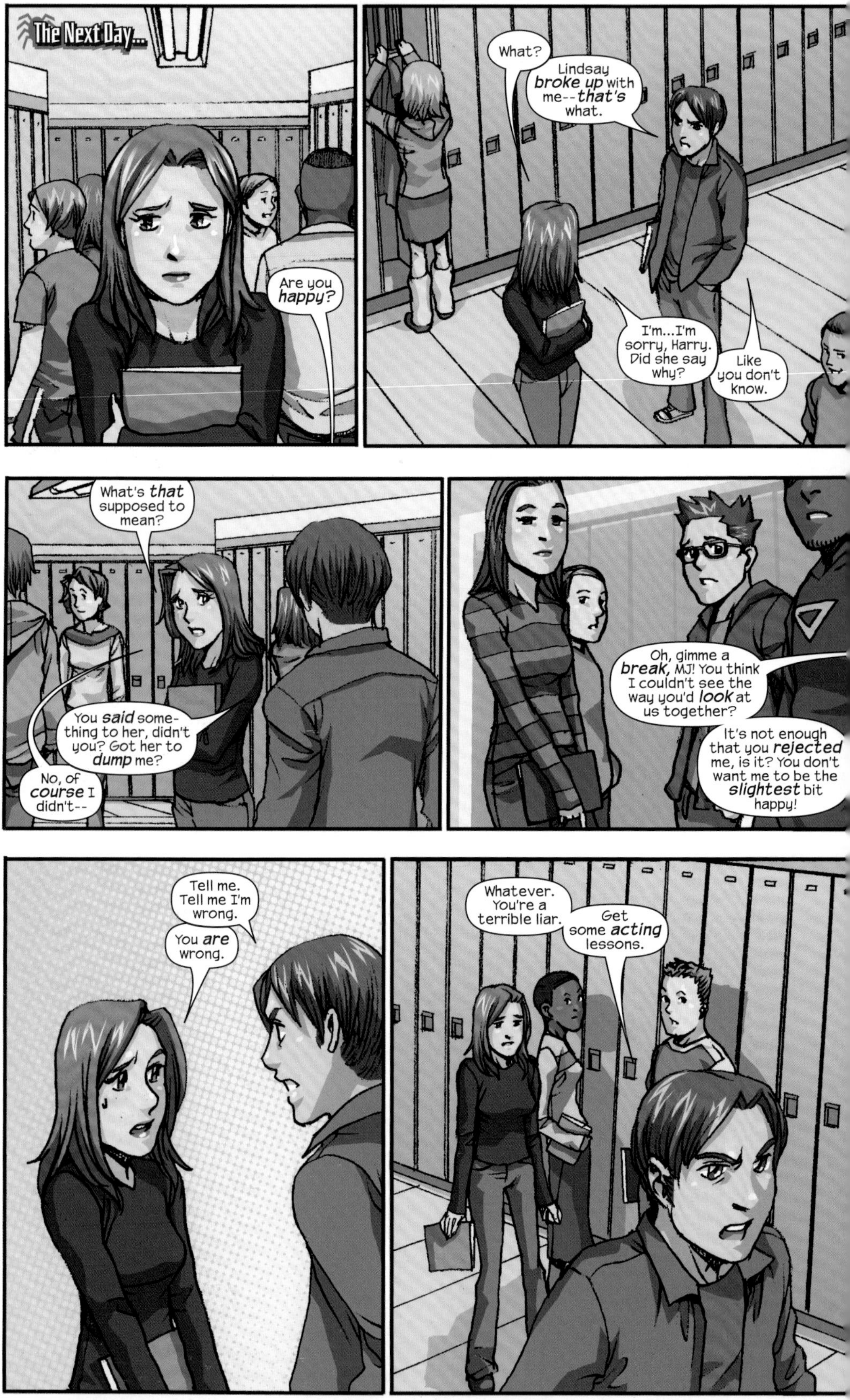

The Next Day...
Are you happy?
What?
Lindsay broke up with me--that's what.
I'm...I'm sorry, Harry. Did she say why?
Like you don't know.
What's that supposed to mean?
You said something to her, didn't you? Got her to dump me?
No, of course I didn't--
Oh, gimme a break, MJ! You think I couldn't see the way you'd look at us together?
It's not enough that you rejected me, is it? You don't want me to be the slightest bit happy!
Tell me. Tell me I'm wrong.
You are wrong.
Whatever. You're a terrible liar.
Get some acting lessons.

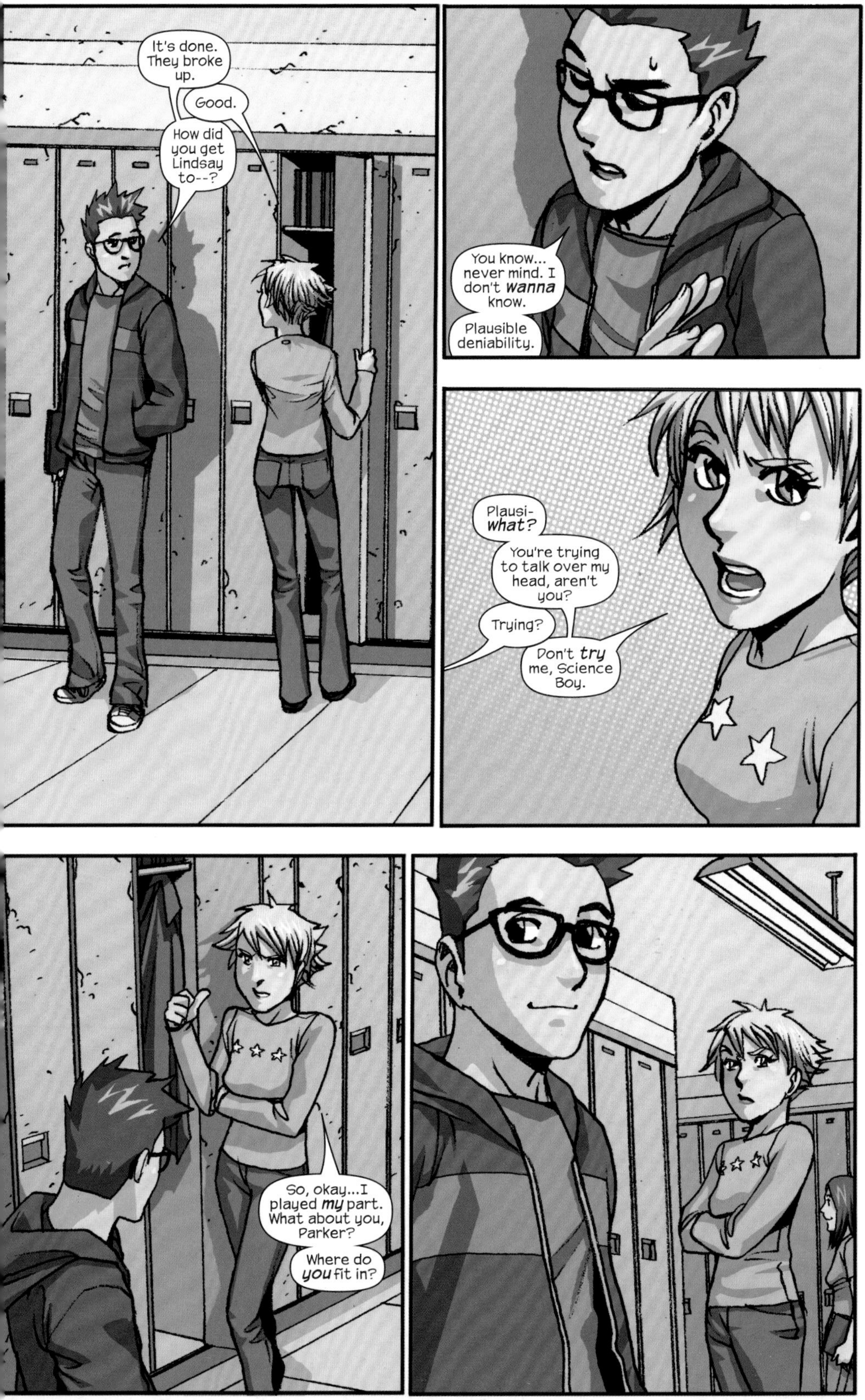
It's done. They broke up.
Good.
How did you get Lindsay to--?
You know... never mind. I don't *wanna* know.
Plausible deniability.
Plausi-*what?*
You're trying to talk over my head, aren't you?
Trying?
Don't *try* me, Science Boy.
So, okay...I played *my* part. What about you, Parker?
Where do *you* fit in?

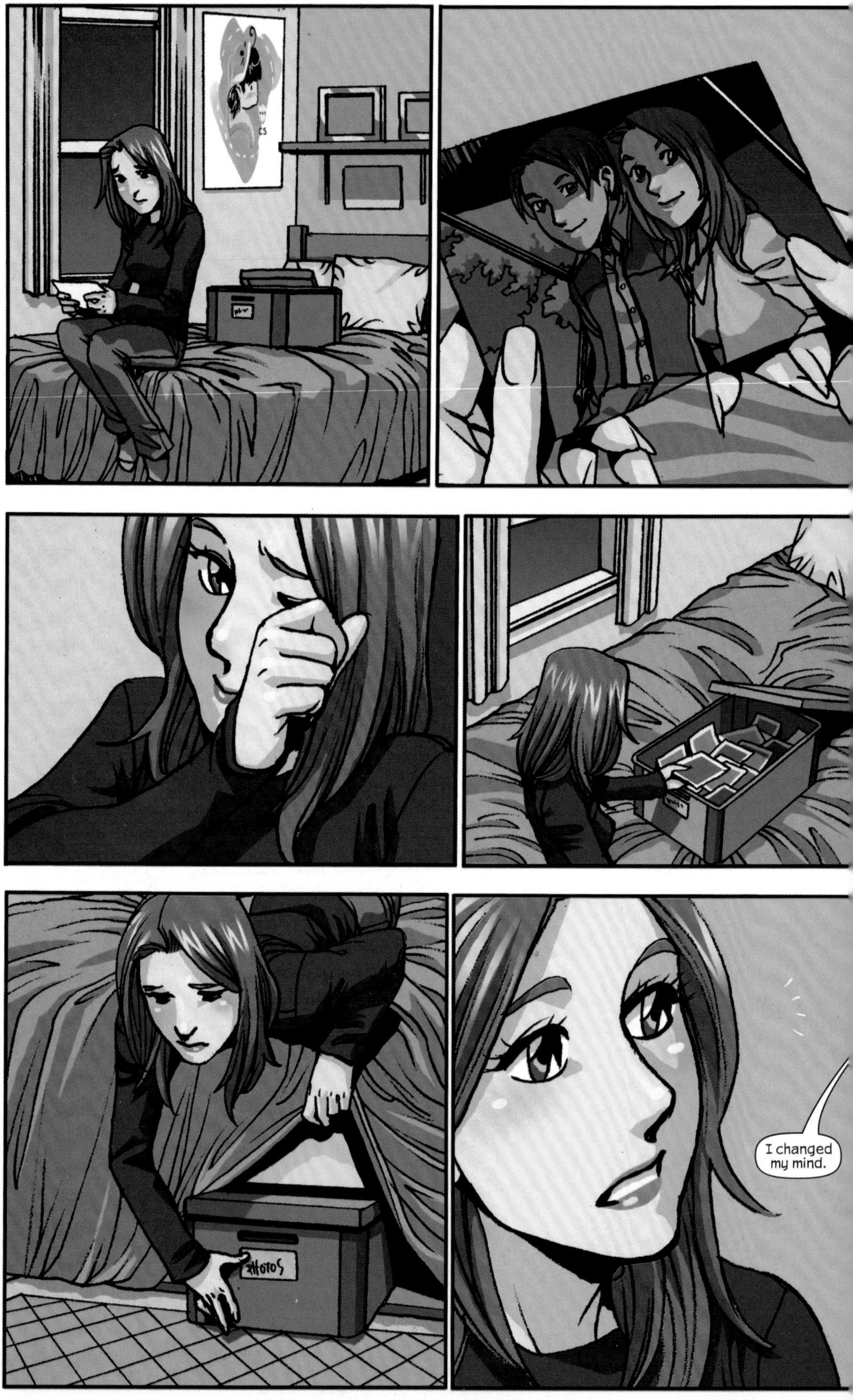
PHOTOS
I changed my mind.

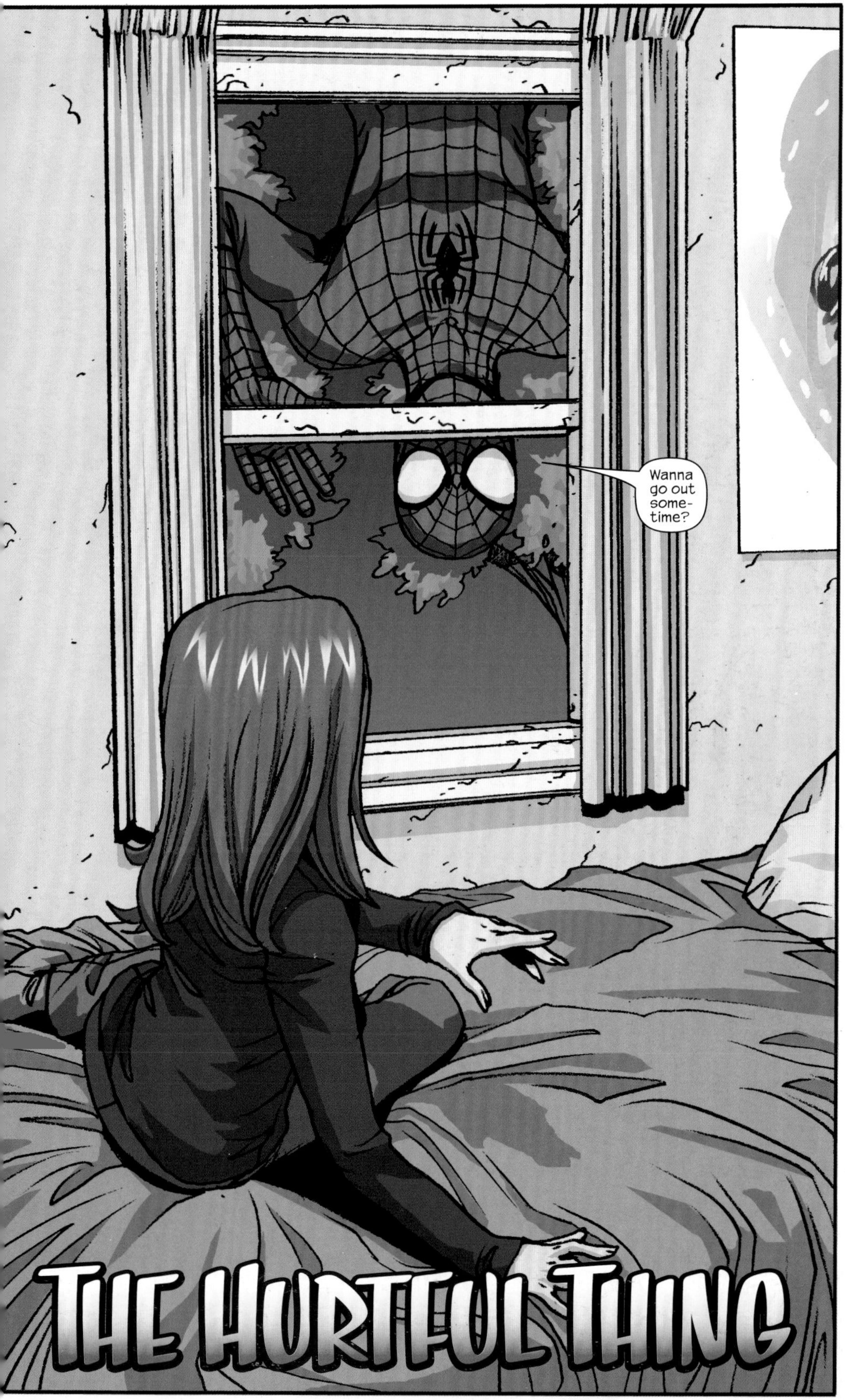
Wanna go out some-time?
THE HURTFUL THING

Character Designs
BY TAKESHI MIYAZAWA

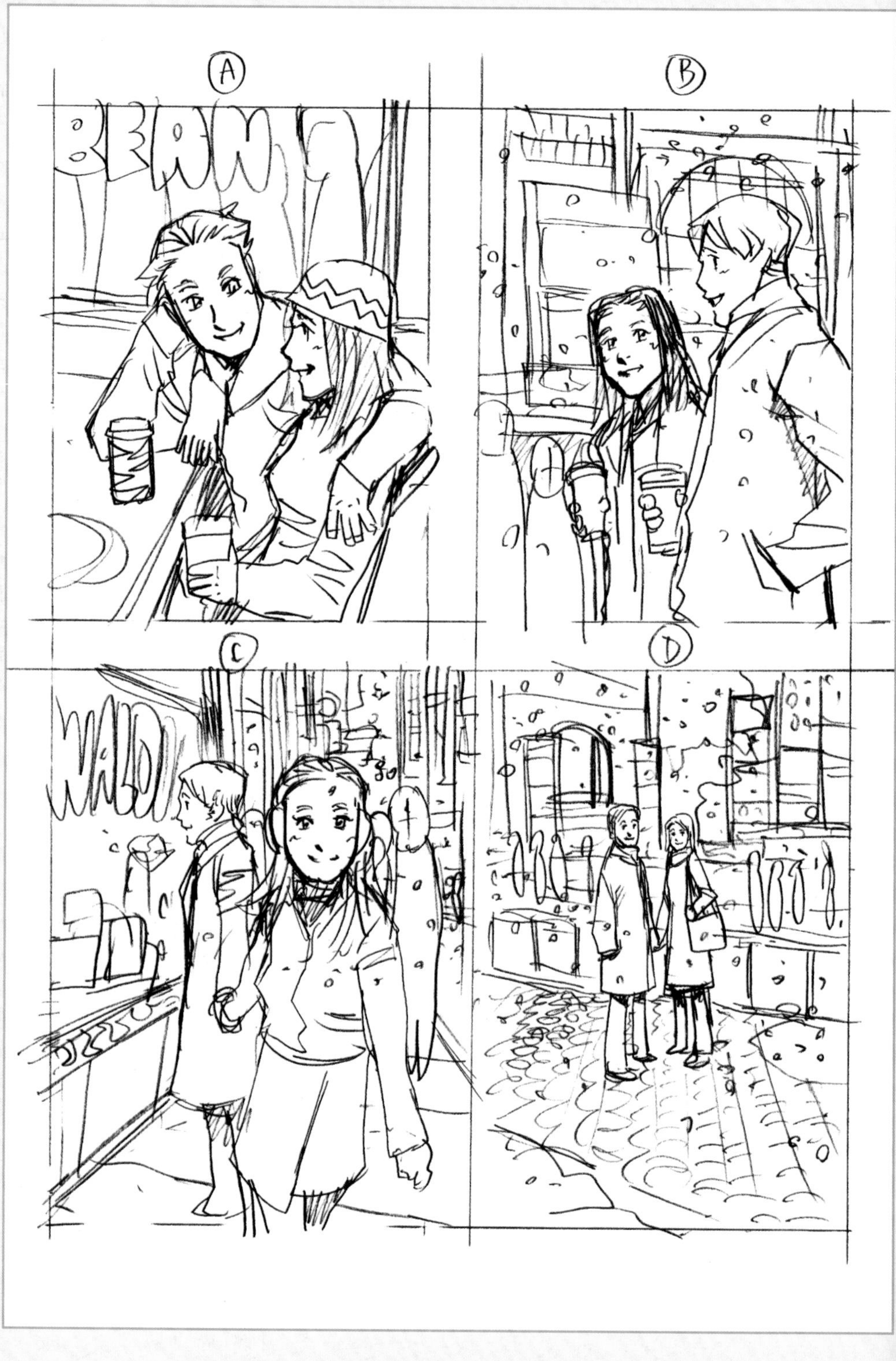
A
B
C
D

Mary Jane: Homecoming #1 Cover Sketches

BY TAKESHI MIYAZAWA

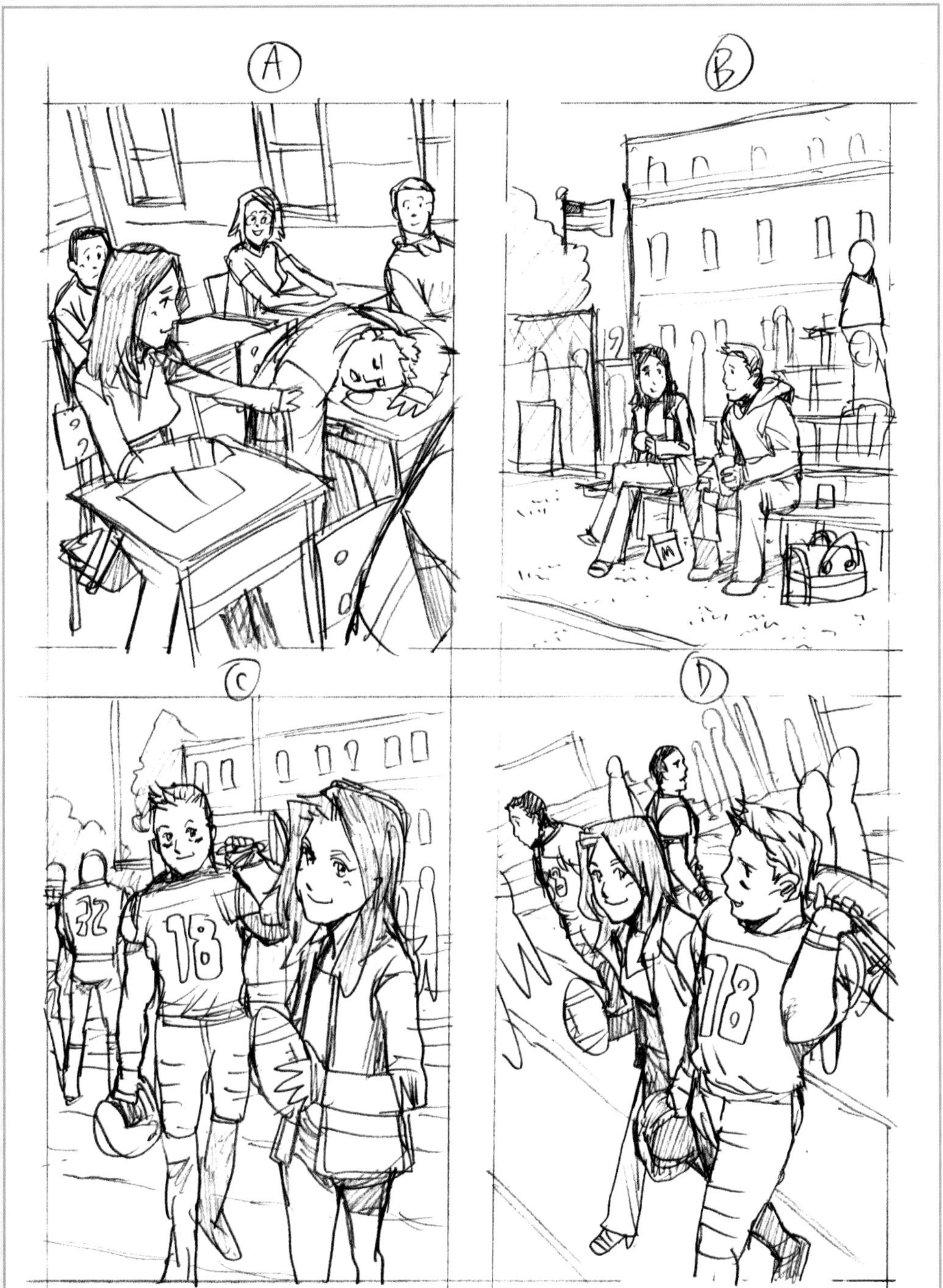
A
B
C
32
18
D
18

Mary Jane: Homecoming #3 Cover Sketches
BY TAKESHI MIYAZAWA

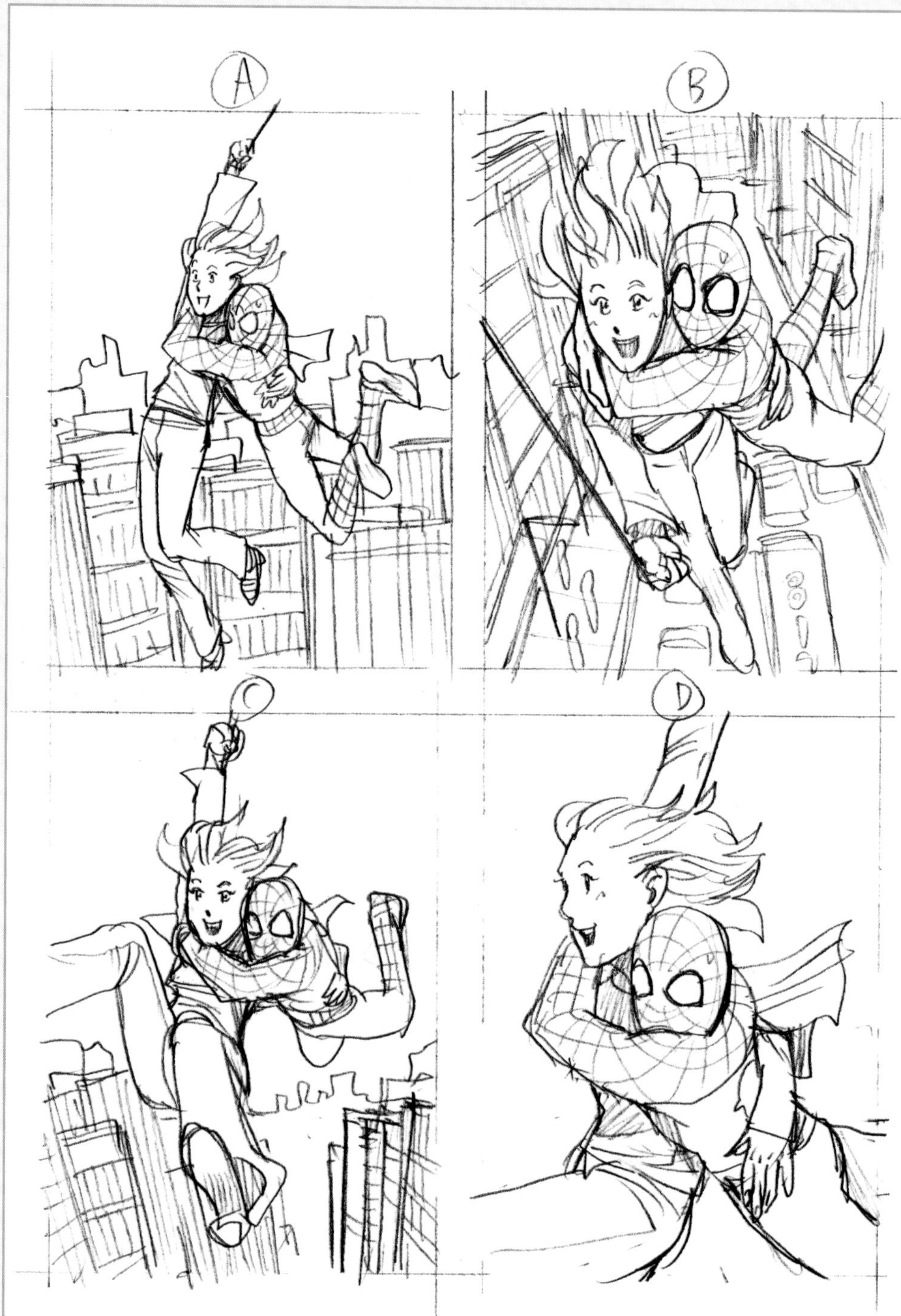
A
B
C
D

Spider-Man Loves Mary Jane #1 Cover Sketches

BY TAKESHI MIYAZAWA

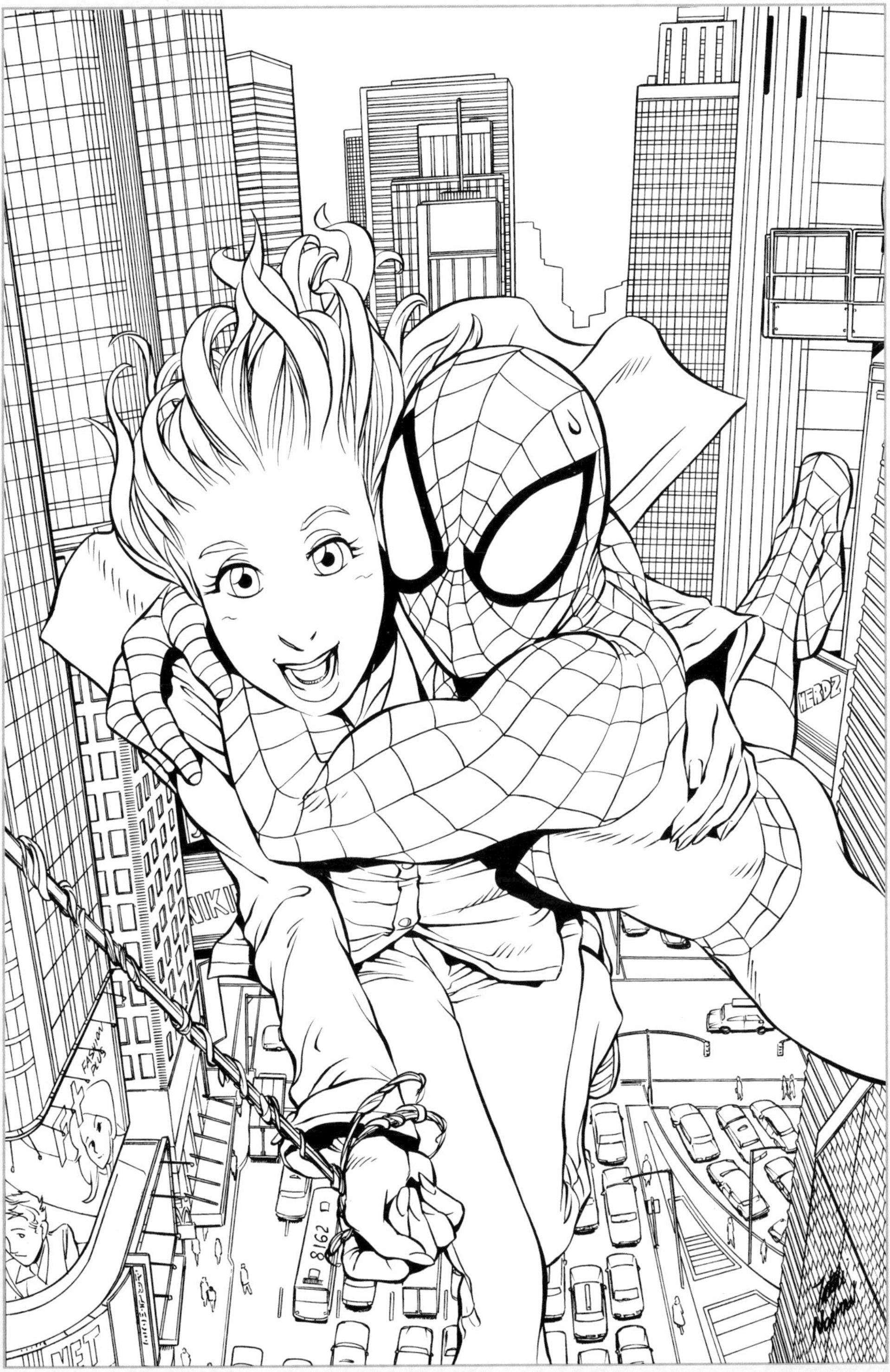
NERDZ

Spider-Man Loves Mary Jane #1 Final Cover Art

BY TAKESHI MIYAZAWA & NORMAL LEE

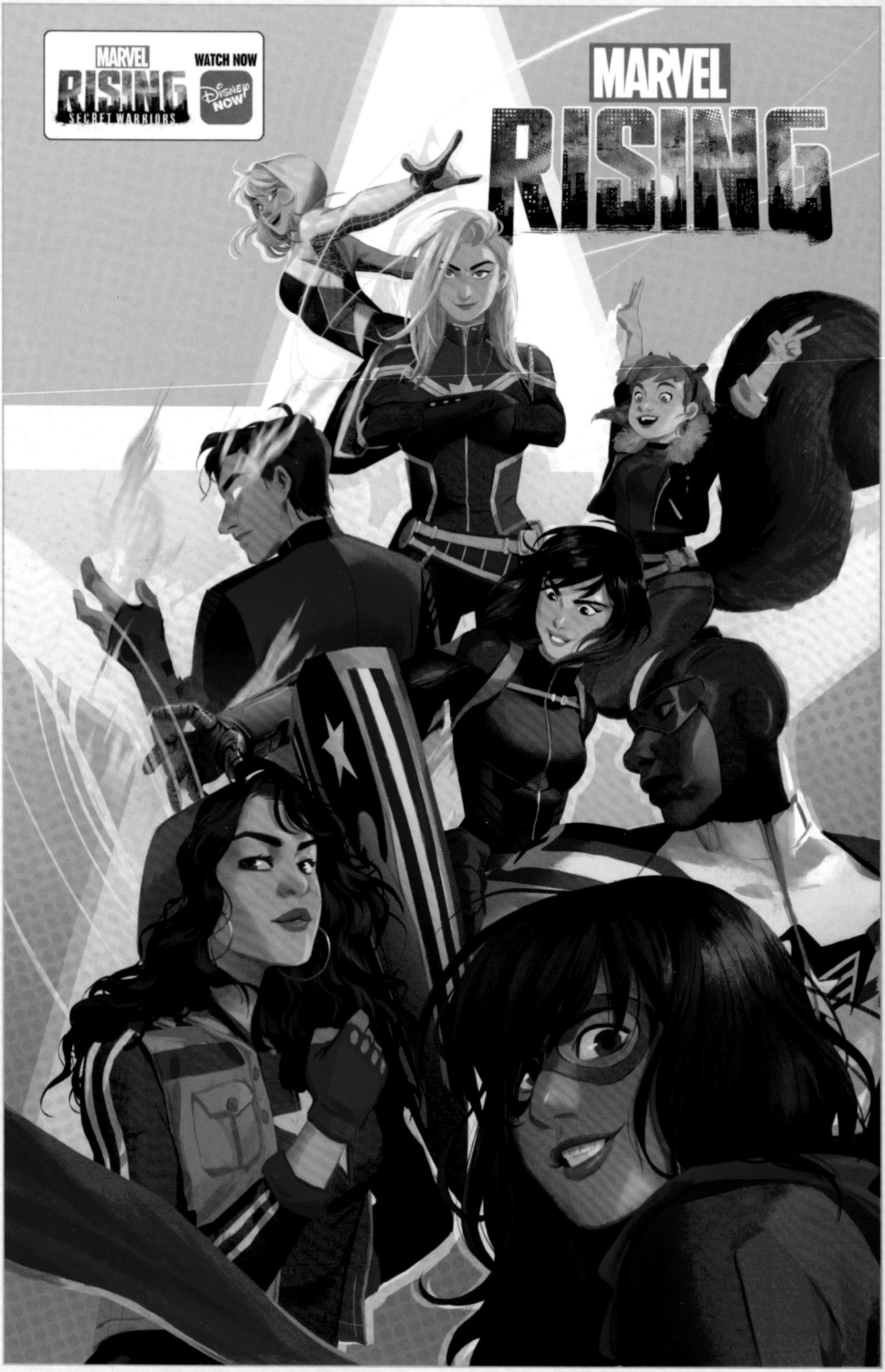
MARVEL RISING SECRET WARRIORS
WATCH NOW
DISNEY NOW
MARVEL
RISING

Marvel Rising Bonus Preview!

MARVEL RISING

THE MARVEL UNIVERSE IS A RICH TREASURE CHEST OF CHARACTERS BORN ACROSS MARVEL'S INCREDIBLE 80-YEAR HISTORY. FROM CAPTAIN AMERICA TO CAPTAIN MARVEL, IRON MAN TO IRONHEART, THIS IS AN EVER-EXPANDING UNIVERSE FULL OF POWERFUL HEROES THAT ALSO REFLECTS THE WORLD WE LIVE IN.

YET DESPITE THAT EXPANSION, OUR STORIES REMAIN TIMELESS. THEY'VE BEEN SHARED ACROSS THE GLOBE AND ACROSS GENERATIONS, LINKING FANS WITH THE ENDURING IDEA THAT ORDINARY PEOPLE CAN DO EXTRAORDINARY THINGS. IT'S THAT SHARED EXPERIENCE OF THE MARVEL STORY THAT HAS ALLOWED US TO EXIST FOR THIS LONG. WHETHER YOUR FIRST MARVEL EXPERIENCE WAS THROUGH A COMIC BOOK, A BEDTIME STORY, A MOVIE OR A CARTOON, WE BELIEVE OUR STORIES STAY WITH AUDIENCES THROUGHOUT THEIR LIVES.

MARVEL RISING IS A CELEBRATION OF THIS TIMELESSNESS. AS OUR STORIES PASS FROM ONE GENERATION TO THE NEXT, SO DOES THE LOVE FOR OUR HEROES. FROM THE CLASSIC TO THE NEWLY IMAGINED, THE PASSION FOR ALL OF THEM IS THE SAME. IF YOU'VE BEEN READING COMICS OVER THE LAST FEW YEARS, YOU'LL KNOW CHARACTERS LIKE MS. MARVEL, SQUIRREL GIRL, AMERICA CHAVEZ, SPIDER-GWEN AND MORE HAVE ASSEMBLED A BEVY OF NEW FANS WHILE CAPTIVATING OUR PERENNIAL FANS. EACH OF THESE HEROES IS UNIQUE AND DISTINCT--JUST LIKE THE READERS THEY'VE BROUGHT IN--AND THEY REMIND US THAT NO MATTER WHAT YOU LOOK LIKE, YOU HAVE THE CAPABILITY TO BE POWERFUL, TOO. WE ARE TAKING THE HEROES FROM MARVEL RISING TO NEW HEIGHTS IN AN ANIMATED FEATURE LATER IN 2018, AS WELL AS A FULL PROGRAM OF CONTENT SWEEPING ACROSS THE COMPANY. BUT FIRST WE'RE GOING BACK TO OUR ROOTS AND TELLING A MARVEL RISING STORY IN COMICS: THE FIRST PLACE YOU MET THESE LOVABLE HEROES.

SO IN THE TRADITION OF EXPANDING THE MARVEL UNIVERSE, WE'RE EXCITED TO INTRODUCE MARVEL RISING--THE NEXT GENERATION OF MARVEL HEROES FOR THE NEXT GENERATION OF MARVEL FANS!

SANA AMANAT
VP, CONTENT & CHARACTER DEVELOPMENT

▶ **DOREEN GREEN** IS A SECOND-YEAR COMPUTER SCIENCE STUDENT – AND THE CRIMINAL-REDEEMING HERO THE UNBEATABLE SQUIRREL GIRL! THE NAME SAYS IT ALL: AN UNBEATABLE GIRL WITH THE POWERS OF AN UNBEATABLE SQUIRREL, TAIL INCLUDED. AND ON TOP OF HER STUDYING, NUT-EATING AND BUTT-KICKING ACTIVITIES, SHE'S JUST TAKEN ON THE JOB OF VOLUNTEER TEACHER FOR AN EXTRA-CURRICULAR HIGH-SCHOOL CODING CAMP! AND WHO SHOULD END UP IN HER CLASS BUT...

▶ **KAMALA KHAN**, A.K.A. JERSEY CITY HERO AND INHUMAN POLYMORPH MS. MARVEL! BUT BETWEEN SAVING THE WORLD WITH THE CHAMPIONS AND PROTECTING JERSEY CITY ON HER OWN, KAMALA'S GOT A LOT ON HER PLATE ALREADY. AND FIELD TRIP DAY MAY NOT BE THE BREAK SHE'S ANTICIPATING...

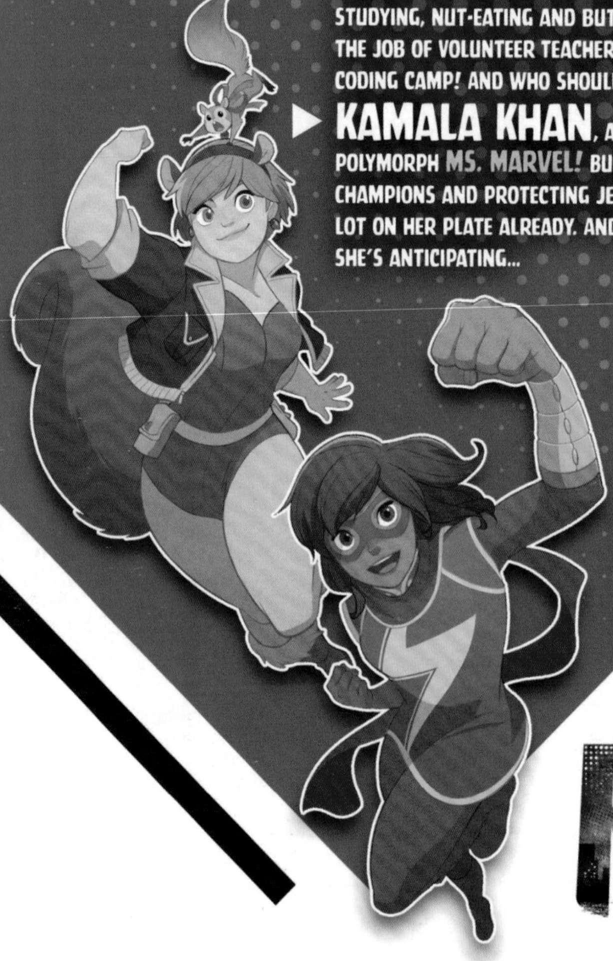

MARVEL RISING

PART 0

DEVIN GRAYSON
WRITER

MARCO FAILLA
ARTIST

RACHELLE ROSENBERG
COLOR ARTIST

VC's CLAYTON COWLES
LETTERER

HELEN CHEN
COVER

JAY BOWEN
DESIGN

HEATHER ANTOS AND SARAH BRUNSTAD
EDITORS

SANA AMANAT
CONSULTING EDITOR

C.B. CEBULSKI
EDITOR IN CHIEF

JOE QUESADA
CHIEF CREATIVE OFFICER

DAN BUCKLEY
PRESIDENT

ALAN FINE
EXECUTIVE PRODUCER

SPECIAL THANKS TO RYAN NORTH AND G. WILLOW WILSON

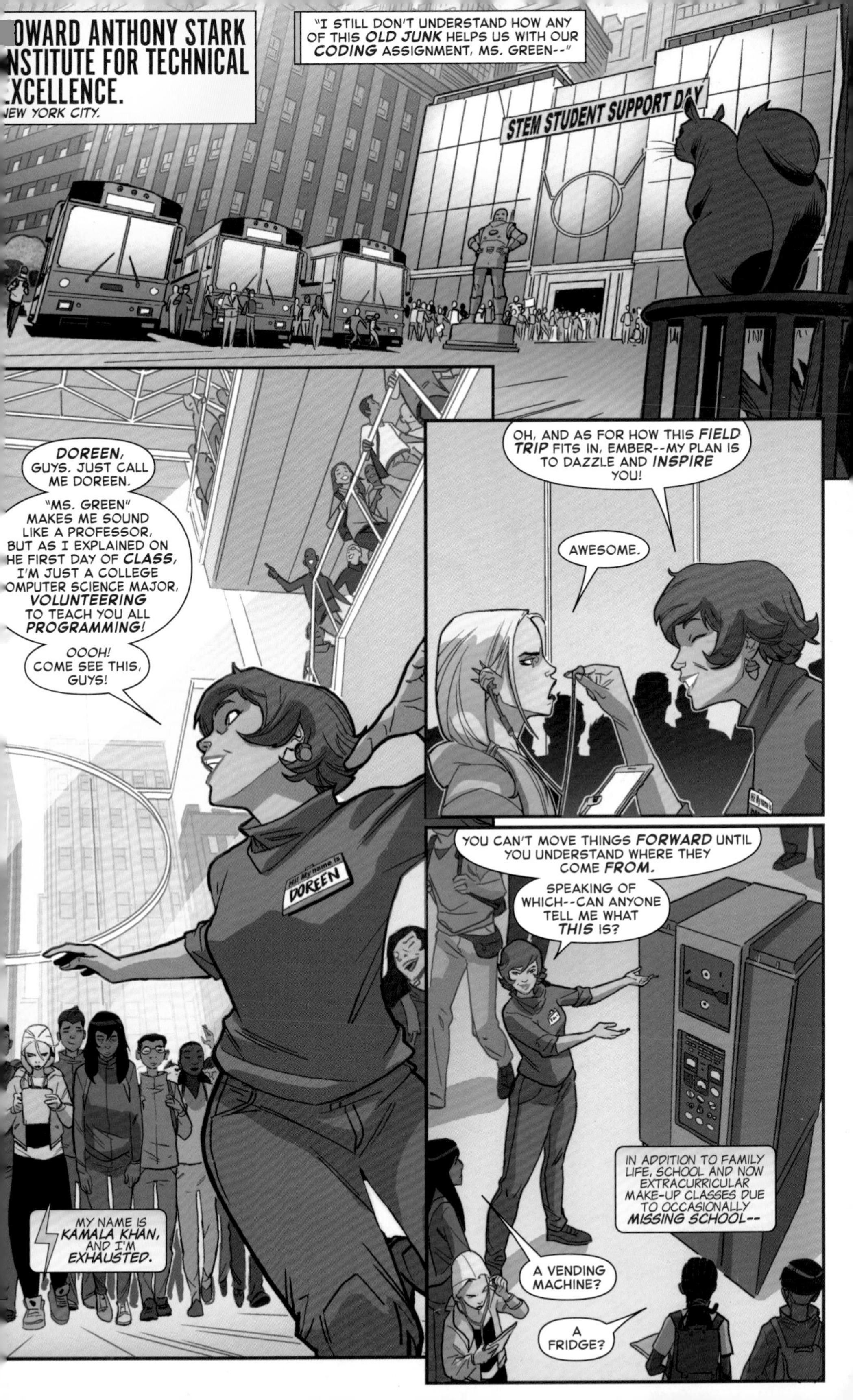

OWARD ANTHONY STARK
NSTITUTE FOR TECHNICAL
XCELLENCE.
NEW YORK CITY.
"I STILL DON'T UNDERSTAND HOW ANY OF THIS OLD JUNK HELPS US WITH OUR CODING ASSIGNMENT, MS. GREEN--"
STEM STUDENT SUPPORT DAY
DOREEN, GUYS. JUST CALL ME DOREEN.
"MS. GREEN" MAKES ME SOUND LIKE A PROFESSOR, BUT AS I EXPLAINED ON HE FIRST DAY OF CLASS, I'M JUST A COLLEGE OMPUTER SCIENCE MAJOR, VOLUNTEERING TO TEACH YOU ALL PROGRAMMING!
OOOH! COME SEE THIS, GUYS!
HI! My name is DOREEN
MY NAME IS KAMALA KHAN, AND I'M EXHAUSTED.
OH, AND AS FOR HOW THIS FIELD TRIP FITS IN, EMBER--MY PLAN IS TO DAZZLE AND INSPIRE YOU!
AWESOME.
YOU CAN'T MOVE THINGS FORWARD UNTIL YOU UNDERSTAND WHERE THEY COME FROM.
SPEAKING OF WHICH--CAN ANYONE TELL ME WHAT THIS IS?
IN ADDITION TO FAMILY LIFE, SCHOOL AND NOW EXTRACURRICULAR MAKE-UP CLASSES DUE TO OCCASIONALLY MISSING SCHOOL--
A VENDING MACHINE?
A FRIDGE?

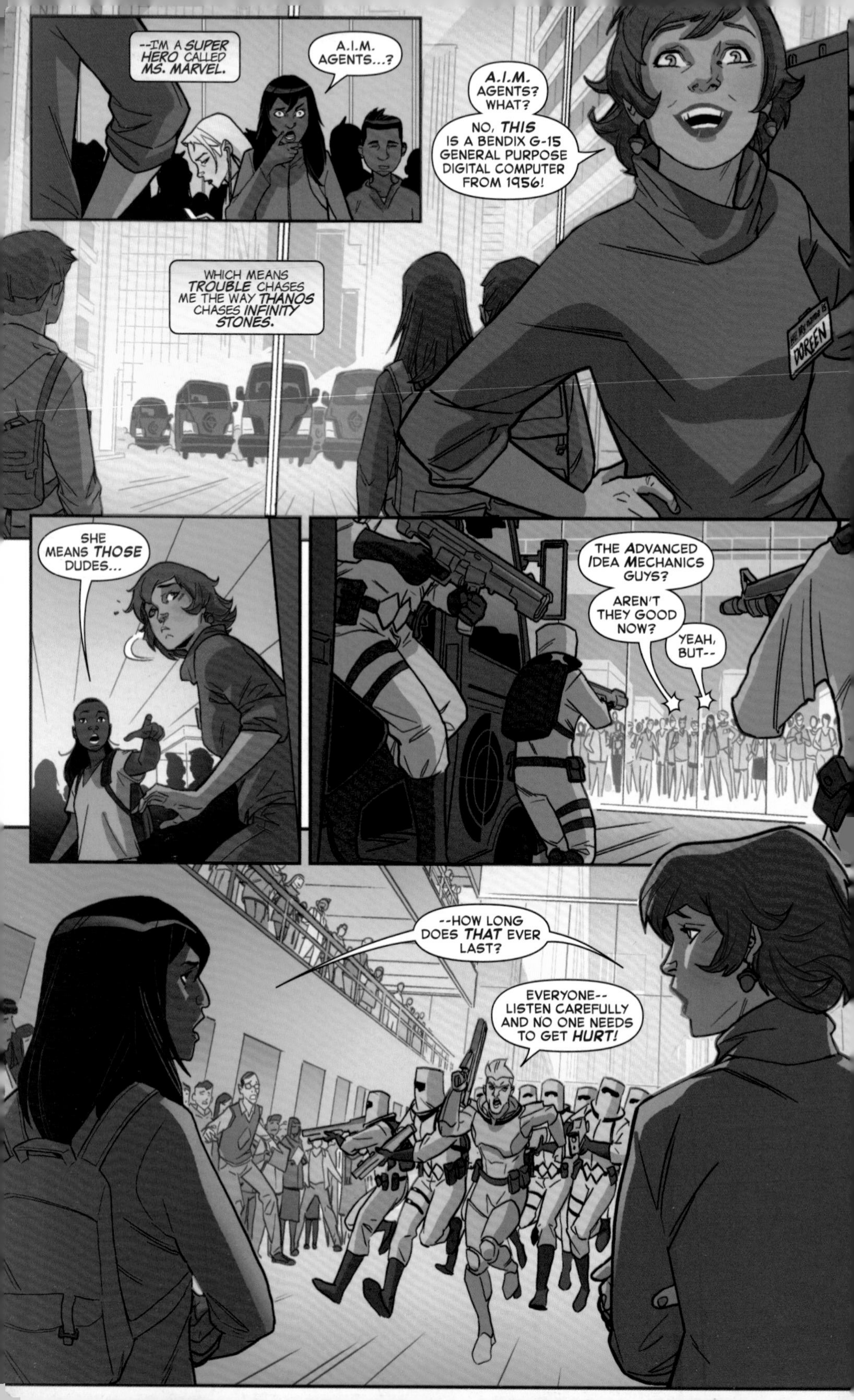
--I'M A SUPER HERO CALLED MS. MARVEL.
A.I.M. AGENTS...?
A.I.M. AGENTS? WHAT?
NO, THIS IS A BENDIX G-15 GENERAL PURPOSE DIGITAL COMPUTER FROM 1956!
WHICH MEANS TROUBLE CHASES ME THE WAY THANOS CHASES INFINITY STONES.
HI! MY NAME IS DOREEN
SHE MEANS THOSE DUDES...
THE ADVANCED IDEA MECHANICS GUYS?
AREN'T THEY GOOD NOW?
YEAH, BUT--
--HOW LONG DOES THAT EVER LAST?
EVERYONE-- LISTEN CAREFULLY AND NO ONE NEEDS TO GET HURT!

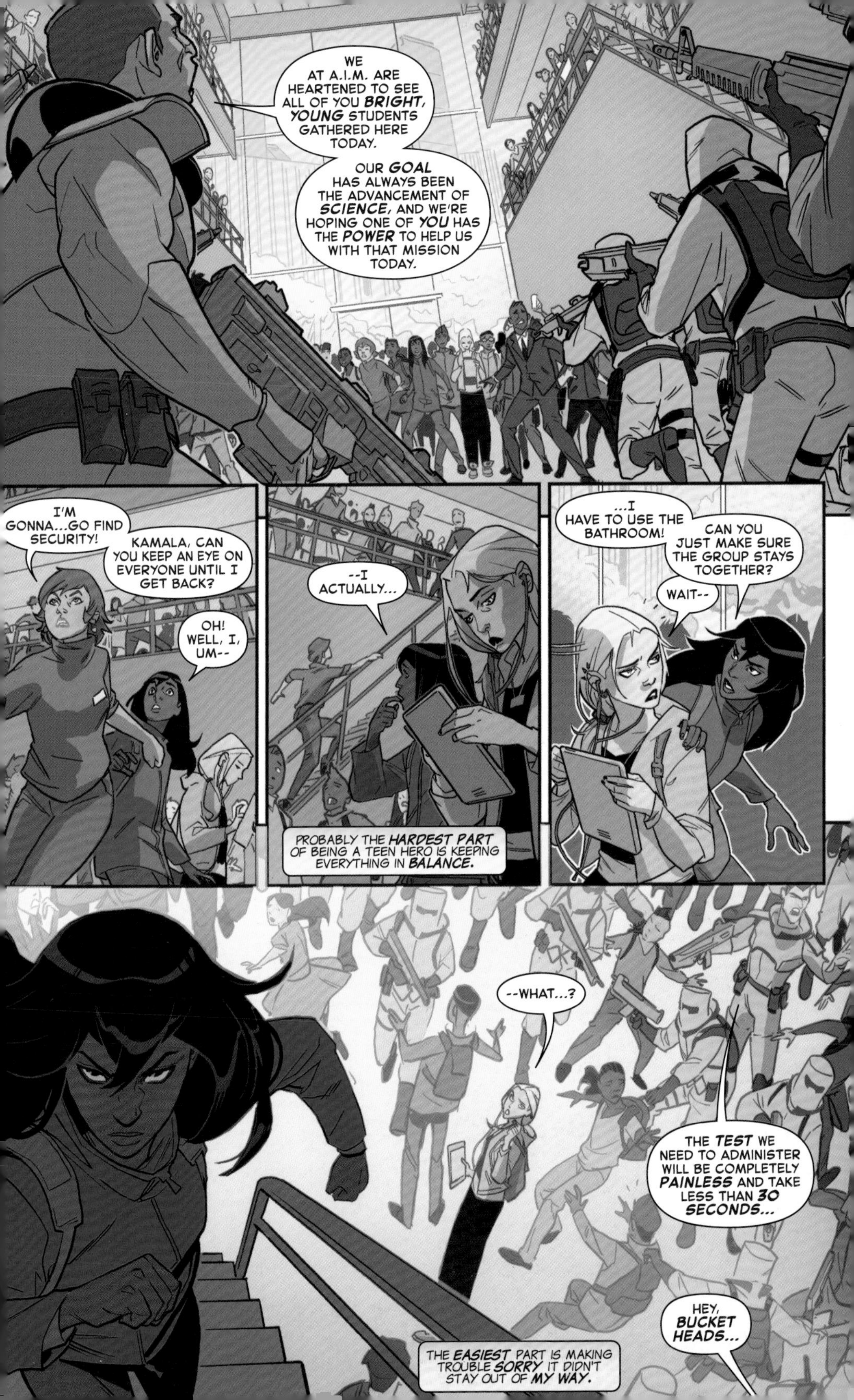

WE AT A.I.M. ARE HEARTENED TO SEE ALL OF YOU BRIGHT, YOUNG STUDENTS GATHERED HERE TODAY.
OUR GOAL HAS ALWAYS BEEN THE ADVANCEMENT OF SCIENCE, AND WE'RE HOPING ONE OF YOU HAS THE POWER TO HELP US WITH THAT MISSION TODAY.
I'M GONNA...GO FIND SECURITY!
KAMALA, CAN YOU KEEP AN EYE ON EVERYONE UNTIL I GET BACK?
OH! WELL, I, UM--
--I ACTUALLY...
PROBABLY THE HARDEST PART OF BEING A TEEN HERO IS KEEPING EVERYTHING IN BALANCE.
...I HAVE TO USE THE BATHROOM!
CAN YOU JUST MAKE SURE THE GROUP STAYS TOGETHER?
WAIT--
--WHAT...?
THE TEST WE NEED TO ADMINISTER WILL BE COMPLETELY PAINLESS AND TAKE LESS THAN 30 SECONDS...
HEY, BUCKET HEADS...
THE EASIEST PART IS MAKING TROUBLE SORRY IT DIDN'T STAY OUT OF MY WAY.

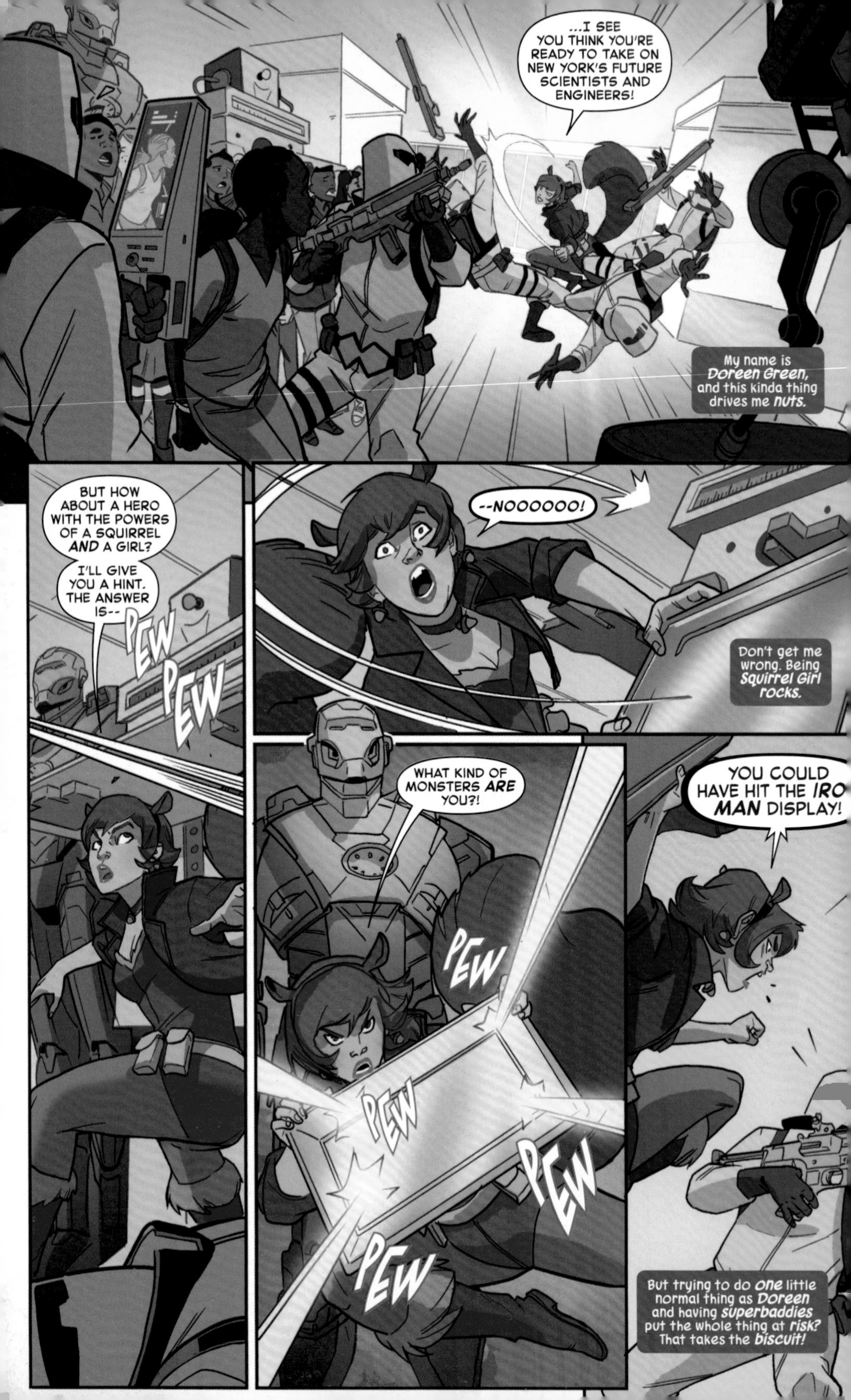
...I SEE YOU THINK YOU'RE READY TO TAKE ON NEW YORK'S FUTURE SCIENTISTS AND ENGINEERS!
My name is Doreen Green, and this kinda thing drives me nuts.
BUT HOW ABOUT A HERO WITH THE POWERS OF A SQUIRREL AND A GIRL?
I'LL GIVE YOU A HINT. THE ANSWER IS--
PEW PEW
--NOOOOOO!
Don't get me wrong. Being Squirrel Girl rocks.
WHAT KIND OF MONSTERS ARE YOU?!
PEW
PEW
PEW
PEW
YOU COULD HAVE HIT THE IRO MAN DISPLAY!
But trying to do one little normal thing as Doreen and having superbaddies put the whole thing at risk? That takes the biscuit!

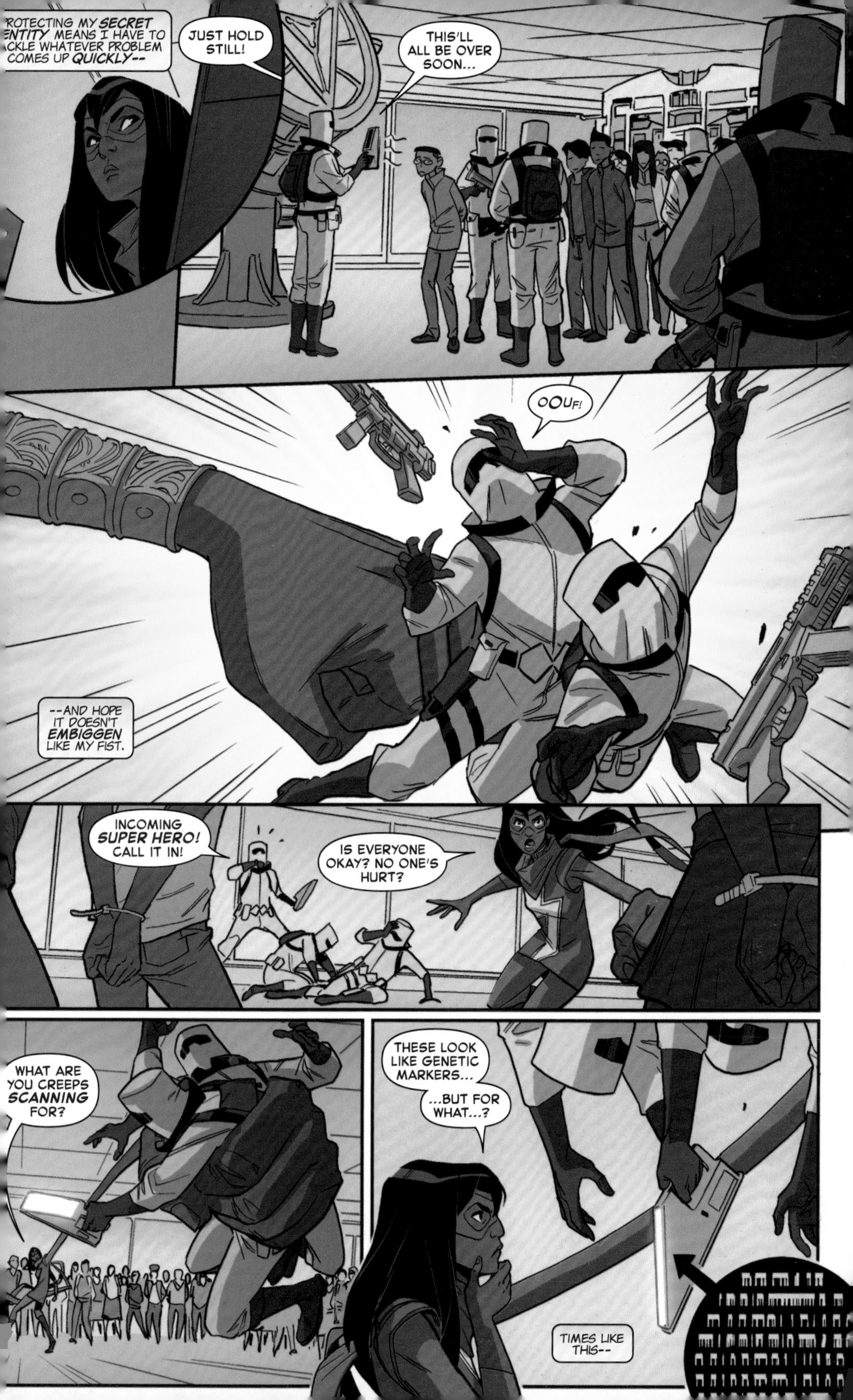

ROTECTING MY SECRET ENTITY MEANS I HAVE TO CKLE WHATEVER PROBLEM COMES UP QUICKLY--
JUST HOLD STILL!
THIS'LL ALL BE OVER SOON...
OOUF!
--AND HOPE IT DOESN'T EMBIGGEN LIKE MY FIST.
INCOMING SUPER HERO! CALL IT IN!
IS EVERYONE OKAY? NO ONE'S HURT?
WHAT ARE YOU CREEPS SCANNING FOR?
THESE LOOK LIKE GENETIC MARKERS...
...BUT FOR WHAT...?
TIMES LIKE THIS--

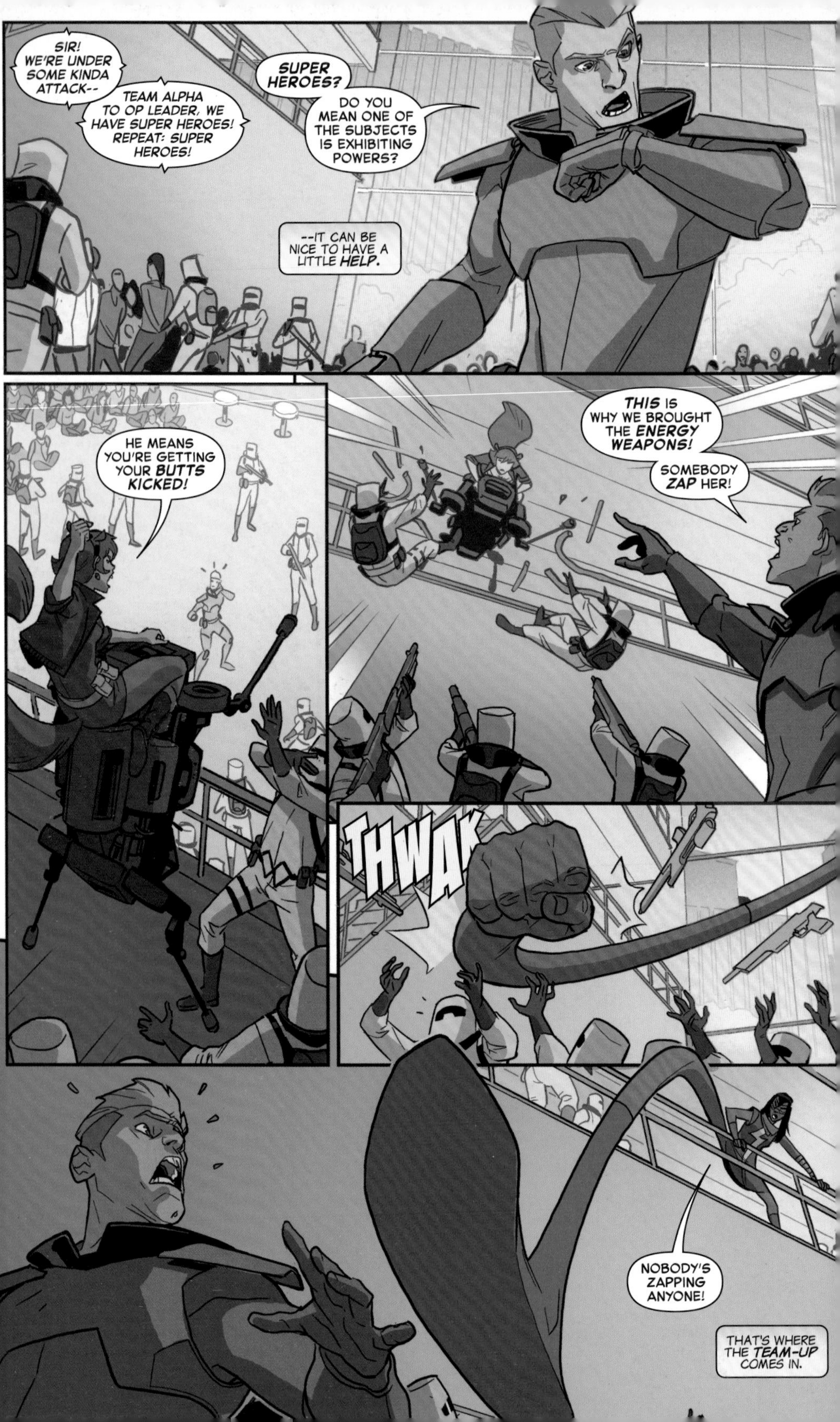
SIR! WE'RE UNDER SOME KINDA ATTACK--
TEAM ALPHA TO OP LEADER, WE HAVE SUPER HEROES! REPEAT: SUPER HEROES!
SUPER HEROES?
DO YOU MEAN ONE OF THE SUBJECTS IS EXHIBITING POWERS?
--IT CAN BE NICE TO HAVE A LITTLE HELP.
HE MEANS YOU'RE GETTING YOUR BUTTS KICKED!
THIS IS WHY WE BROUGHT THE ENERGY WEAPONS!
SOMEBODY ZAP HER!
THWAK
NOBODY'S ZAPPING ANYONE!
THAT'S WHERE THE TEAM-UP COMES IN.

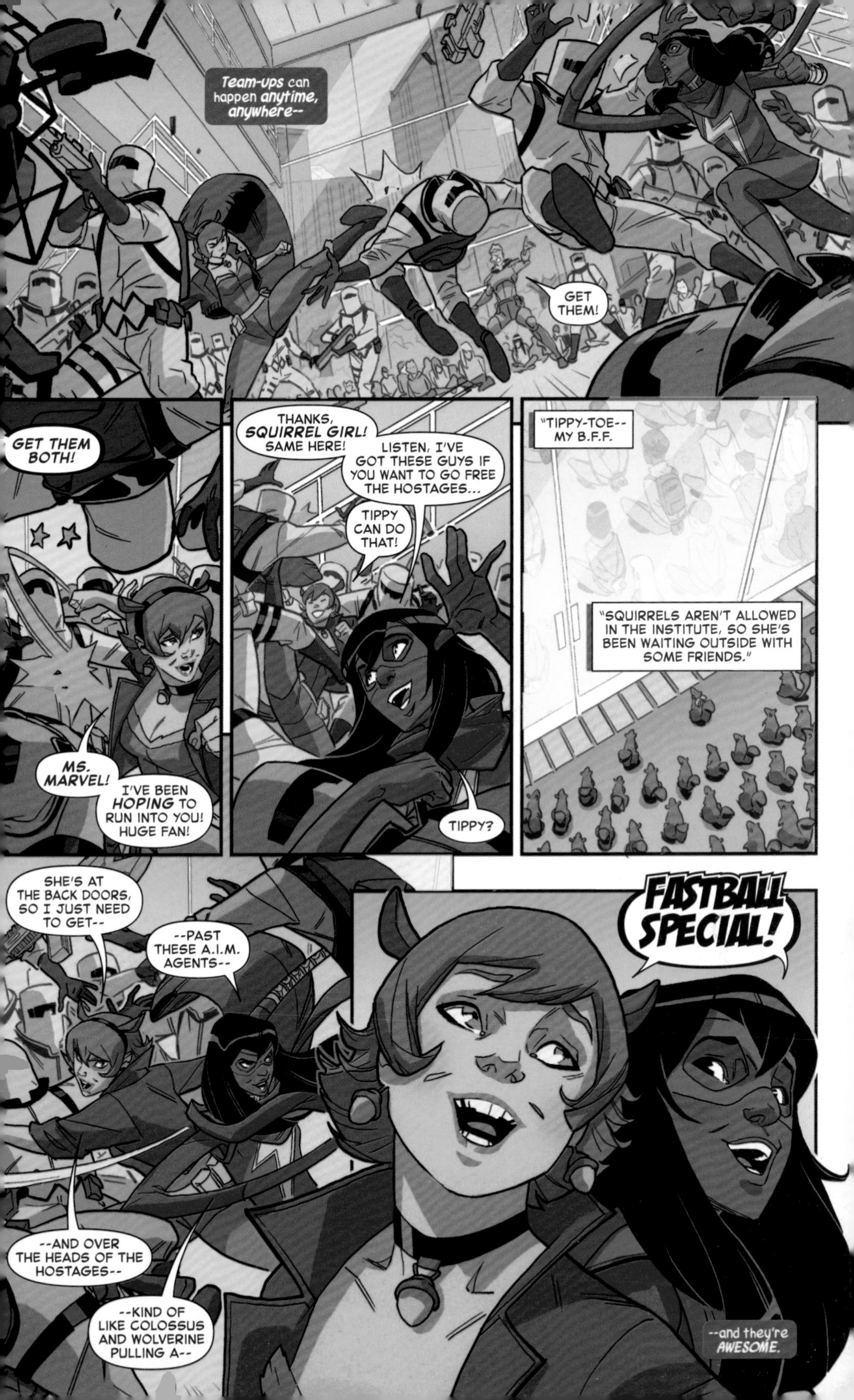
Team-ups can happen anytime, anywhere--
GET THEM!
GET THEM BOTH!
MS. MARVEL!
I'VE BEEN HOPING TO RUN INTO YOU! HUGE FAN!
THANKS, SQUIRREL GIRL! SAME HERE!
LISTEN, I'VE GOT THESE GUYS IF YOU WANT TO GO FREE THE HOSTAGES...
TIPPY CAN DO THAT!
TIPPY?
"TIPPY-TOE-- MY B.F.F.
"SQUIRRELS AREN'T ALLOWED IN THE INSTITUTE, SO SHE'S BEEN WAITING OUTSIDE WITH SOME FRIENDS."
SHE'S AT THE BACK DOORS, SO I JUST NEED TO GET--
--PAST THESE A.I.M. AGENTS--
--AND OVER THE HEADS OF THE HOSTAGES--
--KIND OF LIKE COLOSSUS AND WOLVERINE PULLING A--
FASTBALL SPECIAL!
--and they're AWESOME.

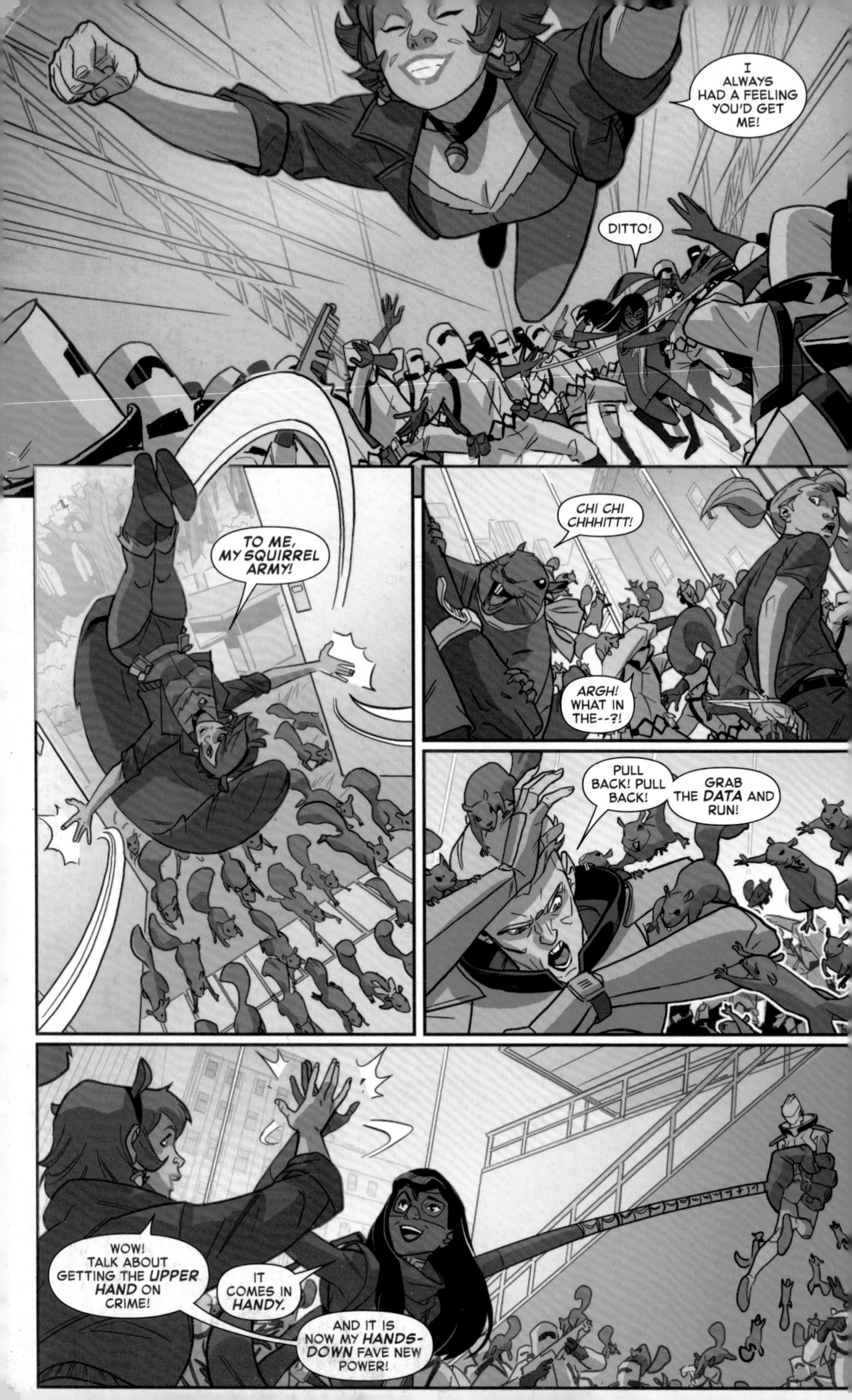
I ALWAYS HAD A FEELING YOU'D GET ME!
DITTO!
TO ME, MY SQUIRREL ARMY!
CHI CHI CHHHITTT!
ARGH! WHAT IN THE--?!
PULL BACK! PULL BACK!
GRAB THE DATA AND RUN!
WOW! TALK ABOUT GETTING THE UPPER HAND ON CRIME!
IT COMES IN HANDY.
AND IT IS NOW MY HANDS-DOWN FAVE NEW POWER!

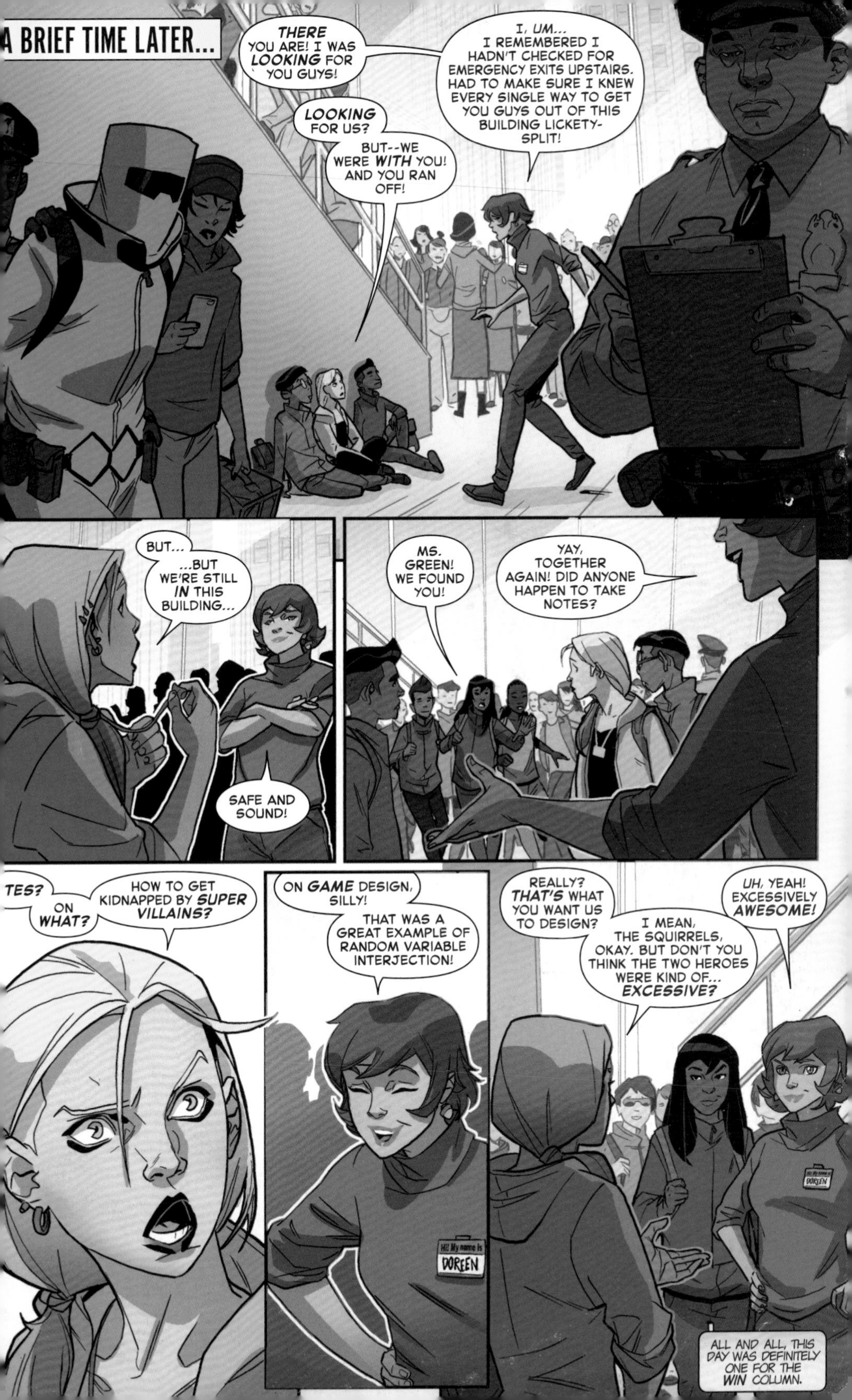
A BRIEF TIME LATER...
THERE YOU ARE! I WAS LOOKING FOR YOU GUYS!
I, UM... I REMEMBERED I HADN'T CHECKED FOR EMERGENCY EXITS UPSTAIRS. HAD TO MAKE SURE I KNEW EVERY SINGLE WAY TO GET YOU GUYS OUT OF THIS BUILDING LICKETY-SPLIT!
LOOKING FOR US?
BUT--WE WERE WITH YOU! AND YOU RAN OFF!
BUT...
...BUT WE'RE STILL IN THIS BUILDING...
SAFE AND SOUND!
MS. GREEN! WE FOUND YOU!
YAY, TOGETHER AGAIN! DID ANYONE HAPPEN TO TAKE NOTES?
TES?
ON WHAT?
HOW TO GET KIDNAPPED BY SUPER VILLAINS?
ON GAME DESIGN, SILLY!
THAT WAS A GREAT EXAMPLE OF RANDOM VARIABLE INTERJECTION!
HI! My name is DOREEN
REALLY? THAT'S WHAT YOU WANT US TO DESIGN?
I MEAN, THE SQUIRRELS, OKAY. BUT DON'T YOU THINK THE TWO HEROES WERE KIND OF... EXCESSIVE?
UH, YEAH! EXCESSIVELY AWESOME!
DOREEN
ALL AND ALL, THIS DAY WAS DEFINITELY ONE FOR THE WIN COLUMN.

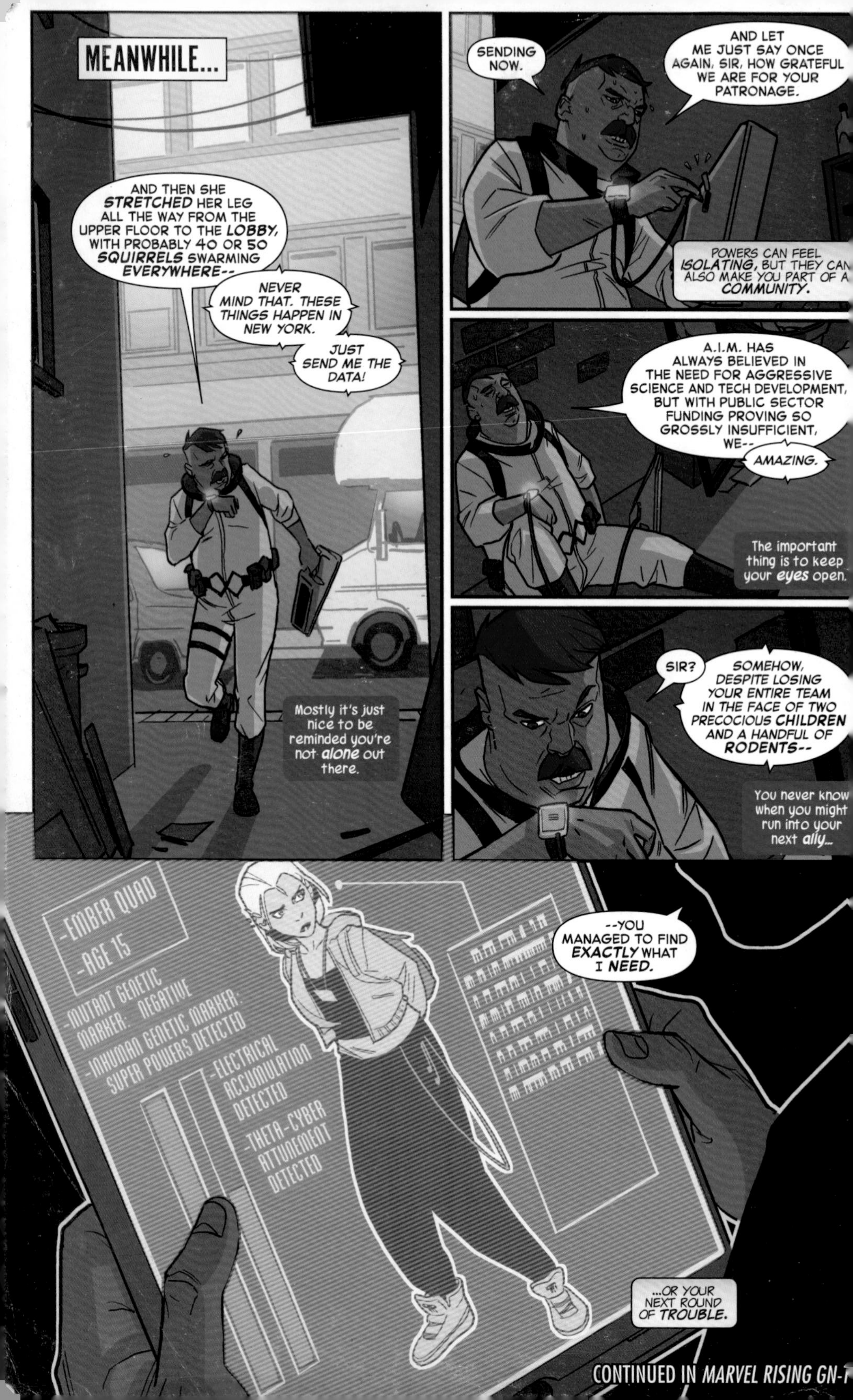

MEANWHILE...
AND THEN SHE STRETCHED HER LEG ALL THE WAY FROM THE UPPER FLOOR TO THE LOBBY, WITH PROBABLY 40 OR 50 SQUIRRELS SWARMING EVERYWHERE--
NEVER MIND THAT. THESE THINGS HAPPEN IN NEW YORK.
JUST SEND ME THE DATA!
Mostly it's just nice to be reminded you're not alone out there.
SENDING NOW.
AND LET ME JUST SAY ONCE AGAIN, SIR, HOW GRATEFUL WE ARE FOR YOUR PATRONAGE.
POWERS CAN FEEL ISOLATING, BUT THEY CAN ALSO MAKE YOU PART OF A COMMUNITY.
A.I.M. HAS ALWAYS BELIEVED IN THE NEED FOR AGGRESSIVE SCIENCE AND TECH DEVELOPMENT, BUT WITH PUBLIC SECTOR FUNDING PROVING SO GROSSLY INSUFFICIENT, WE--
AMAZING.
The important thing is to keep your eyes open.
SIR?
SOMEHOW, DESPITE LOSING YOUR ENTIRE TEAM IN THE FACE OF TWO PRECOCIOUS CHILDREN AND A HANDFUL OF RODENTS--
You never know when you might run into your next ally...
-EMBER QUAD
-AGE 15
-MUTANT GENETIC MARKER: NEGATIVE
-INHUMAN GENETIC MARKER: SUPER POWERS DETECTED
-ELECTRICAL ACCUMULATION DETECTED
-THETA-CYBER ATTUNEMENT DETECTED
--YOU MANAGED TO FIND EXACTLY WHAT I NEED.
...OR YOUR NEXT ROUND OF TROUBLE.

CONTINUED IN *MARVEL RISING GN-T*